Frontispiece: A view of the statue "Let Us Beat Our Swords into Ploughshares," a gift of the Soviet Union to the United Nations, installed in 1959. (Photo courtesy United Nations.)

British Library Cataloguing-in-Publication data are available

Library of Congress Cataloguing-in-Publication Data

Glossop, Ronald J., 1933–
    Confronting war : an examination of humanity's most pressing
problem / by Ronald J. Glossop. — 3rd ed.
        p.   cm.
    Includes bibliographical references (p.   ) and index.   ∞
    ISBN 0-89950-980-0 (lib. bdg. : 50# alk. paper)
    1. War.   2. International relations.   3. Conflict management.
4. International organization.   I. Title.
U21.2.G54   1994
303.6'6 — dc20   94-1409
                                                                            CIP

McFarland & Company, Inc., Publishers
  Box 611, Jefferson, North Carolina 28640

Confronting War

An Examination of
Humanity's Most Pressing Problem

THIRD EDITION

by Ronald J. Glossop

McFarland & Company, Inc., Publishers
Jefferson, North Carolina, and London

Confronting War

For Kent and the other
young people of planet Earth

© *John Trever*
Reprinted with permission of Brick House Publishing Company.

The biggest lesson of all to be learned
about contemporary civilization is that
nothing anyone is doing today makes any
sense unless it is connected to the making
of genuine peace. — *Norman Cousins*

Preface

There was a time when slavery was considered to be a natural and necessary part of human affairs. Then some sensitive and thoughtful persons began thinking of slavery as a social problem. Eventually outright slavery was virtually eliminated from human society.

The same type of evolution may be taking place with regard to the problem of war. For most of human history the only perceived problem related to war was how to win. It is only within the past hundred years that more than a few philosophers and statesmen have regarded war as a social disease, a problem to be solved. As the weapons of war have become more devastating and as the proportion of people affected has increased, it has become clear that war is more than just one of many social problems. The war problem has become the most urgent problem facing the human race. Either the war problem gets solved or humanity risks extinction.

Various efforts have been made to alert humanity to the problem of war and to indicate how the problem might be solved. But just as some people argued that slavery should not and could not be eliminated because it was a necessary part of human society grounded in human nature, so it has also been argued that war should not and cannot be eliminated because it is a necessary part of human society grounded in human nature. On the other hand, just as some persons put forth arguments about why slavery must be ended, so some persons have put forth arguments about why war must be ended. They have also made proposals concerning how to do it.

The purpose of this book is to familiarize the reader with some of the facts, ideas, and arguments related to the war problem and its solution. It is my hope that it will also prove useful to high school and college students and that it will stimulate their teachers to offer formal courses on the subject of war and peace.

As time passes the global situation changes. In 1982 when the first edition of *Confronting War* was written, a main concern of most of humanity was the danger of a nuclear holocaust growing out of the struggle between the United States of America and the Soviet Union. In 1987 when the second edition was written, great changes in the international scene were just beginning to take place because of the policies of "glasnost" (openness) and "perestroika" (restructuring) adopted by Soviet leader Mikhail Gorbachev. Now, in 1994, the Soviet Empire, and even the Soviet Union itself, have been dismantled and the perceived threat of a nuclear holocaust seems much more remote — though the number of nuclear warheads still is only slightly diminished and the number of countries having such warheads will almost certainly increase in the years ahead. Mention of "war" no longer gives rise to the image of a nuclear confrontation between the big powers but rather that of a multitude of "ethnic" and "religious" conflicts, more often within countries than between them and with the killing on a lesser scale. A new edition of this book has become necessary not because the general principles put forth in the earlier editions have proved to be mistaken but because the kind of events to which those principles need to be applied has changed. Because of the greatly changed role of the Russians in world affairs, Chapter VIII on "Ideological Aspects of the Contemporary Situation" has required some revision. Also the historical parts of many different chapters have required updating to include the momentous changes which have occurred within the past seven years.

In connection with this third edition I want to express my thanks to colleagues at Southern Illinois University at Edwardsville from whom I continue to learn much both in the way of facts and in the way of sources of information which I might have otherwise overlooked. In this connection I want specifically to mention William Feeney and Masoud Kazemzadeh of the Department of Political Science, J. Gerald Gallaher and James Weingartner of the Department of Historical Studies, and John Broyer and Carol Keene of the Department of Philosophical Studies. I want to thank David Oughton, former student and now high school teacher and doctoral candidate at St. Louis University, for his ideas and suggestions, especially with regard to the two new sections on the "just war" tradition and on "religion and war." I also want to thank William Feeney and James Elliott for assistance in reading the proofs for this third edition. Assistance from the administration of Southern Illinois University at Edwardsville through the School of Humanities and the Department of Philosophical Studies at Southern Illinois University at Edwardsville, both by means of support for my time to engage in research and writing and by means of photocopying work done by the Humanities Steno Pool, is much appreciated.

For the maps I am indebted to Lora Benedetti and Jeff Ryckaert, students who previously worked with the Regional Research and Development Services at Southern Illinois University at Edwardsville, and to Diane Clements. I am especially grateful to the Brick House Publishing Company for permission to use without cost the John Trevor cartoon on page xv. My thanks also to James Geier for permission to use without cost his "Nuclear Weapons Chart" on page 200 and to the Arms Control and Foreign Policy Caucus to use without cost the map of the former Yugoslavia on page 234.

This book has grown out of my own experience in teaching a course called "The Problem of War and Peace" at Southern Illinois University at Edwardsville (SIUE). During the past twenty years I have learned much from team-teaching this course with many different colleagues. In addition to those mentioned above I would like to express my gratitude to Tetsuya

Kataoka of the Department of Government and Public Affairs; Robert Erickson, Samuel Grant, and Richard Millett of the Department of Historical Studies; Robert Engbretson of the Department of Psychology; Jerome Hollenhorst of the Department of Economics; R. Paul Churchill and Edward Hudlin of the Department of Philosophical Studies; and John Davis, former legal counsel for the University. I have also benefited from hearing a number of guest lecturers for this course: Sugata Dasgupta, Gene Hsiao, Gene LaRocque, Anatol Rapoport, Dudley Weeks, Murray Wiedenbaum, and Jules Zanger. Ideas have also been gathered during the team-teaching of another course, "Global Problems and Human Survival," with Rasool Hashimi of the Department of Economics, Ernest Schusky of the Department of Anthropology, Richard Parker and Marion Kumler of the Department of Biological Sciences, and Deipica Bagchi of the Department of Geography.

Still another source of ideas and stimulation has been conversations with John Danley, Sang-Ki Kim, Tom Paxson, and Gerald Runkle of the SIUE Department of Philosophical Studies, Herbert Spiegelberg of the Philosophy Department of Washington University, and Jean Robert Leguey-Feilleux of the Political Science Department of St. Louis University. My thinking on the subject of war has also been influenced over the years by fellow members of the World Federalist Association including Lawrence Abbott, Harold Chestnut, Eric Cox, Norman Cousins, Tad Daley, Bettie Eisendrath, James Elliott, Walter Hoffman, Myron Kronisch, John Logue, Robert Myers, Sandford Persons, Everett Refior, Scott Tiffany, and Bill Wickersham and by St. Louis area peace activists including Stephen Best, William Eckhardt, Chuck Guenther, James Laue, James McGinnis, Louise Robison, and Bill Stuckenberg. Stan Norris of the Center for Defense Information assisted with the second edition by providing answers to my questions about quantities of nuclear weapons available for use by the United States.

I again wish to express my appreciation to the SIUE Office of Graduate Studies and Research for a Summer Research Fellowship to work on the second edition and to acknowledge the assistance I have received from the staff at Lovejoy Library of Southern Illinois University at Edwardsville, especially Julie Hansen, Linda Carlisle, Charlotte Johnson, and Donald Thompson. I am grateful also to typists Mary Diedam, Karen West, and Ann Morgan for their work on the first edition.

Finally, I again wish to thank my wife Audrey for her patient support and encouragement and more specifically for her help with proofreading.

—Ronald J. Glossop,
January 1994

Table of Contents

xi

List of Illustrations

Part One

Introduction to the War Problem

I. The Nature of the War Problem

War is about power and physical violence. It is about domination and submission between groups of people and their leaders. War is what happens when the leaders of opposing groups of people say to one another, "The only way you will get what you want is over our dead bodies." The result is many dead bodies and one group often being forced to submit to the demands of the other.

War is about physical force being used to resolve a conflict of wills. It is about weapons of increasing destructiveness being used to coerce the other side into agreeing to what they would not otherwise accept. The crucial factor in war is not which of the opposing groups has "righteousness" on its side (both groups are sure that it is on their side) but which group has the power to force the other side to capitulate. As the decades pass, except with guerrilla warfare, the winner is more and more likely to be determined by which side has the most destructive technologically advanced weapons rather than which side has the largest number of fighters. As the weapons become more and more destructive, it also becomes more and more questionable whether anything which might be "won" by war is worth the destruction which occurs during the war. War, which in the past may have been a satisfactory way of dealing with conflict situations, is now likely to be a disaster even for the "winner" and the bystanders.

This book is about war and about alternative ways of resolving conflicts of interest between one group and another. It is about why such conflicts of will occur and about why they sometimes result in the violent struggles we call "war" while on other occasions the conflicts get resolved without violence. It is an inquiry about how war in human society might be reduced or even eliminated.

As was noted in the preface, it is only recently that very many people have begun to think about war as a problem to be addressed rather than as something that just happens, to think about war as a disease of society that needs to be diagnosed and then prevented rather than as a necessary and unavoidable part of the world—like eclipses and earthquakes that will occur no matter what we do. This book is based on the assumption that war is a problem to be addressed, that it is something we can and should try to eliminate from human experience. It adopts the view that we are reasonable and humane enough to want to abolish war, that we are capable of understanding the factors which cause wars to occur, and that we can take

2

action to shape our human attitudes and social institutions, thus replacing war with nonviolent ways of resolving those conflicts of interest which will always be part of human life. Undoubtedly one big obstacle to be overcome is the force of habit and traditional thinking about war which tends to focus only on the issue of how to make the enemy group submit to our group's demands rather than having our group be forced to submit to the enemy group's demands. To see war as a social problem which needs to be solved by means of a cooperative effort requires a major shift in our thinking.

In humanity's earliest days our most urgent problems involved the struggle to survive against the forces of nature—against wild animals and exposure to freezing temperatures, against floods and droughts, against insects and disease. These dangers from nature are by no means completely behind us. And besides we must now also be more careful with regard to misusing our power over nature in such a way that we ourselves become threats to our own future existence. Still the progress of humankind in dealing with threats from the natural world provides a basis for optimism about our capacity to deal with similar kinds of problems in the future. The situation is quite otherwise with regard to the danger of death and destruction from the activities of our own species. There it seems that some fundamental rethinking is in order.

The Importance of the War Problem

Of the many problems facing humanity in the last quarter of the twentieth century, which one is most important? Certainly the great increase in the numbers of people on the earth, largely as the result of the benefits of modern sanitation techniques, new pesticides, and scientifically based medicine, constitutes a problem of the first magnitude. How can all these people be fed? How can the debris from so many people living at even higher levels of consumption be absorbed by nature? How can there possibly be enough nonrenewable resources to meet the demands of larger and larger numbers of persons each of whom uses more and more?

But there is an even more urgent problem for humanity. Perhaps the point can best be made with a story. Suppose that a crew of astronauts has just been launched toward the moon in a space vehicle. At first there are some minor difficulties in getting the spaceship on exactly the right course, but with the aid of ground control the proper maneuvering is accomplished. After a while, as the burden of taking care of the various tasks abates, the members of the crew fall into discussing religion and politics. There are various opposing opinions among the crew, and as the discussion continues it becomes more and more heated. The members of the crew become increasingly absorbed in their dispute. A red warning light begins to glow in the spaceship, but because of their involvement in the religious-political debate the crew members pay no heed. Another light comes on, and then another. There is trouble with the oxygen supply system. There is trouble with the water supply system. There is trouble with some of the waste-removal systems. But the astronauts are so involved in their dispute that they pay no attention to these difficulties. Ground control calls to them in desperation: "Please stop arguing with each other and give full attention to the problems which threaten your survival. And those of you who have plenty of air and water must divert some to those others who soon will become disabled if they don't get any." But there is no cessation of the arguing nor is there any sharing of the air and water. In fact the various members of the crew are now vehemently shouting at each other and trying deliberately to harm one another.

We who are observing this scene from our secure places on the earth would undoubtedly be appalled. We could all see clearly that the priorities of these astronauts have been subverted by their emotional involvement in their dispute. Although these astronauts were having various problems with regard to their spaceship, it would be evident to us who are witnessing this event that their main problem is an overinvolvement in their quarreling with each other. To be sure there are several problems requiring attention such as oxygen supply and water supply and waste removal, but these problems could readily be solved by cooperative action. Their most urgent need is to control their disputations so they can tend to these other problems. They don't necessarily need to come to an agreement on the religious and political issues they are debating. All that is required is that they control their conflicts so that the disputing does not interfere with the fundamental mutual problem of survival. And they don't need to share all resources equally. All that is required is that those who are in desperate need get enough not to die or to be otherwise prevented from making their contributions to the common effort.

In a similar manner, an outside visitor to the earth would be appalled by the stupidity of the people on this planet. We are pouring more and more of our scarce resources and problem-solving talent into a struggle to control or do away with each other while problems crucial to our mutual survival receive only the most marginal attention.[1] Rather than sharing resources, those who have more than others spend huge amounts for ever more destructive weapons so that they can continue to be richer in a relative sense, even though they actually end up having less than they would have if they produced more and shared a bit of it and forgot about the weapons. The people on this planet and their national leaders are as short-sighted as the astronauts on the spaceship in our story.

The end of the Cold War in 1989 has led some people to believe that war is no longer a significant problem for us who live on this planet. It is true that the short-term danger of a nuclear holocaust is much less than it was five or ten years ago, but the long-term danger is not less. In fact, we can be relatively sure that if we do not find a different way of running our world the danger of disaster will be even greater than in the past because nuclear weapons and the knowledge of how to make them have not been eliminated. As time passes additional countries will undoubtedly acquire nuclear weapons, and other new and different kinds of destructive weapons such as those relying on genetic engineering will surely be invented. The current situation is summed up very perceptively by Michael Renner in *State of the World, 1993*: "...[T]he cold war may be dead, but the war system is alive and well: the war-making institutions remain in place, the permanent war economy continues to command large-scale resources, and perhaps most important, the view that military rivalry among states is both rational and inevitable—known in political science as the 'realism' school— still enjoys wide allegiance."[2]

Those who think that environmental problems are more important than the war problem should not forget that ecological leader Barry Commoner has told us that "peace among men must precede the peace with nature"[3] and marine biologist Jacques Cousteau has cogently asked, "Why protect fish if the planet is going to be destroyed?"[4] We do in fact have some significant environmental problems requiring our attention, but as the story about the astronauts above suggests, we should be able to deal successfully with them if we just stop fighting so much among ourselves.

The Four Aspects of the War Problem

There are several aspects to the war problem. So far we have mentioned only the first, the huge expenditure of scarce public funds and research talent getting ready for war. That large expenditure of limited public resources is a great impediment to our quest for survival even if actual war never comes. In 1988 at the peak of the Cold War worldwide military expenditures amounted to $923 billion a year, that is, over $2.5 billion each day![5] That military spending represented 5 percent of the world's gross product or one out of every twenty dollars spent for all goods and services in the world.[6] And that is how much was spent even when no major wars were being fought. During World War II the nations fighting the war spent 40 percent of their gross national product for military purposes,[7] but now some nations spend almost that much just getting ready for war. For example, in 1991 Saudi Arabia was spending 33.8 percent of its GNP, or more than one out of every three dollars spent in the whole economy, on the military.[8] This military spending consumes goods and services that might have been used to meet other human needs. Joshua Goldstein, author of *Long Cycles: Prosperity and War in the Modern Age,* notes that "as a rough rule of thumb, for every 1 percent of gross national product devoted to military spending, overall economic growth is reduced by about one-half a percent."[9] Renowned economist Kenneth Boulding observed that from 1945 to 1978 "the world war industry has probably averaged something like 6 to 10 percent or perhaps even more of the total world product. Summing this over thirty years means that the human race has lost at least two full years, perhaps more, of its total product, which might have been devoted to making everybody richer."[10] That figure is especially tragic when we think of how desperately the poorer countries of the world need financial resources for capital investment, education, and social infrastructure.

The second aspect of the problem of war, the one that came to mind most immediately for most people between 1955 and 1990, is the danger of a nuclear holocaust in which the big powers would unleash on each other the many thousands of nuclear warheads they had ready to launch.[11] With the end of the Cold War this aspect of the war problem has receded from public awareness. The tense moments of the Cuban missile crisis of October 1962[12] seem far removed from the present situation. Nevertheless nuclear-tipped long-range missiles of the U.S., Russia, Britain, France, and China are still in their silos at missile sites and in their tubes on submarines.[13] These missiles can go one-third of the way around the world in just a half-hour. The nuclear warheads on these missiles are at least 20 times more powerful than the bombs dropped on Hiroshima and Nagasaki.

During the last decade of the Cold War, it was noted that a nuclear exchange between the Soviet Union and the U.S. would not only produce an incredible amount of damage to the immediate targets but also would produce so much smoke and soot from the resulting fires that the whole world would experience a "nuclear winter"[14] where plants would no longer grow. This "nuclear winter" would be followed by an "ultraviolet spring" where the ozone layer would no longer be dense enough to protect life from damaging ultraviolet radiation from the sun. Nuclear explosions would destroy that protective ozone layer much more rapidly and thoroughly than do CFCs in the atmosphere. It is possible that all higher forms of life would die from these effects of a nuclear exchange plus the high levels of radioactivity, which would last at least for decades.

We don't like to think about the disastrous consequences of nuclear war, so we are only too glad to suppose that the danger is completely behind us. The danger is certainly less now than it was in the early 1980s, but nuclear weapons have not disappeared, and more and more countries can be expected to acquire them in the years ahead. The danger of a nuclear holocaust would suddenly reappear if tensions again developed among nations which have a substantial number of nuclear weapons.

But the war problem confronting us is not limited to the possibility of a nuclear disaster. The third aspect of the war problem is the occurrence of "conventional" (nonnuclear) wars. It is worth remembering that in the ninety years from 1900 to 1990, 107,800,000 people lost their lives in war,[15] but only about 150,000 of them were killed by nuclear weapons. These wars without nuclear weapons have been rampant since the end of World War II, and all of them which occurred between 1970 and 1990 were fought in the less developed countries.[16] Examples of such "conventional" wars include Israel versus her Arab neighbors, Iran versus Iraq, India versus Pakistan, and China versus Vietnam as well as the more recent fighting among the newly independent republics which were once constituent parts of the former Yugoslavia and the former Soviet Union. Other examples of "conventional" wars are the "wars of liberation" where some "national" group seeks to win its independence such as have occurred and are occurring in Eritrea; among the Kurds in Iran, Iraq, and Turkey; and between the Polisario Front and the government of Morocco in Western Sahara.[17] With the Cold War over, for the next decade or more these conventional wars together with intranational wars will constitute the greatest threat to peace.

Forming a bridge between the second and third aspects of the war problem just discussed is the issue of the proliferation of nuclear weapons. In 1993 nuclear weapons were known to be possessed by the United States, Russia, Ukraine, Kazakhstan, Britain, France, China, and Israel.[18] South Africa built nuclear weapons but has now dismantled them and has converted its nuclear facilities to the building of nonnuclear high-explosive technological devices.[19] India detonated a nuclear device in 1974; it says that it has not yet built any nuclear weapons but will do so if Pakistan does.[20] Pakistan says that it has all the components needed to assemble a nuclear weapon but has not done so.[21] Other countries which seem to be aiming for the capability of building nuclear weapons include Iraq and North Korea.[22] Nations such as Canada, Japan, Germany, Sweden, Italy, South Korea, the Chinese on Taiwan, Argentina, and Brazil undoubtedly could develop the capability of making nuclear weapons rather quickly should they choose to do so.

Beyond the know-how to build nuclear weapons, a nation which wants to construct such weapons must have either enriched uranium or plutonium. The supply of these two crucial materials has so far been fairly well controlled by the present nuclear powers plus Canada and Germany, but the control is not perfect as the cases of Israel and India show. Furthermore, the capability of enriching uranium or producing plutonium can make a country independent of the need for an external supply. The facilities needed to conduct such operations are not easy to hide, but Iraq succeeded in conducting a small plutonium separation program during the 1980s without detection by the United Nations or the International Atomic Energy Agency.[23]

The fourth aspect of the war problem is the occurrence of fighting between groups within one country. These intranational wars are still wars, and in fact it is this aspect of the war problem that is currently most evident. Sometimes the internal fighting is joined by national military forces from outside the country as has occurred in places such as Vietnam, Bangladesh, Afghanistan, Cyprus, and Cambodia. More and more often, however, the fighting within a country has brought the intervention of international peace-keeping forces under the auspices of the United Nations such as has happened in Somalia, Cambodia, and the newly independent republics of the former Yugoslavia. Such intervention by the international community into disputes within countries raises some difficult and significant issues regarding national sovereignty. On the other hand, if the U.N. does not intervene to resolve these disputes, how will they be resolved nonviolently? Discussions of the war problem which deal only with war between different countries are incomplete. Proposed solutions to the war problem must also address the issue of how to deal with these armed conflicts within national boundaries.

In fact, proposed solutions to the war problem must encompass all four aspects of it. Any proposed solution that does not, for example, drastically cut expenditures for the military is not a complete one. Solving the war problem must also deal with conventional wars and civil wars as well as the danger of nuclear war.

The material in this book about the war problem is organized in accord with the steps to be followed in trying to solve any problem. *First,* we need to clarify exactly what the problem before us is. We do this for the war problem by examining the meaning of the key terms "war," "peace," and "justice" (Chapter II). *Second,* we begin gathering information about our problem, which in the case of the war problem means looking at history and noting what we can learn about war from that source (Chapter III). *Third,* we consider and evaluate hypotheses about what causes war, about why wars occur (chapters IV–VII). *Fourth,* we observe the present situation in more detail, being guided to what sorts of things are worth closer observation by our theories about what causes war (chapters VIII–XIII). *Fifth,* we survey various proposals for dealing with the war problem and consider the probable consequences of acting on these proposals; that is, we consider whether they would be likely to help solve the problem and whether they might have some unintended harmful consequences (chapters XIV–XVII). The final step in solving any problem is action guided by the deliberation which has taken place in the previous steps. This concluding phase of the process of dealing with the war problem is up to the reader (Note to the Reader).

II. The Conceptual Framework

What exactly is meant by the terms "war" and "peace"? It should be helpful to the reader to learn how these words are used in this book, and also to consider the meaning of "justice," another term which is crucial to the war problem. Finally, some observations about the relations between peace and justice will be made.

The Meaning of the Term "War"

How shall we use the term "war"?[1] We need a definition broad enough to include both civil wars and international wars but narrow enough to exclude feuds (such as between the Hatfields and the McCoys), riots (such as destroyed the Watts area of Los Angeles in 1965) and intense political action (such as the effort of some persons in Quebec to separate the province from the rest of Canada) which we would not ordinarily call "wars."

The definition of "war" to be used in this book is as follows: *War is large-scale violent conflict between organized groups that are governments or that aim to establish governments.* This definition is important for clarifying exactly what the problem before us is. If we attend to it carefully, it can keep us from running into many blind alleys and wandering off into irrelevant domains.

The first point to be noted is that not all conflict is war but only *large-scale violent* conflict. Those who maintain that the war problem can never be solved often back up their view with the assertion, "You will never be able to get rid of all conflict." A close look at this first part of our definition makes it clear that one need not get rid of all conflict in order to get rid of war. One needs only to manage or control the conflict so that it does not become violent, especially on a large scale. Conflict may in fact be very desirable; it may be a stimulus to needed change. But not all conflict is war.

Of course we sometimes do speak figuratively of "war" between the sexes or of a cold war between countries, but when pushed we are inclined to say that these conflicts are not really wars, but only *like* wars because they are so intense. Consider, for example, how strange it would sound to speak of a "hot war." Wars are necessarily "hot." They necessarily involve violence on a large scale. A "cold war," on the other hand, involves only a readiness to use violence though some scattered cases of violence may actually occur. There may be crises when it seems that the conflict will break into real war, but

9

in a cold war no actual large-scale violence between the antagonists occurs.

In trying to apply our definition of war to actual situations there will be a problem of indicating exactly when a conflict has become sufficiently violent to qualify as a war. What if much property is destroyed but no lives are lost? What if only a few people are killed? Must some minimum number of deaths occur before we say a war is occurring? There are certainly borderline cases in which it is difficult to decide whether there is enough violence to call them wars. Social scientists interested in comparing the amount of warfare in different historical periods or in different geographical regions will be forced to decide somewhat arbitrarily that a violent conflict is to count as a war only if a certain minimal number of deaths have occurred or a certain number of soldiers have been committed to battle.[2] Fortunately, our general discussion of the war problem does not require this level of precision. There are some situations so violent we can unhesitatingly describe them as war. We can focus our attention on these situations and view ourselves as having made considerable headway in solving the war problem if we can successfully deal with these unquestionable cases.

The second crucial idea in our definition of war is that the participants must be members of organized groups. Even the most violent conflict between one person and another is not a war. We might be inclined to make an exception in the case where these two persons are functioning as official representatives of their respective groups and where their one-on-one battle will determine which group is victorious, as was the case in the biblical meeting of David and Goliath; but even then we would want to say that this one-on-one confrontation between selected warriors is a substitute for a battle between two opposing armies. Moreover, if two groups just happen to fall into fighting with each other (as might possibly happen if two groups of different races or nationalities were in the same locale) we would not be inclined to call it a war unless the groups were organized with leaders who give orders and followers who carry them out. War involves the notion of coordinated group action and thus cannot take place without some organization within the groups which confront each other. It should be noted, too, that although the actual fighting is typically done by military forces, the war is not merely between army and army.[3] Especially in modern warfare the military forces are supported by the whole society, which provides weapons, food and medical supplies, new recruits, financial resources, and psychological support. If the military alone fought wars, it would not be necessary to address propaganda to the whole population as is done.

The third crucial idea in our definition of war is the notion that it involves government.[4] A government is a system for group control in which a certain individual or group of individuals is recognized by other governments as well as by those who are ruled by it as having the authority to make decisions which are binding on that whole group.[5] It is only when the governance of some society is at stake that we call a violent conflict a "war."

Violent conflict between opposing groups of hoodlums ("gang war"), for example, falls outside our purview because these groups aim to gain control of illegal activities rather than to acquire the kind of recognized law-making and law-enforcing authority which belongs to governments.

Our definition of war as large-scale violent conflict between groups that are or that aim to establish governments implies that there are two main kinds of wars. The first occurs when one governed society (or a group of them) fights another governed society (or a group of them). This type of violent conflict is *inter*national war (literally, war *between* nations). The second kind occurs when there is a struggle between groups for control of the government within a governed society. This is *intra*national war (literally, war *within* a nation). Further distinctions can be made within these two basic types. For example, international wars may be between nations which are nearly equal technologically and militarily, or they may occur between a technologically advanced nation and a not-so-advanced one. In the latter case the war would be called an *imperialistic* or *colonial* war when the more advanced nation is seeking to establish control and a *war of national liberation* when the less advanced nation is seeking to reestablish its independence. Within the class of intranational wars we can distinguish between a *secessionist war,* in which some region tries to secede from the nation; a *territorial civil war,* in which each of the opposing groups seeking control of the whole nation occupies a fairly well-defined geographical area of the country; and a *revolutionary war,* in which an organized group seeks to overthrow the present government and establish itself as the decision-maker for the whole nation.

It should be noted that a particular war may exemplify more than one type. For example, there may be a struggle for control of the government between two groups within a nation-state where one or both of these groups get assistance from other nation-states. In that case the war is both intranational and international. The wars in Vietnam and Bangladesh were both of this type. In fact, the kind of war which is both intranational and international has become a common situation.

How is terrorism related to war? Terrorism, the carrying out of unexpected acts of violence designed to intimidate or coerce, may be used by various kinds of groups. It has even been, and still is, used by governments to intimidate their own citizens. Political terrorism as the term is usually used today refers to "low-intensity" or "sporadic" warfare carried out by groups so small and weak that they would have no chance of winning a more traditional kind of war.[6] Political terrorists may seek some specific goal such as money for their organization or the release of some of their members who have been imprisoned, but often their aim is to gain public attention and possibly some assistance for their cause, which might otherwise be totally ignored. As in the case of military attacks in war, people tend to evaluate terrorist activities on the basis of their sympathy or antipathy to the aims of the terrorists. In the Middle East, for example, Israelis now condemn the

Palestine Liberation Organization (PLO) for activities similar to what they did before Israel became a nation. Although there may be an inclination to think of terrorism as in some sense "illegal," in fact terrorism *for political purposes* is generally regarded in international law as a kind of warfare in which the terrorists are soldiers for one side.[7] The intermittent violence of terrorists is thus viewed as a scaled-down version of ordinary warfare. Many of the proposals for dealing with the war problem discussed later in this book could be applied to conflicts involving terrorism. Also, since terrorists seek attention for their cause, it seems that a system might be devised whereby small groups seeking political change opposed by those in power would be allowed a continuing opportunity to publicize their view only so long as they do *not* engage in violence.

If we define "war" as "large-scale violent conflict between organized groups that are governments or that aim to establish governments," it should be obvious that the goal of warfare is the acquisition of political power. Each of the groups engaged in a war wants to play the role of decision-maker for some society. Not being able to arrive at some mutually acceptable arrangements by bargaining or negotiation, one group seeks to physically compel the other group to accept its rules for the society in question. The alternative to war thus must consist of some type of *nonviolent* resolution of such conflicts concerning decision-making power. If war is the use of violence to achieve political power, it follows that the implementation of political procedures which are properly responsive to the interests of all groups should make war unnecessary and thus obsolete.[8]

The Meaning of the Term "Peace"

The term "peace" may be taken to mean simply "the absence of war." Some writers on this topic have distinguished between what they call "negative peace" (the mere absence of war) and what they call "positive peace" (a peace in which there is no exploitation of some individuals or groups by others). This distinction is parallel to that which might be made between "negative healthiness" (the mere absence of sickness) and "positive healthiness" (not only the absence of sickness but also physical fitness, good muscle tone, and so on). For those who make this distinction, positive peace is necessarily a good thing while negative peace is not. Consequently, they frequently suggest that the term "peace" be used only for positive peace.[9]

The motivation for using the term "peace" to mean positive peace is admirable. The aim is to ensure that the discussion of how to solve the problem of war is not divorced from the issue of justice. Still, the effort to define "peace" this way seems not to be faithful to our normal use of the term. Also, if the term "peace" is to be reserved for positive peace, what term are we to use to describe negative peace? Furthermore, restricting the term "peace" to positive peace actually interferes with our thinking clearly about the issues of peace and justice and their interrelations. Peace and justice are both desirable things to have in a society, but they are not on that account the same thing. If we were to use the word "peace" to mean only a just peace, we would be forced to overlook certain distinctions which must be made if we are to understand the problems involved in creating an ideal society. In actual social situations "peace" and "justice" often refer to opposing ideals; those who are well off and want to preserve the *status quo* advocate "peace" while those who feel left out and want change call for "justice." This point should become clearer after the discussion of "justice" that lies before us.

Suppose then that we use the word "peace" to mean simply the absence of war, that is, the absence of large-scale violent conflict between organized groups that are governments or that aim to establish governments. Is peace in this sense necessarily a good thing? At first glance it seems to be better than war. In peacetime there may or may not be injustice, but in a war there is bound to be injustice. People are killed or maimed and their property is destroyed simply because they are on the other side or sometimes simply because they are in the way. Bombs and machine-gun fire do not always hit the objects at which they were aimed and they almost always hit other things besides. And even the enemy soldiers at which they are aimed may have had little or no choice about participating in the war. Furthermore, peace tends to make people more humane and sympathetic toward those in other groups, while war tends to make them more suspicious and spiteful toward all persons even remotely related to the enemy group.

Still it is possible for peace to be a very bad thing. A society in which a ruthless dictator rules with an iron hand in an arbitrary and oppressive way may be a peaceful society. There may be an abundance of resentment and hatred, but there still is peace because no one even dares to begin resisting the commands of the dictator. Thus it is quite possible to conceive of a peaceful situation in which there is so much injustice that even war would be better if it meant a chance of getting rid of the dictator. It can be argued that under some conditions injustice becomes so gross that even violence and war are justified. The concept of a "just war" will be explored more fully after our discussion of "justice."

Once it is agreed that even an unjust peace is still peace, the role of government in maintaining peace within the society becomes evident. Government serves many purposes, such as defending the society against other societies and organizing collective action to provide transportation facilities, education for the young, clean water, regulation of trade, and so on, but one of its main purposes is the preservation of public order, that is, the preservation of peace. In order to do this, the government must have some device for keeping conflict among its own members under control. Thus governments have police forces and jails in order to physically subdue those who try to disturb the peace. Usually there are laws so that people will know in advance what types of behavior will be punished by the government. In a republic these laws are made by representatives elected by the people, but in other governments they may be made by a king or dictator or by some group with absolute authority, and may not be "laws" at all. Especially in a republic, but to some extent in most other governments as well, the art of politics develops. This art consists of adjudicating the conflicting interests of different groups when making laws so that peace is preserved within the society. It is especially imperative that injustices severe enough to cause general rebellion be avoided.

Even though governments function as peace-makers within their own domain, they function as potential war-makers in relation to each other. Each government pursues its own interests and, theoretically at least, the welfare of its own people. Thus there is competition between governments for the goods of the earth. Strong governments (in the military sense) will tend to take land and resources from weak governments. As a result, weak governments tend to build up their military might so that they can take from others rather than having things taken from them. In situations where it is not obvious which government is stronger or where the weak government will not merely yield to the stronger, war may occur to settle the issue. Thus governments tend to be war-makers vis-à-vis other governments and peace-makers within their own boundaries.

It should be noted that there could conceivably be peace in a society even though no government exists to adjudicate conflicts between individuals and groups. Conflicting individuals and groups are often able to work out their differences among themselves. In the same way national governments are often able to work out differences among themselves and thus to be at peace with each other. But the fact is that over a period of time there are almost always some intense conflicts which cannot be resolved by the parties involved. Within a government these conflicts are resolved in the political process and by the courts, with the enforcement assistance, if necessary, of the police. When there is no government with law-making and enforcement powers by which conflicts can be resolved, which is presently the case among nations (that is, there is no world government), then violence or threats of violence may be used to try to resolve the conflict. Since this possibility is a very real one, most nations maintain a powerful military force so that they do not need to give in when a conflict reaches the stage where it will be resolved by a contest of force.

Even within nations there may be violent conflict and civil war. The purpose of government is to maintain peace, but it doesn't always succeed. Still it seems to be the case that within a governed society only occasionally does organized violence actually break out while peace is the usual situation; but in the absence of a government which can adjudicate conflicts, violence and readiness for violence are common.

The Meaning of the Term "Justice"

In the present context the term "justice" is being used to refer to a situation where the goods of a society are distributed among the population as they *ought* to be. But how ought they be distributed? What kinds of laws should govern their distribution? It cannot merely be assumed that things should be distributed as they are and that the laws should be as they are. If that were the case, it would never make sense to say that *any* society or *any* law is unjust.

The view that justice is a matter of accepting the existing distribution of goods and obeying the existing laws, whatever the laws say, is not completely without insight, however. We have noticed in our discussion of "peace" that one function of government is to adjudicate in a nonviolent way the conflicts of its members as they individually and collectively pursue their interests. When the government serves as a truly neutral arbitrator in these disputes, each party to the conflict has the obligation to restrain itself in accord with the judgments of the government in order to preserve the peace. If the government really is impartial, each party to the dispute is faced with a choice between living in a society where conflicts about who gets what are peacefully resolved or living in a society where conflicts are resolved by resort to force. Thomas Hobbes, a prominent seventeenth-century English political philosopher, called this latter situation, where there is no government to resolve disputes, a state of war of every individual against every other. Where all conflicts are resolved by the use of force, there is no security of person or possessions for anyone. As Hobbes noted, in such a situation life would be "poor, nasty, brutish, and short."[10] There would be neither peace nor justice. The institution of a truly neutral arbitrator, on the other hand, with the force to subdue those who will not voluntarily obey the laws and judgments of the government, would bring both peace and justice. In this ideal situation, where the government is completely unbiased, justice might well be defined as having goods distributed as they presently are and doing whatever the law requires.

The trouble is that in actual situations the government is usually not a neutral arbitrator either when making laws or when enforcing them. For example, in a Western-style democracy groups and individuals with large amounts of money are usually able to influence the law-making process much more than people with small amounts of money. Thus the laws are more likely to protect and promote the interests of the very rich than of the very poor or even the middle class. On the other hand, after a Communist revolution has occurred, a government will be instituted with the explicit purpose of making laws which favor the poorer "working class" at the expense of the more affluent members of the society, whose property may simply be confiscated by the government. The same kind of bias exists also in the enforcement of the law. In most courtrooms in the West the well-dressed and well-educated are often dealt with less harshly than the poorly dressed and poorly educated. The richer person will probably have a better lawyer representing him. On the other hand, under a newly instituted Communist government a person from a wealthy family can expect harsher treatment than a poor person. So where is justice? Governments are often biased toward some and prejudiced against others.

Whenever we speak of the decisions of a government as unjust, it is implied that we have some independent standard of justice by which we are able to judge. What is this standard of justice? Plato quoted the poet Simonides as offering the suggestion that justice is done when everyone gets what is due him.[11] It seems that there is little with which one can quarrel in this definition, but it still leaves open the question of how we should distribute the goods of society so that all persons have the amount that they ought to have.

This issue of how we should determine what people ought to get is one of the most controversial issues in social philosophy, so it should not be supposed that a short discussion of it can be completely adequate. Still, some basic points can be made. There are two central but opposing principles that must be balanced when this question of justice is being considered. On the one hand there is the *principle of merit,* namely, the principle that *those who are able to accomplish more by virtue of their talents and hard work should reap greater individual rewards and should be able to keep what they have acquired.* The basic belief here is that people need to be encouraged to exert themselves by allowing them to accumulate more than others who do not contribute as much. Supporters of this principle claim that people will work harder over a longer period of time for personal gain than they will when the only motive is the welfare of the whole society. The validity of this principle of merit is supported by the actions of purchasers of goods and services who generally display a readiness to pay more for better quality.

On the other hand there is also another principle of justice, the principle that *everyone should be equal.* The basic belief here is that all people are shaped to be as they are by factors over which they ultimately have no control. People do not choose where they will be born, what traits they will inherit, or what kind of environment they will have as children. People do not choose to be handicapped or to be slow in learning or to be lazy or to be born in a poor undeveloped country rather than a rich developed one. As they grow older, they will make choices, but even then the choices they make will have been determined to a great extent by these other earlier factors over which they had no control. This *principle of equality* displays itself in the claim that workers should be paid based on how many hours they are on the job rather than the quantity or quality of the work completed.

Arguments can be given to support both of these principles. Defenders of the *principle of merit* argue that if talent and hard work are not rewarded then the society as a whole will soon have a lower standard of living. People who have accumulated property must be allowed to keep it. Talented persons won't use their talents, and people will not exert themselves much if they will be just as well off when they loaf. There will be little or no concern for excellence. Competition is required to get people to develop their capabilities. On the other hand, defenders of the *principle of equality* argue that those who are well off are not necessarily more talented or harder working than those who have less. The social system, including the government, has usually been designed to make sure that those persons and groups who have wealth and privileged positions maintain them for themselves and their children. Those who contribute more to society are able to do so only because society or some part of it has first contributed more to them. Cooperation is more essential than competition for promoting the welfare of the society as a whole. Excessive competition tends to destroy human relations and compassion for others.

It might seem that the ideal way of reconciling these two principles of merit and equality is to emphasize *equality of opportunity* for everyone while having actual personal rewards based on the use made of one's opportunities. But even equality of opportunity would not be sufficient to produce justice because some people happen to inherit more talent while others are born with disabilities which they did not choose to have. Also, people do not exist as isolated individuals but live in families and have children. If a husband and wife own things in common, how is it possible to reward one and not the other? And the situation gets even more intricate when we consider children, since one of the things parents most want is a good future for their own children. They usually want their children to have *better* educational opportunities and *better* social opportunities than other children. They want their children to be *more* affluent and *more* influential than other people's children. They are more concerned that *their* children not be threatened by starvation and sickness than that other people's children be preserved from these dangers. It is not that they don't care about other children; they merely care more about their own.

Furthermore, people want this concern about their own children reflected in the policies of their government. For example, think of the outcry from Americans if it were suggested that the United States government make contributions on the order of $50 billion a year to UNICEF or some other agency concerned with the welfare of children in poorer countries in order to modify just slightly the difference in opportunity between American children and the children who live in these other countries. Or consider the outcry which would occur even if the quality of educational opportunities had to be equalized throughout all the schools, public and private, in the United States. Or consider the likely opposition to a law that would prohibit the inheritance of more than $50,000 by any individual on the grounds that such gifts destroy equality of opportunity for everyone. People in positions of privilege do not want equality of opportunity for all children; they feel that one of the important things they have earned by virtue of their talents and hard work is the privilege of sending their children to better-than-average schools and giving them advantages which other children don't have. Yet where is the justice when some children have so much greater opportunities than others? So goes the struggle between the principle of merit and the principle of equality.

It does not take much imagination to see that persons who are well off, either within a society or in relation to the human race as a whole, will see great wisdom in the principle of merit. They will believe that their privileged position is due to their superior intelligence, their greater industriousness, their generally superior genetic make-up, or their better social structure. They have much more than others, but they believe this situation is fair because they deserve to have more. On the other hand, persons who are not so well off, either within a society or in relation to the human race as a whole, will see great wisdom in the principle of equality. They will believe that their inferior position is due to the poverty of their parents, to poor health which is debilitating no matter how hard they would like to work, and to historical developments completely outside their control which have put them in a disadvantaged position. They have much less than others, but they do not believe that it is because they are in any way inferior. In fact it seems to them that they work even harder than the more privileged persons but end up with less.

These differing viewpoints about what principle of justice should be emphasized produce a new basis for the perception of social situations and consequently for social conflict. We will return to these ideas when we consider the ideological aspects of the contemporary world scene. For the moment we can say that different opinions about what is just arise from the fact that people and nations, whether rich or poor, find it difficult to maintain a disinterested point of view. Their own interests always seem much more important than other people's. Furthermore, they do not see how much their own viewpoint is influenced by their present position. The poor believe that if they were rich, they would be much more generous in helping the poor than the present rich are. The rich believe that if they were poor, they would be much less resentful than the present poor are. It is doubtful if either of these beliefs is generally true, either within national societies or within the global society of nations.

Meanwhile, what can be said about justice? It seems that justice involves some kind of delicate balance between the principle of merit and the principle of equality. The fact that people in positions of privilege usually make and enforce the laws would suggest that most governments have overemphasized the principle of merit and underemphasized that of equality. They have been more concerned about maintaining "law and order" and preserving "peace" than about equality of opportunity for everyone. On the other hand, those who are protesting against the injustice of governments may be inclined to overlook the value of merit entirely and to view "justice" as nothing but equality. They tend to be more interested in getting equality, even by violent means, than in preserving a peace which they perceive as designed to maintain an unjust society.

Surely it is not easy to establish just governments, that is, governments which properly balance these two principles of merit and equality, even for national societies. The ultimate challenge of the future, as will become more evident as we proceed, is to establish a governance system on a global basis that will provide a just peace for the whole world. That project will be even more difficult.

The "Just War" Concept

A venerable tradition in dealing with the problem of war is the concern with the question of when it is "just" or "right" to get involved in the violence of war (in Latin *"jus ad bellum"*) and what kinds of use of violence are justifiable once war is going on (in Latin *"jus in bello"*). It should be noted that these questions are only tangential to our central concern of how to eliminate war. In fact, they are addressed to an entirely different issue, namely, what is the morally correct way to behave as long as wars are going to be fought? This whole "just war" tradition assumes that there will be wars; the problem then becomes how to constrain behavior so that wars are not fought when there is no morally good reason for them and so that wars are not more vicious than they should be. Nevertheless the "just war" tradition has been an important part of thinking morally about war, so we want to discuss it briefly.[12]

Historically, the beginning of the just war tradition is traceable back to the Greeks during the Peloponnesian Wars of the fifth century B.C. and then to Cicero in the first century B.C.[13] The source for most modern thinking on this issue is St. Augustine (354–430 A.D.), Christian Bishop of Hippo. The early Church had been totally pacifist, but Augustine argued that sometimes it was morally necessary to use force (violence) in order to combat evil. For example, it would not be right for a Christian to stand by refusing to use force while a criminal was mistreating an innocent defenseless person. The Christian was to be motivated by concern for both the victim and the offender and was not to use more violence than necessary to prevent the evil. Nevertheless, moral duty requires that the offender be stopped from injuring the innocent person, by force if necessary. Extending this pattern of thinking to the arena of international relations, one country can justly go to war against a second country which is unjustly attacking a third country if there is no other way of stopping the evil and if the use of force is only as much as is necessary to stop the wrong.

Augustine's example exhibits the issues usually brought up in discussions about when the use of force or violence is justified. First, there must be a just cause for resorting to force; some evil is to be prevented. Second, the use of force must be done with the right intent; the motive must be to stop evil with no expectation of personal glory or other gain. Third, the amount of force must be no more than what is needed to prevent the wrong. Fourth, which follows directly from the previous point, force is justified only when there is no other way of dealing with the evil. Fifth, there must be a reasonable expectation that the act of intervention taken as a whole will produce more good than evil, which would include the idea that the person trying to stop the evil really has a good chance of accomplishing that goal without inadvertently leading to even more evil happening in the long run. (These last three points are often grouped together under the heading of "the principle of proportionality." Using force is inherently evil and can be justified only if using violence is going to produce more good than evil.) Lastly, in international affairs, this "policing" of unjust actions to prevent evil must be carried out by someone with the political authority to order and control the use of violence, not just anyone who has a weapon or other means of violence available.

The second issue addressed by "just war" theory concerns how war is to be conducted. The first point here is that innocent bystanders (noncombatants, civilians) are not to be harmed ("the principle of discrimination"). The second point is that the particular actions being used during war need to be constrained so that they do not exceed what is needed to accomplish the end and do not result in more evil than good. This second point is an extension of "the principle of proportionality" except that now it is being applied to the problem of how to fight a war rather than trying to decide whether to engage in war at all. In this new context it is called "the principle of double effect," the notion that *each action* performed during a just war has some good effects in stopping injustice but also some bad effects in harming others, and the good must exceed the evil or that particular action is unjust.

The "just war" tradition offers a middle way between pure pacifism (which shuns any use of violence for any reason) and unrestrained realism (which advocates unrestrained use of violence in order to prevail over one's enemy). It is based on the notion that there is a "natural law" or moral order about what is right and what is wrong and that it is legitimate to use force in order to stop violations of the natural law. If those who care about justice are not allowed to use force to stop injustices (to maintain "law and order"), then those who use unrestrained force to advance their own interests will not be held in check. That absence of any kind of check on injustice would lead to even more violence since everyone would be required to use force to protect their own interests.

But there are some difficulties for "just war" theory. First, exactly what does the "natural law" prescribe? Not everyone is in agreement on exactly when injustice is being done. For example, suppose one very small group of people gains possession of almost all the land available in a given area (considerably more than they can actually make use of) and then institutes a government with laws that prevent others from ever owning or using any of that land. Would it be unjust for other people who have been excluded to use force to try to break up or change that system of government so that the land could be more evenly distributed? Does the "natural law" dictate that people should be able to keep whatever they already possess? Or does the "natural law" say that there are other principles of justice which require equality of opportunity and a certain degree of sharing? And of course what makes this kind of situation even more troubling is that those who own the land are going to have one view of what is just while those who are being excluded will have a different view of what is just. We could have a very violent war with both sides quite convinced that they are engaged in a "just war."

Second, there are special difficulties for the "just war" theory in connection with modern society and modern warfare. Can these principles of "just war" be applied in any meaningful way? For example, how can one engage in modern warfare and not kill substantial numbers of "innocent civilians" who just happen to be in the way when explosives detonate or fires spread? Also, are there many "innocent civilians" in a modern war? Aren't the farmers providing the food for the military forces just as much a part of the war effort as the military forces themselves? What about the engineers who are designing new weapons? Are they innocent civilians, or are they perhaps even more important to the war effort than most of the soldiers? What about the educators who are teaching future engineers and soldiers how to read and do mathematical calculations? What about the factory workers who are manufacturing the weapons and the uniforms the military forces will use? In modern "total war" it seems that most of the society is involved in the war effort. Trying to discriminate between combatants and noncombatants seems futile. Besides, people generally do not have much of a choice as to whether they are going to be part of the military forces or not. Why assume that the person in the enemy society who wears a uniform is a more legitimate target than others who are not wearing uniforms? Are not the leaders of the enemy society more likely to be responsible for the war than the soldier on the battlefield? Yet there seems to be a tradition that leaders of the other side are not to be assassinated.

There are also difficulties related to modern weapons, especially nuclear weapons.[14] Is there any way that one can "justly" use nuclear weapons, especially in large numbers? Isn't the destruction caused always going to far exceed any good that could come from their use, especially when one considers the long-lasting radioactivity, the possibility of "nuclear winter," and the enduring effects on the environment—including possibly the end of all life? Can a strategy of nuclear deterrence through the threat of massive retaliation be "just" if the use of nuclear weapons is always unjust? That is, can one justly threaten to use the weapons if it would be unjust to actually use them? On the other hand, if one's enemy has nuclear weapons, isn't it necessary to be prepared to use them in order to deter the enemy from using theirs? In that case, how many nuclear weapons are "enough"? Other kinds of weapons are also becoming ever more cruel and destructive — napalm, chemical and biological weapons, lasers to cause blindness, and so on. Can modern warfare be "just" under any circumstances?

There are so many philosophical and moral dilemmas related to "just war" theory in the modern world that the only sensible course of action appears to be to work as intelligently and energetically as possible to abolish war as a way of resolving social conflict. That is, instead of focusing on *when* it is just to fight wars and *how* it is just to fight wars as "just war" theory does, thought and action concerning the war problem should focus on how to eliminate war altogether.

Further Reflections on Peace and Justice

As we have already noted, the question of justice concerns the proper distribution of the goods and benefits of a society among its members. We have also noted that the general tendency of governments is to be conservative, to preserve the present social order with its greater opportunities for the children of privilege rather than to institute changes which would create more equal opportunities for the less privileged children. A tension exists between the quest for peace (typically viewed as preserving the status quo) and the quest for justice (where violence may seem to be the only way of changing an unjust existing situation). Three additional observations on the relations between peace and justice are in order.

In light of what has been said above, it might be assumed that once government is established there will be less justice with regard to the distribution of goods and benefits than if there were no government because the government will probably be controlled by the powerful to maintain their positions of privilege. But what would the situation be without a government to keep peace? Ruthlessness and violence would be rewarded by gains in possessions and power. Consequently there would be a tendency of the powerful to use their power in an unrestrained way to become even more powerful. Once a government is established, the powerful may use it as an instrument to maintain their power, but in the absence of government the powerful will have other instruments (paid bodyguards and warriors, specially designed weapons, and so on) to maintain their power. The point might be put this way. Government does not necessarily produce justice, but the lack of government probably will allow, and even reward, a great deal of injustice. Whether the injustice with government will be greater or less than the injustice without government is a matter of the particular situation and the particular kind of government to be instituted.

If a world government were instituted over the national governments, would the distribution of the goods of the earth among the various nations be more or less just than it is at present? It can be supposed that such a government would be dominated by the more powerful nations, at least at first.[15] Otherwise, those nations would not even allow it to be formed. Once a government was established, the more powerful nations would undoubtedly try to use it to maintain their positions of privilege. Would the less powerful, poorer nations be better off with such a government or without it? Without it, they are virtually at the mercy of the more powerful nations, which can use their superior economic and military power to impose whatever terms they desire. With it, they are still in a situation dominated by the more powerful nations. Which situation would be more just would depend on specific things such as the acquisition of nuclear weapons and long-range delivery systems by the poorer nations (which would make them less at the mercy of the more powerful nations) and the precise voting arrangements and structure that would exist in the world government (which might be arranged so that the poorer nations were less at the mercy of the richer ones). Only after examining details would it be possible to say whether a fairer distribution of goods among the nations would be more likely with such a government or without it. A critical feature for promoting justice in the long run would be having the kind of government which permits peaceful change to eliminate injustice.

The second point to be considered with regard to the relation between peace and justice concerns the desirability of conducting war to eliminate what are considered to be unjust inequalities in wealth. To understand this point we must begin by noting that there are two different viewpoints that can be taken with regard to the measurement of wealth. People may evaluate their wealth *relatively* in terms of what they have compared to others, or they may evaluate their wealth in *absolute* terms, that is, in terms of what goods and services and burdens they actually have regardless of what others have. In a peaceful situation there may be a great disparity between what the rich have and what the poor have, but the poor may still be better off in absolute terms than they would be if they were to conduct a war against the rich. That is, the poor within a society may unite in a war against the rich in order to end what is perceived as an unjust situation with the result that everyone in the society ends up worse off than before. War can destroy the wealth of the rich, but it cannot by itself make the poor as a whole richer because war does not produce goods but only destroys them. To be sure some of the leaders of the poor may confiscate some of the leftover goods of the rich for themselves, but then all that has happened is that one group of rich persons has been replaced by another group of slightly poorer persons. And that is the situation if the poor *win* the war! If they try to rebel but *lose,* it can be expected that they will be even more oppressed than before.

It could be argued that a violent revolution by the poor against the rich might change an oppressive system and thus would be worthwhile in the long run even if a failure from the short-term point of view. Conceivably such a change for the better is possible. The crucial issue is whether the new leaders will prove to be different from the ones they replaced and whether the new system will put more restraints on the power of the leaders than the old system did. The first one or two generations of leaders after the revolution might well be vividly aware of what they fought to change and might be particularly on guard against special privileges for leaders and their families and friends, but at least by the third generation the leaders are much less likely to be concerned about such issues. Also it is very unlikely that the new leaders will be more restricted in their powers than the old leaders had been because the new rulers will claim that they must be unrestrained in order to make all the changes they feel are so necessary. Nevertheless, it is possible that a violent revolution may result in a society which is more just.

Suppose the poorer nations of the world eventually acquired enough nuclear weapons to be able to cause considerable damage to the richer nations. Suppose they then threatened the richer nations saying that wealth must be shared more equitably or they will use the weapons. The richer nations would probably not yield to such a threat and might even issue a counter-threat. The poor nations could argue, "You have more to lose than we do" (which is true), but the richer nations could argue, "You will be even worse off after a war with us than you are now" (which is also true). Consider the situation if the poor nations were able to launch a surprise nuclear attack destroying a great deal of the wealth of the richer nations and eventually developing a new international system to modify the distribution of goods among nations. Even if things worked out as the poor nations had planned, from an absolute point of view all nations would be worse off than before the war. It is also not certain over the long run that the new system would be more just than the old one. Furthermore, it is really much more probable that in a war the rich nations would prevail over the poor ones. They also might well be provoked by such an attack to be even more oppressive toward the poorer nations than they had been before. A world government which would allow for peaceful change would be a much better alternative for the poorer nations.

The third point to be considered with regard to the relation between peace and justice is that justice in a society produces both peace and prosperity. In a society where there is a general consensus that opportunities are approximately equal, that the goods and burdens of the society are fairly distributed, and that the laws of the society are equitable and impartially enforced there is little likelihood of group violence. Even if a few individuals have some personal gripes, they will be unable to get any substantial following if they try to organize a violent rebellion. Also, when the poorer people who are in greater need of more goods have the money to buy them, the industries of the society are stimulated. Unemployment is reduced, and consequently crime is reduced. As more people work, production is increased and the demand for goods is further increased. Prosperity is promoted by having some wealth in the hands of poorer people.

Let us consider how this principle would work at the international level. Suppose that all tariffs and restraints on international trade now erected by the richer countries were eliminated so that these markets would be opened to the poorer countries. Suppose also that some system were in place to guarantee that a small portion of the income of the richer nations were transferred to the poorer ones. The present resentment felt by the governments of the poorer nations toward the richer nations would be greatly reduced. Although there might be some concern in some of the richer nations as patterns of employment shifted to accord with the new situation, the long-term reaction would be one of satisfaction as the prices for many consumer goods are reduced and the market for exports expands. Unemployment in the less developed countries would decline, and demand for goods from the developed countries would increase. Threats of violence against the investments of those living in richer nations would be virtually eliminated. The gap between poor and rich nations would be reduced, every nation would be better off in absolute terms, and the likelihood of any kind of violence would be greatly reduced. This hypothetical program of peace and prosperity through greater justice can be contrasted with the present world system in which the more powerful nations maintain their positions of superiority through military might and control of the rules of international trade. This present system focuses on preserving the relative superiority of the richer nations, but all nations are poorer in absolute terms than they could be under an international system with greater equality of opportunity.

On the basis of this observation that a just social system produces peace and prosperity, it has been argued by many writers that the best way to produce peace is to promote justice.[16] But there are problems here, too. One person's view of what is just is not the same as another's. Also, for some persons the use of violence can be justified if it promotes justice.[17] Care must be exercised by those who adopt such a view since the quest for justice may itself be the cause of war. On the other hand, leaders concerned about peace but insensitive to issues of justice are not blameless when their maintenance of a grossly unjust social system results in war. As U.S. President John F. Kennedy said, "Those who make peaceful revolution impossible will make violent revolution inevitable."[18]

III. The Historical Framework

The problem which we want to address is the problem of war. We have defined "war" as "large-scale violent conflict between organized groups that are governments or that aim to establish governments." When does the problem of war begin? Since our definition of "war" makes reference to government, there couldn't be war *in this sense* until there were governments; and governments were not developed by humans until they became "civilized," that is, until they changed from a nomadic life-style to living in permanent villages and cities, a change which first occurred in some parts of the world about 10,000 years ago.

The word commonly used to describe pre-civilized nomadic people is "primitive." Evidence indicates that many, though not all, primitive communities did engage in some violent struggles with their neighbors.[1] Primitive peoples apparently used weapons to attack other humans or to defend themselves, the same weapons that they used to kill the animals which they hunted.[2] Thus it seems that there was some armed conflict between precivilized groups of humans (that is, there was some primitive warfare), but it was not at all what we mean by war. As Gwynne Dyer notes, primitive warfare "is an important ritual, an exciting and dangerous game, and perhaps even an opportunity for self-expression, but it is not about power in any recognizable modern sense of the word, and it most certainly is not about slaughter."[3] In other words, primitive warfare was very different from the kind of war which is a problem for us today.

Before the coming of civilization during what is called "the New Stone Age" our nomadic ancestors, like other animals, depended completely on what nature might haphazardly provide. Civilization meant a radical change in their lives, bringing with it not only more organized control over nature in the form of agriculture and domesticated animals but also more organized control over the people living within the society in the form of government. It also brought warfare in the sense of an organized violent struggle for power between one society and another. To quote Dyer again: "Civilization, first and foremost, was the discovery of how to achieve power over both nature and people, and it cannot be denied that it went to our heads: on the one hand, pyramids and irrigation canals; on the other hand, wars of extermination."[4] He goes on to say: "It can never be proved, but it is a safe assumption that the first time five thousand male human beings were ever gathered together in one place, they belonged to an army. That

26

event probably occurred about 7000 B.C. — give or take a thousand years — and it is an equally safe bet that the first truly large-scale slaughter of people in human history happened very soon afterward."[5] In the next two or three thousand years serious warfare spread to more and more societies. Peace researcher William Eckhardt observes that "the evidence is overwhelming that warfare did not come into its own until the emergence of civilization some five thousand years ago."[6] That is, there is overwhelming evidence that government and *the problem of war* emerged together along with civilization. In fact, government and civilization both seem to have come into existence as a result of comparatively peaceful agricultural peoples being conquered by invading nomadic war bands who then organized the resultant society in such a way that their power could be maintained within that society and also could be used against other societies.[7]

The striving for power by the rulers of the most ancient city-states of Mesopotamia is not essentially different from the struggles for power among the leaders of modern nation-states.[8] Nevertheless there is a change in war, a steady increase in the size of the communities involved and a never-ending evolution of the weapons used in fighting these struggles. The continuing occurrence of war in human society, even while the ways in which wars are fought are changing, leads naturally to the question, "Are there any long-range trends with regard to war?" and then to the question, "Is there any reason to believe that a solution to the war problem is more imperative now than it was in past ages?"

The System of Sovereign States

Among the earliest known city-states are those which flourished about 5000 B.C. in the Tigris-Euphrates Valley. The rulers of city-states such as Eridu, Nippur, Ur, Uruk, Assur, Umma, Sumer, Lagash, and Kish engaged in the same kind of struggles for wealth and power that we find among modern nations. Evidence of this exists in the form of peace treaties inscribed in clay about 3000 B.C.[9] Thus the pattern of struggles for power among sovereign states is at least 5,000 years old. At times the struggle is interrupted when one sovereign state establishes an empire by conquering all the others close enough to contend for land and other advantages, but the peace is always temporary. When the leader who has created the empire dies, it may disintegrate as a struggle for power takes place among his previous subjects. Or the newly created empire may come into conflict with other empires built of previously competing states.

One of the earliest recorded empires was brought into being in the Tigris-Euphrates Valley about 2500 B.C. by Lugal-zaggasi of Uruk. This Sumerian empire was then conquered and incorporated into the much larger empire of Sargon of Akkad, which continued until the twentieth century B.C. In the eighteenth century B.C. Hammurabi established a unified Babylonian empire over most of Mesopotamia which lasted 200 years. In the fifteenth century B.C. the Mitanni established an empire which reached from the Mediterranean to western Iran. The Assyrians freed themselves from Mitanni control in the fourteenth century B.C. and then established an empire of their own.

Starting as a separate political entity first unified about 3000 B.C., the Egyptian state eventually spread its influence northward into Syria, where it came into conflict with the Hittites from Asia Minor and the Mitanni living along the eastern shores of the Mediterranean. About 1400 B.C. these three nations entered into a nonaggression pact, and about a century later the Hittites and Egyptians formed an alliance against the expanding Assyrian empire. Nevertheless the Assyrians established control over Palestine in the eighth century B.C. and took control of Egypt in 675 B.C. But the Egyptians and Babylonians revolted and with the help of the Medes from the east destroyed the Assyrian capital of Nineveh in 612 B.C.

The rise and fall of one power after another continued as the Persians conquered Lydia in western Asia Minor and then Babylon (538 B.C.). Under Darius I in the fifth century B.C. the Persian empire reached from the Danube River to the Indus River and from what is now southern Russia to southern Egypt. The city-states of Greece had managed to fight off the Persians even while fighting sporadically among themselves but fell in 338 B.C. to the Macedonians under Philip. Under Alexander the Great the Greeks then extended their domain to include Egypt and the rest of the territory previously held by the Persians (331 B.C.).

To the west the Romans began their expansion in the third century B.C. by defeating the Carthaginians. Then they conquered Macedonia, Greece, and their Numidian rivals in northern Africa. Despite class struggles in Rome which eventually led to the replacement of the Roman Republic by the Roman Empire, Roman power had spread to western Europe, Asia Minor, Egypt, and the east coast of the Mediterranean before the beginning of the Christian era. Although confronted by the Germanic "barbarians" on the north, the Roman government succeeded in maintaining the famous *Pax Romana* in the Mediterranean for 500 years. Nevertheless, as a result of invasions by the Visigoths, Huns, Vandals, and others the western part of the Roman Empire ceased to exist as a political unit after 476. In the seventh century the eastern part of the Empire came under attack as the Muslim Saracens conquered Palestine, Egypt, the rest of north Africa, and Spain. The Muslim advance into western Europe was stopped at Poitiers in 732 by the Franks under Charles Martel. In 800 Martel's grandson, Charlemagne, was crowned Emperor of the new western Roman Empire by the Pope. In the tenth century the Vikings, Varangians, and Norsemen from the north, the Magyars and Bulgarians from the east, and the Turks from the southeast made new incursions into what had been the Roman Empire. The result was a Christian Europe composed of many separate political entities plus the remains of the Byzantine Empire in southeastern Europe.

The largest land empire ever known was then carved out of Asia and eastern Europe by the Mongols under Genghis Khan (1162–1227). But as often happens, the victors were conquered by the culture of the vanquished both in China and in Muslim western Asia. The aggressive Ottoman Turks put an end to the eastern Roman Empire, conquering Constantinople in 1453. The separate Christian kingdoms of Europe banded together to stop the Turkish expansion and won a naval victory at Lepanto in 1571, but when the threat was gone they again went their separate ways.

In western Europe the period 1350–1650 was marked by violence and more violence as peasants fought feudal nobles, townspeople fought feudal nobles, kings fought Emperor and Pope, Protestants fought Catholics, and one nationality fought another. The fighting came to a climax in the Thirty Years War (1618–1648). The Treaty of Westphalia at the end of that war is usually taken to mark the beginning of the European state system which still exists on that continent. National boundaries were established for Spain, France, England, the Netherlands, Denmark, Sweden, Switzerland, Poland, Austria, Hungary, and Russia while the areas which now make up Germany and Italy consisted of many smaller states. At the same time competition among these nations began to escalate with regard to control of territory in the Americas, Asia, and the coasts of Africa. From this point on, the history of these areas, which has not been discussed although it generally reveals the same kind of struggles for power found in Western history,[10] becomes woven into the history of the competition and warfare of the European state system.

The late seventeenth and early eighteenth centuries saw the British successfully checking the expansion of Spanish and French power. The Seven Years' War (called the French and Indian War in America) was ended by two treaties. The Treaty of Paris (1763) gave the British control of all of Canada, all of what is now the U.S. east of the Mississippi, and the east coast of India; the Treaty of Hubertusberg (1763) recognized Prussia as a European power.

The last quarter of the eighteenth century saw two very important revolutions. The United States of America came into existence as British colonists in North America, with help from the French, the Dutch, and the Spanish, successfully revolted against British rule. The second revolution took place in France in 1789 when the middle classes rebelled against the king and the landed aristocracy.

The victorious French revolutionaries became the enemy of the nobility in all the rest of Europe. Napoleon Bonaparte extended French rule over much of the European continent, but eventually the combined forces of Russia, Sweden, Prussia, Austria, and England, aided by nationalistic uprisings against the French in Spain and Austria, put an end to the Napoleonic effort. The Congress of Vienna (1814–1815) redrew the map of Europe with territorial gains for the victors. In America, the Louisiana Purchase (1803) greatly expanded the size of the U.S. while simultaneously many Latin American countries were winning independence from European control. In Europe nationalism became an important factor in the unification of Italy and Germany.

The late nineteenth and early twentieth centuries found the European powers, led by Britain and France, extending their control over Africa and Asia. Only Japan, which had adopted Western industrialism as the result of American prodding, was immune from conquest. In fact Japan embarked on expanding its own sphere of influence and ousted Russia from Manchuria and the Liaotung Peninsula in the Russo-Japanese War (1904–1905). For the most part, however, the big powers negotiated their conflicts with each other while using military power to subdue nonindustrialized societies. While the European powers focused their efforts on Africa and Asia, the United States expanded its territory at the expense of the native American Indians, Mexicans and other Latin Americans, and a declining Spain.

Antagonisms developed in the early twentieth century as the race for colonies and for military superiority became more intense. The Italians, irked by France's takeover of Tunis, joined Germany and Austria-Hungary in the Triple Alliance. The French, still smarting from defeat in the Franco-Prussian War (1870–71), formed an alliance with Russia. The British, concerned about the growing power of Germany, entered into agreements with Japan and then with France and Russia. Competition for influence in the Balkans between Austria-Hungary and Russia provided the fuel for war, and the assassination of the heir to the throne in Austria-Hungary by Serbian terrorists provided the spark that started World War I in 1914. Austria-Hungary, assured of assistance from Germany against Russia if needed, attacked Serbia. The German strategy for fighting an anticipated two-front war against Russia and France (the von Schlieffen plan) called for focusing the main military effort at first against France on the supposition that it would take the Russians some time to mobilize their forces. When the Russians began to mobilize to help the Serbs against Austria-Hungary, the Germans demanded that they stop, but the Russians refused. The Germans then declared war on Russia and its ally France. When the Germans attacked France through neutral Belgium (another part of the von Schlieffen plan), Britain joined the battle against the Germans. As the war continued Turkey and Bulgaria joined Germany and Austria-Hungary while Italy (despite its previous alliance), Romania, Japan, the United States, and some smaller nations joined France and Britain. The Russians withdrew from the war in December of 1917 after the Bolshevik Revolution, yielding a great deal of territory to the Germans and allowing the Germans to throw all of their forces into the fight on the western front. Nevertheless the battle lines across France changed little as large numbers of troops from both sides lost their lives in futile attacks on the entrenched opposing forces. Finally, fresh American soldiers arrived and enabled the Allies to drive the Germans back and bring an end to the war in November 1918.

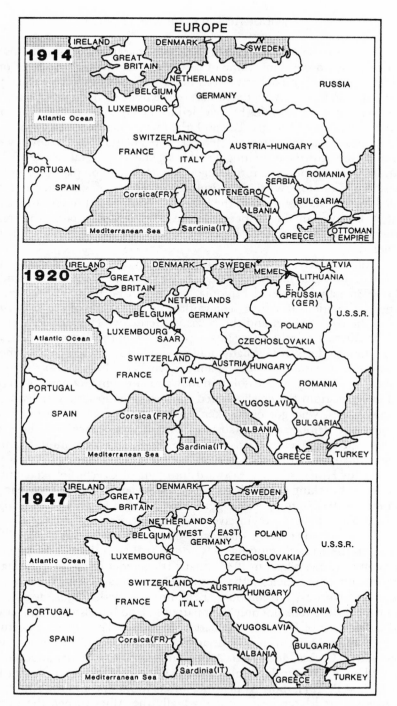

Political boundaries of Europe before WWI, between the wars, and after WWII.

The Treaty of Versailles (1919) provided that Germany should lose all of its overseas possessions, some of its territory in Europe, and most of its military power. Germany was forced to pay reparations to the victors, particularly to France, on whose soil most of the fighting had taken place. The territory which the Russians had yielded to the Germans became the independent nations of Estonia, Latvia, Lithuania (which very briefly included the later autonomous area of Memel), and Poland. Czechoslovakia was created, and Austria and Hungary were separated. Several smaller Balkan nations were combined to form Yugoslavia. (See map on page 31.) At U.S. President Woodrow Wilson's insistence the Treaty of Versailles also provided for the establishment of the League of Nations to preserve the peace, but Wilson was unable to persuade the U.S. Senate to ratify the treaty. Consequently the U.S. never became a member of the organization he had fathered.

Unfortunately, the peace was not preserved, for power politics went on as usual. In 1931, Japan took Manchuria by force from China, and in 1935-1936 Italy conquered Ethiopia, which had been one of the few independent nations in Africa. The worldwide depression of the early 1930s led to the rise of Hitler and the Nazis in Germany. The failure of France and Britain to act decisively against Japan, Italy, or the first militaristic and expansionist efforts of Germany only resulted in further aggressive moves by the fascist nations. In the Spanish Civil War (1936–1939) the fascist Franco, with help from Mussolini in Italy and Hitler in Germany, won control of Spain from the newly elected combined democratic-socialist-Communist forces, who got only token support from France and the Soviet Union. The democratic capitalists in Britain and France and the Communists in Russia each tried to direct Hitler's growing military might against the other. At Munich in 1938 the British and French gave their permission for Hitler to move eastward into part of Czechoslovakia, but he responded by taking the whole country. The Soviets made their move in the summer of 1939, signing a nonaggression pact with Hitler and agreeing to divide Poland between themselves and the Germans.

The German invasion of Poland in September of 1939, usually regarded as the actual beginning of World War II even though the Japanese invasion of China began in 1937, finally triggered a response from France and Britain. Nevertheless, the fast-moving German forces quickly took Denmark, Norway, Luxembourg, Belgium, the Netherlands, and France while the Soviets took not only their part of Poland but also Estonia, Latvia, Lithuania, part of Finland, and part of Romania. The Japanese captured French Indo-China. The Germans continued their expansion into Yugoslavia, Greece, and North Africa. In June of 1941 Hitler attacked the Soviet Union while in December of that same year the Japanese attacked the U.S. at Pearl Harbor. At first the Soviets in Europe and the Americans in Asia suffered large losses, but gradually the Allies turned the tide of battle. Soviet forces began pushing the Germans back on the eastern front while American and British forces crossed the English Channel into France in June 1944. Germany surrendered in May of 1945, and Japan surrendered in August of that same year after the Americans had dropped newly developed atomic bombs on Hiroshima and Nagasaki.

U.S. President Franklin Roosevelt, aware of the U.S. Senate's rejection of Wilson's League of Nations after World War I, led the effort to bring the United Nations into existence even while World War II was being fought. The nations which had fought together to defeat the fascists were to unite to preserve the peace. Within three years after the war's end, however, the Cold War broke out between the Soviet Union and the Western powers. The U.S. had launched a giant relief program, the Marshall Plan, to help Europe recover from the war and prevent the people there from turning to Communism. The U.S.S.R. had kept its military forces in eastern Europe in order to establish a Communist buffer zone. Quarrels developed over the terms of peace, especially in eastern Europe. Stalin did not permit the free elections to which Americans thought he had agreed. In 1948 the Communists staged a coup d'état in Czechoslovakia and then tried to keep the Western powers from moving into or out of West Berlin. The Western powers responded by forming a new military alliance, the North Atlantic Treaty Organization (NATO). When West Germany was allowed to join NATO in 1955, the Communists countered by forming an alliance of the Communist-controlled eastern European countries called the Warsaw Pact.

In China the Nationalists and the Communists continued their civil war which had begun even before the Japanese attack of 1937. The Communist forces under Mao Zedong drove the Nationalist forces from mainland China to the island of Taiwan in 1949. Communist forces in the northern part of divided Korea attacked the non–Communists in the southern part in 1950. South Koreans resisted this attack with the help of American troops and eventually that of many other nations after the United Nations declared the North Koreans guilty of aggression and in violation of the U.N. Charter. As the predominantly South Korean and American U.N. forces pushed northward toward the border of China, Chinese "volunteers" entered the war and drove them back. A truce finally set the border between North and South Korea close to where it had been when the war first broke out.

A prime feature of the period after World War II was the gaining of independence by many former colonies of western European nations. In some cases independence came only after a military struggle against the old colonial power. In Algeria, Indonesia, and Angola the former French, Dutch, and Portuguese rulers were driven out after long battles. The Communist-led Vietnamese drove the French out in 1954 and then the American supporters of non–Communist Vietnamese in 1973. In other cases colonies became independent nations with little or no military action against the former colonial power. In 1946 the U.S. granted the Philippines the independence they had been promised 45 years earlier during the

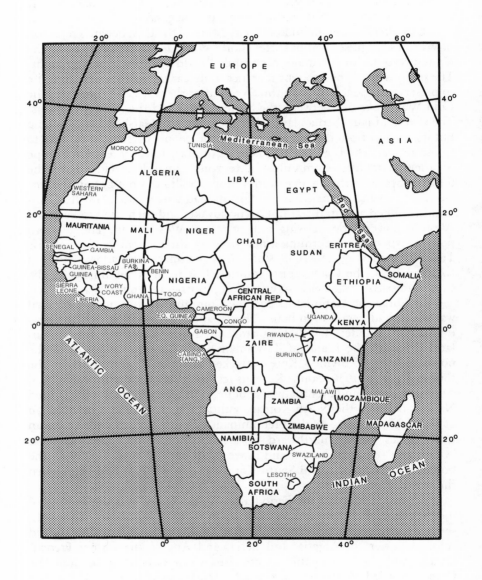

Spanish-American War. In India-Pakistan the British were nudged into leaving, both by sabotage and the nonviolent resistance effort led by Gandhi; but enmity between Hindus and Muslims led to fighting that continued even after Muslim Pakistan was separated from Hindu India.

Another feature of the post–World War II period has been wars within and between newly created or newly independent nations.[11] The creation of the nation-state of Israel in 1947-1948 despite opposition from the Arabs in that region has led to wars in 1948, 1956, 1967, 1973, and 1982. This situation has produced continuing internal conflict in Lebanon among various Christian and Muslim factions as well as intervention by Syria and Israel. In Africa besides the wars for independence there have been violent struggles for internal control in Rwanda, Zaire, Zambia, Algeria, Sudan, Nigeria, Uganda, Burundi, Zimbabwe, Ghana, Chad, Angola, Mozambique, Ethiopia, Morocco, Liberia, and Somalia — with Eritrea winning its independence from Ethiopia in 1993 after 19 years of fighting. In 1971 East Pakistan revolted and with assistance from India became the new country of Bangladesh. In India ethnic and political strife has been occurring off and on since 1983, and in Sri Lanka there has been ethnic violence between Tamils and Sinhalese since 1984. On the Mediterranean island nation of Cyprus fighting began between the Greek and Turkish inhabitants shortly after independence in 1960, and in 1974 there was an invasion from Turkey in support of the Turkish Cypriots. In Indonesia and the Philippines there has been recurring civil strife. In Vietnam, after French forces left in 1954 and American forces in 1973, the civil war between the north and south Vietnamese ended in 1975 with a Communist victory. In Cambodia violent internal fighting starting in 1975 was followed by a Vietnamese invasion in 1978. A year later China, in protest against the invasion of Cambodia, conducted a short campaign against Vietnam, which was renewed briefly in 1987. Ethnic fighting has also broken out in the newly independent republics of the former Soviet Union (especially between Azeris and Armenians) and the former Yugoslavia (especially between Serbs, Croats, and Muslim Bosnians).

But warring has not been restricted to the newly independent countries. Latin America has witnessed violent internal struggles in Bolivia, Argentina, Colombia, Cuba, the Dominican Republic, Guatemala, Chile, Nicaragua, El Salvador, Jamaica, Peru, and Haiti. El Salvador and Honduras fought each other in the "Soccer War" in 1969. In 1982 Argentina and Britain fought over control of the Falkland Islands–Malvinas in the South Atlantic. United States military forces invaded Grenada in 1983 and Panama in 1989. Internal struggle in Afghanistan starting in 1978 led to intervention by the Soviet Union from 1979 to 1989. In Iran in 1978 the Ayatollah Khomeini led a revolution ousting the Shah, and two years later Iraq attacked Iran in a war that lasted until 1988.

Despite all these "local wars" in the less developed countries, the main

Opposite: *Africa*

struggle in the world from 1947 until 1989 was the Cold War between the U.S. and the Soviet Union. These two super-powers were engaged in an intense arms race which included nuclear arsenals with tens of thousands of nuclear warheads. Their military power greatly exceeded that of all other countries, and they were frequently involved behind the scenes on opposite sides in the internal conflicts just listed above. They were unquestionably engaged in a struggle for world domination. The arena of the struggle for power between states had evolved from city-states contending for control of a river valley in 2500 B.C., to nation-states contending for control of a continent in the nineteenth century, to superpowers armed with nuclear weapons contending for control of the whole world during the last part of the twentieth century.

For the moment the threat of a major war possibly resulting in a nuclear holocaust seems to have receded. During the two years from 1989 to 1991 the world witnessed a transformation similar to what typically happens after a war. Fortunately, no nuclear war was necessary to determine the outcome of the Cold War. The Soviet Union, after Mikhail Gorbachev became its leader in 1985, decided to withdraw from the contest. The most dramatic symbol of the end of this "war" occurred in November 1989 with the tearing down of the Berlin Wall which had separated Communist East Berlin from non–Communist West Berlin. By the end of 1991 the Soviet Union had split into its fifteen constituent republics with the biggest one, the Russian Republic, taking the place of the Soviet Union in international bodies such as the United Nations.

The end of the Cold War has produced a very fluid situation in international affairs. It is not clear exactly what kind of "world system" will result, though at the moment it seems that it will be a world with the U.S. very much in charge but sharing global decisionmaking with the other industrialized democracies in western Europe, Japan, and Canada. The United Nations apparently will be used as an instrument for policy but will be kept financially weak and dependent upon these rich nation-states. If past history is an indication of what will happen in the future, we can expect that eventually some other country (China?) or group of countries (a united Europe or a Western Pacific alliance with Japan as leader?) will challenge the U.S. militarily for world leadership. But it is also possible that the long war-filled period of a "civilized" world based ultimately on agriculture and state sovereignty and coercion by physical force is coming to an end and that we are entering a new "post-civilized" world based on industrialization and technology, a system of non-coercive global governance, and the peaceful exchange of goods and services in order to get what we want.[12] It is exciting to be alive during this period of human history which could conceivably see the end of the war problem for human society. The opportunity exists. Will we take advantage of it?

The Changing Nature of War

As we have noted, war is as old as civilization. Yet wars fought in the twentieth century are very different from wars fought four or five thousand years ago. For example, the scope of the world wars of the twentieth century has been much wider than that of the purely regional wars of earlier periods. Even more evident is the difference in the weapons with which wars are fought. The story of the evolution of war is essentially the story of the evolution of weapons.[13]

During the period from 5000 B.C. through the fourteenth century A.D. there were only minor changes in the manner in which wars were fought. The chief weapons were swords, spears, and bows and arrows. The chief defensive strategy was to build a high wall around the city to be defended, while the chief offensive strategy was to prevent those inside the city walls from getting food or other supplies. Those attacking the walled city might also try various devices such as battering rams or catapulted stones for damaging the gates or the walls, while those inside would use devices such as arrows and hot tar or boiling water to keep the attackers away from the walls. Over a period of time methods were developed for protecting the fields outside the walls in order to preserve the food supply; each city equipped an army with shields, swords, and spears to try to maintain control of the land surrounding the city.

All the fighting was done on foot at first, but after about 1000 B.C. horses gradually came into use. Armor was worn both by the foot soldiers and those mounted on horseback. Various special skills were developed — javelin throwing, throwing stones with a sling, shooting a bow while mounted on horseback, fighting from a horse-drawn chariot, and operating a catapult to throw large stones. Field fortifications (walls and trenches) were built. Ships transported troops and supplies. Eventually other ships were designed to ram the transport ships, either sinking or disabling them and leaving them at the mercy of the attackers. In the ninth and tenth centuries the Vikings capitalized on using ships as vehicles for surprise raids on settlements along rivers and sea coasts. Inventions before the fourteenth century such as saddles and stirrups for those on horseback, the crossbow, and the long bow expanded the size of the battlefield but did little to change the overall conduct of war.

Major changes in the way war was fought took place over a 400-year period starting about 1350 when gunpowder was introduced to Europe from China. As a result catapults were replaced by cannons while bows and arrows were replaced by guns and bullets. The first guns were not nearly as effective as bows, but the cannons soon proved to be superior to catapults as devices for bombardment. A crucial victory for gunpowder occurred in 1453 when the Turks used cannons to break openings in the walls of Constantinople, proving to all that a stone wall no longer provided a secure defense against attack. Smaller firearms using gunpowder were gradually being improved and became more widely used during the sixteenth and early seventeenth centuries. Nevertheless the musketeers were still accompanied by pikemen armed with spears who could protect them in close combat. Not until bayonets were mounted on muskets in the late seventeenth century did the pikemen become obsolete.

From the middle of the seventeenth century to the last part of the eighteenth century, war almost took on the character of a game between opposing commanders. The soldiers were trained professionals who were too valuable to lose in battles where rows of men armed with muskets fired volleys at each other from a distance of 50 paces. The spirit of the Enlightenment also suggested that the conduct of war should be rational. Consequently armies tried to maneuver for advantageous positions, and the outmaneuvered commander of a unit might simply surrender before much fighting took place. The majority of the population had little to gain or lose as the result of war games being played between the armies of one king and those of another.

A new age in warfare was ushered in by the American Revolutionary War (1775–1781), the French Revolution (1789–1799), and the Napoleonic Wars (1803–1815). The change came partly as the result of the widespread use of the rifle and partly as the result of the rebirth of the old Greek idea of a state controlled by the citizens rather than a king. The rifle, first used to shoot game, had a longer range than a musket and was much more accurate. It was aimed at a very specific target, not simply pointed in the general direction of the enemy. The participants in these revolutionary wars were different too. They were citizens-become-soldiers who were motivated by loyalty to the national community and government rather than to a king. In the American Revolution colonial legislatures called on citizens to join in the battle for independence from Britain and King George III. In the French Revolution nonprofessionals took up arms against the professional soldiers paid by the king. In the Napoleonic Wars citizen-soldiers fought for the glory of France, and the rest of the citizenry identified with the successes and defeats of that national army.

Since 1815 the changing conduct of war has been largely a case of more of the same; that is, on the one hand new and more destructive weapons are made available by new technology, and on the other participation in war expands both actually and psychologically to greater proportions of the population. The evolution of weaponry includes not only improvement in rifles and artillery but also the development of land mines, wire entanglements, grenades, torpedoes, machine guns, tanks, submarines, and bombs dropped from airplanes. Inventions originally intended for civilian uses — telegraph, railroads, steam-powered ships, trucks, radio, airplanes, helicopters — have been adapted to military uses. Military needs dictated other inventions — tanks and other armored vehicles, poison gas, antiaircraft guns, aircraft carriers, radar, jet-propelled missiles, rocket-powered missiles, nuclear bombs, thermonuclear (hydrogen) bombs, nuclear-powered submarines, artificial satellites for information gathering and navigational assistance, and so on.

War and preparation for war have come to occupy more and more people in more ways, including the building of weapons, the production of food and clothing and medical supplies, the invention of new weapons, and the development of new technologies that may have military uses. The education of young people so they will be able to invent new weapons and otherwise contribute to the war effort is also a part of the national defense program, not only during war but also during peacetime. The distinction between military personnel who are essential to the war effort and civilian personnel who have nothing to do with war, a distinction that was so obvious in the middle of the eighteenth century, no longer seems applicable.

When wars occur, each nation involved commits a great deal of its resources to the fight; even during peacetime the top priority of most national governments is to provide national security. War, which began as localized struggles using primitive weapons and strategies and involving only a small proportion of the population, has now become a matter of worldwide conflict using sophisticated weapons and strategies and potentially involving the whole population.

Overall Trends in Warfare

As one reviews the history of war and the changes which have taken place in the way war is waged, certain questions naturally come to mind. Are wars occurring more frequently or less frequently? Are wars becoming more destructive than they once were? Do more people get killed in wars? Are there any long-term trends of any kind related to the scope, intensity, and general nature of war?

Reliable answers to such questions require a great deal of historical research. Before one can check for trends, details must be known about wars of the past. Ideally one should be able to make a list of all wars ever fought, the nations that were involved, how long each war lasted, how many military personnel were committed to battle, how many casualties were suffered by each side, and so on. To determine the proportion of people involved in a war and the proportion killed, one would need to know the total population both of the nations involved in that war and that of the whole world at that time. There are problems of selection, too. Should civil wars, or only interstate wars, be included? How should one determine whether to include a conflict as a war? On the basis of the number of people committed to battle? On the basis of the number of casualties? On the basis of the size of the states involved? On the basis of whether the participants perceived themselves as engaged in a war? Since different investigators answer these questions in different ways, it is difficult to directly compare one study with another.

Several attempts have been made to list various wars and to estimate the number of persons engaged in battles, the number killed, and so on.[14] These studies provide the raw data from which generalizations must be drawn if they are to have any kind of a factual basis, but a review reveals that much of the data consists more of "guesstimates" than estimates.[15] Furthermore, the most careful of these studies, that done by Melvin Small and J. David Singer, covers a period of only 165 years.[16] Can we trust generalizations about trends based on such a short period of time? That period is so short that it may suggest trends that do not exist over a longer period of time, or it may fail to reveal trends that do exist over a longer period.

In his monumental work *A Study of War,* Quincy Wright compiled data about wars fought from 1480 to 1940. On the basis of this study he concluded that a number of trends can be observed with regard to war.[17]

> It is clear that during the modern period there has been a trend toward an increase in the absolute and relative size of armies whether one considers the peace [time] army, the number mobilized for war, the number of combatants engaged in battle, or the number of military and civil populations devoting themselves to war work.
>
> ... Another general trend has been toward a decrease in the length of wars and in the proportion of war years to peace years.[18]
>
> ... A third trend has been toward an increase in the length of battles, in the number of battles in a war year, and also in the total number of battles during a century.... The number of battles in a war has also tended to increase.[19]
>
> ... A fourth trend has been toward an increase in the number of belligerents in a war, in the rapidity with which a war spreads, and in the area covered by a war.[20]
>
> ... A fifth trend has been toward an increased human and economic cost of war, both absolutely and relative to the population.... [But] the proportion of persons engaged in a battle who are killed has probably tended to decline [from 30–50 percent in the Middle Ages to only 2 percent in the twentieth century]....
>
> The proportion of the population engaged in the armies, however, has tended to become larger, and the number of battles has tended to increase. As a result, the proportion of the population dying as a direct consequence of battle has tended to increase.[21]

Many of these trends cited by Wright are what one would expect as a result of technological advances, especially those made from the nineteenth century on. Changes in communication and transportation made larger armies feasible. These same factors, along with more effective weapons of destruction, suggest that war would break out less frequently, that it would be over more quickly once begun, and that the pace of fighting would speed up. Similarly, a given war would cover a wider area and include more nations, and the cost of war would become greater. The decline in the proportion of combatants who die is readily attributable to advancement in medicine plus the fact that more and more of the armed forces (considered "combatants" by Wright) are not actually engaged in front-line fighting.

Conclusions which are a bit more surprising are drawn by Small and

Singer in their very careful study of international war from 1816 to 1980.

> Is war on the increase, as many scholars as well as laymen of our generation have been inclined to believe? The answer would seem to be a very unambiguous negative. Whether we look at the number of wars, their severity [number of battle deaths for combatants], or their magnitude [number of nations involved multiplied by the number of months each was at war], there is no significant trend upward or downward over the past 165 years *[as long as we make allowance for the increasing population and the increasing number of nations that might get involved in war].*
> ... [T]he number of interstate wars per decade has risen no faster than the number of nations in the interstate system....[22]

It is important to note that these conclusions of Small and Singer are in relative, not absolute, terms and that they are limited to casualties suffered by members of the armed forces. Wars in the central international state system are becoming more bloody, but the number of battle deaths is not increasing much faster than the total population of the nations in the international system.[23] The number of battle deaths for military personnel went from 9,000,000 in World War I to 15,000,000 in World War II, but the total population of the nations in World War II was much greater.[24] The magnitude of wars is increasing, but no faster than the number of nations in the international state system. It should be noted, however, that in certain statistical treatments of the raw data Small and Singer themselves find a downward trend in the number of wars in a given period of time (both absolutely and relatively) and an upward trend in the magnitude and severity of wars (both absolutely and relatively).[25] These conclusions agree with those of Wright cited earlier. Nevertheless, the general conclusion reached by Small and Singer is that with regard to international war there is *no trend* during the last 165 years toward more or less war, larger or smaller wars, and higher or lower casualties among combatants so long as we take account of the growing number of nations and the increase in human population. They draw a similar conclusion about civil war.[26]

Making use of the data gathered by Small and Singer as well as that of others, Francis Beer arrives at a conclusion which agrees with the trends noted by Wright.

> ...[I]f there has been an overall historical trend, it has probably been toward the concentration and aggravation of war. Such a trend implies a decline in the incidence of wars, but an increase in casualties — both in absolute terms and relative to population.[27]

Thus according to Beer's analysis of the data, which agrees with the judgments of others, in more recent times there have been fewer wars with longer intervals of peace between them than in earlier times. When war does occur, however, it is bloodier both with regard to the actual number of persons killed and the percentage of the population suffering death from war. If these trends continue in the future, "long interwar periods may be way stations for subsequent wars which may inflict even greater casualties than the ones which preceded them."[28]

Others studying trends in warfare have also arrived at conclusions which agree with those of Wright and Beer. Jack Levy, who limited his research to wars among the big powers but covered the longer time period 1495–1975, concludes that

> over the past five centuries, wars between the Great Powers have become less frequent but more serious in terms of their extent, severity, intensity, concentration, and (to a certain degree) magnitude.[29]

William Eckhardt argues, on the basis of figures compiled by Bouthoul and Carrère for wars from 1740 to 1974 as well as those of Small and Singer, that even after mathematically taking account of increasing population and the great number of independent nations in recent years, deaths from warfare have been two to three times greater in the twentieth century than during the nineteenth century.[30]

Since the experts do not agree among themselves, even when relying on the same data, and since the data are somewhat limited and in some cases not very reliable, we can only conclude that whether the long-term trends in warfare suggested by Wright do in fact exist is a question which requires still more investigation. The differences also suggest that the 165-year period studied by Small and Singer may be too short to reveal trends that might show up over a longer period.

The Present Urgency of the War Problem

Is the solution of the war problem of any particular urgency at the present time? Has the availability of weapons of mass destruction created a stalemate in which no nation will dare to attack another? Is there any likelihood that scientists will develop new nonnuclear weapons which will make even "conventional" wars much more devastating than they have been in the past? Is there any difficulty for society with regard to the cost of preparing for future wars?

In dealing with the urgency of solving the war problem we need to recall the various aspects of the war problem outlined in the first chapter. The first aspect is the huge outlay of money and effort which presently goes into getting ready for war. As we noted previously, the current worldwide expenditure for military purposes is over $900 billion a year.[31] The expenses are for military personnel, for acquiring weapons, and for designing new weapons. As the weapons of war become ever more sophisticated technologically, it can be expected that military personnel will require more training to learn how to use these weapons and to maintain them in readiness for use. It may be necessary to raise pay levels in order to get enough soldiers with the required capability as well as to induce them to stay in the military in order to reduce training costs. The purchase price of more sophisticated weapons can be expected to be much higher.[32] But the most important financial factor will be the cost of developing ever more sophisticated weapons. The need to keep technologically ahead of potential enemies generates a virtually open-ended demand for more money for new weapons research and development. Even if actual war never comes, if the war problem is not solved the cost of getting ready for war is bound to be an increasing burden. The huge military budgets of the U.S. and the Soviet Union in the tense periods of the Cold War provide a glimpse of what may lie ahead.

We can also look at this issue of how much it costs to prepare for war in terms of the percentage of the Gross Domestic Product (GDP) which is devoted to military spending by these countries which are faced with a possibility of war but which are not actually engaged in war. Here are figures for 1990 or 1991 for some of them:

Saudi Arabia	33.8% of GDP	Yemen	13.1% of GDP
Kuwait	33.0% of GDP	Syria	13.0% of GDP
North Korea	26.7% of GDP	Oman	12.3% of GDP
Iraq	21.1% of GDP	Qatar	12.2% of GDP
United Arab Emirates	14.6% of GDP	USSR	11.1% of GDP
Jordan	14.1% of GDP	Mongolia	11.1% of GDP[33]

The enormous rate of expenditure for "defense" demonstrates the high cost of the war problem even when war itself is being avoided.

The second aspect of the war problem is the danger of nuclear war and its possible disastrous consequences. The destructiveness of nuclear weapons makes it obvious that such a war would be vastly more devastating than anything humankind has previously experienced. One U.S. nuclear-powered submarine carries more destructive power than was unleashed by both sides during all of World War II.[34] The number of nuclear weapons is declining; but even if the goals set by the June 1992 agreement between Bush and Yeltsin are reached by the year 2000, the U.S. and Russia would still together have over 6,000 nuclear warheads on strategic weapons, that is, not counting the nuclear warheads on their tactical weapons.[35] Besides these, Britain, France, China, and probably Israel also have nuclear warheads. So far, none of these countries have made any commitments to reduce the number of nuclear warheads they have. Furthermore, other countries such as Pakistan, North Korea, and Iraq have been trying very hard to develop nuclear weapons and missiles to deliver them in order to counter the nuclear weapons and missiles possessed by their potential enemies. With the U.S. and the former Soviet Union dismantling so many nuclear warheads, a substantial amount of the crucial enriched uranium and plutonium needed to build nuclear weapons will be taken out of existing weapons, and some of it could conceivably end up in the wrong hands. There is also the danger that unemployed Soviet nuclear scientists might sell their knowledge and skills to the highest bidder. It seems likely that several other countries will have nuclear weapons by the year 2000. If protecting one's national interests in the international arena means having more military power than anyone else, how can we suppose that countries which do not yet have nuclear weapons won't try to get them or some other new and even deadlier weapons? Unless the way the world system works is changed, we can expect that there will eventually be a new nuclear arms race, possibly between the U.S. and China.

If nuclear weapons are ever used in very large numbers, even the nations not directly attacked would be adversely affected by the radiation, the atmospheric dust and smoke from nuclear explosions and the resulting fires, and the depletion of the ozone layer. In the past the increasing destructiveness of weapons was much more gradual than is the case with nuclear weapons. The introduction of nuclear weapons and intercontinental ballistic missiles represents a shift in destructiveness and the range at which it can be employed unlike any change in earlier history. It is a vastly greater break from the past than that which occurred when gunpowder was introduced or when airplanes were put to military uses. We are faced with "a qualitatively new situation in relation to war—the possibility and probability of annihilating the human race and all other forms of life on the planet earth."[36]

The notion that big powers possessing substantial numbers of nuclear weapons might get involved in a war but not use their nuclear weapons overlooks the logic of war and the tremendous advantage which comes from using nuclear weapons first rather than second. The aim of war is to use military power to win, to impose one's will on the other side. In such a situation if either side were facing defeat, it would use nuclear weapons rather than surrender. At the same time the side which was winning the war would want to use its nuclear weapons before sustaining such an attack from a desperate opponent. The side facing defeat would know that the prevailing side would feel that way, so it would be led to use its nuclear weapons before the other side expected it. But the same logic would also lead the prevailing side to want to use its nuclear weapons before the losing side tried to launch an unexpected attack. Following this logic through to its end, each side would want to use its nuclear weapons as soon as the situation had deteriorated to one in which the conflict was to be resolved by force. Those who argue for nuclear surgical strikes in a limited nuclear war assume a detachment on the part of the leaders of both sides which, if it existed, would not allow any kind of war to develop. It seems that the only alternative to a nuclear disaster is to prevent *any* war between major nuclear powers from breaking out in the first place.

Our good fortune in making it through the Cuban missile crisis plus the other high points of tension in the Cold War may engender a false sense of security. If there has already been one arms race with each side recklessly building over 20,000 nuclear warheads, a similar thing could happen again. Having played Russian roulette and been lucky enough to have found an empty chamber, we cannot afford to blithely suppose that things would turn out so well again. It would be best to find a way of avoiding that dangerous game.

The third aspect of the war problem is the possibility of conventional war between nonnuclear powers. There is always the danger that the nuclear big powers would get dragged into such a war just as big powers got dragged into World War I as the result of disputes between smaller nations. Also it must be remembered that conventional weapons themselves are becoming more and more destructive. Missiles can be used to carry conventional and chemical warheads long distances as well as nuclear warheads, and the increasing precision of smart bombs and precision-guided missiles means that it is not necessary to have a nuclear explosion to destroy the target. It has been noted that new devices such as cluster bombs and fuel air explosives mean that "both in lethality and in area covered, so-called conventional weapons today approach small nuclear weapons in destructive power."[37] The development of technology is such that more and more countries will obtain these very destructive nonnuclear weapons and will be ready to use them in war if that is what it takes to win. It should be obvious that these "little" conventional wars are small only by comparison with what might be expected in a war using nuclear weapons.

The fourth aspect of the war problem is the occurrence and the threat of the occurrence of civil wars. Indeed, these are the most prevalent kinds of war at the present time. The ready availability of weapons with substantial firepower plus the development of techniques of guerrilla warfare plus the existence of devices for duplicating printed materials and tape cassettes and videocassettes at low cost has given those dissatisfied with a government and its policies a much greater opportunity to promote revolt. Another important factor relevant to civil war is the widespread belief that the government has the responsibility to promote the general welfare of the society. If important problems go unsolved, the government is blamed— even if the matter is outside of its power. Also, the upper classes no longer have a monopoly on knowing how to use weapons or how to read, write, think, and speak out about social issues. Since the poor are now more aware of what will promote their interest and since those interests are usually not the same as the interests of those who hold political power, civil war between these groups with opposing interests is much more likely than in the past.

There is still another way in which the war problem is more urgent today than in the past, at least from the perspective of the ordinary citizen. There was a time, as late as the eighteenth century, when anyone who didn't want to participate in a war could simply ignore it. Armies employed by kings fought against each other and did little to disturb ordinary citizens, who for the most part were completely indifferent concerning whether they were to be subjects of King A or King B. But, as we have noted, that is no longer the case. Now even civilian jobs have military significance, and during a war any citizen is likely to be the subject of an enemy attack. In fact, in modern warfare the number of civilians getting killed typically exceeds the number of military personnel getting killed.[38] World War II meant a gigantic upheaval in the lives of millions of people, but there were some places (part of Latin America and Africa) where the war made little difference, at least directly, to the lives of the people there. If there is a World War III with nuclear weapons, however, no one will escape. Even people in nations which have no involvement in the war will be affected by radioactive fallout, by large amounts of dust and smoke in the atmosphere, and by the alteration of the ozone layer which protects them from excessive amounts of ultraviolet radiation from the sun.

Smaller wars now have a wider impact, too. Americans learned in 1973 that war in the Middle East made a great deal of difference in the availability and price of oil. The same was true with regard to the civil war in Iran in 1978-79 when the price of gasoline again rapidly increased. Civil wars in Central America may have an impact on the prices Americans pay for coffee or fresh fruits and vegetables. On the other hand, such wars may eventually open up new opportunities for people in some less developed countries — education, medical care, and better housing.

The problem of war is more urgent now than in the past also because of the higher cost of war preparations which must be borne by the general public. For example, in the United States, even though the Cold War is over, military expenditures average over $75 per month per person ($300 per month for a family of four),[39] and that does not even count the huge amount needed to pay off the national debt, a large proportion of which is due to past military spending. This cost of preparing for war even in peacetime means less goods for everyone both directly and in terms of less productivity in the long run. In less developed countries as well as more advanced ones, military spending means less much-needed government money for schools, medical care, and other social services.

Today no persons anywhere on earth can truthfully say that solving the war problem makes no difference to their own lives.

Part Two
Causes of War

IV. The Cause of War: Some General Considerations

It is not uncommon to think of war as a disease of society. This analogy has led to the expectation that war could be prevented if we learned more about what causes it. As a result of this pattern of thinking, a great deal has been written and said about the cause of war. In dealing with this issue it is worth pausing to consider exactly what is involved in saying that one thing is a cause of another. Then we need to look at the phenomenon of individual human aggressiveness and to consider what relationship it has, if any, to those violent conflicts we know as war.

Investigating the Cause of War

There are at least four senses in which the word cause can be used: a necessary condition, a sufficient condition, a necessary and sufficient condition, and a contributory factor.

A "cause" in the sense of a *necessary condition* means that the effect cannot occur if the "cause" is not present. If the necessary condition of something is known, one will know how to prevent that thing from happening. For example, the presence of oxygen is a necessary condition for the burning of materials such as wood and paper. It follows that one can put out a fire by using a gas such as carbon dioxide to prevent oxygen from getting to the fire.

A "cause" in the sense of a *sufficient condition* means that the effect must occur whenever the "cause" is present. If the sufficient condition of something is known, one will know how to make that thing occur. For example, the flow of electricity through a wire made of a metal such as aluminum or copper is a sufficient condition to produce heat. It follows that one can make heat (for a toaster or an electric blanket, for example) by having electricity flow through a metal wire.

A "cause" in the sense of a *necessary and sufficient* condition means that the effect cannot occur if the "cause" is not present *and* that whenever the "cause" is present the effect must occur. If the necessary and sufficient condition of something is known, one will know both how to prevent it and how to produce it. For example, the flow of electricity through the filament of an incandescent light bulb is the necessary and sufficient condition of the bulb giving off light. One can stop the bulb from glowing by cutting off the supply of electricity, and one can make it glow by letting electricity flow through the filament.

A "cause" in the sense of a *contributory factor* means that the effect is more likely to occur because of the presence of something, but the relationship is not a necessary one. The cause may be present and the effect not occur, or the cause may be absent and the effect occur anyway. If a contributory factor of something is known, one will be able to make it more probable or less probable but will not be able to guarantee any results. For example, smoking cigarettes seems to be a contributory factor to lung cancer. Some people smoke cigarettes and don't get lung cancer, and others don't smoke but still get lung cancer. Nevertheless, someone who smokes cigarettes is much more likely to get lung cancer than someone who doesn't.

How do these four different senses of "cause" apply to the problem of the cause of war? It seems that if our goal is to prevent all warfare, we will want to know some *necessary conditions* of war. We could then eliminate war by eliminating any one of these necessary conditions. The problem is to discover some necessary condition that we could and would want to eliminate. Consider, for example, that the existence of war as we have defined it requires the existence of groups of people. If we eliminated all people or somehow made it impossible for people to form groups, we would eliminate war. But the proposed cure is worse than the disease.

What about the notion that group conflict is a necessary condition of war? It seems that if we eliminated all conflicts between groups, we would then have eliminated war, that is, *violent* conflicts between groups. The difficulty with this proposal is that eliminating all conflict between groups is more difficult than simply eliminating the violent conflicts which constitute war. Those who think that the only way of eliminating war is to eliminate *all* conflicts of interest between groups set before themselves an even more difficult problem than the one with which they began.

What can be said about the view that since individual human aggressiveness is a necessary condition of war, the way to eliminate war is to eliminate all individual human aggressiveness? Once again, it seems that eliminating all human aggressiveness is a more difficult task than eliminating war. We need not achieve that difficult and in some ways undesirable goal in order to rid the world of war.

When we turn to "cause" in the sense of *sufficient condition,* it seems that what we want to know is not the cause of *war* but the cause of *peace.* Is there anything which when present always produces peace? Theodore Lentz observed that just as medical researchers sometimes focus their attention on unusually healthy groups of people to learn what produces such good health, so peace researchers should focus their attention on peaceful societies to learn what produces them.[1] Efforts in this direction, however, have not yet come up with many promising hypotheses; most of these peaceful societies are pre-industrial.[2] The search has just begun, however, and there are some nations such as Switzerland and Sweden which seem to have very good records in avoiding wars with other countries during the past 200 years. Investigators may also turn their attention to the cause of peace *within* countries. There are many nations which have been relatively free from internal strife for long periods of time, and it would be worthwhile to examine these societies and their institutions to try to discover the cause of peace within governed communities.

The concept of "cause" as necessary and sufficient condition does not involve any issues not already discussed in connection with the separate concepts of necessary condition and sufficient condition, only the concept of *contributory factor* remains to be considered with regard to the issue of what causes war. This sense of "contributory factor" is most likely to be relevant when the causes of very complex phenomena are being investigated, and there can be little doubt that war is a very complex phenomenon. Consequently, when people say that nationalism is a cause of war or that individuals who make profits from selling arms are a cause of war, they are most likely using the word "cause" in this sense of contributory factor rather than in the stronger sense of necessary condition. They can be viewed as claiming merely that if nationalism were reduced, or if the profits from selling arms were reduced, the likelihood of war would be reduced.

One must remember, however, that the mere correlation of one thing with another does not prove that one is the cause of the other, even in the sense of being a contributory factor. Suppose, for example, that one finds a positive correlation between military spending and the number of casualties suffered in war for many different nations over some period of time. Does this prove that high military spending *causes* a nation to get involved in war and suffer many casualties as a result?[3] Saying that a nation with high military spending is *more likely* to engage in war and suffer casualties is different from saying that high military spending *causes* (is a contributory factor to) involvement in war and casualties. There may be tension between two nations which leads them to increase their military spending. A war accompanied by high casualty counts may follow. But this war may have occurred even sooner and been even bloodier if one of the nations had refused to increase its military spending in the face of tension. The correlation between military spending and war may be the reflection of some common cause for both (increased tension) rather than a causal connection between military spending on the one hand and war on the other.

There is still another point related to the issue of causation which needs to be considered by those seeking to discover the cause of war. We have previously noted the analogy which can be drawn between war and disease. Suppose that some physicians were to address themselves to the cause of disease. They would probably begin by noting that there is no cause of disease in general but only particular causes of particular diseases. They would probably note that particular diseases can be put into classes on the basis of their causes — diseases caused by bacteria, diseases caused by viruses, diseases caused by genetic factors, diseases caused by toxic chemicals in the environment, and so on—and that any attempt to make statements about *the cause* of all these various kinds of diseases is bound to fail.

Couldn't a similar point be made with regard to the subject of the cause of war? Perhaps it is inappropriate to try to make judgments about *the cause* of war in general. Perhaps one should begin by examining the particular causes of particular wars and then make an effort to classify these cases on the basis of different kinds of causes. World War I and World War II may be superficially similar in that they are the only two world wars in history, but in terms of their causes they may in fact be very different. Trying to discover some cause of war which is operative in both World War I and World War II (as well as all other wars) may be an exercise in futility.

Once wars had been classified on the basis of their causes, the next step would be to identify symptoms that appear before the war actually breaks out. Only then would there be any chance of using one's knowledge about the various kinds of causes of war to try to prevent wars. Ideally one could learn what type of "medicine" to use when certain symptoms appear so that the threatened war could be avoided. Even if such knowledge became available, however, it is questionable whether a knowledgeable "physician" of society would be consulted by political leaders or that anyone would pay much attention to taking the "medicine" prescribed.

In any case, it is evident that we are far from being able to deal with the problem of war in this manner. Previous efforts to classify wars have usually focused on their size rather than their cause, a situation comparable to classifying diseases in accord with the number of persons who suffer from them. Even studies which start with the examination of the causes of particular wars often end by trying to make generalizations which apply to all wars[4] rather than trying to distinguish different types of wars on the basis of their causes.

Consequently, our situation is that we have little choice but to follow tradition and discuss the cause of war in general. Still, what has been said in this section is relevant to the examination of various theories concerning the cause of war to be undertaken in Chapters V and VI. These theories must be viewed as being about *contributory factors* which are purported to be operative in some wars but not necessarily in all wars. To return to the medical analogy, it might be asserted even on a very general level that bacteria are *a cause* of disease. This statement would not be taken to mean that every single disease is caused by bacteria but only that bacteria are a contributory factor in some diseases. It is regrettable that our discussion of the cause of war should be carried on at such a level of generality, but the present state of our knowledge permits no other approach.[5]

Individual Human Aggression

Aggression can be defined as "behavior whose goal is the injury of some person or object."[6] It is equivalent to violence and therefore seems to be relevant to war, which we have defined as "large-scale violent conflict between organized groups that are governments or that aim to establish governments." It is important, however, to make a distinction between the aggressive behavior of *individuals as individuals* and the aggressive behavior of *individuals as representatives of groups* which are at war with each other. The explanation of the former type of behavior may have very little to do with understanding the latter type of behavior. Giving causes for the aggressive behavior of individuals as individuals is not the same as giving causes for war.[7]

Even though there is some question of the extent to which understanding individual human aggression is helpful for understanding the war problem, it is appropriate to discuss the topic simply because many of those who have dealt with individual human aggression have thought that it is particularly relevant to warfare.[8] Furthermore, even if the relationship between individual aggression and warfare is not as direct as some writers have assumed, whatever relationship does exist can be better understood once the basis of individual aggression is understood.

Three main groups of theories have been advanced to account for individual aggressive behavior. The first group sees aggression as rooted in the biological nature of human beings. The second group sees aggressive behavior as flowing from feelings of hostility which are the result of frustration. The third group of theories sees aggression as the result of one's social conditioning. Let us consider these three types of theories at greater length.[9]

According to the biological-instinctual theories, humans, like other animals, are born with a propensity or drive to be aggressive. Such behavior may be triggered by specific kinds of situations, such as defense of one's territory, but it may also, according to Konrad Lorenz and others, just "explode"[10] with no external stimulation. Sigmund Freud wrote of an instinct of destruction.[11] Robert Ardrey links aggressive behavior with what he calls "the territorial imperative"[12] and writes of the "weapons instinct"[13] which he believes developed in the killer apes from which humans are descended. Another defender of this ethological approach is Desmond Morris.[14] A more recent, quite different version of the same general approach has been put forth by Peter Corning. He emphasizes the evolutionary adaptiveness of the various inborn aggressive responses to specific kinds of situations.[15]

Biological-instinctual theorists rely on studies of animals where aggressive behavior is exhibited primarily in three kinds of situations. First, there is aggressive behavior, primarily but not exclusively among males, for status in the "pecking order" within the group. Second, there is aggressive behavior among males of territorial species for individual territory within the group's territory. Third, there is collective aggressive behavior by males to defend the group and its territory from other groups. Defense of the young, primarily by females, may be mentioned as a fourth specific situation where aggressive behavior occurs, but among the theorists mentioned above only Corning seems interested in this particular manifestation of aggression.

One problem for the biological-instinctual theorists is to indicate in what sense the aggressive instinct is to be regarded as a "cause" of aggressive behavior. Do these theorists want to maintain that the aggressive instinct is a *sufficient condition* for aggressive behavior? In that case they will have a problem accounting for the lack of aggressive behavior in groups of people such as the Tasaday of the Philippines,[16] the Arapesh of New Guinea, the pygmies of Zaïre,[17] the Pueblo Indians of the American Southwest, and the Lepchas of Sikkim.[18] The notion that there is an inborn instinct which is sufficient by itself to produce aggressive behavior in response to certain stimuli is what arouses the antagonism of other theorists. Even those who support the instinctual theory admit that the aggressive instinct can be controlled by civilization.[19]

On the other hand, what is the situation if these biological-instinctual theorists want to maintain merely that the aggressive instinct is a *necessary condition* of aggressive behavior? In this case, why use a term such as "instinct"? It seems more appropriate under these circumstances to speak of a *capacity* for aggressive behavior which must exist as a basis for such behavior, but then it would follow that under some circumstances such a capacity might not be developed. In that case, these biological-instinctual theorists would not be espousing anything different from what is being maintained by social-learning theorists.

A third possibility is that the biological-instinctual theorists want to maintain that the aggressive instinct is only a *contributory factor* to aggressive behavior. Again we must ask: If that is the thesis, then why use the term "instinct," which seems to indicate that there is some inborn drive sufficient by itself to produce aggressive behavior regardless of environmental constraints? If that which is inborn only serves as a contributory factor, it might be more appropriate to speak of a *tendency* or *disposition* for people to engage in aggressive behavior under certain circumstances. The point of the biological-instinctual theory could then be stated in terms of some people having inherited a greater tendency to engage in certain types of aggressive behavior than others. The evidence suggests that there are significant differences in this regard between males and females in humans as well as other animals, but some of these studies also indicate that the tendency to be aggressive can be overcome by training.[20]

A second problem for the biological-instinctual theorists is related to the fact that two of the three aggression-arousing situations on which they focus deal with defense of territory. With territorial animals like some fish and birds, there are many examples of territorial fighting; but when it comes to humans, and even other primates, there is some doubt that they are territorial animals either individually or collectively. David Pilbeam maintains that "territoriality . . . is not a 'natural' feature of human group living; nor is it among most other primates."[21] It might be argued that humans sometimes seem to be very dedicated to defending their homeland or their neighborhood against external invaders, but on other occasions people simply migrate to other lands and other neighborhoods with no desire whatever to defend the territory they are leaving. It is also generally believed that at one time all human life was nomadic. These observations seem to cast doubt on the claim that in humans there is an instinctive drive to defend territory. Furthermore, the fact that American and British soldiers fighting on the mainland of Europe in World Wars I and II did not behave less heroically than French troops fighting for their own homeland suggests that the notion of group territoriality, even if such exists in humans, is not relevant to the problem of modern war.

Some biological-instinctual theorists, recognizing the problems just noted, fall back to postulating a nonterritorial herd instinct that leads people to empathize with members of their own group (the in-group) while being antagonistic to other groups (out-groups). That there is a tendency to such empathy and antagonism is obvious to any observer of human behavior, but that it is instinctive is again questionable. It seems, for example, that one must be taught how far one's in-group extends. It is certainly not instinctual for Americans to feel that residents of Detroit, Michigan, are part of our in-group while residents of Windsor, Ontario, are not. Furthermore, it seems that people must be taught which out-groups to hate, especially since the situation changes rapidly. Consider, for example, American attitudes toward Germany, Japan, and China over the last 60 years. This matter of in-groups and out-groups will be taken up again in the next chapter when we discuss nationalism.

A second group of theories about the cause of individual human aggression are those which view aggressive behavior as the result of hostility brought about by frustration. According to this approach, human beings are viewed as goal-oriented organisms. As long as they are making adequate headway in achieving their ends they do not become frustrated and aggressive, but when they are blocked from reaching their goals they are likely to become more hostile. John Dollard and his colleagues at Yale at one time claimed that frustration was both a *necessary condition* and a *sufficient condition* for aggressive behavior.[22] Later advocates of the theory such as Leonard Berkowitz have made the weaker claim that frustration is merely a contributory factor to aggression.[23]

If the frustration theorists are correct, aggressive behavior will be more readily managed than if either of the other approaches is correct. To produce aggressive behavior, it is much easier to frustrate the person in some way than to alter his genetic make-up or to change habits of responding that have been built up over a lifetime. Alternatively, to control someone's aggression, one would need only to discover what goals are being blocked and then assist the person in making headway toward these goals. If no help can be given with regard to those goals, one might still hope to reduce the aggressive behavior by providing some other substitute satisfactions.

The main doubt to be raised about the frustration-aggression approach concerns the extent to which frustration affects the amount of aggressive behavior displayed. The biological-instinctual theorists emphasize that certain situations will produce aggressive responses of a particular kind whether or not there appears to be any frustration. Those who adopt the social-learning approach note that people learn to accept different levels of frustration in different situations before displaying aggressive behavior. Also there is evidence to indicate that aggressive behavior is displayed in the absence of any frustration or hostility by persons who are merely obeying orders to be aggressive. Stanley Milgrim, whose classic experiment on aggression in the early 1960s showed that people will administer apparently very strong injurious electric shocks to others just because they were told to do so, concluded:

> Although aggressive tendencies are part and parcel of human nature, they have hardly anything to do with the behavior observed in the experiment. Nor do they have much to do with the destructive obedience of soldiers in war, of bombardiers killing thousands on a single mission, or enveloping a Vietnamese village in searing napalm. The typical soldier kills because he is told to kill and he regards it as his duty to obey orders. The act of shocking the victim does not stem from destructive urges but from the fact that subjects have become integrated into a social structure and are unable to get out of it.[24]

Experiments by Milgrim and others indicate that the intensity of aggression displayed by individuals in these experimental situations is totally independent of how frustrated they are.[25] In fact, in some experiments the amount of aggression displayed seems to depend much more on the strength of the attack which triggers the aggressive response and on what kind of response the aggressors expected from those witnessing their aggression.[26] Such evidence challenges the validity of the frustration-aggression theory. It may be that on some occasions frustration produces hostility which produces aggressive behavior, but that viewpoint neglects the fact that aggressive behavior may be brought about by many factors other than hostility.[27] People can behave aggressively without being angry, especially when taking orders from others as they do in the armed forces.

The third group of theories about individual human aggression emphasizes the role of social conditioning in aggressive behavior. According to this approach it is a mistake to assume that humankind has some fixed biological nature that makes people either aggressive or nonaggressive.[28] Human beings have the capability of learning to behave in many different ways depending on what kind of behavior is observed and consequently imitated, as well as on what kind of behavior is rewarded. Although this view is particularly associated with behaviorist psychologists such as John B. Watson and B.F. Skinner, many psychologists of other schools of psychology also favor the social-learning theory. Anthropologists such as Margaret Mead, Ashley Montagu, and Geoffrey Gorer also tend to be supporters of the social-learning approach to explaining human aggressive behavior.

The evidence for the social-learning view of the origin of aggression comes mainly from two sources: psychological studies which show how people's behavior and attitudes can be modified by conditioning and education, and anthropological studies which find very different behavior patterns in different cultures. Anthropologists can point to some societies, such as the Eskimos, where individuals are pugnacious but there is no group warfare; among others such as the Pueblo Indians, individuals are not pugnacious but there is group warfare.[29] This situation would suggest that both individual aggressiveness and group aggressiveness must be learned — separately. The social-learning theory is supported also by the fact that adopted individuals reared from infancy in a culture different from that of their natural parents will display the attitudes and behavior patterns of the culture in which they are reared rather than that of their biological parents.

When the social learning theorists say that the environment causes the presence or absence of aggressive behavior, they seem to mean that the environment is a *sufficient condition* of the behavior. Their claim is that, except in extreme cases of genetic abnormality or the like, the aggressiveness of an individual will be the result of the social conditioning to which the person is exposed. The evidence about sex differences in aggressive tendencies mentioned in connection with the biological-instinctual theory cannot be ignored, but the social-learning theorists claim that these inborn tendencies can be completely overcome by the proper training, as is demonstrated by the existence of the nonaggressive societies mentioned previously.

The casual observer might question the social-learning approach on grounds that certain individuals, even offspring of the same parents, are very different in their aggressiveness though reared in the same environment. The social-learning theorist responds that no two people, even children in the same family, have exactly the same environment. For example, there is a great difference between being a boy with a younger brother and being one with an older brother even when the boys are in the same family. It seems that, even though there may be some slight differences in the inborn tendency to aggressive behavior among individuals and even though people may be more likely to behave aggressively when frustrated, the overwhelmingly predominant factor determining the degree and kind of aggressive behavior displayed by individuals is their social conditioning.

In 1986 an international team of biologists, psychologists, ethologists, geneticists, and others adopted a statement about the biological necessity of war known as the Seville Statement. That statement has subsequently been endorsed by many organizations of scientists around the world, and in 1989 was officially adopted by UNESCO. Here are a few excerpts:

> It is scientifically incorrect to say that we have inherited a tendency to make war from our animal ancestors. . . .
> The fact that warfare has changed so radically over time indicates that

it is a product of culture. Its biological connection is primarily through language which makes possible the coordination of groups, the transmission of technology, and the use of tools. War is biologically possible, but it is not inevitable, as evidenced by its variation in occurrence and nature over time and space. . . .

It is scientifically incorrect to say that war or any other violent behavior is genetically programmed into our human nature. . . . Except for rare pathologies, the genes do not produce individuals necessarily predisposed to violence. . . .

It is scientifically incorrect to say that in the course of human evolution there has been a selection for aggressive behavior more than for other kinds of behavior. . . . "Dominance" involves social bondings and affiliations; it is not simply a matter of the possession and use of superior physical power, although it does involve aggressive behavior. . . . When . . . experimentally-created hyper-aggressive animals are present in a social group, they either disrupt its social structure or are driven out. Violence is neither in our evolutionary legacy nor in our genes.

It is scientifically incorrect to say that humans have a "violent brain." . . . How we act is shaped by how we have been conditioned and socialized. There is nothing in our neurophysiology that compels us to react violently.

It is scientifically incorrect to say that war is caused by "instinct" or any single motivation. . . . Modern war involves institutional use of personal characteristics such as obedience, suggestibility, and idealism; social skills such as language; and rational considerations such as cost-calculation, planning, and information processing. The technology of modern war has exaggerated traits associated with violence both in the training of combatants and in the preparation of support for war in the general population. As a result of this exaggeration, such traits are often mistaken to be the causes rather than the consequences of the process.[30]

Our own investigation of these issues is completely consistent with this very important statement about biology and violence or aggression adopted by scientists from around the world.

Individual Aggression and War

Having discussed various views about the cause of individual human aggression, let us turn our attention to the issue of how such *individual* aggression may be related to that violent *group* conflict we call war. Three rather different situations need to be considered. The first deals with the aggressiveness of group leaders who have a great deal of influence on the behavior of the groups they lead. The second deals with the ways in which hostility, built up in members of a group as a result of frustration, may be directed against other groups. The third deals with the way in which soldiers are conditioned to actually engage in acts of violence.

There is a remarkable incident involving rhesus monkeys that gives support to the notion that a particularly aggressive individual leader can be a cause of war. Robert Ardrey relates[31] how ethologist C.R. Carpenter had transported several groups of rhesus monkeys from India to Santiago Island off Puerto Rico to observe their behavior in a natural environment. One matter which he wanted to study was the dominance relationships of the males in the various groups of monkeys. The usual pattern of dominance among these monkeys is such that the top male monkey prevails in disputes about four or five times as often as the bottom male monkey. While making his observations Carpenter was surprised to find that one group of monkeys began conquering territory from five neighboring groups. In such struggles between groups the usual pattern was much threatening, little actual fighting, and no exchange of territory; but this situation was different. Furthermore, there seemed at first to be no explanation for the expansionist activity since an adequate food supply was distributed to all the groups each day and the size of all the groups was roughly the same.

But Carpenter soon found an explanation. The conquering group was led by an extremely strong, courageous, and domineering male. His factor of dominance over the *second* male in the group was the 5:1 ratio usually found between the top male and the *bottom* male. This commanding leader had a dominance factor of about 50:1 over the bottom male in his group. It was he that led his group on the warpath against the neighboring groups. When Carpenter removed the master monkey from the group, it went back to its own territory and stopped attacking its neighbors. When he returned the master monkey to the group, it again began imposing on the territory of its neighbors. One could not ask for a more striking case of the effect of an aggressive leader on the behavior of a group. In this case the master monkey was both the necessary and the sufficient condition for aggressive behavior on the part of the group as a whole. This incident suggests that the individual aggressiveness of leaders may be a very relevant factor in the causation of war.

When we look at human history, we are struck by the names of individual aggressive leaders who led their people along the path of conquest — Alexander the Great, Genghis Khan, Napoleon Bonaparte, Adolf Hitler, and so on. It may be too simplistic to believe that a single aggressive human leader makes all the difference as was the case with the rhesus monkeys, but the role of the individual leader in determining whether a given human social group will go to war deserves more attention than it usually gets. Having made seven case studies of wars fought in the twentieth century, John Stoessinger in *Why Nations Go to War* concludes:

> *With regard to the problem of the outbreak of war, the case studies indicate the crucial importance of the personalities of leaders.* I am less impressed by the role of abstract forces, such as nationalism, militarism, or alliance systems, which traditionally have been regarded as the causes of war. Nor does a single one of the cases indicate that economic factors played a vital part in precipitating war. The personalities of leaders, on the other hand, have often been decisive.[32]

Bruce Bueno de Mesquita in *The War Trap* succinctly describes the critical role of the leader for initiating war as follows: "the approval of the key leader is necessary for war, while his disapproval is sufficient to prevent his nation from starting a war."[33] Since the aggressiveness of the individual leader may be a significant factor in whether a society goes to war and since women generally are less aggressive than men, an interesting question is whether having more women leaders might mean less war.[34] On the other hand, perhaps even women would need to be aggressive in order to get into leadership positions.

A second way in which individual aggression may be related to the problem of war involves the psychological phenomenon called "displaced aggression."[35] A person who is frustrated may not be able to direct his hostility toward the real source of his frustration and may, consequently, take it out on others. The typical example of displaced aggression is the man who is frustrated in his job by his superiors. He may become angry, but he cannot direct his hostility toward his superiors without losing his job or damaging his chances for promotion, so when he gets home he acts aggressively toward his wife and children.

The phenomenon of displaced aggression can be related to war in the following way. If there is widespread frustration among the members of a society, possibly because economic conditions are bad, a leader may be able to direct the resulting hostility toward some particular group, possibly toward some minority within the country or toward some foreign nation.[36] When economic conditions were very bad in Germany in the early 1930s, Hitler's attacks on the Jews gained a considerable following while just a few years earlier, during prosperity, very few persons paid any attention to him. Today we can expect that when the anticipation of rapid economic advancement in less developed countries is disappointed the hostility toward the richer nations will be great, but since the people of these poorer nations are unable successfully to attack these rich countries their hostility is likely to be directed toward their own leaders or toward their poor neighbors.[37] In fact, the leaders of these frustrated nations may deliberately direct their people's hostility toward neighboring countries in order to keep it from being directed toward themselves. It is an old device of political leaders to protect themselves from troubles at home by starting a crisis abroad, but the 1982 experience of Argentinian leaders with regard to the Falkland Islands–Malvinas indicates why political leaders adopting such a strategy ought to make sure they take on a weak enemy rather than a strong one.

All of the above suggests that prosperity is likely to make peace more probable while economic adversity is likely to produce hostility and war, even though the hostility and war may not be directed against the real source of frustration. It should be noted, however, that this phenomenon of displaced aggression seems to be more closely related to the issue of how leaders get their followers ready to participate in a war than to the issue of how the wars get started. Still, persons who call for aggressive action are more likely to make their way into leadership positions when the population as a whole is frustrated, and leaders are much more likely to embark on a course of action which will lead to war when they feel their followers are ready and eager for the effort.

A third way individual aggressiveness is related to war is in the preparation of soldiers to do the actual fighting of a war. This matter has nothing to do with how wars get started, but only with how individuals are induced to engage in violent behavior once the leaders have decided to go to war. Both the frustration theory of aggression and the social learning theory of aggression are relevant. Much of military training, especially basic training, is based on the principle that a frustrated soldier is more likely to be a hostile person and therefore an aggressive person. The task then becomes one of directing this aggression against the enemy rather than the military leaders in charge of the training or the political leaders who have been responsible for pulling the young person away from his personal pursuits to fight for the glory of his country. A frequently used device is to describe atrocities committed by the enemy. There is also an effort to get the soldiers to view the enemy soldiers as less than human and thus not deserving of the respect usually accorded to humans. A concerted effort is made to get these soldiers to follow orders without questioning them. Of course this military training is supported by a long period of social conditioning leading the young soldiers to identify with their country and to place a positive value on the idea of losing their life for their country. This identification with the national group, nationalism, is one of our subjects in the next chapter.

V. Group Competition and Group Identification

The question of what causes war is an extremely complex one. Part of the complexity is generated by the different meanings of the word "cause" discussed in the previous chapter. But an even more important part of the difficulty is that war itself is a complex social phenomenon. We have defined war as "large-scale violent conflict between organized groups that are governments or that aim to establish governments." Consequently, our question about what causes war can mean (1) "What causes *individual persons* (both leaders and followers) to be so aggressive that they will engage in violent behavior as they do during war?" We discussed that question in the previous chapter. Or the question about what causes war can mean (2) "What causes groups to come into conflict with each other?" that is, *what kinds of things might groups fight about?* That is the first issue we will discuss in this chapter. Or the question about what causes war can mean (3) "What causes individuals *to identify with a group* so completely as to be ready to risk their lives fighting for the group?" That is the second issue we will discuss in this chapter. Our question about what causes war can also focus on other aspects of the social situation which may contribute to the outbreak of violent conflict between groups. We will focus on those possibilities in the next chapter.

Arenas of Group Competition

The main things about which groups may come into conflict with each other are the same things about which individuals may come into conflict: (1) survival, (2) acquisition of goods, (3) wider acceptance of their beliefs, (4) status, and (5) power. The lowest level of competition is for *survival,* to just keep on existing. If an individual is threatened with death, we can expect that person to struggle to survive. Similarly, if a group is threatened with extinction as a group, we can expect that group to struggle to survive. This desire for survival interacting with the broader environmental situation helps explain why *primitive war* is so different from *civilized war.* Our nomadic ancestors, with plenty of unoccupied space in the world, could usually move into some unoccupied territory if their survival were threatened by some stronger group. They might at first put up some kind of fight

61

to stay hunting and fishing and gathering where they already were, but if defeat seemed likely they could just move to some other territory. Societies which never developed a military-type organization to defend themselves survived by migrating to isolated places where they would no longer be pursued by other groups.[1]

Sooner or later, depending on the terrain and the rate of population growth, empty territory into which a group could escape would no longer be available. In this case the defeated group would either be completely exterminated or made into a permanent slave or subordinate class within the victorious society. In that latter case we would have the beginnings of a hierarchical coercive government characteristic of civilized peoples.[2] We would also then begin to have *civilized warfare* among the various triumphant groups for control of even more territory and other kinds of wealth. That is the second level of conflict or competition among societies, *economic conflict.*

Economic competition among groups is focused mainly on acquiring the goods provided by nature: land, good soil and a favorable climate for growing food, access to water, and supplies of raw materials such as wood, metals, and, in the modern world, energy sources such as coal and petroleum. The wants of human beings are virtually limitless and the numbers of them are ever increasing while the goods provided by nature are limited. Over thousands of years humans have learned how to get more of what they want from nature than nature would have provided without human management. The introduction of agriculture and the domestication of animals are two of the earlier developments in this process, while the use of fertilizer for crops and the production of energy from uranium and plutonium are more recent developments. There is a continuing contest between how much is available and the ever increasing desires of an ever expanding population.

Thus there may be a sense in which population growth seems to be relevant to the problem of war in that, when production does not increase as fast as population, the conflict for available goods will become more intense. On the other hand, with the flourishing of science and the resulting industrial revolution during the last two or three centuries, technology has generally allowed the production of goods to more than keep pace with population growth, helped in part by the fact that more industrialized peoples tend to have fewer children. In an industrialized society children are no longer perceived as an asset (low-cost labor) as they were in the agricultural environment. Even if the population were to grow faster than the supply of goods with the result that tensions increased, it is not automatically the case that war would result.[3] There may be resentment on the part of those who are in danger of not surviving; but if they believe there is no chance of getting what they need by group violence, they are not likely to resort to group violence. If there is some other way of getting what they need (producing and selling addictive drugs, selling stolen goods, engaging in prostitution, making simple objects that can be sold to those with money, and so on), then that is what these "left-out" people will do rather than trying to fight a war which they will only lose. It is worth remembering that wars are usually fought by groups which believe they will gain something by engaging in them.[4] The rich and powerful who control the weapons and military forces set the rules for what the non-powerful can and cannot do in order to survive, much as parents set the rules for what young children can and cannot do in order to survive. When there is not enough for everyone, resentment is likely to grow and may produce individual violent acts of protest (such as occurs with terrorism), but it is not likely to produce war. Furthermore, any remedial action by the rich and powerful to help the poor and weak is more likely to be motivated by compassion than by fear of violence, which typically just produces more repression.

After governments are established, the leaders of these governments are better able to pursue their aim of increasing the quantity and kinds of goods available to themselves. Three strategies might be adopted by these leaders. One strategy would be to tax people of their own society in order to get goods for themselves. A second strategy would be to promote the development of technology within their society so that more goods are produced, either for their own use or for trading to other societies for goods which they have. A third strategy would be to organize an army composed of members of their society in order to take goods from other societies by force. The first strategy is limited by the fact that if the people are very poor the leaders will not be able to get much by taxing them. There is also the danger of rebellion if the discrepancy between the supply of goods available to the leaders and that available to others in the society becomes too great. The second strategy of using technology is much more attractive in a scientific-industrial age than it was when human knowledge and technology were more limited, but still today, especially in conflicts among less developed countries, technology may not be able to produce what is wanted more cheaply than it can be obtained by force. Thus the third strategy, war, has been widely used throughout human history as a way of getting more goods, even though the cost can be high when the opposing society is equipped to put up a good fight to keep its goods for itself.

Originally the goods acquired by war (the "spoils of victory") belonged to the leaders and the soldiers who took part in the fighting, but with the development of more democratic societies the government was expected to look out for the welfare of the citizenry generally. Competition between ruling groups in different societies was transformed into competition between nation-state and nation-state, with the government of each seeking to enhance the standard of living of its whole society. Even authoritarian governments now usually define their goal as generating more goods for everyone in the society, not just more for the leaders.

A great deal of ancient war was motivated by the desire to seize the goods of another society, but war for economic gain is by no means confined to the ancient world. From the sixteenth through the early part of the twentieth century there were continuing imperialistic wars in which the technologically advanced European nations were able to gain control over the territory of the less advanced peoples in the Americas, Africa, and Asia. These wars usually did not last very long because the military forces of the European nations were equipped with guns and other modern weapons unknown to the inhabitants of these less developed countries. Conquest by the more advanced nations gave them access to raw materials and to good agricultural land which they could control for their own purposes. The advanced nations were also able to restrict the flow of technological know-how to the native populations of the less developed countries, consequently preserving the arrangements whereby natural resources flowed into the hands of Europeans rather than being converted into manufactured goods within the less developed countries.

Since taking control of the natural resources of less developed countries was a very profitable operation, a new kind of economic competition developed among the imperial nations themselves. Each advanced nation wanted to control as much territory as possible in order to have access to whatever natural resources might be found there. Sometimes nations worked things out peacefully, such as when Spain and Portugal accepted the Pope's decision on how to divide Latin America between them or when Britain and France ended up splitting large segments of Africa and Asia between them, but at other times the competition led to war. Thus competition for the goods of the Earth led to wars not only between technologically advanced countries on the one hand and less advanced countries on the other but also among the advanced countries themselves as each tried to expand at the expense of the others.

As some of the people in the less advanced countries gradually acquired some of the weapons produced by the more advanced countries and as the advanced countries became embroiled in wars among themselves (especially the Second World War), a third kind of war caused by economic competition became a reality. People in the less developed countries were able to fight "wars of liberation" to gain political independence and control over their own natural resources.

At present economic competition among the nations of the world continues. Rich nations compete against other rich nations, but the rich nations as a group also compete against the poor nations as a group. And of course, the poor nations compete among themselves. But now these economic struggles usually take place in a nonviolent way. The more advanced nations for the most part no longer have political control over the less advanced nations, but they control the capital, the technological knowledge, and the markets needed by the less developed countries. Consequently, they are usually able to work out arrangements favorable to themselves. One outstanding exception to control by the advanced countries is OPEC, the Organization of Petroleum Exporting Countries. By forming a producers' cartel, the less developed nations which have petroleum within their territory were able, especially during the 1970s, to greatly increase the price of crude oil, to the great disadvantage of the more advanced countries, which generally were very dependent on imported oil. The cartel still exists, but its influence has been decreased considerably as the result of collective action by the developed countries, by the discovery of oil in territory controlled by the developed countries such as the North Sea and Alaska, and by squabbles among the members of OPEC themselves. The economic struggle to control resources such as oil does still sometimes lead to war, however, as in 1990 when Iraq conquered Kuwait. That conquest led to a military response in February 1991 when Iraq was driven out of Kuwait by a coalition of developed countries led by the United States. This Gulf War was the result of different viewpoints in Iraq and Kuwait about whether to sell oil at "reasonable prices" to the industrialized countries and about how to use the money acquired from the sales.

We should not neglect economic competition as a contributing factor to war *within* nations. We earlier mentioned the possibility of rebellion in a situation where a ruling elite has a great deal more wealth than the rest of the people in the society. The ruling elite are usually able to hire a superior police force armed with superior weapons to maintain control over the rest of the society in much the same way that a technologically advanced nation is able to control its colonies. But a split may occur among the ruling elite which would present opportunities for others in the society to gain some power by agreeing to support one or the other faction. Or some other nation may provide military assistance to the poorer, less powerful people so they have a chance to successfully rebel against the military and economic domination practiced by the elite in that society. In either case it is possible that a civil war will occur due at least in part to the economic competition between groups within that nation-state.

A *third kind of competition* that may lead to war is the effort by groups *to spread their own religious or political beliefs.* A group may have a set of beliefs about the ultimate nature of reality, about how individuals should behave, and or about what kinds of institutions a society should have which they also believe should be adopted by other groups. This "Truth" which they desire to spread may be resisted by other groups, which typically have their own ideas about what is true and good. In modern societies the real issue in this type of conflict is control of information generally and control of the formal education system in particular. People's beliefs and values depend on the information available to them. Children tend to believe whatever ideas they are taught first, and any conflicting ideas they hear later will usually be viewed as false and wrong. Most adults will be influenced in their beliefs by what is believed by others around them. Thus control of the media and education is crucial for promoting a religion or ideology. Competition between groups for control of information and the formal educational system may lead to war.

If the aim of the leaders of a society were simply that people should come to believe what is objectively true and to approve of whatever is objectively good, the appropriate means of accomplishing this aim would be the exposure of both children and adults to the whole range of views that might be held on any topic. The study of philosophy, where people are stimulated to think things through for themselves, would be a central feature of the educational system. There would be a constant effort to challenge prevailing beliefs and values so that mistaken views would be corrected through investigation and debate.[5] Unfortunately, most people, including the leaders of the society, do not want other people to explore ideas and reach their own conclusions. They want their children and other members of their society, and even members of other societies, to believe what they themselves believe and to value what they themselves value. Consequently, in most societies there is an effort to control education and information so that people will come to the "right" (acceptable) conclusions about what is true and what is good. Those who question the accepted beliefs and practices are discouraged, ignored, silenced, or even actively persecuted.

The goal of promoting the views approved by the decision-makers in the society and discouraging those which they disapprove is often not limited to their own society. Two societies with different religions or opposing ideologies are each likely to make efforts to promote their own views in the opposing society as well as in other countries not directly involved in the ideological conflict. Each may even try to make its religion or ideology the prevailing religion or ideology in the whole world. Such ideological conflicts may ultimately lead to war. If the Cuban missile crisis of 1962 had resulted in a war between the U.S. and the Soviet Union, it would have been a war in which ideological conflict was the major factor.

Intense religious or ideological differences may also lead to war *within* a society. People of different religious or ideological persuasions may come to believe that they just cannot continue to live together in the same society. Sometimes a single issue such as the abolition of slavery may become a focal point for intense feeling that contributes to the outbreak of a civil war. A group which advocates a greater sharing of political power or economic wealth may find itself persecuted by the leaders of the society who would be losers if those views were widely accepted. If this group recommending changes uses force to defend itself, a civil war may develop. The 1978 revolution in Iran, the war between the Sandinistas and the Contras in Nicaragua during the 1980s, and the fighting in Bosnia-Herzegovina which followed the break-up of Yugoslavia in 1991 are all examples of how religious or ideological conflict can produce war within a country.

It might be supposed that people would fight more vehemently for physical goods than for abstract doctrines and ideals, but in fact religiously or ideologically motivated wars seem to be especially bloody and unrestrained. Each side believes that it has a holy mission to bring the other side to the "Truth," no matter what the cost or sacrifice. It may be firmly believed by people on both sides that it is better to die than to be forced to live in a society where the religion or ideology of the opposing side prevails. This viewpoint was succintly expressed in the U.S. during the Cold War by the slogan "Better dead than Red." The vehemence of wars motivated largely by religious or ideological differences is evidenced by the nature of the fighting between Christians and Muslims during the twelfth and thirteenth centuries and between Protestants and Catholics in the sixteenth and seventeenth centuries. It has been argued that the destructiveness of modern war makes it likely that if there is a World War III the primary cause will probably be ideological conflict rather than hope of material gain.[6] It seems that many wars taking place within nations in the 1980s and 1990s also involve some kind of religious or ideological conflict.

To anyone who thinks carefully and impartially about the matter, conducting a war to resolve differences in belief about what is true and what is good is as ridiculous as having a fistfight between two individuals to discover whose ideas are best. Beliefs which are true and values which are good will come to prevail if given a chance to be expressed in open inquiry and debate. The notion that the ideas of the winner of a war are closer to the truth and that their values are superior to those of the loser cannot be accepted by anyone who knows how often in human history the speakers of truth have been silenced and the toilers for good imprisoned or killed by those with greater physical force at their command. Violence may be a temporarily effective way of extending one's control over others, but it is not an appropriate method for advancing truth and goodness.[7] The search for truth and goodness requires open discussion of alternative views rather than coercion designed to promote the views of those who happen to be physically in charge at the moment.

A *fourth arena* of competition between groups is for *status*. Status is an abstract concept, but it is also a very real thing. Status is the result of a combination of fear and admiration. It depends on things such as military power, economic power, and scientific or cultural achievements. As in the case of individuals, the group which has status will be deferred to and praised and imitated. Having status means having influence even though that influence may not be formally recognized or authorized in political institutions. An example of status without recognized power is the prestige Japan has acquired in international affairs because of its economic successes while as of 1993 it still has not been made a permanent member of the U.N. Security Council.

Let us consider an example of how status functions in international affairs. Suppose that two nations are negotiating a trade agreement. The richer nation intends to export manufactured goods to the poorer nation while the poorer nation intends to export raw material to the richer nation. As the negotiations proceed the richer nation proposes that all goods moving in either direction be transported in its vessels. The poorer nation does not want to accept such arrangements, but the rich nation takes the position that if the goods are not shipped in its vessels it will simply stop negotiating with this poor nation and work out something with another more cooperative nation. At this point the poorer nation often is trapped because this rich nation is one of the few which can afford to buy large quantities of its raw materials and also supply some of the manufactured goods it needs. Thus the poorer nation is coerced into accepting a trade agreement where all the goods involved will be shipped in the vessels of the richer nation. There has been a struggle concerning which nation will get its way, and the rich nation has prevailed because the poorer nation needs what the rich nation has more than the rich nation needs what the poorer nation has. But this particular trade agreement also means that a situation of dominance has been established. Having yielded to the demands of the rich country on this occasion, the poorer country can expect to be coerced into accepting similar demands in the future.

The example just cited focuses on economic coercion in a struggle for dominance, but one nation might also establish its dominance over another on the basis of military superiority. A militarily weaker nation might be coerced into accepting trade agreements or other policies which it really does not want because of a threat of invasion if it does not go along with the demands of the militarily stronger country. Coercion on the basis of the military superiority is as common as economic coercion. Militarily superiority is also more crucial in a head-to-head confrontation. Since the ultimate test of a nation's strength lies in its capability of defending itself in a war, military superiority is the most crucial aspect of national status.

A good example of competition for status outside the economic and military spheres was the contest between the United States and the Soviet Union with regard to accomplishments in space during the Cold War. Many aspects of the space race such as the size of satellites which can be kept in orbit and the length of time a person can stay in space before returning to Earth have military implications. But one event which had very little to do with military needs was the landing of men on the moon. The Soviets had launched the first satellite in 1957, an event that generated a perception throughout the world that Soviet science was ahead of American science. In response to that situation, in 1961 President Kennedy issued a public challenge to the Soviets to see which country could be first to place a man on the moon. The United States accomplished that in 1969. The Soviet space scientists never did. The landing of men on the moon demonstrated the capability of American science and counteracted the earlier notion that "socialist science and technology" was superior to "capitalist science and technology."

So far we have noted that economic coercion or military coercion or superior scientific accomplishment may be used by one nation or group to establish its superior status or dominance over another. Competition between countries also occurs in other areas such as cultural achievements or winning the most medals in the Olympic Games. Having status means being recognized as superior in some area of competition. But in international affairs there is a general consensus that being "Number One" militarily is much more important than being "Number One" in other ways because ultimately the question of status comes down to who could win a war. That is the ultimate competition. Violent contests of physical force for dominance occur among animals to determine which one is "top dog" of the pack. Similar violent contests of physical force for dominance may take place between nations or between groups within a nation. They are called wars.

In the end, however, the dominant nation or group within a nation wants not only status but also *formal recognition of that status* by means of a treaty or other formal political document. It wants others to formally acknowledge its *authority to determine what policies will be followed* in a particular territory and over a particular population. That is, the dominant group wants not only status but *political power*. Regardless of what other goals are being pursued, acquiring political power is the immediate aim of warfare. Political power (authority to act as a government for the group) is what the winner wins.

It should be noted that although political power may seem to be *an end in itself,* in fact it is essentially *a means* by which other things can be accomplished. A group which has acquired power is able to give orders to accomplish whatever it is that it wants to accomplish, but having power to make decisions for the whole society still leaves open the question of what policies will be adopted. In this respect the quest for political power resembles the quest for money by individuals. Persons who accumulate a great deal of money will be able to buy whatever they want or to give away as much as they want to whomever they wish, but having the money simply provides a means to some other ends. Those who have acquired large amounts of money must still decide how to use it. Similarly, a country or group which wins a war, thus establishing its right to decide what will be done, must still decide how to use that power.

There is another similarity between the quest for money and the quest for political power. People whose aim is to acquire more and more money may at the beginning of their quest have some idea of what they want to use the money for, but after a while the aim of acquiring more money may itself become a goal. While trying to acquire more and more money, these persons may have no idea of what to do with it once it is in their hands. Similarly, leaders of nations or of groups within nations usually aim to acquire more and more political power. At the beginning they usually have some idea of what they want the power for, but in time the aim of acquiring more power may itself become a goal. These leaders may want even more power but have no idea of what to do with it once they have it.

The fact that leaders may not know what to do with their political power once they have it does not stop them from trying to get more power as the recognized decisionmakers over more territory and more people.

Other groups may decide that they will fight rather than lose their decision-making authority, so the desire for political power for its own sake may become a cause of war. Joseph Schumpeter in his book *Imperialism and Social Classes* argues that "objectless" expansionism (expansionism with no reasonable objectives in terms of the welfare of the nation involved) occurs regularly and in fact may be the cause of a majority of international wars that have occurred.[8] At the same time it should be remembered that power can be used to get other things. Beyond assuring survival, power can also be used with regard to the other arenas of competition we have discussed. The nation or group which has political power will be able to use that power to get a larger share of the available goods for its own people, to promote the acceptance of its religion or ideology, and to further enhance its own status. Whether the struggle for political power is instrumental to these other ends or is an end in itself, striving for more political power may be a contributory factor to the outbreak of war.

Group Identification and Nationalism

Groups could not carry out sustained violent conflict with each other if individuals did not commit themselves to fighting for those groups. In earlier times participating in a war may have involved a personal commitment on the part of the soldiers to the king or to some nobleman, but in modern warfare such commitment usually depends on a phenomenon called "identification." People are said to identify with a group when they feel that what is good for that group is good for them and that whatever harms that group harms them. To put it another way, if the group experiences some type of success it will make them personally feel better because the group's welfare is perceived as an extension of their own.

The phenomenon of identification is a common part of human life. For example, students tend to identify with their school and its athletic teams. If the team wins, they feel good. If the team loses, they feel bad. People identify with the religious or ideological group to which they belong, with the racial or ethnic group to which they belong, with their labor unions or professional organizations, with the company which employs them, with their age group, with their gender group, with the local community where they live, with their state, with their nation, and so on. Whenever people think in terms of "we" (for example, "We won" or "We got recognized"), they are identifying with some group.

Group identification seems to be increased by competitive situations, especially when the group or its representatives are experiencing success or confronting a particularly crucial struggle. Winning athletic teams are thought to increase school loyalty. When a representative of a racial group wins a prize, other members of that group experience a greater pride in their racial identity. When a religious or ethnic group faces persecution, other members of that group feel a special awareness of being members of that group. Group identification usually continues, however, even in losing situations and noncritical confrontations.

Since members of a group identify with the success or failure of the group, leaders of the group are under a great deal of pressure to advance the interests of the group. They have a role to play: to do what is best for the group. If they do not succeed or if they seem not to be aggressive enough in pursuing the interests of the group, they are likely to be replaced by other leaders who promise to do better. All groups want to be gainers, winners, the best of their kind. Such a situation necessarily fosters group conflict.

One of the more obvious ways of lessening conflict between two groups is to persuade them both to see themselves as members of the same larger group which is united against some other group. Thus, Catholics and Protestants may experience less tension if they perceive themselves as Christians struggling against Muslims. In turn Christians and Muslims may have less conflict with each other if they view themselves as believers in God struggling against atheistic Communists. Perhaps believers and atheists could in turn see themselves as humans struggling together for survival against the forces of nature, including the psychological forces within themselves, which threaten their continued existence.

Of all the various types of identification, the one most relevant to the war problem in recent times is nationalism. Nationalism is not a necessary condition of war since prior to the last quarter of the eighteenth century wars were fought to a great extent by mercenaries, that is, men who hired themselves out as soldiers. They fought for the king who paid them and felt no nationalistic sentiment. In many wars people were motivated by identification with a religious group rather than a nation. Neither is nationalism a sufficient condition of war since it is possible for people to have strong nationalistic feelings and yet not engage in warfare; the Swedes and Swiss are both good examples. Yet nationalism seems to be an important contributory factor to war, especially in the last 200 years.

To clarify the issue of nationalism as it relates to war, however, we must distinguish three different ways in which this term is used. The first two meanings both involve the psychological phenomenon of *identification* we have just discussed. The third meaning of nationalism refers to a *doctrine* about how governmental arrangements should be based on racial and ethnic considerations.

In order to distinguish the first two types of nationalism we must note the difference between a *nation* and a *nation-state,* a difference which requires special attention because of our tendency to use the term "nation" when we in fact mean "nation-state." A *nation* (or *people*) refers to a group of people who are of the same racial stock, use the same language, share the same religious and cultural traditions, and perceive themselves as a homogeneous group. In this racial-ethnic sense of nation there is no reference to any political unit or nation-state; some nations lack nation-states of their own. Thus we speak of American Indian groups such as the Mohawk nation or the Dakota nation. Another good example is the Jewish nation after the destruction of ancient Israel and before the creation of the modern state of Israel.

A *nation-state,* on the other hand, refers to a population living in a certain territory under the authority of a government. This meaning of "nation" differs from the first meaning, for in some nation-states the people are *not* a homogeneous group. Switzerland is a particularly good example of such a nation-state. It is a political unit, even though it is composed of several different cultural groups with different languages and traditions. Russia and the United States are also examples of nation-states whose populations are composed of several different cultural groups.

Nationalism in the first sense, *racial-ethnic nationalism,* refers to a person's identification with a homogeneous nation or people. This type of nationalism develops naturally when one is reared in a homogeneous group. We tend automatically to identify with other people who look like us, act like us, use the same language we do, and have the same religious and cultural heritage we have. Within a homogeneous ethnic group an intense feeling of group solidarity develops. There is a strong tendency to view people who look different, act differently, use a different language, or who have a different religious and cultural heritage as "strange," "odd," or maybe even "uncivilized."

Nationalism in the second sense, *loyalty to the nation-state* (also called *patriotism*), refers to a person's identification with a nation-state and the people who live within it. This type of nationalism does not develop naturally but comes about as the result of a deliberate effort to inculcate loyalty to the nation-state and its institutions. Symbols such as a flag, a national anthem, and a pledge of allegiance are used as a focus of loyalty. Education of the children emphasizes the history, heroes, and glories of the nation-state and the value of sticking together against outsiders. National holidays are celebrated. A national military force maintains allegiance to the national government, and persons in this force as well as those who hold office in the national government are accorded honor. By such devices the "we" perspective of the people is extended beyond their own cultural group to the heterogeneous nation-state as a whole.

The third definition of the term *nationalism,* what we will call *"doctrinal nationalism,"* is very different from the previous two meanings of the word, both of which are related to the notion of identification with some group. In this third sense, *nationalism* refers to a *doctrine* or *ideological viewpoint,* namely the doctrine that *each racial-ethnic group has a right to have its own independent political nation-state and that all members of this racial-ethnic group should live together in a single political nation-state.* The ideal according to doctrinal nationalism is for each racial-ethnic group to be united in its own "ethnically pure" country. This doctrinal version of nationalism is often associated with the nineteenth-century Italian political writer and activist Giuseppe Mazzini, who used it as the theoretical underpinning for promoting the unification of Italian city-states into the single nation-state of Italy. The basic idea was that the people living in the separate city-states in Italy at that time were all one people (Italians) and thus should have their own nation-state just as the Spanish and the French and the English had. Doctrinal nationalism has also served as a theoretical support for separatist movements among minority racial-ethnic groups within nation-states and for independence movements which promote "wars of national liberation" in territories ruled by foreign colonialists.

Doctrinal nationalism has been behind various movements, earlier in Europe but now also on other continents, which have been intimately connected with violent conflict. In a general way, doctrinal nationalism will almost certainly produce dissatisfaction wherever there are various racial-ethnic groups intermingled in particular geographical areas. Suppose, for example, that there are some enclaves of Italians living within the boundaries of France and some French people living in enclaves within the boundaries of Italy. According to doctrinal nationalism, how is this situation to be handled? Should some small areas of land within France become part of the nation-state of Italy and some small areas of land within Italy become part of the nation-state of France? What should happen to those areas that are about 50 percent French and 50 percent Italian? If these Italians surrounded by French people want to be under the political control of Italy, why shouldn't they move into territory that is already part of Italy? And a similar question could be addressed to the French living in Italy. But why should any people be forced to move to a different geographical area because of a doctrine about "pure" nation-states?

We need to examine the presuppositions of doctrinal nationalism. Why must each racial-ethnic group have its own "ethnically pure" nation-state? Why can't many different racial-ethnic groups live together in a heterogeneous nation-state? The assumption seems to be that in a heterogeneous nation-state one racial-ethnic group (usually but not always the majority) will be in control and will use its political power to discriminate unfairly against other racial-ethnic groups which are less powerful. Undoubtedly, such situations do occur (consider South Africa), but there may be other remedies besides doctrinal nationalism. Why not have ethnically heterogeneous nation-states which aim to protect the rights of all individuals regardless of their racial-ethnic group? Why not have multi-ethnic states where all individuals, regardless of race or ethnic background, have an equal opportunity to get into positions of economic and political power? That seems to be an attractive alternative to doctrinal nationalism.

The main force working against this proposed alternative to doctrinal nationalism is the widespread unquestioned acceptance of the legitimacy of doctrinal nationalism. This situation has become painfully obvious with regard to the break-up of the former multi-ethnic nation-state of

Yugoslavia (see map on page 234). Some Serbs, motivated by the nationalistic vision of a "Greater Serbia," want to unite all Serbs into a single nation-state. Other ethnic groups in the former Yugoslavia such as the Croats don't want to remain a part of a state where the Serbian majority is motivated by doctrinal nationalism rather than the ideal of a multi-ethnic state as existed in Yugoslavia under the leadership of Slovene-Croat Tito. The greatest tragedy of all is in the former Yugoslav republic of Bosnia-Herzegovina. In that state, which declared its independence from Yugoslavia in 1991, the population is 44 percent Muslim, 31 percent Serb, and 17 percent Croat. Some Bosnian Serbs want to become part of "Greater Serbia," and some Bosnian Croats want to become part of the newly independent state of Croatia. But that is not true of *all* of the Serbs and Croats in Bosnia-Herzegovina. Some of them want Bosnia-Herzegovina to be a separate multi-ethnic state. In many cases families and close friends of different ethnic groups have lived together in harmony in the former Yugoslavia. Some of the Bosnian Serbs are in fact fighting in the Bosnian army against other Bosnian Serbs even though they themselves are Serbs! They want to prevent the break-up of Bosnia-Herzegovina into separate ethnic states. But the uncritical acceptance of doctrinal nationalism by people on all sides makes their position almost impossible. Other Serbs view them as traitors because they do not share the vision of a "Greater Serbia." (There is an obvious parallel here to the situation for Jews who oppose Zionism or Quebeçois who do not want Quebec to secede from Canada or Ukrainians who opposed the break-up of the Soviet Union.) At the same time some uninformed Bosnian Muslims treat these Serbs who want a multi-ethnic Bosnia-Herzegovina as enemies just because they are Serbs.[9] It is sad to see how the defenders of a multi-ethnic Bosnia-Herzegovina have been sacrificed on the table of doctrinal nationalism by a world that seems unable to free itself from this war-engendering ideology.

Returning to our examination of the assumptions underlying doctrinal nationalism, why is it essential that all persons of the same racial-ethnic nation live in a single nation-state? The assumption here seems to be that in unity there is strength to be better able to compete militarily and economically against other racial-ethnic groups. The British and French, who got themselves united earlier, were able to establish world empires by the beginning of the twentieth century. On the other hand, when the Italians and the Germans finally got themselves united in the last part of the nineteenth century there were few new areas of the world to colonize. But it becomes obvious here that this side of doctrinal nationalism is based on the assumption that the international system is to remain forever a battleground of different aggressive racial-ethnic groups each in control of a particular state and doing all it can to promote the welfare of this state at the expense of other nation-states. Perhaps that will be the model for the future as it has been for Europe in the past. On the other hand, it is possible that a post–World War II global system will evolve where it is no longer the case that military power is the accepted means by which ethnically pure nation-states battle for domination over each other. In such a revised world order it would no longer be so important for each racial-ethnic group to be united in its own nation-state. Another possibility is that, even if the global system as a whole does not change, the really powerful actors in the international system will be large multi-ethnic nation-states rather than ethnically pure ones. Certainly World War II pointed in this direction.

Before leaving the topic of nationalism we need to at least make mention of the situation of "indigenous peoples," those "native" or "tribal" peoples scattered all over the globe whose very survival is endangered by the spread of industrialized nation-states. Earlier it was noted that the struggle to survive is the most basic kind of competition among groups and that groups which have not been able to prevail militarily have usually migrated to isolated areas to avoid further conflict. There are large numbers of these pre-civilized or pre-industrialized peoples who are being threatened because more civilized industrialized peoples are pushing into these previously isolated areas. Of the 6,000 cultures in the world 4,000–5,000 are indigenous cultures.[10] It has been noted above that one alternative to doctrinal nationalism is the establishment of multi-ethnic nation-states where the rights of minority groups are protected. The fate of indigenous peoples will be determined not just by what protection they are given by the governments of individual nation-states but also by what protection they are guaranteed by the world community. A U.N. Declaration on the Rights of Indigenous Peoples is currently being drafted under the auspices of the U.N. Human Rights Commission. The adoption of such a declaration would be an important development for the preservation of both these indigenous groups and of the ecological systems where they live.[11]

Nationalism as a Cause of War

We have distinguished three meanings of nationalism: (1) identification with one's racial-ethnic group, (2) patriotism, or loyalty to one's nation-state, and (3) doctrinal nationalism, the belief that each racial-ethnic group has a right to have all its members living in its own ethnically pure nation-state. There are four different contexts in which doctrinal nationalism, with its heavy emphasis on racial-ethnic nationalism as the proper basis for political structures, may produce tensions and eventually war. Nevertheless the aspect of nationalism that has probably been most significant in modern international war is loyalty to the nation-state or patriotism. Let us consider more specifically the ways in which nationalism may serve as a cause of war.

According to our definition of war, wars always involve government in some way or other. Consequently, *nationalism as identification with the racial-ethnic group* becomes a causal factor in war only when it is combined with political aims as occurs in doctrinal nationalism. Undoubtedly, racial-ethnic nationalism is a factor in many uprisings and riots and "racial incidents," but unless there are some political aims these events will not be classified as wars.

As noted above, there are four different contexts in which *doctrinal nationalism* may be causally involved in war. First, doctrinal nationalism may provide theoretical support for a *liberation movement* against a country which has conquered a group and made its members into a colony. According to doctrinal nationalism each racial-ethnic group has a right to have its own nation-state rather than being ruled by some other nationality. Thus it follows that this conquered and colonialized racial-ethnic group has a right to become an independent nation-state.[12] The conquered people are likely to develop an intense hatred for the people who have kept them in subjection. They will also tend to regard members of their own nation who cooperate with the conquerors as traitors. When the time is right, the nationalistic feeling of the oppressed people will support a *war of liberation* to throw off the control of the other nation. Since the end of World War II this set of events has occurred in many nations which were once colonies, such as India, Kenya, Algeria, Vietnam, Zimbabwe, Angola, and Mozambique. The same type of resentful nationalism may also be manifested in situations where the foreign political control is more indirect or where the foreign domination is more economic than political. In these cases nationalistic feeling may support a revolutionary movement directed against those native leaders who are viewed as being too cooperative with the foreign oppressor. In Cuba in 1959 and Nicaragua in 1979 such wars of liberation had some success, while both the 1965 uprising in the Dominican Republic and the 1968 uprising in the former Czechoslovakia failed.

The second way that doctrinal nationalism may become a cause of war is by spawning *separatist movements* within a politically unified nation-state. One example of this possibility is the effort of some French-speaking Canadians to get Quebec to secede from Canada and form a separate nation-state. The French-speaking Canadians resent the pro–English bent of the national government and most Canadian business operations. They fear the gradual elimination of French culture and use of the French language. The Canadian government has responded with efforts to try to protect French culture and use of the French language, but there is constant tension because of the two languages. According to doctrinal nationalism French-Canadians should have their own nation-state rather than trying to survive in a multi-cultural Canada.

Separatist movements have actually led to war in many situations because the central government is often ready to fight in order to prevent loss of some of its territory. Two million people lost their lives during the late 1960s when the Ibos of Nigeria unsuccessfully tried to establish a separate nation-state of Biafra.[13] In 1971 the Bengalis of what was then East Pakistan fought a successful separatist war, with help from India, to establish the new country of Bangladesh.[14] In May of 1993 Eritrea won its independence from Ethiopia after a 30-year armed struggle in which over 570,000 people died.[15] Additional examples could be cited. In some situations a racial-ethnic group which wants to have its own independent nation-state is not located within a single nation-state but within the territory of two or three nation-states. An example of this situation is the Kurds, some of whom are living in northern Iraq, some in northern Iran, and some in eastern Turkey. Some Kurds hope to have an independent Kurdistan someday, but that would require a successful separatist movement in at least one of the three countries mentioned, something which is not likely to happen since the other two nation-states in which the Kurds live would probably use their influence to prevent it for fear that a wider separatist movement would also take some of their own territory.

The third kind of movement generated by *doctrinal nationalism* that might lead to war is *irredentism*. This term comes from the nineteenth century. After the nation of Italy was politically unified, the new Italian national government claimed that there were other areas containing cultural Italians which were *not yet redeemed* (in Italian, *irredenta*), that is, which were not yet incorporated into the new Italian nation-state. These areas were within the boundaries of other nation-states. The Italian government did not invite the cultural Italians in these areas to come and live within the political boundaries of Italy but instead claimed that these areas should become part of Italy. The other political nation-states in which the cultural Italians lived did not look kindly on this effort to take some of their territory. It is easy to see how this kind of conflict can lead to a violent confrontation. Some examples of irredentism leading to war are the moves by Germany to control Austria and parts of Czechoslovakia and Poland, which led eventually to World War II, and the claim of Morocco to the Tindouf area of Algeria. In some cases one country claims that culturally and historically the whole of another country belongs to it. Examples are the claim of China to Tibet (which was taken by force by China in 1951 and put more directly under its control in 1959) and of Ghana to all of Togo.

An interesting case of how doctrinal nationalism can lead to separatist and irredentist movements at the same time involves the Somalis of East Africa. The Somalis share a common language and culture, but when the European conquerors drew national boundaries the Somalis were placed in five different political jurisdictions: Italian Somaliland, British Somaliland, Djibouti (under French control), the northeast part of Kenya, and the southeast part of Ethiopia. After gaining their independence, the first two nations united to form Somalia. Uniting the rest of the Somalis has proven more difficult. The Somalis constitute only a small proportion of the population of Ethiopia and Kenya and just over half of the population of Djibouti. The Somalis in Ethiopia are engaged in a separatist effort, while Somalia is engaged in an irredentist effort to expand its boundaries to include all Somalis. The other countries claim that Somalia is merely trying to take from them land which has valuable resources. Furthermore, these other countries resisting the Somali effort have the support of the Organization of African Unity, an organization composed of the present ruling governments in Africa which have decided that all national boundaries should remain as drawn by Europeans because any effort to redraw them could only lead to chaos. This situation apparently leaves the Somali nationalists with a single option for fulfilling their dreams: war. On the other hand, the governments of the newly independent nations of Africa are seeking to promote nationalism in the sense of loyalty to the political nation-state in order to try to overcome the racial-ethnic nationalism that threatens to tear their countries apart.

The fourth kind of movement generated by *doctrinal nationalism* that might also lead to war is that in which an ethnic group within an independent nation-state seeks to have that whole nation absorbed into another nation-state which it culturally resembles. This type of effort is a *reintegrationist* movement. It is similar in a way to irredentism, but here it is the people in the "unredeemed" territory who are actively seeking to be reattached to what they regard as their homeland, rather than the homeland actively seeking to annex the area in which they live. The resistance in this case comes from other ethnic groups in the independent nation-state who do not want to be absorbed into the larger political unit. Cyprus is a good example of this type of situation. Cyprus is presently an independent nation-state, having won its independence from Britain in 1960. Many of its 80 percent ethnically Greek population would like to see it become part of the nation-state of Greece. On the other hand, the 20 percent of the population which is ethnically Turkish is adamantly opposed to such a move. With the nation of Greece ready to defend the interests of the Greek Cypriots and the nation of Turkey ready to defend the interests of the Turkish Cypriots, the potential for violent conflict is obvious. The United Nations peacekeeping force on Cyprus has been able to keep the situation under control most of the time, but there have been many violent outbreaks including an invasion by Turkish troops in 1974 which resulted from Turkish fears that the island was about to be annexed by Greece. Cyprus remains divided with a Turkish-controlled "autonomous republic" in the north and the rest of the island under the control of Greek Cypriots. The desire of Catholics in Northern Ireland to reunite that state with Ireland may be viewed as another example of a reintegrationist movement which has led to violence.

We can now turn our attention to the way in which *patriotism or nationalism as loyalty to the nation-state* is related to war. It is this kind of nationalism that comes into play in most international conflicts.[16] During conflict situations the people of the countries involved are urged not only to love their own country but to hate some actual or potential enemy. During World War II, for example, propaganda in the U.S. urged Americans not only to love their own country but also to hate the Germans and

Japanese. After that war was over and the Cold War had begun, Americans were told that the Germans and Japanese are not really such bad people after all but that the Russians and Chinese, our allies in World War II, are the people we should hate. Recently the Russians have become "good guys" again.

This nationalistic group hatred gets people ready to kill if there is a war. It also distorts people's perceptions of events so that war becomes more likely. Nationalism is nourished by focusing on the good things done by one's own nation and the bad things done by "the enemy," simultaneously ignoring the bad things done by one's own nation and the good things done by "the enemy." It tends to accentuate the differences between "us" and "them" and to dismiss the similarities. In this way, the members of the opposing nations are led to be proud of their own nation and to be indignant about all of the horrible things done by "the wicked enemy."

A particularly good example of nationalistic hatred is the antagonism that developed between the French and the Germans as the result of being opponents in one war after another from the time of Napoleon through World War II. It became difficult for either group to see any virtue in the other. They accentuated their differences in food, drink, language, and so on. Under such circumstances it was relatively easy for the German and French governments to mobilize their people for war against each other.

But in this relationship between Germany and France there may be a lesson concerning the connection between nationalism and war. It may be that nationalism in the sense of hatred of another group is more an effect of war and preparation for war than a cause of it, though it may certainly be both. Because the Cold War created a political situation requiring the Germans and French to cooperate against a possible invasion from the Russians, the nationalistic hatred between these two nations diminished considerably. The shift in American attitudes since World War II toward Germans and Japanese also supports the notion that nationalistic hatred is more the result of wars and indoctrination dictated by political interests than it is a cause of wars. It appears that nationalistic hatred is produced deliberately by leaders and propagandists as the result of opposition to another nation's political policies, and is not the result of some inherent hatred of the people of one nation for the people of another.

Still, we should not overlook the way in which nationalism provides the basis for support of national policies which lead to war. People want their own nation-state to have a high status; they feel good when their country has the highest gross national product or the highest per capita gross national product or the largest number of nuclear warheads. People feel bad when their country falls behind others in these and other categories. They feel good when their country expands its territorial holdings and bad when the extent of territory controlled by their country is reduced. People feel especially good when their country wins military battles or is successful in getting another nation to back down in a head-to-head confrontation, and they feel bad when their country loses a military battle or retreats in a head-to-head confrontation.

These nationalistic feelings support national leaders who aggressively defend the nation-state's economic interests and lead the country to military strength and dominance over other countries. The difficulty is that status is a relative thing. It is impossible for all nation-states to be first, or even near the top, with regard to wealth or military power. Struggles for superiority and "honor" (not backing down) thus take place between country and country. It is nationalism which generates public support for those national leaders who behave aggressively in these struggles. This support for aggressiveness certainly does not decrease the likelihood of international war.

Thus we see that nationalism contributes to war in several ways. Doctrinal nationalism supports liberation movements, separatist movements, irredentist movements, and reintegrationist movements, all of which may lead to war. Loyalty to the nation-state or patriotism supports aggressive national leaders in their struggles for power. It would be difficult to point to any war in the nineteenth and twentieth centuries in which nationalism in one or another sense had not been a significant factor.

VI. Other Views About Causes of War

We have discussed the hypotheses that war is the result of individual human aggression; that it is caused by groups competing for survival, for goods, for control of information, for status, and for political power; and that it is due to group identification, especially identification with the nation. Now we will consider some other views.

Arms Races as a Cause of War

If the ultimate test of a nation's strength is its capacity to defend itself in a war, then any nation which anticipates war seems to have little choice but to build up its military forces to be superior to those of the anticipated enemy. It could even be argued that, in the face of a possible attack from another nation, failure of a nation to increase its military forces might in fact encourage attack because the other nation would be led to expect a quick and easy victory. On the other hand, if two nations confront each other and each aims to make its military forces superior, a steady increase of arms on both sides will result. This escalation of arms construction and deployment will be further intensified if military planners on each side include an extra build-up just in case the potential enemy's forces are stronger than estimated.

This situation in which two potential enemy nations (or groups of nations) each try over a period of time to gain armed superiority over the other is called an arms race. Such a race seems to contribute to the likelihood of war between the nations involved. The temptation to start a war seems to be especially great when one nation possesses a newly developed, significant weapon which its potential opponent does not yet have but will probably acquire in the near future. Why not start a war when the prospect of victory is greatest? Why wait, when waiting might eventually result in the enemy gaining military superiority?

To get a better understanding of what it is like to be a leader of a nation involved in an arms race, the reader is invited to play a simple game.[1] Ideally there should be three participants, but with the proper arrangements and understandings, two can play. When there are three persons, one acts as supervisor, referee, timekeeper, and scorekeeper while the other

81

two represent the heads of nations involved in an arms race. Each player needs a small piece of paper or cardboard which can be concealed under his hand on a flat surface. This piece of paper should have a plus-sign on one side and a minus-sign on the other, so the player can indicate whether he has chosen to increase or decrease the military spending of his nation.

To begin the game, the timekeeper tells the players that they have 30 seconds before they will be required to render their first arms decisions (which can be considered the first annual budget). The players are permitted to communicate with each other and to make "treaties," but as in actual international situations no one enforces any agreements that might be made. As the 30-second deadline approaches, the players place their pieces of paper on the table with either the plus-sign or the minus-sign face up, but conceal it until the timekeeper says, "Now." Players then uncover the papers allowing the others to see the decisions. The timekeeper calculates, records, and announces the score and then informs the players that the next decision is due in 30 seconds. The entire sequence is then repeated. The game can be as long or short as players desire, but for the first game the recommended duration is about 20 decisions.

The scoring of the game is crucial, and the players must understand it before beginning play. Each player receives 10,000 points at the start of the game. This figure represents the average standard of living of the people in each player's country. The object of the game is to score as high as possible, that is, to improve the average standard of living of one's nation as much as possible. Each time a decision is made, scoring depends on the combination of the decisions of the two players. If both players put the minus-sign up, indicating a cutback in military spending, each is awarded 100 points. If both put the plus-sign up, indicating an increase in spending, each loses 100 points. But if one puts the plus-sign up and the other the minus, they receive different scores: the player with the plus-sign gains 500 while the one with the minus-sign loses 500. This scoring represents a situation in which the military superiority of one nation allows it to make coercive arrangements with other nations to the disadvantage of its opponent. The game illustrates the logic of arms races and the difficulty of controlling them even when both parties realize objectively that it would be best for both to disarm.

What strategy should a player use in this game? One might adopt a tit-for-tat strategy, opting each time to do what the opposing player had done on the previous turn. One could adopt a hawkish strategy and increase arms spending every turn, regardless of what the opponent does, on grounds that this would maximize gains and minimize losses whatever decision the opponent made. A player might adopt a dove-like strategy and consistently decrease arms expenditures regardless of what the opponent does on grounds that this seems to be the only way of ending the arms race. (Empirical evidence suggests that this strategy does not work in many situations and in fact often encourages the opponent to be aggressive.²)

Players could also adopt different strategies with regard to communication with the opponent. For example, they might decide to announce what strategy they intend to use and then use it, or they might decide to *say* that they will use one strategy and then actually use another. They must decide whether or not to abide by agreements entered into with the other player. Games like this one have been played and observed with a view to determining which strategies different kinds of people do actually use and which strategies are most likely to succeed in bringing an arms race under control.[3]

In what sense, if any, are arms races a cause of war? It seems that arms races themselves are always an *effect* of some other "cause of war" such as a struggle for power. Nations do not simply fall into arms races against some nations and not against others; there is always some other cause such as economic or ideological conflict which leads to the arms race. For example, before World War I there was an arms race between Britain and Germany but not between Britain and the United States. Why? The difference can be explained at least in part by the conflict of ideology between Britain and Germany while Britain and the U.S. were ideological allies.

Nevertheless, once an arms race begins it may serve as an additional contributory factor to the outbreak of war. It has been argued by Lewis Richardson that the behavior of nations involved in an arms race can be described by a mathematical model.[4] According to this model there are only two circumstances where arms races could be kept from going out of control and ultimately resulting in war: (1) the capability for building more arms is overcome by resistance to military spending, or (2) one side decides to drop out of the arms race and accept domination by the other. Richardson believed that neither of these things would be likely to occur in the twentieth century.[5] Of the wars that occurred between 1820 and 1929, Richardson concluded that arms races were a significant factor in the outbreak of war in about one-ninth of the cases.[6] That result suggests that arms races are sometimes a contributory factor to the beginning of war even though they are also the effect of other causes.

At first glance it may seem that the apparent end of the long arms race between the U.S. and the Soviet Union in 1989 shows that Richardson's mathematical model was mistaken, but actually just the opposite is the case. Richardson had specified two circumstances where an arms race could be kept from going out of control: (1) resistance to more military spending and (2) the readiness of one side to accept domination by the other. He, and many others, believed it unlikely that in the twentieth century either of these circumstances would be realized, but in fact both were. The Soviet leaders did decide that they just could not continue to spend so much for the military while their domestic economy was failing, and they also decided that under the circumstances they could accept domination by the U.S. But it was not generally expected they would do that. In fact, for those who lived through the Cold War it is still somewhat unbelievable that they did. We were very lucky in 1989. Many would say, "Thank heaven for

Gorbachev." What all this means is that improbable events do occur. As anyone familiar with probability theory can testify, improbable events are occurring all the time. Exceptions to generalities do not show that the generalities are mistaken. It is still the case that arms races can contribute to the outbreak of war and that once an arms race gets going it is very difficult to stop it. Don't forget the arms race game.

Particular Villains as a Cause of War

If we look at the problem of crime within a society, it seems reasonable to believe that a good portion of it is caused by a few antisocial people. It seems that the best way to eliminate, or at least greatly reduce, crime is to lock these criminals away so they can no longer harass the rest of society. Some see an analogy between crime and war and believe that the basic cause of war is the existence of a few villains who are ready to use force and violence to exploit the rest of society in order to get wealth and power for themselves. Wars are caused by these war-mongers, it is claimed, and the way to reduce the likelihood of war is to get rid of these troublemakers.

Different versions of this approach point to different types of villains. One view focuses on power-hungry individuals who work their way into leadership positions in nations or other groups which are ready to use violence. A second view sees the troublemakers as groups such as military leaders and weapons manufacturers who stand to realize substantial personal gains as the result of violent conflict. A third view sees the culprits as the elite of a society who are ready and willing to use violence to try to stop inevitable social changes which will eventually eliminate their positions of privilege.

The importance of the aggressiveness of the group leader was discussed earlier in connection with the relation of individual aggressiveness to the outbreak of war. As was noted then, it would be difficult in the human context to defend the view that these aggressive leaders are a necessary or a sufficient condition for war, but the more limited contention that power-hungry leaders are a contributory factor is plausible.[7]

A related thesis claims that particularly aggressive individuals are more likely to get into leadership positions in an authoritarian political system while liberal democratic political systems are less likely to allow such individuals to get to the top or to carry out inordinately aggressive policies when they do get to the top. According to this view, if all governments were democratic rather than autocratic the danger of war would be reduced considerably.[8] Woodrow Wilson's slogans during World War I, that it was "the war to end all wars" and at the same time "the war to make the world safe for democracy," are based on this viewpoint. The difficulty for this thesis is that democratic nations have had their share of aggressive leaders and oppressive foreign policies. It seems that the British, French, and Americans have been just as imperialistic as the Germans, Spanish, and Russians. One can hardly review the policies and practices of the U.S. government toward American Indians, toward Filipinos during and after the Spanish-American War, and toward Central America in the twentieth century and conclude that democratic governments are not aggressive toward other societies. The claim that liberal democracies do not fight wars with other liberal democracies has evidential support but may be due to the fact that countries where the leaders have similar cultural backgrounds and ideological commitments tend not to fight wars with one another.

In evaluating the relationship between democracy and war it should not be forgotten that Hitler came to power in Germany in accord with democratic procedures and that he had public support as long as his various military adventures were succeeding. It is questionable whether democracies have any special advantages in keeping aggressive individuals from gaining positions of leadership. Any restraint on aggressiveness may be due more to the checks on the power of the leader that exist within a democratic system, and even here it must be remembered that there is not much of a check as long as military action results in quick victory. Vietnam was a public relations disaster for the U.S. government, but the reaction to quick military victories in Grenada, Panama, and the 1991 Gulf War shows that the public does not generally disapprove of aggressive military action. In fact they seem to enthusiastically support it as long as victory is achieved quickly and with few casualties.

A second view about particular villains responsible for war is that war is caused by munitions makers, high-ranking military officers and others who profit from war and war preparations. The expression *military-industrial complex*[9] is used to refer to that relatively small group of people who benefit from war and preparation for war, a group that includes not only the professional military and the arms manufacturers but also others such as bankers who finance the arms industry, labor unions whose members produce arms, scientists and engineers engaged in weapons research, politicians eager to promote federal spending in their political districts, and veterans' organizations.

The thesis that arms manufacturers and their allies in the military, the government, and the newspaper-publishing business might deliberately promote war scares to stimulate military spending seems to have been first seriously argued by Richard Cobden in Britain in 1861.[10] He noted the repeated occurrence of a series of events beginning with expressions of concern by high-ranking naval officers (widely publicized by the newspapers) that France was preparing to invade Britain. An increase in appropriations to the navy soon followed, and then the threat disappeared. One event which provides a particularly good piece of evidence to support the view that arms manufacturers have deliberately stimulated arms races occurred a few years before World War I. H.H. Mulliner, the managing director of a British shipbuilding firm, told his friends in the military that he had secret information that the Germans had suddenly speeded up their building of battleships.[11] The story was leaked to the press, who cooperatively published it. The British public demanded that more battleships be built to meet the German challenge. The Germans denied having increased their efforts, but once the British speeded up theirs the Germans felt they had to do the same. After this naval arms race was in motion, Mulliner wrote a series of letters which were published in the London *Times* indicating how he had started the whole thing, but the arms race did not stop and Mulliner himself was fired. Another incident worthy of mention occurred in 1927 when American steel companies sent William Shearer to the Geneva Disarmament Conference for the express purpose of disrupting it.[12]

In the United States the notion that the U.S. munitions manufacturers had been responsible for involving the United States in World War I became popular in the 1930s as a result of public investigations by a Senate committee chaired by Senator Gerald Nye, although the committee failed to prove the allegations.[13] The idea that the military-industrial complex is a possible source of danger to U.S. policy-making was brought to public attention again by President Eisenhower in his 1961 farewell address.[14] During the Vietnamese War some opponents of the war claimed that the military-industrial complex was responsible for U.S. involvement. The notion that the arms race between the United States and the Soviet Union during the Cold War was largely due to the activities of the American military-industrial complex was widespread.[15]

Some observers claim that there was also a military-industrial complex which promoted war and preparation for war in the Soviet Union.[16] Even though there were no owners of arms industries in the Soviet Union, there were managers of such industries whose influence was greatly affected by the importance ascribed to their work. The military and the hawkish members of the political leadership had the same interests as their counterparts in the United States. It was even suggested that the military-industrial complexes of the Soviet Union and the United States kept the arms race going as an informal cooperative enterprise which was very profitable to both of them.[17] With the Cold War ended it has been suggested that the military-industrial complex in the U.S. is searching for some new "enemy" that will keep its services in demand.

What about these claims? Do certain people who profit from war actually cause wars to occur? Even Senator Nye claimed only that American munitions makers had caused the United States to be dragged into World War I, not that they had caused the war in the first place. And even if one took seriously the idea that there was an informal cooperative effort between the American and Soviet military-industrial complexes in support of a gigantic arms race, it does not follow that these groups actually wanted to cause a war or that they could have done so if they had desired that.

We need to use the distinctions about the various senses of "cause" we have previously discussed. Are the advocates of the military-industrial complex theory claiming that these conspirators are a sufficient condition for war or merely a contributory factor? The former claim would suggest that this complex of individuals has so much influence that it can force political leaders to go to war. But even though the military-industrial complex in many countries is more influential than before World War II, it seems far-fetched to believe that this group has greater influence on government policies than the huge nonmilitary sector of the economy and the non-military population.

The claim that the military complex is a contributory factor to war is much more credible. Before the age of the long-range bomber and the intercontinental ballistic missile, high-ranking military officers and owners of arms-producing facilities could be relatively sure that they would not personally be hurt by war and that they stood to gain a great deal by it. Even in an age of intercontinental missiles certain kinds of war can be very profitable for military-industrial complexes in the richer countries. Furthermore, these are just the kinds of wars that have been occurring. The fact that these situations are profitable for the military-industrial complex does not prove that they bring them about, but it does raise suspicions. One such profitable situation is for the country where a military-industrial complex is located to engage in a limited war with an enemy which has no chance of hurting the wealthier country. This is exemplified by U.S. engagements in Korea, Vietnam, and Kuwait and Russian involvements in Hungary, Czechoslovakia, and Afghanistan. A second type of profitable situation for the military and arms producers is a war involving smaller allies of their own country in which the wealthier country supplies military know-how and weapons which need to be replaced again and again as they are destroyed in the fighting. Wars such as those in the Middle East during the Cold War period provided an excellent opportunity for the United States and Soviet Union to test some of their military equipment under actual battlefield conditions. Add to these wars the arms races which occurred in various parts of the world and it is evident that the post–World War II era was a very profitable one for the military-industrial complexes in the United States, Britain, France, and the Soviet Union. Even though the Cold War is over huge amounts of public money continue to flow into the military-industrial complex of the United States and its allies in order to be militarily prepared to fight any "enemy" which may appear on the scene.

Nevertheless, it is more plausible to suppose that national governments struggling for power with each other create the military-industrial complexes than to believe that the military-industrial complexes control the governments. The decision to spend large amounts of government money for military purposes so that arms-making is profitable is a political decision. Governments could make it equally profitable for industry to make computers and tractors to donate to less developed countries. Then a products-for-development complex would come into being which would be as self-perpetuating as the military-industrial complex. Why isn't there an influential products-for-development complex? It is because governments are willing to spend large amounts for weapons to use in the struggle for power against other national governments while they are unwilling to spend large amounts to assist people in less developed countries.

As long as crucial international conflicts are to be resolved by force and threats of force, governments of nations likely to be challenged by others seem to have little choice but to try to make their military forces "second to none." Once a military-industrial complex is created to produce this military superiority, it tends to be self-sustaining and to encourage attitudes and policies which will work to its own advantage. This probably contributes to the existence of arms races and to the outbreak of limited wars, but like the arms race itself, the military-industrial complex seems to be an effect of other, more fundamental causes rather than an ultimate cause of war.[18]

A third view about villains who are responsible for war is associated with the names Karl Marx, Friedrich Engels, and V.I. Lenin. According to this view the villains are the elite of a society who try by force to maintain their positions of privilege in the face of economic and social changes which eliminate the underpinning which gave rise to their status.

Understanding this view will require a brief discussion of some of the basic ideas of Marx, Engels, and Lenin.[19] According to them the most important thing about a society is how its goods and services are provided. A society in which people hunt, fish, and forage for food will be much different from a society in which agriculture and domesticated animals provide the food supply. In fact, they believe that the whole social structure and cultural outlook will depend on the mode of production. In a feudal society where agriculture and domesticated animals are the basic sources of goods, those who own land will be the elite and the culture will develop around their outlook and interests. On the other hand, in a bourgeois society where small-scale manufacturing is the basic means of producing goods, those who own the shops will be the elite and the culture will reflect their concerns. (See chart on pages 124–25.)

According to this theory, if the mode of production continues to be the same, the society will be stable and violent conflict at a minimum. But if the basic mode of production changes, then the situation is different. Consider, for example, what happened at the beginning of the industrial revolution when simple machines were introduced which enabled one person to produce a great deal more than previously could be produced by several persons in the same period of time. The introduction of these machines changed the mode of production from one in which each family milled its own grain and wove its own cloth by hand to one in which machines did this work. Before the introduction of these machines wealth would depend basically on how much land you owned; afterward it would depend basically on how many of these machines you owned. In the old feudal society the big landowners (the nobility) were the elite. A whole social structure and cultural outlook had been built around their interests. The newly rich bourgeoisie did not fit into this structure and outlook. Consequently, a struggle for power resulted. The old landed aristocracy tried to preserve the social structure which supported their positions of privilege while the owners of machinery strove for recognition in accord with their new wealth and power in the society.

If the old elite would have modified their social structure to make room for the owners of machinery, a peaceful transition could have taken place, but the old elite didn't make such a move. Why not? First, they did not intend to surrender their positions of privilege simply because some other people wanted them. Second, the old social structure with which they were familiar was "natural," the only social structure they could imagine. On the other hand, the bourgeoisie had power represented by the productive capability of their machines. If the old nobility wouldn't step aside peacefully, there was no choice but to throw them out of power violently. The French Revolution in 1789 is a good example of the violent overthrow of the old aristocracy by the new middle class.

One might be inclined to say that it was the new middle class rather than the old nobility who caused this violent upheaval. It was, after all, the bourgeoisie and their followers who were the active agents of the revolution. But according to Marx and Engels such a view of the situation overlooks the force used by the old order to try to prevent change. It is true that the repressive violence used by the police was authorized by the laws of the existing government, but that fact merely shows that the government was just one more part of the social structure controlled by the old nobility. The blame for the violence, according to the Marxists, should be placed not on the revolutionaries seeking to establish a social order based on the objective reality of the new dominant mode of production, but rather on the old elite who use force to preserve a social order which is no longer appropriate to the objective situation.

What has been said so far may lead the reader to believe that Marx and Engels were supporters of bourgeois capitalism. In one sense they were. They thought capitalism was a great advance over feudalism and that it was desirable for the bourgeoisie to use force to overthrow the social structures of the landed aristocracy. But in another sense Marx and Engels were opponents of bourgeois capitalism. They opposed the capitalist society in which they lived because they believed that still another qualitative shift had taken place in the mode of production, a shift from small-scale individualistic manufacturing to the social production of goods by cooperative effort in huge factories. The social structure (such as private ownership of factories) and cultural outlook (such as rugged individualism) of the capitalists were built on the foundations of small-scale manufacturing, but Marx and Engels felt that the shift to mass production made these social structures and this cultural outlook obsolete. Thus the capitalists were now to be opposed by the new revolutionary socialists, just as the landed aristocracy had previously been opposed by the revolutionary capitalists. Now it was the capitalists who were using government-sanctioned force to obstruct needed social change. It may seem that the socialist revolutionaries are the instigators of war, but according to Communists the blame belongs to the capitalists who refuse to permit the social changes required by the shift to the collective production of goods. In the nineteenth and twentieth centuries, according to the Marxists, the capitalists who resist the needed change to socialism are the villains responsible for war.

In order to evaluate this view, let us return to our distinctions about the various senses of the word *cause*. Are the present capitalist leaders supposed to be a sufficient cause of war? That is, do they by themselves bring about war? The answer seems to be "No." They might, according to Communists, bring about oppression, but war occurs only when there is also violent resistance to this oppression. Consequently, it does not seem that Marxists maintain that the capitalists are a sufficient condition for war.

Are the capitalist leaders a necessary condition for war at the present time? (Obviously at an earlier time the question would need to be raised concerning the landed aristocracy rather than the capitalists.) It would seem that Marxists answer this question in the affirmative, believing that if all capitalists were out of the way then war would be eliminated. At any stage in history, the Marxists seem to be saying, if the old elite would just step aside when their privileged positions are no longer objectively supported by the mode of production, then there would be no wars.

Such an extreme claim seems difficult to defend. A survey of history reveals many wars in which one feudal society fought against another feudal society and one capitalist society against another. We can even find instances in recent history of one socialist society fighting against another socialist society. If the only basis for war is the unwillingness of the old elite to give way to the new order, why do these nonrevolutionary wars occur? It seems that Marxist thought focuses for the most part on wars *within* societies rather than wars *between* societies, and even *within* societies it is questionable whether the Marxist view adequately accounts for wars such as those resulting from nationalistically motivated separatist movements.

Recognizing that Marxist theory did not seem particularly relevant to the wars taking place between countries in the late nineteenth and early twentieth centuries, Lenin extended Marx's analysis of social conflict to the international sphere.[20] The capitalist countries were engaged in two kinds of wars, he said: colonial wars against less developed countries and wars between themselves. The first type of war could readily be explained by an extension of Marxist principles. The capitalists were countering a possible revolution in their own societies by subjugating distant peoples, exploiting them, and giving some of the benefits to the workers in the home country. This arrangement allowed large profits to continue to flow into the pockets of the capitalists without objection from the working classes at home.

The second type of war, that kind due to economic competition between capitalist nations for control in colonial regions, introduces a cause for war not present in the original Marxist position. This position still ascribes blame to the capitalists for all wars but no longer defines all wars as conflicts between an old elite class and a new revolutionary class. And once Marxist-Leninists concede that economic competition between one capitalist nation and another may be a cause of war, then it would seem that they must also allow that wars may be the result of economic competition between one *noncapitalist* nation and another. They then must also admit that wars within countries can be caused by economic competition between groups which are from the same economic class.

Furthermore, Lenin's revision seems unable to account for more recent wars between one socialist country and another. Were any capitalists involved in the border dispute which developed between China and the Soviet Union in the 1960s? Were any capitalists involved in the Communist Chinese invasion of Communist Vietnam or the Communist Vietnamese invasion of Communist Cambodia in 1979? Once it is admitted that other factors such as nationalism may be involved in these disputes, the question is raised whether nationalism might not be the crucial factor in other wars.

The Marxist-Leninist thesis that the capitalist class is the cause of all war depends on accepting a debatable theory of history which views the ruling class as the cause of all violence. Recent history seems to refute the notion that the capitalists are a necessary condition of war. The most that can plausibly be claimed is that capitalists are a contributory cause of war, a claim that seems to be strongest in the case of colonial wars and efforts to squash liberation movements in less developed countries.[21]

War as an Effort to Suppress Internal Dissension

The famous German philosopher Hegel observed that "peoples involved in civil strife also acquire peace at home through making wars abroad."[22] There seems to be little doubt that when a group or society is engaged in a violent conflict with a common enemy, differences of interest within that group or society are temporarily ignored. For example, in revolutions to overthrow a government such as occurred in Iran and Nicaragua in 1979, the revolutionary forces were able to unite in the fight to overthrow the old regime even though they may have very different views about what sort of new government is to be established after the revolution succeeds. In the same way quarreling groups within a nation tend to forget their grievances against each other when that nation is engaged in a war against another nation. Labor and management perceive that they must work together. Rich and poor see that they must join together in defense or go down to defeat together. Different racial or cultural groups will unite in the common effort even though they might be quite antagonistic toward each other in peacetime.

Under these circumstances it is easy to see that a leader who is being criticized by various factions within a movement or by various groups within a society might be tempted to begin using violence against a common enemy in order to quell the dissent. If internal strife is threatening, a war could be started to keep the internal disturbances under control. The leader must be subtle about accomplishing this outbreak of warfare, however, so that the other side can be blamed for it.

Has this sort of thing ever really happened? Has there ever been a war which was begun with the motive of overcoming internal dissension? One example frequently cited is that of Otto von Bismarck, Chancellor of Prussia and then Chancellor of the German Empire during much of the last half of the nineteenth century. At one time he observed that his various wars had undercut the influence of the left-wing revolutionaries in Prussia, but he never said that he started the wars to accomplish this aim. The wars he started in the middle and late 1860s aimed to bring the previously separate German states under Prussian control. One might be tempted to say that he started wars with external enemies in order to unify the German nation and that he succeeded in accomplishing this goal after peaceful efforts to unite the German states had failed.[23] But it can be asked whether this case is truly an example of wars being started in order to alleviate internal dissension. It seems rather to be a case of a leader being particularly clever at gaining new territory without arousing any resentment among the people who have been brought under his control.

The effort in 1982 by the government of Argentina to take over the Falkland Islands–Malvinas from Britain is viewed by some as an example of a government starting an external skirmish in order to counteract domestic unrest. On the other hand, that effort may have been triggered by the desire of the Argentine government to have control over those islands when a treaty about ownership of resources located on the ocean floor around those islands comes into effect. In any case, the project failed because the British soon recaptured the islands. Furthermore, regardless of the motives in this particular case, attempts to discover any general correlation between internal discord and the fighting of external wars have been inconclusive.[24]

War as an Effort to Eliminate Injustice

We have previously discussed the issue of the relation between peace and justice. It was noted that peace may refer to the persistence of a situation in which some group or some nation is being treated unjustly. If this injustice is flagrant, the resentment may become so intense that people are ready to use violence to change the situation, especially if nonviolent efforts have proved to be unsuccessful.

It is interesting that both Thomas Jefferson and Karl Marx argued that violence is justified in such situations and that both the American and Russian revolutions are examples of wars fought to remove what were perceived to be injustices not removable in any other way. Jefferson even suggested that the use of violence to protect liberty would need to be repeated with some regularity. He wrote in a letter to Colonel Smith in 1787:

What country can preserve its liberties, if its rulers are not warned from time to time, that this people preserve the spirit of resistance? Let them take arms. . . . What signify a few lives lost in a century or two? The tree of liberty must be refreshed from time to time with the blood of patriots and tyrants. It is its natural manure. . . .[25]

Of course, the notion that violence should be used if necessary to combat injustice is not confined to Americans and Russians. In fact, almost all efforts to justify the use of violence, other than the rationale of self-defense, point to the need to remove some perceived injustice. For example, much civil strife has resulted from issues such as opposing claims concerning which person is the rightful ruler of a nation, and even Hitler's earliest aggressive actions were "justified" on grounds that the Treaty of Versailles ending World War I had been unfair to Germany.

A good contemporary example of war being waged in order to remove a perceived injustice is the battle of the Palestinian Arabs against the nation of Israel. This nation was established by Jews in 1947-48 with the aid of Britain and the United States on land inhabited largely by the Palestinian Arabs. When the British relinquished their control of the Middle East after World War II, these Palestinians wanted to establish a new independent nation. They had no objections to Jews already living there joining with them in a secular state, but they did object to the creation of a Jewish state which would be administered in accord with Jewish religious views and which would as a matter of policy try to attract more Jewish people to the area. Why, they asked, should Palestinians be required either to accept second-class citizenship in such a state or to move out of homes their families had occupied for generations? They used violence to try to prevent the establishment of a Jewish state, and they continued to use violence against it after it was created. The Palestinians felt that it was very unjust for such a state to be created, without their consent, on territory which they regarded as their own. A comparable situation for Americans would be to have American Indians, assisted by other nations, reestablish their "nation" where we now live, with the requirement that we abide by the Indian laws or get out. Of course, the Jews and the Indians might feel that they were finally getting back what had unjustly been taken from them at an earlier time. Such are the intricacies of questions of justice. One great problem related to using violence to remove perceived injustices is that different parties have different perceptions of what is just.

Questions of justice are even more likely to be the cause of war *within* nations. We have previously discussed the Marxist view that one cause of war is the unwillingness of the elite to give up positions of privilege when changed conditions indicate they should. We also noted earlier that governments tend to be more sensitive to the problems of people with wealth and power than to the poor and powerless. It is not surprising that sometimes people feel so oppressed that they believe the only viable action is to resort to violence.

Using violence to fight injustice constitutes a problematic situation: The use of violence will probably result in much injustice itself. There is usually a question of whether some nonviolent approach might be effective in alleviating the injustice. There is also a danger that the use of force will fail and make the oppressors even more oppressive. Finally, there is the problem of whether or not one's own perceptions of what is just or unjust are merely biased views reflecting self-interest. Regardless of these considerations, the desire to remove some perceived injustice has been a contributory factor in many wars, especially those taking place within countries.

The Absence of Peaceful Alternatives as a Cause of War

War comes about as a result of conflicts between groups, but such conflict situations need not be resolved by resort to violence. Bargaining, arbitration, and the institutions of government represent some other avenues for resolving conflict. There are some conflict situations, however, where none of these alternatives seems to be a viable option. Bargaining depends ultimately on threats of force and stubbornness. Arbitration depends on the availability of an arbitrator perceived as fair by both parties and also as so strong and independent that he will not be intimidated by either. The institutions of government exist only in the most rudimentary forms with regard to handling conflicts between nations. Even within a nation a fair resolution depends on the government being neutral between the parties to the conflict, a situation which often does not exist. Consequently, it frequently happens that the parties to a dispute decide on trial by force simply because there seems to be no other way.

Within a country, the belief that the conflict cannot be resolved by any approach short of violence produces new sources of antagonism on both sides. Groups intent on overthrowing the government or on establishing an autonomous state for some national minority cease to rely merely on propaganda and peaceful protests to promote their point of view. They inaugurate the use of violence against the police and sabotage against the government generally. On the other side, the government begins arresting and torturing anyone who might in any way be suspected of aiding the revolutionary or separatist forces. Tensions mount. Each incident involving violence calls for more violence by the other side. The perception that violence is the only way to settle the issue thus becomes itself a contributory factor to the outbreak and escalation of violence.

In international conflicts the same situation exists. Once it is believed that the use of violence is the only way to resolve the dispute it follows that if either side momentarily gains a substantial advantage, it should strike at that moment. When it is believed that there will be a war anyway, why not fight it when one has the best chance of winning it? It is apparent that viewing war as inevitable can itself be a cause of war.[26] If such thinking had prevailed, the United States might well have attacked the Soviet Union in the early 1950s when Americans had a marked superiority in atomic weapons and the means of delivering them against the enemy. This type of reasoning seems to have been the basis for the Soviet Union's plans to attack China in 1969 and for earlier American thoughts about attacking China during the Korean War. There is some hope for humanity in light of the fact that this thinking did not result in action on these occasions. Still there is no assurance that restraint and the possibility of third-party intervention will continue to inhibit military action in the international arena.

We must conclude that the absence of trustworthy nonviolent ways of resolving conflicts of interest at both the national and international levels constitutes a contributory factor to the outbreak of war. In the many nations where political and judicial institutions do provide relatively adequate nonviolent means for adjudicating conflicts, peace and a satisfactory degree of justice are maintained even when intense antagonisms exist. The absence of fair and nonviolent instruments for resolving conflict in other nations and at the world level is a particularly important cause of war, because the presence of such instruments would diminish the likelihood of war even in the face of the existence of the other causes of war previously discussed.[27]

VII. The Value of War

The general assumption of our inquiry about war is that human society is now faced with the problem of how to eliminate it. But is war really all bad? Hasn't war, at least in certain respects, been a good thing for human society? Although it would be a mistake to argue that wars occur *because* they serve good purposes such as controlling population and stimulating technological progress,[1] still it might be claimed that we should not seek to prevent them because they do have some favorable results. Let us examine some of the alleged positive values of war.

The Biological Value of War

At the end of the eighteenth century Thomas Malthus first published his thesis that there is a natural tendency for the population of humans to increase in a geometrical progression (or exponential pattern) (2, 4, 8, 16, 32, etc.), while food production tends to grow only in an arithmetic progression (2, 4, 6, 8, 10, etc.). Consequently, population will tend to outgrow food supply, and there must be some devices by which the population growth is checked. According to Malthus, disease, famine, and war are three such devices. Thus war, it is claimed, has a positive value: People are killed off so they and the children they would have produced need not face death from disease or starvation.

Has war been an important factor in controlling human population? The facts seem to suggest not. Even if as many as 51 million people were killed in World War II as some claim,[2] that would have been only 2 percent of the world's population.[3] The people killed in that war were replaced in a single year. In South Vietnam the population actually grew at a rate of 3 percent a year during three years (1964–67) while a war was being fought on its soil.[4] Statistics from earlier wars, all of which were considerably less lethal than World War II, indicate that "during the Christian Era, warfare has not been a major force controlling the size of human population."[5] It is disease, rather than war, which has been the major factor in controlling human population growth, and the surge in population growth during the past 50–60 years can be attributed to the use of DDT, public sanitation projects, and modern medical knowledge rather than any decrease in deaths due to war.

A second view about the biological value of warfare claims that war improves the genetic quality of humans because it provides a means by which

96

the less skilled and less cooperative members of human society are killed or disgraced, while the better warriors win mates and produce offspring. But since such a small proportion of the population is killed even in a war as tragic as World War II, there could be no significant selection of the fittest even if one grants the very debatable premise that war results in the less fit becoming less likely to produce offspring.[6] Anthropologist Frederick Thieme has observed that "racial discrimination, selective immigration policies, imperialistic exploitation of peoples, and a host of other forms of behavior have had a much more significant effect on demography or genetics of many populations than has warfare."[7] It seems then that during the last 5,000 years or so war has not been an important factor in either population control or genetic selection.[8]

What about the future? There has been a steady trend toward more casualties in each war, and the development of modern weaponry, both nuclear and nonnuclear, would not seem to promise any reversal of that trend. An all-out nuclear war between the big powers could in a few hours produce many times the fatalities that occurred during all of World War II, and subsequent deaths from radiation and burns and other causes would swell the death count even further. Conventional weapons are being greatly improved in accuracy and destructiveness so that a much higher number of deaths can be expected even in nonnuclear wars. Thus future wars may have a much greater impact on the population of the earth than recent wars have had. At the same time, the possibility of genetic damage from radiation means that any war fought with nuclear weapons will surely be detrimental from a biological point of view.

The Technological Value of War

Another alleged positive value of war is that it stimulates social change. Societies tend to get into ruts and continue doing things in the same old way until some crisis, such as a war, forces them to adopt a more efficient social system, to do without some resources to which they are accustomed, or to be creative in the development of new weapons. Progress requires challenge, and war serves as the most intense kind of challenge to the society as a whole. Those who advocate this point of view may note the rapid development of aviation, electronics, medical technology, weather forecasting, synthetic materials, and so on during the past world wars. They may point to the large-scale government planning that was nonexistent before World War I and to the changed roles of women, a result of World War II. They may call attention to the changed situations of the former colonies of the Western European nations which have now become independent countries. Their claim is that all of this progress would not have occurred without the stimulus of war.

But it is impossible to say what would have occurred without the world wars. Before World War I the world had been moving toward a global community with a minimum of trade barriers and nationalistic feelings. Within a few decades inventions such as the telegraph, the telephone, the light bulb, the phonograph, the radio, the motion-picture camera and projector, the automobile, the airplane, and the agricultural tractor were brought forth with no stimulus from war. The technique of assembly line production was developed. The Suez and Panama canals were built and put into operation. Remarkable advances were made in controlling malaria, yellow fever, and typhoid. Freud was publishing his theories about the psychological origins of various forms of mental illness, and X-rays were discovered. Einstein published his paper on the theory of relativity in 1905. What would have happened if there had been no World War I? Didn't World War I, with its demand for battleships, submarines, artillery pieces, tanks, and military aircraft, act as a detriment to scientific progress? On the other hand, it was the necessities of war that led the Germans to pioneer the large-scale production of synthetic rubber and use of the Haber process to make the nitrates needed for explosives.

What was the situation between the world wars? New plastics were developed, along with synthetic materials such as rayon and nylon. The effectiveness of penicillin against bacteria was discovered. The basic principles of television, nuclear energy, and rocket propulsion were known before World War II broke out in 1939.[9] During that war, as during most wars, the scientific knowledge already available prior to the war was devoted to technological advancements for the military: nylon parachute cords, radar, V-2 rockets, atomic bombs, and the like. World War II caused a delay of at least five years in the development of nylon clothing, television, and the use of nuclear energy to generate electricity. On the other hand, the war probably hastened the development of antibiotics, DDT, jet engines, helicopters, rockets, and substitutes for petroleum.

The thesis that war and preparation for war yield "spin-offs" that improve human life needs to be countered by the observation that similar investments of money and effort made with the direct aim of improving human life would undoubtedly yield even greater benefits.[10] If it is the case that scientific and technological progress increases during war, it seems due primarily to the willingness of governments to spend large amounts of money on the development of weapons and related research. Suppose that governments were willing to spend similar amounts on medical research, better transportation and communication systems, and eliminating crime. Suppose that governments were willing to undertake massive expenditures to improve the educational levels of their citizens and to research better ways of teaching and learning. It seems safe to predict that the resulting social progress would be several times greater than that which occurs as "spin-offs" from military programs. It is not war and preparation for war that produce technological change. Instead, massive public expenditures for research and development achieve this result. Most governments are willing to pay these costs when stirred up by the threat of external attacks but are less willing to do so simply to improve the lives of their citizens.

It is true that social changes would probably come more slowly without war. Change would tend to be evolutionary rather than revolutionary, but this seems to be desirable because revolutionary change usually involves violence and also tends to elicit more violence later. There is also the issue of whether change is always desirable, a question that especially needs to be considered with regard to the kinds of changes war brings. For example, during war there tends to be a greater concentration of power in the hands of a few leaders, a situation which may continue after the war ends. Is that desirable? During war there tends to be less questioning of public policies and the decisions of those in command, which may also continue after the war is over. Is that desirable? Wars may accelerate social changes, but the changes may be undesirable.

Another aspect of this issue of technological and social progress as a result of war concerns the costs involved. Even if it were granted that more technological and social change takes place during war and that this change is desirable, one must still ask whether the cost of war exceeds the benefits. What might have been accomplished by those killed in a war? What additional things might have been accomplished even by those who survived the war uninjured but who had to devote several years of their early lives to fighting in it? Even in the simplest economic terms the public debt incurred during a war continues long after the war ends, contributing to inflation and taking funds that might be used instead for improving the quality of life. As the destructiveness and costs of war continue to escalate, it becomes more doubtful that war can be justified on the basis of any technological and social progress it might generate.

The Economic Value of War

Closely related to the issue of the technological value of war is the matter of the economic value of war. Especially among Americans there is a widely held view that war promotes economic prosperity. During World War I the U.S. economy did very well. Then, after ten years of peace (the "Roaring Twenties") came a depression, a depression which did not really end until the U.S. economy was stimulated by the outbreak of World War II in Europe. There were also boom times during the Korean and Vietnamese conflicts.[11] Doesn't this history show that war means an abundance of jobs, high wages, and good profits? The situation is somewhat similar for other countries such as Sweden, Switzerland, Canada, and Australia.

This perception that war is good for the economy depends, however, on the war's being fought on someone else's territory. For example, one could hardly say that the American Civil War was good for the U.S. economy of the southern part of the United States or that World War II was good for the economy of European countries such as Germany, Poland, and

Czechoslovakia. When some part of the world is being devastated by war and cannot produce the goods it usually does, there will obviously be a great opportunity for those countries not in the zone of destruction to produce and sell more to those who can no longer provide for themselves. Thus war will mean prosperity for those away from the war as they gain from the misfortunes of those at the center of the fighting. War destroys goods, and only those at a distance from the destruction will profit from it. A specific example of this truth is the devastation of Korea during the Korean War of 1950–53 while the Japanese economy boomed during this period.

Another reason that war seems to produce prosperity is that it leads governments to spend large amounts of money that they don't really have. War serves to excuse a level of government borrowing and spending which would not be tolerated in peacetime. That spending creates demand, thus stimulating the economy. But it should be noted that government borrowing and spending would have the same effect even if there were no war. It isn't only government spending *for war* which leads to more jobs and high profits. *Any* government spending financed by borrowing rather than higher taxes would produce the same results, at least temporarily. Later, of course, when the borrowed money needs to be repaid, there will be a drain on the economy, and that happens also whether the original spending was for the military or some other purpose.

If war isn't a stimulus to economic prosperity, what about military spending when there is no war but only a build-up of military forces? Doesn't that stimulate the economy? Once again, it isn't government spending *for the military* which leads to more jobs and high profits. Any government spending will do it. Large government outlays for education, for highways and public buildings, for medical research, for social welfare — for anything — will produce the same results, especially when it is paid for through deficit financing.

In fact it is now a generally accepted principle that more jobs would be created by nonmilitary spending than by military spending. According to various studies, government spending for military purposes actually causes a loss of jobs because more jobs could have been created if the same amount of money had gone to nonmilitary purposes.[12] It was estimated, for example, that back in 1974 state and local governments could have hired 30,000 more people per billion dollars of spending than could have been hired by the armed forces.[13]

It has also been pointed out that spending for the military is harmful to the economy in the long run. Even people who have benefited from military spending acknowledge that the United States is technologically 20 years behind where it would have been if the money spent on military research between 1950 and 1980 had instead been put into those areas of science and technology promising the most economic progress.[14] Economist Lloyd J. Dumas, having studied the impact of military spending on the U.S. economy, concluded:

> The military system . . . has diverted and continues to divert a substantial fraction of the United States' technological talent and enormous amounts of physical and financial capital, undermining the ability of U.S. producers to operate efficiently and thus to stay competitive with foreign producers.[15]

It has also been noted that among Western industrialized nations there is an inverse relationship between the amount the government spends on military research and the rate of growth of manufacturing productivity.[16]

The conclusion forced on us by the facts is that war, and even military spending without war, is not good for the economy. Similar government expenditures in nonmilitary areas would produce more jobs and more economic prosperity. Furthermore, in the long run expenditures for the military constitute a real hindrance to long-term economic growth.

The Psychological Value of War

Another claim made for the value of war is that it provides a feeling of significance for the individuals who participate, challenging citizens to sacrifice for the welfare of the society as a whole rather than pursuing their own personal welfare. What else besides war can lead individuals to give up the pursuit of their own petty aims and devote their efforts to an endeavor which is crucial for human destiny? It is only during war, some claim, that the existence of the society and its values are really threatened. It is only then that citizens can reasonably be called upon not only to forego certain amenities but perhaps to lose their lives for the sake of a larger good. People are forced to think in terms of the overall course of history and the relative insignificance of their own personal goals and activities. As the German philosopher Hegel put it:

> War is the state of affairs which deals in earnest with the vanity of temporal goods and concerns—a vanity at other times a common theme of edifying sermonizing. . . . War has the higher significance that by its agency, as I have remarked elsewhere, "the ethical health of the peoples is preserved. . . ."
> In peace civil life continually expands; all its departments wall themselves in, and in the long run men stagnate.[17]

Similar sentiments are expressed by World War II Italian Fascist leader Benito Mussolini.

> War alone brings up to its highest tension all human energy and puts the stamp of nobility upon the people who have the courage to meet it. All other trials are substitutes, which never really put men into the position where they have to make the great decision—the alternative of life or death.[18]

That there is some truth in the general point being made by Hegel and Mussolini can be confirmed by talking with persons who have been involved in a war in which they truly believed. Among Americans such persons are more likely to be veterans of World War II than of the Korean or Vietnamese conflicts. These World War II veterans are likely to have fond memories of the war period, when the humdrum existence of everyday life was broken by a new feeling of the significance of every act which contributed to the war effort and thus to the victory of "our" values over "their" values. When discussing such a war, they are likely to tell of a feeling of being a part of something bigger and to confirm the insight that war not only requires self-discipline and self-sacrifice but also provides a psychological lift, a sense that one's life will make some difference in the course of the world.

What can be said in response to this claim concerning the psychological value of war? The American philosopher and psychologist William James recognized the need for self-discipline and self-sacrifice for a larger cause which is met by participation in war, but he also realized that war was becoming too destructive to be a satisfactory way of meeting this need. Consequently, he recommended an alternative. In his essay "The Moral Equivalent of War"[19] James advocated having the government direct a "war" against the injustices of fate and nature, a war for which the young people of the nation would be drafted, trained, and then supported as they attempted to right the wrongs of the world.

James's list of tasks to be performed suggests that he was thinking mainly of requiring the men of the upper classes to get their hands dirty doing the kind of work ordinarily done by people of the lower classes, but his basic idea could be modified by having youth go to work in less developed countries or parts of their own country too poor to pay for their services. These young people would constitute an "army against injustice," something like the Peace Corps or the VISTA program, but James's proposal called for compulsory service for all young people rather than voluntary service for a few. These young people would thus be forced to dedicate themselves to problems beyond their own personal advancement and would find some significance in their lives as a result of being part of a general war on injustice. James realized that the task of establishing this battle against injustice as the moral equivalent of war would be difficult, but he thought it could be done. "It is but a question of time, of skillful propagandism, and of opinion-making men seizing historic opportunities."[20]

The psychological lift which comes from participating in war might also be duplicated by educating people to take a certain attitude toward their own lives. It is the awareness of being completely caught up in a good cause which transcends one's personal fate that makes participation in war such a significant experience. People should be able to become similarly involved in other efforts to advance the welfare of the human community. The problem of developing a human society which is both peaceful and just on the local, state, national, and global levels is a big enough problem to absorb the energies of any who care to join. There may not be danger of losing one's life in the sense of being killed, but there is a challenge to lose one's life in the sense of making continuous personal sacrifices of time and money in order to promote the general welfare. Perhaps we should follow

William James's suggestion and require all our young people to participate in such an endeavor for a couple of years; but an even better approach may be to try to open the eyes of all, young and old, to the challenge of serving humanity, letting them respond as they will. In either case, it is to be hoped that the psychological lift generated by participation in war can be replaced by a similar satisfaction from sharing in the never-ending battle to eliminate injustice, violence, and ignorance.

The Social Value of War

Two theses about the social value of war need to be considered. The first, called "international Social Darwinism," maintains that war is an instrument of struggle among various societies which, like the struggle for surviving among individual organisms, results in the survival of the fittest societies. War is thus an instrument of social evolution. The second thesis maintains that warfare functions as a safety valve allowing the hostility among members of a society to be directed toward an external enemy.[21] War thus promotes social cohesion.

The thesis that war is a useful device by which more advanced societies eliminate less fit societies was popular with Europeans from the fifteenth through the first part of the twentieth centuries, for it provided a rationale for subjugating native populations in the Americas, Asia, and Africa. The question which must be raised here is whether technological superiority in weaponry proves social or cultural superiority. Were those societies which first used iron weapons socially and culturally superior to those which during the same period fought with weapons of bronze? Is the Spartan society to be judged culturally superior to that of Athens simply because it was victorious in the Peloponnesian War? Making weapons and winning wars is but part of the business of a society; an inferiority in this activity does not imply an inferiority in other respects. It seems as inappropriate to evaluate societies on the basis of their capacity to win violent conflicts as to evaluate individuals on this basis.

What about the thesis that war has the positive value of promoting social cohesion by allowing hostility to be displaced onto an external enemy? Other crises such as earthquakes or tornadoes also stimulate group cohesion but do not provide the outlet for hostility that war does. Thus the challenge is to find some other activities which promote group cohesion while at the same time providing a legitimate outlet for aggressive feelings. One obvious substitute for war in this regard is participation in athletic contests, either actually or vicariously through observation. For example, an American basketball team composed of individuals from different racial groups competing against teams from other nations does wonders for reducing domestic tensions between these racial groups. At the same time, however, these contests, like war itself, may stir up antagonisms between nations. In 1969 a three-game series to determine who would represent

Central America in the World Cup soccer championship touched off a short war between El Salvador and Honduras,[22] and in 1985 there was a "soccer riot" in Belgium when British fans attacked supporters of an Italian team.[23] Athletic contests should be a substitute for war, not a stimulus to it. Another possible alternative to war is competition among societies in scientific activities such as the exploration of space or the conquest of disease. Among less developed countries there could be contests to increase the literacy rate, reduce the infant mortality rate, or raise agricultural production.

The possibility of implementing alternative forms of competition is not the only way to respond to the thesis that war is desirable because it creates internal cohesion. It can be noted that even if war was once valuable as a means to this end, it no longer is. The destructiveness of modern warfare is so great that the cost now exceeds any benefits to be expected in terms of group cohesion. Another response is that group cohesion is not always a good thing. Internal dissension is somewhat better than the conformity and uniformity of expressed opinion which is typical of a society at war with an external enemy. Such considerations undermine the notion that war is desirable because of the internal cohesion it maintains within a group.

The Moral Value of War

We earlier noted that a possible cause of war is the desire to eliminate injustice. We have also observed that there is a tendency for people with power to establish institutions by which their privileged positions can be maintained and that this situation exists both within national governments and among national governments at the global level. Frequently political institutions will be used not only to protect power but to extend it. Thus government itself may become an instrument of exploitation. In such a situation ordinary citizens cannot effectively appeal to the government for protection because the government itself is controlled by the exploiters. History is full of instances where people have used violence to overthrow an oppressive government. One of the positive values of war, it is claimed, is its use to gain freedom from tyrannical government. The threat of such a possibility is also useful in checking governments that otherwise might be more oppressive. This same principle seems to apply in the international sphere. If weaker nations possessed no possibility at all of resisting the more powerful nations by some use of force, they would probably be exploited even more than they are.

The use of violence and threats of violence has probably had some influence at times in reducing or eliminating tyranny and the exploitation of weaker nations by stronger ones. An evaluation of the thesis that war and the threat of war is therefore desirable, however, requires taking account of the whole picture. The possibility of violence against the government may serve to keep the government from becoming tyrannical, but a tyrannical government may react to threats of violence by becoming even more oppressive. It may establish secret police to ferret out even the beginnings of protest, and try to control every facet of life so that no revolution can even get started. The possibility of violence against the government thus becomes an excuse for even more tyranny. The same situation exists on the international level. One nation may try to completely dominate another one on the grounds that even a little freedom could be used later to move to total independence and result in less power for the previously dominant nation.

Suppose that a different approach were adopted both by the rulers and the ruled. Suppose that a tradition were established that there would be no armed revolt against the government, and that the government would allow some gradual peaceful change even in opposition to the interests of the privileged people of the society. In this situation the government probably would not be very tyrannical since it would not be fearful of being over- thrown. A new balance would be brought into existence in which distor- tions of justice and exploitation of the poor are kept under control while those not in power would be permitted to publicize their views and even gradually change the social structure. On the international level, a less powerful nation which appears to be somewhat cooperative toward a more powerful nation would probably be allowed more freedom than a smaller nation which constantly rejects all cooperation. The balance here again re- quires the more powerful nation to control its desire to exploit and the weaker nation to forego strident demands for rights.

It is distressing to realize that in these situations power is only partly restrained by considerations of justice and that the claims of the less power- ful for justice must be tempered by a recognition of the realities of power. This type of compromise, widely practiced, is not the morally perfect situa- tion. Yet these situations seem immensely preferable to an unrestrained, violent struggle for power between the privileged and the underprivileged. In the latter situation, the success of a violent revolution may produce a new group of leaders who will themselves become a new privileged group even more oppressive than those they replaced. Cognizant of how it was able to come to power, this group will seek to prevent others from overthrowing its rule. On the other hand, if there is absolutely no possibility of violent resistance by the have-nots regardless of the level of exploitation and op- pression, a real danger of tyranny exists.

The best situation seems to be a system of governance with built-in checks against tyranny. Nevertheless, it must be admitted that despite such efforts the injustice perpetrated by those in power may become so gross and the exploitation of the weak so outrageous that resort to violence seems to be the only reasonable course of action. Peace is desirable, but so is justice. Ideally governments should be vehicles of both peace and justice, but ex- perience shows that they are often merely new instruments by which the privileged extend their power. This analysis suggests that the only way to eliminate the resort to violence as a legitimate means of securing justice is to establish governments which are impartial and which allow for peaceful change. To the extent that this goal is realized, resort to violence as a means of eliminating injustice becomes unnecessary.

Will War Be Missed?

The thesis of this chapter is that none of the claims for the alleged positive values of war can be substantiated. We don't need war to keep the population growth rate down or to eliminate genetically inferior people. We don't need war in order to stimulate new technological developments or social change. We don't need war to avoid economic slowdowns or to guarantee long-term economic growth. We don't need war in order to have something meaningful to do with our lives. We don't need war in order to weed out unfit societies or to sustain social cohesion. We don't need war in order to eliminate injustices in society. There is nothing that we need war for.

Suppose that we could abolish war. Suppose that military careers and military technological challenges and military glory were no longer part of our social life. Would we miss war? Would we be really glad that war was no longer part of human life? Undoubtedly some people would miss the challenges of the ultimate life-or-death contest. Undoubtedly there would be some kind of military-like games and military-like recreational activities for those who miss the old ways. But on the other hand, there would be unparalleled progress in civilized life—in education, in science, in health care, in more participatory social institutions, in the arts. Society would no longer be subject to these spasms of killing and destruction, this periodic wasting of lives and property. Changes, both technological and social, would come more gradually and steadily. There would still be problems to solve and conflicts to resolve, but the problems would be less of our own making and the resolution of the conflicts would be less violent and more enduring.

Will we miss war? I think not. I think the general response to the elimination of war will be "Good riddance."

Part Three

The Contemporary Situation

VIII. Ideological Aspects of the Contemporary Situation

An *ideology* is like a religion except that its main concern is the proper structuring of society rather than the salvation of the individual. It consists of a set of beliefs about the human situation and the way society ought to be organized which guides the thinking and action of a substantial number of persons. Our goal is a better understanding of the ideologies most relevant to the social conflicts occurring in our world in the twentieth century. After reviewing some basic distinctions in the first section, we will focus our attention on the predominant ideology in the United States, Western Europe, and Japan: capitalistic democracy. Then we will deal with the basic tenets of Communism (Marxism-Leninism and Maoism), which has provided the ideological base for twentieth century revolutions in Russia, China, Cuba, and Vietnam and which still influences critiques of capitalistic democracy. In the fourth section we will focus on Fascism and related ideologies opposed to the egalitarianism of both democracy and socialism. In the fifth section we will review the "end of history" thesis of Francis Fukuyama. In the sixth section we will discuss the role of religion and religious movements in war and peace.

Some Basic Distinctions

In our earlier discussion of justice we noted that there are two opposing principles which must somehow be reconciled or balanced in order to have a just (or fair) society. These two principles are *the principle of merit* (that some people deserve to have more than others because they contribute more or are more qualified in some way) and *the principle of equality* (that everyone should have roughly the same amount because how much one can contribute depends ultimately on factors outside one's own control). The *principle of merit* suggests that people should be able to keep whatever they have already acquired, while the *principle of equality* suggests that those who have more should be expected to share with those who have less. These two opposing principles of justice or fairness are so fundamental in social philosophy that adherence to one or the other view is typically used to determine the seating arrangements in the legislative bodies of the world. Legislators who tend to emphasize the principle of merit are usually seated

108

on the right, while those who tend to emphasize the principle of equality are seated on the left. Consequently, to describe someone as a *rightist* indicates that that person emphasizes the principle of merit with regard to what constitutes a fair distribution of wealth and political power within the society, while to describe someone as a *leftist* means that that person is a champion of the principle of equality. It should be evident that rightists will have a high regard for competition and individualism, while leftists will have a high regard for cooperation and collectivism.

In order to get a better appreciation of this distinction between rightists and leftists and a better understanding of the strengths and weaknesses of these two views, let us consider how they could be applied to the problem of giving grades in school. Suppose that we wanted to develop a *rightist grading system which promotes competition by rewarding merit.* If we really want it to be competitive, we should have not just five possible grades or even ten possible grades. We should have *rank-order grading* on each test or assignment. In a class of 30 students, papers would be marked "#1 out of 30" or "#16 out of 30" or "#29 out of 30," and the grades would be posted for all to see. It is not difficult to imagine what would happen with such a rightist system of grading. Competition would be fierce, especially between those at the top of the class. As we know from the rental-car ads, "#2 tries harder." So would #3 and #4. The motivation to work harder to get a better grade would be very great. Much studying would take place, and it could be expected that much learning would occur.

On the negative side of this competitive system we might notice those ranking at or near the bottom of the grading scale dropping out. They would just quit. Who needs constant public reminders that they are near the bottom of the class? The intense competition might also have an adverse effect on human relations. Those who are at the top of the class are likely to feel "superior," while those who are not doing so well even though they are trying as hard as they can are likely to be frustrated. They are likely to resent the fact that others are able to get better grades without spending as much time studying. They would probably complain that the system "just isn't fair" because they are doing as well as they can under the circumstances but not getting much recognition for that effort. They would call attention to the fact that they weren't able to decide whether they would be born smart or not. With regard to the impact of this competitive system on personal relationships, who is going to help someone else to understand the material if that means possibly being one step lower in the class ranking on the next test? Finally, there might be secretive efforts to cheat in some way. Isn't getting the good grade the only thing that really matters much in this system? What difference does it make how much one learns if it doesn't help one get a better ranking?

For contrast, let us consider what a *leftist grading system* would be like where we are trying to *foster equality and cooperation.* If we want equality and cooperation, we should have a system which gives everyone a good chance to succeed and where the class gets graded as a group. We should have a system of *pass-fail grading for individuals* and some kind of *group grade for collective achievement*. We would need to establish some minimum standards that had to be met in order to get credit for taking the course, for example, that you could not be absent more than three times during the term. The group grade would be based on the quality of a class project to be completed during the term. We can imagine what would happen with such a leftist or egalitarian system. Most of the class would probably do nothing except come to class. They might even bring games to play and music tapes to listen to during class time. Why do more than the minimum required for getting credit for taking the course?

On the other hand, a few conscientious students might try to get the class project organized and encourage others to join in and "do their share." Some people might even get very involved with the project, doing extra research in the library to make it better. Those working on the project would try to help each other with regard to whatever was needed to improve the project. An *esprit de corps* might develop as the project progresses, and enthusiasm might build about "our" project and what "we" have been able to do together. Some close friendships might blossom from the joy of working unselfishly together. Some who had not been participating earlier might get involved now in order to be part of what was developing into an exciting and worthwhile project. At the same time, those who had contributed much to the project might feel some resentment toward those slackers who were still not doing anything. They would probably complain that it "just isn't fair" that those who were doing nothing to help would nevertheless be getting the same grade as those who had worked hard. The others could respond that those with more talent and interest should do more and were getting their reward by being able to contribute more to and consequently getting more satisfaction out of the project. In contrast to the competitive system, with this egalitarian system it is evident that there wouldn't be any cheating in order to try to get a better individual grade.

This discussion about rightist and leftist grading systems provides an opportunity to comment on another aspect of the rightist-leftist distinction. The rightist emphasis on competition and merit resembles the "struggle for survival" and the "survival of the fittest" which we find in nature. Therefore we can say that the rightist viewpoint reflects a *"naturalistic"* approach to life. In nature different organisms are born with different inherited traits, and then they compete with each other to see which ones "have what it takes" to survive. Some people "luck out" and happen to be born with superior intelligence or superior athletic ability or superior musical ability. Some people are born of parents who happen to be rich or happen to live in a country where food and shelter and education and health care are readily available. In the competition of life these lucky people will fare much better than those who have not been so fortunate. As the saying goes, "life isn't fair." But that's just the way it is.

Charles Darwin (1809–1882) was a famous English naturalist who emphasized this process of "survival of the fittest" in nature, so this rightist way of thinking is sometimes called "Darwinism." The emphasis on the desirability of competition to see who "has what it takes" to survive can be applied to social policy, and then it is called "Social Darwinism." *Social Darwinism* maintains that the government should *not* sponsor welfare programs to help those individuals who are not faring well in the competition for the goods of life or to help those business enterprises that are not doing so well in the competition to make money. This rightist outlook says that it is desirable in the long run that those who don't "have what it takes" to succeed not be given special assistance. Let them perish before they produce "unfit" offspring like themselves. Let society follow the way of nature.

While the rightist approach is *naturalistic,* the leftist approach is *humanistic* or *moralistic.* The rightist is correct in saying that nature is not fair, but for the leftist it is not appropriate for society to merely follow nature's unfair way. Rather human society should intervene in order to counteract the injustice of an unthinking natural order. If someone is born blind or deaf, the rightist attitude is, "If they can't hack it, too bad." The leftist view is that human society should equalize things by giving special assistance to those who are less fortunate. Society should correct the inhumaneness and randomness of nature. Just as in a family those who happen to have disabilities or debilitating accidents are given extra help, so in the community as a whole those who have not been treated so well by fate should be given extra help by the whole human family.

Here one sees clearly the contrast between the individualistic, naturalistic, scientific, realistic, hard-hearted outlook of the rightist and the collectivist, humanistic, ethical, idealistic, tender-hearted outlook of the leftist. The rightist believes that nature's way is best, especially in the long run. Besides there is no point in trying to change the unchangeable. The leftist believes that nature is often cruel and that the "survival of the fittest" approach must be replaced by a more humane process in which human civilization creates its own just and rational order. This contrast can be applied directly to attitudes toward the problem of war where rightists are more likely to say that "War is nature's way" while leftists are more likely to say "Let's work to replace nature's cruel way of war with a just, humane social order based on reason and compassion."

Let us return to our discussion of the difference between a rightist system of grading and a leftist system of grading in a classroom situation. To get a better appreciation of these two different outlooks you need to think of these alternative systems of grading first in terms of something you are naturally very good at and then in terms of something that you are *not* very good at. You might consider various sports, artistic projects, playing a musical instrument, public speaking, selling things, making things with your hands, fixing mechanical things, dancing, singing, playing chess, and so on. If you focus on something you are good at, the rightist system of grading will probably seem to be the best way. If you focus on something that you are not so good at, the leftist system of grading will probably appeal to you. In other words, we all like to compete in areas where we can expect to do well but would rather have a grading system which is not so focused on competition for those areas where we individually cannot do so well. Applying this point to ideological positions, we can see that those who are doing fairly well in the competition of life are probably going to have a great deal of sympathy with the rightist approach while those who have been "cheated" by fortune will probably have more appreciation of a leftist approach.

So which system is the best system in general? Is a rightist system or a leftist system of grading in the classroom better? Which system is better for encouraging athletic accomplishment? Which system is better for encouraging musical accomplishment? More relevant to the topic of ideology, which system is best for getting people to do the work which society needs to have done? Is it better to follow a rightist system or a leftist system for determining the distribution of goods in society? Is a rightist system or a leftist system better for determining who makes the decisions for the society as a whole? What are the strong points and weak points of each system? Of course, we should not overlook the possibility of trying to find some desirable balance between the two.

Returning to our discussion of ideological terminology, there can be degrees of commitment to the rightist view or to the leftist view. (See chart on page 114.) A person who is intensely devoted to the principle of merit and who may even want to use violence to silence those who favor the principle of equality is an *extremist of the right,* while a person who is similarly committed to the principle of equality is an *extremist of the left. Moderates,* on the other hand, of both the right and left, believe in the use of persuasion and the right of the opposition to be heard. Thus extremists of both right and left often favor authoritarian forms of government while moderates tend to favor Western-style parliamentary democracies where freedom of expression by the opposition is an important part of the political process.

We have noted that social structures, including governments, are usually controlled by the rich and powerful in the society and are consequently usually designed to maintain the privileges which these people and their families enjoy. We have also noted that people in these top positions tend to believe that they hold these positions because they deserve to have them. Thus those at the top of a society are usually defenders of the principle of merit and will want to preserve the *status quo,* that is, they will want to conserve the present values and structures of society which have allowed them to get into the top positions which they occupy. When such rightists take a moderate stance, they are called *conservatives.* On the other hand, moderate leftists who want to reduce impediments to social change and create more opportunity and assistance for those who are not so well off are called *progressives.* (These moderate leftists are sometimes called "liberals," but this term "liberal" is ambiguous because it can also be used to describe all moderates—rightists as well as leftists. The term "liberal"—especially when qualified as "*classical* liberal"—can also be used in a third way to describe those who oppose any kind of government interference with the market forces of supply and demand, so the term "progressive" is the most appropriate term for moderate leftists.) Extreme rightists who strive for even more privileges for those who are specially talented and otherwise well off are called *reactionaries,* while extreme leftists who want to completely uproot the present privileges and existing hierarchical structures of the society are called *radicals.*

These terms are widely used to refer to politicians and others with regard to their views about how society should be organized, but still another distinction needs to be made. This is the distinction between people's *economic ideology* (their views on how the goods of society should be distributed) and their *political ideology* (their views on how the political decision-making power in society should be distributed). (See chart on page 114.) This distinction is useful because it is possible for a given individual to be a rightist with regard to economic ideology (that is, to believe that goods should be distributed on the basis of merit) and a leftist with regard to political ideology (that is, to believe that political power should be distributed on the basis of equality). It would also be possible for a person to be a leftist with regard to economic ideology (that is, to believe that goods should be distributed on the basis of equality) and a rightist with regard to political ideology (that is, to believe that political power should be distributed on the basis of merit). The significance of this distinction becomes more evident when it is noted that the first combination mentioned is precisely what we find in the capitalistic democratic ideology prevalent in the United States and Western Europe while the second combination is characteristic of the Marxist-Leninist view which guided the Soviet Union during the Cold War.

This distinction between economic ideology and political ideology raises another very important issue in social philosophy—the influence of a nation's economic and political systems on each other. One possible view is that the economic system is basic and that the political system is merely a reflection of it. According to this view economic wealth necessarily creates political power. Another possible view is that the political system is basic and that the influence of excessive wealth can be held in check by the government. According to this second view political power assisted by the police power of the state may be used to control and even redistribute economic wealth. Marxist philosophy theoretically opts for the first alternative while Western-style democratic theory has been based on the latter alternative, though in actual practice both Communist states and democratic countries have often acted contrary to their own philosophical foundations. For example, if Marxists want to increase the political power

Ideological Terminology

	Leftist: Emphasizes desirability of *equality* and *cooperation*		*Rightist:* Emphasizes desirability of *merit* and *competition*	
DEGREE OF EMPHASIS	*Extremist* May try to silence opposition.	*Moderate* Use persuasion; let opposition be heard.	*Moderate* Use persuasion; let opposition be heard.	*Extremist* May try to silence opposition.
GENERAL TERM	*Radical* Eliminate all distinctions of rank.	*Progressive* Promote gradual increase of equality.	*Conservative* Preserve present differences of privilege.	*Reactionary* Increase privileges for the elite.
ECONOMIC IDEOLOGY (distribution of goods)	*Communism* Individuals get what they need regardless of how much work is done by them.	*Socialism* Wealth of individuals is based on quantity and quality of work done by them.	*Capitalism* People get wealth from work, ingenuity, and profits on investments.	*Monopolism* Wealth is concentrated in the hands of one small group of persons.
POLITICAL IDEOLOGY (system of governance)	*Direct democracy* All persons participate directly in making decisions for the society.	*Representative democracy* Elected representatives make decisions for the society.	*Oligarchy/Aristocracy* A select small group makes decisions for the society.	*Monarchy/Dictatorship* One person makes decisions for the society.

NOTE: The term *liberal* may mean "moderate" (the opposite of "extremist"). The term *liberal* may mean "progressive" (the opposite of "conservative"). The term *classical liberal* refers to someone who favors freedom of individuals and opposes government control. Consequently, a classical liberal is someone who supports capitalism and a representative democracy in which the powers of government are very limited.

of the working classes and political power depends on economic power, it would seem that they should focus their efforts directly on raising the wage levels of the workers rather than trying to take control of the government through revolution. In the case of democracies, it would seem that they should do more to prevent economic power from being so influential in the political process since such economic influence keeps the state from fulfilling its theoretical function of acting as a check on economic power.

On the chart on page 114 the various economic and political ideologies are arranged from the most egalitarian on the left to the most stratified on the right. With regard to *economic ideologies,* the most leftist distribution of goods is represented by *communism,* aptly characterized by Karl Marx in the famous expression, "From each according to his ability; to each according to his need."[1] It is the kind of situation found in a closely knit family where each member contributes as much as he or she can and where each one gets what he or she needs, but the communists want to extend that kind of familial thinking to the whole society. The next step toward the middle is *socialism,* the view that one's only source of income should be wages for one's labor. That is, one should *not* be able to make money from assets already accumulated as one does when acquiring profit in a capitalistic system, possibly from inherited wealth. In a socialist system, factories and other things like rental property which can be used as a source of income are to be owned by society collectively, that is, by the government. There may be differential pay, however, on the basis of the quantity and quality of work done or on the basis of how critical the work is to the society. Consequently, some people may be a little richer than others, but the huge disparities in wealth which come as a result of inherited wealth, innovation, and other kinds of good fortune in a capitalist system will be eliminated. The next step across the center line into the area of the moderate right is *capitalism.* Here factories, rental property, patented inventions, and the like which can be used to make money (profit) are owned by private individuals. In a capitalistic system people can earn income from wages as in a socialist system, but there also exists the opportunity to make large amounts of money from investments and patents on inventions and figuring out new, more efficient ways of doing things. As a result there may be greater discrepancies in the amount of wealth different individuals have. The final step to the right is *monopolism,* a particular variation of the capitalist system where wealth is allowed to become concentrated in the hands of just a few families. In such a system this small group is able to economically strangle all potential competitors so there is no chance that the concentration of wealth will be changed. As we move from left to right there is less and less equality in the distribution of the wealth within the society and a smaller and smaller group of persons in whose hands the wealth of the society is concentrated.

With regard to *political ideologies,* which focus on who the decision-makers for the society will be, the most leftist or egalitarian system is a *direct (or pure) democracy,* where every person in the group gets to vote on each social issue to be decided. The model here would be the New England Town Meeting where all the citizens of the town come together and can adopt laws by a vote of those at the meeting. Every member of the community is a legislator (lawmaker) for the group. The next step toward the middle is a *representative democracy.* Here the whole group elects a more limited number of persons who will be the decision-makers for the whole community. The system is still democratic, however, since those legislators holding political office must get reelected from time to time by the whole group they are representing. ("Democratic" means "rule by the people.") Crossing the center line and going further to the right we have either *"oligarchy"* (rule by "the few," that is, the well-to-do) or *"aristocracy"* (rule by "the best," by the noble). Here only a small number of persons are the decision-makers for the whole society, and they do not need to worry about getting elected. The ruling group is viewed as above the level of the ignorant and uninformed masses and therefore more qualified to make decisions for the whole society. The final step to the right politically is represented by *monarchy* or *dictatorship,* where one person makes the decisions about what the whole society will do. All the political power is in the hands of that one person. As we move from left to right there is less and less equality in the distribution of decision-making authority and a smaller and smaller number of "more qualified" people who make the decisions for the whole group.

Capitalistic Democracy

The prevalent ideology in the United States, Western Europe, Japan, and many other parts of the industrialized world is capitalistic democracy. As already noted above, capitalism refers to an economic system in which the instruments of production are owned by private persons rather than the government, while democracy refers to a political system in which the decision-making political power is ultimately in the hands of the people as a whole.

The term *capitalism* is derived from the term *capital,* which in this context refers to things such as the machines and factories which can be used to produce more wealth. These "capital goods" which get used to produce things are to be distinguished from "consumer goods," those items which people use to satisfy their own needs and desires. A person who owns some capital goods is a *capitalist,* and the income derived from owning these capital goods is called profit. To be able to earn profit people must save some of their wealth and use it for investment in capital goods rather than buying consumer goods and services for immediate gratification. Thus profit ideally represents a reward for saving rather than spending. Of course, saving money rather than spending it will not automatically produce a profit. The money must be invested, either directly or by an intermediary such as a bank, in something which increases productivity, such as machines. Suppose, for example, that a machine enables a group of employees to produce five times as many consumer goods as they could have produced without it. This larger quantity of goods can then be sold, and part of the money received can be used to pay the workers' wages while another part can provide profit to the investor whose money made it possible to buy the machine in the first place.

A capitalistic system depends on the existence of some kind of capital goods such as machinery that will increase productivity (which is why capitalism comes along with industrialization) as well as on there being some people who are willing to invest their money in productive capital goods rather than spending it on consumer goods for themselves. It also depends on the manufacturer's ability to sell the goods which are produced and on having people who know how to operate the machines. To be able to sell the goods produced, the capitalist must make things of the type and quality which will appeal to potential buyers. A capitalist must pay workers enough that they will work for him or her rather than someone else. Consequently, in theory a system of competition develops among capitalists (or groups of capitalists who have merged their savings to form an enterprise such as a joint-stock company or a corporation). Each capitalist tries to give potential buyers a better bargain than they can get from others. Each capitalist competes for the best workers. Since income depends on the quality and quantity of goods sold, capitalists will pay higher wages to more highly skilled and more efficient workers. Capitalists will also be eager to purchase more efficient machines, which in turn motivates inventors and other capitalists to provide such machines.

The resulting *market economy* rewards inventiveness, good business management, and useful skills. Investing one's money in capital goods rather than spending it on consumer goods will be rewarded with profit. Inefficient and inept businesses will go bankrupt while efficient and proficient ones will prosper and earn more money with which to make further investments and expand their operations. While each person, capitalist and worker alike, aims only to better his or her own personal situation, the system as a whole works naturally to increase productivity and efficiency as well as the quality and variety of consumer goods available. At the same time prices, wages, and profits reflect the supply of and demand for goods, labor, and funds for investment.[2]

The capitalistic system fits well with the view that humans are inherently selfish and lazy but also able to calculate what will be best for themselves in the long run. In a smoothly functioning capitalistic system there is no need for people to be altruistic or even concerned about the welfare of others. They can be confident that acting in accord with their long-term self-interest will do more to help advance human welfare than any deliberately charitable acts. Furthermore, the competitive system of "survival of the fittest" assures that in the long run those capabilities and those ways of doing things which are productive will be preserved and passed along to posterity while those which are not will perish. The capitalistic system motivates people to work hard and be inventive because that is how one acquires wealth in order to be able to survive. Another imperative to be followed in a capitalist system is to save rather than spend, since saving can produce profit which will result in having more goods in the long run.

In actual practice, however, there may be some difficulties in the operation of the capitalistic system. Sometimes one capitalist or a small group of capitalists manages to gain a monopoly in the production of goods of a particular kind; then the competition, which had previously kept prices down, disappears. Another difficulty is that even without monopolies competition is imperfect. Those with very large assets generally have an inherent advantage because they can take greater risks, invest more on the development of new products, buy more expensive machinery, spend more on advertising, and wait longer to realize profits on their investment. Since larger companies and corporations have such competitive advantages, there is a built-in tendency in capitalism toward the development of those very monopolies which can destroy the competitive system.

There are also several other difficulties for the capitalist system. In setting wage levels, the greater assets of the capitalists put them in a much better bargaining position than that of the poor laborers looking for a job, since the laborers need work immediately to get money for food and shelter while the capitalists can wait until someone is found to work at the wages they are willing to pay. Unscrupulous capitalists may produce unsafe products whose defects are not visible to the buyer. Capitalists can hire advertisers, who may be able to persuade people to buy products or services which they really do not need. Also, since products can be sold only to those who have money to pay for them, there is a tendency to produce luxury items which appeal to the whims of the wealthy rather than to make things which meet the basic needs of those who have little or no money. Furthermore, the intrinsic advantage for the richer in bargaining situations, as well as their opportunity to save and invest, produces a strong tendency throughout the system for the rich to get richer while the poor remain poor.

It has sometimes been claimed that capitalism is racist and imperialist. It may well be the case that some capitalists have been racists, but that is not an inherent characteristic of the capitalist system. In fact, racism is foreign to it since the only things which matter in a capitalistic system are competence as a worker or manager or investor plus the possession of money in order to be able to buy as a consumer or to invest as a saver. The race, religion, sex, and age of the individual employee or consumer are irrelevant. It may also be the case that some capitalists have been imperialistic, but nationalistic imperialism is directly contrary to the theoretical basis of capitalism. Capitalists want to be able to make the biggest profit possible on their investments regardless of where that might be. Theoretically they favor a worldwide "free-trade" market economy rather than a system of national tariffs and regulations.

There is only one type of discrimination which is an inherent part of the capitalist system, and that is discrimination against the poor. The poor are discriminated against because they do not have enough money to serve as potential buyers or to be able to invest and earn profits. Capitalism works on the basis of the market forces of supply and demand, and demand is *not* the same as need. *Demand is want plus the money to buy what is wanted.* The poor may be in need but their needs will not constitute part of the demand because they lack money to buy. The other side of this situation is that capitalism won't work well if wealth is too concentrated in the hands of too few persons because then there won't be enough demand to keep the system going.

For the capitalists themselves the biggest problem is the tendency for the whole economy to undergo a continuing cycle of boom followed by bust. During the boom period when goods are selling well, the capitalists invest more in production, hire more workers, and pay each worker more as the competition for labor, especially for skilled labor, increases. Since the workers are getting paid more, they are ready to spend more for consumer goods. Demand increases. The capitalists respond by building more factories to produce still more goods. But the collective value of all the wages paid to all the workers will never be as great as the collective value of all the goods being produced by them. (If it were, there would be no profits left over for the capitalists who own the factories.) Consequently, there is no way the workers can buy all the goods being produced. More goods have been produced than can possibly be sold. Then the bust phase of the cycle begins. The capitalists start laying off workers since there is already an oversupply of what is being produced. These workers no longer have any money with which to buy goods. Others who still have jobs try to keep their expenditures down as much as possible since they fear that they may soon also be laid off. This cutback in purchasing causes sales to decrease even further, leading to more layoffs. Capitalists may then try to sell their machines because they are sitting idle, but no other capitalists will want to buy them when there is no demand for goods. Production eventually comes to a virtual halt. Workers are unemployed, machines are sitting idle, and capitalists are not making any profits. Finally the oversupply of goods is consumed and then the boom part of the cycle can begin again.

In order to deal with the various problems of a completely unregulated or *laissez-faire* capitalistic system, an alternative system has been developed, *government-regulated capitalism*. Under this system the government undertakes certain tasks such as regulating or breaking up monopolies, or establishing laws to protect smaller firms against unfair competition from larger ones, or enacting laws to protect the right of laborers to join unions and bargain collectively with the employer. Agencies are established to protect the public from unsafe products, to protect workers from unsafe working conditions and to keep industries from polluting the environment. The government institutes progressive rates of taxation on income and adopts other measures to try to mitigate somewhat the natural tendency in a capitalistic system for the rich to get richer. Social assistance programs are adopted so the unemployed, the disabled, the very old, children, and others will be able to provide for their basic needs. The government also tries to moderate the boom and bust cycles by controlling the money supply, tax rates, and the amount of government spending. Thus the system of government-regulated capitalism aims to preserve the positive values of capitalism — productivity, efficiency, variety of products, and personal freedom — while controlling its less desirable features.

Let us now turn to the political part of the capitalistic democratic ideology. Democracy refers to a political system in which decision-making power rests ultimately in the hands of the people as a whole. The people determine who their lawmakers and leaders will be. They do this through a system of representatives and elected leaders chosen for limited terms of office. The only way these legislators and leaders can continue to rule is to be reelected when their term of office ends. The political leaders need not be of any particular family, economic class, gender, nationality, religion, occupation, or political party. In the well-known words of Abraham Lincoln, democracy is "government of the people, by the people, and for the people."

The ideology of Western-style democracy includes not only the notion of majority rule but also the principle of minority rights. The right to vote is worthless if there is no chance to be informed about the issues or to hear the arguments offered by persons defending various points of view. Opposition candidates as well as those representing the group in power must be on the ballot, and the voting must be secret so that it is impossible to determine how any individual voted. People must be free to give their opinions, ask questions, hear the opinions of others, form voluntary associations to promote one or another point of view, travel about, and so on. These rights or freedoms are rooted in the notion that in a democracy public policy should be the outcome of rational discussion, debate and deliberation rather than the dogmatic pronouncements of some group.

A fundamental asset of the democratic political system is that it allows for peaceful change. People who don't like a public policy are free to speak against it. They are free to enlist the help of others and even to run for political office themselves. Officials are elected for a limited term and are not allowed to stay in office unless reelected. There is no point in trying to start a violent revolution. It could succeed only if one had the support of many people, and with such support one should be able to win an election. At the same time those in authority have no need to use force except in the case of an attempt to use violence against the government.

Sometimes the question is raised whether in a democracy persons ought to be permitted to openly advocate the overthrow of the government. It is clear that democratic theory requires that such a viewpoint be allowed to be openly expressed. If those who espouse this view can gain enough followers to win elections or to pose a real threat to the government, then the government itself has failed to persuade many people of its value. On the other hand, to try to silence those who advocate overthrow of a democratic government is to resort to an undemocratic approach, which is inconsistent with the rational defense of democracy. Such a course of action would leave this dissatisfied group with no option but to turn to violence to promote their views, the very sort of thing which democracy is designed to make unnecessary.

Capitalistic democracy is sometimes attacked on grounds that, although there are formal freedoms such as expressing a point of view and running for public office, there are in reality only a few wealthy or otherwise influential persons who can take advantage of these freedoms. It is noted that participation in politics requires time both for keeping oneself informed and for the actual political activities and that such time is not available to all persons in the society. Such participation also requires at least minimal amounts of money. There is undoubtedly a great deal of truth in these criticisms. It is obvious that some people are able to exert a great deal more influence on the political process than others. Nevertheless the freedom to participate does exist and many people do participate in various ways that go beyond voting. Furthermore, most people find plenty of time and money for recreational activities and time to watch a great deal of television. It seems that the biggest factor lacking in many cases of non-participation is not so much the opportunity but the inclination. People may complain about the influence of special-interest groups on government policy, but it is their own nonparticipation that permits these groups to have so much influence.

Communism (Marx, Lenin, and Mao)

The ideology followed by the former Soviet Union, by China, by Cuba, by North Korea, by Vietnam, and by many Marxist-Leninists and Maoists throughout the world is popularly known as "Communism." The basic ideas of this ideology were formulated by Karl Marx and Friedrich Engels in the nineteenth century and then supplemented or modified by V.I. Lenin and Mao Zedong in the twentieth century. Marxism-Leninism is one particular variety of *socialism*. The central thesis of socialism is that capital goods, the machines and other means of production, should be owned jointly by the whole society rather than by individuals or private corporations. Marx and Engels called their view *scientific socialism* to distinguish it from earlier socialist views which they regarded as utopian or unrealistic. The *utopian socialists* believed that socialism could be brought into existence merely by convincing people how desirable such a system would be, while Marx and Engels claimed that social change could come about only as the result of the operation of inexorable and inevitable historical forces.

What are these historical forces? The answer to this question is provided by the *materialistic interpretation of history* developed by Marx and Engels.[3] According to this theory the basic factor in understanding historical change is neither divine intervention as Christians believe nor philosophical thought as Hegel had taught, but rather the manner in which the goods of a society are produced, that is, material or economic factors. This *"historical materialism"* or *"economic determinism"* maintains that the predominant mode of production determines all the other aspects of society. Most importantly, the class of people who control the means of production will be in positions of power while those who do the actual physical work required will be the exploited class. If the primary mode of production is small-scale agriculture as in a feudal society, then the landowners will be the ruling class and the serfs who do the physical labor of farming will be the exploited class. If the primary mode of production consists of using machinery as happens after industrialization, then those who own the machines will be the class in control while the workers who run the machines will be the exploited class. (See chart on pages 124 and 125.) The predominant mode of production and resulting social relations will also influence government structure, legal concepts, philosophical views, religion, and the nature of art. It is especially important for understanding the history of conflict to note that the ruling or dominant class will always establish governmental structures and laws which protect its own interests.

According to the Marxist point of view, violent social conflict arises when the predominant mode of production changes and the old ruling class refuses to give up control of the government to those who control the new means of production. Consider, for example, the transition from feudalism to capitalism that took place in Europe in the sixteenth, seventeenth, and eighteenth centuries. The feudal kingdoms, complete with archdukes, dukes, marquesses, earls, viscounts, and others, had established a system of government to serve their purposes and solve their problems. The commercial and productive activities of the up-and-coming bourgeoisie (or burghers, so called because they lived in the towns) did not fit in with the land-centered, manorial system of the feudal lords. In cases of conflict between landowners and merchants, the laws and government structures always favored the landed aristocracy. The bourgeoisie wanted more power and more government concern about the kinds of problems they faced (such as the need for free roads to get from one place to another), but the old dominant class would not willingly surrender control. Although the bourgeoisie sometimes were able to gain political power peacefully, the usual course of events was a violent revolution to overthrow the feudal government.

Marx and Engels argued that by the middle of the nineteenth century a new transition was taking place. Once again a shift in the prevailing mode of production was taking place and the old ruling class was refusing to step aside graciously. Now it was the bourgeoisie that had created laws and government structures to promote their interests; the focus was on protecting private ownership and individual enterprise. But the prevailing mode of production had now shifted from privately owned machines in workshops employing only a few people to corporately owned machines in large factories employing hundreds of workers and usually managed by people other than the owners. Nevertheless the owners were still appropriating for themselves all the "surplus value" of the goods produced. That is, as raw materials were converted into more valuable manufactured items, the owners of the factories sold what was produced, paid the bills (including wages), and kept all the difference for themselves rather than sharing some of that gain in value from the manufacturing process with the workers who ran the machines. The production of the goods had become a social enterprise in which many workers and managers participated, but the owners of the machines viewed the increased value produced in the manufacturing process as belonging solely to themselves.

The workers, the proletariat, were viewed by Marx and Engels as the new up-and-coming class[4] whose interests were being neglected and thwarted by the laws and governments controlled by the bourgeoisie. Although it was conceivable that in some cases the proletariat might be able to gain political power peacefully, in actuality the proletariat would usually need to have a violent revolution to overthrow the bourgeoisie-controlled state just as earlier the bourgeoisie usually had to use violence to overthrow the governments controlled by the landed nobility. Marxists do more than just predict that this will happen, however. Their aim is to make it happen. As might be expected, the Marxists' eagerness to push history along by promoting violent revolutions against bourgeois governments causes such governments to view them as enemies.

Marx and Engels claimed that the system of private ownership which was suitable for the small-scale enterprises of the early bourgeois period is no longer appropriate for the large-scale enterprises of mass production. When a large number of people work together to produce an object such as an automobile, that product should belong to the workers, not to the small group which happens to have enough money to buy stock in the company. Capitalists may argue that those who bought stock made it possible to purchase the machines which in turn provided employment for the workers, but according to Marxists these capitalists were able to accumulate the extra money for purchasing stock only by some previous exploitation. How do these capitalists get their money? They do not need to work but merely make money from the money their families accumulated from earlier exploitation or good fortune. Suppose a person inherits $1,000,000 from rich parents. Without any special talent for investing wisely, the heir should be able to get an 8 percent return on the money. That income of $80,000 per year, year after year, is much more than factory workers can hope to

Marx's Five Stages of Civilization

NAME OF STAGE	PRIMITIVE COMMUNISM	ANCIENT SLAVERY	FEUDALISM	CAPITALISM	SOCIALISM
PREVAILING MODE OF PRODUCTION	Hunting, gathering, and fishing	Slave labor to increase private property	Peasant labor and use of animals for farming	Commerce and small-scale manufacturing	Mass production
MEASURE OF WEALTH	Group welfare	Number of slaves and amount of land	Amount of land	Amount of money	Satisfaction of human needs
RULING CLASS	None	Slave-owners and Emperor	Land-holders and King	Entrepreneurs and capitalists (Bourgeoisie)	Workers (Proletariat)
OPPRESSED CLASS	None	Slaves	Peasants	Factory workers and unemployed persons	None
GOVERNMENT	Communal rule	Emperor and open coercion	King and Court of Lords with personal loyalty to immediate superior	Capitalistic democracy or fascism	People's State governed by Worker's Party

	Collectivism (What is good for the group?)	Pragmatic obedience to those with power (What is commanded?)	Loyalty to immediate superior in exchange for protection (What is expected by my overseer?)	Individualism or totalitarianism (What is good for me?)	Collectivism (What is good for the group?)
PREVAILING PHILOSOPHY					
PREVAILING RELIGION	Tribal gods and personified natural forces	Worship of God who is powerful and demanding	God works through the Church, His intermediary (Catholicism)	God deals directly with individuals (Protestantism)	No Divine Master (atheism)
PREVAILING ART FORM	Decoration of everyday objects	Palaces and monuments for emperors	Art for worship and for the pleasure of the King and Court	Snobbish art for those with money and leisure	Art to advance collectivist attitudes and for edifying the life of the masses

earn, no matter how hard they work. As Marxists see the situation, the laws of the capitalist society protect this continued exploitation of the workers by the capitalists. At the same time, for the most part capitalist-controlled governments do not show an enthusiastic concern for the problems of the proletariat such as unemployment, the availability of affordable health care, and an assured minimum supply of the basic necessities of life such as food and housing regardless of one's financial situation.

The Marxists also claim that the capitalistic free enterprise system, even when regulated by government, is unable to take full advantage of the productive capabilities of mass production. Although each individual enterprise plans its operations with a view to making as much profit as possible over the next few years, there is little or no effort to coordinate the productive capabilities of the whole nation or the whole world for the long-term welfare of the society. During the bust part of the capitalist business cycle, factories sit idle and workers are unemployed even though there are plenty of unmet needs in the society. Even when the system is working rather smoothly, production is geared to what people with money will buy, not to the needs of the general population. So factories still operate well below their maximum capabilities.

Marx and Engels addressed themselves primarily to criticizing capitalism. Workers were encouraged to overthrow capitalist governments, but they were not provided with much guidance about what to do after they gained control. They were told that a transition period would be needed before they could move to the higher phase of Communist society when the slogan "from each according to his ability; to each according to his need" could be implemented.[5] During this transitional "socialist" period private ownership of the means of production would be eliminated but differential pay on the basis of one's contribution to society would continue.

The theories of Marx and Engels are certainly not free of difficulties. They accepted the labor theory of value from earlier writers, a theory which maintains that the value of any product depends completely on the amount of labor required to get it out of nature and into usable form. Even when patched up with questionable notions such as the idea that machines represent stored labor, the labor theory of value has difficulties. Labor is undoubtedly a big factor in the value of most things, but supply and demand seem to be even more crucial factors. Scarce but very useful materials such as petroleum are very valuable even if relatively little labor is required to take them from nature, and the value of a beautiful art object often bears little relation to how much labor was involved in making it.

Marx also made several predictions which have turned out to be incorrect. For example, he predicted that as capitalism progressed the middle class would become smaller and smaller. In fact, it has become larger and larger. For another example, he expected that the proletarian revolutions would occur first in the most advanced industrialized nations such as France and Germany while in fact the first successful revolutions occurred in

Russia, at that time one of the least advanced countries of Europe; in China, a predominantly agrarian and feudal nation; and in Cuba, a semicolonized agricultural country. Furthermore, the revolutions which have occurred seem to be more the result of Marxist philosophy than of any objective historical forces. For a third example, he predicted that capitalists would amass such an abundance of capital that they would be searching around for places to invest. In fact, just the opposite has occurred. Everywhere there is a shortage of capital for investment. From a purely scientific point of view, so many wrong predictions necessarily raise serious doubts about the correctness of the theory.

We have already mentioned, in connection with the discussion of the causes of war, that Lenin made some amendments to Marxist theory in order to use it to explain international war. According to Lenin, capitalists are necessarily going to be engaged in imperialistic ventures as they seek to take over other areas for raw materials and markets.[6] He is also able to explain that the workers' revolutions did not occur first in the most industrialized countries as Marx had predicted because the capitalists in these countries "bought off" their workers by sharing some of the profits from exploiting their colonies. But, as noted earlier, Lenin's view that capitalists can get into wars (such as World War I) as a result of nationalistic economic competition among themselves undermines Marx's contention that all wars are the result of class conflict and opens up the possibility that nationalism may be as important a factor in war as the change in mode of production emphasized by Marx.

Since Marx and Engels had not provided much guidance on what the proletariat should do after they gained power, Lenin had to work out his own program of action after the Bolshevik Revolution in Russia in 1917. He decided to base the government on the soviets, councils of workers, soldiers, and peasants who had been elected by their fellows to serve as representatives. These soviets had been the prime movers in the overthrow of the czar. Nevertheless, it was claimed by Lenin that the soviets needed the leadership of professional intellectual revolutionaries for guidance, so the Communist Party was organized in such a way that it could be controlled by the intelligentsia who had led the revolution.[7]

The procedural arrangement which governed the operation of the Communist Party in the Soviet Union is called democratic centralism. The basic features of democratic centralism are that representatives are elected at the local level; that these lower level representatives then elect higher level ones who elect higher level ones, and so on; that decisions are made by majority rule; that after a decision has been made no further dissent or questioning of that matter is permitted; and that decisions of higher level organs are binding on all lower level organs.[8] It is the last two features which gave the central decision-making bodies so much power in the Soviet system. It is also these two features, plus the fact that the Communist Party was the only political party allowed to exist in the country, which made the political structure in the old Soviet Union so different from Western-style democracies.

When Mikhail Gorbachev introduced the ideas of "glasnost" (openness) and "perestroika" (restructuring) into the Soviet Union in the late 1980s, the whole political system was radically changed. Decisions of the top leaders could be criticized. Persons not in the Communist Party could participate in the discussion of political issues. The system of democratic centralism was modified to be much more like Western-style democracy. Once freedom of expression became the accepted style, even Gorbachev could no longer keep the political and economic changes in check, and the Soviet Union itself eventually came to an end in December 1991.

While discussing Communism, we must also take account of the theoretical modifications introduced by China's Mao Zedong. While Marx and Lenin had focused attention on the class conflict between workers and capitalists as industrialization was taking place, Mao emphasized the conflict between the poor rural peasants and the more affluent elite of the cities, a conflict which existed even before industrialization. From his point of view, one didn't need to wait for industrialization and the development of a proletariat in order to have a revolution to stop exploitation. The peasants could use their superior numbers to take control of the countryside and then strangle the cities which depended on the rural areas for food. Military power was critical, but peasants armed with guns and familiarity with the terrain would be able to outmaneuver troops sent from the cities to subdue them. Furthermore, people living in the rural areas could be recruited for the revolution both by giving them land confiscated from the aristocrats and by threatening them if they did not cooperate.

Mao's focus on the rural poor versus the urban rich extended to his analysis of international affairs. He saw the world as divided between the rich, developed "urban" countries and the poor, undeveloped "rural" countries. He thought that the thrust of Communism on the international level should be to get the poor rural areas to revolt and throw off the control exercised over them by the rich urban areas, just as his revolution in China had begun with the rural areas throwing off the control of the cities. Mao disagreed with Lenin's view that all imperialism was due to capitalism. He claimed that the two superpowers at that time, the capitalistic imperialistic United States and the socialistic imperialistic Soviet Union, were vying with each other for hegemony over the whole world. These two nations constituted what he called the First World. The other developed countries he called the Second World, while the undeveloped countries were called the Third World. Mao believed that the best hope for the Third World countries was to unite with each other under China's leadership and then get assistance from some of the Second World countries to keep the two superpowers in check.

Mao had great faith in the ordinary, unsophisticated, powerless people of the society and was always on guard against any elitist tendency even within the Communist Party of China. He made a special effort to place university students and professors in the fields working beside the poorest peasants, and at the same time he championed the idea that hard-working peasants should be given priority in access to education. One of his main fears was that an elitist group, out of contact with the hard life of the peasants in the rural areas, would again gain control of China and overturn the revolution of the dispossessed which he had led. That concern led him to promote the primacy of ideological training and to be very uneasy about any move toward capitalism. A specific manifestation of this concern was his "Great Proletarian Cultural Revolution" of 1966–69.

At the moment Communism seems to be an ideology with a past but little hope for the future. None of the 15 republics of the former Soviet Union seems to be adhering to that ideology. All of the former Soviet satellite countries of eastern Europe are eager to develop market economies and Western-style democracy. China seems to be moving toward more acceptance of a market economy but under the control of a one-party political system. Even Castro in Cuba now seems ready to allow some private enterprise. There seems to be a general consensus that Communism hasn't worked, but there are still some Marxists and Maoists who feel that Communist ideology is correct and that the difficulties experienced have been due to administrative mistakes and the persistent opposition, both overt and covert, of the powerful United States of America and its allies. Still others have little sympathy with the positive program of the Communists but think that the Communist critique of capitalism is a good stimulant to further thought about that ideology.

Fascism (National Socialism)

For many people the ideology of Fascism seems even less worthy of attention than that of Communism. Fascism (also called "National Socialism") flourished in the 1920s and 1930s led by Mussolini in Italy, a cluster of rebel military leaders in Japan, Hitler in Germany, and Franco in Spain. It was the motivating ideology of all the Axis powers which were defeated in World War II, and is viewed by many as having been destroyed by that defeat. Nevertheless Fascism has recently received some public attention again because of neo–Nazi movements in some countries, especially Germany, and more recently in post–Communist Russia.

What are the central ideas of Fascism or National Socialism? It may be best to begin by considering what a *fasces* is. It is a bundle of rods around an ax handle with the blade of the ax protruding, and it was used by ancient Roman magistrates as a badge of their authority. The point of this symbol is that there is strength in unity, that the fasces cannot be broken as a single ax handle could. The message is that the members of a nation-state must be bound together in order to be able to overpower outsiders.

The Fascist movement can best be understood as a reaction against both Western-style democracy and Marxism. The Fascist accepts the Marxist criticism of Western-style democracy that such a government is just a powerless facade behind which big corporations fight for their private economic interests. These liberal democratic governments have no real decision-making power and no specific aims. They are necessarily weak and lacking in determination. At the same time the Fascist is utterly opposed to the internationalistic loyalty to the proletarian class throughout the world promoted by the Communists. The Fascist regards it as treasonous to try to arouse violent conflict between one part of the nation and another part of it. One's loyalty should be to one's nation and race and culture so that it can prevail in its struggle for dominance against other nations. Fascism is a rightist ideology firmly opposed to both the egalitarianism and moderation of Western-style democracy and the egalitarianism and internationalism of Marxist socialism.

Since Fascists are rightists, one might expect them to advocate the value of competition, and they do. But the focus is not on the competition of individual against individual as one finds in Western capitalism but rather on the competition between one nation-race-culture and the others. That is why it is called "National Socialism." It focuses on the struggle of one national society against other national societies. It sees the world as a struggle between societies not just for survival but even more for dominance. The Fascist emphasizes power and feeling and will rather than law and reason and restraint (which are the values promoted by Western-style democracy). The Fascist emphasizes loyalty to nation and race rather than loyalty to economic class and the oneness of the whole human family (which are the values promoted by Communism). The Fascist glorifies war, discipline, aggressiveness, and violence. Peace is regarded as both boring and contrary to nature; moderation and a tendency to be conciliatory are regarded as weaknesses; and tolerance for different races and cultures is regarded as stupidity.

Fascists or National Socialists believe in the organic unity of their nation and the superiority of their own group. They glorify their own national history, their racial characteristics, their military successes, their language and customs and cultural achievements. The individual is to be totally subordinated to what is good for the whole society. Each individual is like a cell in the organic whole. In actual practice what this means is that the whole society is organized like a military force, and each person is to do his or her duty as determined by those of higher rank. Loyalty to the nation and to the national leader ("Il Duce" or "Der Führer") is supreme and absolute, and individual deliberation about whether the leader might be mistaken is the height of immorality.

One might consider how readily the widespread feelings of patriotism, loyalty to one's nation, hatred of foreigners, and impatience with the deliberative discussions of a democratic government can be used by a charismatic leader to promote a Fascist outlook, especially if economic conditions are bad or other important social problems are not getting resolved. Although Fascism as a recognized ideological movement seems to have been destroyed by World War II, it is easy to see how a dynamic leader in almost any nation facing intractable problems might be able to create the kind of militaristic, aggressive, obedient, intolerant, almost mystical nationalistic movement which could be described as Fascism, whether it carries that name or not.

The "End of History" Thesis

Former U.S. State Department official Francis Fukuyama is the author of a widely discussed article entitled "The End of History?" published in the Summer 1989 issue of *National Interest,* a quarterly journal of foreign policy.[9] That article is very relevant to the issue of ideology and war. Fukuyama builds on the Hegelian view that history is a reflection of the conflict among ideas. His thesis is that during the past two centuries or so the significant wars have been a reflection of a deeper struggle among different ideologies. The American Revolution (1775–1781) and the French revolution (1789–1799) were the historical embodiments of liberal (Western-style) democracy with its ideals of "natural rights" such as life, liberty, and property for all citizens; liberty of action so long as the rights of others are respected; limited government legitimized by consent of the governed; a free economy based on market forces with a minimum of government regulation; equality of opportunity; freedom of thought; and tolerance for individual differences. This liberal ideology has been challenged by the ideologies of Communism and Fascism, but the twentieth century has seen the defeat of both of these opposing ideologies. Liberalism has by no means completely triumphed in Russia and China yet, but Fukuyama is confident that the direction of the flow of events toward acceptance of liberalism will not be stopped. The result is that there are no more ideological challengers to liberalism in sight anywhere. Consequently, the ideological struggles which are embodied in history seem to have come to an end.

Fukuyama points out that he is not saying that there will be no more wars of any kind. There will still be some less advanced areas of the world where ideological struggles and other kinds of conflict will continue for a while, but the situation among the powerful states that might get involved in a major war is different. These advanced areas have reached "the end of history" in the sense that there will no longer be violent struggles for the correctness of some ideology. As Fukuyama himself says:

> There would still be a high and perhaps rising level of ethnic and nationalist violence [in less advanced nations], since those are impulses incompletely played out, even in parts of the post-historical [more advanced] world. Palestinians and Kurds, Sikhs and Tamils, Irish Catholics and Walloons, Armenians and Azeris will continue to have their unresolved grievances. This implies that terrorism and wars of

national liberation will continue to be an important item on the international agenda. But large-scale conflict must involve large states still caught in the grip of history, and they are what appear to be passing from the scene.[10]

It must be remembered that Fukuyama's thesis is by no means accepted by everyone. It can be noted that it is a thesis that an American and West European audience likes very much to hear. After all, it says that Western liberalism (our ideology) has triumphed throughout the world. It says that, at least for a century or so, there will be no major ideological challenges to Western liberalism. But opponents point to factors such as ethnic strife and religious fundamentalism and unresolved tensions within liberalism itself as reasons to be skeptical about Fukuyama's optimism. Doubters note that the apparent triumph of liberalism may be due more to the military and economic power of the U.S. being used to undermine new social experiments in places such as Nicaragua than to the attractiveness of the ideology itself. Still, Fukuyama's article has aroused a great amount of interest and has made a forceful statement for the view that the ideological struggles of the last two centuries have for a while at least been worked out and that a period of ideological stability lies ahead as Western liberalism gets concretely embodied in more and more societies throughout the world, and possibly even at the global level.[11]

Religion and War

Earlier it was noted that an ideology is like a religion except that an ideology focuses on how *society* ought to be organized rather than on what *individuals* ought to do to effect their own personal salvation. It was also noted that wars are large-scale violent conflicts between one *group* and another *group*. Nevertheless, religions can be very relevant to the problem of war. Even though religions focus on the salvation of the individual, the individuals of a given religion are usually clustered together into a closely knit group, so the conflicts between one religion and another are often played out as conflicts between one group and another. Also, even though religions generally do not focus directly on social issues such as capitalism versus socialism or aristocracy versus democracy, their teachings may have rather definite implications about the desirability of one ideology or another. Furthermore, some religions such as Islam do take rather explicit positions on the desirability of particular kinds of social arrangements.

So how is religion related to war? One way is that *religion can motivate individuals to become engaged in warfare.* Even though most religions have taught the desirability of peace and the need to practice the Golden Rule of doing unto others as you would have them do unto you, many of them have also taught that it is important to defend one's faith, using violence if necessary to do so. Indeed religions often promise special rewards to those who lose their lives defending the faith. It is a common teaching of religions that there are just wars, and that for the most part a just war is a war that one's religious (and political) leaders say is a just war. (Religious leaders have often cooperated with political leaders in order to be in a good position to get assistance from the state in prosecuting heretics or proponents of other religions.) Thus religions serve a key role in "justifying" the use of violence by individuals in warfare. The message is that violence is usually not acceptable but that in this particular "just war," violence is not only acceptable but even obligatory. "God" (whose will is known by the religious leaders) not only approves participation in this war but requires it.

The result of this situation is that we can and often do have soldiers motivated by "obedience to God" fighting on opposite sides in a war. History is full of these religious wars — Christians versus Jews, Christians versus Muslims, Catholic Christians versus Protestant Christians, Muslims versus Hindus, Sikhs versus Hindus, Shintoists versus Christians, Muslims versus Jews, Shi'ite Muslims versus Sunni Muslims, and so on. So even though the world's religions talk about peace and brotherly love, they nevertheless often provide the impetus for the most ruthless and unrestrained violence.

Are some religions more likely to support wars than others? It has been suggested that the mystical religions (like Hinduism and Buddhism) which are based more on personal mystical experiences are less supportive of war than the prophetic religions (like Judaism, Christianity, and Islam) which are based more on acceptance of the message of some prophet or prophets.[12] In these latter religions there is a definite tendency to divide people into two groups, those who accept the message and get saved and those who do not and get condemned. Consequently, it becomes very important to determine exactly what the message is, which in turn tends to produce internal divisions in these religions. If one's religion has the Truth which must be accepted in order to be saved, then there is a real temptation to use violence if necessary to convert others for their own salvation. Thus these prophetic religions can more readily be used to promote war than is the case with the mystical religions, where what is important is having certain kinds of experience rather than believing certain ideas.

But it is not just a matter of what religion is being practiced or what ideas are believed. Even more important is the *manner* of believing. As John Stoessinger has pointed out, one can distinguish, even within the prophetic religions, between the dogmatic or authoritarian way of believing and the humanistic or democratic way of believing. To quote Stoessinger:

> The dogmatic or authoritarian way insists that religious belief has a monopoly on truth. The believer possesses the truth and no one else really does. Secondly, God is all-powerful and man powerless, with man's greatest virtue obedience to this all-powerful God. Conversely, the humanistic way of believing is the more democratic one. Religious beliefs are not viewed as having a monopoly on truth. In fact, other belief systems also are recognized as having a part of that truth. Moreover, man

is not totally powerless but is a kind of (forgive the banality) junior partner, together with the deity, in the building of a somewhat better world. Whether one is a Jew, Christian, Moslem, or anything else, if he believes in a dogmatic way, he will tend to contribute to war; if he believes in the humanistic or the more democratic way, he will tend to contribute to peace.[13]

This same general outlook is put forth by Christian theologian Hans Kung in his effort to promote dialogue among the world's religions. He suggests that Christians need to be self-critical about their own religion. They need to prepare themselves to really conduct dialogue with other religions (as well as other denominations of Christians) rather than viewing these others as merely pagans from whom nothing at all can be learned about religion. Such dialogue among religions is essential to peace, since "there will be no peace among the peoples of this world without peace among the world religions."[14] Kung carefully notes that he is *not* saying that *all* war can be stopped by the proper input from religion but only that the right kind of contribution from religion can reduce the amount of war.

Let me say it once more, unmistakably: Religions, Christianity, the Church, cannot solve or prevent all the world's conflicts, but they can lessen the amount of hostility, hatred, and intransigence. They can, first, intervene concretely for the sake of understanding and reconciliation between estranged peoples. And second, they can begin to do away with at least the conflicts of which they themselves are the cause and for whose explosiveness they are partly to blame.[15]

During the last two decades or so, it seems that religious groups have become more prominent in the political arena.[16] The most obvious example was the takeover of Iran in 1979 by Muslim fundamentalists led by the Ayatollah Khomeini. But religious groups are also a major factor in the violent social conflict between Jews and Muslims in the Middle East, between Shia and Sunni Muslims in the Persian Gulf and Pakistan, between Hindus and Buddhists in Sri Lanka, between Catholic and Protestant Christians in Northern Ireland, between Christians and Muslims in Sudan, and between Hindus and Sikhs in India. The Catholic Church has been very much involved in social issues in Poland, the Philippines, and Latin America. In South Africa a leading spokesman for the blacks has been Nobel Peace Prize recipient Bishop Desmond Tutu. Even in the U.S. there has been an upsurge of religious involvement in political issues, especially those related to abortion and homosexuality.

What is behind this greater social activism of religious groups? It would be rash to try to make generalizations which cover all these cases. In some cases, such as the Catholic Christians in Poland, the Sikhs in India, and the various groups in the former Yugoslavia, religion serve as vehicles for national ethnic groups seeking political independence. In other cases, such as the Catholic Christians in Latin America and the Muslim fundamentalists in Iran, the religious fervor reflects a struggle for social justice against an earlier pattern of docile compliance with the dictates of the politically powerful. In many cases — and again Iran is a particularly good example — the religious groups are protesting against modernist secular ideas which are viewed as promoting immorality and shamelessness. Often the religious fervor is heightened by frustration engendered by repeated defeats and continuing subordination. In Iran, however, the previously suppressed religious fundamentalists have gained power, and Christian reformists have had some success against a right-wing dictatorship in the Philippines. In countries such as Algeria, Tunisia, and Egypt, Islamic fundamentalism is a vehicle of the dispossessed to challenge the political and economic elite now in power, and in Haiti some activist Christians are playing a similar role. Whether these various religious groups focused on acquiring political power will be able to gain that power and then use it to develop societies which reflect their religious ideals remains to be seen.

IX. National-Historical Aspects of the Contemporary Situation

As noted earlier, national governments are the main agents relevant to the war problem. They are motivated not only by their ideologies (discussed in the previous chapter) but also by national interests and a national perspective which each has developed as a result of its own history. These diverse national outlooks may contribute to war. From within a given national perspective the actions of the leaders of that country usually appear rational and praiseworthy, while from the perspective of another country those very same actions may seem offensive and detestable. A sensitivity to these different outlooks can help to keep conflicts from becoming so intense that people are ready to resort to violence.[1]

The aim of this chapter is to examine the national perspectives of those countries whose policies are most important in contemporary international politics. We will begin with the viewpoints of the United States and Russia. Then we will turn our attention to the nations of Western Europe, Japan, and China. Finally, we will consider briefly how the world looks to the group of nations known as the less developed countries.

The U.S. Perspective

The ideological outlook of the United States, as mentioned in the previous chapter, is capitalistic democracy. But the American dedication to the economic freedom of a market system and to the political freedom of Western-style democracy is not just an abstract philosophical commitment. It is embedded in and reinforced by the American historical experience.

In the Revolutionary War (1775–1781) the newly settled American colonies won their political independence from Great Britain. Although some people of that day may have questioned the wisdom of that rebellion, no American citizen today doubts that that fight for independence was a good thing. The consequence has been a readiness on the part of Americans to identify with others struggling for their political independence. The Monroe Doctrine (1823) proclaimed U.S. opposition to any recolonization of Latin America by European powers. After World War I (1914–1918) U.S. President Wilson included "national self-determination" as one of his "Fourteen Points" for a peaceful world. After World War II (1939–1945) the

136

United States championed the independence of British and French colonies even though those European countries had been allies in the war. What was viewed as Soviet colonization of Eastern Europe after World War II was a central factor in the development of the Cold War. Domestic opposition to U.S. involvement in the Vietnamese War (1964–1973) also focused on the idea that the people of Vietnam should be allowed to have a Communist system if that was what they wanted.

Knowledge of the early fight for independence also leads to an uneasiness in most Americans about the United States having any colonies, and in fact there were none until 1898.[2] The Philippines, acquired as a result of the Spanish-American War, were an American colony for nearly half a century but were given their independence in 1946; and Cuba was given its independence in 1902 when it could also have been made a colony. The former territories of Hawaii and Alaska have been converted to full-fledged states, and many Americans believe that the same move should be made with regard to Puerto Rico if the Puerto Ricans so choose. Nevertheless it must be noted that U.S. advancement to the level of a world power has come into conflict with the principle of "no colonies." For example, several islands in the Caribbean and others in the Pacific are U.S. colonies, though they are called "self-governing territories" because they are allowed to elect their own governors.[3] It also should be noted that the concern of Americans is generally limited to *political* independence. The problem of continuing *economic* dependency after political independence has been gained, not having been part of the American experience, does not get much attention. Just as it is generally believed that individual persons who have political freedom should be able to take care of their own economic problems, so it is generally believed that nations that have their political independence should be able to take care of their own economic problems.

The American confidence in Western-style democracy is supported by the U.S. experience with its 200-year-old Constitution. American history shows that stable but nevertheless changing governance is possible without tyranny or armed revolution. The main blot on an otherwise good record of stability and internal tranquility was the Civil War or War Between the States (1861–1865). Many persons of diverse national, cultural, racial, and religious backgrounds have been peacefully integrated into a single pluralistic but generally harmonious national community. This experience has led Americans to be very unsympathetic to political violence. It is apparent to them that differences regarding public policy should be resolved by debating and voting. If people in other countries don't have such a system for resolving their differences, Americans believe they should institute a government by which that can be done. The same outlook applies at the world level with regard to disputes among nations. It is quite understandable that both the League of Nations and the United Nations were proposals of American presidents and that just after World War II 63 percent of the American public supported the idea of a federal world government.[4]

Experience has also confirmed for Americans the value of a capitalistic economic system. Even though there have been depressions from time to time, the overall trend has been toward more and more abundance. New inventions, encouraged by the free enterprise system, have kept the United States in the forefront of technological change and increasing productivity. "Rags-to-riches" success stories of new immigrants demonstrate that the opportunity for anyone to succeed still exists. Undoubtedly the outstanding economic record of the United States has been due in part to the presence of good agricultural land, vast natural resources, and the general absence of destruction from war, but most Americans believe that the competition engendered by the market system is a crucial ingredient in the nation's prosperity. They tend to view the spread of American business enterprises into other parts of the world as a good thing, not just for the businesses but also for the people who will get jobs as a result. In fact many Americans are concerned that U.S. businesses are creating too many jobs in other countries while closing down factories in the United States.

Another important aspect of the American outlook is the insistence that there be a moral basis for military action. The first Americans felt that it was necessary to issue a "Declaration of Independence" to morally justify to the whole world their use of violence to achieve independence. The reasoning in that document is based on "natural law" theory, especially as that theory was developed by the English philosopher John Locke (1632–1704).[5] Locke maintained that there is a moral law based on reason (that is, a "natural law") which serves as an unwritten rule of justice to be used by the individual conscience in evaluating governments and the written laws they may adopt. This "natural law" exists as a standard for correct behavior even if no government has yet been established to make laws and enforce them.

When philosophers explore social obligations and the basis of government, they try to imagine what rights and obligations people would have even if there were no government. Such a situation is described as a *state of nature*. Any rights people have in such a situation are called "natural rights," and any obligations are called "natural obligations." These "natural rights" and "natural obligations" together make up the "natural law."

Some "realistic" philosophers such as Thomas Hobbes (1588–1679) maintained that in a *state of nature* people would have a "natural right" to whatever they could acquire and keep for themselves and would have no "natural obligations" whatsoever to anyone else.[6] The state of nature would be an unrestrained survival-of-the-strongest situation. It would be a constant war of everyone against everyone, and the only way out of such a situation would be to establish a very strong government that would adopt some "civil laws" (written laws adopted by a government) and enforce them. According to Hobbes, only after a government was established would it make any sense to talk about any obligations to others, and then the government itself would decide what was obligatory and what was not.

The Americans adopted Locke's much more "idealistic" view of the moral situation in the *state of nature*. As noted above, Locke said that even in the state of nature there would be a "natural law" which would bestow on everyone some "natural rights" and "natural obligations." Locke claimed that everyone has a natural *right* to (a) life, (b) liberty, and (c) property, and therefore everyone has a natural *obligation* (a) not to kill others, (b) not to enslave others, and (c) not to steal from others. That means that life in the *state of nature* would not be nearly as "lawless" as Hobbes had portrayed it. With regard to the question of how the "natural law" would be enforced, Locke maintained that everyone would be entitled to enforce it, and in the end God would make sure that offenders got what they deserved.

Since these rights and obligations exist even in a *state of nature*, no government can take them away. Borrowing from Locke's view, Jefferson wrote in the Declaration of Independence that there are certain "unalienable rights" (rights that could not be taken away), "that among these are life, liberty, and the pursuit of happiness" that no government, including the British government, could nullify. So Locke's ideas about the existence of a "natural law" became the basis of the Declaration of Independence adopted by the Continental Congress of the American colonists in 1776 while they were fighting for their independence.

That "natural law" theory borrowed from Locke has continued to influence American thinking not only with regard to the relations among individual citizens but also has been extended to the relations among nation-states. There is no world government over the national governments, but that does not mean that there is no law governing what it is right and wrong for nation-states to do. Nation-states have a "natural right" (a) to exist, (b) to be free, and (c) to control their own natural resources. That means that they also have "natural obligations" (a) not to attack or destroy other nation-states, (b) not to subjugate or colonize other nation-states, and (c) not to unfairly exploit the natural resources of other nation-states. This "idealistic" view of international relations which is so central in American political thinking means that there is a general antipathy to the Hobbesian "realistic" emphasis on power politics so prevalent among many political scientists and political leaders.

Guided by this "idealistic" perspective as well as by pragmatic considerations, the foreign policy of the United States from the end of the War of 1812 until the time of World War I (1914–1918) was to stay out of European power politics. This policy was feasible partly because of the separation provided by the Atlantic Ocean and partly because it was acceptable to the British, who had the most powerful navy during this period. It also proved to be beneficial for the overseas business interests of American enterprises which consequently faced no nationalistic antagonism. American business also prospered greatly in the United States itself as the country expanded across the continent, assisted by the spoils of the Mexican War (1846–1848). Staying out of European affairs also did not preclude fighting the Spanish-American War (1898) and then a war against the natives in the Philippines (1899–1901) in order to acquire the use of those islands for American business interests.

It was also because of American business interests that the isolation from European power struggles ended in 1917. After World War I broke out in 1914 there was a great demand in Europe for American products, especially arms and ammunition. American businessmen were willing to sell to whoever would buy, but geographical factors plus the British navy made it easier to sell to the Allies.

German submarine attacks on U.S. ships triggered U.S. entry into the war, but U.S. sympathies were already with the British and French, partly because of evidence that the Germans were secretly encouraging Mexico to attack the United States and even more because the Germans were perceived as aggressors who had immorally invaded neutral Belgium. Americans have an animosity toward aggressors[7] that is directly linked to the general acceptance of natural law theory discussed previously. According to that view, nation-states, like individuals, should follow moral principles. They should not physically attack others who have done no harm to them. They should not violate their contracts and treaties. They should respect the property of others. The Germans had violated all these precepts. As aggressors they deserved to be punished. If the British and French could not accomplish that, then it would be completely appropriate for the United States to join the effort to enforce the "natural law." It should be remembered, of course, that the Germans did not perceive themselves as aggressors but as merely doing what had to be done to protect themselves in a war where they would be attacked from both east and west.

After the war Woodrow Wilson proposed a League of Nations where the whole community of nations could collectively determine whether some nation had committed aggression against another. But the U.S. Senate did not provide the two-thirds majority needed to ratify the Versailles Treaty containing the League's Covenant, so the U.S. did not participate in the League. It was argued that since the United States didn't want other nations "meddling" in the Americas, it likewise should not get involved in other nations' affairs. It is difficult to know whether the situation would have been different if the United States had joined the League, but as it was the League did not take forceful action against aggressors, and by 1939 the nations were at war again in both Asia and Europe.

Through 1940 and most of 1941 the U.S. public was not ready to support military action against the all-too-obvious aggression of the Axis powers. That changed quickly when the Japanese attacked the U.S. Pacific Fleet at Pearl Harbor in Hawaii on December 7, 1941. Since that day Americans have been urged to "Remember Pearl Harbor" and to be prepared for an unexpected attack. Pearl Harbor marks the end of an era in American foreign policy. The United States could no longer afford to be indifferent to world affairs. Furthermore, the rapid advances of the Japanese military forces during the first six months after Pearl Harbor made it clear that in the future the United States would need a bigger, better-prepared military force in place before actual fighting begins. The United States had become a full-fledged participant in world power politics.

Even before World War I had ended another event took place which had a great impact on subsequent U.S. foreign policy, namely, the Bolshevik Revolution in Russia. From the beginning the U.S. perceived the Communists as enemies. The opposition of Americans to Communism has three separate but very powerful roots. First, those who are well off financially will obviously be opposed to a movement whose avowed aim is to take their wealth from them and probably even exterminate them. Second, those who are committed to Western-style democracy oppose Communism because of its authoritarian politics and its readiness to use violence to achieve its aims. Third, those who have traditional religious commitments oppose it because of its militant evangelical atheism. It is not surprising, then, that U.S. military forces, along with those of Britain, France, and Japan, intervened in Russia in 1918-1919 to help the pro–Western White Army try to overthrow the new Communist regime.

Despite the negative attitude toward the Communists, in World War II Americans found themselves fighting with the Communists against the Axis powers, who were enemies of both Communism and Western-style democracy. During the war the United States sent much-needed materiel to the Soviets, especially trucks and jeeps, and exactly three months after the war in Europe had ended (May 8, 1945), the Soviets launched an attack on Japanese positions in Manchuria as they had agreed to do.[8] At the end of the war the relations between the Soviet Union and the United States were reasonably good, and the United Nations had been organized on the basis that these two nations together with Britain, France, and China would work together to preserve world peace. But the mood of cooperation changed quickly. From the American point of view the Soviets used their military presence in Eastern Europe to establish Communist governments there instead of permitting free elections. The former U.S. ally seemed to be the same kind of authoritarian aggressor as the Germans who had just been defeated.

In response, on March 12, 1947, U.S. President Truman announced that the United States would provide military assistance "to support peoples who are resisting attempted subjugation by armed minorities or by outside pressures."[9] This "Truman Doctrine" marked a great shift in U.S. policy. It indicated that the United States would be getting involved even in the internal affairs of other countries where military force rather than the ballot box was being used to take control of a country. The policy seemed to work in Turkey and Greece, where U.S. assistance helped anti–Communist regimes to stay in power. A second part of the U.S. response was the Marshall Plan, a program of economic assistance to European countries so they could rebuild quickly and consequently be less susceptible to Communist-inspired uprisings. A third part of the U.S. response, instigated by a Communist takeover in Czechoslovakia (February 1948) and a Soviet cut-off of ground access to West Berlin (June 1948), was the creation of the North Atlantic Treaty Organization (NATO). In that alliance the United States, Canada, and the countries of Western Europe agreed that an attack on any one would be regarded as an attack on all. The Communist expansion in Europe seemed to be under control, and the U.S. program of "containment" seemed to be working.

But the situation was different in Asia. Mao Zedong's Communist forces gained control of all of mainland China in 1949. The most populous nation in the world had come under Communist control. In 1950 the Communist North Koreans attacked non–Communist South Korea, and President Truman, already under attack for having "lost" China by not giving enough support to the anti–Communist forces there, quickly sent U.S. forces to Korea and got the United Nations to declare North Korea an aggressor. After much fighting and much negotiation a truce was signed in 1953. Again Communist expansion had been halted.

In Vietnam, however, a more complicated situation existed. During World War II the French colony of Indo-China had been taken over by the Japanese. After the war the French tried to reestablish their colonial control, but their efforts were resisted by local forces led by Ho Chi Minh. Ho had worked with agents of the U.S. Office of Strategic Services (OSS) against the Japanese during the war and considered himself to be the George Washington of Vietnam. At the same time he was a committed Communist who had spent many years in Moscow. In Vietnam, the American sympathy for national independence movements came into conflict with its opposition to Communism. At first the United States refused to help the French against Ho, but after unexpected gains by the Communists in China the United States changed its policy and started providing materiel to the French. After the French were forced by military defeat to leave in 1954, the part of Vietnam north of the 17th parallel came under Communist control. At this point the United States began to offer assistance to the non–Communist Vietnamese left in control in the south. The number of U.S. advisers was regularly increased in order to help the South Vietnamese government deal with Communist guerrillas. In 1964 the United States sent military forces into South Vietnam. A long, indecisive war ensued, and in 1973 U.S. forces left. Very shortly thereafter the South Vietnamese government surrendered, and the Communists were in control of all of Vietnam and soon also the neighboring countries of Laos and Cambodia.

What was the United States to do in situations like Vietnam? The "hawks" had argued that the Communists had to be stopped in Vietnam or they would soon take over all of Southeast Asia. Military containment had worked in Europe and Korea, and it should also work in Indo-China. The "doves," on the other hand, argued that there was overwhelming support for Ho Chi Minh among the people of Vietnam and that the United

States had no business intervening on the side of a small non–Communist minority. There is still strong disagreement in the United States about what should have been done in Vietnam, and the same conflicting views were evident in debates about U.S. involvement in places such as Nicaragua where apparently popular movements for progressive change had Communists in key leadership positions.

Latin America became a focal point for U.S. resistance to Communism in the late 1970s and 1980s. Fidel Castro had made Cuba a center for exporting Communism to all of Latin America, and especially to Central America and the Caribbean. Many Latin American governments were controlled by right-wing military dictatorships opposed to any kind of liberalization. Opposing them were revolutionary "democratic" forces, many of whom were inspired by Castro's success in Cuba. Democrats and Republicans had very different ideas about what strategy to use to stop the spread of Communism in this area. Democratic President Jimmy Carter tried to persuade the ruling regimes to adopt reforms while simultaneously trying to wean the revolutionary forces away from Communism by showing them that the U.S. was interested in human rights and progressive change. In 1978 he managed to persuade the Senate to ratify the Panama Canal Treaties which would eventually return the canal to the Panamanians. This agreement was to send a message that the U.S. was becoming more sensitive to the concerns of Latin Americans. In 1978-1979 a civil war in Nicaragua led to the overthrow of the corrupt leader Somoza, but a substantial proportion of the Sandinista forces which engineered that revolution were Marxists and their biggest supporter was Castro in Cuba. Even though Sandinista leader Daniel Ortega included non–Marxists in his government, many Americans were convinced that the Communists had just taken control in one more country, which would serve as a base to promote Communist takeovers in other countries such as El Salvador. When Republican Ronald Reagan became president in 1981, he adopted a totally different strategy of giving military and financial support to the counter-revolutionary "Contras" in order to overthrow the Sandinistas. In 1985 Reagan sent U.S. forces to take over the island nation of Grenada after a Communist take-over had occurred there. The message was obvious. No leftist revolutions would be allowed in the Western Hemisphere.

President Reagan also decided to take a more aggressive stance against the Soviet Union, which in 1979 had already shown its disdain for Carter's conciliatory approach by intervening to help Communist forces in Afghanistan's civil war. In the early 1980s Reagan launched a massive military build-up of nuclear forces topped off by the ideal of a Strategic Defense Initiative which supposedly would give the U.S. a protective shield against any Soviet nuclear attack. Reagan had made it clear that the U.S. was going to try to gain military superiority rather than being content with nuclear parity with the Soviet Union.

It is still a matter of debate to what extent this Reagan policy of building up U.S. military forces was what led the Soviet Union to decide to drop out of the arms race with the U.S. and to what extent Gorbachev was going to try to end the arms race anyway because of the sad shape of the Soviet economy. At any rate, significant turning points leading to the end of the Cold War were Gorbachev's accession to the top post in the Soviet Union in March 1985 and Reagan's insistence that he would put U.S. medium-range Pershing II missiles in Europe unless the Soviets dismantled all their intermediate-range missiles aimed at Western Europe. One event which in retrospect can be viewed as the beginning of the end of the Cold War was the summit meeting between Reagan and Gorbachev in October 1986 in Reykjavik, Iceland, where these leaders departed from their prepared agenda and even discussed the possibility of eliminating all strategic nuclear weapons. In December 1987, an agreement was signed that both countries would remove all intermediate-range missiles from Europe, an accord that was put into treaty form in June 1988. The event which most dramatically signified the end of the Cold War was the tearing down of the Berlin Wall in November 1989.

It is virtually impossible to exaggerate the significance of the changes which took place in the international situation between 1986 and 1991. In five years the U.S. went from the Cold War stance of matching the placement of Soviet medium-range nuclear missiles in Europe to seeing its long-time enemy, the Soviet Union, go out of existence, breaking up into its 15 constituent republics. The 40-year-plus Cold War ended with the U.S. as the sole superpower in the world.

In 1991, when the U.S. organized a coalition of military forces to remove Iraqi forces which had invaded Kuwait, U.S. President George Bush could speak of a "New World Order." The Cold War was over, and now the U.S. would take the lead in establishing a world where aggression would not be allowed, where all nations would follow the principles of natural law in their relations with one another. This American ideal, which had been behind the creation of the League of Nations and the United Nations, was now going to be realized under the military leadership of the U.S. The other major Western-style industrialized democracies, the other countries which together with the U.S. made up the G-7 group (Britain, France, Germany, Italy, Canada, and Japan) would have special consultative status. The U.N., especially the Security Council, would be used when feasible. The U.S. would be leader, not autocrat, in the "New World Order."

Since 1991 U.S. military forces have been used primarily to give special help to U.N. peacekeeping forces. This kind of effort began in Iraq after the Gulf War. A large U.S. operation directed toward ending all armed violence was conducted in Somalia starting in December 1992, but all military operations in Somalia were officially turned over to U.N. command in May 1993. Some U.S. personnel have also been involved in U.N. peacekeeping efforts in the former Yugoslavia.

After World War I U.S. President Woodrow Wilson initiated the

League of Nations. After World War II U.S. presidents Franklin Roosevelt and Harry Truman led the effort to create the United Nations. With the Cold War ended, the U.S. is leading the way again in the development of new international institutions. Starting places are NATO, an organization with military capabilities but no longer having a Communist enemy, and the Conference on Security and Cooperation in Europe (CSCE), an organization which was begun during the Cold War to foster cooperation between the opposing sides and which has focused on the protection of human rights. Also existing worldwide organizations such as the U.N. and the International Court of Justice can be reformed to do their jobs better. An International Criminal Court to deal with *individuals* who violate international law could be created. It remains to be seen what will be done with the possibilities.

A prime constraint on what the U.S. can do in its role of world leader is its own poor economic situation resulting from the long-lasting direct and indirect financial drain of the Cold War. Just when financial resources are desperately needed to assist the former Communist countries in their conversion to a capitalistic economy, to support U.N. peacekeeping in several places throughout the world, and to rebuild itself internally, the U.S. finds itself with a large and growing public debt. The conversion to a post–Cold War society will take time and resources, but being able to reduce the huge financial cost of fighting the Cold War should help. The challenge is to create an acceptable new world order without the U.S. carrying too large a proportion of the burden of being the world's policeman.

The Russian Perspective

It is necessary to be clear on the distinction between "Russia" on the one hand and "the Soviet Union" or "Union of Soviet Socialist Republics (U.S.S.R.)" on the other. The present "Russian Federation" is one of the 15 republics that had been united in the Soviet Union before its dissolution in 1991. The country of Russia (sometimes called "the Russian Empire") also existed under the czars before the Communist revolution of 1917 and the formal creation of the Union of Soviet Socialist Republics in 1922. Distinguishing between the Soviet Union and the Russian Federation is not easy because they overlap so much. Before the break-up of the Soviet Union, Moscow served as the capital of both the Soviet Union and the Russian Federation. The Russian Federation comprises 75 percent of the territory of the former Soviet Union, and it is still the largest country in the world in terms of territory. Just over 50 percent of the population of the former Soviet Union lives in the Russian Federation, and almost all of the top leaders of the Soviet Union were Russians. The Soviet Union was a federation of 15 republics, while the Russian Federation is itself a federation of 88 identifiable political subunits. After the dissolution of the Soviet Union, the Russian Federation took its place in the United Nations.

The history of the western part of Russia from the tenth century on follows essentially the same series of social patterns one finds in the rest of Europe: kingdoms established by traders over the areas they were exploiting, then feudal kingdoms based on land holdings, then urban-centered kingdoms based on merchant capital, and then a larger "national" kingdom with an autocratic leader supported by the nobility.[10] But there were some differences. First, the developments in Russia occurred considerably later than in Western Europe. Secondly, and partly as a consequence of the first point, in Russia the landed aristocracy eventually was joined by the new industrial capitalists as rulers of Russia rather than being overthrown by them as happened in the Western European countries.[11] As a result, Russia did not become the kind of capitalistic democracy which had developed in England and France, though it was moving in this direction in the decades just before the 1917 revolution.[12]

A third significant difference between Russia and the countries of Western Europe is the size of the country which eventually came to exist. In the west the expanding populations of the flourishing countries not only came up against each other but before long also reached the shoreline. At this point some of them took to ships and the New World. For the Russians there was land and more land to be taken, especially to the east, and the Russians became "land-sailors" moving ever onward to new lands.[13] The greatest geographical expansion of the borders took place in the seventeenth and eighteenth centuries when all of Siberia and even Alaska were brought under Russian control, and the border to the west and southwest was extended to approximately its present location.[14] In the nineteenth century large numbers of Russians migrated into these new areas, and additional territory was added in the south central region between the Caspian Sea and China. Efforts to expand still farther south brought the Russians into conflict with the British, but in 1907 an agreement on spheres of influence was reached which put Afghanistan into the British orbit.[15] Some observers believe that the desire of the Russians to expand their territory southward did not end then and that the sending of Soviet military forces into Afghanistan in 1979 substantiates that view.[16] On the other hand, alternative interpretations of that action have also been offered.[17]

Although Russian expansion has continued over a long period of time, it also needs to be noted that Russia has been invaded on several occasions from the west, where there are few natural barriers to assist in the defense of the country. In 1812 Napoleon invaded. In 1916 the Germans and Austrians invaded. In 1920-1921 the Poles invaded. In 1941 the Germans under Hitler invaded again. On the first and the fourth occasions, after sustaining massive losses the Russians drove the invaders back and eventually were victors in the war. On the second occasion the Russian government collapsed and was forced to accept a punitive peace settlement. The land lost during the third invasion was taken back in 1939. But the Soviets believed it was time to put an end to these invasions. Consequently, after World War

II they were determined to create a row of friendly "buffer" states in Eastern Europe through which any potential invader would need to pass before reaching the Soviet border. Soviet actions in eastern Europe during the Cold War period are much more readily understood in light of these past invasions.

Another important aspect of the Russian historical experience has been the seemingly never-ending effort to catch up with Western Europe. The Renaissance, the commercial revolution, and the industrial revolution all began farther west and only later reached Russia. The result, as perceived by both Western Europeans and some Russians, has been a long history of Russian "backwardness." Leaders such as Peter I (ruled 1689–1725), Catherine II (ruled 1762–1796), Alexander I (ruled 1801–1825), and Alexander II (ruled 1855–1881) tried to promote Western ways of thinking and acting in Russia, but their efforts only partly succeeded. The Russian "backwardness" was most evident in warfare. The Russians had done rather well in their wars during the first half of the nineteenth century, but the Crimean War (1853–1856) showed they were no match for the British and the French. The Russo-Japanese War (1904–1905) and the first part of World War I (1914–1918) demonstrated that they couldn't hold their own against Japan or Germany. This history of inferiority is important in realizing how important it was for the Soviets to win in their competition with the West during the Cold War, whether the contest was athletic, artistic, scientific, or military. In this context one can appreciate the great concern of Soviet leaders like Gorbachev that in the 1970s and 1980s the Soviets had fallen decisively behind the West with regard to computers, robotics, and other new technologies.

Some other aspects of pre–Revolution Russia are worth mentioning briefly. One is that Russians had been accustomed to an autocratic political system, a system which the fifteenth-century leaders of Moscow borrowed from their Mongol overlords and which was not softened much until the decade before the Bolshevik Revolution.[18] A second is that religiously inclined Russians traditionally thought of Moscow as the center of World Orthodoxy, "the Third Rome," the successor to Rome and Constantinople as *the* holy city of Christendom.[19] The czars and patriarchs served together as protectors of "the Truth" until such time as the rest of the world would be ready to receive it. As custodians of "the Truth" they felt it was altogether appropriate to regulate what the people could read and hear so that they would not be lured away from the true faith. Both of these phenomena have interesting parallels with what happened in the Soviet Union under the Communists.

The Bolshevik Revolution in 1917 brought massive changes in the social order. The leader of the Revolution was Vladimir Ilyich Ulyanov (1870–1923), better known by his adopted name of Lenin. He was a Russian Marxist whose involvement in revolutionary activities got him exiled to Siberia in 1895 and then chased out of the country in 1907. In 1917 he returned by train from Switzerland, aided by the Germans, who hoped that his revolutionary activities would lead to Russian withdrawal from the war. Lenin's writings had served as inspiration to the revolutionaries, and when he arrived in St. Petersburg, the Russian capital, he was recognized as leader of the Bolshevik (majority) faction of the Russian Social-Democratic Workers Party. He led that group in refusing to participate in Kerensky's liberal democratic provisional government set up after the abdication of Czar Nicholas II in March of 1917. He then led them in their own revolution to take control of the Russian government in November of 1917. Under his leadership the new government agreed to peace with Germany; fought to victory against a group of counterrevolutionaries who received assistance from British, French, American, and Japanese military forces; and established the first Marxist state.[20] A Russian government whose aim had been to protect the interest of the nobility and well-to-do was replaced by a Soviet government whose aim was to advance the interests of the workers and the peasants.

Just as Americans generally believe that their historical experience has confirmed the value of their ideology of capitalistic democracy, so Soviet citizens during the Cold War period generally believed that their historical experience had confirmed the value of the Marxist-Leninist ideology. When they compared the Soviet Union with pre–Revolution Russia, they were proud of the differences. Not everything had been perfect, but certainly some great progress had been made, especially in view of the great losses suffered in World War II.

One of the most obvious improvements was the quantity and quality of industrialization which had taken place. Although some progress had been made in the late 1800s and early 1900s,[21] Russia at that time was still a backward country, as the fighting in World War I had demonstrated. During the Cold War the Soviets were able to challenge the United States in the development of the most technologically advanced types of weaponry — nuclear weapons, long-range missiles, surveillance satellites, attack helicopters, nuclear-powered submarines, and so on. Though the Soviet Union was not at the top in the production of consumer goods, still its position relative to the rest of the world was certainly much better than it had been before the Revolution. The Soviet citizenry were convinced that the industrialization pushed so relentlessly by Stalin in the 1930s had given them the capability to defeat the Germans in World War II and that the continued emphasis on industrialization and arms production had enabled them to neutralize postwar U.S. efforts to dominate the world.

A second great improvement was the increased opportunity for everyone in the country. Under the czars many children never learned to read or write, and access to university-level education was generally restricted to the upper classes. National minorities often were not allowed to use their national languages in schools. Health care for peasants and the poor in cities was virtually nonexistent. Taxes on peasants were ten times as high as taxes on landlords.[22] Sports and museums were only for the wealthy. Under

Communism all that had changed. All children had access to education.[23] There was no discrimination against anyone because of her or his nationality.[24] All people could get adequate medical care and participate in the cultural life of the society. Taxes were fair for all. Things such as special training for sports and the arts were provided free to everyone by the government.

A third kind of improvement, claimed the Communists, was the kind of personal outlook developed by individuals living in a socialist system. In pre–Revolution Russia either people would learn to selfishly compete to get all they could for themselves or they would be brought under the influence of the Church, in which case all critical and scientific thinking would be subordinated to the acceptance of superstition and ancient ways of thinking. Under the socialist system people were directed toward social cooperation and progressive thinking directed toward improving the lot of all humanity.

Somewhat related to the above was the understanding of the situation with regard to war and peace. The Communists believed that under the czars Russia got involved in wars in order to advance the interests of its own elite or the interests of foreigners with investments in Russian industry.[25] After the Bolshevik Revolution, it was no longer necessary to fight wars in order to control markets and raw materials for the capitalist class. The wars the Soviets had to fight and get prepared to fight were responses to capitalistic nations which wanted to eliminate the one socialist state strong enough to help protect successful revolutionary movements in other countries from externally supported counterrevolutions.

After World War II Soviet forces were obliged to help the progressive socialist groups in the Eastern European countries maintain control against pro-capitalist groups, groups who not only wanted to put a reactionary government back in control in their own countries but who also would eventually cooperate with other capitalists in trying once again to overthrow the socialist regime in the Soviet Union. Assistance had also been given to progressive groups in other countries, but in no case had Soviet forces ever invaded a capitalist state unless that state had first invaded the Soviet Union, as Hitler did. Soviet military forces were sent into another country only after the proletariat there had succeeded in gaining control of the country and requested Soviet assistance to prevent a counterrevolution. Communists pointed to the existence of a capitalist state like Finland right on the Soviet border to show that capitalist countries no longer needed to fear invasion from the Soviet Union.[26]

The Communists in the Soviet Union proclaimed that their ultimate goal was a world in which all nations had adopted a socialist system. According to their understanding, that was the only way in which capitalist exploitation of some countries by others could be halted. But the Communists' proclaimed strategy was never to use force to take over a country which generally wanted to remain a capitalist country. From their point of view a proletarian revolution would necessarily be a revolution by the majority against an entrenched elite minority, and it could not possibly succeed unless it had widespread public support.[27] After a proletarian revolution had succeeded, as in Cuba, then it would be the task of the Soviet Union to help that regime set up a new socialist society and to prevent any attempted counterrevolution. The Soviets did not perceive themselves as threatening to the U.S. or any other capitalist country because their aim was limited to supporting leftist revolutions which had come about with majority support.

According to the Soviets, the attempt by the United States to portray the Soviet Union as an aggressive country was only a way of diverting attention from what the U.S. itself was doing, namely, maintaining military forces all over the world in order to protect U.S. economic interests as they exploited the raw materials and low-paid workers of the less developed countries.[28] From the Soviet point of view that was the significance of U.S. interventions in Iran in 1953, Guatemala in 1954, Vietnam in 1955–1973, Lebanon in 1958, Cuba in 1961, the Dominican Republic in 1965, Chile in 1973, Grenada in 1983, Nicaragua in 1985, and Panama in 1989. The U.S. proclaimed itself the champion of democracy but in fact was always intervening to prevent revolutions by "the people."

But ultimately the critical issue in the Soviet Union became a question of how democratic that country itself was. Although there were elections, there could be only one party to nominate candidates, the Communist Party. The system of democratic centralism where the decisions of higher level bodies were binding on the lower levels meant that ultimately the real power was in the hands of a very small group of leaders at the top. The Communist Party was supposedly the party of the common people running government for the sake of the masses, but in fact the party itself became the home of a new elite with its own special privileges. They had their own stores for shopping, their own hospitals, their own vacation spots, and so on. They had limousines and chauffeurs at their disposal. They used their positions to get special privileges for themselves and to help their family members and their friends.

Government policy in the Soviet Union reflected the views of the leadership group, and often a single individual. Under Stalin (1924–1953) ruthless terrorism was used to control the population. Control of the economy was centralized, and there was a focus on the development of heavy industry and armaments. Not everyone was enthusiastic about the Communist system, but during World War II the population worked hard for "Mother Russia" in order to defeat the Germans. After the war Stalin's heavy-handedness against those who did not totally obey him became evident again.

Stalin's death was followed by a period of de–Stalinization and reform under the leadership of Nikita Khrushchev. The Soviet space program delivered the first artificial satellite in 1957, an event used by Khrushchev to promote the idea that Communism was proving its superiority over capitalism. On the other hand, the Soviets built the Berlin Wall in 1961 to prevent East Germans from escaping to the freer and more prosperous West. The Cuban missile crisis in 1962 resulted from Khrushchev's push for Soviet military parity with the U.S. Having led the world to the brink of nuclear war, Khrushchev and Kennedy tried to ease the tensions by signing the Partial Nuclear Test-Ban Treaty in 1963. In 1964 Khrushchev was removed from power for making decisions without first consulting with the rest of the leadership, for supporting unscientific theories about the inheritance of acquired characteristics in agricultural policy, for advocating organizational reforms that threatened the position of many people in the party bureaucracy, for inappropriate public behavior such as banging his shoe on a desk at the United Nations and inordinate bragging about the accomplishments of Soviet science, and for being unreasonable in his disputes with the Chinese Communists (such as threatening to launch a nuclear strike on their nuclear facilities if they exploded a nuclear weapon, which they did the day after he was removed from his position[29]).

The Leonid Brezhnev years (1964–1982) saw a return to stable and traditional bureaucracy, a praising of Stalin's accomplishments, a steady growth in military spending, greater assistance to Communist Vietnam in its struggle against U.S. forces while simultaneously following a path of "peaceful coexistence" with the U.S. itself (including signing nuclear arms control agreements like SALT I and SALT II), an effort to develop more technology relevant to the production of consumer goods, and a reigning in of cultural freedom. In Eastern Europe Romania managed to defy the Soviets by trading with the U.S., Western Europe, and China instead of trading exclusively within the Soviet bloc. In 1968 a liberal regime in Czechoslovakia was squashed by an invasion of Soviet and other Warsaw Pact forces in accord with the "Brezhnev Doctrine," the idea that the Soviet Union and its allies reserved the right to use military force to intervene militarily in any Soviet bloc country that seemed to be wavering from orthodox Marxism, thus endangering the whole bloc. In 1979 Soviet forces were dispatched to Afghanistan to help the Marxist side in a civil war there.

When Brezhnev died in 1982, there was a struggle between hardliners who wanted to maintain the Stalin-Brezhnev conservative bureaucratic approach and reformists who wanted to open up the system to new ideas in the Khrushchev anti–Stalin fashion. None of the contenders was young, so it seemed obvious that no one would be in power for long. Yuri Andropov, a reformist, won the contest and used his 15 months in office to promote more discipline in the workplace in order to increase productivity. One of the more significant things he did was to move fellow reformist Mikhail Gorbachev up rapidly in the Party bureaucracy. In fact, when Andropov died it seemed that Gorbachev, even though much younger than the others at the top, would be one of the contenders for the top post. The hardliners, however, were committed to Konstantin Chernenko. At this point Gorbachev apparently struck a deal that he would step aside for Chernenko if it was clear that he would become leader when Chernenko died. The result was that the 73-year-old Chernenko became the Party Secretary for 13 months, but Gorbachev then became the new leader with little resistance in March 1985 after Chernenko died.

Gorbachev was aware that some in the higher echelons of the Party and the government were not enthusiastic supporters of his reform ideas, but he used his position to rapidly replace those people with others who would support him. He started out echoing the ideas of Andropov that there was a need for more commitment to work hard on the job so that the Soviet economy could progress and produce a standard of living more like that found in the West. He initiated penalties for absenteeism and launched an attack on alcoholism. In June 1987 he presented proposals for giving local enterprises more autonomy and having local factory managers elected by the workers. In the international arena Gorbachev indicated strong support for the United Nations and urged diplomats to be more sensitive and less dogmatic in their interactions with other countries. He stressed that the Soviet Union was not going to attack anyone, and indicated a strong interest in arms agreements to reduce both nuclear and conventional weapons. Most striking was his promoting of *perestroika* (restructuring), *glasnost* (openness), and *demokratizatsiya* (democratization). Highly centralized bureaucratic structures were to be decentralized. The media and artists were no longer to be censored for saying things critical of the government. Eastern European countries were to be free to do things in their own way, and in elections in the Soviet Union several candidates would be allowed, not just one as in former years. In the West there was much suspicion that Gorbachev was being deceptively "nice" so that he could catch them off guard.

Looking at the situation in retrospect, it seems that Gorbachev was being completely honest and that if he deceived anyone it was only himself in believing that he could start a reform process that would not ultimately result in the break-up of the Soviet Union. Once people were free to speak out, it became obvious that many of the different nationalities which had been under Russian control did not like that situation. Lithuania was the first to declare its independence from the Soviet Union in March 1990. Gorbachev, now holding the newly created post of President of the Soviet Union, tried to stop this move that might break up the whole Soviet Union by arguing that the separation and its terms would need to be negotiated by both sides. Gorbachev also held back on pushing some of his economic reforms in order to get more support from conservatives, but the result was a negative reaction from Boris Yeltsin, President of the Russian Federation. On August 19, 1991, one day before a Union treaty was to be signed which would end effective control by the Soviet Union over the republics, there was an attempted coup by conservatives to oust Gorbachev with an eye to trying to save the Soviet Union by the use of military force.[30] That attempt was foiled at least in part due to the actions of Yeltsin in Moscow when he daringly and successfully pleaded with the Soviet military forces not to fire on their fellow Russians. The coup attempt failed for lack of support by the military forces, and Yeltsin's courageous actions resulted in his popularity among reformers greatly surpassing that of Gorbachev. The failed coup led to a rash of declarations of independence by the republics.[31] On December 8, 1991, the leaders of the Russian Federation, Ukraine, and Belarus, three of the largest republics, issued the "Declaration of Minsk," which declared that the Soviet Union no longer existed and which invited other former republics of the Soviet Union to join them in the Commonwealth of Independent States (CIS).[32] On December 24, 1991, the Russian Federation was accepted as the successor of the Soviet Union in the United Nations,[33] and on December 25, 1991, Gorbachev resigned from the totally vacuous position of President of the Soviet Union.[34]

Yeltsin is not without his challenges in the Russian Federation. He is a popular reformer president with support from the West ready to lead Russia into becoming an industrialized capitalistic democracy, possibly destined to become in the not-too-distant future part of that small group of leading industrialized democracies which informally govern the world. But Yeltsin's policies are controversial, and at the end of 1993 it was not yet clear what the outcome would be.[35] It should not be forgotten that the Russian Federation has been composed of its own political units and national minorities which might press for independence from the Russian Federation just as the republics of the former Soviet Union fought for and won their independence from that federation. Such a development is a real possibility because of the current dismal economic conditions in Russia and the electoral success of assorted nationalist and Communist political elements in the parliamentary elections of December 1993. Thus it is still to be determined whether Yeltsin's view about the proper future direction of the Russian Federation will get realized.

The Western European Perspective

"Western Europe" refers, of course, not to a single nation but a group of nations of which the largest are Germany, Italy, the United Kingdom, and France. To be able to discuss their outlook in a collective manner is an indication of how much the world has changed since 1945, for before then it was the conflicts among these European nations which led to one war after another, culminating in the two World Wars. They still have their national differences, but in today's world these are minor in comparison to their common situation and outlook: All are capitalist democracies firmly and officially allied with the United States in the North Atlantic Treaty Organization (NATO).

For all of these European countries the past was much more glorious than is the present. In the sixteenth century, Spain, by virtue of her exploitation of the New World, was the chief power in the world.[36] During the next century France became dominant. England challenged France for supremacy in the eighteenth century and became dominant after the defeat of Napoleon in 1815. In the 1880s and 1890s the imperial European powers, led by Britain and France, divided most of Africa and Asia among themselves. By the end of the nineteenth century the British could boast that "the sun never sets on the British Empire," while a recently united Germany was searching for its place in the sun. In 1900 a military force composed of contingents from eight different countries (though almost half the troops were from Japan) was sent into China to put down the Boxer Rebellion there. These industrialized European nations viewed themselves as carrying civilization to the savages of the rest of the world, and in China the main point of dispute was whether each nation should have its own area of control or whether there should be an "open door" policy so that the whole of China would be available for exploitation by all traders regardless of nationality.

Though these European countries were heavily armed with new weapons of war made possible by modern industry and though they were organized into two opposing alliances, it seemed in the early 1900s that they were keeping their contest for power and new colonies under control. But in 1914 they stumbled into World War I, and the war came to a conclusion only after the military forces of the United States put an end to the deadlock on the battlefield. After the war, despite the efforts of President Wilson, the United States declined to become actively involved in the power struggle among nations, so Europe remained the center of world affairs.

Twenty years later the European countries were at war again, and again the United States intervened. By the end of that war in 1945 the European countries were in shambles. The United States and the Soviet Union were clearly the new powers in the world, and though they could not agree on much else they did concur in the view that the European nations should give up their colonial empires. Nevertheless attempts were made by the European nations to regain control over some of their colonies. These efforts often led to battles against local forces seeking independence, and after 15 years most of the former colonies had become independent nations. The European countries had lost most of their colonies as well as their prestige.

After having battled and battered one another for centuries, since the end of World War II the countries of Western Europe have been cooperating with one another and even taking some steps toward unification. The United States helped turn things in this direction when it decided that its postwar economic assistance to European countries (the Marshall Plan) would be coordinated through the Organization for European Economic Cooperation (OEEC). After the rebuilding of Europe was completed, this organization did not go out of existence but continued to give advice concerning economic problems. In 1961 it was expanded into the Organization for Economic Cooperation and Development (OECD).[37]

Another significant development contributing to the unification of Western Europe, also promoted by the United States, was the creation in

1949 of the North Atlantic Treaty Organization (NATO), a military alliance aimed at preventing any further expansion by Communist military forces in Europe. It provided not only for an integrated military command but also for a Council which discussed political issues.[38] Present members of NATO are Belgium, Canada, Denmark, France, Germany, Greece, Iceland, Italy, Luxembourg, Netherlands, Norway, Portugal, Spain, Turkey, the United Kingdom, and the United States.[39]

At the same time the Europeans have been doing some cooperative institution-building on their own. In 1947 France and Britain signed the *Treaty of Dunkirk,* pledging military assistance to each other in the event of another war with Germany and agreeing to strengthen economic relations.[40] The *Brussels Treaty* of 1948, which supplanted the Treaty of Dunkirk, specifically mentions the goal of progressive unification of Europe.[41] The 1954 modification of this treaty produced the Western European Union, composed of seven countries: United Kingdom, France, Belgium, Netherlands, Luxembourg, Italy, and West Germany.[42] This Union still provides an arena for discussing political issues, military policy, and the administration of military forces. It is a forum in which, unlike NATO, France is a militarily involved member, and the United States is not involved at all.[43] In January of 1948 the *Benelux Economic Union* (Belgium, Netherlands, and Luxembourg) initiated an economic program in which customs duties among the three nations were abolished and a common tariff was levied on goods coming into the three-nation region.[44] In 1949 the *Council of Europe* was formed as a diplomatic alliance to promote the unification of Europe. It subsequently has focused on the protection of human rights. It established a *European Court of Human Rights* which acts as an appeal court on civil liberties and which in a couple of cases has even nullified national laws that it found to be inconsistent with its principles.[45] It now has 20 members including Greece, which was expelled in 1969 but readmitted in 1974.

Of greater significance than the bodies mentioned above is the European Community (EC), which has developed out of the *European Coal and Steel Community* (ECSC) created in 1952 by the Treaty of Paris signed by France, West Germany, Italy, and the Benelux countries. The ECSC had a High Authority which could impose binding policies by majority vote on matters related to coal and steel production, including the setting of levies to finance its own operation.[46] It also had its own court, a council (composed of the foreign ministers of the member nations), and an assembly (composed of delegates from the national parliaments).[47] The success of the ECSC led to agreements in 1957 to create two other organizations, the European Atomic Energy Community (Euratom) and the European Economic Community (EEC or "Common Market"), both structured like the ECSC (except that the "High Authority" was given the different title "Commission"). These organizations began operating in 1958. In 1967 the three separate European organizations (ECSC, Euratom, and EEC) were merged into a single European Community (EC) with a single Commission (located in Brussels), a single European Court of Justice (located in Luxembourg), a single Council of Ministers (meets in Brussels), and a single European Parliament (meets in Strasbourg).[48] Originally the members of the European Parliament were selected legislators from the national parliaments, but since 1979 the members have been elected directly by the people. The European Parliament, despite its name, cannot pass laws, though someday it may acquire that power. Like the ECSC before it, the European Community has the authority to raise revenue directly rather than relying completely on assessments on the national governments.[49] Although the European Community originally had the same six members as the ECSC, it now has 12 members: Denmark, Ireland, and the United Kingdom joined in 1973; Greece in 1981; and Spain and Portugal in 1986. In addition to the bodies of the European Community already mentioned, since 1974 there have also been "summit meetings" three times a year of the heads of state of the member nations, meetings which have become institutionalized as the "European Council."

Does all this organization mean that we are moving towards a United States of Europe? Possibly, but not without difficulties. Ironically the end of the Cold War and the reunification of Germany in September 1990 have raised new questions about European unification. During the Cold War Western European countries had a militarily powerful common ideological enemy against which they needed to unite, but with the end of the Cold War the only "outsiders" against which the Europeans must unite are the economic competitors of the U.S. and Japan. Furthermore, a question now gets raised about the possible inclusion of Eastern European countries into a united Europe. Also, the reunification of Germany has ended the earlier relative equality of population and influence in the European Community among Britain, France, Italy, and West Germany. Previously, all four countries had populations between 55 and 61 million, but a united Germany with a population of about 80 million as well as the largest economy and a central geographical location now has a preeminent position.

The decisions facing the European Community are sometimes couched in terms of focusing on "deepening" the community or on "widening" it.[50] "Deepening" refers to making the existing community of 12 nation-states more substantial. This could mean giving more powers to the central authority such as the establishment of a closely integrated financial policy under the direction of an European Monetary Union (EMU) or the adoption of a program for increased redistribution of wealth within the European Community or the selection of "European" rather than national representatives to international conferences and international organizations. "Widening" refers to extending formal membership in the European Community to other European countries. The most obvious candidates are the six countries of the European Free Trade Association (EFTA): Austria, Finland, Iceland, Norway, Sweden, and Switzerland. But beyond that there are several other countries which would like very much to become part of the European Community: Poland, the Czech Republic, Slovakia, Hungary, Slovenia, Croatia, Lithuania, Latvia, and Estonia. Turkey, which is already a member of NATO, would also like to become part of the European Community as its first non–Christian member. There is a definite concern on the part of these countries that not being included in the European Community could present some real economic difficulties for them. It might be noted in passing that if these "outsider" countries are admitted to the official "Europe," Germany's position would become even more central while that of France and Britain would become a bit more peripheral than is the case in the existing European Community.

Before the end of the Cold War and the reunification of Germany, the focus was on "deepening" the community. Jacques Delors, president of the European Commission, has continued to push hard for more deepening. One of his temporary successes was adoption of the Treaty of Maastricht on political and economic and monetary union in December 1991.[51] But the actions required were soon far behind the timetable established by this treaty, including those opening the way for "widening" through the acceptance of new members. A major problem is the reluctance of the national governments and their citizens to transfer national sovereignty to a supranational body, to become Europeans rather than Frenchmen, Englishmen, and Germans.[52] This reluctance is found in varying degrees in different countries in the economic arena, the political arena, the military and "national security" arena, and the cultural arena. There is a struggle between seeking true integration into an economically, politically, militarily, and culturally unified community on the one hand and creating a collection of separate international functional coordinating agencies on the other. There is a struggle between adopting the model of a unified tree or that of a pillared temple, between building a true federation or simply a confederation.[53]

There are two places where this conflict will be played out. One concerns the authority of the European Parliament. So far, there has been a reluctance on the part of the national leaders to give that parliament much power. The decision-making has been focused in the European Commission where the various national governments control the process instead of the European Parliament where national loyalties would get subordinated to party loyalties and Community-wide thinking. The more authority is given to the parliament, the more federal and democratic will be the result. One complaint being voiced about the Maastricht agreement is that it is not democratic enough, that the decision-making has been and continues to be too much top-down from the powers-that-be rather that bottom-up from the voters. One clear sign that Europe has really chosen to integrate would be a decision to give some real authority to the European Parliament rather than keeping all the decision-making authority in the Council of Ministers and the Commission.

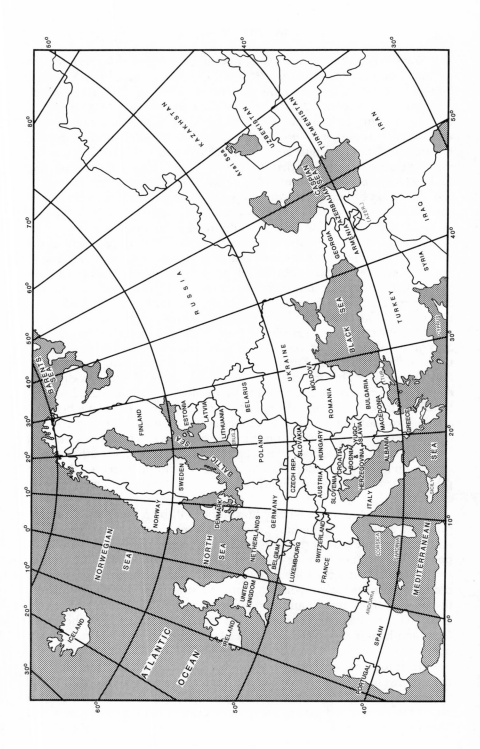

Another place where the true-integration-versus-mere-collaboration battle will be fought out concerns the issue of language. A true integration approach will require a decision to use a single "European" language rather than trying to continue using several different national languages. The European Community, in an effort to be non-discriminatory, has nine official languages for its 12 members. (Ireland agrees to use English while Belgium and Luxembourg agree to use French.) As one can imagine, the cost of translations and interpreting services is huge. In the offices it has been the custom to use English and French, though now the Germans argue with some cogency that German should be given equal status as one of the more privileged languages. As more countries enter the Community, this problem will become more acute. The first other country to enter will probably be Austria with 13 million more speakers of German. But what happens when the Swedes, the Norwegians, the Finns, the Poles, the Czechs, the Hungarians, and so on become members? There is also the problem of language rights for groups within the nation-states such as the Basques and Catalans in Spain. The adoption of Esperanto, a Latin-like European language in use for over one hundred years, would seem to offer a rational and fair solution to the problem of linguistic and cultural integration in Europe. Its official adoption would be a clear signal that the European Community has chosen true integration rather than mere collaboration. It is unlikely that the European Commission would make such a bold antinationalistic decision, but the European Parliament might vote to start teaching Esperanto to all European children as a necessary step in developing a true continental community whose members really would be free to go anywhere and work anywhere and live anywhere in the European Community. As a matter of fact, the European Parliament held a one-day conference on September 29, 1993, in order to discuss the language problem in the European Community and the extent to which a planned language such as Esperanto might contribute to the solution of that problem.[54]

It is still unclear what direction Europe will take. There is a desire for economic integration in order to be better able to compete against the United States and Japan, but there is considerable reluctance to bring about the political integration on which economic integration must be based if it is to be enduring. And now that the Cold War is over there is that difficult question of just where the eastern and southern borders of the European Community should be. Does it make sense to exclude those former Communist countries such as Poland, Hungary, and the Czech Republic which now want to be part of a democratic capitalistic Europe? Why should Mediterranean states like Malta be excluded from a united Europe? Why shouldn't Turkey, which has been a faithful member of NATO, be allowed into the European Community? In the long run might it not be more sensible to aim to integrate Europe (including the former Soviet republics) into

Opposite: *Europe Today*

a wider world community than to try to separate Europe out from the other industrialized democracies in order to be able to compete economically against them?

The Japanese Perspective

As late as 1990 Japan was the only non–Western nation which was listed as belonging to the 29-nation class of "developed countries," that is, highly industrialized nations.[55] Instead of becoming a colony of the Western nations as most of the nations of Asia and Africa did or a semi-colony as China and many of the nations in Latin America did, Japan itself became a colonial power. Though considerably smaller than the United States and though having only about half its population, Japan may equal the U.S. as an economic power by the year 2000.[56] Consequently, Japan is attracting a great deal of attention from those interested in economics, politics, and world affairs.

The critical period for Japan's future occurred between the last years of the sixteenth century and the beginning of the twentieth century.[57] The Japanese reaction to the West during this period can be characterized as readily accepting Western technology while fighting off the intrusion of the Westerners themselves into Japan as long as possible. A long period of internal peace under the Tokugawa shoguns (1600–1868) produced a unified and basically successful opposition to European efforts to forcibly enter the country. The virtual exclusion of Westerners was broken in 1853 when Commodore Perry and his fleet of U.S. ships forced the Japanese to agree to the return of shipwrecked sailors, the opening of fuel ports in Japan for foreign ships, and the development of economic and political relations. During the period called "the Meiji Restoration" (1868–1912) the Japanese worked out compromises which surrendered as little control to the Westerners as possible. At the same time they studied Western science and technology and industrialized their own society. As a result, just over 50 years after the Perry "opening" to the West, the Japanese had so developed their economic and military capabilities that they were able to defeat the Chinese in the Sino-Japanese War (1894–1895) and thus take control of the island of Taiwan (also called "Formosa"), the Pescadores Islands, and the Kwantung peninsula in southern Manchuria. Ten years after that the Japanese were able to defeat Russia, one of the major powers of Europe. While the Chinese, convinced by their superior culture that they had nothing to learn from foreigners, remained under Western domination, Japan had rapidly borrowed Western ways and quickly become a world power.

As a world power, Japan embarked on the task of collecting more colonies just as Britain, France, and the other European powers had done. In 1910 Korea was formally annexed and put under Japanese military control. In World War I (1914–1918) Japan sided with the Allies and used the opportunity to take control of German holdings along the coast of China and some islands in the Pacific which had belonged to Germany. In the years 1918 to 1920 Japanese forces joined the British, French, and American troops fighting against the Communists in Russia, but the Japanese didn't leave eastern Russia until 1922. At Versailles (1919) the Allies gave limited recognition to Japanese influence in China, but a Japanese demand that the Treaty contain a declaration of racial equality was rejected. Nevertheless, in the League of Nations established by that Treaty, Japan was recognized as one of the five big powers granted a permanent seat on the Council.

The imperialist drive of Japan slowed momentarily in the 1920s when a liberal government agreed to limitations on the size of the Japanese navy relative to that of the United States and Britain in accord with the Naval Limitation Treaties of 1922 and 1930. The Japanese already exercised indirect control over Manchuria, but in 1931 the military, unchecked by the civilian government, took direct control of that region. In 1933 Japan withdrew from the League of Nations because that organization had recommended sanctions in response to the takeover in Manchuria. Undeterred, Japan continued taking control of additional pieces of Chinese territory, and open warfare between the two nations began in 1937. The outbreak of war in Europe soon afterwards allowed the Japanese to move into what had been French-controlled Indo-China (now Vietnam, Cambodia, and Laos). They then prepared to attack Burma and the Dutch East Indies (now Indonesia) in pursuit of what they called the "Greater East Asia Co-Prosperity Sphere," a scheme for Japanese hegemony throughout Southeast Asia. The United States refused to accept this militaristic expansion, and the imposition of economic sanctions by the U.S. led to the Japanese attack on Pearl Harbor in December 1941. The Japanese aim was merely to keep the United States from interfering with their expansion; they had no intention of conquering the United States. Unfortunately for them, the American reaction was more uncompromising than they had anticipated.

World War II ended with the dropping of atomic bombs on Hiroshima and Nagasaki and the subsequent surrender of Japan.[58] The United States imposed a democratic political system, at first under strict U.S. supervision but operating on its own after the Peace Treaty of 1951. The new Japanese constitution prohibited armed forces but permitted a national police reserve, which later became a "self-defense force" as the United States came to see Japan less as a past enemy and more as an ally in the Cold War. Nevertheless the Japanese themselves were not eager to rearm. The experience with nuclear bombs had produced a strong anti-militaristic sentiment among the Japanese which still persists.[59]

Having failed in its effort to develop an empire by military means, Japan decided to follow a different path. As Ezra Vogel put it, "Like the Venetians and Dutch in their heydays, the Japanese conceived a vision of economic power without military power."[60] The U.S. use of Japan as a base of operations during the Korean and Vietnamese conflicts provided an additional boost to Japanese economic growth. Between 1950 and 1976 Japan's

GNP increased almost twelvefold while that of the United States increased 2⅓ times and that of Western Europe three times.[61] Japanese per capita income went from $146 in 1951 to $395 in 1960 to over $2000 in 1972.[62] It should be remembered too that during this period Japan had the burden of paying reparations to countries in Southeast Asia for damages done during World War II.[63] This "economic miracle" means that Japan has become a model to be imitated by other countries, especially in Asia.

An important factor in Japan's economic expansion is the relatively small investment in the military sector. During the Cold War when the Soviet Union was spending 13 to 14 percent of its GNP for the military and the United States 5 to 6 percent of its GNP, Japan was devoting about 1 percent of its GNP to the military.[64] As a result Japan had a great deal more of its assets available for capital investment and nonmilitary research and development, two items which are very important for economic growth. These spending figures should not be taken to mean that Japan is militarily weak, however, because Japan's GNP is so large that an expenditure of only 1 percent still makes Japan the seventh largest military power in the world.[65]

A current issue for Japan is whether to make a large investment in the military. The United States has been urging the Japanese to do so in order to counter Russian and Chinese military power in the Pacific area and to assist in U.N. peacekeeping efforts. Of course, it would also be helpful to the United States and Western Europe from the standpoint of economic competition if the Japanese would spend more on the military. On the other hand, a Japanese increase in outlays for the military could be viewed by the Chinese as a threat to them, and presently one of the most promising situations for the Japanese is their blossoming relationship with China. In that country there are over a billion customers for Japanese products, plus raw materials which the Japanese need. Also, the Japanese have thrived under the U.S. nuclear umbrella, so why change anything? Furthermore, even apart from popular opposition, it would not make sense for Japan to try to develop nuclear weapons of its own. Japan would then become a threat to China and a very vulnerable prime target for the nuclear weapons of both China and the Russian Federation.

At the same time Japan needs to protect itself against interruptions in trade. The Japanese economy depends on importing raw materials and exporting finished products. Japan has no oil of its own, and 80 percent of what it imports comes from the often unstable Middle East; it also must import close to 100 percent of its iron ore, bauxite for aluminum production, wool, rubber, and phosphates and about 90 percent of its wheat and soybeans.[66] With no colonies to rely on and no military power that can be readily projected to other parts of the world, Japan desperately needs world peace.

An important development in Japan was the July 1993 election in which the conservative Liberal Democratic Party, which had ruled Japan since the end of World War II, was deposed from power by a coalition of seven reformist parties led by the new Prime Minister Morihiro Hosokawa. Hosokawa is putting Japan on a new course both internationally and domestically.[67] He has publicly apologized to other nations for Japan's military aggression in World War II and has announced his support for the Nuclear Non-Proliferation Treaty, suggesting that Japan is not going to try to develop nuclear weapons despite its accumulation of large supplies of plutonium. He has indicated that Japan is going to deregulate Japanese markets in order to improve the quality of life for its own people and to ease complaints about Japan's huge trade surpluses with the U.S. and other trading partners. Hosokawa also plans major changes in the election system in Japan to try to get rid of the corruption which has been so rampant. It remains to be seen whether he can manage to bring about such radical changes without arousing more resistance than he can overcome.

Internationally in 1990 Japan's gross national product (GNP) was surpassed only by that of the U.S., and its *per capita GNP* was exceeded only by that of Switzerland and Luxembourg.[68] Its financial contributions to the United Nations and related international organizations are exceeded only by those of the U.S.[69] The Japanese are steadily becoming more involved with the United Nations and with U.N. peacekeeping. Japan probably will become a permanent member of the U.N. Security Council, though without a veto. Japan's great dependence on international trade and its tragic history with nuclear weapons provide that country with strong motivation to try to develop more effective world-level political and judicial institutions. The development of such institutions coincides perfectly with Japan's national interests.

The Chinese Perspective

If Japan is the "mighty midget" of the world, China is the "awakened giant." Twenty-two percent of all the people in the world live in this country, and only the Russian Federation and Canada are larger in land area. China also represents one of the oldest continuous civilizations in the world, with a recorded history going back 4,000 years.[70]

For our purposes the history of China can be divided into three periods: (1) the long classical period up to the nineteenth century during which China was the center of Asian culture, (2) the period between 1840 and 1945 when China was dominated by other nations which had already industrialized, and (3) the period of new independence and development since 1945.

During the many centuries of the first period China was known as "The Middle Kingdom."[71] Although the degree of centralization varied from time to time depending on the independence or subservience of the local "warlords," there was always a Chinese Emperor, the son of Heaven, who was the center of power. His dominion extended over the surrounding national groups, who were regarded as inferior peoples, as barbarians whom the Chinese would try to civilize. A "tribute system" existed whereby the leaders of these other peoples would send gifts to the Chinese emperor in recognition of his superiority. Those who presented these offerings would be required to kowtow (kneel and touch their heads to the ground) several times in front of the Emperor, who then would give them some even more valuable things in return as his way of showing that his wealth was greater than theirs. It is important to realize that Chinese superiority was based not primarily on military domination but rather on cultural accomplishments such as literature, philosophy, art, government, and the production of fine goods.

There were some sporadic contacts between China and Europe at least as early as the first century A.D., but more sustained contact did not occur until the sixteenth century when Portuguese traders established a trading colony in Macao just off the Chinese coast.[72] Spanish, Dutch, and British traders followed shortly thereafter, and some Spanish missionaries were even appointed to positions in the Chinese government during the seventeenth century.[73] Nevertheless their impact on Chinese civilization was not lasting.

The rude awakening which marks the beginning of the second major period of Chinese history, the "century of humiliation," came in the form of the Opium War (1839–1842). British traders had opened a base of operations in Canton. They were eager to acquire silks, porcelain, spices, and other goods to take to Europe, but they had difficulty figuring out what to sell the Chinese in return. There was some minor interest in clocks, telescopes, and similar gadgets but not enough to keep the trade going. The Westerners had found, however, that they could supply the Chinese with opium, and once they were addicted they became good customers. The Chinese government had prohibited the sale of opium, but despite continuing efforts could not enforce the prohibition. When a large cache of British opium was seized and destroyed by Chinese officials, the British, arguing that such action constituted interference with their right of free trade, launched an attack and destroyed the Chinese fortifications at Canton. This Opium War ended with the signing of the Treaty of Nanking (1842), which gave the British the right to sell opium, huge reparations for British losses, and the colony of Hong Kong. It also provided for the opening up of four more "treaty ports" for European traders where the principle of "extraterritoriality" would apply, that is, where Westerners accused of violating laws could be tried only in Western courts.[74]

The Opium War was followed by other battles between Westerners and the Chinese government which was trying to control their activities, and each time the military power of the small groups of Europeans allowed them to prevail. New "unequal treaties" were signed giving the Europeans and Americans the right to operate in even more places. Some Chinese, influenced by the teachings of Christian missionaries, tried to overthrow the imperial government. The result was the extremely bloody civil war known as the T'aip'ing Rebellion (1851–1864). The government, eventually assisted by the Westerners who were not sure they would be able to continue their activities if the rebels were to gain control, put down the rebellion. In 1884 and 1885 the French gained control of Vietnam, which had been one of the states paying tribute to China. A new level of humiliation was reached in 1894 and 1895 when the Japanese, an Asian people, used their newly developed Western-style military forces to remove Korea from Chinese control.

In 1900 a group of Chinese called the "Boxers" decided that it was time to use physical force against the Europeans, but their "Boxer Rebellion" was suppressed by a collective force from eight other nations. In 1911 Sun Yat-sen, "the Father of Modern China," led a successful rebellion against the Emperor, but his Nationalist Party could not maintain control of the government and real power remained in the hands of the "warlords." In 1920 the Chinese Communist Party was organized. They adopted the policy of working within the Nationalist Party, but not all of the Nationalists wanted their help. Feuding between the two factions continued throughout the 1930s and 1940s even as they both fought against the Japanese.

The third period of China's history begins with the end of World War II in 1945. The Japanese had taken over the European holdings in China, and now the Japanese were defeated. The way was open for the Chinese to take control of their own country, but which faction would rule? Even before the war ended the United States had been trying to get the Nationalists, led by Chiang Kai-shek, and the Communists, led by Mao Zedong, to come together in a coalition government, but these efforts failed. In the fighting that ensued it seemed at first that the Nationalists would win; but by the end of 1949 the Communists, aided by mass defections, had gained control over all the mainland part of the country. The Nationalists had retreated to the island of Taiwan, where they remain today, still outside of Communist rule.

The Communists' top priority for the new People's Republic of China was industrialization, and with assistance from the Soviet Union the effort moved ahead rapidly. In the countryside the redistribution of land and the establishment of cooperatives were pursued. Education was expanded, and a Marxist-Leninist ideological emphasis was instituted. The aim was to develop the "new socialist man," a person who would be unhesitatingly loyal to the country and the proletarian revolution and who would put those loyalties above pride or self-advancement or love of family and local community.[75]

A top priority in foreign policy was to overcome the image of weakness, of being able to be pushed around by other countries.[76] When China's 1950 warning to the United States that U.N. forces in Korea should stop advancing toward the Chinese border was ignored, a million Chinese "volunteers" entered the fighting to help the North Koreans. At the same time the Chinese sent troops into Tibet to bring that territory under Chinese control.

An uprising there in 1959 was suppressed, and in 1962 the Chinese established their control over some border territory near Tibet which had also been claimed by India.[77] In the early 1950s the Chinese were also able to get the Soviets to return various concessions in Manchuria which had been granted to Russia under coercion at earlier times.[78] Nevertheless the Chinese were thwarted by the United States from achieving their top priority, control over Taiwan.

One of the most fascinating developments in recent world affairs is the break between China and the Soviets which took place between 1958 and 1972. There had always been some conflict between Stalin and Mao,[79] and after Stalin died in 1953 things did not improve, partly because Mao believed that he deserved a higher status in the world Communist movement than the new Soviet leaders, who had not themselves participated in a revolution. Nevertheless in the period 1956–1958 a compromise seems to have been worked out in which Mao agreed not to challenge Khrushchev's doctrine of "peaceful coexistence" in exchange for help in the development of nuclear weapons.[80]

The first serious break occurred in 1958-1959. Mao sought but did not receive Soviet support in his struggles against the Chinese Nationalists on Taiwan in 1958 and in his border disputes with India in 1959.[81] Khrushchev encouraged opposition to Mao within the Chinese leadership,[82] and in June of 1959 he unilaterally canceled the treaty in which the Soviets had promised assistance for the development of nuclear weapons.[83] After a friendly meeting with U.S. President Eisenhower later that year in which the cancellation of the treaty with China on nuclear weapons development probably played a significant role, Khrushchev stopped to see Mao in China. Apparently they quarrelled bitterly not only about "peaceful coexistence" with capitalists but also about Khrushchev's request to set up a radio transmitter in China for contacting Soviet submarines, about Soviet hegemony over Outer Mongolia, and about the location of the Sino-Soviet border.[84] Mao was irked because the Soviets refused to treat the Chinese as equals, while Khrushchev was concerned that the Chinese would pull the Soviets into a nuclear war. In 1960 the Soviets withdrew all forms of aid to the Chinese.[85]

Apparently a new compromise was reached at the end of 1960, but the dispute broke out again at the October 1961 Soviet Party Congress.[86] In 1962-1963 the clashes along the border escalated, though public accusations by each against the other were not made until the fall of 1963.[87] In 1962 the Soviets did not confer at all with the Chinese during the Cuban missile crisis, and the 1963 Soviet-U.S.-British agreement not to test nuclear weapons in the atmosphere may have been aimed at embarrassing the Chinese, who were about to conduct their first nuclear test.[88] In 1964 Khrushchev threatened to destroy the Chinese nuclear facilities if they did detonate a nuclear device, and the Chinese responded that they would then invade the Soviet satellite state of Outer Mongolia.[89] On October 15, 1964,

Khrushchev was removed from his leadership position in the Soviet Union, and the next day the Chinese exploded their first nuclear weapon.[90]

The new Soviet leaders continued their struggle against the Chinese, however, by trying during the next several years to get international meetings of Communists to expel China, but they were unable to accomplish this.[91] In 1968 the Soviets invaded Czechoslovakia, a move which suggested that they might also intervene in other Communist nations such as China.[92] In March of 1969 the Soviets and Chinese reached an agreement on the nonuse of force and continuation of the present boundaries.[93] Nevertheless both sides continued to build up their military forces just in case the agreement was not observed.[94] The border is now quiet but heavily fortified on both sides.

The other half of the shift in China's outlook concerns its relationship with the United States. During the 1960s the Chinese viewed the United States as their arch-enemy. The Americans were the defenders of the Nationalists on Taiwan, the instigators of the military advance toward the Chinese border during the Korean War, and the leaders of the anti–Communist effort in Vietnam. So why did the Chinese suddenly become friendly with the United States in the early 1970s? The Chinese conflict with the Soviets was certainly not sufficient by itself to throw them into the arms of the Americans. The key event in the change of the Chinese attitude toward the United States was the 1969 warning by U.S. President Nixon to the Soviets that an attack on Chinese nuclear facilities would be regarded as an unfriendly act because the radioactive fallout would land on Americans stationed in Korea and Japan.[95] At the same time the United States made sure that the Chinese knew about evidence from U.S. satellites which indicated that the Soviets were prepared to make such an attack if the United States had not intervened. The Chinese responded not only by changing their policy toward the United States and having Nixon come to China but also by inviting Nixon for a second visit even after he had resigned in disgrace from the U.S. Presidency as a result of the Watergate scandal. The Chinese wanted to show their gratitude; they realized that Nixon's strong protest to the Soviets had saved them from an attack on their nuclear facilities. Without nuclear weapons they would have remained at the mercy of a nuclear-armed Soviet Union which had already used its power to impose its will on Communist "comrades" in other countries.

Another aspect of the Chinese experience which merits attention is the shift in outlook after Deng Xiaoping took over the leadership in 1978. Mao's "Great Leap Forward" (1958–1959) — an attempt to increase production by having everyone participate directly in proletarian work, by having "backyard furnaces" for steel production, and by creating "People's Communes" to collectivize work efforts[96] — and his "Great Proletarian Cultural Revolution" (1966–1969) — an attack on the "elitism" and "softness" of Party leaders, professional people, and others in influential positions[97] — had proved to be impediments to the growth of Chinese productivity.[98] The possibility of war against the Soviet Union made it clear that China needed modernization, not ideologically motivated exercises designed to keep everyone equal. The "four modernizations" to be implemented were agriculture, industry, science and technology, and defense. The new leadership claimed that individual effort could be rewarded and decentralized decision-making could be encouraged even in a Communist state. The guiding principle is to be, "What works?" It was also decided that the building up of Chinese society requires peace with the other nations of the world and a decrease in military spending except in the area of new weapons development.

Under Deng Xiaoping's 15 years of leadership, there has been an effort to stimulate economic development while still maintaining the ultimate political control of the Communist Party. Under this "socialist market economy," China has been experimenting, at times permitting fairly unrestrained capitalism and even foreign investment, especially along its southeast coast, but also intervening from time to time with measures of restraint imposed by the Communist Party–controlled central government.

The trend toward less restriction and more freedom started to get out of hand in May of 1989 when university students in Beijing organized a huge demonstration and hunger strike in response to the death of Hu Yaobang, former Communist Party leader who had been removed from office for refusing to take action against a student demonstration in 1986. The previously scheduled visit of Soviet reformer Mikhail Gorbachev to Beijing deterred the Chinese government from clamping down immediately, but on the night of June 3, 1989, the Chinese military moved in forcefully against the students with their large plaster of Paris and styrofoam statue of the "Goddess of Democracy." The resulting "Tiananmen Square massacre" was a demonstration to the whole world that the Chinese leadership under Prime Minister Li Peng and Communist Party General Secretary Jian Zemin was not going to tolerate that much democracy.

When allowed to operate in an open market system, the Chinese show themselves to be very good entrepreneurs. By early 1993 over 70 percent of the economy was outside the centrally controlled state system, and during 1992 the GNP increased by 12.8 percent.[99] But when businessmen become successful, their wealth can be used to undermine the control of the central government. Their businesses not only make them economically independent and politically powerful but also provide jobs which allow their employees to become less and less dependent on state subsidies. As Elizabeth Perry and Ellen Fuller put it in their 1991 article "China's Long March to Democracy" in the *World Policy Journal,* "Increasingly, economic wealth is being translated into political capital."[100] The trends seem to point to a growing tension between the kind of authoritarian political system the Communist leadership wants to maintain and the more open political environment the vigorous economy is likely to produce.

Another factor in the uncertain future of China is the fact that behind-the-scenes leader 89-year-old Deng Xiaoping is likely to die before long, and it is by no means certain who will succeed him as the real leader of the country.[101] At the same time one should keep in mind that if present trends continue, China will have the world's largest economy by the year 2010.[102] The Chinese are also building up their military capabilities both with their own production and by buying planes, missiles, and the like from the former Soviet Union. Their aim is to make China not only the leading economic power in the world but also one of the leading military powers. There is little doubt that China will be an increasingly important player on the world scene.

The Less Developed Countries

The process of industrialization, the change to relying on energy-using machines to help us do our work, began in Britain in the eighteenth century. It represents what Kenneth Boulding in *The Meaning of the Twentieth Century* calls "the second great transition" in human society.[103] The first great transition was the agricultural revolution which began about 10,000 years ago when our distant ancestors changed from their nomadic life-style to relying on agriculture and domesticated animals and to living in permanent settlements. The second equally great transition, industrialization, is based on scientific knowledge of how nature works which is then incorporated into new technology for manipulating the physical world. Industrialization transforms humanity's relationship with nature and with other people because of the incredible new power it puts in the hands of humankind.

Industrialization spread from its starting place in Britain to North America and northern Europe, then to southern and eastern Europe and Japan, and then to Russia and China. Countries which became industrialized earlier used their new power, especially evident with regard to weaponry, to dominate those who had not yet industrialized. At the end of World War II in 1945, one could distinguish between the industrialized or developed countries of Europe and North America plus Japan and Australia and New Zealand on the one hand, and the less industrialized or less developed countries in the rest of the world. Because most of the developed countries were in the northern hemisphere while most of the less developed countries were in the southern hemisphere, one could speak of the "North-South" division in the world.[104] But the spreading wave of industrialization has not stopped; it is still breaking on new shores. That transformation of society that began in Britain over two hundred years ago is now reaching the most remote corners of the world. However, it is still not arriving in all places at the same time.

This section of our chapter on national-historical perspectives deals with the outlook of that large group of countries which are late-comers to the process of industrialization. They are known collectively as the "poorer countries" or the *"less developed countries"* (LDCs). During the time of the Cold War these countries were sometimes described as the *"Third World"*[105] or the *"non-aligned countries"* because they were not allied with either the U.S. and NATO or with the Soviet Union and its Warsaw Pact Organization. They sought to opt out of that East-West conflict, that Communism-vs.-Capitalism contest which they feared could bring a nuclear holocaust which would end their existence as well as that of the protagonists.

How can one describe the LDCs, which together have over three-fourths of the world's population? The *typical* LDC is a poor nation in Africa or Asia and a former colony of some European country, but not all of them fit this description. The oil-rich LDCs of Kuwait, Qatar, and the United Arab Emirates, for example, have higher per capita GNPs than Australia or Britain.[106] Argentina, Brazil, Costa Rica, and Albania are not in Africa or Asia and have not been colonies for a very long time. Many LDCs are very small with populations of less than a million, while India has a population of about 850 million. Some are richly endowed with natural resources, while others have virtually none. What they all have in common is that in 1950 they could not be said to be industrialized countries, and except for a few "Newly Industrialized Countries" (NICs) such as Singapore, Taiwan (technically part of China), and South Korea they *still* cannot be described as industrialized societies. Of course, becoming industrialized happens gradually, so it is difficult to say exactly when a country has arrived at being a developed country. Nevertheless according to a widely accepted classification there are only 28 countries (out of the 140 countries in the world included in the data) which were classified as "developed countries" in 1990.[107]

Traditionally, when dealing with world affairs only the views of a few more powerful countries were considered. The views of the less powerful, less developed countries were largely ignored. But the United Nations has made it technically possible for the less powerful countries to be recognized as legally sovereign nation-states when they become members of that organization. Nevertheless the question of how much influence these less powerful countries can actually have on world affairs is still open. In the last third of the twentieth century a totally new experiment in international affairs is being tried. Through collective action the less powerful nations of the world are trying to make their influence felt on the global scene. The outcome of that experiment is not yet clear, but its unfolding merits at least a brief review.

The effort of these LDCs to exert some kind of collective influence on world events has been focused on a series of international conferences. Although the national representatives of the various LDCs had informally conferred with each other at the United Nations,[108] the first formal meeting for these "Third World" nations was the Bandung Conference held in Bandung, Indonesia, in 1955.[109] All nations of Asia and Africa were invited, and 29 sent representatives. The conference condemned all forms of racism and colonialism and called for peaceful co-existence among all nations regardless of ideological commitment or social system. Plans to convene a second conference of African and Asian countries 10 years later fell apart, largely because of disputes about whether China and the Soviet Union should be allowed to participate.[110]

Nevertheless the Bandung Conference spawned other meetings. In 1961 President Tito of Yugoslavia organized a Conference of Non-Aligned States in Belgrade.[111] His aim was to organize the countries which were not allied with either the United States or the Soviet Union regardless of their geographical location. Twenty-five governments were represented. They agreed that non-aligned nations should work together in opposing colonialism of any kind and should seek to reduce tension between East and West. In 1964 Egyptian President Nasser convened the Second Conference of Non-Aligned States in Cairo.[112] This time 47 governments attended, many of the new ones being black African countries.

The Belgrade Conference in turn inspired another significant meeting for the LDCs, the 1964 U.N. Conference on Trade and Development (UNCTAD) held in Geneva, Switzerland.[113] In advance of this U.N.-sponsored conference, representatives of the LDCs developed a Joint Declaration indicating what they hoped the meeting would accomplish: tariff reductions, opening of markets in the rich countries for products from the poor countries, stabilization of the prices of raw materials, more financial assistance to the LDCs, and a greater share of shipping revenues and the like for the poorer countries.[114] Seventy-five countries signed this declaration. Later three more countries signed and one which had signed withdrew, leaving 77 signers. The association formed by these 77 LDCs was later joined by others but is still called the "Group of 77." For the most part they work within the U.N. framework.

That 1964 Geneva Conference was the first major forum for negotiations on economic issues between North and South. The North refused to grant the LDCs the kinds of changes they were seeking, but the South did manage to make UNCTAD a continuing subsidiary organ of the U.N. General Assembly, where negotiations would be carried on at subsequent conferences. These conferences have for the most part been exercises in futility for the LDCs because of the adamant opposition of the North, especially the United States.

Between 1965 and 1973 the LDCs solidified their two basic associations, the Non-Aligned Movement (NAM) and the Group of 77.[115] The NAM was gradually transformed into a permanent organization with a standing Bureau which met regularly between the summit conferences held every three years.[116] The Group of 77 became the permanent bargaining agent for the LDCs in the United Nations and at the UNCTAD meetings held every three or four years. A challenging task for both these associations was to develop statements of aims which would be acceptable to all the diverse members. The Non-Aligned Movement is a more militant group which serves as a catalyst or motivator for action, while the Group of 77 does the actual negotiating with the North in the United Nations and at UNCTAD meetings.[117]

The quadrupling of the price of crude oil in December 1973 by the Organization of Petroleum Exporting Countries (OPEC) gave the LDCs hope that they would have more success in their negotiations with the North.[118] None of the members of OPEC were industrialized countries, and all were willing to use their new economic power to support the aims of the LDCs. At a special session of the U.N. General Assembly in April of 1974 a pair of resolutions were passed calling for a "New International Economic Order" (NIEO). This new order was to be based on the equality of all nations with regard to decision-making on international economic issues and would recognize the legitimacy of certain principles of special interest to the LDCs such as the right to nationalize privately owned industries exploiting natural resources within their boundaries. The resolutions were adopted despite the protests of the United States and other countries of the North. But resolutions of the U.N. General Assembly are not binding, so the victory was a hollow one. The old international economic order, where the rich countries call the tune, continued. By 1986 even the temporary high oil prices were pushed down below the pre–1973 level (after adjusting for inflation) by the collective action of the developed countries.[119]

The Non-Aligned Movement held its Ninth Summit Conference at Belgrade in 1989. At that time 102 countries were members, mostly from Africa, Asia, and Latin America.[120] The Tenth Summit of the NAM held in Jakarta, Indonesia, in September 1992, was attended by 59 heads of state and U.N. Secretary-General Boutros Boutros-Ghali.[121] The membership was increased to 108 countries. One theme of the meeting was that the end of the Cold War did not end the need for the NAM because the polarization between North and South still had to be addressed. Also the problem of nuclear disarmament had not been solved. Indonesian President Suharto appealed for the "restructuring and democratization" of the U.N. so that LDCs could play a more effective role while Boutros-Ghali said that "the voice of the Third World ... must be represented" at the U.N. because, even though the Cold War has ended, the "temptation to dominate, either worldwide or regionally, remains."[122]

Besides their own conferences, the LDCs can use their voting power in the U.N. General Assembly to convene U.N. conferences on various issues which they believe require some attention, even if the richer countries would rather not address them in such an open forum. Since these conferences are arranged by the General Assembly rather than the Security Council, all countries are represented and there is no veto power for the big powers. One example of a conference where the LDCs were able to have an impact on global policy was the third U.N. Conference on the Law of the

Sea (UNCLOS) which met for one or two sessions each year from 1973 until 1982. The task of that conference was to work out a treaty for the oceans which would embody "the common heritage principle," the principle that the resources of the ocean floor should belong to all of humanity collectively and not just to the rich countries that had the technology to exploit those resources. Another example was the U.N. Conference on the Environment and Development (UNCED) or "Earth Summit" held in Rio de Janeiro, Brazil, in June of 1992. The LDCs wanted such a conference in order to focus attention on the responsibilities of the rich countries to put some restraints on their pollution of the environment and also to provide more economic and technological assistance to the LDCs so that they would not need to despoil the environment in order to get the resources they need for economic development.

A good example of how the LDCs are trying to influence world politics, but also of how they get restrained by the more powerful countries from making much headway in this direction, is the adoption by the U.N. General Assembly in November of 1989 of a resolution declaring the period 1990–1999 to be a Decade of International Law.[123] Traditionally, the LDCs have looked upon international law as merely a facade by which the rich and powerful countries maintained a legal pretense for their exploitation and domination of the poorer countries. But in September 1988, at the NAM ministerial meeting in Nicosia, Cyprus, it was announced that the following June a special NAM ministerial meeting focused on international law would be convened at The Hague, The Netherlands, seat of the International Court of Justice. This change of attitude on the part of LDCs toward international law apparently was inspired by the fact that in June of 1986 the International Court of Justice had rendered a judgment against the U.S. and in favor of Nicaragua in a case involving U.S. mining of the harbors of Nicaragua and U.S. support for the "Contras" against the Sandinista government of Nicaragua.[124] The June 1989 NAM meeting at The Hague adopted "The Hague Declaration on Peace and the Rule of Law in International Affairs"[125] which called for a decade focused on strengthening international law and the International Court of Justice plus holding a peace conference in 1999, the 100th anniversary of the 1899 Hague Conference which had established the Permanent Court of Arbitration. In the fall of 1989 the LDCs introduced a resolution in the U.N. General Assembly to try to implement their "Hague Declaration," but they ran into various objections from the more powerful countries. In order to gain the support of these other countries (all five permanent members of the Security Council became co-sponsors), the resolution was watered down to the point that it called only for the 1990s to be designated the U.N.'s "Decade of International Law" with details to be determined later. It remains to be seen what, if anything, will happen at the U.N. to promote respect for international law and the International Court of Justice and to encourage the further development and codification of international law. It is not clear yet whether or not there will be a 1999 conference focused on how peace and disarmament can be advanced by the strengthening of international law.

Thus we see that the LDCs have managed to maintain their associations for collective bargaining against the rich countries and that they are continuing to try to use the U.N. General Assembly and U.N.–sponsored international conferences to get more "global justice," but they have no clout when negotiating with the North. While the Cold War was on, they had some chance of playing the Russians and Americans off against each other, but now that game is over. Arab oil money gave them a lift in the middle 1970s, but the rich countries developed a coordinated response involving stockpiling and new drilling that ended that threat. The situation is that these LDCs need what the developed capitalist countries have much more than the developed capitalist countries need what they have. At this time threats, whether economic or military, appear ridiculous. It seems that about the only way for these LDCs to have any input in global decision-making is to pass non-binding resolutions in the U.N. General Assembly and set up more international conferences where all national governments are equally represented.[126] Furthermore, just keeping their own LDC associations together is a major challenge in view of the diversity of interests and even some wars among themselves. Past experience has engendered a general pessimism about what can be expected from negotiations with the rich countries. There has been some attempt to focus more attention on what can be done cooperatively among themselves without help from the North, but results are minimal. Nevertheless, the LDCs are still trying to use the U.N. as a means of having some influence on the world scene.

X. Economic Aspects of the Contemporary Situation

The distribution of wealth in society and the ways in which public funds are spent have an impact on the problem of war in various ways. The manner in which the goods of the earth are distributed *among the various nations* raises a question of justice at the *international* level. The maldistribution of wealth *within* nations has implications for the possibility of war *within* countries. The cost of war preparations is another economic aspect of the contemporary situation which must be examined. Both at the international level and within countries, the rich tend to use violence to keep the poor from changing the social order and the poor tend to use violence to try to take power from the rich.

The Rich and the Poor Among the Nations

A widely used distinction in international economics is that between the economically *developed countries* (DCs) and the *less developed countries* (LDCs). To say that a country is developed means that it has a large number of labor-saving machines for the production of goods and services. Labor-saving devices have the effect of increasing the productivity of the workers in the society. The more a machine does, the more can be accomplished by one worker using this machine. Consequently, less developed countries with few machines will have a much lower level of production per person, resulting in a much lower average income compared to that of the developed countries. Experience indicates that less developed countries, because they are poorer and less industrialized, also have lower literacy rates, higher birth rates, less readily available clean water, and a much larger proportion of the population engaged in agricultural production than the developed countries. In general the developed countries consist of the European nations plus the United States, Canada, Japan, Australia, New Zealand, and Israel while the countries of Africa, Asia, and Latin America are less developed countries. Lists of the developed countries usually include 25 to 30 countries[1] while the other countries of the world are considered to be less developed countries.

One of the most significant facts about the world today is the extremely wide gap between the material conditions of life in the developed countries

175

compared to those in the less developed countries. From time to time we hear of thousands of people starving to death in some Asian or African country. These people starve not because of a shortage of food in the world (world per capita grain production was higher in 1984 than at any other time in history, though there has been a slight decline since then[2]) but because they lack money with which to pay for food. No one with money starves to death, in rich countries or poor countries. The basic problem is the distribution of wealth in the world. In 1990 the per capita GNP[3] was $29,009 in Switzerland, $23,053 in Japan, and $19,492 in the U.S. while it was only $498 in Indonesia, $279 in Vietnam, and $109 in Ethiopia.[4] These figures indicate that the average income level in the three developed countries mentioned is 80 times greater than in the three less developed countries mentioned. In the developed countries as a whole the 1990 per capita GNP was $12,809 while for the less developed countries as a group it was $751, a ratio of 17 to 1. In 1982 it had been an 11 to 1 ratio.[5]

How has it happened that some countries are developed and others are not? The answer requires a review of the events of history. In the fourteenth century there was little difference in the standard of living among the various nations of Europe, Asia, and northern Africa, but by the middle of the nineteenth century there were vast differences. The change was a result of the industrial revolution, the making of machines to help people do their work. The coming of the industrial revolution was the result of increasing scientific knowledge about how nature works, coupled with a desire to use this knowledge of nature to serve the goals of people. It started in Great Britain in the late 1700s.[6] To explain precisely why it started there would involve dealing with a complicated combination of factors among the most important of which would be the spirit of liberty and enterprise in England, new scientific knowledge about the natural world, and the availability in one place of crucial raw materials such as coal, iron, and limestone. From Britain the practice of using coal and steam engines made of iron for doing various kinds of work spread to northern continental Europe and North America, then to the rest of Europe, Oceania, and Japan. It is now in the process of spreading throughout the whole world.

To better understand the present gap between the rich countries and the poor countries, one must focus attention on what happened from the beginning of the eighteenth century through the middle of the twentieth century. During this period the newly industrialized countries of Europe, especially Britain and France, were able to use their superior machines of war to bring areas in America, Africa, and Asia under their control. The colonies of the European countries shipped agricultural products and raw materials for industry back to Europe. After the raw materials were converted into manufactured goods, these goods were sold by the colonizing nations to their own people and to other countries. Such sales provided the money for new investment in more machines to make more goods. The activities of gathering raw materials, making goods, selling the goods, and reinvesting in more machinery were all under the control of the leaders of the industrialized nations, and they profited immensely from such an arrangement.

In Africa and Asia this process usually included political control by the European nations coupled with special training and privileges for the native people who assisted them, but in Latin America a slightly different kind of development took place. The United States, having originally been a colony itself, was opposed to the practice of outright political control over other nations. Because of its readiness to guarantee the safety of any foreign investments in Latin America, the United States was able to keep European nations from exercising political control over any land in the Americas except for Canada and a few small colonies. As a result of its policy of protection, however, the United States was forced to establish a new kind of nonpolitical control over Latin America. Latin Americans were thus allowed to control their own countries politically as long as they permitted the foreign investors to operate without interference. The foreign investors established corporations to mine raw materials or to grow agricultural products for sale in the United States or Europe. The aim was to make as much profit as possible, and there was little concern about the impact that the money-making might have on the local population. Latin American political leaders who did not cooperate were replaced by others who did. Apart from the absence of actual foreign political control, this American system of *neoimperialism* was not very different from the more traditional *imperialism* exercised by the European countries over their colonies.

It might be asked why the big businesses operating out of the developed countries didn't build factories in the new colonial areas. One reason is that making manufactured items requires skilled persons to run the machines, and these skills were not possessed by the people in the colonial areas. The native peoples could have been taught these skills, however, if the desire to do so had been present, but it wasn't. The colonizing countries wanted to protect their own industries and the jobs of their own people. Consequently they established tariffs against finished products made in other countries but not against the importation of raw materials from overseas. Entrepreneurs who invested overseas could make money as long as they sent raw materials to the homeland, but if they tried to send finished goods they would find that the tariffs would make those finished goods too expensive to be marketable in the homeland. Thus the tariff arrangements discouraged the industrialization of the colonies while furthering the industrialization of the colonizing powers. The developed countries became more developed while the undeveloped nations remained undeveloped. The situation began to change somewhat only after World War II, when most of the former colonies won their political independence.

Approaches to Economic Development

What can the less developed countries do to move toward becoming developed countries? Three alternative models for development have been noted: the capitalistic or conventional approach, the socialist or radical approach, and the cooperative approach. Regardless of the model to be followed, there are two basic problems: how to get the machines that will increase productivity, and how to develop the know-how to use and repair the machines, market the products, and so on.

The *capitalistic approach* to economic development assumes that the capital for buying needed machinery will be in the hands of private persons or corporations, mostly in the rich countries. The problem for the leaders of a less developed country following this approach becomes one of getting those with money to invest in their country rather than in some other country. The solution is to give investors what they want, including healthy profits, security of investment, and freedom to operate as they desire. When investors are assured that a country will provide these things, they will build the factories needed for development. They will bring the machinery and the highly skilled people needed to manage the factories and market the products, and they will teach the local population how to run and repair the machines. People will be employed and will be paid wages much higher than they could have earned otherwise. The government can tax some of these wages for public improvements, and what the workers spend in the marketplace will provide jobs for others in the society. Economic development will be on its way.

There are, of course, some difficulties for this capitalistic approach. The healthy profits that the investors make are for the most part taken out of the country. Any inclination to impose a substantial tax on these profits conflicts with the fact that investors dislike having their profits taken away in the form of taxes. If the less developed country requires that a certain proportion of the profits be reinvested within the country, the danger exists that the foreign investors may soon control a good deal of that country's economy. Providing security for the private investors may require strict government controls on those within the society who might try to advocate the takeover of all foreign investments by the national government. Giving these foreign firms freedom to operate as they desire also means refraining from passing laws about safe working conditions or pollution controls or the rights of workers to organize unions. These companies may also require the government to provide services such as transportation facilities, water supply, waste removal, and educated workers. In agriculture, foreign investors may buy land and use it to grow crops for export to richer countries while many of that poor country's population starve. Furthermore, the foreign investors may concentrate on capital-intensive rather than labor-intensive production, thus providing a minimum number of jobs for people in the less developed country.

A distinct version of the capitalist model for development was worked out by the Japanese at the end of the nineteenth century. In 1868 a group of reformers gained control of the imperial court and used the young emperor Meiji as the instrument of their reforms. This new government required the feudal lords to sell much of their land to the government for bonds. Then the land was given to the peasants who worked it, and they were required to pay taxes to the government. This money was used to build factories and to educate young people. As the government-sponsored industries became profitable, they were sold, often to the former landowners in exchange for the bonds. Thus many of the old aristocracy became members of the new capitalist class. In less developed countries the rich large landholders often oppose any social changes, but the Japanese approach succeeded in moving the old landed elite into positions of leadership in an industrialized society with little risk for them during the transition. By the time of the Second World War, however, much of the land had again come to be owned by absentee landlords, so after the war a new land reform plan was carried out under the U.S. occupation. This model of using land reform as a way to get capital for economic development has also had considerable success in Taiwan and South Korea.

Another possible source of capital for countries following the capitalistic approach is borrowing from other countries, from foreign banks, and from international development banks such as the International Bank for Reconstruction and Development (the World Bank) and its related organizations, the International Finance Corporation which lends to private enterprise projects and the International Development Association which provides interest-free loans to the poorest of the poor countries. To get these loans, however, the countries and individuals involved must abide by strict regulations. In some situations less developed countries are so deeply in debt that the foreign lending organizations come to control the economic policy for the whole country. The country may complain that it has lost some of its sovereignty, but the lending organizations refuse to give any further financial assistance until specified conditions are met.

The *socialistic approach* to economic development assumes that the needed capital for industrialization will come from within the country and that the investment in new machinery will be made by the government itself. Foreign investment and loans from outside the country are viewed as invitations to foreign meddling and foreign control. The problem for the leaders of a less developed country following the socialistic approach becomes one of finding money in a society where most people are very poor. One device is to confiscate land and other available wealth, especially things owned by foreigners or the very rich within the country. Another is to control the whole economy with the aim of producing a minimum amount of consumer goods so that a good share of the available wealth can be used to build factories and produce machines. The need to cut back on the production of consumer goods is summarized in the expression that "one generation must be sacrificed" for the sake of economic development. Production is to be guided by what is most needed for the long-term welfare of the society as a whole rather than the short-term needs of individuals. The socialistic approach also requires putting a substantial proportion of the society's wealth into education so that people will learn how to read and how to build, use, and repair various kinds of machines.

There are, of course, also some difficulties for this socialistic approach. Those people from whom things have been confiscated will certainly be upset. If they live in other countries, the governments of those countries will exert pressure for payment for the confiscated property. If they are natives, they will feel a continuing resentment toward the government. In fact, governments embarking on the socialist path have little choice but to chase out, kill, or imprison substantial numbers of their own well-to-do citizens from whom they have confiscated property. Furthermore, they will probably need to adopt harsh policies toward the whole population for some time because there will likely be a great many who dislike being part of a "sacrificed" generation. Another difficulty for nations which choose the socialistic path is acquiring those things which they can't produce for themselves. This problem will be much more severe for small countries such as Cuba than for large countries such as the former Soviet Union and Mao Zedong's China. If a country has confiscated property from citizens of many other nations, difficulties may arise when it tries to trade with these other nations. It can perhaps trade with other socialist countries, but if it becomes very dependent on them it risks falling under their domination.

A third approach to economic development is the *cooperative approach*. The basic assumption of this approach is that the less developed countries must work together to change the international pattern of economic relationships which have been carried over from the colonial era. It is claimed that the poorer countries of the world must bargain collectively with the richer countries just as workers bargain collectively to get the best terms they can from an employer. The problem for the less developed countries is how to get the developed countries to pay attention to their demands. As noted in the last section of the previous chapter, the Third World countries have held international meetings and even passed resolutions at the United Nations calling for a New International Economic Order, but little progress has been made in restructuring the international economy.

What the less developed countries want is nondiscriminatory and possibly even preferential treatment with regard to tariffs and restrictions on the manufactured goods they export to the developed countries, a reserve system to stabilize the prices of the raw materials they sell to the developed countries, renegotiation of the terms of their huge debts, regular multilateral foreign assistance from the developed countries amounting to .7 percent of their GNP, a greater voice in making the rules for the world's monetary system, and some internationally approved restrictions on the practices of transnational corporations.[7] What the less developed countries have a chance of getting is a worldwide system of free trade that would eliminate some of the advantages which the richer national governments provide for their own businesses and workers.

One temporary success story for the cooperative approach was the action of the Organization of Petroleum Exporting Countries (OPEC), which at the end of 1973 succeeded in quadrupling the price of crude oil in the world market. By working together some of the less developed countries were able to greatly increase the amount they received from the developed countries for the petroleum they export. Efforts by the less developed countries to raise the price on other raw materials in the same manner by formation of producer cartels have so far not been very successful, and recently OPEC itself has suffered from disagreements among the members.

The main difficulty for the cooperative approach is that the developed countries can and do act together to thwart the efforts of the less developed countries to gain more influence in the international marketplace. Although OPEC gave the less developed countries a temporary psychological lift, the Western developed countries are now in a much stronger position in negotiations because they have developed their own coordinating organization, the International Energy Agency.[8] Working together they have succeeded in stockpiling huge amounts of petroleum, dampening future threats from OPEC. The poor countries need what the rich countries have more than the rich countries need what the poor countries have. Even the suggestion that the poorer countries trade more with each other is not very promising, since the developed countries have the technologically advanced goods which the poorer countries can't provide for themselves. The main hope for the cooperative approach is that more rich countries will respond as the Scandinavian countries have, on the basis of humanitarian concerns.

There is one other hope for a less developed country: that oil would be discovered in its territory. The oil-rich countries have that crucial ingredient for development, money to buy machinery and educate their citizenry. For example, the government share of the revenue from oil in Saudi Arabia at one time amounted to a million dollars every 15 minutes.[9] Recently the price of oil has dropped, and the amount of oil possessed by other oil-exporting countries is not nearly so great, but still oil provides the money that allows some of these less developed countries to look to the future with some optimism.

The Bleak Outlook for the Poorer Countries

Most of the poor countries of the world have no oil, however, so their futures do not look very promising. To see more clearly the situation facing most of the less developed countries, consider some mathematical calculations comparing a poorer developed country (DC) which now has a per capita GNP of $10,000 with an average less developed country (LDC) which now has a per capita GNP of $500.[10]

Suppose that in a given year the DC and the LDC each manage to increase their per capita GNP by 5 percent, a figure which represents a good increase for the DC and a very good one for the LDC, especially in view of the fact that the population growth rate would probably be somewhat greater in the LDC. A 5 percent increase for the DC means that on the average each person in the DC has had a standard of living increase of $500 (5 percent of $10,000) while a 5 percent increase for the LDC means that the average income increased from $500 to $525, an increase of only $25 (5 percent of $500). Thus the *absolute gain* in terms of more income would be 20 times greater in the DC even though the *percentage gain* is the same in both countries. In order to increase the income of its citizens by $500 the LDC would need to experience an unheard-of 100 percent increase in per capita GNP. Because the per capita GNP is already so low in the LDCs even high percentage gains in productivity mean little gain in terms of actual additional income.

The second calculation is based on the supposition that the DC makes absolutely no gain whatever in per capita GNP year after year while the LDC gains at the healthy rate of 5 percent a year. Even making these totally unrealistic suppositions, how long would it take the LDC to achieve a per capital GNP equal to that of the DC? The first year the LDC's per capita GNP would go from $500 to $525. The second year it would go from $525 to $551.25. At the end of 10 years it would be $814.46. At the end of 25 years it would be $1,693.18. Finally, after about 61.5 years the LDC would have a per capita GNP equal to the DC's present $10,000 per year!

The third calculation is based on suppositions that are a bit more realistic but still very implausible. It reflects what might happen *if* the developed countries accepted the full implementation of the program of the New International Economic Order. Let us suppose that the DC's per capita GNP increases at only 2.5 percent a year while the LDC's goes up 5 percent a year. Under these conditions, how long would it take for the LDC's per capita GNP to match that of the DC? During the 61.5 years that it took the LDC to go from $500 per year to $10,000 per year, the DC's per capita GNP would have increased from $10,000 per year to over $47,000 per year. Altogether it would be about 125 years before the LDC would catch up to the DC at a per capita GNP of over $210,000 per year!

As indicated, the last two calculations are based on very unrealistic suppositions. The *absolute gap* between the average income in the developed countries and that in the less developed countries will almost surely continue to widen. There is even a good chance that the *percentage increase* each year will be greater for the developed countries than for the less developed ones (except for those with oil to export) because the richer countries will not need to contend with the large population increases facing most of the poorer countries. In addition, they will probably continue to control the terms of international trade in accord with their own interests and continue to be very niggardly with regard to assisting the less developed countries. Since 1960 the gap in per capita GNP between the developed countries and the less developed countries has continued to widen,[11] and unless something quite unexpected and different occurs, this gap will continue to grow.

It is a grim picture for the poorer nations. Even if they get the New International Economic Order for which they are working, it will be at least 60 years before they can expect to approximate the standard of living which now exists in the poorer developed countries and at least another 125 years before they would near equality with the ever-increasing standard of living of the richer developed countries. Actually the time period would be longer for many countries. In our calculations we have used an LDC with a $500 per capita GNP in 1982 as an example, but there are many LDCs with per capita GNPs under $350. Also, it is very unlikely that much of the New International Economic Order will be implemented.

Furthermore, there are two other significant issues. First, we have been discussing *income* levels rather than *wealth*. In developed countries there are many things such as roads and bridges and public buildings which were built in the past and go on adding to the quality of life even though they are not reflected in data about present levels of income. Second, if the LDCs increased their per capita GNP even halfway to the current level of the DCs, where would the raw materials and resources to provide for higher levels of consumption come from? Depletion of both the renewable and nonrenewable resources of the planet now seems to be a problem even if no one's material standard of living is increased.[12] This very fact may make the developed countries even less willing to assist in any very positive way with the development problems of the less developed countries. The outlook for poorer nations is indeed bleak.[13]

Under these circumstances it seems even more unconscionable that the net flow of money in the world as a whole, largely as the result of the huge debt payments by the LDCs to the industrialized countries, is $25–30 billion a year *from* the *poorer* countries *to* the *richer* countries!

> When the [LDC debt] crisis erupted in 1982 the total debt owed by the developing countries was $700 billion. It is now [in 1991] $1.3 trillion — double the level since the need for international action was recognized. Of more than 100 debtor countries, no more than a handful have been able to win through the long and difficult negotiations with the banks, financial agencies and rich governments for a debt reduction deal. Meanwhile, net transfers from the poor countries to the rich (debt repayment and flight capital less trade earnings, new loans, and private investment) came to about $27 billion in 1990 and a total of $150 billion over the past five years. In 1987 and 1988, in what has to be the unkindest cut of all, the World Bank actually made money on its Third World loan portfolio — i.e., the world's "development bank" took in more in debt servicing than it disbursed in new loans.[14]

Looking at the situation from the other side, however, one could note that the LDCs are cutting their debts and attracting more foreign private investment as a result of their restructuring toward less government involvement in their economies. Furthermore, the fears of the early 1980s that banks in the developed countries would fail because LDCs would not be able to make their payments for debt servicing have greatly subsided. That has been the result of cooperative efforts worked out by the banks, the national governments involved, and the international lending agencies.[15]

The Distribution of Wealth Within the Nations

The very uneven distribution of income among the various nations of the world vividly raises the question of justice. No one chooses where he will be born; yet the very fact of being born in one place rather than another makes a tremendous difference in whether one will face a lifetime of starvation or live in abundance. A similar uneven distribution of income and wealth occurs within nations and similarly raises the question of justice since no one chooses the family into which he will be born. There may be individual Horatio Alger cases where a person from a poor family becomes wealthy because of special talents or special breaks (just as a less developed country may suddenly learn it has rich deposits of petroleum), but there is no doubt that in general persons born into wealthy families can expect a much different kind of life from those born into poor families, even within the same nation.

There are two common ways of measuring the amount of inequality of income or wealth within a group. One is to compare the proportion of the total income or wealth of the society belonging to the richest fifth of the population with the proportion of the total income or wealth of the poorest fifth. A ratio can be determined by taking the percentage of the total belonging to the top fifth divided by the percentage of the total belonging to the bottom fifth. The smaller this ratio, the more equally distributed is the income or wealth of that group. As a specific example, in the United States in 1985 the richest fifth of the population received 41.9 percent of the income while the poorest fifth received 4.7 percent of the income.[16] By dividing 41.9 by 4.7 we get a ratio of 8.91 to 1 as the ratio between what the richest fifth get and what the poorest fifth get. That is, the richest fifth get 8.91 times as much as the poorest fifth. For another example, in Brazil in 1989 the richest fifth of the population received 67.5 percent of the income while the poorest fifth received only 2.1 percent of the income.[17] By dividing 67.5 by 2.1 we get a ratio of 32.14 to 1. Comparing the figures of 8.91 to 1 and 32.14 to 1 reveals that distribution of income in the United States is much more nearly equal than it is in Brazil. Here are the ratios for the income of the top fifth to the income of the bottom fifth in some other countries based on various studies done between 1979 and 1989[18]:

Country	Year of Study	Share of Income to Richest Fifth	Share of Income to Poorest Fifth	Ratio of Top Fifth to Bottom Fifth
Guatemala	1989	63.0%	2.1%	30.00 to 1
Tanzania	1991	62.7%	2.4%	26.13 to 1
Honduras	1989	63.5%	2.7%	23.51 to 1
Chile	1989	62.9%	3.7%	17.00 to 1
Costa Rica	1989	50.8%	4.0%	12.70 to 1
Malaysia	1989	53.7%	4.6%	11.67 to 1
Peru	1985–86	51.4%	4.9%	10.49 to 1
Hong Kong	1980	47.0%	5.4%	8.70 to 1
Switzerland	1982	44.6%	5.2%	8.58 to 1
Thailand	1988	50.7%	6.1%	8.31 to 1
Tunisia	1990	46.3%	5.9%	7.85 to 1
Denmark	1981	38.6%	5.4%	7.15 to 1
Morocco	1990–91	46.3%	6.6%	7.02 to 1
France	1979	40.8%	6.3%	6.48 to 1
Italy	1986	41.0%	6.8%	6.03 to 1
Indonesia	1990	42.3%	8.7%	4.86 to 1
India	1989–90	41.3%	8.8%	4.69 to 1
Sweden	1981	36.9%	8.0%	4.61 to 1
Japan	1979	37.5%	8.7%	4.31 to 1
Poland	1989	36.1%	9.2%	3.92 to 1
Hungary	1989	34.4%	10.9%	3.16 to 1

Another way of indicating the degree of inequality in the distribution of income or wealth in a group is a graph called the Lorenz curve,[19] as shown on the next page. Diagonal line A indicates how the income would be divided if there were absolute equality. That is, the poorest 20 percent of the people would have 20 percent of the income, the poorest 40 percent of the people would have 40 percent of the income, the poorest 60 percent of the people would have 60 percent of the income, and so on. Curve B represents a society in which there is a moderate amount of inequality. The shaded area between line A and B indicates the amount of inequality in that society. Curve C represents a society in which there is a great deal of inequality. As can readily be seen, the area between line A and line C is much greater than the area between line A and line B, reflecting a greater amount of inequality in the society represented by line C.

Using data which have been collected and processed in accord with the two approaches described above, what generalizations can be made about the distribution of income and the distribution of wealth within nations and among the nations of the world? First, the distribution of *income* tends to be more equal than the distribution of *wealth*.[20] Wealth is accumulated over the years while income refers to only one year. Even if less developed countries can bring their per capita GNP (which represents *income*) up to the level of the developed countries, the developed countries will have an accumulation of goods from the past that will still not be matched. The same thing is true of a newly rich family as compared to a family that has had a high income over a period of time. The second family's high income

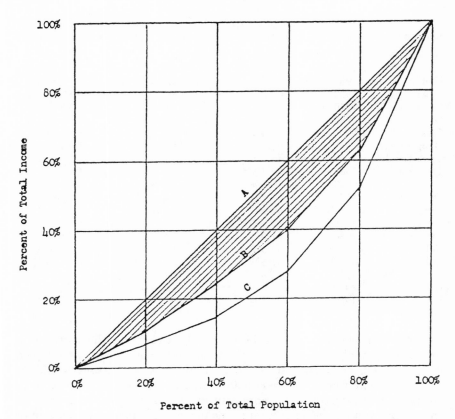

Percent of Total Population

year after year has been used to accumulate wealth which cannot be readily matched by a family that has only recently begun to receive a large income.

A second generalization is that the distribution of income tends to be more unequal in less developed countries than in developed ones. In fact, the greatest level of inequality tends to occur in the early phases of industrialization.[21] As we have noted, in developed countries the ratio between the income of the top fifth and the bottom fifth tends to range between 3 to 1 and 10 to 1, while in the less developed countries it tends to range between 10 to 1 and 30 to 1. It must be remembered, of course, that a tendency is not an absolute rule. As our table shows there are individual differences among both developed and less developed countries, and certain less developed ones may have more equal distribution of income than some more developed ones.

A third observation is that the distribution of income among the nations of the world is even more unequal than the most unequal distribution of income among families in any country. When nations are ranked with regard to per capita GNP, in 1980 the richest fifth of the world's population had a per capita GNP of $7,690 while the poorest fifth had only $170.[22] That means that the ratio of the richest fifth to the poorest fifth of the world's population was 45 to 1. In 1990 the ratio of the income of the richest fifth of the world to the poorest fifth was 55 to 1.[23]

It is certainly not to be assumed that absolute equality of income and wealth would necessarily be a good thing. The point is merely that there are vast inequalities in wealth and income both within nations and among nations and that such inequalities undoubtedly mean inequalities of opportunity for children of different families as well as for children of different nations. If it is believed that these inequalities are due merely to the accidents of history and that they can't be rectified under the existing social order, then there may be resentment and a readiness to use violence to try to change the social order. This desire to change the status quo may occur whether the social order which is perceived to be unjust exists within a nation or among the nations of the world. As more and more poor people within nations and in the world as a whole become capable of reading and learn about their own situations, we can expect this desire for change to become a more and more significant force in social affairs.

Military Expenditures, Social Needs, and Foreign Aid

Another economic aspect of the contemporary situation concerns the amount of public funds being spent for military purposes compared with the amount being used to alleviate poverty and meet the needs of the poor. This matter was mentioned briefly in the first chapter.

Since the poorer countries have massive problems of illiteracy and poor health and a great need to invest for economic development, and since they have no hope of competing militarily with the developed countries, one might expect to find undeveloped countries putting most of their scarce public funds into nonmilitary endeavors. Some less developed countries that are not involved in confrontations with their neighbors are following such a policy. Less developed countries which are devoting 1 percent or less of their GNP to military expenditures are Brazil, Costa Rica, Mexico, Jamaica, Cape Verde, Côte d'Ivoire (Ivory Coast), Ghana, Mauritius, and Nigeria.[24] The usual amount of military expenditures for countries not having conflicts with their neighbors is 1 to 3.5 percent of their GNP. But less developed countries engaged in potential confrontations with their neighbors or struggling with internal turmoil usually have much higher military expenditures. In 1992 military expenditures consumed just over 11 percent of the GNP in Israel and Jordan, 15.8 percent of the GNP in Sudan, 20.1 percent in Ethiopia, 24.1 percent in Croatia, 25.7 percent in North Korea, and 27.8 in Yugoslavia. In 1991 military expenditures amounted to 35.5 percent of Angola's GNP, and no figures are available for 1992. Oil-rich countries are especially fortunate to have money for economic development, but some are putting huge amounts of those resources into the military. For example, in 1992 Kuwait spent 62.4 percent of its GNP on the military! For Oman the figure was 17.5 percent while for the United Arab Emirates it was 14.6 percent. In 1991, the year of the Gulf War, Iraq spent 21.1 percent of its GNP on the military while the figure for Saudi Arabia was 32.5 percent. In 1990 the less developed countries as a group spent $119 billion (3.9 percent of their gross product) on the military. In that same year they spent $115 billion (also 3.9 percent of their gross product) on education.[25] The good news is that the expenditure by the LDCs for education has come up from only 2.4 percent of their gross product in 1960. The bad news is that the percentage spent on the military by the LDCs has not declined; it was also 3.9 percent of their gross product in 1960.

The developed countries have been able to take advantage of the end of the Cold War to cut military spending, from 5.9 percent of their gross product in 1960 to 3.7 percent in 1990.[26] But they have not used these savings to increase the amount of foreign aid they give to the LDCs. Instead, the proportion of their gross product given for aid to the LDCs has decreased, from 0.38 percent in 1960 to 0.33 percent in 1990.[27] If the developed countries had used only half of their 1990 savings from decreased military spending to increase their foreign assistance, they would have given 1.43 percent of their 1990 gross product in foreign aid (that is, the 0.33 percent they did give plus half of the 2.2 percent they cut back from their 1960 level of military spending). That 1.43 percent would be more than four times the amount of foreign assistance they actually gave! The only rich countries which gave a very substantial proportion of their GNP for foreign aid in 1991 are the Scandinavian countries (Norway, 1.14 percent; Denmark, 0.96 percent; Sweden, 0.92 percent; Netherlands, 0.88 percent; Finland, 0.76 percent[28]). But most developed countries are reluctant to give much money to the LDCs because they feel they need these funds in order to meet their own social needs and in order to compete with one another for economic growth. Furthermore, if the poorer countries are just going to continue to use a substantial amount of their limited resources for military purposes, why should the industrialized countries divert their savings from military spending into foreign aid to the LDCs? Of course, the rich countries could distinguish between the poor countries which are pouring resources into the military and those which are not.

A good test of the values of both nations and individuals is how they spend their money. The patterns of expenditure by national governments suggest that most national leaders are more interested in military power than in improving the condition of life for large numbers of people. In the poorer countries especially the resentment continues to build when this occurs. It is hard for mothers and fathers to see their children starving, dying from lack of medical care, or growing up without learning to read. They become angry when they learn that their children wouldn't need to suffer if only a small portion of what is being spent for military purposes was instead used to meet the human needs of the poorer people of the world. This situation should also arouse the indignation of those whose own children are not suffering to the same extent (though their own children may also be short-changed in part because of military spending). Even those without children may be moved to question the priorities presently being pursued by most government leaders.[29]

Economic Conditions and the War Problem

How are the economic conditions we have been discussing related to the war problem? How might the conflict of interest between those in control and those who feel oppressed break out into open violence? One possibility is that the wealthy may use open violence against the poor if the poor seem to be making too many gains by nonviolent means. A second possibility is that the poor will conduct guerrilla warfare, terrorism, or some other type of nonconventional war against those in power. A third possibility is that the frustrated poor may fight among themselves to get whatever resources or power they can manage to grab. Let us consider these possibilities as they relate both to the international scene and to situations within countries.

The possibility of war by the rich against the poor on the international scene almost became a reality in 1974. The previously noted success of OPEC in quadrupling the price of crude oil at the end of 1973 was doubtless a blow to Western Europe, Japan, and the United States. The United States in particular considered a military attack to take over the oil fields in countries such as Saudi Arabia and the United Arab Emirates. These countries had virtually no military forces to resist such an attack. The overt use of violence was a real possibility.

Why didn't the rich countries use their superior military forces to take over the oil fields? Cynics might say that it was because the Western-based oil companies also stood to profit immensely from the price hike, but this suggestion overlooks the fact that many other influential Western-based businesses suffered greatly from the higher prices. This reply also ignores the more significant fact that a complete military takeover would have been even more profitable for the Western oil companies. It could be argued that there was fear that the Soviet Union would intervene to halt a takeover, but the Soviets were not in a position at that time to stop such action. They would have been risking an all-out war over a struggle which, from their point of view, was merely a battle between one group of capitalists and another. It might be argued that the Arabs would have blown up the equipment and pipelines, but it would not take long to repair the damage and start the oil flowing again. From an economic point of view, a quick military takeover would have been cheaper for the United States than all the extra payments made for oil since the price hike.

So why was there no attack? The lack of a military response seems in large part due to public opinion in the developed countries. It should not be forgotten that the United States had just experienced large-scale protests concerning its involvement in Vietnam. Some experts in international relations may not like to admit it, but it seems that in this situation moral considerations influenced public policy. The governments of the Western countries were constrained by the fact that many of their own people would view a military takeover of the oil-rich countries as wrong, as a violation of the principle that the possessions of other nations should not be taken by brute force. Such open international thievery would have made a mockery of the basic notion in Western democratic political theory that force should be restrained by law. Cynics may say that morals don't influence politics and that the policies of democratic national governments are no more moral than those of totalitarian governments, but this striking example from recent history suggests otherwise. This development should also provide some hope to the less developed countries that public opinion in the Western democracies may to some extent restrain these powerful governments in their dealings with weaker, poorer nations.

Nevertheless, there is no guarantee that public opinion will always act as much of a restraint on international policy. Public opinion shifts rapidly, and a short war with a quick victory is not likely to meet with much opposition. Consequently, it is always possible that the poorer nations will find themselves being attacked militarily if they adopt policies which are too damaging to the rich countries. That is especially true if a poorer nation makes the mistake of committing overt aggression as Iraq's Saddam Hussein did when taking over Kuwait in August of 1990. That takeover gave the U.S. the rationale it needed to lead a military attack on Iraqi forces ending with the virtual surrender to the U.S.-led coalition in February of 1991.

The use of violence by those in control can also occur within nations when the poor are making too many gains by nonviolent means. A classic case of this occurred in Chile. Salvador Allende was elected in 1970 and began instituting a socialist program. In 1973 he was overthrown by a military coup which aimed to protect the interests of the rich, including foreigners with investments in Chile. This incident is not unique, but in most situations the poor do not get so far before being repressed. The elite are able to exercise control by using government powers to arrest, imprison, or otherwise silence anyone who might in the future threaten them. This small-scale "authorized" terrorism is carried out against individuals and small groups before their followers become numerous enough to constitute one side in a war. Nevertheless this use of force to prevent peaceful change often serves as a stimulus to the use of violence to overthrow the existing government.

The use of violence by those not in power is the second way that the current economic situation is relevant to the war problem. Since those who control the reins of government usually have sophisticated weapons and well-paid professional military forces, those out of power are not likely to be able to challenge them successfully in a traditional military confrontation. They need to resort to nonconventional efforts. An unlikely possibility might be hidden nuclear weapons or secret biological weapons which can be used to blackmail the richer countries into giving more economic assistance to the poorer ones; a more likely approach is the use of guerrilla warfare. Guerrilla warfare is fought by ideologically motivated citizen-soldiers who use violence in unanticipated settings with the ultimate aim of overthrowing the existing social order.[30] Guerrillas seek not the control of territory but rather the commitment of more persons to the support of their antigovernment activities. They may assassinate or terrorize those in power, but they also engage in acts of sabotage which are likely to produce more government repression and in turn motivate more people to join their struggle. Guerrillas hope eventually to generate enough support to create a regular army capable of defeating the forces of the government.

On the international level guerrilla warfare frequently takes the form of a "war of liberation" to force a colonial power to allow a former colony to become an independent nation. Such wars have been fought in Algeria, Vietnam, Indonesia, and Angola, to name but a few instances of the many which have taken place since the end of World War II. In these situations the guerrilla fighters appeal not only to concerns for economic justice but also to feelings of national pride. The people can readily understand that the guerrillas are helping them to get rid of foreign rulers. Efforts by the colonial power to repress the guerrillas often help the guerrillas by giving them what they most need: more recruits to their movement. Such efforts are also likely to end up providing the guerrillas with more arms, since their major source of military equipment is usually what they can steal or capture from their opponents. Of course, the guerrillas are often also able to acquire arms in the international market or from other national governments which would like to see their revolutions succeed.

When we turn to the situation where the aim of the guerrilla movement is the overthrow not of a foreign colonial power but a native national government, there is no longer a nationalistic component in the struggle. The ideological aspect of the conflict becomes central. As we have noted, within less developed countries there is usually a wide gap between what the rich have and what the poor have, and the government typically strives to preserve this situation. Thus the guerrillas can usually count on support from much of the population, especially in rural areas. The leaders of the government, however, are in a position to use both coercion and enticement to try to get the people to help them against the guerrillas. Consequently the guerrilla fighters cannot succeed unless they are able to persuade the people that the chances of overthrowing the present government are good and that life will be much better if the guerrillas are successful.

It should be evident that the distribution of wealth within a society is directly related to the phenomenon of guerrilla warfare. The guerrilla fighter sees himself as a social reformer in a situation where peaceful change seems impossible. Public support for guerrillas is based on sympathy with that outlook. As more and more people come to know about the great differences in wealth which exist and the role of government in maintaining those differences, we can expect that there will be more and more guerrilla warfare unless governments become much more sensitive to the needs of the poor. Democratic governments which allow for the possibility of peaceful change can be an effective way of defusing guerrilla movements. The U.N.-sponsored process of democratic institution-building in Cambodia provides a concrete example of this process at work. It seems that the ruthless and uncompromising Khmer Rouge guerrilla organization may be falling apart as many members of that movement want to stop fighting and participate in the voting.[31]

The third way that economic conditions may be relevant to the war problem is the possibility that the frustrated poor may fight among themselves for whatever they can get. The point here is *not* that only the poor fight wars. In fact, the big wars are almost always among the rich and powerful for increased status. A poor country is not likely to fight a war against a rich country because it knows it will probably lose the war. But poor countries may fight wars against other poor countries, or there may be wars within poor countries to gain control over the resources and assets which are available. Rich countries or other outside groups may be tempted to assist one side or the other because what is a relatively small investment from their point of view may make a great deal of difference in the outcome of these conflicts in poorer countries.

When we look at the history of war since the end of World War II in 1945, we find that in the period 1945 to 1992 there were 149 wars each with over 1,000 deaths and that 92 percent of them were in the less developed countries.[32] During the Cold War the United States and the Soviet Union avoided any direct conflict with each other, but they were involved in proxy conflicts all over the world which produced many actual wars. Massive supplies of weapons were shipped into the less developed countries to assist one side or the other. Now modern weapons have become readily available on the international market to any group which can afford them or which has an ally who will provide them.

Another manifestation of this situation growing out of the Cold War is the prevalence of militaristic, oppressive governments in the less developed countries, many of which have become independent nation-states since 1945. Of course, there may also be militaristic, oppressive governments in rich countries, but the fact is that in 1992 over half of the less developed countries were controlled by such governments and that these militaristic governments have very poor records with regard to respecting the human rights of their own citizens.[33] Perhaps the end of the Cold War will mean less support from the outside for these militaristic regimes, but weapons can readily be obtained on the open market and money to buy them is often available from oil revenues or drug sales or ideological allies or other sources. As long as these militaristic regimes are able to use force successfully while those who rely on the wider international community for protection are allowed to be robbed and slaughtered, it is not likely that there will be a reduction in reliance on military force in these poorer countries.

XI. Military Aspects of the Contemporary Situation

When nations confront each other in war, military power determines the outcome. Economic power, technological capability, size of population, and morale of the people are relevant only insofar as they can be converted into military power. Military power depends on military leadership, the quality and quantity of ther personnel in the armed forces, and, most importantly, on the weaponry available. Our discussion of the military aspects of the contemporary situation will focus on this last ingredient.

The Post–World War II Struggle for Power

The end of World War II in 1945 left two major powers with strong military forces: the United States and the Soviet Union. The Americans were in a much stronger position than the Soviets, having come through the war without any destruction to their homeland and also having developed the first atomic bombs. The Soviets, on the other hand, had lost 9 percent of their population during the war, and the most densely populated part of their country had served as a battlefield for a couple of years. The United States was eager to forget war and bring its troops back home, but the Soviet Union under Stalin's leadership maintained some military forces to ensure that the newly established governments of Eastern Europe would be friendly to the Soviet Communists. Although the possession of nuclear weapons by the United States allowed American President Truman to be somewhat tough in dealing with the Soviet Union, it should be remembered that the victorious Soviet military forces were concentrated in Europe with a devastated Western Europe before them while the United States had many of its forces scattered throughout the Pacific area. Furthermore, in 1945 the United States had built only three atomic bombs, one by one, and the last two had been dropped on Hiroshima and Nagasaki.[1] Thus no atomic bombs were available for use against the Soviets had war broken out. It is unlikely, however, that the Soviets or anyone else except the highest American officials knew this.

Soviet efforts to create a buffer of friendly governments in Eastern Europe and American efforts to spread Western-style democracy throughout the world soon came into conflict in Poland, Czechoslovakia, Hungary,

194

Greece, Turkey, and conquered Germany. A Communist coup d'état in Czechoslovakia plus a Soviet move to cut off Western access to Communist-controlled Berlin led to the creation in 1949 of the North Atlantic Treaty Organization by the Western nations to prevent any further Communist expansion. The detonation of an atomic device by the Soviets and the takeover of China by Mao's Communist forces in 1949 added to American fears of further expansion by the Communists. The United States detonated a thermonuclear device (a hydrogen bomb) in November of 1952, and the Soviets followed with theirs in August of 1953. In 1957 the Soviets successfully tested an intercontinental ballistic missile and launched an artificial satellite called "sputnik." These events greatly shocked Americans, who for the most part had assumed that American technology was vastly superior to that of the Communists in the Soviet Union. Three months later Americans launched a much smaller satellite, which Khrushchev ridiculed as a "grapefruit." It had now become evident that these two opposing powers would soon be capable of attacking each other with nuclear weapons carried by long-range missiles.

Deterrence Theory

This state of affairs where each side could directly attack the homeland of the other presented a new military situation. Imagine that you are responsible for the military defense of your nation. Previously, you could always protect your nation from attack by defensive military efforts. A protective buffer of other allied countries could be maintained, through which the enemy must proceed before striking, or there might be bodies of water which the enemy must cross before being able to inflict any damage on your homeland. You could count on having some time to launch a defensive effort against attacking enemy forces. Even if the enemy used airplanes, it was at least possible to try to shoot them down before they were able to drop bombs on your cities. With long-range missiles, however, everything was different. How could you hope to stop missiles which are guided to their targets by gravitational and inertial forces and which travel so fast that they can go a sixth of the way around the earth in half an hour? Furthermore, these missiles carry nuclear warheads. One hit could destroy a whole city! If the enemy fired 100 missiles and you could somehow destroy 90 percent of them, 10 of your cities would still be demolished.

Although the notion of some kind of anti-missile missile enjoyed popularity for a time, the prevailing view came to be that there simply was no dependable defense against a missile attack. The only conceivable military strategy seemed to be to try to prevent such an attack in the first place. The aim became one of deterring the potential enemy from launching a missile attack by threatening a retaliatory attack of equal or greater magnitude. It was necessary to persuade the enemy that you had the capability to launch a retaliatory attack even if a surprise attack was launched first, and also that you had the "guts" to do it after your strategy of deterring an attack had failed. Emphasizing a quick retaliatory attack meant that you needed radar units and spy-in-the-sky satellites to detect a missile attack by the enemy, not because anything could be done to stop the incoming missiles, but so that you would know when to launch your own missiles in return.

But the military must consider all the possibilities. What if the enemy were able to somehow knock out or neutralize your radar units and spy satellites? How could you protect your own missiles from destruction by a surprise attack? One solution would be to build hardened silos for your land-based missiles so they would not be destroyed except by a direct hit. Another solution would be to put at least some of your missiles aboard submarines so that the enemy would not know where they are. You might also keep some bombers carrying nuclear bombs in the air at all times so that they could respond to an attack which even wiped out your military airfields. With your own nuclear weapons thus protected, you would have what is called *second-strike capability*. That is, you could absorb a first strike by the enemy and still retaliate. You would desperately want to prevent a situation where an enemy could destroy or neutralize all your own retaliatory capability; that is, you would want to be sure that the enemy does not acquire a *first-strike capability*. If the enemy were to develop systems which could defend against your bombers and detect the whereabouts of all your submarines while at the same time making its own missiles so accurate that they could score direct hits on your missile-launching silos, radar sites, and spy satellites, you would be in deep trouble. Still it would be difficult for the enemy to launch an attack so swiftly and with such a fine degree of accuracy and timing that you would have no chance to launch at least some missiles. Thus what would pose a particularly great threat to your capacity to retaliate would be the development by the enemy of a truly effective anti-missile defense system because then, even if you were able to launch several missiles in retaliation, they could be knocked out before they did any damage.

The doctrine of deterrence through the threat of massive retaliation required that your own missiles be targeted on the enemy's population centers. The enemy theoretically would be deterred from making an attack for fear of suffering a tremendous number of casualties in return. But, asked the military, what if there were some type of limited military engagement and you wanted only one or two of your nuclear weapons to knock out a few of the enemy's military installations? Then you would need to have your missiles targeted on missile sites and military bases rather than on population centers. Such targeting represents what is called *counter-force* targeting rather than *counter-population* targeting. The notion of *limited nuclear war* presumes that you could announce to the enemy that you are not launching a full-scale nuclear attack but are merely going to knock out one or two military bases. According to this way of thinking, you warn them that if they try to respond to your limited attack, an all-out attack will then be launched in response. It is hard to see why the enemy would do anything but lash back with an all-out attack under these circumstances,[2] but during the Cold War some military planners on both sides continued to think in terms of the possibility of a limited nuclear war. The knowledge that some missiles were aimed at military targets which one might want to destroy in a so-called *surgical strike* increased the tension during the Cold War because of the fear that such missiles might in fact be used as part of a general first strike. Missiles aimed at population centers, on the other hand, would be useful only in a retaliatory strike.

There is no reliable defense against a large ballistic missile attack. Up to the end of the Cold War, and even now, the Americans and the Russians both remain vulnerable to a nuclear missile attack by the other. The use of hardened silos for land-based missiles plus the use of submarine-based missiles meant that both sides retained a second-strike capability against the other and that neither could achieve a first-strike capability. Such a situation had a certain stability in it, but it was realized by both sides that the development of an extensive, reliable anti-missile defense by either side would upset this stable situation. That is why the Soviet Union and the United States agreed as part of the 1972 SALT I Treaty to limit the development and deployment of anti-missile missiles. This arrangement for international stability based on each side remaining vulnerable to nuclear retaliation by the other side was called *mutual assured destruction* or *MAD*.

The Cuban Missile Crisis

The closest the world has come to a nuclear holocaust was the Cuban missile crisis of October 1962. Fidel Castro had established a Communist government in Cuba. An invasion attempt by non–Communist Cubans who had fled to Florida was conducted with some U.S. support in 1961, but this effort at "the Bay of Pigs" to launch an anti–Castro uprising failed miserably. Apparently in an effort to discourage future invasion attempts as well as to give the Soviets a chance to equalize U.S. missiles based in Turkey, the Communists decided to put some Soviet missiles in Cuba. Reconnaissance flights by U.S. planes spotted the building of the missile sites. The United States claimed that this presence of a non–American nation's military forces in the Americas was a violation of the long-established Monroe Doctrine, which stated that non–American nations should stay out of American affairs. The United States also succeeded in getting the Organization of American States to endorse this viewpoint. The Soviets could have responded to American complaints by noting that the Monroe Doctrine is simply a U.S. pronouncement which is not international law, even if it had been endorsed by the U.S.-dominated Organization of American States. They might have argued that Cuba was a sovereign state which could legitimately invite the Soviets to put missiles on its soil if it wished to do so. Instead, when confronted with the American accusation, the Soviets denied that they were installing missile bases in Cuba. At a dramatic meeting of the U.N. General Assembly, U.S. Ambassador Adlai Stevenson displayed aerial photos proving to the whole world that the Soviets were liars. President Kennedy sent American ships to intercept the Soviet ships bringing parts needed to complete the missile sites. The world held its breath as the Soviet freighters neared the U.S. Navy ships. It seemed that a nuclear war might begin at any moment. But Khrushchev directed the Soviet ships to turn back, and a nuclear holocaust was averted.

Why did Khrushchev direct the Soviet ships to turn back? It may have been because the two nations had reached an understanding that the United States would not assist any further efforts to overthrow the Castro regime. There may also have been other factors such as an "unrelated" commitment to remove U.S. missiles from Turkey, but an important consideration undoubtedly was the fact that at that time the United States had about a 5 to 1 superiority in the number of atomic weapons which could be delivered by long-range missiles and bombers. The Soviet Union had been coerced into ceasing its missile-building efforts in Cuba even though the Soviets had some missiles capable of delivering atomic warheads onto U.S. cities. It was the overwhelming superiority of the United States in the quantity of available nuclear warheads and delivery systems which had been decisive.

As a result of this incident, the Soviets were convinced that it was not sufficient to have some missiles with nuclear warheads which could strike the United States. They began a massive missile-building effort and increased their defensive capabilities against U.S. bombers. It was the stimulus of the Cuban missile crisis and its outcome that led the Soviets to conclude that military power was necessary not just for defense of the homeland but also for success in international bargaining. In an anarchic world a nation which is obviously second in military power will be coerced into accepting terms dictated by the nation which is first in military power. Since most American leaders also recognize the validity of this principle, as long as world anarchy continues there will be a virtually unlimited arms race to develop ever more destructive weapons and a technological race to try to create some kind of defense against a missile attack. This desire to be able to coerce the other side when negotiating is a more important motive for building nuclear weapons than any intention to actually use them. It has been noted that U.S. presidents have used the threat of nuclear strikes in at least 20 crisis situations.[3] It has also been argued that Israel's possession of nuclear weapons has persuaded its enemies to give up on the possibility of using force to overcome Israel and that the possibility of Arab nuclear weapons in the future is encouraging Israel to negotiate now.[4]

Modern Nuclear Weaponry

Humankind's first weapons, the club, the spear, and the bow and arrow, could kill one person at a time. The invention of the exploding grenade in the fifteenth century meant that a single weapon might kill four or five persons at once. By the beginning of World War I in 1914, artillery shells and torpedoes made it possible for one weapon to kill 10 or 20 people at once, and by the end of that war a single shell from the Germans' "Big Bertha" cannon might kill 40. During World War II, the large bombs dropped by the Allies might kill 60 or 70 persons. But the atomic bomb dropped on Hiroshima in 1945 killed at least 75,000 persons! The first thermonuclear bombs were 20 times as powerful as the Hiroshima bomb, and now some nuclear warheads are available which have more than 1,500 times the explosive power of that first nuclear bomb.[5] Since some of the explosive power will necessarily be wasted because of the physical principles involved in large explosions, it doesn't follow that these newer thermonuclear weapons would kill 1,500 times as many people, or even do 1,500 times as much damage, but there is little doubt that one of these superbombs could kill millions of people in a big city. In fact, atomic weapons generally are so powerful that the primary military problem has been how to make them smaller so that they won't be more destructive than desired.

The quantity of nuclear warheads has generally increased over the years, though secrecy makes it difficult to get exact numbers. It was not until the 1950s that nuclear warheads of many different sizes and kinds came rolling off the assembly lines. By 1960, the United States had 7,000 nuclear warheads in Europe.[6] In 1975 it was estimated that the United States had 8,000 nuclear warheads on its strategic (long-range) weapons and 22,000 on its tactical (battlefield) weapons.[7] (The chart on page 200 compares the destructive power of 1981 nuclear arsenals with the total firepower used in World War II.) Since the radioactive material in nuclear warheads gradually loses its radioactivity, the weapons must eventually be disassembled and the still-active material recycled into new weapons. Thus, even though new warheads are constantly being produced, the quantity of them is not always increasing.[8] Here are the figures for the estimated stockpiles of nuclear weapons, including both those for *strategic* (long-range delivery systems) and those for *tactical* (short-range delivery systems), possessed by the five acknowledged nuclear powers in 1983, 1993, and 2003.[9]

Country	Mid–1983	Mid–1993	2003
United States	23,400	10,500	5,500–8,000
Former Soviet Union*	40,000	15,000	4,000–10,000
Britain	300	200	300
France	280	550	500
China	380	450	300–600
TOTAL	64,360	26,700	10,600–19,400

Includes Russia, Belarus, Ukraine, and Kazakhstan.

Nuclear Weapons

U.S. Senate staff have reviewed this chart and found it an accurate representation.

The dot in the center square represents all the firepower of World War II — total, 3 megatons. The other dots represent the firepower in existing nuclear weapons (in 1981) — 18,000 megatons (equal to 6,000 WW IIs). About ½ belong to the Soviet Union, the other ½ to the United States. The top left circle represents the weapons on just one U.S. Poseidon submarine — 9 megatons — enough to destroy more than 200 of the largest Soviet cities. The lower left circle represents one new Trident submarine — 24 megatons — enough to destroy every major city in the northern hemisphere. (Chart reprinted by permission of James Geier, 2 Howard Street, Burlington, VT 05401.)

In addition to the acknowledged nuclear powers listed above it is generally believed that Israel has as many as 100 nuclear warheads.[10] At one time South Africa had six nuclear weapons, but they were dismantled and melted down before South Africa signed the Nuclear Non-Proliferation

Treaty in July 1991.[11] It is not known whether India and Pakistan have nuclear weapons, but even if they don't have them they "have the capability to produce them in a short time."[12] There is some suspicion that North Korea and Iran may have nuclear weapons, but there is no clear evidence that that is so.[13]

Nuclear warheads are not very useful for strategic military purposes, however, unless a nation has some means of delivering them to the target. It is the long-range bomber and the ballistic missiles as much as nuclear warheads which make today's military situation different from that of World War II. The first delivery system for nuclear warheads was the airplane. By 1948 the United States had bombers with intercontinental range. Then in 1957 came the Russian development of the intercontinental ballistic missile (ICBM). A ballistic missile is started on its way by a rocket engine which does not need oxygen from the atmosphere. The missile goes high above the atmosphere and then free falls onto its target; it is in effect a space shot which does not quite go into orbit. Since it goes so high, its launching is readily detectable by radar, but its speed is so great that the distance between the Soviet Union and the United States can be traversed in half an hour. The first intercontinental ballistic missiles were liquid-fueled, making it difficult to keep them ready for launching on a continuous basis, but before long they were equipped with solid propellants. Solid propellants also made it possible to develop submarine-launched ballistic missiles (SLBMs) which could be launched even while the submarine was submerged. Nuclear warheads have also been placed on artillery shells and bazooka rockets and developed for use as aerial bombs, depth charges, and demolition munitions.[14]

Eventually strategic missiles were armed with more than a single nuclear warhead. At first these separate warheads launched by a single missile simply separated a bit from each other while descending so that the target area would be sprayed with several warheads rather than a single one. Then a system was developed for guiding the separate warheads from a single missile onto different targets: that is, multiple independently targetable reentry vehicles (MIRVs) were developed. The next step was to make the reentry vehicles maneuverable (MARVs) so they could evade anti-missile devices. Later developments relative to long-range ballistic missiles were the use of a mobile rather than a stationary launching pad for land-based missiles and the development of substantially increased accuracy.[15]

In the late 1970s came the development of cruise missiles. They differ considerably from ballistic missiles in that they depend on continuous power after launching until they strike their target. They are in fact pilotless jet aircraft with very small wings. Cruise missiles do not travel nearly as fast as ballistic missiles, but they can fly very close to the surface of the earth, a feature which makes them difficult to detect with radar. Thus they may give an enemy less time to respond than the much speedier ballistic missiles. Cruise missiles are also very maneuverable and can even be called back after they are part way to their target. In addition, they are smaller and much less expensive to build than ballistic missiles. Cruise missiles also pose a special problem for arms limitation agreements because they are much more easily concealed than ballistic missiles and because it is difficult (though perhaps not impossible) to distinguish between short-range and long-range versions of the weapon.[16]

Research and development on new weapons continued in many areas. The range of submarine-launched ballistic missiles was steadily extended. Both land-based and submarine-launched ballistic missiles became much more accurate because of new guidance systems based on the use of more satellites, and the average number of warheads on each long-range missile was increased. Air-launched cruise missiles (ALCMs) were joined by sea-launched (SLCMs) and ground-launched cruise missiles (GLCMs), and long-range "stealth" bombers were developed which because of their design and construction are very difficult to detect by radar. Neutron bombs which produce a great deal of deadly but short-lasting radiation were developed for possible use against military forces, especially those inside armored vehicles such as tanks.

Changes in weaponry required changes in strategy too. For example, before long-range missiles were so accurate, it was feasible to harden ICBM launch-sites and expect that a substantial proportion of them could survive a nuclear attack by the enemy because they could be destroyed only by direct hits. This situation permitted a nation to wait until after an enemy's nuclear weapons actually exploded before launching a retaliatory attack. Now the situation has changed. If a nation waits that long, it may have very few land-based ICBMs left. Consequently, a new strategy was needed, namely, to launch missiles as soon as a warning is received that the enemy has launched its. Since it takes only a half hour at most for the enemy missiles to strike a nation's launching sites, the response needs to be quick. Unfortunately this "launch-on-warning" strategy substantially increases the likelihood of a nuclear war beginning by accident, especially in tense situations.

Strategic Defense

Another development in the nuclear arms race which involved both new technology and a new strategy was the Strategic Defense Initiative (SDI) or "Star Wars Defense" proposed by U.S. President Reagan in 1983. It was believed that the Soviet Union was working on a similar system to defend itself against a ballistic missile attack.

The basic thrust of such systems is to supplement deterrence with a system of defense. According to the earlier widely accepted deterrence strategy, the aim of one's nuclear arsenal was to keep the enemy from attacking, but once an attack had occurred there seemed to be no point in actually launching a retaliatory strike. You could wreak destruction on the enemy, but your action would no longer be a means to any sensible end.

If the United States were attacked, the President would be obliged to order a retaliatory attack which would kill millions of people for no purpose except vengefulness. Strategic defense was designed to give the President an alternative if an enemy nuclear attack were launched; the incoming missiles could be destroyed. At the same time, however, each side viewed the development of a strategic defense by the other side as provocative since it would allow them to launch a first strike and then wipe out any attempted retaliatory strike. That is, the development of an effective defense system by one side would mean the end of the deterrence capability of the other side. The provocativeness of a defense system is especially great if it is not likely to be able to successfully ward off an attempted first strike by the enemy but *is* capable of providing a rather good defense against a retaliatory strike from an enemy significantly disabled by one's own first strike. Unfortunately, the technology is such that it is just this level of capability that a strategic defense system is likely to have.

The operation of a space-based strategic defense system can be understood only if one first understands how ballistic missiles work.[17] The flight of a ballistic missile has four phases. During the "boost phase," which usually lasts about three minutes, the rocket engines get the missile underway. The second phase, the "post-boost phase," begins as the last rocket booster is detached and falls away and the post-booster vehicle (called the "bus") with its low-thrust rocket engine carries the load of nuclear warheads still upward but at a less steep angle. During its five-to-eight-minute trip the "bus" drops off as many as ten reentry vehicles (each with one nuclear warhead) at just the right time and angle to aim them toward their intended targets. It may also drop off decoys and debris to make it more difficult for the enemy to locate the real warheads. This "post-boost phase" is followed by the "midcourse phase" or "coast phase" which lasts about 20 minutes for an intercontinental missile. At this point the reentry vehicles are being carried through space simply by inertia, and gravity eventually begins pulling them back toward earth along a rainbow-like path. The fourth and final phase, called the "terminal phase," begins when the reentry vehicle descends into the atmosphere of the earth. During this phase, which lasts less than two minutes, the reentry vehicle plunges at extremely high speed toward its target, while decoys, which lack the specially hardened protection given the reentry vehicles, burn up or break apart in the atmosphere.

The strategic defense system is multilayered, that is, it is designed to destroy missiles in each of the four phases. Different detection devices and weapons systems are required for each phase of the missile's trajectory. The most important phase is the boost phase because at that point each missile is carrying up to ten reentry vehicles which later will become separate targets. The problem is that hitting the missiles during this phase requires hypervelocity guns, chemical rockets, or directed energy weapons based on satellites (called "battle stations") in lower earth orbit in space. Furthermore, the period of time for detecting the launch, locating the missiles, and destroying them is very short. The sensing system for tracking the missile during the post-boost phase is a bit different, but the weapons used against it are essentially the same as those used during the boost phase. In the mid-course or coasting phase, sorting out the reentry vehicles from the decoys and debris becomes a major problem; but the time period is longer and the defense can begin to rely on ground-based interceptor rockets. In the terminal phase, one can use the same type of ground-based anti-ballistic missiles previously developed by both the United States and the Soviet Union.

There has been much controversy about the Strategic Defense Initiative. Besides the main aim of replacing deterrence with defense, it is claimed that SDI would also permit the United States to protect itself in case of an accidental launch of a nuclear missile. It also could stop an attack from some "crazy" leader who would not be deterred by threat of retaliation. Even if the system were only partly effective, it is argued, it would be very helpful in a limited nuclear war and would greatly limit the amount of damage from an all-out attack. On the other hand, opponents argue that the technological problems are insurmountable, that countermeasures could readily make the system ineffective, that a much simpler system could deal with accidentally launched missiles, and that the many satellites on which the system depends would be very vulnerable if the enemy did in fact want to launch a first strike.[18] It has been argued that a strategic defense system would in fact increase the likelihood of a nuclear war in tense situations because accidental damage to sensitive satellites might be interpreted as the beginning of an attack. There is also the problem that the system would pose a definite offensive threat to any potential enemy since the space-based weapons could be used even if no enemy launch had been attempted. Finally, even if it were possible to make each of the three parts of the defense system 90 percent effective, a launch of 1,400 enemy missiles each carrying ten warheads would result in 14 targets being hit.[19] A separate issue is whether some totally different approach such as having young people from any potential enemy state disbursed throughout the United States might not be a more effective way of preventing an attack at a much lower cost. There is a suspicion that the real motive for developing SDI is not for defense but rather to gain a position of military superiority in order to engage in coercive diplomacy against potential enemies.

Arms Control Agreements

The notion that arms races and the huge expenditures required to continue them might be controlled by an agreement between the adversaries is not new. The 1817 Rush-Bagot Agreement between the United States and Great Britain permitted each side only one lightly armed vessel on Lake Champlain, one on Lake Ontario, and two others on all the other Great Lakes together.[20] In 1902, Chile and Argentina entered into an agreement not to add any more battleships to their fleets and also to disarm and put in dock the three battleships which the two countries between them already possessed.[21] In 1905, Norway and Sweden agreed to establish a permanent demilitarized neutral zone along their border.[22] The Five Power Naval Limitation Treaty resulting from the Washington Conference of 1921–22 set limits on the tonnage of capital ships and aircraft carriers, establishing a ratio of 5 for Great Britain and the United States, 3 for Japan, and 1.67 for France and Italy. At the London Naval Conference of 1930 the same five nations agreed to observe a five-year moratorium on any further construction of battleships, and the first three nations signed an agreement setting limits for each nation on the numbers of cruisers, destroyers, and submarines at the ratio of 10 for Great Britain and the United States to 7 for Japan. These naval agreements were observed until they expired in 1936.[23] The Geneva Protocol of 1925, which is still in effect with 132 signatories, prohibits the use of poisonous gases and bacteriological warfare.

The success of these various arms agreements may be the reflection of other factors rather than an indication of what arms agreements can accomplish. Still, the evidence seems to indicate that if nations can work out arrangements which all involved view as advantageous to themselves, they will tend to observe their agreements. Furthermore, if nations find an agreement becoming disadvantageous, they will usually publicly announce their withdrawal from it rather than trying secretly to take advantage of other parties to the agreement, a course of action which would lead to special difficulties if they later wanted to enter into other international agreements. In other words, nations generally do not enter into arms control agreements (or most other kinds of agreements) unless they intend to abide by them. This fact is confirmed by the hard bargaining which goes on when nations strive to reach arms agreements. If there were no intention to abide by the agreement, why struggle so intensely over the terms?

Before reviewing the various arms control treaties adopted since the end of World War II, let us consider briefly how such treaties may be classified. First, some treaties are bilateral (between two countries) while others are multilateral (among more than two countries). Second, we can classify the treaties according to the type of weapons they seek to control: nuclear weapons and the accompanying delivery systems, biological weapons, chemical weapons, and conventional weapons. Third, we can classify the treaties on the basis of whether they completely prohibit something, such as the deployment of weapons of a particular kind, or merely limit the number permitted. Fourth, we can classify the treaties as zonal (applying only to certain geographical areas) or general (not limited to particular regions). Finally, we can distinguish among those treaties which focus on the development and testing of weapons, those which focus on the deployment of weapons, and those which focus on the transfer of weapons from one nation to another. We shall review existing multilateral arms control agreements and then the bilateral arms agreements which have been made between the United States and the Soviet Union/ Russia.

A good example of a multilateral zonal arms prohibition agreement is the *Antarctic Treaty,* which was signed in 1959 and which got enough signatories to go into effect in 1961. This treaty covers nuclear and other kinds of weapons and prohibits both their development and their deployment in the Antarctic. At the end of 1992, it had been acceded to by 40 countries including the United States, Russia, the United Kingdom, Japan, and France.[24]

The *Partial Test Ban Treaty (PTBT)* (1963) prohibits the testing of nuclear weapons in the atmosphere, in outer space, under water, or anywhere else where the radioactive debris may enter the territory of a nation other than the one which exploded the device. In effect this agreement prohibits all aboveground testing of nuclear devices. It is a multilateral treaty which applies only to the testing of nuclear weapons, a step which is crucial for their development. One aim of this treaty is to hinder the development of nuclear weapons capability by countries which do not already have it. This treaty has been acceded to by 120 countries, including the United States, Russia, the United Kingdom, and Japan, but not France and China. In March 1986 China announced that it would no longer carry out nuclear tests in the atmosphere, but it has still not signed the treaty.

Might the Partial Test Ban Treaty (PTBT) become a total or *Comprehensive Test Ban Treaty (CTB)?* That is one of the key issues to be determined in the 1990s. One provision of the 1963 PTBT is that if one-third of the signatories call for a conference to consider amending the treaty, such a conference must be convened by the three "Depositary Governments" where the text of the treaty has been deposited—the U.S., the Soviet Union, and the United Kingdom. Despite U.S. stonewalling, such a conference was held in New York in January 1991 to consider amending the PTBT to make it a comprehensive test ban. In order to be adopted amendments must get the approval of a majority of signatories and of all three of the PTBT's "Original Parties"—the U.S., the Soviet Union, and the United Kingdom.[25] Realizing that the U.S. would simply kill any actual proposed amendment for a CTB by voting against it, the countries at the 1991 conference which favored a comprehensive ban adopted the alternative strategy of introducing a two-part resolution calling for (a) continued consultation on the complex issues related to verification of compliance and sanctions for non-compliance and for (b) resuming the conference at an appropriate time in the future. Of the 95 countries participating in the conference, 74 voted for this resolution, 19 abstained, and only the U.S. and Britain voted against it.[26] It will be up to the president of that 1991 conference, Ali Alatas of Indonesia, to determine when to try to reconvene it. Meanwhile a self-imposed moratorium on nuclear testing has been adopted by all the nuclear powers except China, which set off underground nuclear explosions on May 21, 1992,[27] and October 5, 1993. China nevertheless says that it favors a "complete prohibition on nuclear tests within the framework of effective nuclear disarmament"[28] and that it "will work in common with the other countries towards a comprehensive nuclear test ban at an early date."[29] At the same time it was reported in 1993 that "the United States said 'the rapid completion of a Comprehensive Test Ban Treaty (CTBT)' was a major U.S. objective and an important change in policy by the new [Clinton] Administration."[30] These are promising statements, since the viewpoint of the governments of the U.S. and China will be critical in determining whether or not the CTBT becomes a reality.

The *Outer Space Treaty* (1967) prohibits placing nuclear weapons or other weapons of mass destruction in outer space, including celestial bodies such as the moon. It also forbids the establishment of any military bases, the testing of any kinds of weapons, and the conducting of any kind of military maneuvers on celestial bodies. It is a multilateral treaty which has been signed by 93 countries, including the United States, the Soviet Union, the United Kingdom, Japan, and France.

Another multilateral zonal treaty is the *Latin American Nuclear-Free Zone Treaty* or *Treaty of Tlatelolco* (1967) which prohibits the testing, manufacture, production, acquisition, receipt, storage, installation, deployment, or possession of nuclear weapons in Latin America. The second Protocol to this treaty allows non–Latin American countries which have nuclear weapons to pledge themselves not to contribute to acts involving a violation of the treaty and not to use or threaten to use nuclear weapons against Latin American nations which have signed the treaty. This treaty has been ratified by 23 Latin American countries, and the Protocol indicating cooperation on the part of nations possessing nuclear weapons has been signed by all five nuclear-weapon states.

The *Nuclear Non-Proliferation Treaty (NPT)*, which will be getting much attention in the 1990s, is a multilateral treaty which was signed in 1968 and came into force in 1970. Its aim is to prevent the spread of nuclear weapons to countries which do not already possess them (what has been called "horizontal proliferation"). At the same time the nuclear powers pledge to pursue negotiations to control the increase of nuclear weapons among the countries which already possess them (what has been called "vertical proliferation") and to work for a treaty on general and complete disarmament. During the Cold War little progress was made toward checking vertical proliferation because the West insisted that it needed nuclear arms in order to balance the superior conventional military power of the Soviets. But now that the Soviets are no longer challenging the U.S. and its allies militarily, it is widely expected that the nuclear powers will also become serious about reducing their stockpiles of nuclear weapons. On the other hand, some countries such as India are insisting that the NPT be revised in order to eliminate all nuclear weapons rather than merely extending a situation where some few countries are allowed to have nuclear weapons while others are not. The Non-Proliferation Treaty has 160 signatories including all the nuclear powers and Japan but not including Israel and India. One provision of this treaty is that there can be a review conference to examine the operation of the treaty every five years if requested by a majority of the signatories, and such review conferences have in fact been held every five years in Geneva, Switzerland. Article X specifically says that a review conference will be held after 25 years (that is, in 1995) to determine whether "the Treaty shall continue in force indefinitely. . . ." That twenty-fifth anniversary meeting scheduled to convene in New York from April 17 to May 12, 1995, should be one of the most important arms control conferences ever held. Some non-nuclear countries are threatening to vote against extending this Non-Proliferation Treaty unless the nuclear states first sign a Comprehensive Test Ban Treaty (CTBT) which would put an end to all nuclear testing by all countries. As noted above, the January 1991 conference called to consider amending the Partial Test Ban Treaty to make it a comprehensive ban on all nuclear testing was unable to accomplish this goal because of opposition from the U.S. and Britain. On the other hand, that conference to consider the possibility of amending the Partial Test Ban Treaty will probably be reconvened sometime before the 1995 meeting on the Non-Proliferation Treaty in an effort to find out whether the U.S. and Britain are still opposing a total ban on nuclear testing.

The *Sea-Bed Treaty*, signed in 1971 and in force since 1972, prohibits the placement or storage of nuclear weapons or other weapons of mass destruction on the floor of the ocean beyond the 12-mile territorial waters of coastal states. It is a multilateral treaty designed to prevent nuclear powers from using the sea-bed as another place from which nuclear weapons might be fired. This treaty has been acceded to by 88 countries including the United States, Russia, the United Kingdom, and Japan, but not including China or France.

The *Biological Weapons Convention,* signed in 1972 and in force since 1975, prohibits the development, production, and possession of biological agents or toxins as well as devices for delivering such agents or toxins for hostile purposes. Any such materials on hand must be destroyed within nine months from when the convention enters into force or from when a nation accedes to the treaty. This multilateral convention has been acceded to by 126 countries, including the United States, Russia, the United Kingdom, and Japan, but not including China or France.

The *Environmental Modification Convention,* signed in 1977 and in force since 1978, prohibits military or other hostile use of environmental modification techniques to manipulate natural processes in a way which would be harmful to other countries. This multilateral treaty has been acceded to by 57 countries including the United States, Russia, the United Kingdom, Japan, China, and France.

The *Inhumane Weapons Convention,* signed in 1981 and in force since December 1983, contains three protocols addressed to prohibiting weapons which cause fragments not detectable by X-rays when in the human body;

restricting the use of mines, booby-traps, and the like; and restricting the use of incendiary weapons. This multilateral treaty has been signed by 35 countries including the United States (but not yet ratified by the Senate), Russia, the United Kingdom, China, France, and Japan.

Multilateral zonal treaties to keep nuclear weapons out of particular areas of the world are becoming popular. The *South Pacific Nuclear-Free Zone Treaty (SPNFZ)* was adopted in 1985 and has 11 signatories.[31] Following the model of the nuclear-free treaty for Latin America (Treaty of Tlatelolco), there is a protocol for nuclear states to sign indicating that they will not use nuclear weapons or threaten to use them or conduct tests with them in this part of the world. Turning from a zonal treaty that already exists to one that is likely to come into existence in 1994 or 1995, let us consider the situation in Africa. Now that South Africa has renounced both apartheid and nuclear weapons, it seems probable that the U.N. and the Organization for African Unity will be able to work together to develop a treaty for an African Nuclear-Weapon-Free Zone (ANWFZ) which excludes nuclear weapons while still allowing for the nuclear power generation which African countries need for development.[32]

Another approach to nuclear arms control is to focus on the missiles which could be used to deliver nuclear warheads. The *Missile Technology Control Regime (MTCR)* was formed in April 1987 by the G-7 leading industrialized democracies (Canada, France, Germany, Italy, Japan, U.K., and U.S.) in order to restrict the transfer of equipment and technology useful in building missiles capable of carrying nuclear warheads.[33] Twenty-five industrialized democracies are now formal members, and China, Israel, Romania, and Russia have committed themselves to abiding by the restrictions even though they are not formal members of the Regime.

Multilateral treaties are also being used to control chemical and biological weapons. The *Australia Group,* formed in 1985, is composed of a variety of industrialized countries which have agreed to restrict the export of "precursor" chemicals from which chemical weapons might be made.[34] In December 1992 new restrictions with regard to various items and equipment which might be used in making biological weapons were adopted. There are now 26 countries which belong to this group.

In January of 1993, 130 countries signed the very sophisticated *Chemical Weapons Convention (CWC)* designed to replace and move beyond the 1925 Geneva Protocol.[35] This new treaty not only bans the use of chemical weapons but adds the restriction that such weapons cannot be developed, produced, acquired, stockpiled, or transferred to any other country. Present stockpiles must be eliminated in 10 to 15 years. Furthermore, an Organization for the Prohibition of Chemical Weapons (OPCW) which has three organs (the Conference of State Parties, the Executive Council, and the Technical Secretariat) was created to oversee implementation and enforcement and to set up review conferences for the first, fifth, and tenth years of the treaty. There are now 147 signatories,[36] but the convention does not come into force until 180 days after it has been ratified by 65 countries, and in no case can it come into force before January 13, 1995. This important agreement was possible only after the U.S. and Soviet Union reached a bilateral agreement in June 1990 to end production of chemical weapons and to reduce their stockpiles of such weapons to no more than 5,000 metric tons by the end of the year 2002.[37]

Multilateral actions to monitor military activities involving conventional weapons are also being taken. For example, in February 1990 when it was becoming evident that the Cold War was ending, the members of the Conference on Security and Cooperation in Europe (CSCE) adopted *"Vienna Document 1990."* The CSCE was originally established by the Helsinki Accord of 1975 in order to reduce tensions in Europe between West and East. The CSCE is made up of members of NATO, former members of the Soviet-organized Warsaw Pact Organization, and other "neutral" European states. During the Cold War one of its main functions had been holding meetings to monitor human rights violations. The post–Cold War "Vienna Document 1990" establishes a range of "confidence-building measures" (CBM) to be carried out by the members.[38] These include (1) giving notification of military exercises exceeding a specified size, (2) allowing a limited number of inspections of the military facilities of some other country, (3) evaluation (including verification visits) of the annual reports submitted by each country concerning its military activities, and (4) visits arranged by each country to its airfields at least once every five years. This agreement has been very useful in furthering the transition from the Cold War outlook to the perspective of an undivided Europe.

Although not really a treaty, another important development with regard to possible future control of weapons is the *U.N. Register of Conventional Arms* instituted by U.N. General Assembly Resolution 46/36L adopted in December of 1991.[39] This resolution called on member-states voluntarily to report by April 30, 1993, and annually thereafter their previous year's imports and exports of major armaments such as tanks, armored vehicles, artillery systems, combat aircraft, attack helicopters, warships, and missiles and missile launchers. Seventy-one countries, including all five permanent members of the U.N. Security Council, had reported by the fall of 1993.[40] Of course, the reporting is purely voluntary and some countries which are major arms traders have not yet complied, but this is a clever device for putting pressure on those doing a great deal of trading in arms. The Register will be reviewed in 1994, and some modifications can be expected, including new categories of weapons to be reported.

Another non-treaty event related to the control of weapons is the expected advisory opinion of the International Court of Justice, possibly in 1994, on the issue of whether the use of nuclear weapons by any national government, even during war, is a violation of international law. The World Health Organization has requested the World Court to address this issue, and it is expected that the General Assembly will do the same.[41]

Bilateral Agreements During and After the Cold War

Let us now direct our attention to the history of those very important bilateral arms control agreements, mainly on nuclear weapons, which were worked out between the U.S. and the Soviet Union during the Cold War. The Cold War is over now, but a review of these agreements nevertheless deserves our attention since they may provide some guidance if we confront other nuclear arms races in the future. Though there were earlier agreements between the United States and the Soviet Union regarding a "hot line" between the two countries and measures to reduce the likelihood of a nuclear war beginning by accident, the first and most important bilateral arms control agreement was the SALT I agreement of 1972.[41] "SALT" stands for "Strategic Arms Limitation Talks" and the SALT I agreement was actually composed of two separate treaties. The first was the *Anti-Ballistic Missile* (ABM) *Treaty* which limited each country to two sites at which ABMs could be deployed and limited the number of ABMs at each site to 100 missiles. It also limited the number and characteristics of radar installations related to the ABM systems or to surface-to-air missiles (SAMs) that might be used against ballistic missiles. Each side pledged not to develop, test, or deploy ABM systems or components which are seabased, air-based, space-based, or mobile land-based. In 1974 a protocol to the ABM Treaty was signed reducing the number of ABM sites allowed for each country to one. After building an ABM site in North Dakota, the United States decided not to spend the funds needed to keep it in operation.[42] The Russians maintained their ABM system near Moscow at least through the end of the Cold War.

The second part of the SALT I agreement was the *Interim Agreement on the Limitation of Strategic Offensive Arms.* This interim agreement was originally scheduled to expire in July 1977, but was extended beyond that date by both parties in anticipation of the signing and ratification of a new treaty, SALT II. The aim of the Interim Agreement was to set limits on the number of long-range missiles and missile-firing submarines each side could have. It should be noted that this agreement did not cover tactical (shorter range) missiles but only those with intercontinental range and it said nothing about long-range bombers or the number of warheads that could be placed on each missile. In all these areas not covered by the treaty the U.S. had a great advantage, but in the number of missile launchers covered by the treaty the Soviets were allowed a slight numerical advantage.

The *Threshold Test Ban Treaty* of 1974, formally called the Treaty on the Limitation of Underground Nuclear Weapon Tests, is a bilateral agreement between the United States and the Soviet Union to limit the size of underground nuclear explosions for the purpose of testing nuclear weapons. No such explosion is to be over 150 kilotons (more than ten times as large as the bomb dropped on Hiroshima!). A protocol to the treaty indicates that each side will provide the other with certain information that will assist in verifying compliance with the treaty.

The *Treaty on Underground Nuclear Explosions for Peaceful Purposes* was signed by the United States and the Soviet Union in 1976 in order to extend the 150-kiloton limit to nuclear tests for peaceful purposes. This treaty provides for on-site inspections to ensure compliance.

One of the most complex arms control treaties ever negotiated was SALT II,[43] signed by the United States and the Soviet Union in June of 1979 but never ratified by the U.S. Senate. The SALT II agreement went far beyond SALT I in that it limited the number of all kinds of long-range delivery systems each side could have as well as indirectly setting a limit on the number of nuclear warheads permitted on strategic weapons. Unlike SALT I, the numerical limits to be put into effect were the same for both sides. Each side was permitted a total of 2,400 delivery systems until the end of 1980 and a total of 2,250 after that. Within this aggregate limit there were limits for particular types of weapons. The maximum number of land-based ICBMs was 820, while the maximum number of MIRVed missiles (whether land-based ICBMs, SLBMs, or ASBMs) was 1,200. The maximum for MIRVed missiles *plus* heavy bombers was 1,320, with each heavy bomber being restricted to carrying a maximum of 20 long-range (more than 600 kilometers) air-launched cruise missiles (ALCMs). In counting these systems, if any launcher had been tested with a MIRVed missile, then all launchers of this type would be counted as being equipped with MIRVed missiles whether they were or not. Both parties agreed not to start construction of any new nonmobile ICBMs; not to relocate present nonmobile ICBMs; not to make major modifications in the size of the missiles to be fired from a given launcher; not to put extra ICBMs near launching tubes for quick second launches from the same tube; not to develop, test, or deploy systems for rapid reloading of launching tubes; not to develop or test or deploy any ICBMs heavier than what that nation already had; and not to flight-test or deploy any larger number of warheads on any given type of missile than was already available on that type of missile. Each side was permitted to test and deploy one new light ICBM system. Both sides agreed to notify the other of any planned ICBM launches where the trajectory would extend beyond the launcher's own national territory, and both sides agreed not to impede verification of compliance by the other side. The treaty also indicated that both sides would work toward another agreement further limiting strategic offensive arms. Even though SALT II was never ratified by the U.S. Senate, its limits were observed by the U.S. until 1986 when President Reagan indicated that the U.S. no longer intended to abide by it.

In 1977 the Soviet Union began building medium-range missiles targeted on Western Europe. Such missiles were not prohibited by SALT I or SALT II, which dealt only with strategic missiles, that is, missiles having intercontinental range. In 1979 NATO responded by deciding to deploy some of its own intermediate-range missiles in Western Europe. The focus on increasing the number of these medium-range missiles aroused great concern among some Europeans that a limited war, possibly using nuclear weapons, might be fought just in Europe between the two superpowers. U.S. medium-range missiles in Europe could reach some targets in the Soviet Union, but many Western Europeans doubted that the U.S., which had a veto over use of nuclear weapons by NATO, would risk the possibility of a nuclear attack on its own cities in order to try to save Western Europe from a Soviet attack. Since the Soviets apparently had superior conventional forces in the European theater, it seemed possible that they might make use of those superior forces while neutralizing the threat of nuclear weapons from the U.S. The British and French had their own nuclear weapons, but they were obviously no match for the Soviet nuclear weapons.

In 1981 newly elected U.S. President Reagan, in an effort to counteract this situation, proposed the "zero option" (no intermediate-range missiles for either side in Europe) and indicated that there would be a massive build-up of U.S. medium-range missiles in Europe (despite widely publicized public protests) if the Soviets did not eliminate all of theirs.[44] In 1983 Reagan announced the Strategic Defense Initiative (SDI), a space-based defense system that supposedly would allow the U.S. to defend itself against a strategic nuclear attack rather than relying on deterrence. In March 1985 Mikhail Gorbachev took over leadership of the Soviet Union. Gorbachev and Reagan had summit meetings in Geneva in November 1985 and in Reykjavik, Iceland, in October 1986. Throughout 1986 and 1987 the Soviets tried to link the elimination of the intermediate-range missiles in Europe to the elimination of all nuclear weapons and to the end of the SDI program being researched by the U.S., but the issue of the elimination of all intermediate-range missiles was finally separated from these other issues and the *Intermediate-Range Nuclear Forces (INF) Treaty* was signed December 8, 1987, and ratified by both countries in May 1988.[45] The treaty calls for the elimination of all U.S. and Soviet intermediate-range land-based nuclear weapons (ranges of 300 to 3,500 miles [500 to 5,000 kilometers]) anywhere in the world.[46] The INF Treaty was the first which actually resulted in the destruction of any nuclear weapons (though the warheads were removed for use on other weapons), and its revolutionary provisions for on-site inspections for verification provided an important base for later agreements.

The December 1987 Reagan-Gorbachev summit in Washington where the INF Treaty was signed laid the groundwork for the first *Strategic Arms Reduction Treaty I (START I),* which was signed July 31, 1991, in Moscow at the third summit meeting between U.S. President Bush and Soviet President Gorbachev.[47] This treaty commits the Soviets to reducing their strategic weapons by more than 35 percent (from 11,000 warheads to 7,000) and the U.S. to reducing its strategic weapons by about 25 percent (from 12,000 warheads to 9,000).[48] It limits both sides to 1,600 strategic nuclear *delivery vehicles* (ballistic missiles plus bombers); 6,000 "accountable *warheads*" (warheads on bombs and cruise missiles count for less than one "accountable warhead" since it takes them 10–20 times as long to get to their targets); 4,900 *ballistic missile* warheads; and 1,100 warheads on *deployed mobile* ICBMs. The Soviet Union had to cut the number of its huge land-based SS-18 missiles by half since a limit is imposed of 1,540 warheads on 154 heavy intercontinental ballistic missiles (ICBMs). The total arsenal limits do not apply to sea-launched cruise missiles (SLCMs) because it is so difficult to verify their existence, but there are to be annual declarations for five years with regard to the number of *long-range* SLCMs with each side being restricted to 880 of them. The treaty continues for 15 years, and then is renewable for successive 15-year periods. START I was ratified by the U.S. Senate October 1, 1992,[49] and by Russia November 4, 1992.[50]

The ratification was delayed because the Soviet Union, one of the signatories of the treaty, went out of existence in December 1991. The Soviet Union was succeeded by the Commonwealth of Independent States (CIS) whose dominant member was Russia. At a meeting of the CIS in April 1992, Russia proposed that it alone become the successor to the Soviet Union with regard to START I, but the other republics with nuclear weapons—Belarus, Kazakhstan, and Ukraine—rejected that proposal.[51] In May 1992 a meeting called to resolve the problem of ratification by the former Soviet republics resulted in a protocol to START I (called the *"Lisbon Protocol"*) in which the three republics other than Russia agreed to either destroy their nuclear weapons or transfer them to Russia and also to become signatories of the Nuclear Non-Proliferation Treaty (NPT).[52] Kazakhstan ratified START I, including the protocol, in July 1992, and Belarus did the same in February 1993.[53] But at the end of 1993 Ukraine still had not ratified START I, and this postponement is also delaying action on START II—even though Ukraine has indicated that it intends to become a non-nuclear state.[54] At least part of the problem seems to be that the nuclear weapons have a great financial value and removing them is very costly while at the same time the Ukrainians are having financial problems. They also are suspicious that if they lack nuclear weapons some post–Yeltsin Russian leader might try to reassert Russian control over Ukraine.[55] Ukraine would prefer that the nuclear weapons of the former Soviet Union be controlled by the Commonwealth of Independent States rather than by Russia.

The *START II* agreement of January 3, 1992, between the U.S. and Russia aims to reduce the number of strategic nuclear weapons on both sides below the limits established by START I.[56] Each side would be limited to a total of 4,250 nuclear warheads on ICBMs, SLBMs, and heavy bombers with sublimits of 2,160 warheads on SLBMs, 1,200 on multi-warhead ICBMs, and 650 warheads (including ALCMs) on heavy bombers. After both sides have reduced their weapons to these limits, a further reduction is to be implemented before January 1, 2003. The new limit would be 3,500 warheads on strategic weapons with a sublimit of 1,750 on SLBMs. All deployed ICBMs and all heavy ICBMs will be limited to one warhead each, and all production or purchasing or testing of ICBMs with more than one warhead will be forbidden. One of the main positive points of this treaty from the point of view of the U.S. is the elimination of all of Russia's SS-18 heavy multi-warhead ICBMs. One of the concerns of some Russians is that the treaty is very favorable for the U.S. because SLBMs, of which the U.S. has many more than the Russians, are still allowed to carry more than one warhead. On the other hand, the Russians will not need to make any reductions in the number of warheads on their more modern SLBM-launching submarines while the U.S. will. It is worth nothing that the restriction of one warhead for each ICBM encourages the development of a defense system which does not need a space-based component as is envisioned in the U.S.'s SDI system since there would no longer be a great advantage to destroying a missile on its way up as there is in the case of multi-warhead missiles. As already noted, both START I and START II are being delayed by Ukraine's reluctance to ratify START I until it gets more financial assistance and also some assurance that Russia wouldn't take advantage of its proposed nuclear monopoly in its relations with Ukraine.

The dissolution of the Soviet Union at the end of 1991 also created problems for other treaties, including the *Treaty on Conventional Forces in Europe (CFE)*. Strictly speaking this treaty is not a bilateral treaty between two countries, but it is between two opposing *groups* of countries, the countries of NATO and those of the Warsaw Pact. Its aim is to cut back not on nuclear weapons but rather on the huge build-up of *non-nuclear* weapons that had occurred during the Cold War. It was originally signed in Paris on November 19, 1990, at a summit meeting of the member-states of the Conference on Security and Cooperation in Europe (CSCE).[57] The CFE Treaty set limits on the numbers of conventional weapons each of the opposing sides could have between the Atlantic Ocean and the Ural Mountains: 20,000 tanks, 20,000 artillery pieces, 30,000 armored combat vehicles, 6,800 combat aircraft, and 2,000 attack helicopters. It also permitted on-site reduction inspections. In February 1991 NATO proposed suspending talks to implement the CFE agreement on grounds that the Soviet Union was seeking to circumvent the spirit and letter of the agreement by doing such things as moving large quantities of military equipment east of the Urals.[58] In June 1991 the U.S. announced that it had reached an agreement with the Soviets on what needed to be done to comply with the treaty,[59] and in November 1991 the U.S. Senate ratified the treaty while also approving a half billion dollars to help the Soviets with the destruction of tactical nuclear weapons.[60] But a month later the Soviet Union was dissolved, so the constituent republics of what had been the Soviet Union had to work out the details of their military relations to each other, which they did at the Tashkent (Uzbekistan) Summit of May 15, 1992.[61] This agreement paved the way for the signing on June 5, 1992, of a revised CFE Treaty (known as CFE1A) calling for sharp reductions in conventional weapons and troop levels.[62] It was ratified separately by Moldova, Ukraine, and Russia in the early part of July and came into force on July 17, 1992, after an extraordinary agreement for "provisional appliance" of the treaty based on the anticipated ratification by Armenia and Belarus.[63] The first 120 days of the operation of the treaty constituted a "baseline validation period" during which inspections were made (without major incident) to determine the existing number of items of each kind which are subject to the treaty, so it will be known how many of each must be eliminated to reach the acceptable limits.[64]

The *"Open Skies" Treaty* was based on an idea first proposed by U.S. President Eisenhower in 1955 and resurrected by U.S. President Bush at a meeting of NATO in May 1989. It also began as a proposed treaty between NATO and the Warsaw Pact countries. The treaty allows countries to make observation flights over the territory of the other countries which are signatories of the treaty. The aim is to eliminate concerns that some other country might be preparing for some kind of military action. The negotiation of this treaty was intertwined with that of the Conventional Forces in Europe (CFE) Treaty just discussed. The "open skies" idea was agreed to in principle by all concerned parties in February 1990, but because of concerns of the Soviet Union and then the break-up of the Soviet Union the treaty was not put into final form and signed until March 24, 1992, in Helsinki at a meeting convened by CSCE.[65] It now has the form of an agreement between individual NATO members and the individual countries which once made up the Warsaw Pact Organization, including the various separate republics of the former Soviet Union. The treaty is to enter into force 60 days after it has been ratified by 20 countries. As of July 1993 27 countries had signed the treaty but only seven had ratified it.[66]

The context for arms control agreements since the end of the Cold War is much different from the situation that existed previously. Instead of great tension between the opposing sides, the attitude now has become one of cooperation. The likelihood of war between what had been opposing sides is approaching zero. There is some residual fear, but nevertheless the atmosphere is one of pragmatic problem-solving on how to cut back on the huge quantities of these weapons that are no longer needed while simultaneously discouraging the selling of the weapons or the knowledge of how to produce them to countries in other parts of the world.

Before concluding this section on arms control agreements, let us try to make some observations about the bilateral arms control agreements made between the U.S. and the Soviet Union during the Cold War period. *First,* we can note that such agreements were possible in part because the superpowers could use the new technology of high-flying reconnaissance aircraft and satellites to keep track of each other's activities with some confidence that they wouldn't be greatly deceived about what the other one was doing. *Second,* treaties such as the Partial Test Ban (PTB) Treaty and the Non-Proliferation Treaty (NPT) show that even though the superpowers were engaged in a struggle against each other, they could still engage in a cooperative effort to discourage other nations from becoming viable competitors. *Third,* the two superpowers were quite willing to restrict the area of competition between themselves as is shown by their acceptance of the Antarctic Treaty, the Outer Space Treaty, the Latin American Nuclear-Free Zone Treaty, the Sea-Bed Treaty, the Biological Weapons Convention, the two parts of the SALT I agreement, the Threshold Test Ban Treaty, the Treaty on Peaceful Nuclear Explosions, the Environmental Modification Convention, SALT II, the Inhumane Weapons Convention, the Intermediate-Range Nuclear Forces Treaty, and START I. *Fourth,* despite strident rhetoric in the U.S. about how the Soviets were violating arms control agreements, even the "hawks" in the Reagan administration agreed to abide by SALT II for more than five years even when the agreement had not been ratified by the U.S. Senate, and the same suspicious administration also went on to negotiate other arms control agreements with the Soviets. *Fifth,* in negotiating arms control agreements each side sought agreements which they thought would be advantageous for themselves. For example, in SALT I the U.S. didn't want the treaty to deal with the number of warheads or the number of bombers because it had an advantage over the Soviets in those areas. For that same treaty the Soviets, counting on their ability to soon put multiple warheads on a single missile just as the Americans were already doing, negotiated for a superiority in the number of launchers. *Sixth,* until Gorbachev and the winding down of the Cold War, the aim of the agreements was not to cut back on the number of weapons but rather to control the future increase in weapons of particular kinds. The effect was to channel research and development into those areas not restricted by the agreements. That is how we arrived at the contest over medium-range missiles in Europe: the number of long-range strategic weapons was restricted by SALT I and SALT II, but no limits had been placed on the number of medium-range missiles one could have. *Seventh,* if there hadn't been arms control agreements, the Cold War probably would have been even more costly and more dangerous than it was.

Modern Non-Nuclear Weaponry

When discussing the destructive potential of modern war, there is a tendency to think mainly of nuclear weapons. Sometimes in arms control agreements special attention is given also to chemical and biological weapons while the remaining weapons tend to be lumped together into a miscellaneous class called "conventional weapons." But a separate class of "chemical and biological weapons" is not always easy to distinguish. For example, is napalm a conventional weapon or a chemical weapon? Are incendiary bombs conventional weapons or chemical weapons? This section will deal with all kinds of non-nuclear weapons. These are the weapons typically used in warfare, and they are rapidly becoming more sophisticated and deadly.[67] At the same time it should not be forgotten that even in World War II more people were killed in Tokyo in a May 1945 raid using "conventional" incendiary bombs than were killed ten weeks later at Hiroshima by an atomic bomb.[68]

In Vietnam, the U.S. introduced many new weapons designed mainly to kill or seriously impair individual persons.[69] Besides using napalm and white phosphorus, which had been developed earlier, the U.S. used fragmentation bombs loaded with difficult-to-detect plastic fragments and also asphyxiation bombs that released a cloud vapor which, when ignited, quickly consumed all the oxygen in the area. Such new antipersonnel weapons, plus others being developed, promise that the number of injured people and the severity of their wounds will be much greater in future wars than has been the case in the past. Lasers now being used to guide weapons may accidentally blind enemy soldiers, and it is likely that efforts are already being made to develop them further with the aim not only of nullifying optical sensors being used to find targets but also of deliberately blinding enemy personnel, either temporarily or permanently.[70]

The biggest difference in the new weapons is the improved range and accuracy of projectiles made possible by radar, television cameras, heat-seeking devices, infrared devices, radio beams, radio control, and tiny computers as well as the lasers just mentioned. In earlier times soldiers practiced for hours to be better able to hit what they were aiming at. A huge proportion of the firepower delivered in battle did not hit the target. But that situation is rapidly changing. The new precision-guided munitions (PGMs) or "smart weapons" are much more likely to hit the target. The targets at which these devices are aimed are very unlikely to escape destruction. For example, during the Vietnam War two bridges which had escaped destruction during many regular bombing attacks were knocked out in the first effort using smart bombs.[71] The great accuracy of these new precision-guided munitions means that during future battles it will not be safe to be in an airplane or a tank or a ship or anything else that is easy to locate. The military answer to this situation is pilotless aircraft and eventually crewless tanks. An airplane equipped with television cameras and the proper control systems can be flown by a "pilot" on the ground and can take greater risks of being shot down than would be reasonable with a pilot aboard. It could even be used for kamikazi missions where the plane itself is crashed into the target, which in essence is what cruise missiles do.

The automated battlefield is the prospect of the future.[72] It can be expected that we will even see robotic killing machines, "weapons programmed to kill without reference to human authority."[73] The outcome of battle will depend on the technological capabilities of the weapons, which will necessarily have been designed and produced well before the war begins. The development of the automated battlefield and the training of personnel to use such equipment will be very expensive for nations that want to participate in preparing for such battles, but any nation that does not get involved in the use of the new weaponry will be as helpless against this military technology as primitive peoples with bows and arrows were against Europeans equipped with guns. The cost of developing and producing these new weapons will obviously be high, and the contest for superiority will be unending.[74] The military has never been particularly enthusiastic about nuclear weapons, since they are too powerful to require much need for complex strategy, but with the new electronic, unmanned conventional weapons the game of war becomes very challenging. The military-industrial complex will also gain new significance because the outcome of battles is likely to depend as much on the weapons available as on the ingenuity of the military leaders.

Chemical and biological weapons are likely to be important in the future not so much because of their likely use on the battlefield (they are difficult to control) but because of their possible use against large populations by those countries (and terrorist groups) which lack the capability or the financial resources to build nuclear weapons. These kinds of non-nuclear weapons are much less expensive to build than nuclear weapons, and the facilities for building them are much easier to hide from "enemy" inspectors. Retired Green Beret commander Colonel William Wilson observes:

> Biologial weapons come cheap. A panel of experts told the United Nations that in a large-scale operation against a civilian population, casualties might cost $2,000 per square kilometer for conventional weapons, $800 for nuclear weapons, or $600 for nerve gas, but only $1 for biological weapons. In the not-too-distant future, countries throughout the world will learn how to produce [through genetic engineering] an enormous variety of large biological molecules, including toxins, on a scale that was previously inconceivable.
>
> Gene-splicing's potential to facilitate the large-scale production of biological and toxin weapons raises another danger—proliferation. Unlike the complex and expensive technological infrastructure required to design and produce nuclear weapons, a sophisticated recombinant-DNA facility can be set up without a large capital investment. Since 1982, U.S. Army scientists have made increasing use of gene-splicing to study and prepare defenses against extremely hazardous biological toxins. Between 1980 and 1984 the number of Pentagon-funded projects using recombinant-DNA technology grew from zero to more than forty, including eleven projects under way in army and navy laboratories and thirty-two others contracted out to universities and private technology firms in Israel, Scotland, and the United States.[75]

It seems that biological weapons, and to a lesser extent chemical weapons, may become the weapons of choice—especially for deterrence and terrorism—for poorer countries which can't afford long-range ballistic missiles and nuclear weapons.

XII. Institutional Aspects of the Contemporary Situation

There are many kinds of international institutions in the world today, but the one most obviously relevant to the problem of war is the United Nations. It will be our first topic, and we will discuss it in four sections: its structure, its peacekeeping activities, the influences on it, and its accomplishments. Other international institutions also require some attention even though their relation to the war problem may be less direct. For example, there are many government-sponsored *global administrative or functional agencies* which are important to our study because of their roles throughout the world in solving social problems. We also need to consider *regional functional and political organizations* formed by national governments. (An administrative or functional organization is limited to dealing with one particular kind of problem, such as regulating the use of a river or controlling disease, while a political organization addresses any kind of issue of interest to the member nations.) Finally, we need to discuss international *nongovernmental organizations,* that is, international organizations formed by individuals and private organizations rather than by representatives of national governments.

The Structure of the United Nations

The first effort to create a global political institution was the formation of the League of Nations after World War I. Forty-two nations were original members of the League, and 20 others became members at one time or another, including all the major powers except the United States. The main structures of the League were the Assembly (one representative from each nation), the Council (permanent representation for the Great Powers and elected representation from other nations), and a Secretariat (civil servants employed by the League). There were also a number of specialized functional agencies to handle particular international problems, all of which in one form or another have now become specialized agencies of the United Nations. One of the basic principles of the League was that no nation surrendered any of its sovereignty over its own affairs when it became a member. Measures other than those dealing with procedural issues required unanimous support in both the Assembly and the Council.

World War II seems to have come about partly as the result of the League's failure to act decisively when powerful nations such as Japan and Italy began to engage in expansionist military activities. Great Britain and France in particular seemed to be guided more by balance-of-power thinking than by the provisions of the Covenant of the League, which they tended to regard as good for public relations with their own citizenry but too idealistic for use in the real world.[1] In 1933 the Assembly of the League adopted a resolution condemning Japan for its invasion of Manchuria, but Japan responded by quitting the League. In 1936, when the League did nothing to protect Ethiopia from being taken over by Italy, several countries withdrew, and Italy itself withdrew near the end of 1937. The Soviet Union was expelled in 1939 for attacking Finland. After the German conquests of 1939–40 (which included France), Great Britain was the only great power remaining and very few other nations continued as members. For all practical purposes the League ended in June of 1940 when Secretary-General Avenol resigned, though a final "funeral session" was held in 1946 after the United Nations had been formed.

The formation of the League's successor, the United Nations, began even while World War II was still being fought. President Franklin Roosevelt, aware of the fate of Wilson's plan for U.S. participation in the League of Nations, decided not to wait until the war was over to involve the United States in an organization to preserve the peace. In January of 1942 representatives from 26 nations met in Washington, D.C., and adopted a "Declaration by the United Nations" to fight together against Germany, Italy, and Japan and to accept the democratic and anti-imperialist principles enunciated in the Atlantic Charter, which had been approved by Roosevelt and Britain's Prime Minister Winston Churchill in August of 1941. A resolution calling for the creation of a general international peace-keeping organization was adopted by the United States, the Soviet Union, the United Kingdom, and China at the Moscow Conference in October of 1943. At Washington in August of 1944 and at Yalta in February of 1945 representatives of the big powers agreed on the general structure of the United Nations. The actual final wording of the Charter of the United Nations was worked out by delegates from 50 nations[2] in San Francisco in April, May, and June of 1945. (Germany surrendered, ending the war in Europe, on May 8, 1945.) The Charter was signed on June 26, 1945, and acquired sufficient ratifications to go into effect on October 24, 1945, the date generally recognized as the beginning of the United Nations. (Japan surrendered, ending World War II, on August 15, 1945.) The first session of the U.N. General Assembly was held in London in January 1946. Among other things, it decided to establish permanent headquarters in or near New York City. Most of the subsequent meetings of the United Nations were held in temporary facilities in and around New York until 1952, when the organization moved into its present building along the East River in Manhattan.

The structure and principles of operation of the United Nations are similar to those of the League of Nations.[3] Each nation retains its national sovereignty; that is, each nation decides for itself what it will or won't do and can withdraw from the organization whenever it so desires. Disputes between nations are to be resolved by negotiation rather than war. Aggression by one nation against another is to be stopped by collective security, that is, by collective action of all the other nations against the aggressor, using economic measures primarily but including military action if necessary. In both the League and the United Nations, the primary bodies have been the all-inclusive Assembly and the smaller Council in which the big powers have more influence. The greatest difference is that the United Nations has more machinery devoted to promoting economic and social progress in the poorer nations of the world.

The main body of the United Nations is the General Assembly, in which each member nation may have five representatives but only one vote. The General Assembly has the power to make decisions concerning the operation of the United Nations, such as determining the budget of the organization and electing representatives to various U.N. bodies including the Security Council, but with regard to other matters it can only make recommendations to the member governments. Actions are taken on the basis of majority rule (two-thirds majority on certain important issues) rather than requiring unanimity as was the case in the League of Nations. The General Assembly cannot pass laws for the world as a legislature could, but neither is the Assembly merely a "debating society" as it has sometimes been called, for it does govern the operation of the U.N. organization itself. The number of nations in the United Nations has increased from the original 51 members to 184 in 1993.

The primary function of the Security Council is the maintenance of peace. The five major powers who fought together to win World War II were expected to work together to preserve the peace. Thus the United States, the Soviet Union (the Russian Federation after December 1991), the United Kingdom, France, and China are permanent members of the Security Council. Any one of them can prevent Security Council action by casting a veto. Originally the Security Council had six other nations elected to the Council by the General Assembly, but the Charter was amended to increase that number to ten in 1965. A measure can be enacted by the Security Council only if it receives an affirmative vote of nine of the 15 members and no permanent member is against it. All members of the United Nations, upon joining the organization, commit themselves to accepting and carrying out the decisions of the Security Council. In principle, then, decisions of the Security Council are binding in a way that resolutions passed by the General Assembly are not.

A third major organ of the United Nations is the Economic and Social Council. The main function of this body is to coordinate efforts to promote economic and social welfare throughout the world. It does this by working with the many specialized agencies of the United Nations and by establishing its own committees and commissions. For example, it has commissions on the status of women, on statistics, on population, on social development, on narcotics, and on human rights. Originally the Economic and Social Council consisted of 18 representatives selected by the General Assembly, but the number was increased to 27 by an amendment which became effective in 1965 and then to 54 by another amendment which came into effect in 1973.

The fourth main organ of the United Nations, the Trusteeship Council, has been very successful in its task of supervising the transition of Trust Territories from being dependent territories under the control of larger nation-states to being independent nation-states. Of the original 11 "strategic" Trust Territories, all have already become independent except one Pacific island mini-state, Belau (sometimes called "Palau"), which formerly was one of the four components of the U.N. Trust Territory of the Pacific administered by the U.S. The other three components of that territory were the Federated States of Micronesia, the Marshall Islands, and the Northern Mariana Islands; and in 1982 they signed compacts of free association with the U.S. granting them internal sovereignty and U.S. aid while the U.S. would control their defense and foreign policies. Belau also signed such a compact, but it could not be implemented because of U.S. objection to the clauses in the Belau constitution which "banned the entry, storage, or disposal of nuclear, chemical, or biological weapons."[4] A referendum to allow easier amending of the constitution passed in 1992, so it seems that Belau also is on the way to leaving the category of "Trust Territory." At that point the Trusteeship Council would have discharged all its responsibilities and perhaps could be converted into a Council for the Rights of Indigenous Peoples[5] or into a wider-scope Human Rights Council.

The fifth main organ of the United Nations is the International Court of Justice, the revised version of the Permanent Court of International Justice which had been created by the League of Nations. Like the earlier Court, the International Court of Justice meets in the Hague, Netherlands, and has 15 judges. Every three years five new judges are selected for nine-year terms, and no country may be represented by more than one judge. The aim of the Court is to render legal decisions in cases involving international law, the interpretation of treaties, and the like. Although the Court can give advisory opinions when asked to do so by the General Assembly or the Security Council, only nations can be parties in any actual case to be decided by the Court. Furthermore, all nations which may be directly affected by a decision of the Court must agree in advance to abide by the decision before the Court will consider it.[6] Naturally, it is difficult to persuade an alleged violator to make such an agreement.

The sixth main part of the United Nations is the Secretariat, the employees of the United Nations under the directorship of the Secretary-General. The Secretary-General not only is in charge of all the personnel employed by the United Nations but also has special responsibilities such as making an annual report to the General Assembly and bringing to the attention of the Security Council any matter which he believes threatens world peace. The Secretary-General is elected by the General Assembly after being recommended by the Security Council. Although no term of office is stipulated in the Charter, the first General Assembly decided that a Secretary-General should serve for five years and could be reappointed. The Secretary-Generals of the United Nations have been Trygve Lie of Norway (1946–52), Dag Hammarskjöld of Sweden (1953–61), U Thant of Burma (1961–71), Kurt Waldheim of Austria (1972–81), Javier Pérez de Cuéllar of Peru (1982–91), and Boutros Boutros-Ghali of Egypt (1992–   ).

Peacekeeping by the United Nations

According to the provisions of the Charter of the United Nations, international peace is to be maintained by a system called *collective security*. According to this strategy if any member nation of the United Nations is attacked, all the other member nations are to help the victim nation against the aggressor. This approach to keeping the peace goes beyond the traditional alliance system in which a particular group of nations agree that if any one of them is attacked by a potential enemy state or alliance they will all fight together. With a system of collective security, on the other hand, it is assumed that all member nations of the *whole international community* will work together, militarily if necessary, against *any* country or group of countries that attack any one of them. For such coordinated action to take place, some person or body must be able to indicate when aggression has taken place and what kind of action (for example, diplomatic sanctions, economic sanctions, deployment of military forces) should be taken against the aggressor. In the U.N. the responsibility for indicating when aggression has taken place and coordinating the effort against the aggressor belongs to the Security Council.

The League of Nations had been committed to this same collective security approach to peace, but the strategy had failed miserably when Japan attacked Manchuria in 1931 and again when Italy attacked Ethiopia in 1935. Even when there is agreement that aggression has occurred and that military action should be taken, it is difficult for national leaders to act in accord with the collective security principle. Each nation-state realizes that military action is risky and that some of the soldiers involved in the fighting will probably be injured and killed. At the moment of truth national leaders and their citizenry are likely to ask themselves, "Why should soldiers of *our* country get killed to help protect some *other country?*" The answer to that question is that participating in military action against an aggressor is part of one's responsibility as a member of the United Nations, because that is the system by which the U.N. is supposed to keep the peace. But that is a hard answer to sell to the public when it is members of their families who will be getting injured and killed. The leading members of the League of Nations were not ready to make the required sacrifice in 1931, nor in 1935, nor in the critical years after that leading up to World War II. Nevertheless the United Nations, which was established after World War II, was based on trying the strategy of collective security again. Near the end of World War II the U.S., at that time the undisputed leading world power, believed that Woodrow Wilson's League of Nations had failed only because the U.S. had not become a member. The Americans were confident that under U.S. leadership collective security would work for the United Nations.

During the first few years of the U.N., the United States and Britain tried to use the organization as a tool for opposing Communist moves in Eastern Europe, but these efforts failed because the Soviets simply used their veto in the Security Council to prevent any action by the U.N. When Communist troops from North Korea invaded anti–Communist South Korea in 1950, however, the U.N. Security Council, prodded by the U.S., declared North Korea to be an aggressor and called on U.N. members to help the South Koreans and their U.S. allies. This action was possible only because the Russians were boycotting the Security Council at the time to protest China's being represented at the U.N. by Chiang Kai-shek's appointees, even though Communist revolutionary forces led by Mao Zedong had conquered all of China except the island of Taiwan. Sixteen other nations sent troops in response to the call of the Security Council, but the brunt of the fighting was borne by South Korean and U.S. forces. Nevertheless this action by the U.N. marked the first time in history that an international organization had organized a collective military force to resist armed aggression.

At first the forces defending South Korea were driven back, but eventually a counter-attack was launched. The U.N. forces, commanded by U.S. General Douglas MacArthur, pushed northward past the 38th parallel, which had been the boundary between North and South Korea. As they pushed farther north, the Chinese Communists warned that they would enter the war if the northerly advance was not halted. The warning was not heeded. Using large numbers of troops, the "volunteer" Chinese forces pushed the U.N. forces back toward the 38th parallel. After two more years of indecisive fighting, in 1953 a truce was worked out, and the boundary between North and South Korea was set not far from where it had been before the war.

An important development took place at the U.N. during this Korean conflict. After the Security Council had declared North Korea to be an aggressor, the Soviet Union returned to its seat in the Security Council in order to veto any further resolutions for U.N. action. The U.N. General Assembly responded by passing the "Uniting for Peace Resolution." This resolution declared that the General Assembly can make recommendations to the member nations (including recommending the use of armed forces) whenever the Security Council fails to act in cases where peace is threatened or aggression has occurred. This tactic of taking action in the General Assembly when the Security Council fails to act has been utilized two other times. It was used in 1956 with American and Soviet approval after an attack by Britain, Israel, and France against Egypt; and it was used again in 1960 to authorize the continued use of U.N. troops in the Congo when the Security Council which had originally authorized the mission failed to support its continuance.

The only time that a heavily armed military force has been used in a U.N.-supervised collective security action against a specified aggressor was in Korea, but during the Gulf War in 1990-91 the U.N. played a less direct role in a military "collective security" effort to stop aggression. In August 1990 the military forces of Iraq under the leadership of Saddam Hussein invaded and conquered the small neighboring oil-rich country of Kuwait. Iraq had several complaints against the Kuwaiti leadership, some of them tangentially related to the Iran-Iraq War of 1980–1988, and decided to use military force to put an end to its control of territory which Saddam Hussein claimed really belonged to Iraq anyway. Western countries, led by the U.S., were concerned that Saddam was gaining control over more of the world's oil supply and might try to acquire even more by taking over the oil fields of Saudi Arabia too. Furthermore, the Iraqi conquest of Kuwait was the very kind of naked aggression that the U.N. was supposed to prevent, and it was quickly condemned by the U.N. Security Council. U.S. President Bush sent American military forces to Saudi Arabia immediately to stop any further advances by Iraqi forces and then proceeded to organize a large-scale multi-national "collective security" effort to take economic and, if necessary, military action against Iraq. The U.N. Security Council passed a resolution authorizing member states to use "all necessary means"[7] to get Iraqi forces out of Kuwait and set a deadline of January 15, 1991, for the forces to be removed. When the deadline passed without an Iraqi withdrawal, massive air attacks by the U.S.-led coalition were carried out against Iraq for the rest of the month and into February. On February 24, 1991, a ground attack began which ended only 100 hours later with a very one-sided victory for the coalition forces.[8] The fighting ended when Saddam Hussein agreed unconditionally to all U.N. demands. The aggression against Kuwait had been stopped under the authority of the U.N. Security Council, but the military action itself had been directed by the U.S. and not by the U.N.

Most of the U.N.'s efforts to keep the peace, however, have not involved military action guided by the strategy of collective security. The main response of the U.N. to conflict situations has been to implement what has come to be called a *"peacekeeping operation."* Such an operation traditionally consisted of sending an observer mission to some area of tension or sending lightly armed soldiers to police a truce between previously warring parties, but especially since the end of the Cold War in 1988 (when U.N. peacekeepers were awarded the Nobel Peace Prize) these peacekeeping operations have expanded in concept to include a wide range of activities such as monitoring elections and protecting those providing humanitarian assistance to refugees.[9] It is worth noting that even though this new approach of setting up peacekeeping operations has become the usual U.N. response to conflict situations (instead of relying on collective security as a way of keeping the peace), such operations are not explicitly authorized by the Charter of the U.N.[10]

The Middle East has been the scene of several peacekeeping operations.[11] (See maps on page 228.) In 1947 the U.N. General Assembly passed a resolution calling for the partition of Palestine into a Jewish state and an Arab state with international status for Jerusalem. This arrangement was to go into effect after British forces left the area, but even before that withdrawal the Arabs and Jews were engaged in war with each other as the Arabs tried to prevent the establishment of a separate Jewish state in an area where much land was privately owned by Arabs. The Security Council established a Truce Commission to try to prevent violence. On May 14, 1948, the Israelis proclaimed the independence of the state of Israel, and fighting expanded as Arab nations in the area used their armies to support the Palestinian Arabs. The Security Council called for a cease-fire but it lasted only four weeks. Then the Security Council called for another cease-fire and made an effort to enforce it with its own Truce Supervision Organization (UNTSO). Eventually a truce was made in 1949 which left the Israelis in control of slightly more territory than they would have had according to the 1947 U.N. resolution calling for partition.

In 1956 Egypt nationalized the Suez Canal which had been operated by the Suez Canal Company, chief shares in which were owned by the British government and French private companies. The British and French governments tried to work out a plan for internationalization of the Canal, but the Egyptians rejected this proposal. Then Israel, Britain, and France attacked Egypt. Eager to keep the Soviets from sending troops into the region as they had threatened to do, U.S. President Eisenhower condemned the attack against Egypt, and the United States and the Soviet Union worked together in the U.N. to stop further aggression against Egypt. After Britain and France vetoed the idea in the Security Council, the General Assembly authorized the U.N. Emergency Force (UNEF) to supervise the cease-fire under the provisions of the "Uniting for Peace Resolution" previously discussed. Israel refused to allow the UNEF troops on the territory it controlled, so they were stationed only on the Egyptian side of the border.

In 1967 Egypt's Nasser asked Secretary-General U Thant to remove the U.N. troops from Egyptian territory. Then, having already excluded Israeli ships from the Suez Canal, Nasser inaugurated a blockade of the Gulf of Aqaba, Israel's only access to the Red Sea. Unable to get much help from its allies in overcoming the blockade, the Israelis launched a lightning attack on Egypt, Syria, and Jordan. In six days the Israelis gained control of the whole Sinai peninsula, the Gaza Strip, the West Bank, all of Jerusalem,

ISRAEL

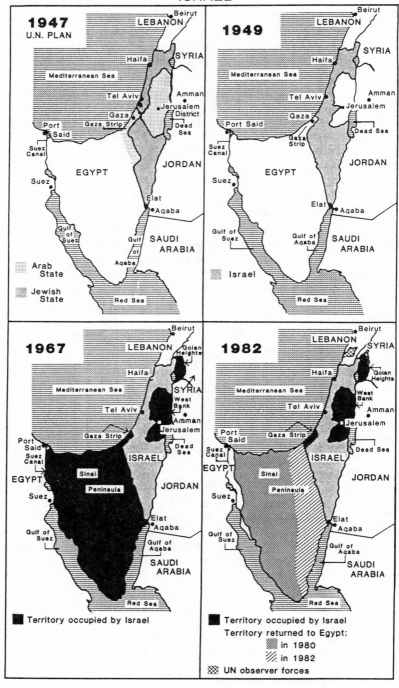

and the Golan Heights. The U.N. Security Council called for a cease-fire, and the call was soon accepted. This time, however, the Israelis maintained control over most of the territory they had taken. In November of 1967 the Security Council passed the crucial Resolution 242, setting down principles for the solution of the Middle East conflict. It called for withdrawal of Israeli forces from territory taken in the recent war, an end to war in the area, free navigation for all ships through international waterways such as the Suez Canal, resolution of the problem of what to do with the Palestinian Arab refugees, and maintenance of the territorial integrity and political independence of all countries in the area.

In October 1973 war broke out again, initiated this time by Arabs who had become impatient with the lack of progress in getting land back from the Israelis. The Israelis were pushed back at first but soon regained all the territory they had lost, and more. Once again the Security Council called for an end of military activities and sent in a U.N. force to supervise the truce. The U.N. Emergency Force (UNEF II) was stationed between Israeli and Egyptian forces, while the U.N. Disengagement Observer Force (UNDOF) was stationed between Israeli and Syrian forces. The establishment of these U.N.-sponsored peacekeeping forces was significant because for the first time the Soviet Union actively supported a U.N. peacekeeping effort and troops from a Communist country (Poland) were a part of the peacekeeping force. The Camp David accords of September 1978 led to the Egyptian-Israeli peace agreement of March 1979 wherein Israel returned occupied territory in the Sinai peninsula to Egypt in exchange for Egypt's recognition of Israel's existence as a nation.

Near the end of 1976 Syrian forces took over much of Lebanon in an effort to stop fighting between Muslims and Christians in that country. The Israelis did not want hostile forces along their northern border, however, and gave strong military support to the Christian, anti–Muslim forces in the southern part of Lebanon. In 1978, after over a year of civil war in Lebanon, the U.N. Security Council voted to send in the U. N. Interim Force in Lebanon (UNIFIL) to try to maintain some public order in the southern part of that country. This peacekeeping operation in the midst of civil strife without well-defined borders between the belligerents was a new role for U.N. forces and did not work out well. The Israelis complained that terrorist attacks were still being launched by Palestinians in Lebanon, and in June 1982 they invaded Lebanon in an effort to eliminate all military activities of the Palestine Liberation Organization (PLO) in that country. In June 1985 Israeli forces were pulled out of Lebanon except for a narrow strip of land just north of the Israel-Lebanon border and south of the area in Lebanon patrolled by U.N. forces. When Iraq was defeated in the Gulf War in February 1991 and a new Israeli government was elected in June 1992, the situation seemed ripe for a new settlement between Israel and the Palestinians. After much negotiation a "Declaration of Principles" was signed by Israel and the Palestine Liberation Organization in September 1993.

The Middle East is by no means the only part of the world in which U.N. peacekeeping efforts have been implemented. Even though it is not generally considered to be a "peacekeeping operation," in October 1946 the U.N. General Assembly, responding to complaints by Greece that Communist guerrillas were infiltrating from the north, authorized the creation of a U.N. Special Committee on the Balkans (UNSCOB) to monitor the situation.[11] This commission made annual reports supportive of the Greek viewpoint from 1947 until 1951. Armed conflict in Kashmir between Pakistan and India led in 1948 to the establishment of the U.N. Military Observer Group in India and Pakistan (UNMOGIP) to monitor a cease-fire worked out with the assistance of a commission appointed by the U.N.[12]

In 1958 the U.N. Security Council authorized the establishment of the U.N. Observation Group in Lebanon (UNOGIL) to investigate charges that the United Arab Republic (a temporary union of Egypt and Syria) was attempting to overthrow the Lebanese government.[13] In 1960 the Security Council authorized the establishment of the U.N. Congo Force (ONUC) to assist the newly independent nation of the Congo (now called "Zaire") in suppressing a rebellion in the mineral-rich province of Katanga.[14] This rebellion was not merely an internal affair, however, because many of those fighting for Katanga's secession from the new government were European mercenaries flown into the area by foreign planes to keep foreign mining operations out of the control of the new national government. The first aim of the U.N. was to get all foreign mercenaries out of the country. After several military skirmishes lasting until 1963, the local leaders of the rebellion were persuaded to accept control of the province by the national government of the Congo. It was 1964, however, before all of the U.N. forces were removed.

When a dispute arose in 1961 between the Netherlands and Indonesia concerning whether or not the western part of New Guinea (West Irian) was to be considered a part of the newly independent Indonesia, the U.N. Security Force (UNSC) was sent in to bring order. In September 1962 the U.N. Temporary Executive Authority (UNTEA) took charge of administering the area until the sentiments of the local population could be determined.[15] In 1963 the U.N. Yemen Observation Mission (UNYOM) was sent into Yemen during a civil war between forces supported on the one hand by Saudi Arabia and on the other by the United Arab Republic; its recommendations were not accepted and it withdrew in 1964.[16] Near the end of 1963 fighting broke out between the Greek and Turkish residents of the newly independent nation of Cyprus, and in 1964 the U.N. Peacekeeping Force in Cyprus (UNFICYP) was sent there to maintain order.[17] They have remained, though they were unable to do much except to maintain control of the Nicosia Airport during the 1974 conflict when armed forces from Turkey invaded the island. In 1965 war again broke out between India and Pakistan, this time not only in Kashmir but all along the border. The U.N. Security Council reacted by expanding the size of UNMOGIP already on the scene in Kashmir and by creating the new U.N. India-Pakistan Observation Mission (UNIPOM) to supervise the cease-fire along the rest of the border for six months.[18] After that the U.N. observers were withdrawn except from Kashmir itself. In 1965 the Mission of the Representative of the Secretary-General in the Dominican Republic (DOMREP) was sent to that country to observe the tense situation resulting from armed conflict between leftist revolutionary forces and the government plus the subsequent intervention by U.S. Marines.[19] DOMREP worked in cooperation with the Inter-American Peace Force (IAPF) coordinated by the Organization of American States.

One of the most successful of all U.N. operations was the supervising of the withdrawal of South African forces from Namibia (formerly called Southwest Africa), the bringing together of opposing racial and ideological groups to establish a new constitution, and then the election of a new democratic regime for that country.[20] The U.N. team was called the U.N. Transition Assistance Group (UNTAG). The project began with a Security Council resolution in 1978, but implementation did not occur until April 1989 after Cuban and South African involvement in the fighting in Angola was ended. A Constituent Assembly was elected in November 1989, a new constitution was adopted by the Constituent Assembly in February 1990, and independence was declared on March 21, 1990.[21] The next month Namibia became a member of the U.N. It has become a model of what a racially integrated southern African country can be.[22]

Having successfully put a government together in Namibia, the U.N. decided to try to do it again in Cambodia.[23] There the process started with the small U.N. Advanced Mission in Cambodia (UNAMIC) moving into the country during November 1991 to supervise a truce agreed to by the three warring factions the month before. The U.N. Transitional Authority in Cambodia (UNTAC) set up its operations in March 1992 and then conducted elections in May 1993.[24] There was uncertainty concerning whether the party which had been in power would accept its defeat in the election, but eventually the two opposing sides who had participated in the election process agreed to serve as co-chairmen of a transitional government under the leadership of former monarch Prince Norodom Sihanouk.[25] Even the non-cooperating Khmer Rouge guerrillas have indicated that they want to join the newly formed government, but they are still trying to use military force against government forces in an effort to get into a better bargaining position for a truce. Also it seems that long-term stability in Cambodia will require economic development as well as political peace.[26]

The end of the Cold War in 1988 meant that the operation of the U.N. Security Council was no longer hampered by the threat of vetoes from the U.S. and the Russians. The result was that 17 new U.N. peacekeeping operations were authorized from 1988 through 1993.[27] The U.N. Iraq/Kuwait Observer Mission (UNIKOM) was established in early 1991 at the end of the previously discussed "collective security" action known as the Gulf War. The U.N. Security Council had approved the terms of the truce which brought the military action against Iraq to an end. Consequently, it sent in its team of U.N. inspectors to monitor the Iraq-Kuwait border and to guarantee that the halt in arms production agreed to by Iraq was implemented. In addition to those U.N. efforts mentioned elsewhere in this section on "Peacekeeping by the United Nations," the following should also be mentioned: (1) the U.N. Good Offices Mission in Afghanistan and Pakistan (UNGOMAP) created to monitor the Afghanistan/Pakistan border as the Soviets withdrew their forces in 1988; (2) the U.N. Iran-Iraq Military Observer Group (UNIIMOG) established to monitor the Iraq-Iran border after their war ended in 1988; (3) the U.N. Angola Verification Mission (UNAVEM I) set up in Angola as the Cubans were withdrawing their forces in 1989, and then UNAVEM II established in June 1991 to supervise peace accords between two opposing domestic factions in Angola and subsequent elections; (4) the U.N. Observer Group in Central America (ONUCA), set up in 1989 to verify on-site inspections in the carrying out of the Guatemala Agreement (Esquipulas II) to stop cross-boundary shipping of arms to guerrilla groups in El Salvador, Honduras, and Nicaragua; (5) the U.N. Observer Mission in El Salvador (ONUSAL) set up in El Salvador starting in July 1991 to oversee the stalled peace process there and to provide a civilian-controlled military force for El Salvador; (6) the U.N. Operation for Mozambique (UNUMOZ) set up in Mozambique in 1992 to not only monitor an agreement ending the civil war there but also to prepare the way for elections conducted by the parties themselves; (7) the U.N. Observer Mission Uganda-Rwanda (UNOMUR) set up along the Uganda/Rwanda border in July 1993 to prevent military assistance coming into Rwanda from Uganda; (8) the U.N. Observer Mission in Georgia (UNOMIG) set up in August 1993 in the former Soviet republic on the eastern coast of the Black Sea in order to monitor a cease-fire agreement between opposing military forces in the Abkhaz section of the country where some factions are seeking independence from Georgia[28]; and (9) the U.N. Observer Mission in Liberia (UNOMIL) established in September 1993 to oversee a July peace agreement signed between the warring opposing political factions in that country.[29]

The U.N. has also been called on more and more often to monitor elections where there is an international dimension relevant to the stability or security within that region of the world.[30] In 1989 the U.N. Observation Mission for the Verification of Elections in Nicaragua (UNOMVEN) was set up to monitor the important February 1990 elections in Nicaragua in which the leftist Sandinistas lost control over Nicaragua.[31] In December 1990 and January 1991 observers from the U.N. helped monitor the two-stage elections in Haiti, but some of the military leadership in that country have prevented the newly elected Jean-Bertrand Aristide from taking office. As a result the U.N. Mission in Haiti (UNMIH) was authorized to operate in Haiti starting in September 1993. In September 1991 the U.N. Mission for a Referendum in Western Sahara (MINURSO) was dispatched to Western

Sahara to prepare for a referendum to determine whether the people in that region claimed by Morocco want to be part of Morocco or want to become a separate independent country.[32] Elections supervised by U.N. personnel (UNAVEM II) were held in Angola in September 1992, but the UNITA Party would not abide by the results.[33] Thus one can see that a growing problem for the U.N. is the refusal of military armed factions to accept the results of U.N.-monitored elections.[34]

Also the U.N. has embarked on coordinating programs of humanitarian assistance, a task that often requires subsequent protection to be furnished by U.N. peacekeeping forces. One example of such an operation that began with a humanitarian focus is that being carried out in Somalia. The first involvement was by the U.N. Operation in Somalia (UNOSOM I) in April 1992. Then, in response to concern about the continuing level of armed violence in that country, U.S.-led heavily armed military action came to Somalia as part of the U.N. United Task Force (UNITAF) in December 1992.[35] In May 1993 a new larger U.N. force involving participants from more countries (UNOSOM II) began being deployed with a focus on disarming the fighting factions and protecting relief workers.[36] The killing of some members of the U.N. forces in August, September, and October of 1993 has led to an effort to focus more attention on a political solution rather than a military one.

One of the most difficult and complex missions for U.N. peacekeeping has been in the former Yugoslavia. (See map on page 234 for borders and other information as of December 1992.) Yugoslavia was a multinational state ruled by Marshal Tito (born Josip Broz) and the Communist Party until Tito's death in 1980.[37] After his death the country gradually began to fall apart,[38] partly because of ethnic conflicts which were not kept under control and partly because of the disintegration of one-party rule as the result of Gorbachev's opening up of the Communist system in other Eastern European countries such as Hungary and Czechoslovakia. In trying to understand what has been happening it is wise to keep a number of facts in mind. *First,* Tito was a minority Slovene-Croat in a Yugoslavia where the Serbs were the majority, so other minorities could trust him to look out for their minority interests in a way that would not be expected from any Serb leader. *Second,* during Tito's rule ethnicity was not very important to better educated Yugoslavs so there were many cross-ethnic marriages. *Third,* the northwestern republics (Slovenia and Croatia, which declared their independence from Yugoslavia in June 1991) are more industrialized, wealthier, and more "Westernized" than the rest of Yugoslavia, so they were much more eager to replace the state-controlled egalitarianism of Communism with a system which relies on market forces. *Fourth,* some Serbs feel that, as a majority, they have a right to be the dominant group in Yugoslavia, or what they sometimes called a "Greater Serbia." *Fifth,* the Yugoslav National Army has been under the control of the majority Serbs, and the power of that army has been used to try to keep the former

Slovenia
Capital: Ljubljana
Population: 2.0 million
Ethnicity: 91% Slovene; 3% Croat; 2% Serb; also Italians and Hungarians
Religion: primarily Roman Catholic
Refugees: 65,000
Military Status: Serbian-led federal army intervened after secession, but withdrew following cease fire.

Croatia
Capital: Zagreb
Population: 4.8 million
Ethnicity: 79% Croat; 12% Serb; 2% Yugoslav
Religion: Primarily Roman Catholic, with Eastern Orthodox
Refugees: 650,000
Military Status: One-third of territory controlled by Serbian irregular forces; Croatian forces control about one-third of Bosnian territory.

Federal Republic of Yugoslavia

Serbia
Capital: Belgrade
Population: 5.8 million
Ethnicity: 85% Serb; 5% Yugoslav; 3% Muslim; 2% Montenegrin; 2% Gypsy
Religion: Primarily Eastern Orthodox
Military Status: Continues to exert power over Serb irregular forces in Bosnia and Croatia.

Vojvodina
Capital: Novi Sad
Population: 1.9 million
Ethnicity: 65% Serb; 20% Hungarian; 5% Croat; 3% Slovak; 2% Rumanian
Religion: Primarily Eastern Orthodox, with Roman Catholic.

Kosovo
Capital: Pristina
Population: 2.0 million
Ethnicity: 82% Albanian (State Department says 90%); 10% Serb; 3% Muslim, 2% Gypsy
Religion: Primarily Muslim

Bosnia-Herzegovina
Capital: Sarajevo
Population: 4.4 million
Ethnicity: 44% Muslim; 31% Serb; 17% Croat
Religion: Muslim, Eastern Orthodox Christian, and Roman Catholic
Refugees: 600,000
Military Status: Two-thirds of territory controlled by Serbian irregular forces; one-third controlled by Croation forces; approximately 1,000 UN peacekeepers in Sarajevo to protect relief operations.

Macedonia
Capital: Skopje
Population: 2.0 million
Ethnicity: 69% Macedonian; 20% Albanian; 5% Turk; 2% Muslim; 2% Serb; 2% Gypsy
Religion: Primarily Eastern Orthodox, with Muslim
Refugees: 30,000
Military Status: Albanians threatening to secede.

Montenegro
Capital: Tito
Population: 610,000
Ethnicity: 69% Montenegrin; 13% Muslim; 7% Albanian; 5% Yugoslav; 3% Serb
Religion: Primarily Eastern Orthodox, with Muslim
Refugees: 50,000

About the map: Solid lines on the map represent boundaries of republics which have international recognition; dotted lines represent boundaries of republics considered part of the Federal Republic of Yugoslavia by the international community. Population and ethnic data is from the CIA and U.S. Census Bureau. Yugoslavians were given a choice in the 1981 Census of listing their ethnicity as "Muslim," although technically it is not an ethnic group. Refugees listed in a country are from all areas of the former Yugoslavia. Estimates are made from UNHCR data as reported in the press.

EUROPE, showing former YUGOSLAVIA (shaded area)

Source: Arms Control and Foreign Policy Caucus

Yugoslav republics of Slovenia, Croatia, Bosnia-Herzegovina, and Macedonia from seceding from Yugoslavia.

The U.N. first got involved in the conflict in the republic of Croatia, where about 12 percent of the population are Serbs. The government of Croatia moved to declare its independence from Yugoslavia, but the Serbs living in Croatia didn't want their republic to secede from Yugoslavia.[39] The Yugoslav Army was determined to use military force to support these Serbs living in Croatia who now wanted to declare the regions where they lived independent from Croatia and still part of Yugoslavia. But Croats living in these regions generally supported the independence of Croatia from

Yugoslavia. The United Nations Protection Force (UNPROFOR I) was established in March 1992 to demilitarize the three U.N. Protected Areas in Croatia where there is a mixed population of Serbs and Croats and to protect all the people living there.[40]

In June 1992 part of the U.N. Protection Force (sometimes subsequently referred to as UNPROFOR II) was authorized to move from bases in Croatia into Bosnia-Herzegovina in response to intensified fighting near the city of Sarajevo, capital of Bosnia-Herzegovina.[41] Here the ethnic issue is more complex as there are Bosnian Muslims living mostly in urban areas, Bosnian Serbs, Bosnian Croats, and Bosnian ethnically mixed families. Furthermore, Bosnian Serbs themselves are divided on the issue of whether they want to become part of a "Greater Serbia," and some Bosnian Croats identify more with Bosnia than with Croatia. The Serbian-controlled Yugoslav Army is the strongest military force and is being used to keep as much of Bosnia as possible under Yugoslav (Serbian) control, but Croatia also has its own army now and can give military assistance to the Bosnian Croats. The task of UNPROFOR II is to facilitate the delivery of humanitarian aid to all parties and to protect civilians in several "safe areas" around cities such as Sarajevo, Tuzla, Zepa, Gorazde, Boihac, and Srebrenica from attacks by Serbian military forces.[42] Negotiations have focused on trying to divide Bosnia-Herzegovina into ethnic areas. Each ethnic group wants to control as much territory as possible, and the Serbs have used their superior military forces to gain control of more territory than they would get if the division was based simply on population. They refuse to give up what they have gained by tough fighting. On the other hand, the other groups, and especially the Bosnian government leaders, say that such aggression should not be rewarded. Furthermore, they argue that any territory given to Bosnian Serbs will soon get attached to "Greater Serbia" and any territory given to Bosnian Croats will get attached to Croatia, so there won't be much territory left for the multiethnic country of Bosnia. Furthermore, since the Bosnian Muslims live mainly in the cities, if the country of Bosnia is divided up along ethnic lines, the various segments of what is left of Bosnia will not even be attached to each other, so the country will not be a viable entity. That doesn't bother the Serbs at all because from their viewpoint it just shows that all this territory should be part of "Greater Serbia." As the various factions fight to gain control of more territory and as various diplomats from the U.N. and the European Community try to work out a diplomatic settlement, the U.N. forces try to do their job of assisting in providing humanitarian aid and protecting those living in the "safe areas."

Before 1985, the world did not think much about U.N. peacekeeping, but in the 1990s the situation has changed completely. Now when there is a trouble spot anywhere in the world, one question to be considered is whether a U.N. peacekeeping force might be able to help. In October 1993 17 separate U.N. peacekeeping projects were being carried out with more than 80,000 personnel. The annual U.N. peacekeeping bill was over

$3 billion for the year 1992,[43] and the total annual budget for the 17 1993 operations was $4.392 billion.[44] That, of course, brings up one of the big problems confronting U.N. peacekeeping: Who will pay for it? In some of these peacekeeping efforts the funding comes from regular assessments on the member nations of the U.N., but in other cases where some opposition might exist there has been a reliance on appeals for voluntary contributions. The response to such appeals has not been overwhelming. The problem of funding has become ever more critical because of the readiness of the U.N. to create ever more peacekeeping operations in situations where the big powers have no great stake in the outcome (for example, Somalia, Cambodia, Liberia, Bosnia). If the richer, more powerful countries do not have an immediate interest in these places, are they going to put out the money needed to keep the peacekeeping operations going? (On the other hand, might it be possible to establish a new funding system whereby the big multinational corporations which need a peaceful world for their money-making activities could bypass the national governments and contribute directly to a U.N. peacekeeping fund?[45]) It is worth mentioning that the peacekeeping idea has now become so popular that other international organizations are getting into the act. In 1993 peacekeeping operations were being carried on by the European Community, the Conference on Security and Cooperation in Europe (CSCE), the Economic Community of West African States (ECOWAS), and the Commonwealth of Independent States (CIS) as well as independent groups of countries focused on dealing with a particular conflict.[46]

In June 1992 U.N. Secretary-General Boutros Boutros-Ghali issued *An Agenda for Peace* in which he called for several modifications in the way that the U.N. deals with threats to the peace.[47] He proposed that the U.N. do more in the way of taking preventive action before fighting begins. He proposed that the U.N. do more of its own information gathering and that all countries accept the compulsory jurisdiction of the International Court of Justice without reservations. He further suggested that the U.N. could create demilitarized zones in areas between countries where it is suspected that fighting might occur and that U.N. forces could be placed in a country which believes that it might be attacked by another. That last idea was implemented for the first time in Macedonia in December 1992 when the U.N. Security Council authorized sending a U.N. "preventive" peacekeeping force to Macedonia (UNPROFOR M) to forestall possible military action by Yugoslav forces such as already had occurred in Bosnia-Herzegovina,[48] and in July 1993 the U.S. agreed to send some of its troops to bolster the forces already there.[49]

The Secretary-General's *An Agenda for Peace* also suggested that nations earmark and train certain forces for U.N. peacekeeping work, that certain kinds of equipment be pre-positioned for quick use in U.N. operations, that there be a Peace Development Fund to provide instant financing for new U.N. peacekeeping operations, and that there be more cooperation between the U.N. and regional organizations in coordinating peacekeeping efforts. He called for the U.N. to have more heavily armed "peace enforcement" units to go into situations where resistance might be expected. He also noted the need to do more in the way of post-conflict peace-building so that instigations to restart the fighting are replaced with incentives for the previous opponents to work together. At the same time, he called on the Security Council members to initiate negotiations to be prepared for the typical kinds of collective security operations mentioned in Articles 43 and 47 of the U.N. Charter. So Secretary-General Boutros-Ghali showed that he wants the U.N. to be ready to make use of the provisions for collective security in the Charter but also that he does not want U.N. efforts for maintaining peace to be restricted to what is explicitly spelled out in the Charter.

Dominant Influences in the United Nations

If we look at the U.N. not just from the viewpoint of what the structures are but from the viewpoint of who actually influences what happens at the U.N., we can delineate three periods in the history of the organization. The first period, the time of U.S. dominance, lasted from the signing of the "Declaration by the United Nations" in 1942 through the San Francisco Conference to draw up the Charter in June 1945 to the crucial vote in 1971 which decided that the Chinese Communists would finally be allowed to appoint China's representatives at the U.N. The second period, the late Cold War period during which the U.S. and the Soviet Union nullified each other's efforts in the Security Council while the less developed countries built up their membership and their influence in the General Assembly, came to an end in 1988 with the end of the Cold War (marked by withdrawal of Soviet forces from Afghanistan) and the end of proxy wars between the superpowers throughout the Third World. The third period has been characterized by U.N. involvement in peacekeeping efforts throughout the world with general support from the whole international community but with new questions arising about financial resources and the extent to which the world community can legitimately involve itself in intranational conflicts. Of course, these transitions from one period to the next occurred gradually and did not take place all at one moment.

At the beginning the U.N. was basically a child of the U.S. It was conceived by U.S. President Franklin Roosevelt as a replacement for the League of Nations. The U.N. was brought into existence during World War II by the U.S., with major support from Britain and acquiescence by the Soviet Union. When the U.N. was formally created in 1945, Europe and Japan had been devastated by World War II, and the U.S. had about 40 percent of the gross world product and a monopoly on nuclear weapons. Of the 51 original member nation-states of the U.N., two-thirds (Western European countries, Latin American countries, members of the British Commonwealth, China, Iran, Iraq, Lebanon, Liberia, the Philippines, Saudi Arabia, and Turkey) could usually be expected to vote in accord with what the U.S. wanted. The U.S. could get anything it wanted passed in the General Assembly (such as the Universal Declaration of Human Rights in 1948), and in the Security Council its desires were blocked only by Soviet vetoes (though the Security Council was even able to declare Communist North Korea an aggressor in 1950 when the Soviets were boycotting its meetings). During that early period the Soviet Union cast veto after veto while the U.S. never had to cast a veto because what the U.S. didn't want never even came up for a vote.

A big change occurring in the U.N. during this first period was the admission of a large number of new members, many of them former colonies of European countries. Between 1945 and 1955, only nine countries were admitted to membership in the U.N., but in 1955 there were 16 new members in one year. In 1960 U.N. membership reached 100 countries with the admission of 17 new members, all but one being former African colonies. The U.S. and the Soviet Union both strongly supported this official recognition of the end of colonialism, so it was not difficult for the newly independent countries to get the U.N. General Assembly in 1960 to pass a resolution supporting the idea that all territories have a right to self-determination which overrides any claims advanced by colonial powers.[50]

But this increase in the number of U.N. members from Africa and Asia together with new Marxist-inspired attitudes of opposition to U.S. economic domination on the part of most less developed countries culminated in the crucial 1971 vote on China which marks the end of the first period of U.N. history. The Chinese Communists under the leadership of Mao Zedong had taken control of all of mainland China in 1949. The Soviets argued that Mao's Communist government should now appoint the Chinese representatives at the U.N., but the U.S. argued that the Chinese Nationalists led by anti–Communist Chiang Kai-shek were still the legitimate government of China even if they had been pushed off the mainland and onto the island of Taiwan by the Communist revolutionaries. The issue of who should appoint the U.N. representatives from China came up regularly in the General Assembly, but year after year the U.S. position prevailed. In 1971, however, things were different.[51] In 1969 the U.S. under President Nixon's leadership had shifted its own policy toward China in an effort to get the Chinese Communists to side with the U.S. against the Soviet Union. At the same time, the U.S. did not want to abandon its old ally, Chiang Kai-shek and his Chinese Nationalist Party. A good compromise seemed to be to allow Taiwan to become a separate member of the U.N., an approach that was called the "two Chinas" policy. But both the Chinese Nationalists and the Chinese Communists opposed that proposal. Consequently, the U.S., in an effort to keep its Nationalist Chinese ally from losing its representation at the U.N., opposed the 1971 resolution which said that the Chinese Communists should appoint China's delegates at the U.N.

just as it had opposed similar resolutions previously. But the General Assembly voted in favor of the resolution to unseat the representatives of Nationalist China to make room for representatives appointed by the Chinese Communist regime. For the first time in the history of the U.N. General Assembly, an important resolution opposed by the U.S. had been adopted. But it is worth noting that the U.S. had been so dominant at the U.N. during this first period that the Chinese Communists had to wait 22 years before they were permitted to appoint China's delegates at the U.N.

That 1971 vote made it evident that the U.N. was into its second period marked by the control of the General Assembly by the less developed newly independent anticolonial countries while the Security Council was immobilized by the U.S.-Soviet confrontation which meant that one or the other would veto every significant resolution. Having an international organization dominated by the poorer, less developed countries was definitely a new kind of situation in international affairs. The General Assembly could not pass binding resolutions as the Security Council could, but it did control the operation of the U.N. itself, including the adoption of the budget for the organization. On the other hand, during this period the prevailing attitude of the big powers was to ignore the U.N., to try to keep it poor and powerless, and to conduct their business with each other bilaterally or through other international organizations such as NATO and the Warsaw Pact Organization.

The big problem for this new controlling group of less developed countries at the U.N. was that they lacked economic power. Contributions to the U.N. are assessed by the General Assembly on the basis of ability to pay, and none of these former colonies made very large contributions to the support of the U.N. In fact, over a third of the U.N. budget came from the United States on grounds that the United States had over a third of the world's gross income. This situation allowed the United States to score a point against the less developed countries in response to the 1971 vote on China. In 1972 the United States successfully requested that the General Assembly set 25 percent of the U.N. budget as the maximum any single nation could be assessed. The United States did nothing to contradict rumors that if this proposal to reduce its own contribution was not passed it might just quit the U.N. altogether. The message from the United States was clear: Don't push your voting advantage too far, or you may lose a substantial portion of the money coming into the U.N. On the other hand, the less developed countries realized that neither the United States nor the Soviet Union was likely to withdraw from the U.N. because this would clear the way for the other to maintain a close working relationship with those very nations in which the ideological battle between Communism and democratic capitalism was being fought.

The financial threat to the U.N. from the United States was temporarily diminished at the end of 1973 when the Organization of Petroleum Exporting Countries (OPEC) quadrupled the price of oil. This event not only demonstrated the vulnerability of the developed countries to economic pressures; it also meant large amounts of money in the coffers of those oil-rich Arab nations with sparse populations on which to spend their new-found wealth. These countries could now provide some of the foreign aid which the United States might threaten to withhold from nations which voted against it in the U.N. They could replace U.S. contributions to the U.N. if the United States were to withdraw from the organization. This new situation provided the impetus for the less developed countries to become even bolder in the U.N. They passed a resolution calling for a New International Economic Order to replace the existing system of trading arrangements which favored the developed countries (1974) and another resolution declaring that Zionism is a form of racism (1975). The passage of this last resolution shows how Arab oil money was influencing U.N. voting. Since the U.S. had always supported the existence of Israel and now Arab countries opposed to Israel were using their financial influence to get anti–Jewish resolutions passed by the U.N., many Americans who had supported the U.N. began to have doubts about the organization. To many observers interested in international affairs the U.N. had become an anti–U.S. organization controlled by less developed countries overly sympathetic to Communist ideology and readily swayed by Arab oil money to thumb their noses at the U.S.

During this Cold War period there was little the U.N. could do to end armed conflicts along the borders of and within the less developed countries. Every conflict in these poorer countries became an opportunity for the opposing superpowers to pour in weapons and military assistance to try to gain some increased influence in that part of the world. In places such as Ethiopia and Somalia, there were even switches with regard to which superpower was giving assistance to which fighting group. In 1987 there were 22 wars where more than a thousand people a year were dying, and all of them were in less developed countries.[52] In 1990 it was observed that "without exception, the wars of the last two decades have all been in the developing world."[53] The situation seemed to be that the superpowers did not want peace but rather victory in war for the group they were supporting, no matter how long it might take to prevail. This kind of proxy fighting was also very profitable for arms manufacturers and a possible source of glory for military advisers.

The transition to the third period in U.N. history has come as a result of the end of the Cold War between the U.S. and the Soviet Union. It is difficult to say precisely when that conflict ended, but one significant point indicating that the international situation had changed was the April 1988 agreement leading to Soviet withdrawal from Afghanistan. Then in June 1988 the INF Treaty was signed eliminating all medium-range missiles from Europe, in November 1989 the Berlin Wall was torn down, and in December 1991 the Soviet Union ceased to exist. During this rapid transformation of the international landscape, the U.N. was being called on to monitor truces or elections in Afghanistan, Angola, Guatemala, and Nicaragua, thus bringing an end to conflicts where one side had been supported by the Communists and the other side by the U.S. The plan to create a new government in Namibia also started moving forward at this time.

For Americans the existence of a "new" U.N. became evident during the 1990–91 crisis in the Persian Gulf when U.S. President Bush used the U.N. Security Council, no longer hampered by the threat of a Soviet veto, to condemn Iraq's invasion of Kuwait and to authorize U.S.-led military action against Saddam Hussein's Iraq. The President talked of a "new world order" where international aggression would no longer be permitted. After the Gulf War ended, the U.N. was called on to make sure that Iraq lived up to the terms of the truce and also to assist with temporary humanitarian assistance to the Kurds being attacked by Saddam Hussein's forces in northern Iraq. New U.N. peacekeeping operations were being established all over the world. Many people, both within the U.S. and elsewhere, were voicing the opinion that the U.N. "is finally working as it was designed to work."[54]

Buoyed by the quick, one-sided victory in the Gulf War and by successful U.N. peacekeeping operations in Namibia and Cambodia, Americans were ready to support more participation in U.N. efforts in places such as Somalia. But the U.S. domestic budget crisis, the existence of obviously difficult and dangerous situations such as that in the former Yugoslavia, and the deaths of some Americans in Somalia combined to raise questions about how much the U.S. should support the U.N. All these new peace-keeping operations have caused the U.S.'s bill for U.N. peacekeeping to skyrocket, from $61.1 million in 1987 to $794 million in 1993.[55] That seems a miniscule amount compared with the $278 *billion* budgeted for U.S. national military expenditures in 1994,[56] but some American leaders seem to be more ready to cut millions from international peacekeeping than to cut billions from national military spending. From their viewpoint too much of the U.N. peacekeeping is not relevant to U.S. national interest. One must ask, however, why it was in the national interest to support all that military assistance to less developed countries during the Cold War while it now seems not to be in the national interest to prevent wars in those same countries.

In this post–Cold War period of the U.N. one of the big questions to be answered is the extent to which not only the U.S. but also other countries will focus their attention on their own domestic problems while ignoring problems in other parts of the world. Other countries such as China and some of the less developed countries would undoubtedly be happy to see the U.S. and its "Westernized" allies being less supportive of U.N. involvement in international issues such as peacekeeping in support of democratic approaches to governance, defending human rights, and protection of the environment. Their concern is that their own national sovereignty may be compromised by an active U.N. too much influenced by Western values.

Accomplishments of the United Nations

The United Nations came into existence October 24, 1945. It has not been particularly successful in its announced aim "to save succeeding generations from the scourge of war." Yet the rest of that first sentence of the U.N. Charter makes reference to the two world wars, and the fact is, regardless of whether the United Nations is responsible for it or not, there has been no World War III. The League of Nations was formed in 1919 and 20 years later another world war was being fought. The United Nations has already existed for almost 50 years without another world war. Furthermore, a look at its record reveals that it not only has accomplished several of its aims to some degree but also has brought about other desirable developments.

One of the U.N.'s major accomplishments is simply that it has managed to maintain its existence and even to extend its membership to practically all the nations of the world. Survival is no small task for a political organization. Even a national-level political institution which maintains its existence for 50 years is considered a stable institution. Over half the nations which now belong to the United Nations did not have independent national governments at the time the United Nations was formed; the United Nations is older than they are! Continuing existence produces expectations and traditions. The longer the United Nations survives as an organization with almost universal membership, the more difficult it becomes for anyone to conceive of a world without it or for national leaders to conceive of their own nations as nonmembers.

With regard to the war problem, the United Nations has been the agency by which multilateral arms control agreements have come into existence as well as the vehicle for many peacekeeping operations. The United Nations has established various committees to further arms control. With regard to peacekeeping efforts, one can only conjecture about whether any of the situations in which the United Nations intervened might have otherwise developed into a large-scale war. The U.N.'s role in Korea should not be forgotten, even if it is very unlikely that there will ever again be a similar operation. At least the precedent was set for an international organization coordinating an effort to resist aggression in accord with the idea of collective security. One should also consider whether in the absence of the United Nations there could be a situation such as the one that occurred at the time of the Gulf War when the major military power in the world sought the approval of the international community before launching a military attack to punish an aggressor nation and then turned over the task of enforcing the truce to the international community.

A third area of achievement for the United Nations consists of providing opportunities for formal and informal exchanges between diplomats in times of crisis and for planning cooperative efforts to resolve conflicts. The existence of the United Nations makes possible meetings in the hallway or the lunchroom which may produce important diplomatic exchanges that would never have taken place if formal arrangements for such meetings had been required in advance. Diplomats from smaller countries may be able to take part in discussions to which they otherwise would not have been invited. The Secretary-General and other U.N. personnel can participate in negotiations as representatives not of this or that nation, but of the world community. How much difference this opportunity for ready contact between diplomats has made toward preventing war cannot be determined with precision, but it is hard to believe that it hasn't helped.

Fourth, the United Nations has been developing a whole new tradition in international politics, one of conferring and debating and appealing to disinterested third parties rather than making military threats and issuing ultimatums. This new tradition involves a shift from a situation where interaction between nations is only bilateral and coercive to one where it is also multilateral and persuasive. The United Nations is thus serving as a school at which national governments and their leaders are learning how to participate in a democratic parliament. Even representatives from nations with autocratic governments are learning that different points of view must be allowed to be expressed, that the opinions of third parties are important, that appeals to reason rather than force can be influential, and so on.

Unfortunately, the United States, which prides itself on being a democratic nation, seems to have trouble at times functioning within this democratic forum. As a nation Americans have yet to learn the very important lesson that on the world scene they are a minority, less than 5 percent of the world's population. They have yet to learn that democracy means listening as well as talking, appealing to reason rather than being coercive, and abiding by the decision of the majority even when the United States doesn't agree. They must learn that there are others in the world who care about freedom and justice just as much as the United States does.

A fifth area of achievement for the United Nations is its supervision of the relatively smooth transition from a world of colonizing nations and their colonies to a world of independent sovereign countries. We have already noted that the Trusteeship Council has monitored the shift to independence of many lands and that over half the nations of the United Nations were colonies at the time the United Nations was formed. Even if the United Nations had accomplished nothing else, its supervision and legitimation of the decolonization of much of the world makes it one of the greatest success stories in human history.

Obviously one cannot claim that the United Nations accomplished this transition alone. There can be no down-grading of the sacrifices made by millions in wars fought for the independence of their homelands. At the same time, it can be noted that the process would undoubtedly have been much slower and much bloodier without the United Nations. Many nations have won their independence without bloodshed, and the existence of the United Nations has often facilitated this development. The United Nations provides a ready means by which the independence of a nation can be registered as an objective fact. A country may declare itself to be independent, but that independence is publicly recognized by the rest of the world when it becomes a member of the United Nations, equally sovereign with every other nation.

The United Nations has not only helped these new nations to achieve recognized independence; it has also helped them to survive once they have become independent. This is its sixth area of achievement. Most of these former colonies are poor and short of the skills needed to run businesses, schools, hospitals, and governments. They need loans and other forms of development assistance. The United Nations has helped to provide these. The less developed countries have been successful in the past in using the United Nations as a vehicle to procure and secure their *political independence.* Their expectation now is that it will assist them further in their *economic development.*

A seventh area of accomplishment for the United Nations is its progress in carrying out the aim stated in the second paragraph of the Charter, namely, "to reaffirm faith in fundamental human rights." The various declarations and covenants on this subject serve as an ideal for the world's governments and peoples to pursue even though they are often far from being actualized. Their role in the development of standards may be compared to that played by the Declaration of Independence and the Bill of Rights in the formation of public opinion in the United States. The three main U.N. human rights documents (the Universal Declaration of Human Rights adopted by the General Assembly in 1948; the Covenant on Economic, Social, and Cultural Rights passed by the General Assembly in 1966; and the Covenant on Civil and Political Rights also passed by the General Assembly in 1966) were all adopted without a dissenting vote.[57] Even national governments which do not honor these rights in practice feel bound not to vote against them as public statements of the ideals toward which humankind should be moving.

The Covenant on Civil and Political Rights contains an optional Protocol which nations may also adopt when they ratify that Covenant. The Protocol indicates that the nation acceding to it recognizes the right of its citizens to file complaints about violations of their rights directly to the U.N. Human Rights Committee, a committee formed of representatives elected by those nations who have ratified the Covenant. As more and more nations accede to this very special Protocol, the pressure on the others who have not adopted it will mount. The accusations of human rights violations made against each other by potential enemies do not carry much weight because each is known to be merely attacking an opponent, but failure to ratify the Protocol of the Covenant on Civil and Political Rights will eventually be viewed as a self-accusation before the whole world. Unfortunately, the media in most of the world have not paid much attention to these Covenants and the all-important Protocol, so the pressure of world public opinion has not yet been brought to bear on this issue.

In addition to the three basic documents on human rights, the United Nations has also adopted several treaties on specific human rights such as the prevention of genocide, protection of refugees, political rights of women, abolition of slavery, the nationality of married women, the status of stateless persons, consent to marriage, elimination of racial discrimination, elimination of religious intolerance and discrimination, and the rights of children. Most of these efforts to further human rights would not have occurred without the United Nations.

An eighth accomplishment of the United Nations is directing the attention of the whole world to crucial global problems so that action can be taken toward solving these problems. The technique which has been used to focus attention on an issue is the convening of a world conference devoted to that problem. Experts from all over the world, governmental representatives and sometimes private citizens too, get together to discuss this problem and possible solutions to it. The first of these world conferences was on the environment. It was held in Stockholm in 1972 and led eventually to the creation of the U.N. Environmental Programme with headquarters in Nairobi, Kenya. In 1973 the first session of the U.N. Conference on the Law of the Sea was held in New York. Many subsequent sessions were held in Caracas, Geneva, and New York over a period of nine years, and a treaty on the governance of the oceans was signed in 1982 by 117 nations. In 1974 the World Conference on Population was held in Bucharest and the World Food Conference met in Rome. Starting in 1975 and continuing into 1977, the Conference on International Economic Cooperation in Paris dealt with the relationship between the developed and the less developed countries. In 1976, Vancouver, British Columbia, Canada and Geneva were the sites of conferences on human settlements and employment. In 1977 the World Water Conference was held at Mar del Plata, Argentina, and a conference on the nuclear fuel cycle was held in Salzburg, Austria. In 1978 the Conference on Technical Cooperation among Developing Countries was held in Buenos Aires. In Vienna in 1979 a conference was held on Science and Technology for Development. In 1981 a conference was held in Nairobi on New and Renewable Sources of Energy. Vienna was host again for the 1982 Conference on the Peaceful Uses of Outer Space. In July 1985 a Conference to Review and Appraise the Achievements of the U.N. Decade for Women was held in Nairobi, Kenya. In June 1992 the U.N. Conference on Environment and Development (also called "the Earth Summit") was held in Rio de Janeiro, Brazil. This list of U.N.-sponsored world conferences is by no means complete. The success of the earlier conferences in drawing attention to a given problem has in fact led to such a multiplication of conferences that they no longer attract as much attention as they once did. But even though the general public may not be so well informed about some of the more recent conferences, experts in the various fields involved are aware of them and appreciate their importance in focusing efforts on the solution of these problems.

A ninth area of accomplishment of the United Nations is most evident to social scientists and government officials. The United Nations secures and maintains data on societies all over the world and publishes yearbooks and statistical records containing comparative information from these societies. The information-gathering capabilities presently vary widely from country to country, so the data is not yet so standardized as desired, but the existence of the United Nations as an information-gathering and information-dispensing agency will undoubtedly lead to increasing reliability of this information as the years go by. These data about what has happened and what is happening all over the world are crucial for planning for the future whether the planning is done by private parties, by national governments, or by the United Nations itself.

The tenth contribution of the United Nations is actually a whole collection of achievements of a collection of organizations, some of which are subsidiary organs of the United Nations and some of which are fairly autonomous agencies which report to the U.N. Economic and Social Council. The subsidiary organs of the United Nations, whose work constitutes part of the U.N.'s accomplishments, include the U.N. Conference on Trade and Development (UNCTAD), the U.N. Children's Fund (UNICEF), the Office of the U.N. High Commissioner for Refugees (UNHCR), the U.N. Commission on Human Rights (UNCHR), the World Food Programme (WFP) (a combined effort with the Food and Agriculture Organization), the U.N. Institute for Training and Research (UNITAR), the U.N. Development Programme (UNDP), the U.N. Environmental Programme (UNEP), the U.N. Population Fund (UNFPA), the U.N. University (UNU), the U.N. Special Fund, and the U.N. Relief and Works Agency for Palestine Refugees in the Near East (UNRWA), the U.N. Disaster Relief Office (UNDRO), the U.N. Centre for Human Settlements (Habitat), and the International Research and Training Institute for the Advancement of Women (INSTRAW). The more autonomous specialized agencies, several of which existed before the United Nations and some even before the League of Nations, will be discussed in the next section.

Worldwide Functional Agencies

National governments are one of the most prominent features of social life on the earth. The boundaries of their control often mark the limits within which a certain language or a certain currency is used. But national boundaries are not inscribed on the surface of the earth, and they do not stop the flow of air and water and animals and radio waves and goods and people from place to place. As a result, problems frequently arise which cannot be handled by national governments acting separately. The League of Nations and the United Nations represent two different efforts to create a supranational organization dedicated to dealing with world problems in general. On the other hand, each of the international organizations now to be discussed aims to perform a specific function. Such organizations consequently are called *functional agencies* or *specialized agencies.* They are also sometimes called *administrative agencies* because they aim to do what needs to be done to solve a particular kind of international problem without confronting political and ideological issues.

The first permanent international functional agency was the Central Commission for the Navigation of the Rhine, created in accord with the Final Act of the Congress of Vienna in 1815. The Commission contained representatives from all countries which border the Rhine, and its task was to facilitate and regulate river traffic. It established the first group of international civil servants and even provided pensions for them. Except for periods of war the Rhine Commission has continued to function to the present day.

The next permanent international functional agency was the European Commission of the Danube, created in 1856. It developed a system of tolls and licenses which permitted the lower Danube to be kept navigable without all the expense being borne by Romania. It also provided a single licensing agency for all users of the river regardless of what country they might be in or go through. The Commission proved to be a success, lasting until World War II. After that war a new Danube Commission was formed. Similar international commissions have been established to supervise navigation on other waterways which flow through more than one country. These functional agencies are regional rather than worldwide in scope, however, and consequently are more directly related to the next section below, which deals with regional functional agencies.

Another example of an early international organization, one which is global in scope, is the International Red Cross. This organization grew out of the efforts of Jean-Henri Dunant, a Swiss humanitarian who had organized emergency aid services for both French and Austrian wounded soldiers at the Battle of Solferino in 1859. The Geneva Convention of 1864 committed the nations who signed it to caring for war wounded, whether friend or enemy. National Red Cross Societies (or Red Crescent Societies in Muslim countries) have been created to provide humanitarian assistance not only in time of war but also during peacetime, especially when natural disasters occur. The international coordination is provided by the International Committee of the Red Cross, a group of 25 citizens, and by the League of Red Cross Societies which has a secretariat in Geneva.

The first of the worldwide functional agencies which eventually became incorporated into the present U.N. system was the International Telegraphic Union established in 1865. The agency was created by a multilateral convention which enunciated the general principles of the organization and set the rules to be followed by those signing the convention. The International Telecommunication Convention of 1932 brought together the International Telegraphic Union and the International Radiotelegraphic Union, which had been established by a separate convention in 1906. The new International Telecommunication Union became effective in 1934 and became a specialized agency of the United Nations in 1947. Its task is to encourage international cooperation in the use and further development of communication by telegraph, radio, cable, telephone, and television. Regulation of the use of various radio and television frequencies is one of its main functions.

One of the better known worldwide functional agencies is the Universal Postal Union. To facilitate international postal communication without each nation trying to throw the burden of postal charges for this international mail on the other, the General Postal Union was formed in 1874-75. A single scale of charges for all international mail was to be established, and transit charges through any given nation were to be based on weight and mileage. The legislative body is the Postal Congress which meets every five years. New policies are adopted by majority vote, but each nation must then separately ratify its concurrence with the change. It is so advantageous to each nation to belong to the Union that a tradition has been established of virtually automatic ratification of any changes proposed by the Congress. The Congress elects an Executive Council of representatives from 40 different countries to supervise the system between Congresses. The name of this organization was changed to the Universal Postal Union in 1878, and it became a specialized agency of the United Nations in 1948.

There are so many worldwide functional agencies that it would be tedious to try to discuss each one. We can, however, mention those that are officially a part of the U.N. system. Most of the specialized agencies are funded through assessments on their members; the International Telecommunication Union (ITU) and the Universal Postal Union (UPU) discussed above are two of these. The International Atomic Energy Agency (IAEA) aims to promote the safe and peaceful use of atomic energy. The Food and Agriculture Organization (FAO) aims to improve the quantity and quality of the world's food supply by assisting in agricultural research programs, irrigation projects, pest control activities, development of fishing techniques, and the like. The International Fund for Agricultural Development (IFAD) aims to provide resources for agricultural and rural development in the poorest rural areas. The International Maritime Organization (IMO) aims to improve ship safety and navigation procedures on the high seas, minimize environmental damage from shipping activities, and insure that damages to private property or the environment are paid for by those who do the damage. The International Civil Aviation Organization (ICAO) aims to promote safe and efficient international air travel by regulating aircraft operation, safety equipment, pilot training, and language use for communications related to international flights. The International Labor Organization (ILO) aims to improve the workplace environment for laborers by setting international standards for safety and working conditions so that employers in one country cannot argue that they are disadvantaged compared to employers in another country who need not meet the same standards. The U.N. Educational, Scientific, and Cultural Organization (UNESCO) aims to increase international cooperation in the areas of education (especially literacy programs), scientific research, and the preservation and exchange of culturally and historically important buildings and objects. The World Health Organization (WHO) aims to prevent the spread of disease (especially across national boundaries), to promote health education, and to encourage medical research. The World Intellectual Property Organization (WIPO) aims to promote international cooperation in respecting copyrights, patents, and trademarks. The World Meteorological Organization (WMO) aims to coordinate the gathering and exchange of weather information from all over the world. The U.N. Industrial Development Organization (UNIDO) aims to assist the less developed countries of the world in their efforts to industrialize. The General Agreement on Tariffs and Trade (GATT), a step toward the creation of an International Trade Organization, is a treaty designed to lower tariffs and reduce restrictions on international trade; countries who have signed the treaty maintain a staff in Geneva to deal with alleged violations and new trade issues.

Four specialized agencies dealing with financial matters are officially part of the U.N. system. The International Monetary Fund (IMF) aims to promote the stability of exchange rates between different national currencies and to promote international cooperation with regard to monetary policies. The International Bank for Reconstruction and Development (IBRD), also known as the World Bank, provides loans and other assistance for economic development. The International Development Association (IDA) is affiliated with the World Bank and focuses on helping the poorest nations by arranging loans at extremely low rates of interest. The International Finance Corporation (IFC) is also affiliated with the World Bank, but it aims at promoting private business in less developed countries. As affiliates of the World Bank, both IDA and IFC can borrow from the Bank and thus are able to loan much more than if they were limited to the funds actually given to them by national governments. The World Bank system as a whole provides a means by which richer countries can provide foreign assistance to less developed countries without confronting issues about whether the projects being proposed are in fact promising, and without getting into the position of funding worthless projects just because of the political consequences of not funding them.

In a sense, all these global functional agencies which form part of the U.N. system constitute what would be departments if a fully developed world government existed. For example, WHO would be the Department of Health, FAO would be the Department of Agriculture, and UNESCO would be the Department of Education. These agencies are busy solving real world problems and improving the quality of life for the whole human race. For example, as the result of the work of WHO, smallpox has been eliminated from the face of the earth.[58]

Regional Functional and Political Organizations

Although our discussion of functional agencies has so far been directed mainly to those which are *global* in scope, we did mention the commissions for the Rhine and Danube rivers, which are examples of *regional* functional organizations. There are many more of these international regional functional organizations than of those with a worldwide scope. Although regional functional organizations carry on many different specific kinds of tasks, the most important ones fall into one of two classes. First, there are those regional organizations whose primary function is military cooperation against a prospective opponent. Second, there are those regional organizations whose primary function is economic cooperation. In addition to these *functional* organizations there are regional *political* organizations which aim to peacefully resolve any kind of conflict among their members and to adopt a common policy toward nations outside the organization.

Regional *military* organizations may look at first glance like simple military alliances, but there is a difference. A regional military organization includes a governing council, which meets on a regular basis, and an integrated military staff, which functions at all times, not just during crises or war. In other words, an actual organization is created to implement a military agreement rather than just having a commitment to join in the fighting in case of an attack. The most obvious example of such a regional military organization is the North Atlantic Treaty Organization (NATO).

Regional *economic* organizations usually seek to develop a free trade area or common market among the nations which belong. Tariffs and quotas between member states are eliminated, and a common tariff policy is adopted toward nations or groups of nations outside the regional group. These regional economic organizations also seek to promote economic cooperation and development among their members. In the case of Benelux (an economic union of Belgium, the Netherlands, and Luxembourg) cooperation includes provisions for the free flow of capital and labor across national boundaries and for common tax laws, welfare policies, and postal and transport rates.

The outstanding example of regional economic integration is Western Europe. The European Coal and Steel Community was created in 1952 to integrate the coal and steel industries in France, West Germany, Italy, and the Benelux countries. The European Economic Community (the EEC or "Common Market") was created by the same countries in 1957 to establish a free trade area among them and a common economic policy toward other nations. Denmark, Ireland, and the United Kingdom joined in 1973, Greece in 1981, and Portugal and Spain in 1986.

The success of the European Economic Community in promoting economic growth in Europe led to the formation of other international economic organizations such as the European Free Trade Association (EFTA) consisting of the capitalistic European countries not in the European Economic Community, the Latin America Free Trade Association (LAFTA), the Andean Development Corporation (the Andean Group within LAFTA), and the Caribbean Free Trade Community (CARICOM). There are also several regional development banks modeled on the World Bank.

Some economic international organizations are less than global in scope but also are not regional. One example is the Commonwealth of Nations made up of Britain and many of its former colonies. Another example is the Organization for Economic Cooperation and Development (OECD). That organization began in 1948 as the Organization for European Economic Cooperation (OEEC) whose aim was to coordinate American assistance to a devastated Europe. The United States, Canada, and Japan joined with these Western European countries in that organization, whose name was changed in 1961 to the Organization for Economic Cooperation and Development and whose aims included the further development and economic stability of the developed capitalist countries, the coordination of aid to the less developed countries, and the promotion of world trade. Still another example of an economic international organization which is not global but which is also not regional is the Organization of Petroleum Exporting Countries (OPEC).

Continuously increasing economic cooperation within a group of countries usually will eventually lead to problems of a political nature. For example, there are frequently differences among member countries with regard to tax policies, agricultural subsidies, and benefits for the unemployed. As economic integration proceeds, it becomes necessary to decide how to reconcile these different policies. Economic cooperation reaches a point where it cannot be expanded without some type of political integration. The European community seems to have reached this point.

Consequently, it should not be surprising that when we turn our attention to international *political* regional organizations, it is Western Europe which is farthest along the path to significant political integration. The European Union (formerly called "the European Community") has a decision-making Council, a Commission, a Court of Justice, and a Parliament. In the spring of 1979 the people of Western Europe for the first time elected representatives to the European Parliament. The powers of the European Parliament are quite limited now, but they can be expected to grow as this institution matures.

Although Europe leads the way in political integration, there are several other regional political organizations which are much weaker in nature but are nevertheless dedicated to dealing with the problems of the region in a general way and not serving as merely functional or administrative organizations. The basic aim of these organizations is usually to keep nations outside that region from intervening in what are viewed as regional matters. If the nations in the region are able to settle any disputes among themselves, then action by other nations or by the United Nations will be unnecessary.

For example, the Organization of American States (OAS), which includes all the countries of the Americas except Cuba and Grenada, serves to continue the Monroe Doctrine of the United States, according to which nations in other parts of the world are to refrain from interference in American affairs. Similarly, the newly independent nations of Africa have created the Organization of African Unity (OAU)not only to work together in moving out of their colonial status but also to settle conflicts between African nations without the involvement of either the developed capitalist states or the Communist bloc. All African nations except South Africa belong. The Arab League was established to foster Arab unity but has found little agreement except in anti–Israel sentiment, and even on the issue of how to deal with Israel there has been much disagreement. One regional international political organization which seems more interested in promoting cooperation among its members than in keeping outsiders out is the Nordic Council, composed of Denmark, Finland, Iceland, Norway, and Sweden. That Council aims to promote more uniform legal and economic practices among its members. Another regional group which is focusing more on cooperation than opposing outsiders is the recently formed South Asian Association for Regional Cooperation (SAARC) composed of Bangladesh, Bhutan, India, the Maldive Islands, Nepal, Pakistan, and Sri Lanka. With the Cold War ended an organization which is likely to become a focus for cooperation between all states of Europe, the republics of the former Soviet Union, the U.S., and Canada is the Conference on Security and Cooperation in Europe (CSCE). It now has 52 members and a Secretariat in Prague.

It is possible that one or another of these or other regional international political organizations will become more significant in the future, but so far only the European Union seems to have developed a higher level of integration than that found at the global level in the United Nations. Meanwhile, it is distressing to see that in many regional organizations the motive of keeping outsiders out usually seems to be much more important than that of furthering positive cooperation among the nations of the region.

International Nongovernmental Organizations

When we look at the international institutions which reflect a developing global community, we tend to concentrate so much attention on those institutions created by and for national governments that we may overlook the international institutions created by individuals and groups other than national governments. Yet these *nongovernmental* international organizations play a crucial role in promoting those attitudes and perspectives which are essential if there is ever to be peace and justice on a global scale. The United Nations has recognized the importance of these nongovernmental organizations (NGOs) by permitting many of them to have a special affiliation with the United Nations and its agencies through the U.N. Economic and Social Council as provided in the U.N. Charter.[59] At present over 700 nongovernmental organizations are so affiliated.[60]

Among the NGOs affiliated with the United Nations, the ones most directly relevant to the problems of peace and justice are those whose efforts are focused on issues such as human rights and disarmament. Amnesty International, which won the Nobel Peace Prize for 1977, conducts independent investigations of violations of human rights and consequently has been permitted to present its findings to the U.N. Human Rights Commission (UNHRC). The same privilege has been extended to the International League for Human Rights. In fact, these two NGOs have been so successful in bringing violations of human rights to the attention of the public that certain national governments have tried to deprive them of consultative status with the Economic and Social Council. In the disarmament area it was the nongovernmental U.S. National Resources Defense Council which worked out an agreement in May 1986 with the Soviet Academy of Sciences whereby scientists were allowed to set up monitoring stations near where the other side conducts nuclear tests.[61] This arrangement showed that adherence to governmental agreements restricting nuclear tests can be verified.

An historic moment occurred at the United Nations when, during the 1978 Special Session on Disarmament, representatives from some of the nongovernmental organizations interested in disarmament were allowed to address the Assembly.[62] These representatives seemed to be much more eager to move toward a disarmed world than the government representatives of many of the nations. This is why the NGOs are so important. They speak for the interests of humanity, for peace and justice. Many of the national governments and their representatives, on the other hand, are interested primarily in protecting national interests, the interests of powerful groups in their countries, and the status quo. U.S. President Eisenhower once remarked, "I like to believe that people, in the long run, are going to do more to promote peace than are governments. Indeed, I think that people want peace so much that one of these days governments had better get out of the way and let them have it."[63] If citizen effort is ever going to succeed, it will need to be channeled through NGOs dedicated to peace, justice, and the common good.

One large group of NGOs affiliated with the United Nations consists of the international religious organizations. These affiliated religious groups include representatives from Catholic and Protestant Christianity, Judaism, Islam, Buddhism, and Hinduism as well as smaller groups such as the Baha'is, the Friends, and the Unitarian-Universalists. Religious groups are important to peace because of their role in the development of attitudes. Some religious institutions have been promoters of the grossest kind of parochialism and nationalism, leading war combatants on both sides to believe that God is on their side and that opponents should be utterly destroyed because they are the incarnation of evil. Other religious institutions, however, have been instrumental in inculcating a devotion to peace and justice and the welfare of the whole human family. Which of these attitudes is promoted by religious groups makes a great deal of difference concerning what kind of world we live in and will live in.

Other international nongovernmental organizations consist of professional or vocational groups. Still others focus on special hobbies and interests. Many service organizations have an international scope. There are also athletic organizations which transcend national boundaries. Organizations such as the Club of Rome seek to promote the independent study of problems facing the global community. Only a minority of these numerous international organizations are formally related to the United Nations, but they nevertheless are global institutions which accordingly tend to break down the nationalism and parochialism which have been so prominent a factor in modern warfare.

Another very important kind of nongovernmental international institution is the transnational business enterprise. These companies, frequently called "multinational corporations," tend to promote feelings of human unity. National differences in regulations, tax laws, systems of measurement, language, and the like are nuisances to these companies. Although transnational businesses are motivated by a desire for profit and may in some ways be perceived as instruments of imperialism, in other ways they facilitate the development of a global perspective and a positive attitude toward human cooperation which is free from nationalistic and other kinds of biases.

A significant problem for many nongovernmental international organizations is the absence of an international language. Governmental organizations and some transnational business enterprises operating at the international level are able to provide the equipment and personnel to make quick translations available to the participants at their meetings, but this is not true for many of the nongovernmental international organizations. For example, when the World Conference on Religion and Peace holds a world assembly, what language or languages should be used? Such organizations are usually not able to afford the equipment and personnel needed to furnish translations and copies of written material in several different languages; and if English alone is used, speakers of other languages do not have an equal opportunity to participate in the proceedings. Generally the leaders of the national governments, who are provided with translations when they get together, have not shown much interest in this problem, but in 1954, 1985, and 1993, UNESCO passed resolutions urging national governments to teach their students about the world language problem and the international language Esperanto which has been developed to deal with it.[64] Nevertheless solving the problem seems to depend primarily on the work of a nongovernmental organization, the Universala Esperanto-Asocio. Obviously, when Esperantists have a world conference they do not have the kind of language problem which other international organizations do because they all speak Esperanto.

XIII. Legal Aspects of the Contemporary Situation

We are likely to suppose that laws can exist only when there is some authorized person or body to make the laws and see that they get enforced; that is, we may believe that there cannot be law without government. Since there is no government above the nations (the United Nations is not a full-fledged government even though it is a political organization), we may conclude that there cannot be anything such as international law which nations are obliged to obey. But such a conclusion would not be correct. International law exists and is recognized by national governments even though it is not always obeyed. We will begin our discussion of the legal aspects of the contemporary situation by reviewing how international law has evolved. We will then turn to the laws of war as an example of international law. After considering the sources of international law, we will discuss the issue of how effective international law can be expected to be in regulating the behavior of nations.

The Nature of International Law

International law rests on the presumption that the relations between nations are somewhat different from the relations between individual persons. Individual persons are not self-sufficient. They need other persons to bring them into existence, to care for them when young, to exchange goods and services with them (no person can take care of all his own needs), and to keep them company. They have sexual desires which lead them to mate with others and parental feelings which cause them to care for their offspring. Nations, on the other hand, are presumed to be relatively self-sufficient "organisms." They usually can survive if necessary without any interaction with other states. They do not need other states to bring them into existence or to take care of them when young. They do not need other states to help them provide for their needs or to keep them from being lonely. They do not have sexual desires which lead them to interact with other states, nor do they produce son and daughter nations which must be cared for. People must live in societies, but nations do not need to live in a society of nations; they are able to survive in relative isolation from other nations with few adverse effects.

256

Since people must live in societies to survive and meet their various needs, they can be expected to abide by certain restrictions on their behavior in order to remain in the society. As societies evolve, these restrictions are codified as the law of the society, and the laws are maintained by religious and political authorities. This law of the society over its own citizens is called *municipal or domestic law* as opposed to the very different type of law, *international law,* which regulates the behavior of nations with regard to each other. Because of their very different situations, individual persons are born into a society and are subject to the laws of that society, while nations are subject to no laws except those which they have explicitly accepted as binding on themselves. Another way of saying that states are subject to no externally imposed law is to say that nations are *sovereign.*

Although nations are not subject to any laws but those to which they have deliberately and explicitly subjected themselves, they may nevertheless be conquered and destroyed by other nations. Many nations that once existed no longer do. Thus a struggle for survival and power exists among the various nations presently existing. In this context for survival and power, nations may find it advantageous to enter into agreements (treaties) with other nations. For example, consider a situation where there is an aggressive state more powerful militarily than each of two other neighboring states but not more powerful than both of them together. In this situation the two weaker nations may enter into an agreement not to attack each other and to fight together if the stronger one should attack either one.

What assurance is there that these two nations will live up to their agreement with each other? The situation is somewhat different from a contract between two citizens of the same state where the government will use its power to penalize any party which fails to fulfill its agreement. There is no government over the states to enforce the agreement if either side should try to back out. Still nations make such agreements, and most of the time they live up to them. Why? Because it is in the self-interest of each state to do so. Let us consider the situation in detail. Suppose that you are the leader of the state which finds its treaty partner being attacked. It is in your self-interest to abide by your agreement even though it means going to war. That is because if the more powerful enemy state overcomes your partner, which is likely if you refrain from fighting, then that victorious nation will probably attack you after it has solidified its conquest of your former partner. Consequently, it is better to join in the battle as soon as your partner is attacked than to wait and let the more powerful state devour your partner and you, one at a time.

There is also some motivation to join in the battle in accord with the treaty merely to establish the fact that your country can in general be counted on to live up to its agreements. If your country should get a reputation for not fulfilling its treaty obligations, then other nations will be reluctant to make other treaties with you in the future. Furthermore, since each nation enters into only those treaties that it wants to make, your country need not make any commitments which it does not intend to keep. Of course, there are cases where states have not lived up to their agreements, but in such cases the governments involved are very eager to provide some justification for not keeping their commitments, thus preserving their honor as treaty-keeping countries. States tend to abide by the treaties into which they enter because it is in their long-term self-interest to do so.

One of the most basic kinds of agreements nations make with each other is that which provides for reciprocal benefits; that is, each nation agrees to do for the other exactly what the other one agrees to do for it. For example, Nation A may agree to allow the citizens of Nation B to travel through Nation A unhindered if Nation B allows the citizens of Nation A to travel through Nation B unhindered. A good deal of international law depends on this principle of reciprocity. It is the basis, for example, of the law of diplomatic immunity, whereby each nation agrees not to harm or arrest or otherwise interfere with diplomats sent into its territory by other nations. Without such an agreement diplomats might be harassed, put in jail and held for ransom, or even killed. Under such circumstances no diplomats would go to other countries and international communication among nations would be severely handicapped. The principle of reciprocity is also the basis of the laws of war to be considered below. Such rules governing conflict are obeyed because each nation finds it beneficial to abide by them, because only then can the other side also be expected to abide by them.

Certain agreements, such as that providing for the immunity of diplomats from arrest, have become so common that nations may feel it is no longer necessary to stipulate that such an agreement exists when they begin dealing with each other. These and similar widely accepted arrangements in the dealings of countries with one another have come to be viewed as the rules of international *customary law*. To avoid possible misunderstandings about exactly what these customary rules are, however, they were codified in 1961 in the Vienna Convention on Diplomatic Relations.

The sovereignty of the nation is basic in all international law. Even though the rules of international customary law have the weight of wide acceptance and tradition behind them, any country which wishes to renounce them or to join with another nation in some agreements which are not consistent with the customary law may do so. As sovereign, any nation can decide which other nations it will recognize. It can decide to take on obligations to another nation or to an international body such as the United Nations. It can unilaterally declare a previous agreement with another state to be void if in its own opinion the other party has not fulfilled its obligations under the agreement! Furthermore, no nation can be bound by the agreements of other nations. Consequently, even if all nations but one agreed to follow certain principles (for example, that all should completely disarm), that single sovereign nation could still refuse to go along. If other countries were determined to make the agreement universal, their only option would be to physically subdue the recalcitrant country, consequently depriving it of its existence as a sovereign nation. This example also illustrates how some nations may be subject to coercion by other more powerful nations even though, in principle, all nations are sovereign. The reality is that nations are sovereign, but only so long as they can maintain their existence as independent nations.[1]

The Evolution of International Law

It should be evident that international law is not static, but is instead a changing body of obligations which may even differ from nation to nation. Although the counterpart of modern international law was developed among the Greek city-states, present international law has grown out of the dealings of European states with each other in the Middle Ages when nations were generally much smaller than those of today. At one time it was supposed that nations were at war with each other unless they had specifically entered into an agreement to be at peace. Unless there were specific agreements to the contrary, rulers could do as they pleased with any foreigners in their territory. To assure that a treaty would be kept, one party frequently provided the other with hostages who could be killed or otherwise abused if the provisions of the agreement were not fulfilled.

As the European community grew in wealth and technology, certain traditions and expectations with regard to international behavior developed. Frequently, principles of municipal law were extended by analogy to the international situation, especially when the ideologies and institutions of the nations involved were similar. Different views about the nature of international law were used to support efforts to argue for or against the adoption of certain proposed rules. Some philosophers appealed to *natural law,* that is, to the dictates of reason, as a guide to what is required of nations in their relations to each other. Others took what has come to be known as the *positivist position,* maintaining that countries had no obligations to each other except what they had specifically agreed to do in formal treaties. Still others appealed to *custom and tradition* as the basis for determining present obligations of one nation to another.[2]

Regardless of what philosophy of law might be used to provide a rationale for the principles of international law which came to be followed in the European system, the principles adopted were those which were acceptable to the more powerful nations. Thus, freedom of the seas became an accepted principle. Likewise the notion that the discoverer of a land was entitled to claim it for his own country was generally accepted. Any kind of claim which was not challenged by other nations would be regarded as legitimate. The right of conquest over "inferior" native peoples was accepted without question. As these European nations extended their control over the Americas, Africa, and Asia, they took these concepts of international law with them. Needless to say, if the peoples being subdued could have learned about this "international law" which was being used to justify their subjugation, they would not have regarded it as very desirable. It merely served as a device by which the powerful could exploit the weak, all the while maintaining that this was done by a legal process. It also functioned, however, to regulate the dealings of the European countries with each other, so that the danger of war between the colonizers would be minimized.

By the nineteenth century Europe had become a society of nations where interactions were not just between one state and another but frequently among several countries. After World War I, President Wilson persuaded the Europeans of the desirability of an international organization to regulate international affairs. The creation of this League of Nations, which was intended to include not only European nations but also nations of other parts of the world, was conceived as being completely consistent with the notion of national sovereignty on which international law was based. Any nation which wanted to join could do so without giving up any of its sovereignty, since all decisions of the League were to be unanimous. No nation could be compelled to join the League or to remain in it once it had joined.

Although the League of Nations in no way encroached on the principle of national sovereignty, it did develop a new principle in international relations, the notion of collective security in the face of an aggressive attack. Until the creation of the League, war had been regarded as a natural and legitimate way of expanding national power and any nation that was attacked was expected to defend itself. The League introduced a new idea in international law, namely, that launching a military attack against another nation was a reprehensible act and that it was the responsibility of sovereign nations to assist other sovereign nations in the enforcement of this principle, even when they were not themselves victims of the aggression.[3] It is obvious from history that nations found ways of avoiding this responsibility when it did not serve their own interests, but nevertheless the principle of the illegitimacy of military aggression and of the responsibility of all nations to act against an aggressor had been stated and at least nominally accepted by the nations which joined the League.

Another important development in international law came when the League established the Permanent Court of International Justice. For the first time an international tribunal was established to interpret international law as it applied to particular cases. If there were any dispute about what was required by international law in a particular situation, the nations now had a third party to which they could turn for an answer if all the disputants involved agreed to do so. This development also meant that there would be some pressure on every nation to accept principles of international law that had been accepted by most other nations. Strictly speaking, however, it was still true that no principle could be applied by the Permanent Court to a nation which had not accepted it.

The establishment of the United Nations after World War II also marked new developments in international law, at least in terms of what nations committed themselves to doing. The Security Council, composed of representatives from a small group of countries, was authorized to decide what kind of action should be taken with respect to threats to the peace, breaches of the peace, and acts of aggression. It was also given the right to determine what actions member nations and their military forces should take in such circumstances!⁴ Although any countries supplying forces must ratify arrangements made by the Security Council, there seems to be an important move away from the notion of national sovereignty in these provisions. The principle enunciated in the U.N. Charter is no longer simply that of collective defense as found in the League Covenant, but rather *internationally organized* collective defense under the direction of the Security Council and its Military Staff Committee. To be sure, no country is compelled to join the United Nations, but once it has signed the Charter it takes on a new kind of obligation not previously found in international law. The existence of such a commitment has led Switzerland to stay out of the United Nations itself, even though it belongs to most of the U.N.'s specialized agencies.

A second new development in international law ushered in by the United Nations concerns the commitment to human rights mentioned in the Charter and developed by the Universal Declaration of Human Rights and two later treaties, the International Covenant on Economic, Social, and Cultural Rights and the International Covenant on Civil and Political Rights. Especially significant for the development of international law is the Protocol to the Covenant on Civil and Political Rights.⁵ Nations which adopt this Protocol give their citizens the opportunity to appeal directly to an international body, the U.N. Human Rights Committee, if they feel their human rights are being violated by their own national government. Here, for the first time, the possibility exists of a nation entering into an international agreement which restrains the sovereignty of that government over its own citizens.

A third development in international law since the end of World War II has been the much greater emphasis on violations of international law by individual persons. There has been an effort to delineate and prescribe penalties for those individuals who have broken international law. The wide and early acceptance of the principle of the freedom of the seas resulted in pirates being considered international criminals some time ago, and the problem of piracy at sea was virtually eliminated in the nineteenth century. The new problems are piracy in the air in the form of hijacking airplanes, taking of international hostages, crimes by individuals against diplomats and citizens of other countries, and terrorism by individuals. International conventions have been adopted defining these crimes and indicating what national governments may do when such crimes are committed. The effort to penalize individuals for breaking international law got a big boost from the Nuremberg trials after World War II, where Nazi leaders were tried as individuals for war crimes.[6] Although one can be cynical about whether the persons tried in these cases were really any more responsible than others not brought to trial and about whether these trials are not simply a device used by the victors to humiliate the vanquished, one can also see them as part of a trend toward singling out for punishment those individuals who break international law. In this connection it is worth noting that a few of the German defendants at Nuremberg were found *not guilty* of violating international law.[7] The Nuremberg example has not been forgotten. In May 1993 the U.N. Security Council decided to establish an international war crimes tribunal in The Hague, The Netherlands, to prosecute war crimes and human rights violations committed after January 1, 1991, in the former Yugoslavia.[8] The U.N. General Assembly is also actively considering the possibility of establishing a Permanent International Criminal Court (a standing court rather than an *ad hoc* court) to try individuals for violating international law. If such a court is established, it will be a breakthrough in international law because until now all international courts dealing with individuals have been set up after the fact to deal with only one particular situation.[9]

This brief survey indicates that international law is developing gradually in the direction of world law, a law which is above the national governments and which puts some restrictions on national sovereignty.[10] Consider the changes that have taken place: While it was once assumed that nations are at war with each other unless they had explicitly signed a truce, it is now assumed that nations are at peace unless they have declared war on each other. Furthermore, fighting a war is now viewed as acceptable behavior only if it is in response to aggression either against the nation itself or some other nation.

The old presuppositions on which international law was based no longer hold. In a modern technological world, nations are no longer self-sufficient. Even a large and powerful nation such as the United States must import large amounts of oil and other raw materials from abroad, and it must sell some of its goods to other nations. In the present world the behavior of every nation makes a great deal of difference to all the others, whether it consists of testing nuclear weapons, adopting new tariffs to protect domestic production, adjusting the exchange rate of its currency, raising the prices on its exports, broadcasting propaganda, or building up its armed forces. Consequently, it no longer makes sense to conceive of nations as essentially isolated "organisms" which once in a while come into contact with their immediate neighbors. A society of nations has been developing and, along with it, a code of conduct suitable for such a society.[11]

Laws of War

One of the most interesting aspects of international law is that even when nations are engaged in open hostilities against each other they still follow rules, the laws of war, which restrain their behavior. How is this possible? It stems from the same principle as all international law, namely, mutual self-interest. For example, in war both sides will experience situations where some of their military forces are so outnumbered that they will want to surrender rather than be slaughtered. Consequently, a rule of war exists by which armed forces are permitted to surrender rather than being killed. Furthermore, it is to the advantage of each side to keep observing this rule. If one side starts slaughtering opponents who have surrendered, it can expect the same to happen to its own personnel who are trapped. Consequently, the rules of war are designed to keep war from becoming any more brutal than it already is.

A fundamental distinction made in the rules of warfare is that between military personnel (combatants) and civilians (noncombatants). It is presumed that the contest in war is between the military forces of the nations involved and that the aim of warfare is military victory. According to this way of thinking, there is no point in killing civilians because it does not contribute to military victory to do so. Since the governments on both sides want to preserve their civilian populations from any more harm than necessary, the rules of war indicate that it is acceptable to try to kill military personnel (as well as to destroy the armaments they use or could use) but that it is improper to try to kill civilians (or to destroy the equipment they use for farming or other civilian pursuits). Trains and ships and airplanes carrying military personnel or military supplies are fair game, but others are not. Following this same outlook, prisoners, wounded military personnel and those who care for them, pilots who have parachuted from their aircraft, survivors of sunken ships, and the like are not to be attacked since they no longer constitute a military threat.[12]

In modern warfare the distinction between military and civilian sectors of a nation's wartime efforts has become very blurred. Whole nations are mobilized for warfare. The high school student of today is the soldier of tomorrow, so why wait until he gets into uniform before trying to kill him? Some of the food which the farmer grows may go to civilians, but part also goes to the military, who would have a hard time continuing the war without it. The workers who are producing tanks, airplanes, ships, and ammunition are civilians, but the goods they produce are as crucial to the continuation of the fighting as the soldiers who use them. The wounded soldier of today is the already-trained functioning soldier of tomorrow, so why wait until he has recovered before trying to kill him?

Also, if we look at war carefully, we see that it is the governments rather than the military forces which are ultimately responsible for carrying on the war. If the civilian population is bombed and otherwise intimidated, won't they eventually pressure their own government to stop the war by surrendering? Why not make the population of the other side suffer just as the other side will cause suffering to one's own population if the area where they are living were to be conquered? Such questions came to the fore especially during World War II when aerial bombing made it possible to attack far behind the front lines. Furthermore, now that nuclear weapons with their extensive destructiveness are available, it becomes hard to see how an attack could any longer be pinpointed on military targets even if the attacker wished to do so. The present planning for the use of strategic nuclear weapons is not inhibited very much by any wish not to harm civilians. The traditional distinction between military targets on the one hand and civilian areas and personnel on the other is in danger of being lost completely. Yet, if this distinction is eliminated, then those international laws protecting prisoners and the wounded on grounds that they are no longer active members of the enemy's military forces would seem to lose their justification too.

If there cannot be humane war, why not try to prohibit war itself as inhumane? An effort to renounce war as an instrument of national policy was made in 1928 in the form of the Treaty for the Renunciation of War (also called "The Pact of Paris" and "The Kellogg-Briand Pact"). Unfortunately, this treaty did not stop World War II from occurring (though it did serve as a basis for some of the indictments of German leaders at the Nuremberg trials). The U.N. Charter also contains statements renouncing war, and even renouncing the *threat* of using force![13] The trouble is that international laws of war have not always been obeyed during war, and there is no basis to expect that an international law against starting a war would be observed any more faithfully. In the final analysis, nations tend to act in terms of their perception of their own national interest; and when obeying international law comes into conflict with national interest, it is national interest which prevails.

The Sources of International Law

We have already noted that international law differs from municipal law in that there is no authorized person or body which enacts or enforces it and that international law evolves as other things change. We have mentioned in passing some of the sources of international law, but will now explore this issue in more depth. Suppose that you were a member of the International Court of Justice hearing a case. Since there is no world legislature whose acts would produce world law, where can you turn to discover what the international laws are that might bear on the case at hand?

Article 38 of the Statute of the International Court of Justice spells out precisely what sources are to be used.[14] First, you could turn to "international conventions [including treaties], whether general or particular, establishing rules expressly recognized by the contesting states." Note that it does not matter what principles of international law may have been accepted by other nations. All that counts are the principles explicitly acceded to by the parties involved in the present dispute.

Second, you could refer to "international custom, as evidence of a general practice accepted as law." As we noted earlier, there are certain principles involved in the relationships between nations which have become so common that they are assumed rather than being written into treaties; these rules of international customary laws were codified in the 1961 Vienna Convention on Diplomatic Relations.

Third, you could use "the general principles of law recognized by civilized nations." An example of such a general principle is the idea of reciprocity, the principle that whatever rights a nation claims for itself must also be recognized as rights for other nations too. It is understood that this source of law is to be used only when the matter cannot be resolved using the first two sources. It is only the very general principles of law which are accepted by all the major legal systems of the world that are relevant. The main point of specifying this source of international law is to preclude a situation where the Court could not decide an obvious issue because the principle involved had not come up for consideration in earlier treaties or conflicts.

Fourth, appeal could be made to "judicial decisions" previously rendered by international, and even national, courts and to "the teaching of the most highly qualified publicists of the various nations." Scholars of international law are constantly publishing arguments for one or another position, and if there were a consensus among these experts on international law from various legal traditions, then their opinions might be used to support a judgment. Still, it must be remembered that appeals to previous judicial decisions and to the opinion of experts are "subsidiary means for the determination of rules of law" and consequently become significant only when the first three sources leave the issue unresolved.

One of the most interesting sources of international law is that which grows out of treaties and covenants in a secondary way. For example, states which have joined the United Nations have signed a treaty (the U.N. Charter) upon entering the organization. The Charter establishes the whole U.N. structure, including the General Assembly. Suppose the General Assembly unanimously passes a resolution dealing with a particular aspect of international law, for example, that the oceans are "the common heritage of mankind" rather than the property of any nation. If none of the nations protested or voted against this principle when given the opportunity to do so, it can be assumed that all have accepted it, just as if they had signed a treaty containing this declaration. No nation could later claim during a judicial proceeding that it had not accepted it. On the other hand, if a given nation had voted *against* that declaration, it would not be obliged to conform to that declaration no matter how many other nations in the General Assembly had voted for it. Thus, there is no assumption that the General Assembly can make international law. The situation is rather that nations put themselves on record when they cast their vote in the U.N. and that these votes might later be taken by the International Court of Justice to indicate acceptance of a measure acted on by the General Assembly.

Enforcing International Law

Just as there is no legislature or other authority to make international law, so also there is no police force or other agency to enforce it. What is to be done if a decision has been rendered by the International Court of Justice and a nation refuses to abide by the decision? Ideally, the U.N. Security Council should coordinate enforcement efforts, but it is also conceivable that the U.N. General Assembly might recommend measures to the member states of the U.N. or that individual nations might act on their own. In any case, efforts to enforce the decision might include cutting off trade, severing diplomatic relations, eliminating international exchanges with regard to mail or transportation, or initiating military action.

How effective would such enforcement efforts be? It seems to depend a great deal on the power and self-sufficiency of the "outlaw" country and the level of support among the more powerful nations for enforcing the sanctions. If the country which refused to abide by the Court's decision was a weaker nation and there was enthusiastic support for enforcement among all the big powers, the actions suggested above would undoubtedly be effective; there probably would be no need to go beyond the imposition of economic sanctions. On the other hand, if the country which refused to abide by the Court's decision was a powerful country or had even a single powerful ally who would not support sanctions against it, efforts to enforce the decision would be vetoed in the Security Council or thwarted in some other way. Another aspect of trying to enforce a decision against a nation-state is the fact that carrying out sanctions, such as cutting off trade, might be more disadvantageous to the other nations than to the nation supposedly being punished.

Even though we might abhor the fact that international law will be much more of a constraining factor on weak nations than on strong ones, we should not forget that unfortunately the same thing is true to some extent even within domestic legal systems. Very wealthy individuals, politically influential people, corporations, labor unions, and the like have enough power that legislatures and courts are much more protective of their interests than of the interests of poor, powerless, unorganized people. What makes the national political and judicial systems as workable as they are is that even the most powerful individuals and groups constitute only a small proportion of the nation as a whole and thus their capacity to resist the dictates of the common interest is restricted. On the other hand, on the international scene the United States alone accounts for about a quarter of the world's production of goods and services. Its allies in Western Europe and Japan account for another quarter. How could any world organization hope to endorse decisions to which the United States and its allies were intensely opposed? Perhaps the only hope for either international law or world law is to deal with individual persons rather than large groups or nations. Then the problem of enforcement becomes much more manageable.

We should not suppose, however, that the only motivation which national governments have for obeying international law is the possible coercive activities of other nations. As noted previously, another important motive is long-range self-interest. International law has been built on the basis of agreements which are mutually satisfying to the nations entering into the treaties. Any loss which may come from the application of international law in one situation will probably be small compared with the gains that can be made in the long run by making use of international law. Consequently, although nations can be expected to struggle to their utmost to advance their national interests, they can also be expected to exercise some restraint instead of openly violating international law. For the smaller, less powerful nations the gains from a strengthened system of international law will be even greater than for the more powerful countries. In this connection it is worth mentioning that the U.N. General Assembly, at the instigation of the less developed countries, has declared the 1990s to be "The Decade of International Law."

A third motivation which national governments have for obeying international law is furnished by the relation of such governments to their own citizens. In many democratic nations, and even in some non-democratic ones, there is a concern for the morality of law which will be marshalled against any national government which blatantly transgresses it. In the 1930s when the governments of Great Britain and France were making deals with Mussolini to try to lure him onto their side against Hitler, even though the Covenant of the League of Nations required them to resist Italy's aggression in Ethiopia, they had to keep what they were doing secret.[15] They knew that a substantial proportion of their own citizenry backed the League and its principles of collective defense against nations engaging in aggression. In 1974, when OPEC quadrupled the price of oil, there was some talk of using military force to conquer the oil fields of the Middle East, but such a blatant use of force and indifference to international law would have generated mass protests in the United States and other Western democracies.

National governments must also keep up at least the appearance of abiding by international law because of the dangerous example they would provide to their own citizens if they openly defied established principles of international law. Although there is a considerable difference between municipal law and international law, the subtleties of this distinction will not be apparent to most of the citizenry. Consequently, most national governments will do everything they can to avoid being perceived as violators of international law because they do not wish to provide an example of lawlessness to their own people.

Finally, it should be kept in mind that there is one way in which the enforcement of international law is not as much of a problem as the enforcement of municipal law, namely, that in international law each nation is subject only to those rules which it has explicitly accepted as binding, while in municipal law individual persons are subject to rules which they did not personally consent to obey but which were imposed on them by the government. A nation need not commit itself to any rule that it doesn't intend to follow. This situation means that nations will have fewer legal obligations but will usually abide by the ones to which they have committed themselves. An obvious exception, however, is the situation where nations have just lost a war and are coerced into signing agreements which they would not make voluntarily. Under such circumstances they may not feel obliged to fulfill the terms which have been imposed on them.

Regardless of theoretical considerations, however, one cannot be very optimistic about the enforcement of international law after what happened with regard to Iran in 1980. The Iranian government acquiesced in the seizure of American diplomatic personnel and property by some of its own citizens in direct violation of the principle of diplomatic immunity, one of the oldest principles of international law. The International Court of Justice ruled unanimously that Iran had violated the 1961 Vienna Convention on Diplomatic Relations, which Iran had signed. Nevertheless, no international sanctions were adopted against Iran, even though it was not a superpower or the close ally of a superpower and all diplomats everywhere were threatened by the weakening of this particular international law. The fact that many countries were dependent on Iran for oil may have also been an important factor. Nevertheless, the failure of the international community to enforce the decision of the International Court against Iran was a disaster from the point of view of promoting future reliance on international law and the International Court of Justice. At the same time it should be recognized that the decision of the Court may have been a factor in Iran's being persuaded by Algeria to finally release the American hostages they had taken.

Part Four

Proposals for Solving the War Problem

XIV. Reforming the Attitudes of Individuals

In Part IV we are making an important shift from focusing on facts about what has happened and is happening to a new kind of question: *What should be done to deal with the war problem?* It seems that any *prescription* about the proper remedies should be based on a *diagnosis* of why wars occur. We have already discussed the causes of war in Part II. The information in Part III should help you to evaluate those various theories about why wars occur. In a general way, we can classify the various alleged causes of war into four groups: (1) wars begin in the minds and with the attitudes of those *individuals* who decide to participate in or support wars; (2) wars result from the *basic structure* or *ideological foundations* of some war-prone, unjust *national governments;* (3) wars occur because of the *policies,* foreign and domestic, followed by national governments; and (4) wars are due to the law-of-the-jungle *nature of the international system* in which national governments must operate. Of course, wars may have more than one cause and even more than one kind of cause. But regardless of what particular view one takes on the issue of the cause(s) of war, it seems that one's *prescription* of what should be done to deal with the problem needs to be connected to one's *diagnosis* of why the problem exists.

The four chapters which make up Part IV are arranged according to four general *classes of prescriptions* on how to deal with the war problem, each related to one of the classes of alleged causes mentioned in the previous paragraph. Within each class or group of prescriptions you will find *particular prescriptions,* some of which might be combined with each other and some of which are blatantly incompatible with each other. Our aim is to explore all the alternatives so that you are in a better position to evaluate particular proposed prescriptions. In fact examining these various prescriptions may even lead you to reexamine your thinking about the causes of war. As noted above, there should be a direct relation between what you maintain causes wars and your prescription(s) for dealing with the war problem.

This chapter on which you are now embarking is focused on modifying the *attitudes of individuals* as a way of dealing with the war problem. There are different specific proposals about what attitudes need to be developed, and you might very well agree with some proposals and disagree with others. You might also think that none of these proposals are worthwhile

270

because you might believe that the *attitudes of individuals* are not a very important factor in war. In that case, you will be more interested in the subsequent chapters on what should be done to promote peace. Chapter 15 discusses three specific prescriptions which are quite different from each other but all of which fit into the general category of prescriptions addressed to changing the *basic structure* or *ideological basis* of *some national governments* which are alleged to be the trouble-makers who cause war. Chapter 16 contains a wide range of proposals, some of which are diametrically opposed to each other but which nevertheless fit into the category of prescriptions focused on what *policies national governments should follow* in order to avoid war. Chapter 17 also contains a variety of proposals, but they have in common the fact that they are addressed to the issue of changing *the way the international system works* as the key to having a peaceful world.

The preamble of the constitution of the United Nations Educational, Scientific, and Cultural Organization says: "Since wars begin in the minds of men, it is in the minds of men that the defenses of peace must be constructed." In one way or another, education seems to be at least part of the solution to almost any social problem. But when we speak of education, we must beware of jumping to the conclusion that education is for young people alone or that it refers only to what happens within classrooms in schools. Education refers to all teaching of some by others in all kinds of situations. Most of our attitudes come from our parents, our close associates, and the mass media. Teachers are close associates of their students only for a brief period of time. Consequently, although it is to be hoped that teachers and the formal educational system of which they are a part can be instrumental in furthering the objectives discussed below, it would be a gigantic mistake to believe that the institutionalized educational system, by itself, can do a great deal to reform the attitudes of individuals. If the attitudes of individuals are to be reformed in a manner that will make war less likely, many persons in the society will need to take part. The efforts of the mass media will be especially important, and several kinds of attitudes will need to be addressed. Furthermore, it is not only the attitudes of the masses which need to be reformed but even more importantly the attitudes of the leaders.

Interest in Social Issues Including International Affairs

Attitudes about the importance of certain kinds of events are affected by how much we know about them. It is true that when we think that something is important we make an effort to find out about it, but it is also true that we tend to regard as unimportant anything about which we know very little. Consequently, the development of attitudes and interests depends to some extent on the knowledge we acquire, especially when young. If this knowledge is only about our own immediate family and close friends, we may unconsciously come to believe that what is happening to others in other places is unimportant. The same holds at another level, too: If we learn only about our own nation and its history and traditions, we may unconsciously come to believe that what has happened and is happening to people in other lands is unimportant. Interest in the problems of the larger society and of the global community is not inborn. It must be developed in younger people and nurtured in older people.[1]

Most injustice that exists in society is the result not of malevolence but of indifference. People are very much aware of their own personal and family problems, but a special effort is required to develop a sensitivity to the problems of others and to the problems faced by the society as a whole. The beginning of social injustice is the attitude of indifference on the part of large numbers of people. Consequently, a just society requires that its members acquire an interest in the problems of others and the problems which confront the group as a whole.

It is important for peace and justice at the global level that this interest go beyond domestic issues.[2] People need to be informed about international affairs and about the problems being faced by other nations as well as those confronting their own country. They need to know about governments and other institutions and about the various ideas and ideologies that motivate people. If we never learn about the competing interests and the various outlooks which guide social decision-making, we probably will never understand the significance of the individual events which are reported in the news. Also if we have never been encouraged to think of war as a problem for humanity to solve, we will probably not be aware of how particular political decisions help or hinder the solution of this problem.

Skepticism and Tolerance

Developing awareness about social issues, the problems of different nations and different groups, social philosophy, and the war problem is not sufficient, however. It is also important that certain attitudes be developed if the war problem is to be solved. A crucial one is an attitude of skepticism toward what others tell us and toward the beliefs we have already adopted. We are credulous creatures. We tend to believe whatever we are told unless there is some good reason to doubt it, and sometimes we believe what we are told even when there is reason to doubt it. We are also creatures of habit. If there should be a conflict between one idea and another, we tend to believe that the idea we heard first is the correct one. We find it difficult to discard any belief we have once held, and the longer we have held it the harder it is to give up.

It is because of our natural credulity and our natural dislike for changing our views that we must make a special effort to develop a skeptical outlook in ourselves and others. Although what people tell us is generally a reflection of what they believe to be true, no one is infallible. Consequently, at least part of what we are told by others is false. We are not infallible, either. Thus it follows that at least some of our own present beliefs are mistaken. Of course, if we knew which of our ideas are false, we would discard them. The only rational procedure is to be somewhat skeptical both about our own beliefs and the beliefs conveyed to us by others.

Skepticism is especially important for solving the problem of war because wars often have an ideological basis. There is usually an effort by the leaders of each nation or social group to impose their "obviously correct" views about religious, economic, political, or other matters on the rest of their own group as well as on other societies. In each nation or group, people come to be convinced of the correctness of their own beliefs because those beliefs were the ones they heard first and most often from persons most dear to them. They just *know* that their own views about religion and about the ideal political and economic arrangements in a society are true. The views of "the enemy," on the other hand, have come to their attention only late in life, if at all. These views are unfamiliar and are often conveyed by strangers or books written by unknown authors, so it is assumed that they are mistaken. Thus each side, being composed of people who are credulous creatures of habit, is sure that it is fighting for truth and justice. Most people in each nation or social group believe themselves to be the agents of good and the enemy to be the embodiment of evil. Even violence seems justified since the issue is perceived as a struggle of truth and justice against falsehood and wickedness.

One way of trying to prevent this situation is for all people everywhere to develop skeptical attitudes toward all their beliefs and toward the "information" which is being conveyed to them. Prejudices which differ from our own and the propagandistic nature of devices used to spread ideas with which we disagree are obvious to us. What is necessary is that we be alert to the fact that we also have our own prejudices (most of them learned in our earliest years), and that the ideas which we have been led to accept may also have been spread by propagandistic devices. We need to examine even our most basic beliefs to determine whether they have a sound foundation or are merely reflections of prejudices. Even after we have critically examined our beliefs, we must continue to keep in mind that we may be mistaken.

Closely related to the attitude of skepticism is the attitude of tolerance for beliefs and practices which are different from our own. If we are absolutely sure of the correctness of our own beliefs and practices, then it may seem appropriate to impose these beliefs and practices on others even if they are not willingly accepted. If we happen to be in a position where we cannot impose them on others, we still are tempted to make fun of different beliefs and practices. But we need to combat these inclinations. Just learning about the various beliefs and practices of others at an early age will help to make them seem less strange, but special efforts should also be made to develop an attitude of appreciation of the different perspectives of others. Such an attitude does not develop automatically. It is the natural inclination of people to be intolerant of beliefs and practices different from their own, and this tendency supports a readiness to engage in wars against foreigners or others who differ in some way. Consequently, the deliberate development of an attitude of tolerance for those who are different is one instrument for making wars less likely.

Reluctance to Use Violence

Another attitude which needs to be fostered to promote peace is the reluctance to resort to violence in situations of disagreement and conflict. Each of us has ideas of what is true and right and good (with what is good usually being taken as equivalent to what is good *for me*). We regularly find others disagreeing with us. When we are in a position to do so, it is tempting to coerce the other party into following our point of view. The mistreatment of children, old people, minority groups, and women testifies to the readiness of people to use violence to impose their will on others. But the attitudes of skepticism and tolerance just discussed imply another way of handling conflict situations. The use of violence overlooks the possibility that our own ideas may be mistaken. It also neglects the consequence that resentment is aroused in those who are coerced into acting against their own will.

A nonviolent approach to conflict situations will involve a recognition that one's own beliefs about what is true or right may need to be corrected, as well as an effort to appreciate the point of view of the other party. The conflict situation can thus be viewed as an opportunity for learning and developing a wider range of concern. The opportunity for learning can best be exploited if each party can state not only its position but also the grounds or reasons for this position. Each party to the conflict should be free to raise objections to beliefs which it thinks are mistaken. Ideally, the parties would become aware of the weaknesses in their own positions and the strengths in those of their opponents. Eventually a compromise of some sort may be possible. Each party should also develop a sensitivity to the concerns of the other. In conflict situations it is desirable to engage in role-playing where each party argues for the opponent's position. This exercise helps develop an awareness of the interests of the other party. Undoubtedly, this nonviolent approach to conflict situations is not one which will occur automatically. If we want life to be more peaceful, we will need to make an effort to have both children and adults learn about it and want to use it.

Although peace requires that people learn to develop a reluctance to use violence in conflict situations, many young people today are being taught just the opposite. Boys are still often told that the "manly" way of resolving differences of opinion is to use their fists against those who disagree. Propagandists urge their followers to stop at nothing in promoting their cause. On television and in movies violence is glorified as the quick and proper way of resolving conflict, and the long-term consequences of using violence in conflict situations are conveniently neglected. In discussing international relations, many government leaders and media representatives assume without even considering alternatives that the use of force and threats of force is the only proper way to handle conflicts between nations. The question of what is right or just is often not asked; the only issue is how to coerce the other party into accepting one's own terms. When many people feel that violence and threats of violence are the proper way to resolve differences among them, there is little hope of avoiding war and eliminating arms races. On the other hand, if there were a general feeling that conflict situations should be resolved by nonviolent means, the chance for peace would be much greater.

One way of reducing the readiness to use violence in social situations would be to expand public knowledge about the philosophy and techniques of nonviolent resistance and to promote a wider awareness of some of the situations where nonviolent actions have brought about social change. A widespread familiarity with the teachings and lives of Mohandas Gandhi and Martin Luther King, Jr., would provide a good beginning.[3] Peace on all levels will be furthered if people develop a negative attitude toward the use of violence in conflict situations.

Unselfishness

It is a commonplace that warfare would be greatly reduced if people were less greedy and selfish. It seems that no matter how much people have, they always want more. The situation is aggravated in a society where advertising creates wants in order to sell goods and services to those who have the money to buy them. People who never thought about a midwinter vacation of a week or two in Hawaii or the Caribbean may, as the result of advertising, find themselves not only wanting such a vacation but positively needing one. Furthermore, the vicissitudes of life are such that it is impossible for most people to have enough insurance and savings to take care of all the emergencies that might arise. Faced with what appears to be unlimited "needs" for our own welfare, it is difficult for most people to be much concerned about the welfare of others. The expenditure of $1,000 or more for a vacation seems sensible, while a gift of half that amount to educate illiterate people in other parts of the world might lead some to think that the giver had lost his sense of the worth of money. Our own "needs" seem pressing and urgent, while those of others seem insignificant and remote. It is certainly natural to be more concerned about ourselves than others, but a peaceful world will require people to develop more concern for others and a more realistic appraisal of their own needs than what is generally found at present among the affluent persons of the world. Those who are well off need to remind themselves often that they did not choose where to be born and thus could just as well be living in a poor country where the threat of starvation and death from disease is a daily reality.[4]

It is not only individual selfishness which must be tempered but group selfishness as well. One of the interesting aspects of society is the existence of small groups, such as families, whose members display the greatest unselfishness toward each other but who are reluctant to assist those outside this group. For example, parents may sacrifice so that their children can acquire a college or university education but will be reluctant to give a penny so that other children can learn the very basic skills of reading and writing. They will make sure that their own parents are cared for but at the same time display complete indifference toward other old people who may be in much more desperate need of help. In this situation, the individuals may be very unselfish, but the family group could well be described as selfish. While generosity confined to the family group is a natural human trait, peace will be much more likely when not just individuals but also families (and other larger groups such as nations, too) become much less selfish.

Globalism and Humatriotism

We have just considered the needs for families and other groups to become less selfish not only as individuals but also as groups. Another way of handling what is essentially the same problem is to expand the "we" group, the group with which we identify. The attitude of identifying with members of our family and with close friends seems to develop naturally. With a bit of effort, nations are able to extend the group with which the individual identifies. When there is a single language, a single cultural heritage, and a racially homogeneous group, the identification with the nation is likely to be easily established, but even in nations such as Switzerland, where a variety of languages and cultures exists, it is possible to develop a sense of "we" which extends to the whole country.

An obvious question arises. If people can be taught to identify with all the others in a heterogeneous nation, why can't the same devices be used to stimulate identification with all the people of the world? If a national flag can be used in helping to develop a sense of identification with the nation, why not use the U.N. flag to help develop a sense of identification with the whole global society? If nationalism can be furthered by a pledge of allegiance to the national government, why not use a pledge of allegiance to the whole world in order to further a commitment to globalism?[5] If nationalism can be developed by celebrating national holidays, why can't a sense of globalism be developed by celebrating world holidays?

A step in the direction of a world holiday has already been taken by the United Nations General Assembly. In December of 1971, a resolution was adopted 63–6 proclaiming U.N. Day, October 24, to be an international holiday and recommending that it be observed as a public holiday by all nations which are members of the U.N. Dorothy Schneider of St.

Louis, who was instrumental in persuading delegates from various nations to introduce this resolution, has now shifted her efforts to getting the United States to follow the recommendation and make U.N. Day a national holiday in the United States.[6] A somewhat related annual event in the United States and some other countries which helps to develop an attitude of globalism is the annual collection for UNICEF conducted near the end of October.[7]

Of course, the fact that such devices *can* be used to develop a sense of globalism does not mean that they *will* be used. In fact, the persistence of the system of sovereign nations and the enduring possibility of war mean that national governments, schools, and mass media which are directly or indirectly under their control will probably continue to try to develop *patriotism* (loyalty to the homeland) rather than *humatriotism*[8] (loyalty to the human race). National governments can't afford to have their soldiers hesitating to kill enemy soldiers just because they are also human beings. In case of war they need young people who are unquestioningly loyal to them, not to the whole human race. If a world government were instituted over the national governments, the situation would be different. Then an effort could more readily be made to develop humatriotism because national governments would no longer have a potential need for soldiers. It is worth noting, for example, that the state governments in the United States formally control the educational system but do not need to develop intense loyalty to their own state governments because they have no need for soldiers to fight against other states. The irony of the situation is that a world government probably will not be feasible until there are large numbers of people who have already adopted an attitude of loyalty to the world community. It seems then that the development of humatriotism cannot wait until after a world government is formed. Loyalty to the whole human race is needed now.

It is sometimes argued that creating a sense of globalism will not work in the same way as creating a sense of national loyalty because there will be no out-group or enemy to serve as a stimulus for group cohesion. It is claimed that the love for one's own group (amity) must be accompanied by the hatred of some enemy group (enmity). For example, Robert Ardrey says, "The primate amity-enmity complex cannot exist without enemies."[9] Earlier, Sigmund Freud had observed, "It is always possible to unite considerable numbers of men in love towards one another, so long as there are still some remaining as objects for aggressive manifestations."[10] Historically, nationalism seems to have been strongest when there has been a traditional enemy, such as occurred when Germany and France confronted each other in the nineteenth and first half of the twentieth centuries. On the other hand, there are cases where national pride and patriotism are strong even in the absence of any recent external enemies; Switzerland and Sweden are but two examples. Also, in a study directed specifically to the topic of loyalty, Harold Guetzkow concluded: "Although an out-group is often useful in serving as a foil in the development of in-group solidarity, it is not a necessary condition for the development of group loyalty."[11] It is at least possible that people can learn to view war, huge military expenditures, wasted resources, pollution, diseases, and natural disasters as "the enemy" of the human race against which they can direct their aggressive tendencies.[12]

In our earlier discussion of nationalism, we noted that the existence of different languages within a country, though not an insurmountable obstacle to building a sense of national identity, nevertheless constitutes a hindrance to that goal. Not being able to communicate directly with other people because of language differences tends to block the process of identification. If people cannot read the same materials or listen to the same radio and television broadcasts, they may develop very different attitudes and beliefs about the world. There is also a basis for suspicion when some people are speaking to one another and others cannot understand what they are saying. It follows that one thing which might help a great deal to develop a sense of community among all the peoples of the world is the use of the same language everywhere.

It is unlikely that people will stop using the language with which they are familiar and start using another. What seems more realistic is that people all over the world could concentrate on learning the same second language. In that way people everywhere could retain their own native languages but at the same time speak directly with people from other countries without the assistance of a translator. In the late nineteenth century, with this very thought in mind, a Polish oculist named L.L. Zamenhof developed an international language called Esperanto. This artificially constructed language is based on a vocabulary drawn from a mixture of European languages and has an easily learned, completely regular grammar and phonetic spelling. Interested individuals and groups worldwide have devoted themselves to spreading the use of Esperanto. It is also used in some international broadcasting and international publications. Efforts to have Esperanto adopted as an official language at the League of Nations did not succeed. Similar efforts at the U.N. have so far met with a similar fate, but UNESCO has shown some interest in the work of the Esperantists.[13]

Whether it be Esperanto or some other language, it would be helpful in the long-term development of the world community if the United Nations would take action, declaring some single language to be the one official language of the future.[14] It could be determined that at some definite future date (perhaps 25 or 50 years hence) this language would be the only one to be used at the United Nations and in official inernational communications. Starting immediately, young people all over the world could be taught this language in addition to their own. Costly translation facilities and multiple printings of all documents could then be avoided. Maximum use of the technological capabilities of worldwide communication and transportation systems would no longer be hindered by the absence of a single language. Everyone in the whole world could communicate directly with everyone else.

In the absence of such deliberate action by the United Nations it is still possible that some single world language may develop. In fact, English is rapidly becoming such a language not only because it is the official language in many countries but also because of the present influence of American technology and business. The difficulty with English as the world language, in addition to its eccentric spelling and other irregularities, is that such a development carries with it overtones of cultural imperialism. Not only the English language, but also the cultural traditions and values which are carried in the language, would be thrust on everyone. A global ethnically neutral language like Esperanto would avoid this problem. Even though its vocabulary is fundamentally European, Esperanto has from the beginning carried with it a spirit of international cooperation and has been accepted enthusiastically by Japanese, Chinese, Koreans and other non–Europeans.

The crucial point, however, is the central role that a single world language, whether Esperanto or some other language, would have in creating a sense of world community. If somehow a single world language could be decided upon, the development of a sense of "we"-ness which includes the whole world would develop much more rapidly. It is a sad commentary on the absence of vision of the political and educational leaders of the nations that so little attention has been directed to this significant problem of a single language for the whole human family.[15]

Before leaving the topic of patriotism and humatriotism, we should take note of how perceptions of international affairs would be different if nationalism were subordinated to globalism. Such a change could be expected to at least partially erode the double standard of morality which now is frequently manifested in the perception of foreign relations. For example, at the time of the Cuban missile crisis in October of 1962, Americans generally believed that it would be very wrong for the Soviets to install missiles even though the Cuban government wanted them and even though the United States had its own missiles in Turkey not far from the Russian border. For another example, Americans generally believe there is something wrong about some other countries having nuclear weapons, but at the same time feel it is quite proper for the U.S. to have thousands of them. On what basis can it be argued that it is bad for these other countries to have nuclear weapons but that it is good for the U.S. to have them? If the predominant nationalistic point of view is replaced by a global perspective, this double standard of morality will no longer go unquestioned.

Of course, it is not only American nationalism that leads to the adoption of a double standard of morality in international affairs. Russian nationalism, Israeli nationalism, Palestinian nationalism, Vietnamese nationalism, and so on—all of the nations find it easy to excuse themselves for the very things they find reprehensible if done by other nations. Such a distortion of perceptions provides a fertile ground for wars. An attitude of globalism could serve as a welcome corrective to the double-standard mentality of nationalistic thinking in international affairs.

Even many of those involved in the academic study of international relations could benefit from adopting a global framework which would override the nationalistic perspective which is so automatically assumed in their work. Many scholars in the field of foreign affairs have been unable or unwilling to see world politics from a perspective where the problem to be addressed is one of governing the whole world for the welfare of the whole human race. They tend to consider global issues strictly from the standpoint of how knowledge of international affairs can be used to help their own national leaders to promote the welfare of their own particular nation. Some scholars do not even ask how a human problem such as the problem of war can be solved. Fortunately, there are others who have adopted a global perspective and have come to see that political science need not forever remain the handmaiden of national governments. Humatriotism is needed by everyone, including scholars in the field of international relations.

World Citizenship

It is not sufficient, however, that people begin to identify with all other human beings. People need to take on a readiness to work for the world community and its further development. Such an attitude would lead to more citizen support for globally minded organizations in their efforts to solve global problems. An acceptance of one's role as a world citizen would lead to personal actions such as learning a global ethnically neutral language, conserving resources, eating less meat (which would free more grain for use as human food), and making financial contributions to international agencies such as the International Red Cross and UNICEF and to the international relief organizations of churches and other groups. A good example of what can be done by committed world citizens is the "Live Aid" global rock concert and telethon telecast from Philadelphia and London in July of 1985 which featured the new song "We Are the World." That event not only raised millions of dollars to aid famine victims in Africa but also increased awareness of the reality of a single world community.

The development of a positive attitude toward world citizenship does not preclude taking on responsibilities at the local or national level of community. Just as a good citizen of Illinois or California or Texas can also be a good citizen of the United States, so a good citizen of the United States can also be a good citizen of the world. In fact, citizenship at the various levels of community is important.[16] It would be inappropriate for a citizen of Illinois or California or Texas to seek to promote the interests of that state in a manner detrimental to the larger community of the United States. In the same way, it is inappropriate for a citizen of any nation to seek to promote the interests of that nation in a manner detrimental to the larger world community. A good national citizen will also be a good world citizen, and a good world citizen will also be a good national citizen.

Looking Forward Rather Than Back

When dealing with social problems, human beings have a tendency to look back rather than forward. Consider how often in a conflict between individuals one person says, "You started it; you did X" while the other says, "It's not my fault, you did Y." This same thing happens in social conflicts: Group A remembers that at some time in the past Group B did this dastardly thing to their ancestors while Group B focuses on some other unforgivable deed done by the ancestors of Group A.

Looking back to what has been done is a sure formula for *not* solving problems. A most obvious fact is that no one can change the past. The most that one could do under such circumstances is to say "I'm sorry," but that is going to be very hard to say if the action was not yours but something done by some group of your ancestors. Looking back also involves making both sides return to the very frame of mind which produced the antagonistic actions. That makes it more difficult to resolve the conflict. Digging into the past to try to get more information about who was right and who was wrong may be appropriate in a courtroom where guilt or innocence must be determined, but in a social conflict situation it just accumulates more facts from the past that can't be changed and generates more antagonistic feelings that make resolving the conflict more difficult.

In order to deal with problems constructively, people should learn to focus on *what can be done in the future* rather than what was done in the past. In conflict situations, the best approach is to consider not merely what one party can do (although that may be necessary in some situations) but rather to have both parties to the conflict work together with the attitude "What can *we* do to get from the present situation to another situation which will be better for both of us?" The notion of "clearing the air" by discussing the past is totally wrong-headed. What is past is past and can't be changed. The appropriate approach is to rule out talk about the past and focus on the present and the future. Attend not to feelings about the past but to goals for the future.

There is no doubt that looking toward the future is in some ways more difficult than focusing on the past. When one looks at the past, there are details and realities. When one looks toward the future there are only imprecise goals and shadowy ideals. With reference to the earlier proposal that there should be world holidays to celebrate global events comparable to national holidays to celebrate significant events in the nation's history, how can one establish holidays to celebrate goals that are yet to be realized? How can one decide on an appropriate date for celebrating something that is going to happen in the future? It is difficult, but it is not impossible. It does require a shift from our usual way of thinking, but it can be done. This proposal says that if we can get more people to make that shift from focusing on the past to focusing on the future, it is more likely that we can do something constructive in the way of solving the war problem.

Overcoming Defeatism and Apathy

One attitude which needs to be overcome not only for solving the war problem but for solving all kinds of social problems is the attitude that the problem is so big that there's nothing anyone can do about it. Many people regard it as practically impossible to make any significant social changes, even in a small community. They tend to think that it would be even more difficult to make such a major change as abolishing war. Therefore they do nothing to even help with such an effort.

A number of observations can be made to counteract this kind of attitude. First, it can be noted that some very significant social changes have been made in the past, so social change is possible. From 1787 to 1789 the United States of America was created through the adoption of a totally new constitution. The persons mainly responsible for that change numbered less than a hundred. Non-governmental organizations such as the International Red Cross, Amnesty International, and Greenpeace which have had a significant impact on society were originally started by a handful of persons. Religions which have influenced millions of people have usually been started by one individual or a very small group. We see the tremendous impact of these efforts and tend to think that there was not much effort required and that their success was more or less a sure thing; but if we see the world as it was when those movements were just getting started, we can readily imagine almost everyone predicting that the effort could never succeed. After changes have occurred, they seem completely natural and almost foreordained; but at their small beginnings success seems to be impossible. Modern chaos theory tells us that the flapping of the wings of a butterfly may eventually influence the weather in a major way halfway around the world, so we can conclude that what one person does or doesn't do also may have a significant impact. All too often people get off track by asking, "What about others? They don't seem to be doing anything to help solve this problem." The proper response to that comment is that what other people do is their business, and what you do is your business. Are you as an individual doing what is helpful, or are you part of the problem?

Second, we should note that there is a big difference between concluding, "I can't do anything that will make much of a difference" and "I can't do anything at all." We need to keep in our minds the oft-quoted words of Edward Everett Hale:

> I am only one, but still I am one.
> I cannot do everything, but still I can do something.
> And just because I cannot do everything
> I will not refuse to do the something that I can do.

Along the same lines we have the verse "Stubborn ounce person" by Bonaro Overstreet:

> You say the little efforts that I make will do no good,
> That they will never prevail to tip the hovering scale where
> justice hangs in the balance.
> Well, perhaps I never thought they would,
> But I am prejudiced beyond debate in favor of my right to
> choose which side the scale shall feel the stubborn ounces
> of my weight.

Third, when thinking about dealing with the war problem, one can discard the *predictive* mode of thinking in favor of the *prescriptive* mode of thinking. Instead of focusing on the question *"Will* war ever be abolished?" (as if what we do could never have any bearing on the outcome), people could learn to ask *"Should* war be abolished?" and *"What needs to be done* in order for that to happen?" If we do not think of ourselves as agents whose actions can make a difference, then we are not likely to make a difference. On the other hand, if we view ourselves as free agents who can decide what should be done and who can then act to bring about what should be, then we are likely to make a difference. We need to promote that outlook reflected in the words of Robert Kennedy (borrowing from George Bernard Shaw's *Man and Superman*): "Some people see things as they are and ask 'Why?' I dream things that never were and ask 'Why not?'"

XV. Reforming the Internal Operation of National Governments

We have considered one approach to promoting peace, modifying the attitudes of individuals. A different strategy is that of reforming the internal operation of national governments. National governments are crucial to the war problem, whether we consider international wars or civil wars. In international wars, the national governments not only carry on the wars; it is also their policies which generate the conditions which may result in war with other nations. In civil wars the national government will be one party in the war, and its policies will have been instrumental in producing the conditions which lead to revolt. Consequently, it is plausible to argue that if national governments operated properly, the problem of war would be solved. There are, of course, various proposals about how national governments should be changed in order to make war less likely.

"The Western approach" assumes that the existence of war is due to nondemocratic national governments. If all national governments were democracies, it is claimed, warfare, both international and intranational, would be eliminated or greatly reduced. On the other hand, "the Marxist approach" assumes that the existence of war is due to capitalist-controlled national governments. If all national governments were socialistic, it is claimed, warfare, both international and intranational, would be eliminated or greatly reduced. A third view, the Gandhi-King approach, assumes that any kind of government is likely to perpetrate injustices and that the proper way of countering unjust governmental decisions is to mobilize large-scale nonviolent protests. It claims that if people everywhere could be organized and trained in the techniques of nonviolent resistance, then not only warfare, but also gross injustice, would be eliminated or greatly reduced.

The Western Approach

Defenders of the idea that democracy in every nation is the way to peace generally suppose that international wars are caused by power-hungry dictators who want to expand the area of their domination. As noted in our

284

discussion of the causes of war, the aggressiveness of leaders may be a significant factor in whether the groups they lead will behave aggressively toward other groups. It is claimed by supporters of this Western approach that extremely aggressive persons are more likely to gain control of the government in a dictatorship than in a democracy, because when people elect their leaders they will not vote for persons who advocate war or follow aggressive policies which are likely to lead to war. Furthermore, in a democracy there will be more restraints on what an aggressive leader can do. Authoritarian leaders, on the other hand, are accustomed to using ruthless force to subdue dissenters even in their own countries. Such individuals, it is argued, can be expected to use military means to try to increase the area of land and the number of people over which they have control. Consequently, it can be concluded that democratic nations will tend to have governments which seek peace and compromise, while countries with authoritarian rulers will tend to be militaristic, aggressive, and imperialistic.[1]

In the eyes of most Americans, World War II was a perfect illustration of the correctness of this view. Hitler established his authoritarian rule within Germany before being able to use his militaristic approach to subdue people in other countries. Mussolini began by silencing dissenters in Italy. The Japanese military allowed no public criticism of its policies in Japan. These nations thus were able to launch aggressive attacks on their neighbors without worrying about objections from their own people. If there had been a democratic government, it is argued, at least some of the people in Germany would have protested against Hitler's military expansion into Austria, Czechoslovakia, Poland, Belgium, France, Denmark, and Norway. Some persons would have protested against attacking Britain and Russia and declaring war on the United States. If there had been a democratic government in Japan, surely there would have been some protests against the attack on the United States at Pearl Harbor. Also, the Soviet Union headed by the dictator Stalin was able to reach an agreement with Hitler to divide Poland between them. Would the Russian people have approved that move if they had been allowed to express their views?

According to the adherents of this view, it is not only international war which would be ended if all nations were democracies. Such a change would also mean an end to wars within countries. If people can change their rulers at the ballot box, there seems to be no point in engaging in a violent struggle against the government. Dissenters can wait until the next election and try to generate enough support for their views to vote a different government into power. Under such a system, it is claimed, there is no justification for forceful action against the government in power. Even the motivation for trying to organize a violent revolution against the government is removed because it seems to be easier and less dangerous to exert the effort needed to win an election than to launch a successful military revolt.

But historical realities raise some questions about the theory that the institution of democratic governments everywhere would mean the end of war. Democratic governments in Great Britain, France, and the United States seem to have been as imperialistic and to have fought as many wars as the authoritarian governments in Spain, Portugal, and Russia. The involvement of the United States in the Mexican War and then the Spanish-American War can hardly give support to the notion that democratic governments don't engage in expansionistic, aggressive wars. There may have been some protesters, but they did not prevail. More recent American involvement in Asia and Latin America also raises doubts about the inherently pacifist nature of democracies. Furthermore, even if it were the case that democratic governments do not deliberately seek to bring about wars, they might still inadvertently make war more probable because of the policies they follow in international affairs as a result of their voters focusing on domestic affairs and fearing entanglement in the affairs of other nations.[2] Also, regardless of the apparent cogency of the argument about the needlessness of revolutions in a democracy, the historical reality is that even democratic governments do experience violent revolutions and civil wars. One of the bloodier examples is the American Civil War.

The historical record thus forces us to reexamine the argument that the institution of democratic governments would mean the end of war. A basic assumption of the argument was that ordinary people want peace. The problem is that the people of a nation also want other things. They want a high standard of living and will support policies that give it to them, even though these policies may arouse antagonism in other countries. Furthermore, the identification of people with their nation leads them to support wars which add to the territory and glory of the nation. What the people generally oppose is not war but a losing war or a long drawn-out indecisive war.[3] A war which can be won quickly and which adds to the national territory or prestige will generally have popular support. Even in Germany in World War II, Hitler was quite popular as long as the German forces were winning. In the United States, the invasion of Grenada in 1983 was quite popular though widely protested in the rest of the world as a most blatant violation of international law.

With regard to war within a country, the "revolution through the ballot box" argument neglects the fact that a minority group may suffer from the tyranny of the majority. In such a situation, an appeal to the ballot box is almost certain to end in defeat for the mistreated minority. The minority may have no wish to rule over the majority, but may simply want to withdraw and form a separate government in order to be free from domination. Having no chance of winning an election, they may feel that resort to violence is the only means of changing the situation, even in a democracy.

A Marxist reading this discussion would object that the whole presentation has been incredibly naive. It is based on the assumption that there are democratic governments where the people really have the power to elect the leaders they want and to follow the policies they approve. In reality, says the Marxist, so-called democratic governments are in fact controlled by capitalists and politicians who are subservient to them. Decisions on whether or not to engage in war are made on the basis of its being advantageous to capitalists. Imperialistic wars against weaker nations will be "sold" to the public through an appeal to nationalism, even though the real motivation is to give capitalists access to raw materials and control over markets. As for a revolution through the ballot box, the capitalists will make sure that the process by which candidates are nominated will be under their control. They will make sure that the mass media and the educational system indoctrinate people to admire capitalism and hate socialism. People who openly advocate socialist ideas will be harassed by the FBI and the local police and ignored by everyone else. Consequently, the Marxist argues, the so-called democratic system can be changed only if working classes use violence to remove the capitalists from their position of behind-the-scenes control.

Even though the argument that democracy in all countries would reduce warfare apparently has some deficiencies, perhaps something can still be said for it. The Marxist critique can actually be used to help undercut the historical cases used previously to show that democracy doesn't stop war. If the Marxist analysis is correct, then the cases cited do not refer to truly democratic nations but only to pseudo-democratic national governments. It could be claimed that it was a small ruling clique that sold the American public on the Mexican War and then on the Spanish-American War, and that the protesters of those wars were not given sufficient opportunity to express their views. What would have happened in a true democracy? It is hard to say. Nevertheless, it is worth noting how so-called democratic governments have had to keep some of their militaristic adventures secret from their own people. One distressing example of such secrecy occurred prior to World War II, when the governments of Britain and France concealed their secret agreements with Mussolini concerning Ethiopia.[4] Another illustration is the U.S. government's concealment from its citizens of events during the Vietnamese War. These cases of government secrecy suggest that government leaders in democracies realize that some of their war-oriented policies would not be generally approved by their own people. Perhaps leaders in truly democratic governments would be less inclined to follow militaristic, aggressive policies than those national leaders who are not obligated to explain or defend their policies before the public.

Peace researcher R.J. Rummel wants to take this argument in favor of democracy and against dictatorships (what he calls "absolutist" governments) one step further. He agrees that absolutism is "the major factor causing war,"[5] but more important than that is the fact that the toll of deaths resulting from *absolutist governments killing their own citizens* has been much greater than the total number of people getting killed in wars, both international and civil! To quote from Rummel himself:

And the worst type of these absolutist governments is communist. It is a killing machine, responsible for the massacre, executions, starvation, deaths from forced exposure, slave-labor, beatings, and torture of at least 95,153,600 people in this century or 477 people per 10,000 of their population. By contrast, the number of battle casualties from all wars in this century is 35,654,000 or 22 per 10,000 people of the populations involved. On a per capita basis, communism is at least 20 times deadlier than war. Communism in this century has killed even more people, aside from the communist wars, than the 86,000,000 that perished in all the wars and revolutions since 1740.[6]

The problem, however, is not only Communism but any kind of totalitarianism and absolutism.

Hitler killed from 4,200,000 to 4,600,000 Jews, but he also killed (aside from military action) 425,000 Gypsies, 2,500,000 Poles, 3,000,000 Ukrainians, 1,400,000 Belorussians, and 2,500,000 to 3,000,000 Soviet prisoners of war.[7]

The absence of democratic procedures regularly brings disaster and death.

Where the government is totalitarian, as under Soviet communism or the current Muslim ayatollahs of Iran, or absolutist as under Idi Amin of Uganda or Francisco Macias of Equatorial Guinea, the ruling elite have the same effective power over their people that slave masters have over the slaves. Mass killing, executions, forced privation, and the like then become a practical means to maintain power, eliminate opposition, punish disobedience, and pursue political, economic, social, and religious policies. Without the restraints of opposing power foci, regular competitive elections, free speech, and a pluralistic social system, it is natural that human life will be secondary to a regime's desire for self-preservation, power, and the success of its policies.[8]

So, concludes Rummel, not only is democracy effective in avoiding war but even more importantly it saves lives within one's own society during what is supposedly "peacetime." On the other hand, one of the most embarrassing facts for advocates of democracy is that notorious dictator Adolf Hitler originally came to power in Germany as a result of an election in which his Nazi Party got more votes than any other party.

The Marxist Approach

From the Marxist point of view, it is not authoritarian national governments that cause war, but rather countries where control is in the hands of capitalists. It is assumed that capitalists will subordinate all other interests to that of making money. According to Marxist theory, capitalists make money by exploiting the workers who operate their machines. As more goods are produced and sold, the capitalists make more profit. Consequently, the Marxist sees capitalists as desiring to gain control over more and more resources, workers, and consumers. The capitalists in the more technologically advanced countries are able to extend their control over less developed countries either directly by turning them into political colonies, or indirectly by supporting native leaders who will be cooperative. Capitalistic or imperialistic wars break out between capitalistic countries as they compete with each other for control of these less developed countries. Wars of national liberation break out when less developed countries struggle to rid themselves of control by foreign capitalists and their native lackeys. There is also the possibility of war between advanced capitalist and advanced Communist countries if the capitalists seek to reestablish capitalism in the Communist country.

According to Lenin, World War I is a good example of a war fought between advanced capitalist countries as they struggled with each other for control of colonies in Africa and Asia. By then the British and French had worked out agreements with each other regarding colonial holdings, but Italy, Japan, and Germany were just getting ready to go colony hunting. In World War I, both Italy and Japan correctly determined that they would better extend their territorial holdings by fighting against Germany and Austria-Hungary and with the French, British, and Russians. Although that war was touched off by conflict in the Balkans, it was Germany's rapidly increasing military power that had led to the opposing alliances which caused the war to spread rapidly once fighting began. World War II is also viewed by Communists as primarily a struggle between the capitalist classes in Germany, Italy, and Japan on the one hand and those in France, the United Kingdom, and the United States on the other. The battle in eastern Europe between Germany and the Soviet Union, however, is taken to be the result of capitalist Germany trying to eliminate socialism in Russia. Examples of wars of national liberation are the Algerian War, when the French were expelled, and the Vietnamese War, in which the Vietnamese Communists drove out first the capitalists of France and then the U.S.-supported Vietnamese capitalist government of South Vietnam.

Marxists also claim that capitalists are to blame for civil wars, because capitalistic governments make laws which justify the exploitation of workers, and workers have no opportunity to gain fair treatment other than through a violent revolution. "Democratic procedures" may be devised to create the illusion that it is possible for the masses to inaugurate changes in policy, but the capitalists ensure that anticapitalist candidates have virtually no chance of getting elected. If such a candidate should somehow be elected, the capitalists will use the military to engineer a coup d'état to remove the elected anticapitalist from power. Events in Chile in the years 1970–73, when the Marxist Allende was democratically elected and then overthrown by a rightist military group, follow this pattern exactly. These events, say the Marxists, show that the possibility of a lasting peaceful socialist takeover of a capitalist country by a revolution at the ballot box is an illusion. Consequently, according to the Communists, revolutionary war is the only course open to those who desire social justice for the masses. Castro's more enduring revolution in Cuba illustrates the proper Marxist way to get rid of an oppressive capitalist regime and then establish a socialist society, but the capitalists seem to be succeeding in using their economic power to undermine Castro's experiment in socialism in Cuba.

Once again, however, there are historical realities that raise doubts about the correctness of the Communist doctrines put forth. If simply instituting socialist governments will end war, why is it that the Communist regimes in Russia and China engaged in battles with each other? Why is it that Vietnamese and Cambodian Communists fought each other? Why have the Chinese and Vietnamese Communists engaged in warfare against each other? According to Communist doctrine socialist regimes should never have such wars.

Also, civil disorders do not seem to cease when Communist governments take over. Consider the revolts in Hungary in 1956, in Czechoslovakia in 1968, and Afghanistan since 1980 as well as the uprisings that occurred at various times in East Germany and Poland. If Communism ends the problem of injustice within a society, why was it necessary to take extreme measures to prevent large numbers of people from fleeing these nations? Even very repressive totalitarian governments weren't able to completely silence dissenters or to completely stop defectors from finding asylum in other countries.

The historical record thus suggests that there is something wrong with the Marxist argument. Where does it go awry? A basic assumption of the Marxist view is that capitalists want profits and nothing else, but in fact capitalists are people with other interests, too. They can be, and sometimes are, interested in political freedom and the welfare of the human race as well as their own profits. Marxists also assume that workers always identify with other members of the working class from all over the world, as if nationalism were nonexistent. In fact, the ineffectiveness of the socialist pacifist movement at the beginning of World War I, the conflicts between the Russians on the one hand and the Yugoslavs and Chinese on the other, and the conflict between Vietnam on the one hand and Cambodia and China on the other all indicate that nationalism is a stronger social force than any anticipated class solidarity among the workers of the world.

With regard to civil war, it seems a mistake to assume, as the Marxist does, that a government will be dedicated to justice simply because it is controlled by noncapitalists. Why suppose that socialists will be completely unselfish leaders, dedicated only to the welfare of the society? The Marxist tends to neglect the fact that the desire for political power can make a person indifferent to the concerns of others as surely as the desire for profit can.

The defender of democracy would object that the Marxist analysis concentrates too much on the economic aspects of the social system without paying enough attention to political aspects or to the psychological principles which apply to the behavior of leaders. Some Marxists think that the rise to power of autocratic leaders such as Stalin and Mao was merely an accident, while in fact the system of centralized political control which is practiced in Communist countries may make the concentration of power in the hands of one authoritarian person almost inevitable.

Even though the Marxist view that ending capitalism will end war has been shown to be questionable, we should note that the desire of those with wealth to expand their profits and their area of control has been an important factor in many past wars. It is the capitalistic part of Western ideology, rather than the democratic part of it, which has led the European peoples to exploit others who had less technological knowledge. It is the capitalistic part of Western ideology which has led to wide differences in income, wealth, and power within Western societies. The Marxist criticism that capitalism has not been particularly concerned about social justice seems to some extent correct. But so far, there is little evidence that the socialist systems controlled by Communists abound in justice or freedom, and in the international sphere socialists seem to be as subject to nationalistic enmities as capitalists are. Furthermore, developments in both the now defunct Soviet Union and Maoist China suggest that a socialist-type planned economy is much less productive and progressive than a capitalist-type market economy, and shared poverty is still misery.

The Gandhi-King Approach

A third approach to reforming the internal operation of national governments focuses on the problem of justice rather than directly on the problem of war. It assumes that a major cause of war is the resort to violence or threats of violence by those who want to eliminate the injustices perpetrated by those in power. Injustice stems from the fact that, both within nations and on the global level, people with economic, military, and political power use that power to advance their own personal and group interests at the expense of those who lack such power. This unjust behavior on the part of the powerful, for the most part, is not the result of a conscious and deliberate effort to harm other people, for they, like all people, are merely more aware of their own interests than of the interests of others. Injustice is the result of indifference to the interests of those being exploited.

The natural reaction of exploited people is to feel resentment and hatred toward those who exploit them. They become ready to use violence to overthrow and destroy their oppressors. But, argued Gandhi, to react in such a resentful, hateful, and aggressive manner is to become a perpetrator of injustice oneself. Reducing the situation to a mere struggle for power between oppressors and oppressed leaves no room for moral considerations. The side which wins the contest of force will simply impose its will against the other side. Even if the formerly oppressed group wins the struggle for power, it will simply become a new ruling group using threats of violence to control those who lost the fight. It is unlikely that there will be any more justice than before.

In order to escape from round after round of conflict in which oppression begets violence which begets counter-violence, an entirely different approach is required. A means must be found which is appropriate to the goal of furthering justice. Instead of relying on physical force, Gandhi believed that the champion of justice must appeal to a different kind of power, the power of love and commitment to truth. *"Satyagraha"* means "the power of truth," and a person committed to using that power is called a *satyagrahi.* *Satyagrahis* will feel no ill will against those whose interests conflict with their own, no matter how oppressive and unjust they may seem to be. Instead of seeking a situation in which they can impose their will on those who have coerced them, they will try to do what will be beneficial for everyone. *Satyagrahis* will dedicate their whole being to the removal of injustice, but they will not hate anyone, even the perpetrators of the most gross injustices. Their attitude will be one of trying to help oppressors to rid themselves of their insensitivity to the concerns of others.

What technique might the victims of social oppression use to stop the injustices being committed against them without in turn becoming oppressors? In the development of his own thinking, Gandhi's first answer to this question was to use reason. He thought that if the oppressed party could state its case so clearly and dispassionately to the oppressors that the injustice would be evident to any rational observer, then the oppressors would see their error and change their ways. But while practicing law in South Africa, Gandhi discovered by personal experience that this appeal to reason accomplished virtually nothing toward changing the oppressive policies of the ruling groups. Something else was needed.

The new technique Gandhi developed to give power to truth is known as *nonviolent resistance.* Sometimes his approach is mistakenly called "passive resistance," but the technique he advocated is anything but passive. Gandhi insisted that those who were suffering from injustice must be active in their resistance to it. If they did nothing, the oppression would continue. The oppressed must be committed to the removal of injustice by an appeal to the oppressor's sense of justice. They must act to dramatize their plight and show their willingness to suffer even more, if necessary, to change the situation. Although individuals should do whatever they can to protest injustices, the likelihood of success in changing unjust conditions is much greater when large numbers of people are willing to unite their efforts in nonviolent resistance. Some particular techniques of collective nonviolent resistance are demonstrations, boycotts, strikes, and refusals to comply with orders given by the ruling group. An important part of the Gandhi approach is the openness of the planning for nonviolent resistance. Those whose injustices are being protested are permitted to give their side of the story and are told in advance what types of nonviolent activities will be undertaken, as well as details of when and where they will occur.

It is claimed that nonviolent resistance can end war because it provides a means other than violence by which oppressed people can eliminate injustice. The case of India shows how it can be used by the people of a nation to rid themselves of domination by the government of another nation. The civil rights movement in the United States, led by Martin Luther King, Jr., shows how it can be used within a nation as a substitute for violent revolution. But the big question for nonviolent resistance is whether it can succeed in eliminating government-supported oppression when there is no threat of violence in the background. The detractors of the nonviolent approach argue that in the cases of India and the United States, there was a real threat of violent action if the nonviolent approach didn't work. Without the threat in the background, neither Gandhi nor King would have succeeded. Furthermore, it is argued that the British and American governments are not among the more ruthless and oppressive governments the world has ever known. Could the Jews have used nonviolent resistance against Hitler's Nazi government? Could Russian dissidents have used nonviolent resistance against Stalin's ruthless rule? Can massive nonviolent resistance even get started when there is a government which prevents potential dissenters from meeting with each other? Such questions arouse skepticism about how effective nonviolent resistance can be against an extremely determined oppressive government.

The defenders of nonviolent resistance respond that even ruthless governments eventually become reluctant to use violence against nonviolent protesters because the ruthlessness becomes so evident, even to the people who have previously not been protesting against it.[9] Gandhi believed that there is a basic decency about most people that would rebel against obvious oppression. The task is for oppressed people to make their oppressed state obvious to people who are otherwise indifferent. Members of the oppressed group who have been indifferent to trying to change the situation and even some others outside the oppressed group will join the resistance effort once the unjust situation is sufficiently dramatized. To be sure, organizing nonviolent resistance so that it can be effective is not easy. Gandhi liked to compare the need for strategy and for courage required for nonviolent resistance to that required in a military confrontation. The "soldier" of nonviolent resistance needs to be trained and disciplined and should be regarded as just as much a hero as any guerrilla fighter who uses violence to try to eliminate oppression. In fact, participants in nonviolent resistance would be even more worthy of admiration than the guerrilla fighters because they would not be drawn into defiling their own human nature by killing and injuring others in the name of justice.[10]

In the end, however, it seems that the basic assumptions of the Gandhi-King approach can still be called into question. Even if people do have some basic sense of justice, it seems to be a weak motive for action compared with self-preservation. It seems almost self-evident that sufficiently ruthless government leaders can keep most dissenters silent by the use of threats of death and injury, if not to the individual then to those that person loves. It is also very questionable whether all or even most wars are the result of the use of violence to eliminate the oppressive policies of some dominant group. In fact, in international affairs it seems that wars are usually fought between one powerful nation or group of nations and another powerful nation or group of nations. The truly poor nations, economically and militarily, realize that any attempt to use force will bring on defeat. It seems that nonviolent resistance may offer an alternative to violence as a way to remove some injustices in some particular kinds of situations, but it is debatable whether even the widespread use of nonviolent resistance to protest oppression by ruling groups would do much to reduce the frequency of war. In fact, such activity might even lead to more ruthless oppression by those in power.[11]

Nevertheless in some situations nonviolent resistance has been an important factor in bringing about change. The overthrow of the Shah in Iran in 1979 was largely nonviolent.[12] The February 1986 expulsions of Duvalier from Haiti and Marcos[13] from the Philippines were both largely the result of nonviolent efforts. The nonviolent movement led by Bishop Tutu in South Africa was instrumental in calling world attention to that country's continuing policy of *apartheid*. In 1989 the uprisings against the Soviet army in eastern Europe showed how successful nonviolent resistance can be.[14] The impact of the Gandhi-King approach on world events is gradually growing. On the other hand, the suppression of the nonviolent "Democracy Movement" by the Chinese Communist armed forces in Tiananmen Square in Beijing in June 1989 seems to have been a defeat for nonviolence, but possibly not in the long run.

XVI. Reforming the Policies of National Governments

In the previous chapter, we considered various ideas about how the internal operations of national governments might be changed to lessen the likelihood of war. In this chapter we will examine proposals concerning the policies national governments might adopt to reduce the likelihood of war. Most people interested in politics and international relations believe that it is in this area that solutions to the war problem must be found even though they might disagree vehemently about which of these policies are the right ones to follow. Our focus will be mainly on courses of action which might be adopted in relation to other national governments, but in many cases these same approaches might also be applied to relations with antagonistic groups within the nation.

It may be worthwhile to reiterate the point made in the previous chapter, namely, that national governments and the policies they follow are crucial to the war problem. International wars are the result of interactions between various national governments, and wars within nations are usually the result of reactions of various groups to the policies of their own national governments. It seems that war could be eliminated if national governments followed the proper policies. Of course, there may be contextual factors which make it difficult for national governments to follow these ideal policies, but a discussion of that point must be postponed to the next chapter.

As we discuss these various proposals, we need to keep certain points in mind. *First,* our point of view is to consider policies that might be adopted by any national government. There will be a natural tendency for those who live in the United States to think only in terms of policies that might be adopted by this country, but our aim is to maintain a broader perspective. Some policies that might not seem very attractive to a superpower may make a great deal of sense for other nations. *Second,* we are engaged in a normative or evaluative enterprise, not a descriptive or factual inquiry. Our focus is on what *should be* done, not on what *is* being done or what policies leaders are currently pursuing. We may refer to cases where a particular policy is being used or was used by way of example, but the fact that a policy is being used or was used does not settle the issue of whether such a policy is a good one. *Third,* it is not to be supposed that these various

295

policies which we will be considering are mutually exclusive of one another. Some of them are incompatible with others, but there are many others which could readily be followed simultaneously. *Fourth,* we need to keep in mind that the problem of war currently confronting humankind has four aspects: the threat of nuclear war between big powers, the threat of conventional war between nations, the threat of war within nations, and the expenditure of huge amounts of money and effort for military purposes. Certain proposals may be directed primarily to one or another of these aspects of the war problem. Even a proposal which promises to deal successfully with one aspect of the problem will probably need to be supplemented by other proposals to deal with other aspects of the problem. *Fifth,* some of these proposals have received a great deal more attention in the past than others. There may be an unconscious tendency to think that some proposals which are unfamiliar are for that reason insignificant. Here the reader is advised to be on guard against the natural tendency to dismiss new ideas as ridiculous just because he has not previously heard of them.

Peace Through Military Strength and Alliances

The most common national policy for avoiding war is to be so strong that no potential enemy will risk an attack. The Latin phrase *para bellum* (prepare for war) is often used to describe this approach. It applies both to international relations and the situation within a nation. War with other countries breaks out, it is maintained, when stronger nations let weaker ones entertain the hope that they might win in a contest of force. War within a country breaks out when some subservient group comes to believe that it might be able to successfully revolt against the national government. The secret of preserving peace is for those with power to have such an overwhelming amount of it and such an obvious resolve to use it that no other government or group will be tempted to test their strength. This policy of *peace through strength* focuses primarily on building up the military and secondarily on forming alliances.

Military Superiority. In order to fully appreciate the attractiveness of the peace through strength position, it is important to realize that wars very seldom, if ever, happen by accident. Wars occur when the leaders of at least one government or organized group estimate that they will gain more from fighting a war than they can gain by other means such as diplomatic bargaining.[1] If a national government is weak, other governments outside and organized groups within are likely to try to take advantage of it. A weak government will regularly be in a position of either peacefully yielding some of its interests to aggressive enemies or being attacked militarily if it does not yield enough to placate its stronger opponents. The only way of avoiding such an unpleasant situation is to be strong. In the modern world being strong means not only having a well-trained and well-equipped military but also supporting research to develop new and better weapons.

In the United States, many advocates of the peace through military strength approach are very critical of the policies followed by the U.S. government since the end of World War II. At that time the United States had a monopoly in nuclear weapons, an overwhelming superiority in arms production, and well-trained armed forces. It was a great mistake, claim the supporters of this view, to disarm so rapidly when it should have been obvious that the Communists would be making moves all over the world to try to expand the territory they control. If U.S. military power had been maintained rather than dismantled, U.S. forces could have saved at least some of eastern Europe from falling under Communist domination. An all-out effort in China could have kept that country from falling to Mao's Communist forces. In the Korean War, the United States should have used its superior military might to attack China itself when the forces from that country began assisting the North Koreans. If the United States had given more aid to the French in Indo-China when the war first started and had put more resources into the struggle after the French pulled out in 1954, the Communists would not have gained control of that area. According to this view the United States was consistently too restrained and too reluctant to use its military power, leading the Communists to be more daring than they would otherwise have been. It resulted in U.S. retreat and Communist advances in both Europe and Asia. The only time that Communist expansion was halted was when the United States indicated its readiness to use all its military force, as in Europe after the formation of the North Atlantic Treaty Organization and as in Cuba in 1962 when the Russians were coerced into removing their missiles.

Supporters of the peace through military strength approach maintain that the Cold War came to an end because of U.S. President Reagan's commitment to this approach. Reagan made it clear that the U.S. was willing to spend more and more on "national security" in order to give the U.S. overwhelming military superiority rather than continuing to have a stand-off with the Soviets. He launched the "Strategic Defense Initiative" or "Star Wars" program in order to escape the mutual assured destruction situation in nuclear weapons. He realized that if the Soviets could neutralize U.S. strategic nuclear weapons, they might think they could use their superior conventional forces in Europe to take over Western Europe or at least engage in coercive diplomacy against the countries of that region. Consequently, he announced a program designed to give the U.S. strategic superiority. It was sold to the American public as a defense system, but the Russians fully understood that the U.S. was going for first-strike capability. When the Russians started deploying medium-range missiles that could strike Western Europe, Reagan responded by deploying U.S. Pershing II missiles based in Europe and aimed at the Soviet Union. He insisted that the only thing that would halt deployment of the U.S. missiles was the "zero" option, that is, absolutely no medium-range missiles for the Soviets or the U.S. After much bluster the Soviets backed down and accepted the "zero" option. The Soviets also began to realize that it would be impossible for them to match the kind of buildup of military forces that Reagan had planned. According to this outlook, that is why the Cold War ended with the Soviets in effect capitulating to the U.S. (An alternative point of view is that the crucial change in the Soviet position was due to the accession to power of Mikhail Gorbachev in the Soviet Union.)

So far we have been considering this policy of peace through military strength only from the U.S. point of view, but it is a policy that could be pursued by any nation. During the Cold War, it was being pursued by the Soviet Union as well as the U.S. That is why there was such an intense arms race between those two superpowers who were contending for global supremacy during that period. But also in regional disputes such as those between Israel and its Arab neighbors or between India and Pakistan, both sides typically put as many resources into building up their military forces as they think they can afford, not only to defend themselves but also to be able to be tough in negotiating sessions. Nations do not want to find themselves in a position where their critical interests must be sacrificed because the opponent is militarily stronger. In a world where conflicts of national interest are ultimately settled by force and threats of force, being militarily strong is a good way of avoiding being forced into accepting "agreements" which you don't really like as well as preventing others from attacking or threatening to attack you.

There are some problems, however, with the peace through military strength approach. The nation which is very strong militarily can be fairly confident that it won't be attacked, but can other nations be confident that they won't be attacked by it? Strong military forces may make a nation more secure from attack, but its forces then constitute a threat which makes other nations less secure. The leaders who build up the military might of their countries may be thinking in terms of using those forces to deter an attack on their own country, but once the forces are available it is very tempting to use them to launch an attack on another country. Peace through military strength may thus lead to attempted conquest through war.

A second problem for the peace through military strength approach concerns the actions required of a national government which pursues this policy to its final logical implications. If all conflicts are ultimately to be decided by force, then force should be used to eliminate competitors while they are weak. In the international sphere, this approach would require a dominant nation to seek to extend its control over potential enemies by attacking them and conquering them before they become militarily strong enough to offer much resistance. Within a country, peace through military strength would require a national government to seek to silence all criticism and dissent before it has a chance to spread and possibly lead to a revolution. Peace through military strength ultimately means maintaining the status quo by means of the most forceful suppression of any efforts to challenge the power of those who presently are in control. Such an approach seems fitting only for a totalitarian regime bent on eliminating all opposition, whether from some other country or from within.

A third problem for the peace through military strength approach concerns what happens when rival parties both adopt this approach. In the international arena, the result is an unrestrained arms race which consumes more and more of the resources of the countries involved. When the contending nations have nuclear weapons, a balance of terror results which is threatening even to other countries. Rather than solving the war problem, the peace through military strength approach intensifies one aspect of the problem, the huge cost of preparations for war. The same result occurs within nations when opposing groups commit themselves to the use of military force to resolve their differences. Guns and ammunition are stockpiled by those not in power for the day when they may be able to revolt against the government. The government, on the other hand, builds up its forces and tries to imprison anyone who might participate in a revolt. Ruthlessness begets more ruthlessness in the continuing struggle for power. Even those who would prefer to remain neutral and stay out of the struggle cannot escape the violence. Nations which had been peaceful thus become battlegrounds in which both their human and material resources are consumed. This tragedy has occurred in recent decades in countries such as Lebanon, Angola, Afghanistan, Cambodia, and El Salvador.

Thus, the view that peace should be preserved by building up military strength runs into some significant difficulties. It seems to be more a policy for trying to maintain the power of those who now have it than a policy which promotes peace. The peace through military strength advocate must be ready to resort to more and more force to try to thwart any effort to modify the present social order, both international and domestic. This attempt to prevent peaceful change may in fact be a major contributory factor to the eventual outbreak in violence. The leaders may begin with some sensitivity to issues of justice and the possible need for change, but the logic of their reliance on force pushes them to assume that their own control must be maintained. Furthermore, when opposing groups both adopt this same approach, an all-out race for military superiority is the result, aggravating rather than solving the war problem. The peace through military strength approach, when carried to its logical conclusion, even encourages violent attacks against potential enemies while they are weak. A proposal which is put forth as a policy to promote peace actually turns out to be a policy which blocks efforts for peaceful change and leads to arms races and opportunistic use of force.

Alliances. A country which seeks peace through strength need not rely solely on its own military forces. It can form alliances with other countries which will provide military assistance if war comes. States with a common interest can enter into a mutual defense pact which declares that an attack on either will be considered an attack on both. By such an alliance both nations have strengthened their power relative to others. Weaker countries will be much less vulnerable to an attack from a potential enemy if they have formed an alliance with a much stronger nation. This situation is not unlike that of a small boy who finds a big, strong friend who will help him resist a bully who has been harassing him. The idea of increasing one's strength by making alliances also applies in the case of conflicting groups within nations. It is not unusual for a revolutionary effort to succeed because of an alliance of dissatisfied groups which nevertheless begin fighting against each other once the old regime has been toppled. At the same time, ruling governments may themselves be the result of an alliance of groups working together to preserve the basic structure of the present order.

Though a country which has alliances with other countries may be stronger as a result, the question remains whether it will be less likely to get involved in a war. Some potential enemies that might otherwise consider attacking will probably be deterred, but the stronger nation in the alliance may try to control the policies of the weaker, possibly even resorting to military force to do so. There is also the possibility of a country being dragged into a war if its ally is attacked or of being attacked simply because it has entered into the alliance with the other country. Finally, there is a danger that a country's ally, knowing that it will have assistance, will deliberately act in such a way as to invite an attack. Thus, entering an alliance does not necessarily mean that a nation will be more likely to remain at peace. Consequently, upgrading national strength through alliances has drawbacks not found in the strategy of increasing strength by building up one's own military forces. Nevertheless, strength through alliances is likely to be much less expensive.

Separate from the issue of whether a country entering an alliance is more or less likely to get into a war is the issue of whether alliances in general make peace more probable or less probable. It can be argued that World War I was a major war rather than a minor war because of the system of alliances existing before the war began. On the other hand, there is a widely held view that peace is preserved by a *balance of power* between opposing alliances. It is generally believed that if one nation or group of nations acquires an overwhelming military superiority over another nation or group of nations, it will be inclined to make unreasonable demands or possibly even start a war to convert its military supremacy into economic and political gain.

There are several different kinds of situations where the balance of power concept is relevant. There may be two opposing blocs of nations, neither of which has obvious military superiority over the other. This situation is called a *bipolar balance of power*. Each of the sides is likely to try to gain superiority by various means including recruiting new allies; but peace will be maintained, according to the balance of power view, if neither side gains a great superiority over the other. A second type of situation is the *tripolar system* where there are three opposing nations or groups of nations. In this situation the two weaker states or group of states will form an alliance against the more powerful state or groups of states. If two of the three states or blocs of states are nearly equal in power, the third state or group of states may act as a "balancer," shifting its support from one group to the other in order to maintain the balance. Many historians believe that Britain played just such a role as "balancer" in Europe from 1815 to 1914, thus keeping most conflicts from degenerating into wars during this period of the *Pax Britannica.*[2] A third situation is a *multipolar system* where there are many different nations and groups of nations which keep shifting alliances with each other, thus keeping any nation or group of nations from gaining an overwhelming military superiority. Similar balance of power situations can also be found in the struggles among groups within nations.

The basic premise of the balance of power view of maintaining peace is that wars occur when one side has overwhelming superiority over another. It is assumed that under such circumstances the more powerful side is likely to start a war because it is confident it can win. This basic supposition of the balance of power view is very questionable. When a nation or group of nations has obvious military superiority, other nations and groups of nations tend to be conciliatory and even subservient in order to try to avoid a war they are likely to lose. Of course war might eventually occur if they came to the view that they had to fight to protect what they had not already surrendered. On the other hand, when there is a balance between powers, it might well be that a crucial conflict situation will develop and neither side will back down because neither perceives itself as weaker than the other. War then seems a likely result. It is surprising that the balance of power view is so popular when it is so debatable whether war is more likely when there is an imbalance between powers than when there is a balance. Nations can be expected to seek to form alliances with other nations, especially against nations and groups of nations which seem threatening, but this behavior is more readily explicable on grounds that the nations are protecting their own national interests by getting help against a potential enemy than on grounds that they are trying to preserve peace by maintaining a balance of power.

Seeking peace and security through strength is the prevalent approach among the national governments of the world. The most popular path to strength has been the building up of military forces, but entering into alliances is also widespread. In a world where conflicts of national interest may ultimately be settled by war, there seems to be no substitute for military strength. How else can a country keep from becoming coerced by other nations which have built up their strength? Though the peace through strength approach has some real deficiencies from the point of view of solving the war problem, it seems destined to remain one of the most popular policies for national governments to follow unless there is a substantial modification of the international system.

Peace Through Neutrality and Economic Self-Sufficiency

A very different approach which national leaders may adopt to keep out of wars is to concentrate on solving the domestic problems of their own nation while seeking to isolate themselves from the conflicts of other nations. They will avoid all alliances and refrain from military interventions. Their military forces will be such that they pose absolutely no threat to any other nation. At the same time a country pursuing this strategy will usually be committed to using research, technology, and conservation measures to avoid economic dependency on other countries. For example, a country which is dependent on imported oil for energy could be expected to make a massive effort to develop alternative energy sources on the assumption that in the long run this approach will be less expensive than building up military forces in order to try to guarantee the availability of oil.

A good example of a nation which has followed a policy of neutrality for some time is Switzerland. The Swiss have steadfastly refrained from entering into any kind of military alliances. They even obtained an explicit exemption from participation in any military sanctions against other nations before joining the League of Nations, and they have been reluctant to join the United Nations because of the collective security provisions of its Charter. They have tried to mind their own business, not developing any close ties with any other particular nations, but not making any enemies either. Under this policy they have managed to stay out of both world wars. They have military forces, but these forces are single-mindedly devoted to defending the homeland against any possible invasion. For the Swiss this policy has worked well, and they presently have the world's highest per-capita income. Sweden is another example of a country which has done very well by following a neutralist policy.

The success of a neutralist policy, however, may depend on factors outside the control of the national leaders. Switzerland and Sweden are countries where much of the land is mountainous. For the most part they do not provide good travel routes for armies of other nations bent on conquest, and the Swiss and Swedes could fairly readily blow up bridges and tunnels which would frustrate would-be invaders. The situation is quite different for countries such as Belgium and Poland. These nations have also tried to stay out of wars, but with little success. Their relatively flat land is very inviting to militant leaders looking for good routes for getting at their enemies. Switzerland and Sweden also have been assisted in their policies of neutrality by their lack of readily exploitable scarce natural resources. It would seem that a small country with crucial natural resources such as the oil-rich United Arab Emirates would be well advised not to try to defend itself without relying on any allies.

For a good part of its history, the United States tried to follow a policy of neutrality with regard to Europe. Nevertheless it found itself dragged into both world wars. After World War II, the United States followed just the opposite of a neutralist or isolationist policy, forming alliances and intervening militarily all over the world in an effort to stop the spread of Communism. The Vietnamese War raised some doubts about the desirability of playing "world policeman," but the success in the Gulf War has led to renewed support for the "world policeman" role. At the same time U.S. financial problems have increased reluctance to play that role. With the Cold War over, there are some calls for a return to isolationism, but it is unlikely that the U.S. will or can go back to that policy.

A country may also find it difficult to follow a strategy of neutrality and self-development if it is very short of resources. Japan is a good example, for it must import almost all the oil it uses. Development of hydroelectric, solar, and nuclear energy can provide a bit of self-sufficiency, but the need for energy and other natural resources is too great to be met by current technology. Japan's objective situation seems to preclude a policy of national self-sufficiency and noninvolvement in international conflicts.

It seems then that the desirability of a policy of neutrality and economic self-sufficiency depends on particular circumstances. A country which is a major power may find it hard to refrain from helping ideological allies when they are in danger of being conquered by a powerful ideological enemy. A country which depends greatly on others for resources must take an interest in the outlook of those nations. A small country with readily exploitable resources is likely to be quickly conquered by aggressive powers if it relies only on its own defensive efforts. A country which provides a good route for conquering armies may not be able to stay out of wars. And the fact that a nation decides not to intervene in the affairs of other nations does not automatically assure that other nations will forego the use of force to conquer it or damage its vital interests.

Do neutrality and isolationism promote peace? It certainly seems that a country which is following a policy of neutrality will not be a threat to other nations. Consequently, it is less likely to be attacked. Its lack of alliances means that it is also less likely to be dragged into wars between other nations. On the other hand, if there are other nations committed to the use of military force in expanding their power, a policy of neutrality may play right into their hands by allowing them to conquer one country at a time. Even the case of Switzerland needs to be reexamined from this point of view. If Hitler had been successful in maintaining control for some time over all of the rest of continental Europe, would not Switzerland sooner or later have been converted by one means or another into a German-speaking fascist country swearing its allegiance to *der Führer?* If so, Switzerland was saved not by its isolationist policy but by the Allies who put an end to Hitler's rule. Similarly, other countries following an isolationist policy may escape from war for a time, but they face the possibility of being swallowed up by those interested in expanding their power by military means unless they are saved from disaster by others. If there are powers bent on spreading their control without limit by military means, it seems prudent to join with others in resisting such expansionism at its beginning. Isolationism would be a good policy if all other nations would always mind their own business, but there often are national leaders who feel that they should control more than they already do. The same kind of considerations apply to groups within countries which seek to stay out of political issues. Whether they can preserve their own interests and ideology by noninvolvement in political conflicts will depend on the policies pursued by the other groups in that society. The fate of the Baha'is in Iran shows that political noninvolvement does not necessarily save a group from being persecuted.

Peace Through Strictly Defensive Strength

We have noted that a national policy of neutrality does not necessarily prevent a country from being attacked. Such a country may thus need some kind of defense. Nations not committed to neutrality may also want to adopt a system of defense which will not be threatening to their neighbors. There are two possible approaches to a purely defensive program for national security.[3] The first relies on a *strictly defensive military capability for the armed forces*. The second is a radically different approach called *civilian-based defense* which involves training the whole population in techniques of nonviolent resistance to be used against an invader.

Defensive Military Forces. The approach of relying on purely defensive military forces for national security builds on the fact that some kinds of weapons will be threatening to other nations while others will not. For example, weapons such as bombers and tanks will make other countries feel less secure because such weapons have an offensive capability. On the other hand, if a country refrains from building offensive weapons while nevertheless stockpiling defensive weapons such as land mines and anti-tank weapons, other nations will not feel threatened by its military capability. Of course, countries typically say that *all* their weapons are defensive. The crucial test of whether a weapon is really defensive, however, is whether the potential adversary views it as defensive.[4] The basic idea of the purely defensive military approach is that relying on weapons that have only a defensive capability allows a country to acquire a very strong military defense without leading other countries to become concerned that they may become victims of an attack. A nation can build up its own security without making other countries feel insecure.

What are some of the main characteristics of a strictly defensive military effort? Obviously one would need to build obstacles and protected weaponry which an invader would need to get past in order to get into the country. Any weapons which are mobile would need to be small and have limited range so they would not be threatening to neighboring countries. A purely defensive force would not contain any nuclear weapons because there is no way to use these weapons in one's own territory without destroying what one is trying to protect.[5] An effective defense force would need to be dispersed throughout all parts of the country rather than concentrated in certain areas which could be readily destroyed by a few nuclear weapons. In fact, defensive forces should be especially well trained in guerrilla fighting (paramilitary defense) so they would be able to continue to harass an invader even if the conventional defensive forces were defeated.[6]

A great asset of a policy which shifts away from offensive weapons and builds up defensive capabilities is that a country can increase its own security without needing any kind of prior agreement with the adversary. The elimination of all offensive weapons means the availability of more resources for defensive weapons while the adversary becomes less threatened and therefore less likely to remain antagonistic. In fact, according to this approach, if a country were able to develop some relatively inexpensive but effective weapons that could be used only for defense, it should share the knowledge of how to build such weapons with the opponent and encourage him to make these weapons rather than offensive devices.[7]

It is to be noted that this defensive military approach in effect seeks to deter the enemy from attacking, but *not* in the sense of threatening retaliation as in the doctrine of nuclear deterrence. Rather one deters the enemy by decreasing the likelihood that an attack will be successful because one has strengthened one's defensive capabilities. To apply this defensive approach to the area of strategic nuclear weapons a country would need to dismantle all its nuclear warheads and delivery systems and rely completely on a missile defense system. Needless to say the Strategic Defense Initiative proposal of U.S. President Reagan did not fit this model because it did not call for getting rid of all U.S. offensive weapons.

Would such a strictly defensive military effort be a good way of promoting peace and security? There might be some minor problems such as determining whether certain defensive weapons might not be able to be used offensively in some situations and making sure that widely dispersed and somewhat autonomous defensive units remain loyal to the central government.[8] One's capability of helping friendly countries would be severely limited. The biggest problem, however, would be that restricting oneself to defensive weapons means that enemies could attack repeatedly knowing that no counterattack would occur. They could continue to build newer offensive weapons while destroying the defensive weaponry the other country already has and its capability to build more. They would know that they could never lose more than their own attacking forces. How long could a purely defensive effort be successful under these circumstances?

The response of the advocate of the strictly defensive approach would be to raise the issue of why the enemy wants to attack. Doesn't one country attack another because it fears being attacked itself? If the opponent has no offensive weapons, wouldn't that fear be eliminated? So why would a country attack another country which has purely defensive forces?

Here we reach the questionable assumption on which the proposal for a strictly defensive system is based, namely, that the only reason one nation would attack another is the fear of being attacked itself. The whole history of war indicates that some groups attack others even though there is no fear whatever of being attacked by them just as some individuals attack others even though there is no fear of being attacked by them. To secure valuable assets, to spread an ideology, to gain status, to dominate — these are the reasons one group attacks another. It is naive to suppose that these motives will disappear just because other groups have decided to rely on strictly defensive weapons. It is true that we would have a more peaceful world if *all* nations would give up their offensive weapons and rely instead on strong defensive forces, but some groups have expansionist aims and will continue to build up their offensive capabilities until they can overcome the defenses of others. This offensive capability will make other groups feel insecure, but that is exactly what the expansionist group intends. It can then coerce other groups into accepting a situation which they don't like but can't resist. If they do try to resist, the aggressive group will resort to war and force compliance.

If no other groups actively challenge the aggressive group, it can be expected to continue its aggressive ways, probing here and there to find places where the defense of some other group is not sufficient to resist it. In a system of collective defense, other groups would come to the assistance of the weak; but if each group is relying only on its own defensive efforts, a strong aggressor will be able to overcome them one resisting group at a time.[9] Even if the nonaggressive groups unite in a common collective-security effort, they will be at a great disadvantage because they can do nothing to destroy the capability of an aggressor to build even more powerful offensive weapons while the aggressor is able to destroy their capability of building defensive weapons. Groups which rely on strictly defensive efforts are destined to be overcome eventually by aggressive groups with superior offensive capabilities. It just isn't true that groups prepare for and engage in war only because they are fearful of being attacked by others.

Civilian Defense. The second kind of purely defensive effort which has been proposed as a way of promoting peace is to rely on the civilian population of the society rather than military forces. This civilian-based system of defense could be used as a backup for the military defense just discussed,[10] but it could also be used by itself. The basic idea of a civilian-based system of defense is to train all the citizenry of a country in techniques of nonviolent resistance which can be used to frustrate an invader even though he may have an overwhelming superiority of military force. Gene Sharp, the primary spokesman for this idea, notes that the people of a society need to be equipped with a means of fighting so that they can defend themselves rather than relying solely on that small part of the population which constitutes the armed forces of the country.[11] Even if a country has an army of professional soldiers, the people of that country should not be defenseless if their army is defeated. And once a nation dedicates itself to developing a full-fledged system of civilian defense, it may find that building up traditional military forces is superfluous. Such a system of national defense also has the advantages of not being threatening to one's neighbors and of being useful for resistance even to an internal group which attempts to take over the government by force. Consequently, it seems to be an especially appropriate type of defense for a democratic country.

Exactly how could a civilian population defend itself nonviolently against an invading army? It might begin by destroying anything that would be useful to the invaders. Explosives might be used to blow up key bridges, harbor facilities, airports, mines, factories, radio broadcasting towers, and the like. Automobiles could be parked in rows to block highways and streets. Human chains 20 or 30 people deep, unarmed but backed up by reinforcements and determined not to move, could be formed to stand in the way of the advancing enemy. Work which the enemy wanted done simply wouldn't get done. The people would obey no commands but those given by their own leaders, and the leaders would give no commands that would assist the invaders.

The strategy of civilian-based defense depends on the principle that invading military leaders can succeed in accomplishing their goals only if others cooperate by following their orders. If the whole civilian population just refuses to do what they are told, if they refuse to work or provide supplies, then the invading army will be stymied. The army will be in the country but they will have no control over it. They may make threats and even carry some of them out in order to try to get their commands obeyed; but if the whole population stubbornly refuses, then they cannot be subdued regardless of the violence that may be used against them. If their resistance is completely nonviolent, the commanders of the invading army may eventually even have difficulty trying to get their own troops to follow orders to use violence against these nonviolent people.

It may be argued that once the invading force kills a few people the others will be frightened into obeying, but that reaction is precisely what training in civilian defense must overcome. Soldiers do not stop fighting just because some of their buddies have been killed. In fact, such an event may make them more determined than ever to fight. Civilian defenders need to be taught to react in the same way except that their fighting will be done nonviolently. They must also realize how important it is that no one turn traitor and cooperate with the invader and that no one begin to use violence, thus undermining the nonviolent resistance. Most important of all, they must be taught to keep firmly before their minds the truth that no matter how many of their friends and family are killed or tortured, the number of casualties would probably have been even greater if they had tried to rely on military resistance and thus invited massive destructive attacks.

The notion of civilian-based defense as an alternative to a traditional military defense system may not seem a very attractive possibility to a superpower such as the United States, or even to countries such as Russia, the

United Kingdom, France, and China which have nuclear-tipped missiles to launch at any country which attacks them. But what about countries such as Sweden, Japan, Mexico, and Nigeria, not to mention smaller countries? They do not have a nuclear deterrent. What sort of defense can they hope to develop against a possible attack by a nuclear power? Even if they could develop nuclear weapons and missile launchers, they might not want to do so since the presence of such weapons in their country might invite a nuclear attack. Even a big buildup of conventional weapons might make them a target for attack when they otherwise might not be bothered. Consequently, the civilian-based defense system constitutes an attractive possibility. The governments of Sweden, Norway, Lithuania, Latvia, Estonia, and the Netherlands have sponsored official studies of the possibilities of this approach.

Would a system of civilian-based defense work? Advocates point to the partial success of resistance movements in the Ruhr Valley in 1923 when the German population resisted a French-Belgian takeover attempt, in Norway and in Denmark where Hitler's forces were shunned and ignored during World War II, and in the Czechoslovak uprising against the Russians in 1968. In 1920, the German Weimar Republic was saved from an attempted internal takeover by strikes and refusal of the population to cooperate. In these cases there had been no advanced preparation for the resistance effort. It is claimed that a civilian population trained in advance and equipped with hidden resources such as duplicating machines and radio transmitters could be much more successful. If there can be partial successes against military forces without advanced preparation, one could expect even better results with planning and special training in civilian defense.

The skeptics remain unconvinced, however.[12] The crucial issue is human nature. Will people refrain from reacting violently when under violent attack? Will people stand up to threats of violence when they see their own family members being threatened and tortured? As some people yielded to threats and revealed secret hiding places and secret codes, it would become more and more difficult for others to keep up their resistance. There might even be some persons who for ideological or other reasons would want to help the invaders. Another problem is that the enemy would also be in a position to use nonviolent techniques against them. For example, the invaders could shut off supplies of electricity, food, petroleum, medical care, and so on unless the captured citizenry cooperated. The approach of civilian-based defense, its detractors argue, does not have enough respect for the influence of physical force, especially in an age of mind-altering drugs and brainwashing techniques. The mind is too dependent on the body, too much a part of the body, too dedicated to the continuation of one's own personal existence. Some people may be committed enough to suffer greatly and possibly die, but it is doubtful that such commitment would be the prevalent response regardless of advance training and preparations. Furthermore, there is always the gruesome possibility that the invading nation would simply slaughter huge numbers of people and then move some of its own population into the conquered country. Some domestic revolutionary movements have massacred substantial proportions of their own people, so the possibility of murdering large numbers of foreigners should not be dismissed too readily.

The advocate of civilian-based defense might still maintain that, especially for smaller countries, this system of defense makes more sense than other alternatives. But is this true? Doesn't an alliance with other countries offer more security than civilian-based defense? Furthermore, even though a traditional military buildup might not constitute much of a deterrent to a big power, it might nevertheless be a good policy to follow for opposing other small and middle-sized countries, especially when one considers the influence of military power on international relations. Also a civilian defense system won't help much to assist in the defense of an ally. It seems that relying on a civilian-based defense system alone is not a particularly attractive strategy though it may be worth planning in advance to follow such an approach if and when one's military forces have been subdued. If all nations were committed to using civilian-based defense rather than building up their military forces, war might be less probable; but it seems that few nations are ready to rely solely on a type of defense whose success seems so questionable.

Peace Through Arms Control and Renunciation of War

As previously noted, two rival nations pursuing a policy of peace through military strength are likely to find themselves engaged in an arms race. We earlier noted that arms races are sometimes a contributory factor to the outbreak of war. It would seem that anything which could keep arms races in check would make war less likely. It is the aim of arms control agreements to promote peace by slowing and possibly even reversing arms races.

Arms Control. One of the main problems for those contemplating arms control agreements is being able to know whether the other side is keeping its part of the bargain. Treaties governing the testing of nuclear weapons and limiting the number of strategic weapons were possible because of technological developments which permitted each side to know what the other was doing without needing to rely on "on-site" inspections. Probably the most important advance in this regard has been the development of spy-in-the-sky satellites which carry sophisticated photographic equipment. By means of these satellites it is not difficult to locate the complex of radars and antiballistic missiles which constitute an ABM site or the launching pads for intercontinental ballistic missiles. The problem of inspection can still be a major obstacle, however, with regard to smaller weapons such as cruise missiles. Consequently, agreements limiting these smaller weapons are not to be expected unless some system of on-site inspection can be worked out.

Such a system is not likely, however, as long as each side fears the other will use such inspections not merely to make sure that agreements are being kept but also to gain valuable information about military installations which could be used when planning an attack. Even the notion of a neutral on-site inspection team is not likely to be acceptable in a tense situation because the adversaries may not trust neutral observers to be clever enough not to be duped or neutral enough not to pass valuable information to the other side.

Another problem for arms control agreements is that new kinds of weapons are always being deployed. This situation is especially acute in the age of modern science. Arms control agreements are going to be addressed to the kinds of weapons which exist at the time the agreements are made. As new kinds of weapons are developed, they generally are not restricted by earlier agreements. For example, agreements to limit nuclear weapons, possibly even prohibiting the testing of them, do not restrict laser weapons or bacteriological/viral weapons and the research directed to their future development.

Somewhat related to this problem of new-weapon development is the problem that arms control agreements may serve only to divert military spending and research from one kind of weapon which is restricted to another kind which is not. Consider what happened with SALT I. That treaty put limits on the number of long-range nuclear weapons launchers each side could have, but it did not put any limits on the number of warheads each missile could carry. The result was to divert efforts away from building more launchers but to increase the effort to put more warheads on each missile. Also both SALT I and SALT II limited only intercontinental range missiles, so both sides were free to engage in a new arms race focused on building medium-range missiles.

A cynic will note that during the Cold War the arms agreements between the U.S. and the Soviet Union put restrictions on weapons which both sides had decided wouldn't be very effective anyway (such as pre–1980 antiballistic-missile missiles) or on weapons which both sides decided they already had in more than adequate quantity (such as intercontinental ballistic missiles). Also when many tests had already been done with large-yield nuclear weapons and when it became apparent that the military needed smaller, not larger, nuclear weapons, then an agreement was made to ban the testing of large nuclear devices with a yield of over 150 kilotons. Furthermore, there was always some consideration given to the situation of other countries. After the U.S., Britain, and the Soviet Union had learned how to test nuclear weapons underground in 1963 but the French and Chinese did not yet have that capability, a treaty was adopted banning nuclear explosions in the atmosphere. In fact, part of the motivation for that treaty probably was a desire to embarrass the Chinese if they tried to explode a nuclear device, but they did it anyway in 1964. The treaty to ban large nuclear explosions may have had somewhat the same kind of motivation since the U.S. and the Soviet Union no longer needed more information about such large weapons but newer nuclear powers would. And the Non-Proliferation Treaty is obviously an effort to keep countries which do not already have nuclear weapons from obtaining them.

The major difficulty with arms control agreements as a road to peace, however, is that even if successful in slowing arms races they do very little to eliminate the danger of war. Suppose, for example, that through arms control agreements all of the nuclear weapons and all the ballistic missiles which now exist could be eliminated. Suppose that even the knowledge of how to build such weapons were eliminated. Would such a development mean the end of war? Obviously not. We would simply regress to something like the pre-nuclear world of 1945. Almost 40 million people were killed in World War II, and nuclear weapons accounted for less than 250,000 of the deaths. And the nonnuclear weapons of today are much more destructive than those available in the 1940s. In fact, one could even argue that the elimination of nuclear warheads and ballistic missiles would make war *more* likely. Without the threat of such weapons, we might already have had World War III. In fact it has been argued that the presence of nuclear weapons has produced a *Pax Atomica*.[13] Those who want to eliminate all nuclear weapons need to ask themselves whether the goal they seek is really desirable.

Renunciation of War. If agreements limiting certain kinds of weapons do not do much to reduce the likelihood of war, perhaps national governments could go further and renounce any use of force or threats of force to settle their differences. The most obvious example of an effort in this direction was the General Treaty for the Renunciation of War, commonly called the Kellogg-Briand Pact, of 1928. In it the signing parties agreed to renounce war "as an instrument of national policy in their relations with one another."[14] It stated further that "the high contracting parties agree that the settlement or solution of all disputes or conflicts, of whatever nature or of whatever origin they may be, which may arise among them, shall never be sought except by pacific means."[15] Sixty-one nations had signed this pact by the end of 1930, the only important nonsigners being Argentina and Brazil. However, the agreement did not state what should be done if some nation did violate the agreement, which Japan, Paraguay, and Italy had all done by 1936. It is questionable whether the agreement had any influence on the behavior of the nations which had signed it. Still, at the Nuremberg Trials after World War II, this treaty was appealed to as setting forth international law which had been violated by the Nazi leaders.

Another example of an international agreement renouncing the use of force is the Charter of the United Nations. Article 2 says in part:

> 3. All Members shall settle their international disputes by peaceful means in such a manner that international peace and security, and justice, are not endangered.
>
> 4. All Members shall refrain in their international relations from the

> threat or use of force against the territorial integrity or political independence of any state, or in any other manner inconsistent with the Purposes of the United Nations.[16]

But once again there is no indication of what should be done if this pledge is violated. It is also doubtful whether national governments act much differently because they have joined the United Nations. By becoming members of the United Nations, however, nations do indicate that they accept these principles as international law.

A more recent example of the use of this approach to peace is the 1973 Agreement Between the United States and the Soviet Union on the Prevention of Nuclear War. In this agreement

> The Parties agree . . . to proceed from the premise that each Party will refrain from the threat or use of force against the other Party, against the allies of the other Party, and against other countries, in circumstances which may endanger international peace and security.[17]

This agreement also indicates that whenever there seems to be a risk of nuclear conflict, the two governments "shall immediately enter into urgent consultations with each other and make every effort to avert this risk."[18]

How much either side felt bound by this agreement is a matter for speculation. Still, it seems pointless to sign such an agreement unless there is at least some expectation by each side that the other will abide by it.

The technique of maintaining peace by renouncing the use of force suffers from a number of deficiencies. The most obvious one is the absence of provisions for enforcement. No punishment is stipulated for those who violate the pledge, no arrangements are made for deciding whether punishment is warranted, and no structure is established to oversee the punishment of violators. Any agreement not to use force to resolve disputes cannot be expected to work until there is also agreement on some alternative trustworthy way of settling differences. About all that can be said for pledges by national governments not to use force is that it is probably better for them to make such pledges than to refuse to make them.

The approaches of arms control and the renunciation of force can be joined in a single effort to try to achieve general and complete disarmament. The reader may be surprised to learn that in 1961 the United States, represented by John McCloy, and the Soviet Union, represented by Valerian Zorin, reached an agreement on principles to govern negotiations aimed at general and complete disarmament. Among them were the following:

> (1) The aim of negotiations should be general and complete disarmament accompanied by the establishment of reliable procedures for the peaceful settlement of disputes.
> (2) When the process is completed, all armed forces will be disbanded, all stockpiles of weapons will be destroyed, all military training will be ended, and all military expenditures will cease.
> (3) The disarmament programme should take place in stages with

verification of compliance at each stage by an international disarmament organization created within the framework of the United Nations.

(4) During the disarmament process institutions for the peaceful settlement of international disputes should be strengthened and a U.N. international peace force should be developed to keep the peace.[19]

These principles were also approved by the U.N. General Assembly.

Unfortunately, there was a significant difference of opinion concealed in the agreement that there would be verification concerning compliance. The Soviets took this to mean that the process of destroying weapons would be verified, while the United States insisted that the verification must extend also to what arms still remained. This difference received more attention than the areas of agreement. It seemed that the governments involved did not really want to reach a workable agreement. The leaders of national governments have difficulty imagining a world where they will have no military forces to try to protect their national interests, and their distrust of possible enemies is too great to allow them to seriously consider the notion of complete disarmament. Part of the difficulty, of course, is the lack of any clear idea of how international disputes would be resolved in the absence of those military forces which at present give the more powerful nations a superior position in bargaining situations.

Although the prospect of general and complete disarmament seems remote, the value of arms control agreements which have been reached should not be disparaged too much. With the Cold War having ended, START I and START II are actually leading to the dismantling of large numbers of nuclear weapons. The CFE (Conventional Forces in Europe) Treaty is providing the framework for large cutbacks in weaponry and forces along the previous battle line between East and West in Europe. Without the tradition of earlier arms control agreements it would have been difficult to move suddenly to these very significant agreements for backing away from war readiness. Also procedures and traditions have been established that can serve as a basis for new agreements such as a Comprehensive Test Ban (CTB) Treaty.

Nevertheless, arms control agreements are directed more to controlling the symptoms of conflict than to preventing war. The arms control agreements during the Cold War did not help end that tense situation. They only seem to have kept arms expenditures and weapons development somewhat under control. Perhaps they didn't even do much to restrain military spending since the restrictions established by earlier agreements may have merely resulted in larger expenditures for the research and development needed for unprohibited kinds of weapons. With the Cold War ended, the arms control agreements provide a good device for winding it down. But the Cold War ended because of other factors, not because of arms control agreements. The new arms control agreements that are leading to a decrease in the numbers of weapons are an effect of the end of the Cold War, not a cause of it. Arms control agreements are undoubtedly more desirable than not having them, but they do not seem to have had much bearing on preventing war.

Peace Through Conciliatory Moves and Gradual Tension Reduction

Arms control agreements and eventually general and complete disarmament seem to be moves in the right direction in the struggle against war, but sometimes tensions and distrust are so great that negotiations between opposing parties cannot even get started. What, if anything, can be done to move toward peace in situations where neither side trusts the other enough to even contemplate the possibility of arms control agreements?

The best known suggestion for action in this kind of situation is the GRIT proposal of psychologist Charles Osgood.[20] GRIT stands for "Graduated Reciprocation in Tension-Reduction" or "Graduated and Reciprocated Initiatives in Tension Reduction."[21] The aim of GRIT is to convert a situation of intense tension and distrust into one where it is possible to have negotiated settlements made in good faith. The general idea is for one party to make a series of conciliatory moves announced in advance with a public invitation for the opponent to make reciprocal gestures of his own choosing. At the same time defenses continue to be maintained in case the opponent misinterprets the moves as signs of weakness.

Osgood's very detailed proposal, published in 1962, was addressed specifically to the confrontation between the United States and the Soviet Union. In his book *An Alternative to War or Surrender* he suggested that even while making conciliatory moves the United States would need to maintain its capacity to launch a nuclear retaliatory attack and be ready to meet an attack using conventional weapons with adequate conventional weapons of its own. He proposed that the announced conciliatory gestures be carried out regardless of whether the other side indicated it would reciprocate, and they would need to be continued over a long period of time, not just for a month or two. Conciliatory moves were to be planned which would promote cooperative enterprises, which would encourage the transfer of sovereignty from the national to the international level, which would reduce the imbalance between have and have-not nations, and which would strengthen democratic ways of life. If successful, this strategy would lead to reciprocal conciliatory moves by the Soviets, a lessening of tension, and some serious bilateral negotiations.

Would such a policy of unilateral conciliatory moves work? At the height of the Cold War would the United States even be willing to try such a policy in its dealings with the Soviet Union? It seems that a policy of this sort was attempted by President Kennedy in 1963 and with some good results, the most obvious one being the adoption of the treaty to stop nuclear testing in the atmosphere signed in August of 1963.[22] The main conciliatory moves consisted of a unilateral U.S. halt to nuclear tests in the atmosphere and U.S. approval of the sale of a large amount of wheat to the Soviet Union.

> For each [conciliatory] move that was made, the Soviets reciprocated. ... They participated in a "you move–I move" sequence rather than waiting for simultaneous, negotiated, agree[d]-upon moves. Further, they shifted to multilateral-simultaneous arrangements once the appropriate mood was generated. ...
>
> ... A danger that seems not to have been anticipated by the United States Government did materialize: the Russians responded not just by reciprocating American initiatives but by offering some initiatives of their own ... Washington was put on the spot: it had to reciprocate if it were not to weaken the new spirit, but it could lose control of the experiment.[23]

Why was such an apparently successful move for peace which began in June of 1963 not continued past November of 1963?

> The reasons were many: the Administration felt that the psychological mood in the West was getting out of hand, with hopes and expectations for more Soviet-American measures running too high; allies, especially West Germany, objected more and more bitterly; and the pre-election year began, in which the Administration seemed ... [to want to make sure that] even if all went sour—if the Soviets resumed testing, orbited bombs, etc.—no credible "appeasement" charge could be made by Republicans.[24]

Another relevant factor may have been President Kennedy's assassination on November 22, 1963, but some additional conciliatory moves were made by Lyndon Johnson after he was elected in 1964. He continued them for about a year. Increasing U.S. involvement in Vietnam may have made the Russians less ready to respond to conciliatory moves on other fronts. It is also relevant that Khrushchev was removed from his leadership position in the Soviet Union in 1964. Kennedy and Khrushchev had gone through the Cuban missile crisis to the brink of nuclear war in October of 1962 and then led their countries through the détente of 1963, but by the end of 1964 neither man was any longer part of the international decision-making process.

Another example of a unilateral conciliatory move to resolve a conflict was Anwar Sadat's dramatic trip to Jerusalem to address the Israeli Knesset in December 1977. The long-term consequences of that move are still not complete, but there is no doubt that it led to negotiations and an agreement between Egypt and Israel in 1979 that would otherwise have been unthinkable. Sadat's move does not fall within the strategy outlined by Osgood, however, because there was not a series of moves but simply one dramatic gesture. Sadat was not operating from a position of military strength, and he seems to have been motivated partly by the hope of influencing public opinion in the United States, a country which could be expected to act as a mediator in the dispute. Still, Sadat's act was an example of making a conciliatory move to loosen a deadlocked confrontation.

It would be a mistake to assume that unilateral conciliatory moves will always be successful. The success of Kennedy's initiatives in 1963 may have resulted from the fact that Kennedy and Khrushchev had come face-to-face with the possibility of nuclear war during the Cuban missile crisis a few months earlier. The success of Sadat's move seems to be due to the fact that he gave the Israelis what they had wanted all along: the recognition of Arab countries that Israel had a right to exist. It is quite conceivable, however, that conciliatory moves could have other results. When the stronger party in a conflict situation makes a conciliatory move, the other party may view this as an opportunity to catch up or surpass the other side in strength. When the weaker party makes a conciliatory move, the stronger may view this as an act of desperation which signals that a complete victory can be won by becoming more aggressive.

Advocates of the gradual tension-reduction approach can reply that there is some risk in any situation. One must also take account of the risk involved when tensions continue to mount and actual fighting breaks out using today's devastating weaponry. Furthermore, the GRIT proposal as worked out by Osgood preserves a retaliatory capability. The gradualist is not suggesting unilateral disarmament, only unilateral conciliatory moves which may induce the other party to reciprocate. The other party may not reciprocate, but how can this be known until the attempt is made? Although our discussion of the peace through tension-reduction approach has been focused on international relations, this same type of strategy could also be applied to group conflicts within nations.

Peace Through Good Relations, Morality, and Cooperation

Although there are obvious differences between international relations and interpersonal relations, there may nevertheless be some principles operative in the interaction between individuals which can also be applied to the interaction between nations. The GRIT proposal discussed in the previous section is a case in point. It was developed not by an expert in international relations but by psychologist Charles Osgood. The presumption made by Osgood is that some principles effective in reducing interpersonal conflict might, with suitable modification, be applicable to reducing international conflict. Undoubtedly one must be careful in making such a move. Nevertheless certain kinds of behavior which tend to keep interpersonal conflict under control should be considered in terms of what they may suggest for more peaceful international relations.

One kind of behavior which seems to promote good interpersonal relations is *communicating* with those who speak or write to you. In international affairs, the parallel of such politeness would be the maintenance of diplomatic relations with all other countries which indicate a desire to have them. Even if their interests and ideologies are different, nothing is to be gained by refusing to have official dealings with them. Such a response can only create bitterness and almost guarantee unfriendliness in return. Communicating with another person does not mean that one approves of that person's life-style, and in a similar way maintaining diplomatic relations with other countries need not indicate approval of the governments or policies of those countries. In both interpersonal and international relations, the frank and open exchange of views seems more fruitful for preventing violent conflict than the refusal to respond to communications. The courtesies and rituals of diplomatic exchanges can take some of the edge off even the most bitter disputes. One way of promoting peace would be the maintenance of proper diplomatic relations with all other governments that desire them, regardless of their ideologies.

At the same time sometimes in interpersonal relations strong antagonistic feelings develop, and then peace may best be achieved by a separation of the feuding parties. If two persons have found they cannot tolerate each other, perhaps the best course of action is for each to have nothing to do with the other. Similarly, in international relations peace may be furthered if two antagonistic countries simply ignore each other. Unfortunately, such a solution often is not possible in international affairs because of geographical or other factors.

Another important aspect of interpersonal behavior which may provide some ideas about how to solve the problem of violent international conflict is *morality*. In interpersonal relations morality provides a basis for individual restraint. It is based on notions of reciprocity (don't do things to others that you wouldn't want them to do to you) and the benefit to each person of a peaceful social order (rather than having a situation where each person pursues his own self-interest without regard to the interests of other individuals or the welfare of the group as a whole). Similarly, in international relations morality based on reciprocity and the benefit to all nations of a peaceful international order might serve as a welcome restraint on the actions of national governments.

Many, perhaps most, scholars of international affairs would consider any attempt to apply moral principles to the behavior of nations as completely misguided.[25] They would contend that nations are quite different from individual persons. They would argue that the very purpose of national governments is to promote the interests of the nation while people do not exist merely to promote their own interests. Individuals are necessarily part of a social order while nations are not necessarily part of a community of nations. Leaders of nations, they contend, must think purely in terms of the preservation of their own nation and the furthering of its interests. To determine policy on the basis of some notion of international morality would be to act contrary to their duty to the nation they lead.

Regardless of how widespread this view is, it must be questioned. The view that the national governments should be concerned only about the people of their own nation neglects the fact that nations are composed of people who have a species-kinship with people of other nations. Those living in other countries are people too, and our empathy with them does not end at the nation's borders, no matter how much some national governments may try to promote such a limitation of concern. Furthermore, nations more and more *do* live in a community of nations. Only a few of the larger nations of the world are even close to being self-sufficient communities. The main point to be made in connection with the view that national governments should not be restrained by any kind of moral considerations, however, is that this doctrine of the absence of morality in international relations is itself at least partly responsible for the prevalence of war in the world. If individuals were to be guided in their behavior by a like principle that each person should pursue only personal interests regardless of the effects on others, then the same prevalence of animosity and violence which is found in international relations would be observed in interpersonal relations. A widespread recognition of the need for morality among nations based on the principle of reciprocity and the value to all nations of a peaceful international order would undoubtedly reduce the amount of war in the world. National leaders would be free to promote the interests of their state, but only within the limits permitted by international morality.

Has there ever been anything like moral behavior on the part of nations? A few examples may help to refute the notion that moral behavior is completely unheard-of in international affairs. One of the more outstanding cases occurred in 1956 when U.S. allies Britain, France, and Israel attacked Egypt, then ruled by Nasser and supplied with military equipment by the Russians. Surely expediency dictated that the United States would support its allies against a nation generally regarded at that time as being at least partly in the Communist camp, but the United States following principle rather than expediency (and also eager to keep the Soviets from having an excuse to put their military forces into Egypt), worked with the Soviet Union in the United Nations to stop the attack made by its own allies on grounds that it violated the U.N. Charter's prohibition against aggression. One could also point to the Marshall Plan undertaken by the United States after World War II to assist Western Europe in rebuilding itself economically. This plan was undoubtedly motivated in part by a desire to keep the Communists from gaining control in these countries, but the United States might have tried to achieve that aim by continued military occupation and policies similar to those followed by the Soviets in eastern Europe. Economic assistance to the less developed countries of the world should also be mentioned, especially that which comes through the United Nations with no strings attached, as well as international disaster relief efforts and the acceptance of refugees from other countries. It seems that humanitarian concerns at least sometimes extend beyond national boundaries.

The debate in the United States concerning the ratification of the new Panama Canal treaties in 1978 reveals the kinds of arguments which can be advanced for and against a foreign policy based on moral restraint. The Carter administration's morally oriented policy was based on the assumption that the United States should be sensitive to the national interests of Panama and to the attitudes of Latin Americans toward the United States. The heavy-handed manner by which the United States had gained control of the Canal Zone in the first place was considered somewhat questionable. The opponents of Carter's moral approach appealed to the national interest of the United States. They argued that the United States was a powerful nation and should not yield anything to a small Latin American country ruled by a dictator. Furthermore, they argued, the decision on the Canal treaties should be evaluated strictly from a military point of view and in the context of the worldwide struggle against the Soviet Union.

These two views on the Canal treaties dramatize how a moral or idealistic approach which takes account of the interests of other countries and the attitudes of people in those countries differs from a so-called realistic approach which appeals solely to national self-interest and militaristic considerations. The realistic approach is consistent with the peace through military strength strategy previously discussed, but it tends to arouse resentment and hatred. The other nation may not respond militarily at that moment, but a readiness to use violence has been created and may be manifested when the opportunity presents itself. The moral or idealistic approach, on the other hand, tends to stimulate friendship and increase the long-term prospects for peace. It may, of course, also encourage the oppressed to be more vocal about their other complaints, but in the long run this reaction seems preferable to ongoing suppressed indignation.

Another principle from interpersonal relations that seems applicable to international relations is that *working together* on mutually beneficial projects tends to promote friendship.[26] Of course, it is possible that such joint efforts may also produce tension, so it is important to choose the right kinds of projects. An example of the wrong kind of project was the Apollo-Soyuz Test Project in 1975 in which American and Russian spacecraft were joined in space. The Russians and Americans involved shook hands in space as well as conducted a few joint experiments, and the events were jointly televised to the peoples of both countries and to the rest of the world. Nevertheless, this joint space venture was not a good choice for a cooperative project because of the close connection between space technology and military technology. There were those of both nations who suspected that the other side was using the project to find out more about its technology. The whole project also seemed to be more an artificial propaganda stunt than an effort to accomplish something really useful. A better possibility for a joint space project would be a global peace-monitoring system.[27] That idea may be implemented now that the Cold War is behind us.

Of course, it is not only with regard to the U.S. and the former Soviet Union that relations could be improved by carrying out joint projects. In the Middle East the Israelis and Arabs could undertake joint development projects which cross their national boundaries. Such joint projects might also be worked out by India and Pakistan. On the island of Cyprus, projects could be undertaken which would help both the Greek and Turkish communities. This strategy can be used within countries when the leaders of groups between whom there is tension can establish some projects on which the opposing groups can work together. It is undoubtedly difficult to get such projects started, but experience shows that when carefully planned and implemented they do work to decrease tension.

Closely related to the idea of joint projects is the idea of the mutual exchanges of people between communities. An extreme example of this approach is the practice of exogamy among some primitive peoples. Since young people are required to marry outside their own group, kinship relations are built up among individuals in the different groups. Under such circumstances the likelihood of war among these groups is greatly reduced, especially since even the leaders then have these extra-group kin.[28] Exogamy does not seem very workable in the modern world, but something like it was practiced not too long ago among European royalty. It is still possible, however, to encourage exchanges of entertainers, athletes, artists, teachers, engineers, students, and other groups. Such exchanges promote an awareness that foreigners have skills, interests, and attitudes which are not unlike those of the people in one's own country. As more and more individual friendships are built up across national boundaries and between ethnic groups, there is more and more resistance to the possibility of war between them.

Another kind of exchange is exchange of information. Governments can encourage the exchange of books and magazines, films and tapes, lecturers and educators. One possible development would be for news broadcasters and journalists from different countries to have regular programs on local stations. With modern communication equipment it is possible to hear radio broadcasts from other countries, to talk by phone to people in other countries, to participate in worldwide computer networks, and to send faxes back and forth. And of course when people travel to other countries, as is now possible for an ever increasing number of people, there is a two-way exchange of information between traveler and local residents.

Our discussion of cooperative projects and exchanges has now gone from dealing with *government-to-government* relations to a dealing with *person-to-person* relations. Modern transportation and communication systems, the existence of a global economy, and more interest in matters beyond the borders of one's own country mean that more and more individuals not connected with the government are meeting other individuals from different countries and different ethnic groups. Deliberate efforts of groups of individuals to "build peace" by reaching out personally to "enemy" groups, independently of what their national governments or ethnic leaders might want to do, have become widespread enough to be given a name. It is called "Track-Two Diplomacy," a term first used by Joseph Montville of the U.S. State Department in 1981.[29] Not all of these "citizen-diplomacy" efforts are as highly structured as his own version of how such an exchange between "opposing groups" should be organized. Montville's model contains three key components: (1) an informal problem-solving three- to five-day workshop composed of small numbers of politically influential members from the "opposing" groups mediated by a small cadre of psychologically sensitive trained facilitators, (2) a "grand strategy" worked out in the workshop to influence public opinion to be supportive of efforts to move toward more harmony, and (3) the implementation of a project which is economically advantageous for both of the "opposing" groups.[30] Even though Montville is from the U.S. State Department, he does not propose this as a government-sponsored activity but rather as one that non-governmental groups can promote.

Citizen diplomacy to promote cooperative projects and exchanges seems to be a worthwhile approach to peace whether it is sponsored by governments or by non-governmental groups. If it were promoted by governments it would fit nicely into our present subject of policies national governments might follow to promote peace. On the other hand, if it were promoted by non-governmental groups, it would seem to require a different place in our discussion of proposals for solving the war problem, probably in the chapter on reforming individual attitudes. Montville himself ties citizen diplomacy to the idea of functionalism as a road to peace, a topic which we will discuss in the next chapter. Track-Two Diplomacy has been placed in this chapter because it is so closely tied to the idea of cooperative projects as a way of improving relations between societies in conflict, even though the exchange may be sponsored by non-governmental groups as well as by governments.

The great difficulty for joint projects and mutual exchanges as a road to peace is how to get them started when tensions are high. Even if it becomes possible to work out such projects or exchanges during a period of high tension, they might well be sabotaged in one way or another by a few individuals, leading to more antagonism than if there had been no joint project or exchange efforts in the first place. But once there is a break in a confrontation situation, these joint projects and mutual exchanges can do much to solidify the new spirit of cooperation, either in the international situation or between groups within a nation-state. Respect for the other group, a sensitivity to the interests of the other group and to the advantages of peace, and the implementation of cooperative projects can be expected to promote peace. On the other hand, coerciveness, hard-nosed selfishness, and a refusal to undertake joint projects can be expected to increase the probability of violent conflict in the long run.

Peace Through Third-Party Involvement

When a conflict arises between two parties, there are various devices for trying to resolve it. One, of course, is a contest of force. But in most situations the parties can agree in advance that they do not want to use force to settle the disagreement if another way can be found. One of the most common approaches is to bargain. When both parties have a great deal to lose if they cannot come to some kind of agreement, there is a great deal of pressure to be conciliatory. On the other hand, in most negotiating each side tries to get the best bargain it can, and this factor tends to make each party unconciliatory. A bargainer who is "hard-nosed" tends to be rewarded while one who is too conciliatory gives up more to the other side than necessary. Consequently, the bargaining process itself is usually very tense as each side tries to get all it can. Most of the interaction between nations takes place by bargaining. In some situations, however, bargaining does not resolve the issue and the conflict continues. Is violent conflict the necessary outcome? Not necessarily. There are other ways of trying to resolve the dispute. One important alternative is the introduction of a third party to try to help the two sides come to an agreement. This third party may intervene on its own because it wants the dispute settled or it may be invited to participate by the parties in the conflict.

We can distinguish four different roles a third party might play in trying to resolve a conflict: (1) provider of "good offices," (2) mediator, (3) arbitrator, and (4) adjudicator. To *provide "good offices"* means to assist the parties in a conflict to communicate with each other in a situation where bargaining has not even begun or where it has ceased because of its apparent hopelessness. The "good offices" may consist of conveying messages between parties who have refused to talk to each other or of providing a neutral meeting place for representatives of the two sides so neither one needs to agree to meet at a place favorable to the other.

Mediators do more than facilitate communication; they actually make proposals which they then encourage both sides to accept. In their proposals they are able to bring in an outside perspective about what seems to be a fair agreement. With a mediator on the scene negotiators for the opposing sides can explain any conciliatory actions to their constituents on grounds that they are merely reacting positively to the efforts of the mediator while still being adamantly opposed to the other party. This point is important because the negotiators need to be able to assure the people they represent that they are getting everything they can for their group. Sometimes mediators may even offer some rewards of their own to the disputing parties to try to get them to accept the proposed solution. Still, the mediator must get both sides to accept explicitly all aspects of the proposed agreement before the conflict is resolved.

In arbitration, the two parties who can't reach an agreement on the issues which divide them are at least able to agree in advance that they will abide by the decision of an *arbitrator* they both view as neutral. They each present their case to the arbitrator who then renders a judgment about how all aspects of the dispute are to be resolved. The obvious difficulty of this approach is finding an arbitrator whom both sides can really trust.

Adjudicators differ from arbitrators in that they concern themselves only with the legal aspects of the case. They are concerned not with making a decision that will be perceived as acceptable by both parties involved but only with rendering a judgment about what the law dictates in this particular case. Some sorts of disputes are best handled by an arbitrator while others, where laws are already prescribed to govern the situation, may best be handled by an adjudicator or judge.

How does this discussion apply to conflicts between nations and between groups within nations? Sometimes one national government will act as provider of good offices, mediator, or arbitrator in a dispute involving other national governments. On other occasions a particularly respected individual or group of individuals may be called on to act as a third party to help settle a dispute between nations or between groups within a nation. International organizations may also serve as third parties in dispute settlement, especially in the areas of mediation and adjudication, but discussions of their role will be postponed to the next section in which the use of international organizations to promote peace will be the theme.

A good example of third-party intervention on the initiative of the third party itself is U.S. participation in the conflict between Israel and its Arab neighbors. The U.S. would like to see this dispute completely resolved. The U.S. has been the main supporter of the state of Israel since its creation in 1948, but it also wants to be on good terms with the Arabs because of how much oil they supply to the U.S. and its allies. During the Cold War most of the Arab countries were strong allies against the Soviet Communists. The U.S. is in a good position to act as a mediator in this dispute because both the Israelis and the leaders of most of the Arab governments regard the U.S. as a friend. President Carter offered large financial incentives to both sides in order to bring about the Camp David accords between Israel and Egypt in 1978. That led to a formal land-for-peace treaty between those countries in 1979. In 1982 the U.S. played a major role in preventing a fight to the finish between the Israelis and the Palestine Liberation Organization in Beirut, Lebanon. More recently the U.S. has been pushing the Israelis to settle their differences with the Palestine Liberation Organization, and a "Declaration of Principles" was signed by both parties in September 1993 in Washington.

Of course, many other instances of efforts to settle international disputes through the efforts of third parties can be cited. In 1871 the U.S. and Britain signed the Treaty of Washington which established the Geneva Arbitration Tribunal to settle what was known as the *Alabama* claims. These claims of the United States against the British were made on grounds that the British had illegally sold warships, including the *Alabama,* to agents of the Confederacy during the American Civil War. The arbitration panel decided that Britain should pay the United States $15,500,000 in damages, the British paid it, and the dispute was ended.[31] In 1904 Russian warships fired on some British trawlers in the North Sea. The British demanded reparation. A Commission of Inquiry, consisting of naval officers from Britain, Russia, France, the United States, and Austria-Hungary, was formed to settle the dispute. It decided that the Russians should pay the British 65,000 British pounds. Once again the payment was made and the dispute was over.[32] In 1905 U.S. President Theodore Roosevelt offered to assist in ending the Russo-Japanese War. His offer was accepted, and the United States played a major role in mediating the conflict, which ended with the signing of a peace treaty.[33]

More recent cases can also be cited. In 1949 Egypt and Saudi Arabia successfully mediated a dispute between Syria and Lebanon which arose from the killing of some Lebanese civilians by Syrian soldiers and which had led to a harmful cessation of trade between the two countries.[34] Turkey and Iran served as mediators in a border dispute between Pakistan and Afghanistan which began in 1947, when Pakistan gained its independence from Britain, and which lasted until 1963.[35] In 1967 President Hamani of Niger successfully mediated a dispute between Chad and Sudan which had occurred as a result of Sudanese assistance to Muslim insurgents in Christian-ruled Chad.[36] In 1958, an unhappy conflict flared up between Chile and Argentina concerning the possession of three islands at the southern tip of South America, and the British were called upon to act as arbitrators but without much success.[37] In 1977 Queen Elizabeth II rendered her judgment, based on the opinion of expert legal advisers, that all three of the disputed islands belonged to Chile, but the Argentinians refused to accept this judgment even though they had earlier agreed to abide by whatever decision was made.[38] In 1984, however, the dispute was resolved through the mediation of the Pope with the three islands still going to Chile but with Argentina getting control over most of the ocean around them.[39] In 1980 Algeria played a key role in getting U.S. hostages out of Iran.

The notion of third-party settlement of disputes can also be applied to conflicts within a nation. Sometimes the third party in such disputes may be another nation. For example, a civil war in Yemen from 1962 to 1970 which saw Egyptian and Saudi Arabian intrusion to help the opposing sides was eventually settled with the assistance of Sudan and Saudi Arabia. At one point, representatives from Iraq and Morocco also helped oversee the withdrawal of foreign troops.[40] For another example, the United Kingdom took an active role in negotiating between blacks and whites in its former colony of Rhodesia (now called Zimbabwe) in order to work out a constitution acceptable to both groups and to supervise the first elections.[41] Of course, the mediators in intranational conflicts are not always, or even usually, persons from another country. Individual arbitrators acceptable to both sides can frequently be found within the society involved.

From a broader point of view, in democratic societies where there is a large middle class, this class in effect functions as an ongoing mediator between the rich and the poor, between the ultraconservatives and the revolutionaries. In fact, it can be argued that in many less developed countries the situation is explosive just because there is no sizable middle class to serve as mediators. Consequently, the rich, who want to preserve their positions of privilege, and the poor, who are pressing hard for a more equal sharing of wealth and power, may both feel that only violence and the complete domination of one group by the other can bring the conflict to an end.

It should be evident that third-party mediation has proved to be an effective approach for resolving some difficult conflicts. In order to be successful, the third party must be perceived as impartial and as having a real desire to have the conflict resolved. When the third party also has power and influence which it is willing to use to help enforce an agreement and economic resources which it is willing to use to "sweeten" the agreement, success is even more likely. Of course, there is always the possibility that the third party who seeks to resolve a conflict may end up being viewed as an enemy by both the disputing parties. Nevertheless, it is to be expected that third-party involvement will become more widely used in the future to try to keep conflicts, both international and intranational, from becoming wars. As we will see in the next section, the third party in international disputes often is an international organization or its representatives.

Peace Through International Conflict Management

A relatively new approach to peace which has attracted the attention of many persons interested in international relations is that of controlling or managing conflicts through the use of international organizations such as the United Nations and the International Court of Justice.[42] The use of regional international organizations like the Organization of American States, the Council of Europe, the Arab League, and the Organization of African Unity to control conflict among members is also part of this approach,[43] but our discussion will focus on the use of the United Nations and the International Court of Justice.

This idea of peace through international conflict management began with the development of the League of Nations after World War I and has become much more widespread with the development of the United Nations after World War II. In a very general way one could say that this approach to peace uses an international organization as a third party to deal with conflicts between members of that organization. An organization such as the United Nations can be used in many different ways: to allow for a public airing of differences between disputants, to furnish trained individuals for private mediation, to send special commissions to determine the facts of a conflict situation, to provide armed forces to guard against violations of agreements that have been reached, and so on. The International Court of Justice can render legal judgments about the application of international law to particular conflict situations. In using this approach nations surrender none of their national sovereignty, but yet they make use of the forum and the machinery of international organizations in order to resolve their conflicts.

The way in which the United Nations has operated to promote peace is not exactly what was envisioned at the time that this organization was created in 1945. The plan for preserving peace put forth in the U.N. Charter is called *collective security*. The basic idea of collective security is that any nation which is attacked by an aggressor can expect all the other members of the United Nations to join it in fighting against the aggressor. The closest approximation to this type of response occurred in 1950 when North Korea attacked South Korea. Sixteen nations sent at least some forces to assist South Korea in the battle against North Korea, which had been labeled the aggressor by the United Nations. But even this noteworthy case was far from the type of response that should have occurred according to the doctrine of collective security. Most of the fighting in Korea was done by South Korean and American troops. Even the other nations which responded sent relatively small contingents. The U.S.-led coalition fighting against Iraq in the Gulf War had support from 29 countries.[44] Although the military action was authorized by the U.N., it was organized and directed by the U.S. and most of the troops were furnished by nine countries.[45] It is questionable whether that military action should be described as "collective security." It certainly wasn't carried out in accord with the U.N. Charter's provision for collective action by the U.N.[46]

On the basis of past experience with the League of Nations as well as the United Nations, collective security does not seem to be a very trustworthy system for stopping aggressive attacks. Nations want the benefit of collective security if they are attacked, but they don't want to take on the costs of making their contribution to collective security if some other nation is attacked. Although the United Nations has solved the very difficult problem of working out a very precise definition of "aggression," the even more difficult problem remains of determining in a particular situation whether a given nation is an aggressor or not. Furthermore, even if there is general approval of the notion that a given country is an aggressor, there still may be little response to an appeal for help to fight against that aggressor.

Meanwhile, the United Nations has in actual practice developed an approach to controlling conflict not envisioned at the time of its founding, namely, the policing of agreements arrived at by the parties to the conflict after the Security Council (or in some cases the General Assembly) has passed a resolution calling for a cease-fire supervised by U.N. forces. Our earlier chapter on the United Nations included a discussion of this type of effort called *peacekeeping* and described the many peacekeeping operations presently being carried out by the U.N. In peacekeeping there is no effort to brand one country or another as an aggressor. The attempt rather is to stop the fighting and persuade the countries to resolve their differences in a nonviolent way. It should be evident, however, that this approach can be used only in those circumstances where all the big powers in the Security Council agree or where the General Assembly, in view of inaction by the Security Council, passes a resolution calling for a cease-fire under U.N. supervision. Of course, in situations where emotions run high, appeals by the United Nations may simply be ignored.

The formal peacekeeping operations of the United Nations are not the only device which that organization has for promoting peace. Peacekeeping activities come into play only after a situation has become tense and fighting has broken out. Ideally, other kinds of U.N. efforts can keep a potential conflict from reaching the fighting stage. The Secretary-General may confer privately with parties which seem to be heading for a conflict. Fact-finding commissions can be appointed. The General Assembly or the Security Council can pass resolutions which serve as indicators of international public opinion. As a result, national governments may be more restrained than they otherwise would be. The existence of the international organization serves at least to some extent to inhibit its members from pursuing their national interests without regard to consequences for other nations and for the international community as a whole.

It is not possible to evaluate exactly how successful the United Nations has been in defusing conflict situations because some potential conflicts are kept from even coming to public attention by behind-the-scenes meetings of diplomats at the United Nations. It is possible, however, to look at the U.N.'s record in handling disputes which have reached the stage of public awareness. In a 1978 study of the effectiveness of the United Nations in managing conflict in various types of situations R.L. Butterworth concluded that the United Nations

> has been involved in the growth of conditions for world order. . . . It has done so by acting as a generalized resource for states to try to use in conducting international politics. . . . Shared norms, perceptions, and habits of cooperation have been stimulated and facilitated through the U.N.'s conflict management activities.[47]

Still, he observed, the United Nations has frequently not been successful. He noted that ". . . the U.N. is usually effective only when substantial collective resources are mobilized"[48] and that "the U.N.'s effectiveness was strongly linked to American leadership."[49] If the United States backs away from a leadership role at the United Nations, that organization may become even less effective than it has been in the past.[50]

It would seem that if nations were really interested in promoting peace, they could make better use of the United Nations and the International Court of Justice than they do now. Instead of thinking simply in terms of how they can use the United Nations to advance their short-term national interests, they could focus their attention on how to make the United Nations more effective as a peacemaking and peacekeeping organization. Some moves to make the United Nations more effective may require changes in the Charter. We will consider those possibilities in the next chapter. For now let us consider some things which could be done without changing the Charter.

A good beginning point for such a discussion is U.N. Secretary-General Boutros-Ghali's *An Agenda for Peace* issued June 17, 1992.[51] One of the most important new ideas the Secretary-General put forth in this report is the idea of *preventive diplomacy*. Until now official U.N. efforts have generally been confined to what happens after fighting has already taken place and a truce has been worked out. The Secretary-General says that the United Nations should become involved in crises *before* fighting occurs. Such an outlook means that the U.N. would be engaged in more of its own information gathering. There would be greater use of U.N. fact-finding missions. There would be the possibility of the deployment of U.N. peacekeeping forces within the boundaries of a country which believes that it may be attacked by another country. The U.N. forces would go in, with the approval of the Security Council, to forestall an anticipated attack. Or in a situation where two countries are mutually suspicious of each other, there could be a demilitarized zone between the two possible adversaries with U.N. forces in that zone. The big difference from the present situation is that the U.N. peacekeeping forces would be put in place *before* any actual fighting breaks out. Another aspect of preventive diplomacy is that the Secretary-General would be authorized to go to the International Court of Justice to get an advisory opinion on the legal aspects of a conflict before any military action occurs.

An Agenda for Peace also calls on member nations to earmark particular national military units for U.N. peacekeeping. It recommends the pre-positioning of military equipment needed for peacekeeping operations so that when peacekeeping forces are created the needed equipment will be ready. One of the more controversial ideas in the report is that the U.N. should have a new type of enforcement unit, more heavily armed than the lightly armed units which have thus far taken part in U.N. peacekeeping. Such forces would be ready to go into more volatile situations where U.N. forces have not previously been prepared to go such as the former Yugoslavia. He calls for cooperative peacekeeping operations where the U.N. and regional organizations such as the Organization of American States, the Organization for African Unity, and the European Community work together. Such cooperation between the U.N. and regional organizations has already begun in Latin America and the former Yugoslavia. In addition the Secretary-General proposes that humanitarian relief be coordinated under the U.N., not just where fighting has already occurred but also where there is a danger of armed conflict as a result of starvation or the absence of adequate housing or adequate health care, and so on. One recommendation already implemented is the creation of a Humanitarian Revolving Fund of about $50 million for emergency situations.

With regard to the financing of U.N. peacekeeping, one suggestion is the creation of a Peace-keeping Reserve Fund so that money would be available during the initial stages of a peacekeeping operation. Then starting up a new peacekeeping operation would not be hindered by a lack of financial resources exactly when they are most desperately needed. Another recommendation is that a U.N. Peace Endowment Fund of a billion dollars be created with the proceeds from the fund being used to finance various facets of peace-keeping. Another recommendation is that U.N. member nations start paying for U.N. peacekeeping out of the national military budget instead of the foreign affairs budget. It is also suggested that money could be raised for peacekeeping by some kind of a tax such as a levy on arms sales or a levy on international air travel.

The Secretary-General also indicates that all member nations should accept the compulsory jurisdiction of the International Court of Justice — without reservations. Many countries have not even committed themselves to accepting the jurisdiction of the Court. Of those that have made such a commitment, many have hedged their commitment with reservations. For example, the U.S.'s commitment to the authority of the Court is compromised by the "Connolly Reservation" attached to U.S. acceptance of the Court's authority. The "Connolly Reservation" says that the U.S. will decide for itself what is and what is not a domestic issue and will not accept the authority of the International Court of Justice to make that determination. The Secretary-General is saying that it is time for all countries to withdraw their reservations so that such loopholes to accepting the decisions of the International Court of Justice can be closed. When some countries make such reservations to their acceptance of the Court's authority, then other countries feel that they also can adopt their own particular reservations. As a result the Court's utility for resolving international legal disputes is undermined.

What else might be done to make the U.N. more effective as a keeper of the peace? *An Agenda for Peace* called for more fact-finding by the U.N. What the Secretary-General did not specifically say is that the U.N. needs its own "intelligence" agency, including its own satellites for information-gathering. At present the U.N. is dependent on being given information from national satellites operated by a very few countries. As early as the 1978 U.N. Special Session on Disarmament France proposed that the U.N. should have its own U.N. surveillance system and the idea has been explored by the organization, but during the Cold War progress toward any kind of implementation was blocked by both superpowers.[52] Such an information-gathering agency might be integrated into a U.N. Arms Control and Disarmament Agency that could verify compliance with arms control agreements using the satellites as well as random on-site inspections. Such an agency might provide the impetus for more arms control agreements and possibly a plan for gradual and total disarmament.[53]

The Secretary-General's proposals called for some heavily armed U.N.

units that could be used in situations where armed resistance is expected. Events in the former Yugoslavia and Somalia suggest that there is a real need for such forces. But this proposal is not likely to be effective unless it is modified a bit. The Secretary-General seems to be thinking of contingents from national armed forces that would engage in this dangerous mission, but national governments are not likely to send their soldiers into such a situation when their own national interest is only remote. What is needed is a standing force of individually recruited volunteers directly under U.N. control.[54] With this arrangement national leaders would not be put on the spot for risking the lives of the soldiers in their national armed forces. A force of individually recruited soldiers could operate in places like the former Yugoslavia to promote the world interest rather than being restrained by concerns of short-term national interest.

An Agenda for Peace recommends the establishment of a U.N. Peace Endowment Fund of a billion dollars, but where will the financing come from? Instead of relying completely on national governments for money, why not allow and encourage private individuals and private corporations to contribute to this fund? Perhaps some peace-oriented non-government organizations would want to collect money for such a fund. Consider too that many consumer-oriented multinational corporations make a great deal of money when there is peace, and they lose money when there is war. The U.N. could encourage these corporations to put their economic weight on the side of peace just as some of them have put it on the side of national military establishments in the past. All that is required is some safeguards to make sure that the money is contributed with no strings attached.[55]

With regard to the use of courts as a way of dealing with international conflict we should mention again a proposal discussed earlier in connection with legal aspects of the contemporary situation, that of creating an International Criminal Court where *individuals* can be held accountable for violations of international law. In the Persian Gulf War President Bush said that the U.S. had nothing against the people of Iraq but only Saddam Hussein. But what happened? The coalition forces led by the U.S. killed a hundred thousand Iraqis, but Saddam Hussein is still in charge of the country of Iraq. Where is the problem? The difficulty came from attributing guilt to the *country* of Iraq rather than to Saddam Hussein, the *individual*. The same problem exists in the former Yugoslavia where the focus should be on individuals who are violating international law rather than on this or that ethnic group. In conflict situations the violence is often due to a few specific individuals. We could change the way we operate at the international level so that we focus on violations of international law by individuals rather than focusing just on national governments.

Peace Through Peace Research and Peace Education

As we have earlier noted, worldwide expenditures for military purposes amount to about $2.5 billion a day. As weapons become ever more sophisticated, the cost of developing and producing them can be expected to continue to increase. Under these circumstances it seems that the national governments should be interested in promoting peace research and peace education so that these huge outlays of resources for the military would become unnecessary.

From the point of view of cutting their own future costs, it is hard to imagine what better investment could be made by national governments than support of peace research, especially when it is recalled that national governments are responsible for maintaining peace among opposing groups in their own society as well as preventing wars with other countries. It seems that nations cannot afford *not* to invest some of their resources in learning how to promote peace.

Despite the desirability of supporting peace research, few national governments are contributing much to such efforts. In fact, in 1979 the number of people all over the world actively engaged in peace research was estimated at 5,000.[56] The financial support for peace research comes from many different sources, such as foundations, trust funds, special grants, membership contributions, university budgets, and direct government contributions.[57] The funding of peace research from all these sources was less than 1 percent of the amount spent for military research in Canada and Sweden, less than 2 percent in the United States, and less than 5 percent in West Germany and India.[58] National governments in countries such as Sweden, Denmark, Finland, France, West Germany, Japan, Norway, and the United Kingdom have given some direct support to peace research.[59] Sweden's Stockholm International Peace Research Institute is probably the outstanding example of a nationally supported institution devoted strictly to the study of peace from an international point of view. (The International Peace Academy in New York, the United Nations University with headquarters in Tokyo, and the University for Peace in Escazu, Costa Rica, all are internationally supported and do not focus their efforts mainly on peace research.) In 1984 the U.S. Congress authorized the creation of a U.S. Institute of Peace, and the Institute began functioning in 1986.[60]

What specific kinds of problems might peace researchers consider? One obvious task would be the evaluation of proposals for solving the war problem, such as those discussed in this book. Research could try to determine how various approaches could be made more effective and to learn how particular approaches could best be applied to particular kinds of situations. Peace researchers could examine periods of peace as well as the beginnings of wars in order to try to learn what factors promote peace and what factors undermine it. The problem of how to educate people to promote peace could be investigated. The various topics discussed in this book provide only a beginning list of the issues which peace researchers need to study.

Peace research can also develop new proposals and techniques for resolving group conflicts and then test their effectiveness. Let us look at but one technique which has been developed to be used when an arbitrator has been enlisted to try to resolve a conflict. It is called the *last-best-offer technique*. After the regular bargaining process has gone as far as it can go, each side is asked to give its "last best offer" to the arbitrator, that is, to indicate the most conciliatory agreement it can bring itself to make. The arbitrator must choose one or the other proposal, whichever one is felt to be most fair, as the final settlement. It is not permissible to "split the difference" between the two offers, a different mediating technique which has the adverse effect of encouraging each side to be more excessive in its demands so that it will be better off after the difference is split evenly. With the last-best-offer technique, each side is led to be as conciliatory as possible in hopes that its proposal will be the one accepted by the arbitrator. Peace researchers could investigate how this and other techniques might be applied both to international disputes and to disputes between groups within countries.

Although peace research involves discovering and evaluating techniques for resolving conflict which are immediately applicable, it must also deal with the more general issue of the relation between justice and peace. It needs to focus on the problem of peace not merely from the point of view of how to preserve the status quo without violence, but also from the point of view of how to remove the injustices and resulting resentments which prompt people to resort to violence. If peace research is not to be simply another instrument in the hands of those with power and privilege, it must focus on the processes by which peaceful change can take place. It needs to address itself to investigating alternatives to violence for those who are presently being treated unfairly by the social system as a whole. On the international level, peace research must be concerned with the plight of the less developed countries and how the international order can be changed in a peaceful way to accommodate the interests of these countries without ignoring those of the more technologically advanced countries. On the domestic level, peace research must deal with the situation of the poor and dispossessed and how the social system can be changed in a peaceful way so that it takes account of their interests as well as those of the rich and powerful.

It seems obvious that supporting peace research would promote justice as well as peace both within nations and among them. In fact, economist and peace scholar Kenneth Boulding maintained that there is nothing that can be done that would more dramatically increase the probability of the survival of humanity than a massive effort in peace research.[61] Such an effort might make the difference of whether or not we all die in a nuclear holocaust. It could save governments large sums of money now being spent for military forces, weapons, police forces, prisons, and special personnel for suppressing riots. It is distressing to note that national governments are so wedded to resolving conflict by force that they are generally unwilling to fund the efforts to learn about other techniques of conflict resolution.

What about peace education? Here national governments face a difficult problem. As much as they might like to educate their people to be more informed about and committed to peace, they realize that the present international system may require them to resort to force to protect their national interests. As Gwynne Dyer observes, "To be a state is also, in practice, to fight wars...."[62] Thus every nation must prepare its citizens so they will be ready to participate in wars. Under such circumstances it is not surprising that most national governments are less than enthusiastic about promoting peace education. Substantial support for peace education on the part of national governments is not likely until the system of sovereign nations is changed. How that system might be changed to promote peace is the topic of the next chapter.

XVII. Reforming the International System

So far we have reviewed proposals for promoting peace by reforming the attitudes of individuals, by reforming the internal operations of national governments, and by reforming the policies of national governments. We turn now to another set of proposals based on the view that, as helpful as some of these other proposals may be, there can be no lasting solution to the war problem until the present anarchy among nations is replaced by some kind of system at the international level that puts some limits on national sovereignty.

The present international system consists of over 180 sovereign nations, each devoted to the pursuit of its own national interests. When we say that these nations are *sovereign,* we mean that there is no higher authority to which they are subject. As we have previously noted, even the most significant international organization which presently exists, the United Nations, is based on acceptance of the principle of national sovereignty. Although there are some parts of the U.N. Charter which suggest that the Security Council can require member nations to do certain things, no nation can be forced to yield its sovereignty. If an effort were made by the United Nations to coerce a nation to do something it doesn't want to do, it could withdraw from the organization and then would no longer be legally subject to its jurisdiction.

Those who believe that the system of sovereign nations must be changed before an enduring and dependable peace can be established argue as follows: There are bound to be conflicts of interest between different nations. These conflicts may be resolved by bargaining, mediation, arbitration, and adjudication; but if the conflict is intense and the nations involved have approximately equal military power, it can be expected that situations will arise in which each of these nations will insist on having its own way. So long as there is no higher authority which can settle the dispute, the nations will use threats of force, and ultimately war itself, to try to resolve the conflict in accord with their own interests. The only way to avoid these wars and the military buildups which are related to them, it is claimed, is to place some restriction on national sovereignty. Those who want disarmament by the nations first and *then* a consideration of alternative nonviolent ways of resolving disputes are hoping for something that can never be. It is only *after* trustworthy nonviolent means of resolving disputes which limit the sovereignty of nations have been developed that one can expect the national governments to seriously consider disarming.

According to those who maintain that the international state system must be changed, part of the difficulty with the present system is the roles that national leaders are required to play. National leaders are expected to do everything possible to promote the national interest. Any conciliatory move with regard to the concerns of other nations is likely to be taken as a sign of weakness and a betrayal of the nation they lead. A great deal of the power in the world is in the hands of national leaders who must play this role. On the other hand, who has the role of looking out not just for this or that nation but for the whole human race? Who has the job of being concerned more about promoting world peace than about promoting national interests? The present international system lacks anyone with power to play this role. The Secretary-General of the United Nations comes closest to having such a position, but even he serves at the pleasure of the national governments and dares not say or do anything that might offend the more powerful ones. The representatives of the national governments at the United Nations for the most part view themselves as having a responsibility not to solve world problems but only to protect the interests of the national governments they represent. Under such a system, it is claimed, enduring peace is not likely. It is necessary to change the structure so that the power of those concerned about purely national interests is more limited while the power of those concerned about the welfare of the broader human community is strengthened.

Another difficulty with the present international system, it is claimed, is that the notion of national sovereignty is not consistent with the realities of the modern world. National sovereignty is based ultimately on the two assumptions that nations are self-sufficient social units and that national governments are capable of protecting their citizens from any harm which might be done to them by other groups. But in today's world neither assumption is true. No nation exists which is not at least somewhat dependent on the events that take place in other national societies. Even the largest nations have needs which they themselves cannot meet. National governments also are no longer able to completely protect their citizens from any harm that might be done by other groups. It is obvious that the governments of the smaller and weaker nations are "sovereign" only in theory. Furthermore, even the superpowers cannot protect their own people completely. They cannot stop intercontinental missiles tipped with nuclear warheads from falling on their cities. Even if such an attack were deterred by threat of retaliation, governments cannot save their own citizens from the radioactivity of a nuclear war in which their own nation is not involved. What could the United States do to protect its citizenry from radioactive fallout in the event of a nuclear war between Russia and China? All the deterrent weaponry in the world would not help. It is no longer true that nations are self-sufficient and that national governments are capable of protecting their citizens from all dangers originating in other societies. As a consequence, it is argued, it is now necessary to move beyond an international system based on the obsolete idea of unlimited national sovereignty.[1]

How might such a change be accomplished? One possibility would be limiting or bypassing national sovereignty with regard to specific international situations. A second possibility is the consolidation of groups of nations into larger political units on the basis of geography, culture, or ideological commitments. A third possibility would be the establishment of a world government over the national governments so that the kinds of political and judicial institutions for resolving conflict now found within nations would be created at the global level.

Those who would like to see the establishment of a world government may differ on which of three possible approaches is most likely to succeed in producing such an institution. The *federalist approach* to world government advocates the deliberate decision by national governments to transfer certain powers (such as maintaining armed forces) to a world government while retaining other powers (such as establishing laws concerning the ownership of property) for themselves. The *functionalist approach* to world government advocates the creation of more and more global agencies (such as the World Health Organization, the Food and Agriculture Organization, and the Universal Postal Union) to handle particular global problems until such agencies collectively constitute a world government handling the problems of the global community. The *populist approach* to world government advocates a grass-roots people's movement to establish a democratic world government directly responsible to the people of the world, a global political institution which would control national governments rather than being subservient to them.

Limiting National Sovereignty in Specific Situations

There are many particular ways in which national sovereignty might be limited or bypassed in order to reduce the likelihood of violent conflict.[2] In order to give some organization to our discussion we will consider them under seven headings: developing supranational agencies for governing territory not already controlled by nations; modifying voting arrangements in the United Nations in order to diminish the influence of the principle of national sovereignty and increase the importance of the United Nations in conflict resolution; allowing the United Nations to have sources of revenue other than contributions from national governments, thus making the United Nations less dependent on national governments; extending the powers of the International Court of Justice so that it can assist in the resolution of more conflicts; allowing the United Nations and the International Court of Justice to interact directly with private parties to help resolve international conflicts; developing a standing autonomous international peace-keeping military force which could intervene in conflict situations; and using direct action by a nongovernmental group to try to stop the use of armed force by national governments. This discussion aims to call attention to some of the ways in which the principle of national sovereignty might be eroded in order to promote the peaceful resolution of conflicts.

One of the more promising approaches to limiting national sovereignty is to prevent it from spreading beyond its present limits. There are still parts of the world, such as the oceans, which so far have not been claimed to be under the jurisdiction of national governments. Traditionally international law has maintained that the oceans cannot be claimed by any nation or made subject to the laws of any country. "The freedom of the seas" has meant that ships could go anywhere on the oceans. It has meant that one could take out of the oceans fish, whales, or whatever else was wanted and dump into the oceans garbage, sewage, radioactive wastes, or whatever else wasn't wanted. In order to protect their coasts, nations were allowed sovereignty over an area out to three miles, called the territorial sea because it was regarded as the territory of the coastal nation. But beyond this three-mile limit, the seas belonged to no one.

Unfortunately, since World War II nations have been expanding their area of control of the oceans. In 1945 the United States, having discovered oil in its continental shelf (the ground which slopes away from land but which is under water), claimed ownership of all natural resources in the shelf, even beyond the earlier three-mile limit.[3] Chile, Ecuador, and Peru, not having much of a continental shelf but having many fish upon which their economies depended in the waters off their coasts, in 1952 joined together in the Santiago Declaration claiming ownership of the resources in the ocean itself out to a distance of 200 miles.[4] Other nations also began claiming resources off their coasts beyond the three-mile limit.

To try to prevent further grabs of ocean resources and to eliminate possible violence from conflicting claims, the U.N. General Assembly in 1969 passed a resolution calling for a moratorium on efforts to exploit the resources of the sea-bed under the oceans until an international regime was established to control such exploitation, and in 1970 it passed another declaring the oceans to be "the common heritage of mankind" and another calling for a Conference on the Law of the Sea.[5] The U.N. Conference on the Law of the Sea (UNCLOS) held its first session in New York in December of 1973 and then had one or two sessions each year until the text of the Law of the Sea Treaty was finalized in 1982. Before the end of 1984 the treaty had been signed by 158 nations and international bodies.[6] It is scheduled to go into effect one year after it has obtained 60 ratifications. The sixtieth ratification occurred on November 16, 1993, so the treaty should enter into force on November 16, 1994, even though the U.S. has not yet ratified it.[7] The treaty provides for a territorial sea twelve miles in width instead of three; for the preservation of the international status of straits even as the width of the territorial sea is otherwise extended; for an economic zone under the control of the coastal state extending out to 200 miles; and for an International Seabed Resources Authority to control exploitation of the resources of the sea-bed beyond the economic zone of the coastal states.

From the point of view of the issue of sovereignty, it is this International Seabed Resources Authority which is especially interesting. For the first time in human history a region of the earth will come under the control of an international regime with law enforcement capabilities. Once such a supranational government is organized and functioning, it is not hard to imagine a gradual extension of the area for which it is responsible or the creation of similar agencies to govern other areas such as Antarctica[8] and outer space, including the moon and planets.[9] At any rate, the effort to create an international agency to control the resources of the sea-bed represents a first step in ending the expansion of territory controlled by national governments.

A second situation where national sovereignty could be eroded is in the voting arrangements in the Security Council and the General Assembly of the United Nations. In the Security Council each of the five permanent members (the United States, Russia, China, the United Kingdom, and France) has the power to cast a veto, thus blocking action even if all other members of the Security Council favor the action. The extravagant degree of sovereignty granted these five nations could conceivably be trimmed if there were certain situations in which the veto could not be used. For example, the veto power could be eliminated on votes concerning the establishment of fact-finding commissions, the interposition of peacekeeping forces to preserve the status quo, or the admission of nations into the United Nations. Perhaps some limitations on the veto would be accepted by the big powers in exchange for modifications on the voting arrangements in the General Assembly.

In the General Assembly at present, each nation, no matter how large or small, powerful or weak, gets one vote. The number of people in a nation and the amount of economic wealth and military power it has make a great deal of difference in the actual conduct of international relations, but these factors are not reflected in the voting of the General Assembly. It is theoretically possible that a resolution could be passed in the General Assembly on the basis of votes of countries which have less than 5 percent of the world's population and less than 1.5 percent of the gross world product.[10] Under such circumstances, who is going to pay much attention to votes in the General Assembly? Resolutions have no binding authority anyway, but the one-vote-per-nation arrangement means that their moral influence is minimal too.

A change in the voting rules to take account of factors such as population and economic power could be viewed as putting some constraints on the notion of national sovereignty, especially that part of the doctrine which holds that every nation is equal to every other nation. One well-known proposal is that put forward by Grenville Clark and Louis Sohn in *World Peace through World Law*. In this first system proposed in 1966 the four most populous nations—China, India, the Soviet Union, and the United States—would each have 30 votes. The 10 next populous nations would have 12 votes each, the next 15 would have 8 votes each, the next 20 would have 6 votes each, the next 30 would have 4 votes each, the next 40 would have 3 votes each, and the others would have one vote each.[11] This arrangement approximates a system of representation in which the number of votes is proportional to the square root of the nation's population, which itself is another possible system.[12] But if one were to rely on population alone as a basis for representation, at that time China with 22 percent of the world's population and India with 16 percent would have had considerably more votes than the Soviet Union with 6 percent and the United States with 5 percent. Such a system would have deviated too much from the realities of power in the world, so Clark and Sohn proposed that all four of these countries have the same number of votes. Under their proposal the General Assembly would become a law-making parliament with very restricted powers.

A later proposal for changing the voting in the U.N. General Assembly is Richard Hudson's "binding triad" idea.[13] Each country would continue to cast one vote as it does now, but the votes would be tabulated three times. On the first tabulation each nation would be credited with one vote as at present, but on the second computation the vote of each country would be multiplied by its population, and on the third computation it would be multiplied by that country's contribution to the U.N. budget (an amount based roughly on its GNP). Any measure which received at least a two-thirds (or some other specified proportion) favorable vote on all three tabulations would become binding international law. Thus, the General Assembly theoretically would become a law-making body, though there might be considerable difficulty in working out measures which could garner the required number of votes.

A third situation where national sovereignty could be eroded concerns the financial arrangements for the United Nations. At present the only source of funds for the United Nations is assessments and contributions from national governments.[14] This arrangement means that those governments which make substantial contributions can exert considerable pressure on the United Nations by threatening to refuse to pay certain assessments or to withdraw from the organization entirely if displeased. The United Nations would be much less susceptible to such threats if it had its own source of funds. When the International Seabed Resources Authority created by the Law of the Sea Treaty discussed above becomes operative, it could tax the resources being taken from the ocean floor and pass some of the revenue along to the United Nations. A small tax might also be levied on all resources taken out of the economic zones of the oceans on the principle that all parts of the oceans, even that part which makes up the national economic zones, have been declared to be the common heritage of mankind. It might even be possible to tax arms that cross national boundaries or to assess a proportional tax on any nation's military expenditure that exceeds 3 percent of its GNP. Perhaps the United Nations could collect fines for violations of regulations it might adopt governing air or water pollution which crosses national boundaries. In any case, if the United Nations had its own source of funds, it would be less vulnerable to economic threats from national governments.

The fourth situation where national sovereignty could be eroded concerns the International Court of Justice. At present only national governments can be parties in cases before the Court, and the Court will accept a case only if all parties to the dispute agree in advance to abide by its decision. Only the Security Council, the General Assembly, and other U.N. organs and agencies which first get the approval of the General Assembly can get *advisory* opinions from the Court. Under these circumstances the Court has not been very busy. Why not expand the powers of the Court? One possible change would be to allow the Security Council to get binding decisions from the Court rather than merely advisory ones. A second possible change would be to allow the Secretary-General and regional international organizations such as the Organization of American States to ask for advisory opinions. A third possible change, one which would have a much greater impact on national sovereignty, would be to allow a national government to get an advisory opinion from the Court in a conflict situation even though the other governments involved have refused to accept the jurisdiction of the Court. Other changes of the same sort are possible. The point is that the International Court of Justice would take a much more active role in resolving international conflicts if such changes were made.

A fifth way of making national sovereignty less of an obstacle in international conflict resolution would be to permit greater interaction between individuals on the one hand and the United Nations and the International Court of Justice on the other. As the United Nations was originally conceived, the only place in which there was to be any interaction between the United Nations and individuals was the Secretariat, where persons are hired as employees of the United Nations. The Economic and Social Council was permitted to consult with nongovernmental organizations concerned with matters related to its activities. Otherwise, the United Nations and the International Court of Justice could do business only with national governments and their representatives. But some changes toward more direct interaction between the United Nations and private parties are already taking place. In the area of human rights, the International Covenant of Civil and Political Rights contains an optional Protocol by which a national government can give its citizens the right to appeal directly as individuals to the U.N. Human Rights Committee when they feel that their rights granted by the Covenant have been violated. Another significant development occurred at the U.N. Special Session on Disarmament in 1978 when representatives of nongovernmental organizations interested in disarmament were allowed to address the session.

What further changes might be made in permitting the United Nations and the International Court of Justice to interact directly with individuals and nongovernmental organizations? One idea is to let the United Nations directly recruit individuals to serve in the U.N. peacekeeping forces rather than relying on contingents of armed forces from national governments. Another idea is to have the General Assembly create a second, advisory assembly composed of representatives from national legislatures or nongovernmental organizations which could propose resolutions to the main assembly.[15] With regard to judicial issues, there already exist international conventions which prohibit certain activities such as hijacking airplanes on international flights or using violence against diplomats, activities carried on by individuals rather than national governments. The International Court of Justice could create a separate International Criminal Court to deal with those individuals who are accused of violating these international laws.[16] It could also establish international courts to handle civil cases between private parties from different countries or between a private party and a foreign government. Among other things, such courts would provide a setting for resolving legal disputes between governments and transnational corporations.

A sixth way to move toward limiting national sovereignty is to develop a standing international peacekeeping force ready to participate in peacekeeping efforts. At present international peacekeeping forces are organized by the U.N. Secretary-General *after* the Security Council has called for them. Nations which are enthusiastic about collective peacekeeping could join together to create their own separate Active Peacekeeping Organization[17] or Peacemakers Association of Nations.[18] The peacekeeping police force created by this new international organization would consist of soldiers drawn from all member nations, and they would serve as individuals in a unified force rather than as members of national contingents. In every member country there would be stationed some soldiers from all other member states. Each member nation of the peacekeeping organization would know that the newly created force would automatically provide assistance to it under specified conditions such as an attack by another country. Policies concerning the use of the peacekeeping force would be promulgated by the political assembly of the new organization, and the force could also be used for peacekeeping efforts of the United Nations. Such a peacekeeping association of nations would allow its member states to reduce their expenditures for defense while increasing their national security and their participation in international peacekeeping. It would also represent a step away from world anarchy and reliance solely on one's own national military forces for security.

A seventh approach to limiting national sovereignty involves the use at the international level of the Gandhian idea of nonviolent resistance. This approach involves the creation of a nongovernmental organization composed of individuals from all over the world who are willing to participate in unarmed and nonviolent activities at points of conflict anywhere in the world. These people would be dedicated to direct nonviolent action to oppose the use of force by national governments. Such a World Peace Brigade was organized in 1962 but lost its momentum by 1964 because of financial difficulties and differences of opinion on whether to emphasize reconciliation of the opposing sides from an impartial point of view or confrontation to advance the interests of oppressed people. Another difficulty was that action seemed always to be related to issues of justice within a country rather than being addressed to international conflicts. Nevertheless, Robert Johansen has proposed the creation of a nongovernmental, international nonviolent police force which would engage in mediation as well as nonviolent direct action, and the World Peace Brigade has been rehabilitated under the new title Peace Brigades International.[19] Such an international group committed to nonviolent intervention could serve as a moral force which might act as a check on national armed forces when they are used for purposes such as suppressing people in other countries.

There are, then, many changes that could be made to limit or bypass the sovereignty of national governments that would facilitate the peaceful resolution of conflicts. There are many ways of eroding national sovereignty which are more modest than the grander schemes to which we now turn.

Consolidating Nations into Larger Units

When nations decide to associate with each other to carry on joint activities, they can work out different structural arrangements for their collective enterprise. They may decide on a looser organization called a "confederation" or "league," or they may prefer a tighter organization called a "federation" or "federal union." (See chart on page 343.) In a *confederation* or *league* each nation retains complete sovereignty. The central body composed of representatives from the member nations may make recommendations for collective action, but each country retains for itself the right to act or not act in accord with the recommendations of the central body. Each member nation is free to leave the association at any time and for any reason. Furthermore, the central body has no right to deal with the individual citizens of the member nations but rather must confine itself to dealing with the governments of the nations which belong to it. International organizations such as the United Nations and the Organization of American States exemplify this confederate type of organization.

In the tighter kind of organization called a *federation* or *union* the structure is different. In this system certain areas of decision-making are given to a new central "federal" government and the member nations surrender their power to make decisions regarding these matters. However, the power to make decisions in all other areas is retained by the members. In

Comparison of Confederation and Federation

Confederation or League	*Federation or Union*
Each member state retains its complete sovereignty, including having its own independent armed forces.	Split sovereignty: member states possess authority in some areas while other powers are delegated to the central federal government.
Each member state has a right to withdraw at any time for any reason.	No seceding from the union is allowed; commitment is to stay in the central organization.
Individual citizens of member states have no right to interact with the central organization.	Individual citizens may interact with the central government in those areas where it has authority.
Individual citizens of member states cannot be arrested or tried by the central organization or its officials.	Individual citizens can be tried as individuals in federal courts for violating federal laws and in state courts for violating state laws.
Primary loyalty of citizens is to their own state; no expectation of loyalty to the central organization exists.	Primary loyalty is to the central federal government while secondary loyalty to one's state or province is permissible.
All financial resources for the central organization come as contributions from the member states.	The central federal government has its own independent sources of revenue, including authority to tax individuals.

a federal system there is, then, a divided sovereignty. The central government has the authority to make laws concerning certain types of issues, while the member nations have the authority to make laws concerning all other issues. On those issues where the central government has authority, laws will be made on the basis of some agreed-upon procedure usually involving voting by representatives. Each member nation will be obligated to abide by the decisions made by these procedures on these delegated issues regardless of its own interests. Furthermore, in a federal arrangement members usually are not free to dissociate themselves from the central government once they have joined. If they were free to leave, the central organization would be reluctant to make any decision which any member nation didn't like and the result in practice would be similar to the loose association found in a confederation. Finally, in a federal structure the central "federal" government will have the authority to arrest, judge, and imprison individual persons who violate those laws made by the central government. The member nations, of course, will have their own particular laws and will have the authority to arrest, judge, and imprison individual persons who violate these laws. The governments of the United States and Mexico as well as those of many other nations are examples of this federal type of organization.

The history of the United States furnishes an excellent opportunity for appreciating the differences between a confederation and a federation.[20] Even though 1776, the date of the Declaration of Independence, is usually taken to mark the beginning of the United States of America, the fact is that there was no federal government until 1789, when George Washington became the first President. The Revolutionary War (1775–81) was fought by 13 sovereign states joined in a collective war effort against British rule. The participants thought of themselves as New Yorkers or Pennsylvanians or Virginians rather than Americans. During the period 1781 to 1788, they cooperated together under the Articles of Confederation with an organization structurally very similar to the present United Nations. Each state had one vote in the Continental Congress, and the Congress could pass resolutions making recommendations to the states but could not make binding laws. In 1787, at a meeting in Philadelphia whose announced purpose was to formulate amendments to the Articles of Confederation, a Federal Constitution was drawn up to replace the Articles. The Federalists, under the leadership of Hamilton, Madison, and Jay, led the state-by-state battle for ratification of the Constitution which would convert the confederate structure then existing into the federal structure of the United States of America. The main argument for federation was that many problems facing the states (maintenance of good currency, payment of war debts, restrictions on trade and travel between states, foreign relations with European countries, growing tension between some states, threat of successful insurrections) could not be solved without a federal government.

After the creation of the federal government in 1789, the precise limits of the powers of the federal government had to be worked out in practice. Eventually the American Civil War (1861–65) was fought to determine whether states could secede from the federal union when they felt that the federal government was exceeding its authority. Those who favored secession claimed that states were totally sovereign and had the right to determine their own policies free from interference by the federal government. On the other hand, the defenders of the Union claimed that if some states were allowed to secede it would be the end of the federal government and the states of North America would revert to a confederacy. The outcome of the war was the preservation of the federal nature of the central government and the firm establishment of the principle that no state could secede from that union.

Returning to the present international situation, some thinkers claim that it would be desirable for various groups of nations of the world to join together in a common effort to advance the welfare of their people and to protect themselves from exploitation and conquest by outside nations. For example, how many countries in Africa or Latin America are in a position to defend themselves against exploitation and domination by more developed countries? For another example, how can the countries of Western Europe expect to compete economically with the United States if each acts separately in terms of its own national interest? It seems that the best hope for many nations of the world is to unite with other countries in a larger, more powerful organization. Such organizations may be based on geographical proximity, similarity of culture, ideological agreement, or some combination of these.

We have previously mentioned the existence of various regional political organizations such as the Organization of American States, the Organization of African Unity, and the Arab League. They are all examples of loose confederations formed basically to keep outside nations from intervening in their part of the world. Even the European Community, which has changed its *name* to "European Union" and which may someday become a real union or federation, is still largely a confederate organization. These confederate structures do not basically alter the present system of sovereign nations because they do not limit the sovereignty of their members. In our present discussion the notion of consolidating nations into larger units as a road to peace will be limited to the forming of federations.

The argument for such federations is that they alone in the long run will be strong enough to protect the nations involved from being dominated by others. The federal structure promotes peace by decreasing vulnerability from outside attack and by providing political and judicial institutions for the nonviolent resolution of conflicts among their own members, and it promotes justice by decreasing vulnerability to exploitation. A United States of Western Europe, for example, should be able to protect itself militarily even without U.S. assistance and could be more effective at preventing domination of its economy by the United States or Japan. It could also help control conflicts among its own members.

The development of regional federations in Africa and Latin America would also be significant. A united Africa could be more effective in keeping non–Africans out of Africa, thus preventing both military and economic exploitation. It could help to keep peace among the various nations in the region and possibly even help control violence within nations. A united Latin America would be more effective in resolving conflicts among its members and in protecting itself against economic exploitation by American, Japanese, and European businesses. In both instances, however, the nationalistic attitudes, the disparity in size and wealth of the countries involved, and the competition among the nations of the region with each other make the creation of such federations very unlikely. For example, in Latin America Brazil conceives of itself as a future superpower. It would be reluctant to join any Latin American federation unless it was given a commanding role in the organization, but the other nations of that region probably would not join any federation in which Brazil was given a commanding role.

Although federations are usually based on geographical proximity, they can also be based on other factors such as ideology. Some champions of capitalistic democracy have suggested that all "free nations" should join together in a federation in order to preserve their way of life from both Fascists and Communists. In 1938 when Hitler was threatening Europe, Clarence Streit advanced the idea of an Atlantic Union, a federation of the mature democracies on both sides of the North Atlantic plus the nations which at that time made up the British Empire.[21] Other nations could be admitted to the Union of the Free as they demonstrated their capability for conducting their affairs in a democratic way. Streit and his followers see this Union of the Free as a step toward eventual world government, since it could grow to include more and more nations. The Union of the Free can't *start* as a world government, however, since there are too many nations in the world who are not committed to or experienced enough in the system of democratic government. If a world government were to be established at present, the people who understand how democracy works would be outvoted by national governments with autocratic systems. But a Union of all the mature democracies would create an extremely powerful supernation which could dominate the world scene and the United Nations in the same way that the United States dominates the Western Hemisphere and the Organization of American States. This Union would be a much more effective way to stop the spread of totalitarianism, whether of the left or right, than the present international system in which the sovereign national democracies often are competing with each other rather than working together. On the other hand, a federation limited to the European democracies would be a mistake, since it would tend to accentuate differences between the United States and Europe rather than bringing them together as the Union of the Free would do.

In response to the point that such a Union might well provoke those left out of the federation to form a countervailing *union of nondemocracies,* defenders of the Federal Union of the Free note that even a union of the states left out of the original nucleus would be very weak compared with the economic and military power of the advanced democracies. Also nondemocratic countries do not have the bonds of shared values to support a federation. Their only motivation for uniting would be to oppose the advanced democracies, and that kind of negative goal cannot be an enduring basis for union. Furthermore, these other countries know that once they individually adopt a democratic political system and a free market economic system, they will prosper and will become eligible for acceptance into the Union of the Free. Finally, the demise of the Soviet Union has led to a situation where hardly anyone now believes that an authoritarian centrally controlled system can be a good system for a country to adopt. The Union of the Free has not only economic and military power but also the psychological power of an attractive ideal.

What can be said in the way of evaluating this proposal for a Federation of the Free? First, it can be noted that the attempt to create such a union might in fact lead to dissension among the advanced democracies because it would force them to focus on their differences as they tried to work out rules for the union. Who would get how many votes in the central parliament? Would the leader be selected by parliament as is done in most of the countries of Europe, or would there be a separate election for a president as is done in the U.S.? What language or languages would be used? Might the union be dominated by one or two countries? Informal cooperation among the democracies might be a better approach than trying to get them formally federated.

Second, with regard to the issues of peace and justice at the global level, it seems that the establishment of a Union of the Free would accentuate antagonistic feelings between the mostly white, rich, Christian countries of Europe and North America and Australia on the one hand and the mostly nonwhite, poor, and largely non–Christian countries of Asia and Africa on the other. The fact that only the "core" "democratic" countries which are in the federation from the beginning would be involved in drawing up the rules raises questions about how *democratic* this project is. In fact, the countries which form the nucleus of the union seem like a private "club" which will allow others to get in only after they are ready to conform to the rules established in advance by the elite ruling clique. That would be especially true if poor democracies like India were not allowed to be a part of the original core. It seems that the union may be called "democratic" while in fact it is rich, capitalistic, Euro-centered, and very *nondemocratic.* This perception is further strengthened by the fact that when Streit originally made his proposal in 1938 he included the segregated Union of South Africa as one of the advanced democracies which should be part of the original nucleus.[22]

In response the defenders of the Union of the Free would reject the racist charge by noting that Japan would be included in the original nucleus, and so too would be all the nonwhite people living in the advanced industrialized democracies. The criterion for inclusion is not race but having experienced life in a liberal capitalistic democratic system for a long enough period of time that it has become part of the way of thinking of most people in the society. Champions of the Union of the Free argue that having a large immature democracy like India in the nucleus might inadvertently undermine all the progress which has come over the centuries as a result of Western liberalism. It is safer to let the mature democracies make the rules and then bring in the other countries when they are ready and in such a way that they cannot wreck the system which even those in the poor countries so much admire and want to be a part of. For those who believe that Western democratic capitalism represents the last word in social justice and social progress, the creation of a Union of the Free which can gradually grow into a world federation seems to be the ideal way to bring about a global federation without endangering the principles of Western liberal democracy in the process. Others who are less confident about the ultimate wisdom and justice of contemporary Western democratic capitalism will be more skeptical about whether this proposal provides the best way to a peaceful and just world.

World Government Through Federation

In the previous section the difference between a confederation and a federation was discussed. It was also noted that the United States of America began as a confederation but was then converted to a federation by the states because the confederate structure was unable to adequately handle many of the problems facing the emerging American community. World federalists argue that the national governments of the world should follow a similar course of action and convert the United Nations into a federal-type central government because its present confederate structure does not adequately handle many of the problems facing the world community — problems such as pollution control, planning for a global language, and management of the international financial system as well as nonviolent resolution of international disputes. Essentially, this approach to world peace proposes that national governments delegate certain powers (such as the authority to own and control the production of weapons of war) to a central federal government while retaining for themselves other powers (such as the making of laws governing property ownership, education, and family relations). Some world federalists would like to see many powers shifted to the central government so that it could deal with all the various global problems facing the world community; they are called *maximalist* world federalists. Others would want to shift only those few powers directly related to the problem of war and disarmament; they are called *minimalist* world federalists. In either case there would be a drastic change in the international state system. National governments would transfer authority to deal with certain kinds of issues to a new world government, a government which would be quite different from present national governments not only because of its extensive scope and the heterogeneity of the people it governed, but also because there would be no external enemy against whom defense would be needed.[23]

In this respect a federal world government would be quite different from the federal union of democratic nations previously discussed. The advocate of a federal world government argues that a union of any part of humanity against some other part of humanity is going to leave unchanged the fundamental situation of sovereign entities aligned against each other. Force and threats of force would then still be the determining factors in conflict situations. The basic argument of the advocate of the Union of the Free is that democratic capitalism will prevail if the free nations will only unify their efforts and take advantage of their superior power. Peace will come as a consequence of that strategy. The advocate of world federalism, on the other hand, focuses on the need to change the method by which ideological conflicts are resolved. The federalist wants conflict to be settled within a political and judicial structure which makes resort to violence unnecessary and unacceptable and which holds individuals, not national governments, accountable for violations of the law.

World federalists claim that the institution of government which has been somewhat successful at providing for the peaceful resolution of conflict within villages, within city-states, within provinces, and within nations should now be extended not merely to geographical regions or groups of nations with a common ideology but to the whole world.[24] They claim that modern technology has created a global community which needs global political and judicial structures. Fast postal service, air transportation, and television and other communications services have linked people more closely with some in other nations than with many in their own country. More and more the national boundaries marked on maps make less and less difference to the everyday lives of people and the associations they form. These national boundaries are already less significant for the world community than the boundaries between the states were at the time the federal government of the United States was created. The world is ready, the world federalist says, for world government.[25]

One obvious question to be raised is whether there is any hope whatsoever that such a federal world government could possibly be brought into existence in the very near, or even the distant, future. We will turn to that issue shortly. For the moment, let us suppose that such a federal world government could be created. Would it put an end to war? It should be recalled that there are two kinds of war, those between governments and those within a governed territory, that is, civil wars. If all the peoples and territory of the Earth were under one government, there would be an end to "external" wars unless a violent conflict arose with visitors from another planet. But the possibility of civil war would remain. In fact, civil wars might become more common just because there would be no external enemy which might otherwise inhibit any movement toward disunity. Even the United States, which the world federalist likes to point to as an ideal example of a federation which evolved from a confederation, had a brutal civil war. If federation did not prevent war among the states of the United States, what likelihood is there that it would prevent war among the nations of the world? In response to this challenge, an advocate of a federal world government would argue that one war in 200 years is a much better record than probably would have developed had there been no federal government in the area of the world that now makes up the United States. The establishment of a federal government for the United States promoted a coordinated expansion to the West and led the various state governments to converge in their structure and ideology. Completely sovereign states probably would have competed with each other for control of the West and may well have diverged more and more from each other in their structure and ideology. Wars probably would have been as common as they have been in Europe. The American experience thus suggests that federal world government would probably greatly reduce the probability of war even if it would not necessarily eliminate it entirely.

But, the opponent of federal world government will argue, one cannot put much confidence in a generalization drawn from a single instance. Furthermore, it is claimed, there are some instances which suggest that sometimes nations live more peacefully together under separate national governments than they would if an effort were made to bring them under a single central government. For example, Norway and Sweden seem to have had more peaceful relations with each other after they decided to establish separate governments than when efforts were being made to bring them under a single government.[26] Canada and the United States, Sweden and Finland, Spain and Portugal, and many other neighboring but sovereign nations live in peace with each other with no expectation of war between them even though there is no government uniting them. It seems that where nations are peacefully inclined toward each other a government over them is not needed, while if they are not peacefully inclined toward each other it would be impossible to form such a government.

One response which the defender of world federalism would make to this point is that nations which are peacefully inclined toward one another at one time may not always be so inclined and that a common government over them would help to cement a community of interests between them and make it more likely that any conflicts which do arise are fought out in the political and judicial arena rather than with arms. Other federations such as Switzerland, Germany, Brazil, and Mexico show that the experience of the American federation in maintaining peace is not unique. Another response would be that most individual persons get along peacefully with others most of the time but no one would conclude from this situation that government over individual persons is not needed or undesirable. Government is needed not so much for the many who would live together in peace anyway, but for the few who will go on a rampage if they are not stopped by force mobilized by the community as a whole. Also, the existence of the government as an agency for conflict resolution through its political and judicial processes tends to keep adversaries from thinking in terms of using violence to resolve their differences.[27] Furthermore, a federal world government would make it feasible to enforce arms control measures since enforcement would involve action against those individual persons who possess and make weapons of war rather than seeking to regulate whole national governments as must be done in a confederation. That is why world government is the best hope, not only for ending actual war but also for ending the military buildups that are an important part of the war problem.

One of the main concerns voiced by opponents of a world government is the worry that such a government might become a vehicle for a world dictatorship from which there would be no escape. This same kind of concern was voiced by those who opposed the Constitution of the United States of America as a replacement for the Articles of Confederation. The advocate of federal world government would use the same response which was used in connection with the creation of the American federation, namely, that tyranny can be prevented by creating a government with checks and balances both within the central government and between the central government and the member states as well as by incorporating into the constitution of the central government a Bill of Rights limiting its power over individuals. Perhaps the constitution of a world government could also contain a Bill of Rights for member nations limiting what the central government could do with regard to them. Another factor which could be expected to help keep a dictatorship from developing at the world level is the absence of any external enemies. If we look at national governments, we see that the restriction of the rights of citizens is often justified on grounds that it is necessary to protect the nation from its external enemies. Such an appeal would not be available to the leaders of a world government. With regard to this issue of protecting the rights of individuals, advocates of world federalism can even advance an additional argument for their position, namely, that the presence of a federal world government would tend to undermine national totalitarian and militaristic governments because they would no longer be able to victimize their own populations on grounds that such suppression is necessary for national security.

The opponent of world federalism might also raise the question of whether it is desirable to have still another layer of government when many people feel that there is already too much government spending and too much government bureaucracy.[28] The world federalist's response to this objection is two-fold. First, a large proportion of spending by the national governments is due to funding for military establishments in order to be prepared to fight wars and to maintain military superiority for diplomatic purposes. With a federal world government these huge expenses would disappear, just as within the United States the state governments do not need to maintain military establishments. Second, the most efficient arrangement is to have social problems being tackled by the lowest level of government that can deal with that problem effectively. There are global problems such as destruction of the ozone layer and control of international drug-trafficking which by their very nature must be dealt with at the global level and which would involve less bureaucracy when addressed by a global agency than when they are addressed by many different national governments trying to coordinate their efforts by diplomatic means. The present international system where nation-states compete against each other economically, militarily, and in every other way has generated a situation where national governments are expected to deal with every kind of problem. A global-level government would not increase the total amount of government but would permit a better distribution of responsibility for dealing with social problems at the appropriate level.

Another problem which the advocate of world federation must address for people living in the industrialized democracies is whether the federal world government would be supportive of democratic capitalistic ideology. Might it not be sympathetic to authoritarian and socialist governments? Once again the response is two-fold. First, the federalist principle means that each nation-state would be free to have whatever kind of political system and whatever kind of economic system it wants *within its borders.* People do not need to have complete ideological agreement in order to live together in peace; they need only agree on what nonviolent procedures will be used to resolve their conflicts with each other. Second, the global system itself would need to be democratic and permissive of free enterprise. A world federation must be established by consent, not by conquest, and it can be expected that no nation-states will agree to enter a system which does not allow them an appropriate involvement in the decision-making for the world community. The particular kind of voting system to be established must be worked out, but it is assumed by all world federalists that there will be a democratic system based on voting. The democratic procedures already practiced at the United Nations also point in this direction. The question of whether the global government would allow free enterprise at the world level might have been a legitimate concern before the demise of the Soviet Union, but now there seems to be a consensus that a market economy is a better system than a centrally controlled economy. If particular nation-states want to have a socialist system within their countries they could do that, but the idea of a centrally controlled economic system at the global level is no longer an attractive possibility and will not be acceptable. In fact, another argument that might be marshalled in favor of world federation is that a worldwide system of free trade requires such a global government in order to establish common rules for the global system which cannot be undermined by some national governments having lax standards on environmental protection or worker safety.[29]

Assuming that the development of a federal world government might be desirable, is there any chance that such a government could be established? From a theoretical point of view, the transition would involve a change from resolving disputes on the basis of military power, where what counts is the size of armed forces and the destructive efficiency of weapons, to one of resolving disputes on the basis of political power, where what count are the number of votes and the skills of legislators. The crucial task would be to work out a voting system which would be fair to all and which would protect the interest of every nation-state at least as much as that interest is protected now. Since the smaller countries of the world are presently generally at the mercy of the larger, more powerful countries, they would have much to gain by joining a world federation which provides legal protection from exploitation by other nations. The middle-sized countries would also gain more control over their own destinies than they have under the present system, where critical issues may be decided without much input from them.

But what is the situation for the big powers with their nuclear weapons and formidable economic capability? The U.S. and its allies can pretty much determine what is going to happen in the international arena and how much opposition to what they want will be tolerated. Consider the response to the Iraqi invasion of Kuwait. On the other hand, their power is not unlimited, and they must consider the costs of military action as the U.S. learned in Vietnam and the Soviet Union in Afghanistan. Certainly these experiences have led to some restraint with regard to military action in the former Yugoslavia. The U.S. and the Russians also learned about the long-term adverse effects of huge military expenditures as their economies fell relative to those of other countries such as Japan, which did not spend so much on the military. Under these circumstances it seems advantageous for the big powers to work out arrangements which put restraints on their arms races and at the same time to institutionalize to some extent their present predominant position in world affairs.

That is what is happening at the United Nations. The big powers apparently want to make the U.N. Security Council more effective in its efforts to resolve international disputes. This concern is evidenced by the unprecedented January 1992 meeting of the heads of state of the 15 countries on the Security Council and the *Agenda for Peace* issued six months later by Secretary-General Boutros Boutros-Ghali in response to their request for proposals.[30] The question which must be addressed is whether the U.N. can be made effective for the big powers without changing the U.N. Charter. If there were a general consideration of modifications in the Charter, many of the less powerful nations can be expected to raise questions about whether there is not a need to restrict or even eliminate the veto in the Security Council for the five permanent members. But the big powers see the Security Council as a forum where they can deal with global conflicts on the basis of what they want without too much influence from the other countries.

Under these circumstances, is there any likelihood that a world federation would be implemented? We should note that there have been efforts to modify the U.N. Charter in the direction of a world federation. In 1974 the U.N. General Assembly created an ad hoc Committee on the Charter and on Strengthening the Role of the Organization, and in 1975 the General Assembly voted to make this a Special Committee of the General Assembly. The General Assembly has succeeded in keeping this committee functioning despite the opposition of the big powers. It should also be noted that there are interest in and support for "global governance" from very knowledgeable and experienced people in the area of international relations. A specific example is the Stockholm Initiative on Global Security and Governance adopted by a group of former national and international leaders on April 22, 1991.[31] The final two recommendations of that report are "that a World Summit on Global Governance be called" and for "the establishment of an independent International Commission on Global Governance." This led in turn to the formation in September 1992 of a 28-member Commission on Global Governance co-chaired by Ingvar Carlsson, former Prime Minister of Sweden, and Shridath Ramphal of Guyana, former Secretary-General of the Commonwealth.[32] The U.S. Congress authorized a 16-person U.S. Commission on Improving the Effectiveness of the U.N. to study the problem of how to improve the U.N. After holding hearings in six cities, it issued its final report in 1993.[33] Modifications in the way the U.N. operates are proposed, but as might be expected none of these bodies is recommending the conversion of the U.N. into a world federation in the near future.

Although no move toward a federal world government seems near at hand, some possibilities for action can be noted. It is conceivable that a coalition of countries such as Japan, India, Canada, Germany, Australia, Mexico, Nigeria, Argentina, and maybe even China could promote a strengthening of the United Nations or the development of a new organization as a way of gaining more control over their own destiny. It is always possible too that some U.S. president will lead the way toward the development of a federal world government. It was U.S. presidents, after all, who were responsible for the League of Nations and the United Nations. Another U.S. president, sincerely committed to world peace through world law, might be able to make the seemingly distant dream of a federal world government a reality in a rather short period of time, especially if pushed along by something like the shock of Japan or China passing the United States in GNP as the U.S. economy continues to be retarded by large military expenditures.

Even the most optimistic advocates of world federalism do not see such a government coming into existence in the next 25 years. Yet many see such a development as inevitable. A crucial question is how best to structure such a government so that it will maintain peace and still allow for the peaceful change which is necessary if injustices are to be corrected. The various national governments need to be studied to learn which of the different existing political structures and procedures best promote justice and the resolution of group conflicts. The strong emphasis on political justice embodied in the ideology of the West and the strong emphasis on economic justice embodied in the statements by those in the poorer countries both need to be incorporated into the coming world government. The advocates of federal world government believe that the absence of real security in a world where national conflicts are resolved by force and threats of force will cause leaders to see that it is in their nation's interests to develop a federal world government to adjudicate their disagreements by political and judicial means and to police their agreements by focusing on individual law violators.

World Government Through Functionalism

Many of those who recognize the need to change the international system agree with the world federalists that problems need to be considered on a global basis but do not agree that a structured federal world government brought into existence by the deliberate action of the national governments is the best or most feasible way to make the shift away from international anarchy. These thinkers emphasize the interdependence of the nations of the world and the desirability of building structures to solve various global problems on a problem-by-problem basis. They believe that many decisions about global problems can be made on a consensual basis without emphasizing voting if discussions can be focused on solving specific global problems rather than on abstract principles.[34]

Earlier, when dealing with presently existing international institutions, we discussed the various functional agencies associated with the United Nations such as the World Health Organization, the International Labor Organization, and the Universal Postal Union. Functionalists believe that the best way to change the international system is to continue to create more and more such agencies to work on the various particular problems facing humanity. In the long run, they claim, this approach is much more likely to lead to a gradual limiting of national sovereignty than is an effort to try to get the various national governments to agree explicitly to limit their sovereignty. If functional agencies are created, they will gradually develop the competence and authority to deal with the particular problems to which they are devoted. The national governments will find these functional agencies and the bureaucracies they have developed extremely helpful in carrying on the actual business of international problem-solving. Gradually, the functionalist notes, the agencies will make more and more of the decisions which need to be made concerning international issues while the national governments will find it less and less important to concern themselves with these matters. There will be no need for an explicit transfer of sovereignty because real power and authority will gradually have shifted to the global functional agencies.

To better understand this functionalist approach, let us consider what happens within national governments. Many important decisions are now made by individual bureaucrats. In the United States, for example, the President and Congress cannot keep track of every decision concerning government action. The President delegates authority to Cabinet officers, who in turn delegate it to others, who in turn delegate it to others. Guidelines for action may be given by the President or a Cabinet member, but there are many decisions not governed by guidelines, and with others there is considerable room for judgment about how the guidelines should be applied to a particular case. People not at the top of the bureaucracy know more about some situations than those of higher rank and consequently must advise the higher-ups concerning what should be done in specific cases. As long as things are running smoothly, those higher up in the bureaucracy don't want to be bothered with such decisions. In the same way, international functional agencies can build bureaucracies of experts to handle the practical problems of the international community. As long as these agencies adequately perform the tasks for which they were established, the national governments are not likely to intrude. As the functional agencies handle many of the real day-to-day problems of the global community, they will gradually become the "departments" of a developing world government.

Critics of the functionalist approach object that this proposed way of proceeding overlooks the areas of intense conflict between nations. They claim that national governments will use their power to keep functional agencies from carrying out any policies which they find contrary to their own interests and allow the agencies to do only what doesn't offend any national government. Otherwise, the offended national government will withdraw its support of the functional agency or try to obstruct its activities.[35] An actual example of this type of reaction was the withdrawal of the United States from UNESCO in 1984. But, functionalists will reply, in most cases the national governments will find the functional agency too useful to themselves to take such negative actions. For example, it would be difficult even for a large and powerful nation to withdraw from the Universal Postal Union and work out separate agreements for transfer of international mail with all the other countries in the world. Furthermore, even if some nations don't want to belong to a particular international functional agency (for example, the former Communist countries previously did not want to belong to the International Monetary Fund), the agency can still serve others who do want to participate. International interdependence is such that nations which stay out or withdraw from an international functional agency will probably hurt themselves more than they will hurt the agency.

But will the development of global functional agencies help solve the problem of war? Even if these agencies successfully handle their particular assignments, won't the arms race continue? Won't the issues vital to the interests of national governments still be resolved on the basis of force and threats of force? To this point functionalists will make two responses. First, it may not be possible to do everything at once, but over a period of time the success of functional agencies will make it clear to all nations that they have more to gain by working together than by engaging in confrontation tactics. The number of issues viewed as worth fighting about will gradually diminish to zero. Second, the functionalists will note that the problem of arms control and disarmament should be handled by a functional agency deliberately designed to take care of this problem. Such an agency might develop its own system of surveillance satellites to keep track of the military activities of all nations.[36] It might also develop proposals for arms limitation. The representatives of the various nations on the International Arms Control and Disarmament Agency could work to develop disarmament policies on which they could all agree. Once policies were adopted the functional agency could see that they were implemented. If any nation failed to carry out its part of the disarmament plan, the International Agency could announce this fact to all other countries and delay any further disarmament until the offending nation complied. Obviously, if some powerful nation refused to continue to cooperate, the disarmament could not go on. But what alternative could there be? Would the other nations of the world or a world government try to use military force to force the reluctant country to disarm? Disarmament is possible only when all the nations, and especially the more powerful ones, are ready to take this action together.

We can readily imagine a debate between a world federalist and a functionalist concerning the functionalist approach to disarmament. The federalist would make two main points. First, he would go back to his basic thesis that disarmament cannot be expected until an effective judicial system is in place to resolve intense conflicts of interest. To this point the functionalist could reply that some kind of arms control might be possible even if the situation did not yet permit complete disarmament. Furthermore, he would argue, it is the existence of various kinds of functional agencies, including one for arms control, that would best prepare the way for a situation where formal political and judicial systems for resolving conflict could be developed and accepted.

The second argument of the federalist would be the claim that a functional arms control and disarmament agency could not be as effective as a disarmament plan carried out by a world government because only under the federalist approach could individual violators of the disarmament agreement be arrested and penalized. A functional agency could deal only with the national governments. The functionalist would reply that it is not individuals but national governments which purchase modern weapons and hire people to use them. As long as these governments want weapons and armies, they will not permit the arrest of their citizens who make them and practice using them. It may be true that national governments would not need arms to protect their interests if there were an effective world government which protected them, but, the functionalist claims, it is also the case that the national governments would not need arms to protect their interests if the various functional agencies were successfully solving the various global problems to which they were addressing themselves. The functionalist argues that either the national governments would find cooperation more satisfying than military confrontation (in which case a formal world government is merely icing on the cake) or they would not (in which case even a federal world government could not prevent a war). The federalist would respond that there are possibilities between these extremes. Nevertheless, the functionalist would reply, the gradual transfer of power to global agencies is much less threatening to national governments than the federalist plan for a sudden and explicit transfer of particular powers from national governments to a new central world government.

This hypothetical debate concerning the desirability and feasibility of trying to establish a functional International Arms Control and Disarmament Agency points up the basic differences between the federalist and functionalist approaches. Both have as their ultimate goal a governing structure for the world community, but they advocate different means for achieving that goal. The federalist wants to make a frontal attack on unrestricted national sovereignty because he believes that national leaders, whose primary responsibility is to deal with international problems, should be able to see the desirability, and even the necessity, of transferring some of the powers of national governments to a central limited world government. That government could then use its powers to enforce a disarmament agreement by dealing with actual individuals who might try to violate it. This federalist approach seeks to create a world community from the "top down." The functionalist, on the other hand, maintains that the world community must become more accustomed to working together through the development of many different functional agencies before a full-fledged world government can be created. This functionalist approach maintains that one must work from the "bottom up," from a sense of world community to the development of a formal political structure to govern it. Of course, there is no reason that both of these approaches could not be tried simultaneously.

World Government Through Direct Citizen Action

There are still other thinkers who agree with the world federalists and the functionalists that the present system of nations with unlimited sovereignty must be replaced by the development of some global institutions, but they differ about how this can best be accomplished. They think that the federalists are naive to believe that national governments are going to voluntarily and explicitly transfer even a few of their powers to a central world government. They also think the functionalists are naive to pay so little attention to power politics and the drive of national governments to promote their own interests at the expense of other nations. The more powerful nations will cooperate with the global functional agencies only so long as they can use them to preserve the advantages which they have over other nations. National leaders are too clever to allow their positions of superior power to be gradually eroded in those areas which are important in the struggle for goods, power, and status. It is true that there cannot be a transformed peaceful world until the national governments are made at least somewhat subordinate to a world government, but the national governments themselves will never initiate efforts which require them to give up any power. Consequently, the only hope for a peaceful world is for citizen action to create a globally oriented social and political system directly, that is, by somehow bypassing the national governments. There are several different ideas about how to do this.

One approach focuses on changing the attitudes and patterns of behavior of individuals without making any particular effort at present to construct a fully developed global political structure. Each person can be encouraged to think and act as a world citizen. Any laws or commands of national governments which are inconsistent with this outlook are to be ignored. A notable example of someone who advocates such an approach is Garry Davis. In 1948, he pitched a tent on the grounds of the Palais de Chaillot in Paris where the U.N. General Assembly was meeting and declared himself to be a world citizen and consequently not subject to the jurisdiction of national laws.[37] He has also encouraged others to adopt the view that their primary loyalty is to the whole of humanity rather than to a nation and to openly declare themselves to be world citizens loyal to the "government" Davis has established.[38] Many persons have signed statements indicating that they consider themselves to be world citizens, though only a few of them totally reject the jurisdiction of national governments as Davis has done. A list of world citizens is also being kept in Paris and Palo Alto, California, by the International Registry of World Citizens.[39] A related effort is the holding of a convention, a World Citizens Assembly, every two or three years with the next one planned for San Francisco in 1995.[40]

Another version of the "world citizen" approach focuses on cities and organizations rather than individual persons. An effort is made to get city councils or boards of aldermen to adopt resolutions declaring all people in their community to be world citizens.[41] A city which has adopted such a resolution is said to be "mundialized" (from the Latin word "mundus" meaning "world"). The adoption of a resolution of mundialization may include related provisions such as flying or displaying the United Nations flag, forming sister-city relationships with cities in other countries, making a regular contribution to the U.N. Special Account in lieu of world taxes, and urging educational institutions in the community to promote a global outlook among their students. The idea of adopting statements of mundialization has also been extended from city councils to other organizations such as universities, schools, churches, and lodges as well as to other political units such as state governments. For example, in the U.S. proclamations of world citizenship have been issued by political leaders in Minnesota, Illinois, and Iowa. The basic idea of the mundialization effort is to develop and give concrete expression to a global outlook without working through national governments.

A third version of the "world citizen" approach is represented by W. Warren Wagar's call for the development of a world civilization.[42] Wagar is addressing himself mainly to young social activists whose concern for justice leads them to protest against wars, military spending, draft registration, and the various activities of "the establishment." The obstacle to justice, he says, is not some particular "establishment" in some particular national society, not capitalism or Communism, but the anarchic system of sovereign nations. The way to overcome it is to form a worldwide political party which will work behind the scenes until the moment is ripe to take power and establish a world government. What is required, he says, is the building of a new global civilization based on common concerns for justice on a worldwide scale, for personal freedom for all people, for preservation of the earth, and for truth and meaning. It is to the building of such a world civilization that everyone should be devoted.

A second general kind of populist approach to world government focuses on the idea of creating some kind of council or committee of outstanding individuals from all over the world which will serve as a concrete embodiment of the conscience of the world community. This approach is also committed to a global orientation, but it recognizes a need for a focal point for generating pronouncements and possibly concerted action. According to one plan proposed by Joseph H.C. Creyghton of the Netherlands,[43] a citizens' group asks over 100 outstanding persons from all over the world to form an "Emergency World Council." This Council then asks nine highly respected persons from various countries to form a provisional world government. At the appropriate time, this group would announce that they are assuming worldwide political authority. Within three years they would announce the procedures for direct election of the members of a world parliament by all citizens of the world *without any prior approval from national governments*. Once the world parliament is convened, it would draft a constitution for a permanent world government. The only power possessed by the provisional world government or by the permanent one to follow it would be the support given by the citizenry who voluntarily follow its directives. The hope is that at the critical moment a large proportion of the people of the world would follow the directives of the world government even if the national governments tried to stop them. For example, some national governments might forbid their citizens to participate in the elections of representatives to the world government. The key test would then be whether people in those nations would try to vote anyway. The difficulty with this approach, of course, is the improbability that many people would follow the world government directives when national governments ordered them to do otherwise and backed up those orders with police power.

A second version of this approach in which a world council is established would emphasize the ethical dimension rather than the legislative one. French philosopher Jacques Maritain suggested that a small council of persons deemed to be especially wise, disinterested, and trustworthy be selected to speak out as the conscience of humanity on social issues.[44] Such persons might be nominated by religious organizations, universities, and governments and then elected by the people of all nations. Those elected would lose their national citizenships and would have no power of any kind with which to enforce their judgments. Unlike a court, no individual or nation could bring questions before the group. The council would give moral judgments concerning what is just on issues of its own choosing only. Such a council could influence the formation of public opinion in those situations. Maritain was especially concerned that individual citizens be given guidance concerning whether a war in which their own country is involved is a just war. The world council he proposed could give a disinterested answer, as compared to the biased answer citizens would get from their own government. Once again, the problem is how many people would pay attention to the world council.

British philosopher Bertrand Russell went beyond proposing a council of this kind. He established the Bertrand Russell Peace Foundation to cast the public spotlight on institutionalized violence, and this Foundation in turn organized public tribunals to examine cases of gross violation of human rights by national governments.[45] Tribunals have been held to hear evidence and render verdicts concerning matters such as war crimes committed by the United States in Vietnam, repression in Chile after the overthrow of the Allende government, and the exclusion of persons from public employment in West Germany on grounds of their political views. The Russell Foundation has also held public hearings on the invasion of Czechoslovakia by Russian and East German military forces and the relationship between World Bank policies and problems of development in the poorer countries. The members of what is now called "the People's Permanent Tribunal" are selected by the Russell Foundation from among leading thinkers of various nations. The evidence uncovered and the verdicts rendered are published in the hope of influencing world public opinion.

Another proposal along these same lines is Gerald Gottleib's call for the establishment of a "Court of Man."[46] Noting that history reveals several instances where courts operated without any governmental power to enforce their decisions, Gottleib claims that the same thing could be done for the global community. This approach can work, he claims, because people have a tendency to obey law which they regard as fair even if there is no coercive enforcement of it. The jurisdiction of the Court of Man would be "crimes against humanity and against the peace,"[47] but it would approach these matters as civil rather than criminal cases; that is, aggrieved individuals, groups, and states could appeal to the Court for judgments concerning what restitution is due them because of violations of international law. The justices on the Court would be drawn from various cultural, racial, geographical, and religious backgrounds, and regional subcourts might be established if the number of cases warranted. At first the only device for enforcement would be the publication of the judgment of the Court, but eventually national governments and the United Nations might lend support to enforcing the judgments. Such a Court would directly promote the development of world law but would not be a world government. Still, its existence might be instrumental in changing the international system because an aggrieved state could appeal to the Court rather than threatening to use force to protect its interests. Unlike the International Court of

Justice, in the Court of Man the state accused of wrongdoing would not need to consent to participate before the case would be heard. Once again the big question is how many people would pay any attention to the decisions of this Court.

A third general approach for direct citizen action consists of getting a worldwide assembly of "world citizens" to draft a "World Constitution" which is then presented to the people of the world for their acceptance.[48] This effort derives from a World Constituent Assembly held in Interlaken, Switzerland, and Wolfach, Germany, in 1968 which began drafting a "Constitution for the Federation of the Earth." A subsequent Assembly held in Innsbruck, Austria, in 1977 adopted the Constitution and approved long-range plans for generating support for its ratification by votes of the people in national referendums. An effort is being made to get universities, town councils, other organizations, and individuals to indicate their acceptance of this Constitution and the bills passed by the three sessions of the Provisional World Parliament held in Brighton, England (1982), New Delhi, India (1985), and Miami, Florida, USA (1987). Ultimately the success of this effort depends on the authorization of referendums by national governments for the ratification of the proposed Constitution and the bills which have been adopted, but this plan differs from the traditional approach of world federalists because it contains a grass-roots program for pushing the national governments into action. A separate effort focused on developing and promoting a comprehensive Charter amendment to convert the United Nations into a world federation is being carried out by a newly formed group called "One World Now."[49] The big question, as always, is whether there will be enough citizen involvement to create much of a response.

The most recent effort to move toward world government by bypassing the national governments is a frankly political project called "Philadelphia II."[50] Led by former U.S. Senator from Alaska Mike Gravel, who now lives in California, this effort is a grass-roots political program which has been launched in California and Missouri, two states that permit a referendum where the people can make a law by a direct vote rather than relying on the state legislature. The issue to be put on the ballot is not a general resolution in favor of world government but rather a measure asking for the calling of a world constitutional convention and providing for use of some state revenues to conduct and promote additional referendums in other states and other countries of the world. When a stipulated critical mass of citizens throughout the world have voted to have a world constitutional convention, the convention will be held with delegates to the convention being elected in accord with the rules accepted in the referendums. This project relies on worldwide direct democracy and the idea that the people, *not* the national governments, are sovereign. Getting a world constitution by this means would not require any action by any state or national governmental body. Just as the U.S. Constitution drawn up in Philadelphia in 1787 contained within the document the procedure for its ratification (an assembly of elected representatives in each state, with an affirmative vote in nine of the 13 states being required for the Constitution to be ratified), so the world constitution would stipulate the rules for its ratification. The expectation is that its ratification would also depend on elected assemblies throughout the world, so approval by national parliaments and national executives would not be needed. And that is as it should be, according to this view, because national governments, overly enamored of their own power, are the main obstacles to progress toward a world government which the world community so desperately needs.

Although the federalist, functionalist, and populist approaches to world government may seem to be in competition with each other, they can also be viewed as complementing each other.[51] Those who wish to avoid emphasizing one or another particular approach may even drop the term "world government" in favor of the term *world order*. This expression indicates that the desired global political order must promote the values of social justice, economic well-being, human rights, and ecological balance as well as peace.[52] Some advocates of world order have become reluctant to use the term "world government" because they feel that such an expression suggests a political institution designed to protect the interests only of those who already have power. Nevertheless, they believe that the present system of sovereign nations must give way to a new global political order.

The federalist, functionalist, and populist approaches all seem to be necessary if a new global political order is ever to become a reality. Since the national governments now have the highest level of political power, it seems that the federalists are right in saying that a global system of governance cannot be established without the acquiescence, sooner or later, of these national governments. It seems that the functionalists are right in saying that, at least for the near future, it is easier to erode sovereignty by building up global functional agencies than by launching a direct attack on unlimited national sovereignty. Finally, it seems that the direct-citizen-action advocates are right in saying that most national governments are not going to move toward a new world political order until they are pushed very hard in that direction by a substantial grass-roots movement.[53]

A Note to the Reader

We have now come to the final step in solving the problem of war—action guided by the deliberation which has taken place in our inquiry thus far. There are many things you might do to be part of the solution. Some "proposals for solving the war problem" have been presented in the last four chapters of the text. As you review these proposals you should be able to find some that you find particularly worthwhile. One possible place to begin is with reforming the attitudes of individuals—including yourself.

However, most of the proposals discussed deal with modifying social policies and institutions, and such changes are not likely to be accomplished by individuals working alone. Consequently, if you are really serious about doing something to help solve the war problem, you need to associate yourself in a formal way with some of the many organizations working against war. Most of these organizations publish a regular newsletter or other literature, and after you join you will receive materials which will continue to keep you informed and motivated. You will be alerted about when to write letters to public officials in order to have maximum impact on public decision-making. You will be able to mesh your own particular talents with those of others in an integrated effort. You will be helping to promote peace by financially supporting the work of paid employees working for peace organizations. Your membership will also help the organization you support to be noticed by political and media leaders. There would be a great deal more interest in dealing with the war-peace issue if the membership of peace organizations grew to four or five times its present level.

One of the more informative organizational newsletters is *The Interdependent,* the quarterly newsletter of the United Nations Association of the United States of America (485 Fifth Avenue, New York NY 10017). If your interest is in political action related to global issues, you may want to get the "Global Statesmanship" ratings published every other year by the Campaign for U.N. Reform (713 D Street SE, Washington DC 20003). If you believe that the best hope for world peace is the development of global political and judicial institutions, you may wish to join the World Federalist Association (418 Seventh Street SE, Washington DC 20003) or contribute to the UN Office of the World Federalist Movement (777 U.N. Plaza, New York NY 10017). You could also provide support for the Center for War/Peace Studies (218 E. 18th Street, New York NY 10003) in order to receive

365

its *Global Reports*. If you are interested in the populist approach to world government, you may want to get information about the Conferences on a More Democratic United Nations (CAMDUN, 301 E. 45th Street, #20B, New York NY 10017) or the World Citizens Assembly (2671 Southcourt, Palo Alto CA 94303). Or you may want to join the Association of World Citizens, 110 Sutter Street, Suite 708, San Francisco CA 94104) or subscribe to *World Citizen News* (113 Church Street, Burlington VT 05401). Or you may want to contact the World Constitution and Parliament Association, 1480 Hoyt St., Suite 31, Lakewood CO 80215 or One World Now, P.O. Box 1145, Houston TX 77251. If you like the idea of a grass-roots political action like "Philadelphia II" to get things moving toward a world constitutional convention, you may want to join One World, P.O. Box 2566, Monterey CA 93942. If you want to be up-to-date on what the parliamentarians of the democratic countries of the world are doing to deal with the war problem, you should make a contribution to Parliamentarians for Global Action (211 E. 43rd Street, Suite 1604, New York NY 10017) in order to receive their newsletter. If you like the idea of getting a world federation by starting with a nucleus of the industrialized democracies, you may want to join the Association to Unite the Democracies (1506 Pennsylvania Avenue, Washington DC 20003).

An umbrella membership peace organization which connects peace educators with peace activists is the Consortium on Peace Education, Research, and Development (COPRED, Institute for Conflict Analysis and Resolution, George Mason University, Fairfax VA 22030-4444). For those interested in education about peace and other global problems a good organization is Global Education Associates (475 Riverside Drive, Suite 456, New York NY 10115). On the academic side we should mention the U.S. Institute of Peace (1550 M Street NW, Washington DC 20005), the International Peace Research Association (Prof. Paul Smoker, Antioch College, Yellow Springs OH 45387), the World Policy Institute (777 U.N. Plaza, New York NY 10017), and the Joan B. Kroc Institute for International Peace Studies (University of Notre Dame, P.O. Box 639, Notre Dame IN 46556-0639).

Some peace organizations focus on disarmament and the wastefulness and inappropriateness of high levels of military spending. A valuable source for up-to-date facts on the thinking and planning of the U.S. military establishment from a critical point of view, one on which even members of Congresspersons rely, is *The Defense Monitor* published monthly by the Center for Defense Information (1500 Massachusetts Avenue NW, Washington DC 20005). Another good critique of U.S. military planning is *Defense and Disarmament News* published by the Institute for Defense and Disarmament Studies (2001 Beacon Street, Brookline MA 02146). For information about military strategy related to missiles and space weaponry a valuable source is the newsletter of the Institute for Space and Security Studies, 5115 Hwy A1A South, Melbourne Beach FL 32951.

Many peace organizations emphasize the need for social justice as well as for peace. One such worldwide organization is the Women's International League for Peace and Freedom (1213 Race Street, Philadelphia PA 19107). Amnesty International (322 Eighth Avenue, New York NY 10001) has received much acclaim for its work in writing letters and staging demonstrations in support of political prisoners who have not advocated the use of violence but who nevertheless have been imprisoned and tortured for opposing some of the oppressive policies of their governments. Other organizations working in the area of the advancement of human rights are the International League for Human Rights (236 E. 46th Street, New York NY 10017) and Helsinki Watch (36 W. 44th Street, New York NY 10036).

Nonviolence is a central theme in the work of peace organizations such as the War Resister's League (339 Lafayette Street, New York NY 10012), Clergy and Laity Concerned (198 Broadway, New York NY 10038) and the Fellowship of Reconciliation (Box 271, Nyack NY 10960). One group which deserves special mention because of its fine newsletter concerning the legislative scene in Washington is the Friends Committee on National Legislation (245 Second Street NE, Washington DC 20002).

Some organizations focus their efforts on the development and distribution of peace-oriented literature. World Priorities (Box 25140, Washington DC 20007) publishes the very valuable *World Military and Social Expenditures* as well as other materials. The World Without War Council (175 Fifth Avenue, New York NY 10010) seeks to mobilize public concern about the war problem and does this partly by operating a bookstore (421 South Wabash, Chicago IL 60605) from which a great variety of peace-oriented literature can be purchased.

It should be evident that there is no shortage of organizations and activities. What is needed is more people to support them. For most organizations the annual membership fee is $25 to $40, and most of them offer a reduced rate for students, retired persons, and others on limited income. The mention of contributing money, even a small amount, may dampen the enthusiasm of some people. They want peace, but not *that* much. Yet we must recognize that what we really value is indicated not primarily by what we say but by how we spend our time and money.

We are living during a momentous period of human history, a time of transition from a world of separate national communities to a new global community in which war will become obsolete. Our task is to help develop the attitudes and build the institutions which this new world community needs. Everyone's help is needed—including yours.

Appendix: Relevant Dates

5000–3000 BC	First cities and beginning of wars between city-states.
3000 BC	Political unification of Egypt (Menes).
2500–2350 BC	Sumerian Empire in Mesopotamia (Lugal-zaggasi).
2350–2000 BC	Akkadian Empire in Mesopotamia (Sargon I).
2200–1750 BC	Hsia Dynasty in China.
1800–1600 BC	Old Babylonian Empire in Mesopotamia (Hammurabi).
1766–1122 BC	Shang Dynasty in China.
1350–640 BC	Assyrian Empire (Tiglath Pileser I, Sargon II, Sennacherib, Ashurbanipal).
1122–221 BC	Chou Dynasty in China (Wen Wang, Huan Kung).
626–539 BC	Chaldean (New Babylonian) Empire (Nebuchadnezzar II).
538–338 BC	Persian Empire (Cyrus, Darius I, Xerxes I).
334–323 BC	Macedonian Empire (Alexander the Great).
202 BC–AD 220	Han Dynasty (Liu Pang, Liu Hsiu).
146 BC–AD 395	Roman Empire (Julius Caesar, Augustus Caesar, Trajan, Diocletian).
(AD) 330–1204	Byzantine (Eastern Roman) Empire (Justinian, Basil I).
618–880	T'ang Dynasty (Li Yüan, T'ang T'ai Tsung, T'ang Hsüan Tsung).
632–945	Islamic Caliphate Empire (Umar I, Mu'āwiyah I, al-Walīd, Al-ma'mūn).
960–1279	Sung Dynasty (T'ai Tsu, Tseng Tsung, Shen Tsung, Kao Tsung).
1215–1367	Mongolian Empire (Genghis Khan, Kublai Khan, Timur).
1337–1453	Hundred Years' War between France and England.
1354–1918	Ottoman Turk Empire (Murad I, Mehmed II, Süleyman I).
1368–1644	Ming Dynasty (T'ai Tsu, Ch'eng Tsu).
1453	Cannons using gunpowder break openings in walls of Constantinople.
1571	"Christian League" destroys Ottoman navy at Battle of Lepanto.
1588	English navy destroys the Spanish Armada.
1600–1868	Tokugawa Shoguns rule Japan.
1618–1648	Thirty Years' War, ended by Treaty of Westphalia.
1640–1649	Civil War in England between forces of Cromwell and those of Charles I.
1644	Ch'ing forces take Beijing; rule of Manchu Emperors in China begins.
1756–1763	Seven Years' (French & Indian) War, ended by Treaties of Paris and Hubertusberg.
1775–1781	American Revolutionary War, ended by Treaty of Versailles (1783).

369

1789–1799	French Revolution overthrows Louis XVI.
1792–1815	Napoleonic Wars, ended by Congress of Vienna.
1817	Rush-Bagot Agreement limits military vessels on Great Lakes of North America.
1839–1842	Opium War, ended by Treaty of Nanking.
1846–1848	U.S.-Mexican War.
1851–1864	T'aip'ing Rebellion in China.
1853	U.S. intervenes to open Japan to Western influence.
1853–1856	Crimean War, ended by Treaty of Paris.
1861–1865	U.S. Civil War.
1870–1871	Franco-Prussian War, ended by Treaty of Versailles.
1884–1885	West Africa Conference in Berlin.
1894–1895	China-Japanese War, ended by Treaty of Shimonoseki.
1898	Spanish-American War, ended by Treaty of Paris.
1898–1901	Boxer Rebellion in China.
1899–1902	Transvaal (Boer) War, ended by Treaty of Vereeniging.
1904–1905	Russo-Japanese War, ended by Treaty of Portsmouth.
1911–1912	Chinese revolution ends Manchu/Ch'ing Dynasty.
1914–1918	World War I, ended by 1919 Treaties of Versailles, Saint Germain, Neuilly, and Trianon.
1917	U.S. enters World War I.
1917	Bolshevik Revolution institutes Communism in the Soviet Union.
1919–1920	Russo-Polish War, ended by Treaty of Riga.
1920	League of Nations begins operating.
1921–1922	Washington Naval Conference limits numbers of large warships.
1922	Mussolini and Fascists come to power in Italy.
1926–1935	Civil War in China, Nationalists vs. Communists.
1931–1933	Japan attacks Manchuria and establishes hegemony.
1933	Hitler selected to be Chancellor of Germany.
1935–1937	Italy attacks Ethiopia and subdues it.
1936–1939	Spanish Civil War; Franco gains control.
Aug 1937	Japan attacks China, start of World War II in Asia.
Mar 1938	German forces occupy Austria.
Sep 1938	Munich Conference on Czechoslovakia.
Oct 1938–Mar 1939	German forces take control of Czechoslovakia.
Apr 1939	Italian forces take control of Albania.
Aug 1939	Soviet-German Nonaggression Pact signed.
Sep 1939	Germany attacks Poland; World War II begins in Europe.
Nov 1939–Mar 1940	Russo-Finnish War, ended by Treaty of Moscow.
Jun 1941	Germany attacks the Soviet Union.
Dec 1941	Japan attacks Pearl Harbor, Hawaii; U.S. enters World War II.
May 1945	World War II in Europe ends.
Jun 1945	U.N. Charter signed at San Francisco Conference.
Jul 1945	First atomic bomb detonated at Alamagordo, New Mexico.
Aug 1945	U.S. drops atomic bombs on Hiroshima and Nagasaki in Japan.
Sep 1945	World War II ends.
Jan 1946	U.N. begins operating.
Jul 1946	Unrestrained Civil War in China begins.

Dec 1946	Indo-China War against French control in Vietnam begins.
Jun 1947	U.S. announces Marshall Plan for European recovery.
Aug 1947–Mar 1949	First India-Pakistan War after partition of Indian subcontinent.
Dec 1947	London Council of Foreign Ministers ends efforts of U.S. and U.S.S.R. to negotiate differences on future of Europe.
Feb 1948	Soviets assist in Communist coup in Czechoslovakia.
Mar 1948–May 1949	Berlin blockade by Communist forces in Germany.
May 1948–Feb 1949	First Arab-Israeli War following U.N. partition of Holy Land.
Jun 1948–Aug 1957	British are driven out of Malaysia.
Aug 1949	North Atlantic Treaty Organization (NATO) established.
Oct 1949	People's Republic of China established.
Jun 1950–Jul 1953	Korean War with intervention by U.N. forces.
Oct 1950–May 1951	Occupation of Tibet by China.
Mar 1953	Stalin dies leading to temporary thaw in the Cold War.
Jul 1954	Geneva Agreement establishing divided Vietnam and ending French control over Indochina.
Nov 1954–June 1962	Algerian War of Independence from France.
Apr 1955	Conference of Asian and African nations at Bandung, Indonesia.
May 1955	Warsaw Treaty Organization established.
Sep 1955–Oct 1959	Cyprus War of Independence from Britain.
Oct 1956–Dec 1956	Second Arab-Israeli War with British & French intervention.
Oct 1956–Nov 1956	Intervention by Soviet forces in Hungary.
Dec 1956–Jan 1959	Castro leads Communist revolution in Cuba.
Mar 1957	Treaty of Rome creates European Economic Community.
Oct 1957	U.S.S.R. launches first artificial satellite (sputnik).
Jul 1958	U.S. forces intervene in Lebanon conflict.
Nov 1958–Feb 1960	Belgian Congo (Zaire) wins independence from Belgium.
Jul 1960–Sep 1966	Civil War in Congo (Katanga Province) with U.N. intervention.
May 1961	"Bay of Pigs" invasion of Cuba is repulsed.
Oct 1962	Cuban missile crisis; Soviets remove missiles.
Aug 1963	Partial Nuclear Test-Ban Treaty signed.
Nov 1963	President John F. Kennedy assassinated.
Dec 1963–Dec 1967	Civil War in Cyprus with U.N. intervention.
Aug 1964	U.S. Congress passes Gulf of Tonkin Resolution authorizing Presidential action against North Vietnam.
Apr 1965–Jun 1966	Intervention in Dominican Republic by U.S. forces.
Aug 1965–Jan 1966	Second India-Pakistan War.
Nov 1965–Apr 1969	Chinese "Cultural Revolution" against elitism.
Jan 1967–Jan 1970	Biafran Civil War in Nigeria.
Jun 1967	Third Arab-Israeli War (Six-Day War).
Jul 1968	Treaty on Non-Proliferation of Nuclear Weapons.
Aug 1968	Intervention in Czechoslovakia by Warsaw Pact forces.
Oct 1968	Civil War in Northern Ireland begins.
Mar 1969	Russian-Chinese clashes along Ussuri River border.
Jul 1969	U.S. astronauts land on the moon.
Mar 1970–Feb 1990	Cambodian Civil War with Pol Pot's Communists gaining control in 1975 and Vietnam intervening in Dec 1978.

Mar 1971–Dec 1971	Pakistan Civil War; Bangladesh becomes a separate country.
Jul 1972	SALT I Arms Control Treaty between U.S. and U.S.S.R.
Mar 1973	Last U.S. forces leave Vietnam.
Oct 1973	Fourth Arab-Israeli War (Yom Kippur War).
Apr 1975	South Vietnam forces surrender to North Vietnam.
Apr 1975–	Civil War in Lebanon with Israel intervening (1982–85).
Nov 1975	U.N. adopts "Zionism is racism" resolution.
Sep 1976	Mao Zedong dies prompting struggle for leadership in China.
Jan 1978–Nov 1989	Civil War in Nicaragua; Somoza deposed by Sandinistas in 1979 and U.S. intervention (1981–89).
Apr 1978–	Civil War in Afghanistan with U.S.S.R. intervening (1979–89).
Jan 1979	Iranian Shah Mohammed Reza Pahlavi overthrown by forces loyal to Ayatollah Ruhallah Khomeini.
Feb 1979–Mar 1979	Chinese invasion of Vietnam under Deng Xiaoping's leadership.
Sep 1980–Jul 1988	Iraq-Iran War.
May 1980	Tito dies, raising doubts about governance of Yugoslavia.
Apr 1982–Jun 1982	Falkland Islands/Malvinas War between Argentina and Britain.
Jun 1982–Jun 1985	Fifth Arab-Israeli War; PLO ousted from Beirut, Lebanon.
Mar 1985	Gorbachev gets top leadership position in Soviet Union.
Oct 1985	U.S. forces invade Grenada and overthrow Marxist government.
Feb 1986	Philippine nonviolent revolution ends Marcos regime.
Apr 1986	U.S. attacks Libya in retaliation for supporting terrorist attacks.
Oct 1986	Reagan-Gorbachev summit in Reykjavik.
8 Dec 1987	Reagan and Gorbachev sign INF agreement in Washington.
14 Apr 1988	Agreement to withdraw Soviet forces from Afghanistan.
1 Jun 1988	Intermediate-Range Nuclear Forces Treaty signed in Moscow.
18 Jul 1988	Cease-fire agreement in Iran-Iraq War.
15 Feb 1989	Last Soviet troops leave Afghanistan.
4 Jun 1989	Chinese forces put down pro-democracy demonstration in Tiananmen Square, Beijing.
14 Sep 1989	F.W. deKlerk elected President in South Africa on platform of evolutionary change to eliminate apartheid.
10 Nov 1989	Berlin Wall torn down.
20 Dec 1989	U.S. forces invade Panama and remove Noriega from leadership.
25 Feb 1990	Violeta Chamorro wins in Nicaraguan election monitored by U.N. and O.A.S. ending Sandinista control in Nicaragua.
11 Mar 1990	Lithuania declares independence from U.S.S.R.
2 Aug 1990	Iraq invades Kuwait.
7 Aug 1990	U.S. troops land in Saudi Arabia.
15 Aug 1990	Iraq accepts Iran's terms for peace.
3 Oct 1990	East Germans vote to accept rule of West German government.

9 Oct 1990	U.S.S.R. ratifies Threshold Test Ban Treaty and Peaceful Nuclear Explosions Treaty after U.S. ratification on 25 Sep 1990.
19 Nov 1990	Member states of NATO and Warsaw Pact sign Conventional Forces in Europe Treaty.
16 Dec 1990	Aristide wins U.N.-monitored election in Haiti.
20 Dec 1990	Shevardnadze resigns as Foreign Minister of U.S.S.R.
16 Jan 1991	U.S.-led air strikes on Kuwait begin.
23 Feb–28 Feb 1991	U.S.-led coalition forces liberate Kuwait and invade Iraq.
3 Apr 1991	U.N. Security Council sets terms of cease-fire in Iraq.
27 May 1991	Last Cuban troops leave Angola.
12 Jun 1991	Yeltsin becomes first democratically elected President of Russia.
17 Jun 1991	U.N. peace-monitoring forces arrive in Angola.
25 Jun 1991	Slovenia and Croatia declare independence from Yugoslavia.
26 Jul 1991	U.N. sends peacekeeping forces to El Salvador.
31 Jul 1991	U.S. and U.S.S.R. sign START I Treaty.
19–21 Aug 1991	Attempted coup to oust Gorbachev from leadership in U.S.S.R.
20 Aug 1991	Estonia declares independence from U.S.S.R.
21 Aug 1991	Latvia declares independence from U.S.S.R.
23 Aug 1991	Gorbachev agrees to Yeltsin's demand for Russian control of all natural resources and U.S.S.R. assets within Russia.
23 Aug 1991	U.N. sends monitoring team into Cambodia.
5 Sep 1991	Ceasefire monitors from EC and CSCE arrive in Yugoslavia.
17 Sep 1991	U.N. accepts into membership Estonia, Latvia, Lithuania, North Korea, South Korea, the Federated States of Micronesia, and the Marshall Islands.
21 Sep 1991	U.N. referendum supervisors arrive in Western Sahara.
8 Dec 1991	Formation of Commonwealth of Independent States by Russia, Ukraine, and Belarus.
11 Dec 1991	Treaty of Maastricht adopted by European Community members.
15 Dec 1991	U.N. Security Council votes to send monitors into Yugoslavia.
16 Dec 1991	U.N. General Assembly repeals "Zionism is racism" resolution.
24 Dec 1991	Russia takes Soviet Union's place as member of the U.N.
25 Dec 1991	Gorbachev resigns marking end of U.S.S.R.
31 Jan 1992	First summit meeting of the heads of state of members of U.N. Security Council calls for strengthening the U.N.
15 Feb 1992	Israel moves into U.N.-patrolled area of Lebanon to stop guerrilla attacks by Hezbollah.
2 Mar 1992	U.N. accepts into membership San Marino, Armenia, Azerbaijan, Kazakhstan, Kirgizstan, Moldova, Tajikistan, Turkmenistan, and Uzbekistan.
9 Mar 1992	U.N. peacekeeping forces to Croatia and Bosnia-Herzegovina.
22 Mar 1992	Bosnia-Herzegovina, Croatia, and Slovenia accepted into U.N.

23 May 1992	Protocol to START I Treaty makes Russia, Ukraine, Belarus, and Kazakhstan official successors to U.S.S.R.
3–14 Jun 1992	UN Conference on Environment and Development (Earth Summit).
17 Jun 1992	U.N. Secretary-General Boutros Boutros-Ghali issues "An Agenda for Peace."
31 Jul 1992	Georgia (formerly part of U.S.S.R.) accepted into U.N.
29–30 Sep 1992	First multiparty elections in Angola held under U.N. supervision.
1 Oct 1992	U.S. Senate ratifies START Agreement.
4 Nov 1992	Russia ratifies START Agreement.
9 Dec 1992	U.S. forces enter Somalia to assist U.N. peacekeeping forces.
1 Jan 1993	Czech Republic and Slovakia become separate countries.
3 Jan 1993	START II Treaty between U.S. and Russia signed (but can't go into effect until START I is ratified by all parties).
15 Jan 1993	Signing of Chemical Weapons Convention.
19 Jan 1993	Czech Republic and Slovakia accepted into U.N.
22 Feb 1993	U.N. Security Council establishes war crimes tribunal for former Yugoslavia.
7 Apr 1993	Former Yugoslav Republic of Macedonia accepted into U.N.
23–28 May 1993	U.N.-monitored elections in Cambodia.
28 May 1993	Eritrea and Monaco admitted to U.N. membership.
18 Jul 1993	Liberal Democratic Party loses control of Japanese government.
25 Jul 1993	Andorra admitted to U.N. as 184th member.
13 Sep 1993	Israel and PLO sign "Declaration of Principles."
18 Nov 1993	U.S. votes to adopt North American Free Trade Agreement.
12 Dec 1993	Russians approve Yeltsin's new constitution.

Chapter Notes

Chapter I. The Nature of the War Problem

1. In 1991 the U.S. was still spending just over 5 percent of its Gross Domestic Product on military purposes even though the Cold War was over. See the International Institute for Strategic Studies (IISS), *The Military Balance 1992–1993* (London: Brassey's, 1992), p. 218.

2. "Preparing for Peace" in Lester R. Brown (ed.), *State of the World, 1993* (New York: W.W. Norton, 1993), p. 140.

3. Barry Commoner, "Ecosystems Are Circular: Part II," *American Forests,* Vol. 80, No. 5 (May 1974), p. 60.

4. St. Louis *Post-Dispatch,* Apr. 12, 1985, p. 2.

5. Ruth Leger Sivard (ed.), *World Military and Social Expenditures (WMSE), 1991,* 14th ed. (Washington: World Priorities, 1991), p. 50. This figure reflects the value of a dollar in 1987.

6. Sivard, *WMSE 1991,* p. 50.

7. Kenneth Boulding, *Stable Peace* (Austin TX: University of Texas, 1978), p. 28.

8. IISS, *The Military Balance 1992–1993* (see note 1), p. 219.

9. Josua S. Goldstein, "How Military Might Robs an Economy," *New York Times,* October 16, 1988, p. F3.

10. Boulding, *Stable Peace,* p. 29.

11. In the middle of 1988 at the height of the Cold War it was reported by *The Defense Monitor* (published by the Center for Defense Information, 1500 Massachusetts Ave. NW, Washington DC 20005), Vol. 17, No. 5 (1988), p. 1, that the U.S. could "explode more than 16,000 nuclear weapons on the Soviet Union" while "the Soviets can explode over 11,000 nuclear weapons on the United States." These figures include more than 12,600 U.S. strategic (long-range) weapons (about half of which are on submarines) and about 10,500 Soviet strategic weapons.

12. For an insider's view of the Cuban missile crisis, see Robert F. Kennedy, *Thirteen Days* (New York: W.W. Norton, 1969).

13. "The U.S. nuclear stockpile is at its lowest level since late 1958 or early 1959. ... [T]he current operational stockpile ... contains some 10,500 warheads." So reported *The Bulletin of the Atomic Scientists,* Vol. 49, No. 5 (June 1993), p. 57. That same report noted that "the operational stockpile will eventually drop to 5,100 warheads — 3,500 strategic and 1,600 non-strategic weapons."

14. A history of the discussions of "nuclear winter" can be found in Thomas F. Malone, "International Scientists on Nuclear Winter," *The Bulletin of the Atomic Scientists,* Vol. 41, No. 11 (Dec. 1985), pp. 52–55. For a complete bibliography on the subject, see *World Armaments and Disarmaments, SIPRI Yearbook 1985,* pp. 127–29.

15. Sivard, *WMSE 1991,* p. 20.

16. Sivard, *WMSE 1991,* p. 20.

17. For an overview of the world's conventional wars going on near the end of 1992 including both struggles for independence and other intranational wars see *The Defense Monitor,* Vol. 21, No. 6 (November 1992), especially p. 8.

18. It is uncertain how many nuclear weapons Israel has, but it has been noted that "Mordecai Vanunu's revelations suggest that Israel may possess about 200 warheads, some of them 'boosted' weapons with H-bomb power." See Pervez Hoodbhoy, "Myth-Building: The 'Islamic' Bomb," *The Bulletin of the Atomic Scientists*, Vol. 49, No. 5 (June 1993), p. 45.

19. David Albright, "A Curious Conversion," *The Bulletin of the Atomic Scientists*, Vol. 49, No. 5 (June 1993), pp. 8–11.

20. David Albright, "A Proliferation Primer," *The Bulletin of the Atomic Scientists*, Vol. 49, No. 5 (June 1993), p. 22.

21. Albright, "A Proliferation Primer," p. 22.

22. Albright, "A Proliferation Primer," pp. 14–23.

23. Albright, "A Proliferation Primer," pp. 16–18.

Chapter II. The Conceptual Framework

1. For an historical overview of some attempts to define "war" see Donald A. Wells, *The War Myth* (New York: Pegasus, 1967), pp. 17–31.

2. Lewis Richardson in *Statistics of Deadly Quarrels* (Pittsburgh: Boxwood, 1960) used 317 (that is, $10^{2.5}$) deaths as the minimum. Quincy Wright in *A Study of War* (Chicago: University of Chicago, 1942) relied on the number of troops involved rather than the number of casualties and decided that a conflict would be counted as a war if at least 50,000 troops were committed to the fighting or if the war was recognized as a war in the legal sense (Vol. 1, p. 636). J. David Singer and Melvin Small in *The Wages of War, 1816–1965: A Statistical Handbook* (New York: Wiley, 1972) worked out very precise criteria for deciding whether to count an armed conflict as a war. An inter-state war is taken into account only if there were at least 1,000 battle fatalities (p. 35), while imperial and colonial wars are taken into account only if the imperialistic or colonial power suffered at least 1,000 battle fatalities per year (pp. 36–37). Small and Singer did not consider civil wars in their first study, but they did in their revised edition, *Resort to Arms: International and Civil Wars, 1816–1980* (Beverly Hills CA: Sage, 1982). The same criteria for including a war in the study are given in the new edition on pp. 54–56.

3. On the relation between the society, the military, and war see Keith F. Otterbein, *The Evolution of War: A Cross-Cultural Study* (New Haven CT: Yale University-HRAF, 1970), pp. 17–23, 63–64.

4. Jean-Jacques Rousseau makes this point in *The Social Contract*, Book I, Chapter 4 where he says, "War is therefore not a concern between man and man but between State and State...." This passage can be found in John Somerville and Ronald E. Santoni (eds.), *Social and Political Philosophy* (Garden City NY: Doubleday, 1963), p. 210.

5. This definition of government might need to be modified just a bit if one were dealing with noncentralized political communities such as bands and tribes which engage in primitive warfare. See Otterbein, *The Evolution of War*, pp. 17–19.

6. See all the articles but especially the editor's introduction in Yonah Alexander (ed.), *International Terrorism: National, Regional, and Global Perspectives* (New York: Praeger, 1976).

7. See Abraham D. Sofaer, "Terrorism and the Law," *Foreign Affairs*, Vol. 64, No. 5 (Summer 1986), pp. 901–22.

8. Note that this view of the relation between war and politics generally coincides with that of Carl von Clausewitz, *On War*, edited with an introduction by Anatol Rapoport, trans. by J.J. Graham (New York: Penguin, 1968), pp. 119, 402, 405. The crucial difference in emphasis is that von Clausewitz, influenced by the international situation of his day, viewed war as an appropriate way for a nation to try to get what

it wanted when it could not accomplish this through diplomacy, while our observation is influenced by the fact that any conflicting groups can be viewed as being members of a larger society to which war is generally disastrous. In this context war would become unnecessary if the same kinds of political procedures now found within most nations which have stable governments were duplicated in other nations and also developed for the global society.

9. See for example Johan Galtung, "Violence, Peace, and Peace Research" in the *Journal of Peace Research,* Vol. 6 (1961), pp. 167–91.

10. See Thomas Hobbes, *Leviathan,* Chapter XIII in *The English Works of Thomas Hobbes,* edited by Sir William Molesworth (London: John Bohn, 1839, reprinted 1966), Vol. 3, p. 113.

11. Plato, *Republic,* Book I, pp. 331e and 332c.

12. Three of the better known modern books in this tradition are Paul Ramsey, *The Just War: Force and Political Responsibility* (Paterson NJ: Littlefield Adams, 1968, 1983); James Turner Johnson, *Can Modern War Be Just?* (New Haven: Yale University Press, 1984); and Michael Walzer, *Just and Unjust Wars: A Moral Argument with Historical Illustrations* (New York: Basic Books, 1977).

13. See John Brinsfield, "The Origins of the Just War Tradition," reprinted in Dick Ringler (ed.), *Dilemmas of War and Peace: A Sourcebook* (Madison WI: Board of Regents of Univ. of Wisconsin System and Corporation for Public Broadcasting, 1993), pp. 406–10. The original article "From Plato to NATO: The Ethics of Warfare" was published in *Military Chaplain's Review,* Spring 1991.

14. There are so many books and articles addressing the moral issues of nuclear war that it seems inappropriate to list only a few of them. Nevertheless, here is a short list, most of them anthologies: Russell Hardin, John Mearsheimer, Gerald Dworkin, and Robert E. Goodin (eds.), *Nuclear Deterrence: Ethics and Strategy* (Chicago: University of Chicago, 1985); William V. O'Brien and John Langan (eds.), *The Nuclear Dilemma and the Just War Tradition* (Lexington MA: Lexington Books, 1986); Joseph C. Kunkel and Kenneth H. Klein (eds.), *Issues in War and Peace: Philosophical Inquiries* (Wolfeboro NH: Longwood Academic, 1989); Charles W. Kegley, Jr. and Eugene R. Wittkopf (eds.), *The Nuclear Reader: Strategy, Weapons, and War* (New York: St. Martin's, 1985); John B. Harris and Eric Markusen (eds.), *Nuclear Weapons and the Threat of Nuclear War* (San Diego: Harcourt Brace Jovanovich, 1986); and Edward J. Laarman, *Nuclear Pacifism: "Just War" Thinking Today* (New York: Peter Lang, 1984). See also the *Journal of Social Philosophy,* Vol. 18, No. 2 (Summer 1987) and *The Monist,* Vol. 70, No. 3 (July 1987) where a single number of these periodicals is totally dedicated to this topic. Ringler's sourcebook mentioned in the previous note also contains many relevant selections.

15. Harrop A. Freeman, "Pacifism and Law" in Robert Ginsberg (ed.), *The Critique of War: Contemporary Philosophical Explorations* (Chicago: Henry Regnery, 1969), pp. 284–96, presents the interesting thesis that once government machinery is in place, the less powerful will gradually become able to make use of that machinery to protect themselves from oppression by the powerful. See pp. 291–93.

16. For example, see Riseri Frondizi, "The Ideological Origins of the Third World War" in Ginsberg, *The Critique of War,* pp. 77–95, especially p. 89 and pp. 93–95.

17. Kenneth E. Boulding, *Stable Peace* (Austin, Texas: University of Texas, 1978), p. 67.

18. Quoted by Frondizi in Ginsberg, *The Critique of War,* p. 94.

Chapter III. The Historical Framework

1. Quincy Wright, *A Study of War* (1942), Vol. 1, p. 61. Wright devotes a whole chapter to primitive warfare (Vol. 1, pp. 53–100) as well as an appendix on the "Relation

between Warlikeness and Other Characteristics of Primitive Peoples" (Vol. 1, pp. 560–61). On the other hand, Margaret Mead notes that the Eskimos and the Lepchas of Sikkim do not understand the notion of war, "not even defensive war." Her article "Warfare Is Only an Invention—Not a Biological Necessity" was originally published in *Asia*, Vol. 40, No. 8 (Aug. 1940), pp. 402–05 and has been reprinted in various collections including Leon Bramson and George W. Goethals (eds.), *War: Studies from Psychology, Sociology, Anthropology*, rev. ed. (New York: Basic Books, 1968), pp. 269–74, and Charles R. Beitz and Theodore Herman (eds.), *Peace and War* (San Francisco: W.H. Freeman, 1973), pp. 112–18. The phrase quoted above is from the third paragraph of this article. Behavior which we might describe as warfare has even been observed among chimpanzees. See Jane Goodall, "Life and Death at Gombe," *National Geographic*, Vol. 155, No. 5 (May 1979), pp. 592–621.

2. Maurice R. Davie, *The Evolution of War: A Study of Its Role in Early Societies* (Port Washington NY: Kennikat Press; originally published in 1929 by Yale University Press, reissued in 1968 by Kennikat Press), pp. 2–4.

3. Dyer, *War* (Homewood IL: Dorsey Press, 1985), p. 6. The first chapter of Dyer's book entitled "Roots of War" which contains this quotation is reprinted in Melvin Small and J. David Singer, *International War: An Anthology*, 2nd ed. (Chicago: Dorsey Press, 1989), pp. 3–17 and in Dick Ringler (ed.), *Dilemmas of War and Peace: A Sourcebook* (Madison WI: Board of Regents of the University of Wisconsin System and the Corporation for Public Broadcasting, 1993), pp. 53–69.

4. Dyer, *War*, p. 11.

5. Dyer, *War*, p. 11.

6. William Eckhardt, *Civilizations, Empires, and Wars: A Quantitative History of War* (Jefferson NC: McFarland, 1992), p. 2.

7. Davie, *The Evolution of War*, pp. 160–75, especially 174–75.

8. Charles S. Gochman and Zeev Moaz, "Militarized Interstate Disputes 1816–1976: Procedures, Patterns, and Insights," *Journal of Conflict Resolution*, Vol. 28 (1984), p. 615.

9. Frederick L. Schuman, *International Politics*, 7th ed. (New York: McGraw-Hill, 1969), p. 34. This text contains a relatively brief history of international politics and war from 5000 B.C. to A.D. 1945 on pp. 33–99. The subsequent account of post–World War II history is much more detailed.

10. Schuman, *International Politics*, pp. 38–39.

11. For more information on casualties in wars in the twentieth century in which there were 1,000 or more deaths per year see Sivard, *WMSE 1991*, pp. 20–25.

12. Kenneth Boulding, *The Meaning of the Twentieth Century* (New York: Harper, 1964), pp. 2 and 5–23. See also Harlan Cleveland, *Birth of a New World* (San Francisco: Jossey-Bass, 1993).

13. Robert Ardrey in *African Genesis* (New York: Dell, 1967) suggests that man should be defined as the weapon-making animal. See pp. 185–207. For a somewhat satirical treatment of the history of warfare and the development of new weapons see Richard Armour, *It All Started with Stones and Clubs* (New York: McGraw-Hill, 1967).

14. An excellent critical review of these attempts can be found in Singer and Small, *The Wages of War, 1816–1965*, pp. 7–11 and in the revised version, *Resort to Arms*, pp. 25–29. See also Francis A. Beer, *How Much War in History: Definitions, Estimates, Extrapolations, and Trends* (Beverly Hills, CA: Sage, 1974) and Francis A. Beer, *Peace Against War: The Ecology of International Violence* (San Francisco: W.H. Freeman, 1981), pp. 20–49. For reports on another recent effort to list all major conflicts from 1740 to 1978 see the following articles by Gernot Köhler: "Gaston Bouthoul and René Carrère: A List of the 366 Major Armed Conflicts of the Period 1740-1974," *Peace Research*, Vol. 10 (1978), 83–108, and "Gaston Bouthoul and René Carrère: Major Armed Conflicts, 1965 to 1 July 1978," *Peace Research*, Vol. 11 (1979), 183–86.

15. The investigators themselves tell us that in many cases the evidence for their estimates is very weak. See Singer and Small, *The Wages of War, 1816–1965,* p. 4; Beer, *How Much War in History,* pp. 7 and 30; Wright, *A Study of War,* Vol. 1, pp. 101–103; and Sivard, *WMSE 1982,* p. 36.

16. Small and Singer, *Resort to Arms.*

17. Wright and his fellow researchers focused on wars from 1480 to 1940, but he did not limit himself to that more recent period when making judgments about long-term trends.

18. Wright, *A Study of War,* Vol. 1, pp. 234–35. Wright considers the points of agreement and disagreement between his own generalizations and those drawn by Lewis F. Richardson in *Statistics of Deadly Quarrels* in his introduction to Richardson's work. See pp. vii–xiii of the edition edited by Wright and C.C. Lineau (Pittsburgh: Boxwood, and Chicago: Quadrangle Books, 1960).

19. Wright, *A Study of War,* Vol. 1, p. 236.

20. Wright, *A Study of War,* Vol. 1, p. 237.

21. Wright, *A Study of War,* Vol. 1, p. 242.

22. Small and Singer, *Resort to Arms,* p. 141.

23. Small and Singer, *Resort to Arms,* pp. 139–41.

24. Small and Singer, *Resort to Arms,* pp. 89–92.

25. Small and Singer, *Resort to Arms,* pp. 130–32.

26. Small and Singer, *Resort to Arms,* pp. 261–67 and 275.

27. Beer, *How Much War in History,* p. 20; see also Beer, *Peace Against War,* pp. 38–39, 41, and 46.

28. Beer, *How Much War in History,* p. 31.

29. Jack S. Levy, "Historical Trends in Great Power War, 1495–1975," *International Studies Quarterly,* Vol. 26, No. 2 (June 1982), p. 298.

30. William Eckhardt, "The Task of Peace Education," *Peace Research,* Vol. 18, No. 2 (May 1986), p. 16.

31. See note 5 for Chapter I.

32. Sivard, *World Military and Social Expenditures, 1991,* pp. 12–13.

33. International Institute for Strategic Studies (IISS), *The Military Balance 1992–1993* (London: Brassey's, 1992), pp. 219–21.

34. Sivard, *World Military and Social Expenditures, 1981,* p. 15. See also the chart on p. 200 of this book.

35. IISS, *The Military Balance 1992–1993,* pp. 225–28.

36. John Somerville, "Scientific-Technological Progress and the New Problem of Preventing the Annihilation of the Human World," *Peace Research,* Vol. 11 (1979), pp. 11–18. The quotation is from page 17.

37. Sivard, *World Military and Social Expenditures, 1991,* p. 13.

38. Sivard, *WMSE 1991,* pp. 22–25.

39. IISS, *The Military Balance 1992–1993,* p. 218, gives the per capita defense expenditure for the U.S. as $902.

Chapter IV. The Cause of War: Some General Considerations

1. Theodore Lentz, "Introduction," in Theodore Lentz (ed.), *Humatriotism* (St. Louis: The Future Press, 1976), p. 28. (Publisher's address: 6251 San Bonita, St. Louis, MO 63105.)

2. See for example Matthew Melko's *Fifty-Two Peaceful Societies* (Oakville, Ontario: Canadian Peace Research Institute Press, 1973). Melko has made some modifica-

tions of his original data as the result of comments received from others. See his "Note on the Dating of the Phoenician Peace" in *Peace Research*, Vol. 7 (1975), p. 108. For a more recent refinement of this effort see Matthew Melko and Richard D. Weigel, *Peace in the Ancient World* (Jefferson NC: McFarland, 1981). For a study of seven peaceful contemporary groups see David Fabbro, "Peaceful Societies: An Introduction," *Journal of Peace Research*, Vol. 15 (1978), pp. 67–83. Using a statistical approach rather than starting with particular peaceful societies, R.J. Rummel has argued that democracies have fewer wars, external and internal, than totalitarian regimes. See his "Political Systems, Violence, and War" in W. Scott Thompson and Kenneth M. Jensen (eds.), *Approaches to Peace: An Intellectual Map* (Washington: U.S. Institute of Peace, 1991), pp. 350–70, especially pp. 351–52.

3. For an example of such an inference see Norman Alcock, *The War Disease* (Oakville, Ontario: Canadian Peace Research Institute Press, 1972), pp. 152–53. It is remarkable that Alcock nevertheless takes note of Lewis Richardson's care in concluding that arms races are only sometimes the cause of war. See pp. 70–71.

4. See for example John Stoessinger, *Why Nations Go to War*, 5th ed. (New York: St. Martin's, 1989). After analyzing the beginning of seven recent wars, in the final chapter Stoessinger provides several "common themes" which he believes can be extracted from his case studies. The kind of detailed case studies he conducts seem to be necessary in order to proceed to the classification of wars on the basis of their causes.

5. Mention should be made of the "Correlates of War" project being carried out by J. David Singer, Melvin Small, and their associates. They attempt to check various theories about the cause of war by trying to calculate the correlations between the presence of the purported causes of war and the actual occurrence of wars. See J. David Singer (ed.), *Correlates of War I: Research Origins and Rationale* (New York: Free Press, 1979); J. David Singer (ed.), *Explaining War: Selected Papers from the Correlates of War Project* (Beverly Hills CA: Sage, 1979); and J. David Singer (ed.), *Correlates of War II: Testing Some Realpolitik Models* (New York: Free Press, 1979). Even this project, however, looks for factors correlated with *all* wars rather than seeking to *classify* wars on the basis of their causes as is done with disease.

6. Leonard Berkowitz, "The Concept of Aggressive Drive: Some Additional Considerations" in L. Berkowitz (ed.), *Advances in Experimental Social Psychology*, Vol. 2 (New York: Academic, 1965), p. 302.

7. For a forceful statement of the view that the causes of individual aggression are different from the causes of war see Ralph L. Holloway, "Human Aggression: The Need for a Species-Specific Framework" in Morton Fried, Marvin Harris, and Robert Murphy (eds.), *War: The Anthropology of Armed Conflict and Aggression* (Garden City, NY: Natural History Press, 1967), pp. 29–48, especially pp. 29–30. For an earlier statement of this view, see Bronislaw Malinowski, "An Anthropological Analysis of War," *American Journal of Sociology*, Vol. 46, No. 2 (Jan. 1941), pp. 521–50, especially pp. 523–33.

8. A good collection of excerpts from selections relating individual aggression to warfare can be found in William A. Nesbitt (ed.), *Human Nature and War*. This booklet for students was published by the State Education Department of New York, 99 Washington Ave., Albany, NY 12210, in 1973.

9. For a good collection of three selections, one dealing with each type of theory about human aggression, see Richard A. Falk and Samuel S. Kim (eds.), *The War System: An Interdisciplinary Approach* (Boulder, CO: Westview, 1980), pp. 77–156.

10. *On Aggression* (New York: Harcourt Brace Jovanovich, 1966), p. 52. The relevant passage is reprinted in Nesbitt, *Human Nature and War*, p. 9.

11. *Civilization and Its Discontents* (New York: Norton, 1930), p. 67. The relevant passage is reprinted in Nesbitt, *Human Nature and War*, p. 14.

12. *The Territorial Imperative* (New York: Atheneum, 1961).

13. *African Genesis*, p. 325.

14. *The Naked Ape* (New York: McGraw-Hill, 1967).

15. "Human Violence: Some Causes and Implications" in Beitz and Herman, *Peace and War*, pp. 119–43. This article contains a rather extensive bibliography on the physiological basis of aggression. Corning would probably object to being grouped with Lorenz, Ardrey, and Morris because his views are considerably different from theirs. Still, his emphasis on the physiological basis for aggressive behavior seems to require classifying his view as one that emphasizes the biological rather than the cultural or psychological aspects of aggression. At the same time it should be noted that for Corning, as well as for others such as Freud who emphasize the biological or instinctual basis of aggression, the solution to the war problem is to be found in politics rather than biology.

16. Peggy Durdin, "From the Space Age to the Tasaday Age," *New York Times Magazine*, Oct. 8, 1972, pp. 14ff., partially reprinted in Nesbitt, *Human Nature and War*, pp. 45–47.

17. Geoffrey Gorer, "Man Has No 'Killer Instinct,'" *New York Times Magazine*, Nov. 27, 1966, pp. 47ff., partially reprinted in Nesbitt, *Human Nature and War*, pp. 49–52.

18. Mead, "Warfare Is Only an Invention—Not a Biological Necessity." See Note 1 for Chapter III.

19. Ardrey, *African Genesis*, pp. 359–60. Also see Freud's response to Einstein in *Why War?* (Paris: International Institute of Intellectual Cooperation, 1933), reprinted in Peter Mayer (ed.), *The Pacifist Conscience* (Chicago: Henry Regnery, 1967), pp. 235–48; see especially pp. 247–48.

20. Corning, "Human Violence" in Beitz and Herman, *Peace and War*, pp. 131–43.

21. "The Fashionable View of Man as a Naked Ape Is: 1. An Insult to Apes, 2. Simplistic, 3. Male-oriented, 4. Rubbish," *New York Times Magazine*, Sept. 3, 1972, pp. 10ff., partially reprinted in Nesbitt, *Human Nature and War*, pp. 29–33. See also Sally Carrighar, "War Is Not in Our Genes," *New York Times Magazine*, Sept. 10, 1967, pp. 74ff., reprinted in *UNESCO Courier*, Vol. 23, No. 8 (Aug.-Sept. 1970), pp. 40–45, and partially reprinted in Nesbitt, *Human Nature and War*, pp. 23–28. But in defense of group territoriality in primates see Ardrey, *African Genesis*, pp. 46, 77, 82–85, and 107–10 and Jane Goodall, "Life and Death at Gombe," *National Geographic*, Vol. 155, No. 5 (May 1979), p. 599.

22. J. Dollard, L.W. Doob, N.E. Miller, O.H. Mowrer, and R.R. Sears, *Frustration and Aggression* (New Haven: Yale University, 1939). See especially p. 1.

23. Leonard Berkowitz, "The Frustration-Aggression Hypothesis Revisited" in L. Berkowitz (ed.), *Roots of Aggression* (New York: Atherton, 1969), pp. 1–28.

24. Stanley Milgrim, *Obedience to Authority: An Experimental View* (New York: Harper and Row, 1974), p. 166.

25. Arnold H. Buss, *The Psychology of Aggression* (New York: Wiley, 1961), pp. 20–23.

26. Richard J. Borden, "Social Situational Influences on Aggression: A Review of Experimental Findings and Implications," *Peace Research*, Vol. 7 (1975), pp. 97–107.

27. William Eckhardt, "A Conformity Theory of Aggression," *Journal of Peace Research*, Vol. 11 (1974), pp. 31–39.

28. For a good general statement of this approach see John Dewey, "Does Human Nature Change?", *The Rotarian*, Feb. 1938, reprinted in Mary Mothersill (ed.), *Ethics* (New York: Macmillan, 1965), pp. 83–91. Another good general statement of this view is Mark A. May's "War, Peace, and Social Learning" in Bramson and Goethals, *War: Studies from Psychology, Sociology, Anthropology*, pp. 151–58. See also Stoessinger, *Why Nations Go to War*, pp. 202–203.

29. Mead, "Warfare Is Only an Invention—Not a Biological Necessity." See Note 1 for Chapter III.

30. *UNESCO Courier,* Feb. 1993, p. 40. For more information about the Seville Statement, including the full text, see David Adams, "The Seville Statement on Violence: A Progress Report," *Journal of Peace Research,* Vol. 26, No. 2 (1989), pp. 113–21.

31. *African Genesis,* pp. 107–10.

32. Stoessinger, *Why Nations Go to War,* 4th ed., p. 206.

33. Bueno de Mesquita, *The War Trap* (New Haven CT: Yale University, 1981), p. 21.

34. Peter A. Corning, "Human Violence: Some Causes and Implications," a paper prepared for the symposium "Value and Knowledge Requirements for Peace" at the 138th meeting of the American Association for the Advancement of Science in Philadelphia, December 1971. The paper is reprinted in Charles R. Beitz and Theodore Herman (eds.), *Peace and War* (San Francisco: W.H. Freeman, 1973), pp. 119–43. The discussion concerning women leaders occurs on pp. 129–30. For another discussion of the desirability of having women leaders because of sex differences in aggressiveness, see Melvin Konner, "The Aggressors," *New York Times Magazine,* Aug. 14, 1988, pp. 33–34.

35. See E.F.M. Durbin and John Bowlby, "Personal Aggressiveness and War" in Bramson and Goethals, *War: Studies from Psychology, Sociology, Anthropology,* pp. 94–95. See also Edward C. Tolman, "Drives Toward War", pp. 165–68.

36. Ross Stagner, *Psychological Aspects of International Conflict* (Belmont, CA: Wadsworth, 1967), pp. 109–10.

37. Stagner, *Psychological Aspects of International Conflict,* pp. 148–49, and Kenneth Grundy, "The Causes of Political Violence" in Beitz and Herman, *Peace and War,* pp. 50–68.

Chapter V. Group Competition and Group Identification

1. Keith F. Otterbein, *The Evolution of War: A Cross-Cultural Study,* pp. 20–21.

2. Robert L. Carneiro, "A Theory of the Origin of the State," *Science,* Vol. 70 (1970), p. 735.

3. For a good discussion of how population growth is only tangentially related to the problem of war see Quincy Wright, *A Study of War,* abridged ed. by Louis Wright (Chicago: University of Chicago, 1964), pp. 278–95.

4. This thesis is demonstrated convincingly by Bruce Bueno de Mesquita in *The War Trap* (New Haven CT: Yale University, 1981).

5. Anatol Rapoport in *Fights, Games, and Debates* (Ann Arbor MI: University of Michigan, 1960), pp. 9–12 makes some excellent points about the differences between the three different activities mentioned in his title. He notes, however, that even in debates it is assumed that the aim is to get the other person to come over to accepting one's own opinion. The continuing search for what is true, which is our present concern, must take a different form. It must be what Rapoport calls an argument (p. 273). It consists of a dialectic of eliminating errors within one's own thinking rather than of defending a particular theory no matter what objections are raised. In his later work *The Origins of Violence: Approaches to the Study of Conflict* (New York: Paragon House, 1989), pp. 510–11, Rapoport again distinguishes between fights, games, and debates. His discussion of "Objective Criteria" on pp. 516–17 comes closer to the situation of trying to discover what is true but is still considered in the context of a conflict situation between opposing parties rather than the context of a single individual trying to discover what to believe by considering all the facts and arguments which might be used to support various possible views. That dialectical process in which one argues within oneself to ferret out erroneous beliefs is the basis of philosophy and the appropriate alternative to ideological struggle among different social groups.

6. Risieri Frondizi, "The Ideological Origins of the Third World War" in Ginsberg, *The Critique of War,* pp. 77–95, especially pp. 81 and 87–88.

7. Harrop Freeman, "Pacifism and Law" in Ginsberg, *The Critique of War*, pp. 284–96, especially pp. 293–94.

8. Schumpeter, *Imperialism and Social Classes* (Cleveland: World, 1955), pp. 6 and 24–25.

9. See Jonathan S. Landay's article "Loyal Serbs and Croats in Sarajevo See Woe in Partition of Bosnia," *Christian Science Monitor*, July 30, 1993, pp. 1, 4.

10. See Alan Thein Durning, "Supporting Indigenous Peoples" in Lester R. Brown (ed.), *State of the World 1993*, pp. 80–100. The statistics are from p. 81.

11. Durning, "Supporting Indigenous Peoples," in Brown, *State of the World 1993*, pp. 80–100.

12. It should be noted that on some occasions the group which has been subjugated is in fact a *multi-ethnic* group rather than all being of the same race and ethnic background, so that strictly speaking in some wars of liberation the appeal is not to doctrinal nationalism but rather to another principle, namely, that no potential territorial nation-state should be under the control of another nation-state. But such a distinction is too refined to receive much attention in ordinary political discourse.

13. Sivard, *WMSE 1991*, p. 25.

14. See Stoessinger, *Why Nations Go to War*, 4th ed., pp. 128–37.

15. *Keesing's Record of World Events, 1993*, p. 39450 and Sivard, *WMSE 1991*, p. 25.

16. For a more extended discussion of this aspect of nationalism by a psychologist see Stagner, *Psychological Aspects of International Conflict*, pp. 17–83.

Chapter VI. Other Views About Causes of War

1. This "Arms Race Game" is an adaptation of the "Prisoner's Dilemma" game. See Rapoport, *Fights, Games, and Debates*, pp. 173–74, and Ralph M. Goldman, "Political Distrust as Generator of the Arms Race: Prisoners' and Security Dilemmas" from *Arms Control and Peacekeeping* (New York: Random House, 1982), reprinted in Burns H. Weston (ed.), *Toward Nuclear Disarmament and Global Security* (Boulder CO: Westview, 1984), pp. 90–94.

2. Alcock, *The War Disease*, pp. 169–70.

3. See Alan G. Newcombe, "A Foreign Policy for Peace," *Gandhi Marg*, Vol. 16 (1972), pp. 254–65. A slightly revised version of this article is reprinted in Israel W. Charny (ed.), *Strategies Against Violence: Design for Nonviolent Change* (Boulder CO: Westview, 1978), pp. 3–18. See also Alcock, *The War Disease*, pp. 164–73.

4. Lewis F. Richardson, *Arms and Insecurity* (Pittsburgh: Boxwood, 1960), pp. 12–36. See also Alcock, *The War Disease*, pp. 70–83 and 200–212.

5. Lewis F. Richardson, "Could an Arms Race End Without Fighting?", *Nature*, Vol. 168 (1951), pp. 567–68 and Richardson, *Arms and Insecurity*, pp. 35–36 and p. 76.

6. Richardson, *Arms and Insecurity*, p. 70.

7. Ziegler, *War, Peace, and International Politics*, pp. 123–24, argues that the view that individual aggressive leaders are a cause of war cannot be correct because there are many wars in which there seem to be no villains. Ziegler's argument is cogent only against the view that individual aggressive leaders are a *necessary condition* of war. It does not apply to the thesis that individual aggressive leaders are a *contributory factor* to war. The view that national leaders play a key role in determining whether or not their countries will engage in war is convincingly defended by Bueno de Mesquita in *The War Trap*, pp. 19–29.

8. See Kenneth Waltz, *Man, the State, and War* (New York: Columbia University, 1959), pp. 8–9. A primary advocate of the thesis that democracies are less likely to get involved in wars, especially with each other, is R.J. Rummel. A recent statement of

his view can be found in "Political Systems, Violence, and War" in W. Scott Thompson and Kenneth M. Jensen, *Approaches to Peace: An Intellectual Map* (Washington: U.S. Institute of Peace, 1991), pp. 350–70. For the opposing viewpoint on this issue see Steven Chan, "Mirror, Mirror on the Wall...," *Journal of Conflict Resolution*, Vol. 28, No. 4 (Dec. 1984), pp. 617–48.

9. The term "military-industrial complex" was coined by Malcolm Moos and popularized by President Eisenhower when he used it in 1961 in his farewell address. See Alvin R. Sunseri, "The Military-Industrial Complex in Iowa" in Benjamin F. Cooling (ed.), *War, Business, and American Society: Historical Perspectives on the Military-Industrial Complex* (Port Washington NY: Kennikat, 1977), p. 158. For a recent publication on the military-industrial complex in the U.S. see Gary Chapman and Joel Yudken (eds.), *Briefing Book on the Military-Industrial Complex* published by the Council for a Livable World Education Fund, 110 Maryland Ave NE, Washington DC 20002 in December 1992.

10. Anne Trotter, "Development of the Merchants-of-Death Theory" in Cooling, *War, Business, and American Society*, p. 96.

11. Trotter, "Development of the Merchants-of-Death Theory" in Cooling, *War, Business, and American Society*, pp. 97–98.

12. Trotter, "Development of the Merchants-of-Death Theory" in Cooling, *War, Business, and American Society*, p. 94.

13. Trotter, "Development of the Merchants-of-Death Theory" in Cooling, *War, Business, and American Society*, pp. 101–103.

14. Benjamin F. Cooling, "Introduction" in Cooling, *War, Business, and American Society*, p. 3.

15. See for example Seymour Melman (ed.), *The War Economy of the United States* (New York: St. Martin's, 1971).

16. See C. Wright Mills, *The Causes of World War Three* (New York: Simon and Schuster, 1958), pp. 17–19, 47–50, and 86–89.

17. Stagner, *Psychological Aspects of International Conflict*, p. 137.

18. For a good critical discussion of the thesis that war is caused by a few individuals seeking personal gain see Bernard Brodie, *War and Politics* (New York: Macmillan, 1973), pp. 283–302.

19. The best source for these basic ideas is *The Communist Manifesto* by Marx and Engels. The *Manifesto* along with other relevant selections can be found in *The Marx-Engels Reader*, ed. by Robert C. Tucker (New York: W.W. Norton, 1972) and in *Karl Marx: Selected Readings* (Oxford: Oxford University, 1977), ed. by David McLellan. See also Frederick Engels, *Herr Eugen Düring's Revolution in Science*, tr. by Emile Burns (New York: International, 1939), especially pp. 292–310.

20. V.I. Lenin, *Imperialism: The Highest Stage of Capitalism* (New York: International, 1939), especially pp. 9–14 and 76–98.

21. It has been argued by a Chinese Marxist, Chen Qimao, that the presence of multinational corporations has generated a new situation where wars between capitalist countries have become very unlikely and that such wars are no longer inevitable as Lenin maintained. See Chan Qimao, "War and Peace: A Reappraisal," *Beijing Review*, Vol. 29, No. 23 (June 9, 1986), pp. 18–25, especially pp. 19–22.

22. *Philosophy of Right*, tr. by T.M. Knox (Oxford: Clarendon, 1942), p. 295.

23. For a brief account of Bismarck's efforts and views see Ziegler, *War, Peace, and International Politics*, pp. 7–20.

24. For an attempt to show that there is a correlation between external war and domestic conflict in "polyarchic" (democratic) states see Jonathan Wilkenfeld, "Domestic and Foreign Conflict Behavior of Nations," *Journal of Peace Research*, Vol. 5 (1968), pp. 56–69. Wilkenfeld cites various earlier studies that had concluded that there was

no correlation between foreign conflict and domestic conflict such as Rudolph J. Rummell, "Dimensions of Conflict Behavior Within and Between Nations," *General Systems,* Vol. 8 (1963), pp. 1–50.

25. This letter is reprinted in John Somerville and Ronald E. Santoni (eds.), *Social and Political Philosophy* (Garden City NY: Doubleday, 1963), pp. 259–60.

26. Quincy Wright, *A Study of War,* abridged edition by Louise Leonard Wright, p. 428.

27. See Emery Reves, *The Anatomy of Peace* (New York: Harper, 1945; republished by Peter Smith, Publisher, Gloucester MA, 1969), pp. 144–47.

Chapter VII. The Value of War

1. It is surprising how widespread the tendency is to assume that since wars may have some supposed good consequence they are therefore fought in order to achieve that end. For example, in the list of 14 theories about the cause of war discussed by Walter S. Jones in *The Logic of International Relations,* 5th ed. (Boston: Little, Brown, 1985), pp. 396–435, two of them (the eleventh and the thirteenth) involve this mistake.

2. Frank B. Livingstone, "The Effects of Warfare on the Biology of the Human Species" in Fried, Harris, and Murphy, *War: The Anthropology of Armed Conflict and Aggression,* p. 5.

3. Some nations suffered more than others with the Soviet Union losing 9 percent of its population during that war while Germany lost 5 percent of its population, England and France about 1 percent, and the U.S. only .2 percent. See Livingston, "The Effects of Warfare" in Fried, Harris, and Murphy, *War: The Anthropology of Armed Conflict and Aggression,* p. 5.

4. Livingstone, "The Effects of Warfare" in Fried, Harris, and Murphy, *War: The Anthropology of Armed Conflict and Aggression,* p. 5.

5. Livingstone, "The Effects of Warfare" in Fried, Harris, and Murphy, *War: The Anthropology of Armed Conflict and Aggression,* p. 5. Frederick P. Thieme, discussant of Livingstone's paper at the 1967 symposium of the American Anthropological Association on the effects of war on the human species, agreed with Livingstone's judgment on this matter. See p. 16 on the Fried, Harris, and Murphy book.

6. Livingstone, "The Effects of Warfare" in Fried, Harris, and Murphy, *War: The Anthropology of Armed Conflict and Aggression,* pp. 6–8. Interestingly Livingstone is making the point that the genetic consequences are so slight that one need not be concerned that modern war has an *adverse* effect on the gene pool, an effect which might be expected when it is supposed that there is a tendency for the *better fit* persons to be called to serve in combat situations during war. Our concern in the text is the opposite view that war is *good* because then the less *fit* are less likely to survive and reproduce.

7. "The Biological Consequences of War" in Fried, Harris, and Murphy, *War: The Anthropology of Armed Conflict and Aggression,* p. 18.

8. The situation in earlier times among more primitive people may have been somewhat different. In fact, primitive warfare may have been an important factor in both population control and genetic selection. See Livingstone, "The Effects of Warfare" in Fried, Harris, and Murphy, *War: The Anthropology of Armed Conflict and Aggression,* pp. 8–11; Corning, "Human Violence" in Beitz and Herman, *Peace and War,* p. 126; and Stanislav Andreski, "Evolution and War," *Science Journal,* Vol. 7 (Jan. 1971), p. 91.

9. John Nef, "Political, Technological, and Cultural Aspects of War" in Ginsberg, *The Critique of War,* pp. 120–37, especially pp. 130–31.

10. "Military Research and the Economy: Burden or Benefit?", *The Defense Monitor,* Vol. 14, No. 1 (1985), pp. 1–8, and Lloyd J. Dumas, "The Military Burden

on the Economy," *Bulletin of the Atomic Scientists,* Vol. 42, No. 8 (Oct. 1986), p. 24.

11. See the graph on the inside front cover and the graph on page 80 of Paul A. Samuelson and William D. Nordhaus, *Economics,* 12th ed. (New York: McGraw-Hill, 1985).

12. See for example Marion Anderson, *The Empty Pork Barrel,* a booklet published by Employment Research Associates, Lansing, Michigan, in 1978, especially page 1, where it was noted that one billion dollars spent by the government would, on the average, generate 58,000 jobs for defense but would generate 76,000 jobs for teachers. For a critique of this study and others which denigrate military spending as a means of stimulating the economy, see Gordon Adams and David Gold, "Recasting the Military Spending Debate," *Bulletin of the Atomic Scientists,* Vol. 42, No. 8 (Oct. 1986), pp. 26–32. For an extended discussion of the impact of military spending on the economy see Ann Markusen, "The Militarized Economy," *World Policy Journal,* Vol. 3, No. 3 (Summer 1986), pp. 495–516, especially pp. 499–503.

13. Anderson, *The Empty Pork Barrel,* p. 1.

14. See the statement of Simon Ramo, cofounder of TRW, Incorporated, a company with heavy military involvement, cited in Lloyd J. Dumas, "The Military Burden on the Economy," *Bulletin of the Atomic Scientists,* Vol. 42, No. 8 (Oct. 1986), p. 25. The original source is Simon Ramo, *America's Technology Slip* (New York: Wiley, 1980), p. 251.

15. Dumas, "The Military Burden on the Economy," p. 25.

16. "Military Research and the Economy: Burden or Benefit?", *The Defense Monitor,* Vol. 14, No. 1 (1985), p. 4.

17. *Philosophy of Right,* p. 295.

18. From *The Political and Social Doctrine of Fascism* (tr. by Jane Soames) as reprinted in Somerville and Santoni, *Social and Political Philosophy,* p. 431.

19. Reprinted in Bramson and Goethals, *War: Studies from Psychology, Sociology, Anthropology,* pp. 21–31.

20. William James, "The Moral Equivalent of War" in Bramson and Goethals, *War: Studies from Psychology, Sociology, Anthropology,* p. 29. James seems naively optimistic in supposing that a government with so many people at its command would have them disinterestedly pursue justice rather than its own national interest. American Peace Corps volunteers are frequently disillusioned to find that they have become agents of American foreign policy rather than disinterested workers for justice. It is difficult to believe that things would be different under the program James proposes.

21. See Andrew Vayda, "Hypotheses About Functions of War" in Fried, Harris, and Murphy, *War, The Anthopology of Armed Conflict and Aggression,* p. 88.

22. *Newsweek,* Vol. 74, No. 4 (July 28, 1969), p. 54 and *Time,* Vol. 94, No. 4 (July 25, 1969), pp. 29–30.

23. Richard Lacayo, "Blood in the Stands," *Time,* Vol. 125, No. 23 (June 10, 1985), pp. 38–41.

Chapter VIII. Ideological Aspects of the Contemporary Situation

1. This phrase from *Critique of the Gotha Program* can be found in David McLellan (ed.), *Karl Marx: Selected Writings* (Oxford: Oxford University, 1977), p. 569 and in Robert C. Tucker (ed.), *The Marx-Engels Reader* (New York: W.W. Norton, 1972), p. 388.

2. Adam Smith (1723–1790) in *An Inquiry into the Nature and Causes of the Wealth of the Nations* (ed. by J.R. McCulloch, Edinburgh: Adam and Charles Black,

1863), Book IV, Chapter II, p. 199, poetically describes this operation of the market system as the working of an "invisible hand." The basic ideas of capitalism and the implications of its natural international dimensions are described by Smith in this work.

3. Although this view of history is fundamental in Marx's thought, the most sustained discussions of historical materialism occur in Frederick Engels, *Herr Eugen Düring's Revolution in Science,* trans. by Emile Burns (New York: International Publishers, 1939), pp. 292–310 and Frederick Engels, *Ludwig Feuerbach and the End of Classical German Philosophy* (trans. by Anonymous, Peking: Foreign Languages Press, 1976), pp. 38–59.

4. Marx and Engels seem to assume without argument that the dominant class in a mass-production society will be the factory workers (the proletariat). They fail to consider an alternative possibility, that the new dominant class will be the managers. The important role played by managers in both capitalist and socialist countries gives some plausibility to this alternative view. Such a view would also make the shift from individualistic capitalism to the collectivist type of production analogous to what Marx and Engels claim happened during earlier transitions. In no earlier shift did the oppressed class of the previous stage become the new ruling class. The new dominant class was always a new class brought into existence by the new mode of production. In the shift from small-scale manufacturing to mass production the new class which arises with decision-making power upon which both stockholders and factory workers depend is the managerial class.

5. This phrase from *Critique of the Gotha Program* can be found in David McLellan (ed.), *Karl Marx: Selected Writings* (Oxford: Oxford University, 1977), p. 569, and in Robert C. Tucker (ed.), *The Marx-Engels Reader* (New York: W.W. Norton, 1972), p. 388.

6. V.I. Lenin, *Imperialism: The Highest Stage of Capitalism* (New York: International, 1939), especially pp. 9–14 and 76–98.

7. David Lane, *Politics and Society in the U.S.S.R.* (New York: Random House, 1971), pp. 11–14.

8. Lane, *Politics and Society in the U.S.S.R.,* p. 129.

9. For a booklet which contains the original article plus a summary of the discussion of it held in July 1989 at the U.S. Institute of Peace see *A Look at "The End of History?"* edited by Kenneth M. Jensen, published by the U.S. Institute of Peace, 1550 M St. NW, Washington DC 20005.

10. This passage is on page 26 of the booklet mentioned in the previous note.

11. Fukuyama hints at this last point on page 34 of the aforementioned booklet.

12. Hans Kung, *Christianity and the World Religions* (New York: Doubleday, 1986), p. 353.

13. John G. Stoessinger, "The Great Religions in Peace and War," *Religious Humanism,* Vol. 15, No. 3 (Summer 1981), pp. 108–13.

14. Hans Kung, *Christianity and the World Religions,* p. 443.

15. Hans Kung, *Christianity and the World Religions,* p. 442.

16. See the *Journal of International Affairs,* Vol. 36, No. 2 (Fall/Winter 1982/83), pp. 187–328, which is devoted to the topic "Religion and Politics."

Chapter IX. National-Historical Aspects of the Contemporary Situation

1. See Robert Jervis, *Perception and Misperception in International Politics* (Princeton NJ: Princeton University, 1976), especially chapter 6. See also Ross Stagner, *Psychological Aspects of International Conflict* (Belmont CA: Wadsworth, 1967).

2. John A. Garraty, *A Short History of the American Nation* (New York: Harper and Row, 1971), pp. 346–47.

3. For details see *World Almanac, 1985*, pp. 656–58.

4. David W. Ziegler, *War, Peace, and International Politics*, 3rd ed. (Boston: Little, Brown, 1984), p. 139.

5. See Locke's *Second Treatise of Government: An Essay Concerning the True Original, Extent, and End of Civil Government*. It can be found as the second part of John Locke, *Two Treatises of Government*, edited by Peter Laslett, revised ed. (New York: The New American Library, 1965), pp. 305–477.

6. Hobbes's views on the absence of obligations to others in the state of nature are given in chapters 13–15 of his *Leviathan*. See *The English Works of Thomas Hobbes*, edited by Sir William Molesworth (London: John Bohn, 1839, reprinted 1966), Vol. 3, pp. 110–47.

7. Walter S. Jones, *The Logic of International Relations*, 5th ed. pp. 49–51. See also Michael Walzer, *Just and Unjust Wars: A Moral Argument with Historical Illustrations* (New York: Basic Books, 1977), pp. 51–63.

8. Frederick L. Schuman, *International Politics: Anarchy and Order in the World Society*, 7th ed. (New York: McGraw-Hill, 1969), pp. 198 and 449.

9. Jones, *The Logic of International Relations*, p. 62.

10. See Mikhail N. Pokrovskii, *Russia in World History*, ed. by Roman Szporluk, trans. by Roman and Mary Ann Szporluk (Ann Arbor: University of Michigan, 1970), pp. 95–102.

11. Pokrovskii, *Russia in World History*, pp. 78–80.

12. Donald W. Treadgold, *Twentieth Century Russia*, 5th ed. (Boston: Houghton Mifflin, 1981), pp. 76–84.

13. Treadgold, *Twentieth Century Russia*, pp. 20–21.

14. For maps showing Russia's expansion see *Encyclopaedia Britannica*, 15th ed. (1974), Vol. 16, pp. 55 and 80.

15. Sergei Pushkarev, *The Emergence of Modern Russia, 1801–1917*, trans. by Robert H. McNeal and Tova Yedlin (New York: Holt, Rinehart, and Winston, 1963), p. 363.

16. See Hedrick Smith, "Russia's Power Strategy: Reflections on Afghanistan" in *New York Times*, reprinted in *The Conduct of Soviet Foreign Policy*, 2nd ed., ed. by Erik P. Hoffmann and Frederick J. Fleron, Jr. (New York: Aldine, 1980), pp. 737–47, especially pp. 738–41.

17. See Helmut Sonnenfeldt, "Implications of the Soviet Invasion of Afghanistan for East-West Relations" in *NATO Review*, April 1980, reprinted in Hoffmann and Fleron, eds., *The Conduct of Soviet Foreign Policy*, pp. 748–55, especially pp. 749–50. See also the subsequent article in that volume, "Detente and Afghanistan" (pp. 756–61) by Raymond L. Garthoff.

18. Treadgold, *Twentieth Century Russia*, pp. 7–9.

19. Otto Hoetzsch, *The Evolution of Russia*, trans. by Rhys Evans (New York: Harcourt, Brace, & World, 1966), pp. 56–58.

20. Michael T. Florinsky, *Russia: A Short History*, 2nd ed. (Toronto: Collier-McMillan, 1964), pp. 417–20, 435–37, and 446–73.

21. Pokrovskii, *Russia in World History*, pp. 120–29.

22. Pokrovskii, *Russia in World History*, p. 114.

23. *Encyclopaedia Britannica*, 15th ed. (1974), Vol. 6, p. 426.

24. Vladimir Mshvenieradze, *Political Reality and Political Consciousness*, trans. by Margot Light and Ludmila Lezhneva (Moscow: Progress, 1985), pp. 308–310.

25. Pokrovskii, *Russia in World History*, pp. 204–10.

26. See Pertti Pesonen, "Living Beside the Soviets," *World Press Review*, Vol. 33, No. 8 (Aug. 1986), pp. 34–36.

27. John Somerville, "Marxism and War," in Robert Ginsberg (ed.), *The Critique of War: Contemporary Philosophical Explorations*, pp. 138–51.

28. For a presentation of the view that American foreign policy is based on U.S. economic interests see Harry Magdoff, *The Age of Imperialism: The Economics of U.S. Foreign Policy* (New York: Monthly Review, 1969).

29. Immanuel C.Y. Hsü, *The Rise of Modern China*, 2nd ed. (New York: Oxford University, 1975), p. 817.

30. For details see *Keesing's Record of World Events, 1991*, p. 38368.

31. For details see *Keesing's Record of World Events, 1991*, pp. 38372–73.

32. For details see *Keesing's Record of World Events, 1991*, p. 38654.

33. See *Keesing's Record of World Events, 1991*, p. 38656.

34. See *Keesing's Record of World Events, 1991*, p. 38655. For a good review of five informative books dealing with the events leading to the end of the Soviet Union, see Michael Mandelbaum, "The Fall of the House of Lenin," *World Policy Journal*, Vol. 10, No. 3 (Fall 1993), pp. 97–109.

35. Daniel Sneider, "Yeltsin's New Deal Reneges on Promises to Republics," *The Christian Science Monitor*, Nov. 5, 1993, pp. 1, 4, and Daniel Sneider and Wendy Sloan, "Yeltsin Stays the Course on Market Reforms, but Offers to Soften the Shock," *The Christian Science Monitor*, Dec. 23, 1993, pp. 1, 4.

36. For a history of Europe which perceptively observes the various shifts in ideas and powers see René Albrecht-Carré, *One Europe: The Historical Background of European Unity* (Garden City NY: Doubleday, 1965).

37. For more information see James R. Huntley, *Uniting the Democracies: Institutions of the Emerging Atlantic-Pacific System* (New York: New York University, 1980), p. 340 and pp. 66–74.

38. Huntley, *Uniting the Democracies*, pp. 56–66.

39. Huntley, *Uniting the Democracies*, p. 350. Spain joined in 1982. France withdrew in 1965 but has now rejoined. See Huntley, p. 112, note 56, for details.

40. Huntley, *Uniting the Democracies*, pp. 329–30.

41. Huntley, *Uniting the Democracies*, p. 99.

42. Huntley, *Uniting the Democracies*, pp. 99, 335, 351–52.

43. Huntley, *Uniting the Democracies*, pp. 99–103.

44. Huntley, *Uniting the Democracies*, pp. 103–04, 332, 346–47.

45. Huntley, *Uniting the Democracies*, pp. 87–92, 339, 341, 343, 348–49.

46. Huntley, *Uniting the Democracies*, pp. 129–30, 336, 350–51.

47. Ziegler, *War, Peace, and International Politics*, pp. 379–80.

48. Huntley, *Uniting the Democracies*, p. 355.

49. Huntley, *Uniting the Democracies*, p. 77.

50. For a scholarly discussion of the issues involved see George Ross, "After Maastricht: Hard Choices for Europe," *World Policy Journal*, Vol. 9, No. 3 (Summer 1992), pp. 487–513.

51. For a detailed discussion of the Maastricht meeting, see *Keesing's Record of World Events, 1991*, pp. 38657–38659.

52. See Godfrey Hodgson, "Grand Illusion: The Failure of European Consciousness," *World Policy Journal*, Vol. 10, No. 2 (Summer 1993), pp. 13–18.

53. See Ross, "After Maastricht," p. 501.

54. See István Ertl, "Lingva politiko debatita ĉe la Europa Parlamento," *Esperanto*, October 1993, p. 161.

55. Ruth Leger Sivard, *World Military and Social Expenditures, 1991*, pp. 50–59.

56. See Ezra F. Vogel, "Pax Nipponica?", *Foreign Affairs*, Vol. 64, No. 4 (Spring 1986), pp. 752–67.

57. Edwin O. Reischauer and Albert M. Craig, *Japan: Tradition and Transformation* (Boston: Houghton Mifflin, 1978), pp. 74–76, 79–80, 89–91, 116–24, 128–30, 135–36, 142–89. See also Herschel Webb, *An Introduction to Japan,* 2nd ed. (New York: Columbia University, 1957), pp. 24–35.

58. It is worth noting that even after the two atomic bombs and the entry of the Soviet Union into the war there was still some opposition to surrendering among the Japanese leaders. See Reischauer and Craig, *Japan: Tradition and Transformation,* p. 277.

59. Reischauer and Craig, *Japan: Tradition and Transformation,* pp. 280, 298, and 327–28 and Webb, *An Introduction to Japan,* pp. 53–54.

60. Vogel, "Pax Nipponica?", *Foreign Affairs,* Spring 1986, p. 755.

61. Jones, *The Logic of International Relations,* p. 92.

62. Reischauer and Craig, *Japan: Tradition and Transformation,* p. 285.

63. Webb, *An Introduction to Japan,* p. 84.

64. U.S. Arms Control and Disarmament Agency, *World Military Expenditures and Arms Transfer, 1985,* pp. 68, 81, and 85.

65. Vogel, "Pax Nipponica?", *Foreign Affairs,* Spring 1986, p. 756.

66. Reischauer and Craig, *Japan: Tradition and Transformation,* p. 323.

67. See Clayton Jones, "Hosokawa Speech Sets New Path for Japan," *The Christian Science Monitor,* Aug. 24, 1993, p. 3.

68. Ruth Leger Sivard, *World Military and Social Expenditures, 1993,* pp. 43–51.

69. *United Nations: Image and Reality* (New York: U.N. Dept. of Public Information, 1986), p. 18.

70. Immanuel C.Y. Hsü, *The Rise of Modern China,* 2nd ed. (New York: Oxford University, 1975), p. 3.

71. For a good brief description of this period see Jones, *The Logic of International Relations,* pp. 136–37.

72. Hsü, *The Rise of Modern China,* pp. 6–7, 130–31.

73. Hsü, *The Rise of Modern China,* pp. 131–41.

74. Jones, *The Logic of International Relations,* pp. 139–40.

75. Hsü, *The Rise of Modern China,* pp. 709–92.

76. Hsü, *The Rise of Modern China,* pp. 792–93.

77. Schuman, *International Politics,* pp. 349–50.

78. Schuman, *International Politics,* p. 550.

79. For details see Hsü, *The Rise of Modern China,* pp. 805–06 and 809–10. The Soviets even told American diplomats that Mao and his followers were not "real Communists." See Schuman, *International Politics,* p. 543.

80. Alberto Ronchey, *The Two Red Giants,* trans. by Raymond Rosenthal (New York: W.W. Norton, 1965), pp. 13–14, and Hsü, *The Rise of Modern China,* p. 794.

81. Ronchey, *The Two Red Giants,* p. 14, and Hsü, *The Rise of Modern China,* p. 815.

82. Hsü, *The Rise of Modern China,* pp. 832–34.

83. Ronchey, *The Two Red Giants,* p. 14 and Hsü, *The Rise of Modern China,* p. 815.

84. Hsü, *The Rise of Modern China,* pp. 812–13.

85. McNeill, *The Contemporary World,* p. 130, and Ronchey, *The Two Red Giants,* pp. 17, 46.

86. Ronchey, *The Two Red Giants,* pp. 17–18.

87. Ronchey, *The Two Red Giants,* pp. 73–74.

88. Ronchey, *The Two Red Giants,* pp. 18–19.

89. Hsü, *The Rise of Modern China,* p. 817.

90. Hsü, *The Rise of Modern China,* p. 817.

91. Hsü, *The Rise of Modern China,* pp. 817–18.

92. Hsü, *The Rise of Modern China,* p. 821.

93. Hsü, *The Rise of Modern China,* pp. 820–21.

94. Hsü, *The Rise of Modern China,* pp. 822–25.

95. Hsü, *The Rise of Modern China,* pp. 821, 823–34. For more details see Joseph Alsop, "Thoughts Out of China—I: Go Versus No-Go," *New York Times,* March 11, 1973, Sec. 6 *(Magazine),* pp. 31 and 100; also H.R. Haldeman, *Ends of Power,* p. 92. It is worth noting that the idea of attacking China's nuclear facilities may have earlier originated with U.S. President Kennedy! See page 31 of the Alsop article.

96. Hsü, *The Rise of Modern China,* pp. 786–89, 796–97.

97. Hsü, *The Rise of Modern China,* pp. 829–55.

98. Hsü, *The Rise of Modern China,* pp. 789, 831, 851–52.

99. Gerald Segal, "The Coming Confrontation between China and Japan," *World Policy Journal,* Vol. 10, No. 2 (Summer 1993), pp. 27–39.

100. *World Policy Journal,* Vol. 8, No. 4 (Fall 1991), p. 676.

101. See Sheila Tefft, "China's Leaders Vie for Place as Deng's Heir," *The Christian Science Monitor,* Aug. 23, 1993, pp. 1, 14.

102. Segal, "The Coming Confrontation between China and Japan," p. 27.

103. *The Meaning of the Twentieth Century* (New York: Harper and Row, 1964), pp. 1–2.

104. The term "North-South" has even been incorporated into the titles of special studies such as *North-South: A Program for Survival,* "The Report of the Independent Commission on International Development Issues Under the Chairmanship of Will Brandt" (Cambridge MA: MIT, 1980).

105. See John Cruickshank, "The Rise and Fall of the Third World: A Concept Whose Time Has Passed," in the *Toronto Globe and Mail,* reprinted in *World Press Review,* Feb. 1991, pp. 28–29.

106. Ruth Leger Sivard, *World Military & Social Expenditures, 1993,* pp. 46–49.

107. Sivard, *WMSE 1993,* pp. 43–45 designates as "developed countries" in 1990 the following: United States, Canada, Belgium, Denmark, France, Germany, Iceland, Italy, Luxembourg, Netherlands, Norway, Spain, United Kingdom (Britain), Bulgaria, Czechoslovakia, Hungary, Poland, Romania, Soviet Union, Austria, Finland, Ireland, Sweden, Switzerland, Israel, Japan, Australia, and New Zealand. A note indicates that new classifications are likely in the future, particularly for countries in Eastern Europe.

108. Robert A. Mortimer, *The Third World Coalition in International Politics* (New York: Praeger, 1980), p. 15, and Mario Rossi, *The Third World: The Unaligned Countries and the World Revolution* (New York: Funk and Wagnalls, 1963), p. 161.

109. Mortimer, *The Third World Coalition,* pp. 6–9.

110. Mortimer, *The Third World Coalition,* pp. 20–22.

111. Mortimer, *The Third World Coalition,* pp. 11–15.

112. Mortimer, *The Third World Coalition,* pp. 18–20.

113. Mortimer, *The Third World Coalition,* pp. 15–18.

114. Mortimer, *The Third World Coalition,* p. 16.

115. Mortimer, *The Third World Coalition,* pp. 2, 24–42.

116. For a list of all the LDC conferences held through 1979, see Mortimer, *The Third World Coalition,* pp. 143–44.

117. Mortimer, *The Third World Coalition,* pp. 33–34, 41, 70–71.

118. Mortimer, *The Third World Coalition,* pp. 43–73.

119. See John Tanner, "The Ogre of Deflation," *World Press Review,* Vol. 33, No. 10 (Oct. 1986), p. 15.

120. Instituto del Tercer Mundo (Juan D. Jackson 136, Montivideo 11200, Uruguay), *Third World Guide 93/94* (published in 1992), p. 80.

121. *Keesing's Record of World Events, 1992,* p. 39122.
122. *Keesing's Record of World Events, 1992,* p. 39122.
123. Dieter Heinrich, "World Federalists Welcome Adoption of U.N. Decade of International Law," *World Federalist News,* Nos. 14 & 15 (Dec. 1989), five-page "Special Report" inserted between pp. 6 and 7. (Published by WFM, Leliegracht 21, 1016 GR Amsterdam, The Netherlands.)
124. Lynn H. Miller, *Global Order: Values and Power in International Politics,* 2nd ed. (Boulder CO: Westview, 1990), pp. 85–86.
125. Heinrich, "World Federalists Welcome Adoption of U.N. Decade of International Law."
126. Miller, *Global Order,* pp. 146–52 and 163–67, especially pp. 164–65.

Chapter X. Economic Aspects of the Contemporary Situation

1. See for example Sivard, *WMSE 1993,* pp. 42–51.
2. Lester Brown and others, *State of the World, 1993* (New York: W.W. Norton, 1993), p. 11.
3. The ready availability of data for many countries leads us to use the "per capita GNP" even though it is not a wholly satisfactory measure of the material conditions of life. It will tend to exaggerate the differences between the developed and less developed countries because the Gross National Product (GNP) does not include goods made or services provided where no payment was made. The "per capita GNP" also gives no indication of how evenly or unevenly the income is distributed within a country. In order to have a better measure of the quality of life in less developed countries the Overseas Development Council, a nongovernmental organization in Washington, DC, has developed a new measure of welfare called the "Physical Quality of Life Index." The PQLI is a composite figure based on indexes for three widely used social indicators: the infant mortality rate, the life expectancy of a one-year-old child, and the literacy rate in that country. For more information about the "Physical Quality of Life Index" see Martin M. McLaughlin et al., *The United States and World Development: Agenda 1979* (New York: Praeger, 1979), pp. 129–44 and Morris D. Morris, *Measuring the Condition of the World's Poor: The Physical Quality of Life Index* (New York: Pergamon, 1979). To see the difference between per capita GNP and PQLI in measuring the gap between DCs and LDCs see John W. Sewell et al., *U.S. Foreign Policy and the Third World; Agenda 1985–86* (New Brunswick NJ: Transaction Books, 1985), pp. 213–29, especially p. 228. A question has also been raised about the appropriateness of using exchange rates to calculate the GDP of less developed countries. The U.N. International Comparison Programme (ICR) has developed an approach using the purchasing power of currencies (PPCs) instead of exchange rates for comparing economies. For details see World Bank, *World Development Report 1993* (World Bank, 1818 H St. NW, Washington DC 20433, 1993), pp. 307–08 and 296–97. The U.N. Development Programme (UNDP) in turn has combined these purchasing power figures with data on life expectancy and literacy to create a "human development index." For details and a critical evaluation of this effort (which puts Spain ahead of the U.S. and North Korea ahead of Brazil) see "Development Brief: The Human Condition" in *The Economist,* May 26, 1990, pp. 80–81.
4. These figures are from Sivard, *WMSE 1993,* pp. 46–51.
5. For the 1990 figures see Sivard, *WMSE 1993,* pp. 46–51. For the 1982 figures see Sivard, *WMSE 1985,* p. 38. Even though a division is made between developed and less developed countries, it should be realized that in actuality there is a continuum of different levels of development and wealth.

6. For a detailed account of the beginning of the industrial revolution see Christine Vialls, *The Industrial Revolution Begins* (Minneapolis: Lerner Publications, 1982).

7. For an extended account of the rationale for a New International Economic Order from the point of view of the less developed countries, see Jan Tinbergen (Coordinator), *RIO: Reshaping the International Order* [A Report to the Club of Rome] (New York: E.P. Dutton, 1976) and James B. McGinnis, *Bread and Justice: Toward a New International Economic Order* (New York: Paulist, 1979).

8. See James R. Huntley, *Uniting the Democracies: Institutions of the Emerging Atlantic-Pacific System* (New York: New York University, 1980), pp. 95–98.

9. William A. Rugh, "Saudi Arabia," *The Wilson Quarterly,* Vol. 3, No. 1 (Winter 1979), pp. 60–61.

10. In 1990 the per capita GNP was $12,797 for Britain, $9,160 for Ireland, $625 for Bolivia, and $498 for Indonesia. Sivard, *WMSE 1993,* pp. 46–51.

11. McLaughlin, *U.S. and World Development: Agenda 1979,* p. 176 and Hughes, *World Futures,* p. 85. According to data provided by Sivard, *WMSE 1993,* p. 42, the ratio between the per capita GNP of the developed countries as a group and the LDCs as a group can be calculated to be 15.38 to 1 in 1960, 16.16 to 1 in 1970, 15.34 to 1 in 1980, and 17.06 to 1 in 1990.

12. Lester Brown, *The Twenty-Ninth Day* (New York: W.W. Norton, 1978), especially pp. 242–71.

13. One of the most optimistic forecasts of the future of the less developed countries is that given by Herman Kahn and his associates at the Hudson Institute in their book *The Next 200 Years* (New York: William Morrow, 1976). In that book it is argued that the less developed countries will develop much more rapidly than the present developed countries did. Kahn's optimistic forecast is "that the current 100–1 ratio of per capita product between the wealthiest 10 percent and the poorest 20 percent of the world population could shrink to about 5–1 after 200 years, give or take a factor of two or three" (pp. 55–57). Mention of a factor of three suggests that it might take 600 years to get this ratio! And if we look at the absolute figures projected by Kahn rather than merely the ratios, we get a very different perspective. In 1975 the average income for the wealthiest 10 percent of the world's population was about $7,000 while for the poorest 20 percent it was about $70 per person, a difference of $6,930. According to the very optimistic projections of Kahn and his associates, in 200 years the figures would be $45,000 per person for the richest 10 percent and $9,000 per person for the poorest 20 percent, a difference of $36,000. The ratio would be less but the *gap* between the rich and poor would be much greater *in absolute terms* than it was in 1975. Incidentally, these figures are in constant dollars, so the projected upward shift is due entirely to increased productivity and not inflation. It should be noted that the authors of this forecast admit (p. 57) that population growth in the less developed countries might not fall off as rapidly as projected so that the 100 to 1 ratio between richest and poorest might persist for 200 years! Even Kahn's optimistic forecast does not portray a very bright future for the poorer countries.

14. Nicholas Raymond, "The 'Lost Decade' of Development: The Role of Debt, Trade, and Structural Adjustment," *The U.S. National Committee for World Food Day,* October 1991, pp. 1–14; reprinted in Robert M. Jackson, ed., *Global Issues 93/94* (Guilford CT: Dushkin, 1993), pp. 112–21.

15. William R. Rhodes, "Third-World Debt: The Disaster that Didn't Happen," *The Economist,* Sept. 12, 1993, pp. 21–23; reprinted in Robert M. Jackson, ed., *Global Issues 93/94,* pp. 138–40.

16. World Bank, *World Development Report 1993* (World Bank, 1818 H St. NW, Washington DC 20433, 1993), p. 297. In 1970 the ratio was 5.79 to 1. See McLaughlin, *U.S. and World Development: Agenda 1979,* p. 182.

17. World Bank, *World Development Report 1993*, p. 297.

18. World Bank, *World Development Report 1993*, pp. 296–97.

19. For further explanation and more examples see Paul A. Samuelson and William D. Nordhaus, *Economics*, 12th ed. (New York: McGraw-Hill, 1985), pp. 565–70.

20. Samuelson and Nordhaus, *Economics*, pp. 564, 568–70.

21. Samuelson and Nordhaus, *Economics*, p. 568.

22. Sivard, *WMSE 1982*, p. 19.

23. Sivard, *WMSE 1993*, pp. 5 and 25.

24. These and other figures in this paragraph are from *The Military Balance 1993–1994* published by the International Institute for Strategic Studies, 23 Tavistock St., London WC2E 7NQ, 1993, pp. 224–28. Six developed countries also spend less than 1 percent or less of their GNP for military purposes (Austria, Estonia, Japan, Kyrgystan, Latvia, Lithuania) while Iceland has no military expenditures of any kind.

25. Sivard, *WMSE 1993*, p. 43.

26. Sivard, *WMSE 1993*, p. 43.

27. These percentages are calculated from the raw data on economic aid, $19.103 million in 1960 and $49.928 million in 1990, provided by Sivard, *WMSE 1993*, p. 43.

28. World Bank, *World Development Report 1993*, p. 274. The proportion the U.S. gave to foreign aid in 1991 was 0.2 percent of GNP, the lowest rate for richer countries except for Ireland which gave 0.19 percent.

29. For a recent statement on the problem of the distribution of wealth at the global level see *North-South: A Program of Survival*, the report of the Independent Commission on International Development Issues under the chairmanship of Willy Brandt (Cambridge MA: MIT, 1980). On page 4 of this report it is noted that "the military expenditure of only half a day would suffice to finance the whole malaria eradication programme of the World Health Organization. . . ."

30. A good succinct statement on the relation between poverty and guerrilla warfare is Vladimir Dedijer's "Guerrilla Warfare: The Poor Man's Power" in Beitz and Herman, *Peace and War*, pp. 41–49.

31. *World Press Review*, January 1994, p. 5.

32. Sivard, *WMSE 1993*, p. 20.

33. Sivard, *WMSE 1993*, p. 21.

Chapter XI. Military Aspects of the Contemporary Situation

1. Sheldon Novick, "The Secret of the Atom Bomb," *Environment*, Vol. 18, No. 6 (July/Aug. 1976), p. 10. The first bomb had been used in the test at Alamagordo, New Mexico. Novick notes that two other bombs were made and then immediately exploded in 1946 (pp. 11–12). The U.S. had only a very few atomic bombs on hand in 1947 and didn't have a model suitable for mass production until 1948 (p. 16). This same information is presented by Novick in his book *The Electric War: The Fight Over Nuclear Power* (San Francisco: Sierra Club, 1976), pp. 15–17 and 24–30. The information that the U.S. had no atomic bombs in reserve after dropping two on Japan is also given by Bernard Brodie in *War and Politics*, pp. 51–52. For more information on the slow buildup of the U.S. atomic arsenal see Michio Kaku and Daniel Axelrod, *To Win a Nuclear War: The Pentagon's Secret War Plans* (Boston: South End, 1986), pp. 43–44.

2. For a discussion of this point see *World Armaments and Disarmament: SIPRI Yearbook 1981*, pp. 38–45.

3. Gwynne Dyer, *War* (Homewood IL: Dorsey Press, 1985), p. 181, quotes Mar-

shal Oleg A. Losik of the Malinovsky Armored Forces Academy in Moscow as saying in 1982, "We know that since 1945 nineteen nuclear strikes have been considered in Washington—four against the Soviet Union." Joseph Gerson, *The Deadly Connection: Nuclear War and U.S. Intervention* (Philadelphia: New Society, 1986), p. 11, says, "The public record now reveals more than twenty occasions when U.S. Presidents threatened to resort to nuclear war during crises." The specific occasions are discussed by Gerson on pp. 10–13 of that book as well as by Barry M. Blechman, Stephen S. Kaplan, and others in *Force Without War: U.S. Armed Forces as a Political Instrument* (Washington: Brookings Institution, 1978), pp. 47–49.

4. Avner Cohen, "Did Nukes Nudge the PLO?" *The Bulletin of the Atomic Scientists,* Vol. 49, No. 10 (Dec. 1993), pp. 11–13, especially p. 13.

5. Nuclear weapons are measured in terms of the equivalent explosive power of a given number of tons of TNT. The Hiroshina bomb was equivalent to 12,000–14,000 tons (12–14 kilotons) of TNT. Some hydrogen bombs have been produced which have an explosive force equivalent to 25,000,000 tons (25 megatons) of TNT.

6. Novick, "The Secret of the Atom Bomb" in *Environment,* p. 16.

7. *The Defense Monitor,* Vol. 4, No. 2 (Feb. 1975), p. 1.

8. The U.S. total of nuclear warheads peaked at 32,000 in 1967. See William Arkin, Thomas Cochran, and Milton Hoenig, "The U.S. Nuclear Stockpile" in *Arms Control Today,* Vol. 12, no. 4 (April 1982), p. 2. The peak for the Soviet Union was probably 1986. See Sivard, *WMSE 1993,* p. 16.

9. Sivard, *WMSE 1993,* p. 16.

10. International Institute for Strategic Studies, *The Military Balance 1993–1994,* p. 118.

11. David Albright, "South Africa Comes Clean," *The Bulletin of the Atomic Scientists,* Vol. 49, No. 4 (May 1993), pp. 3–5 and David Albright, "A Proliferation Primer," *The Bulletin of the Atomic Scientists,* Vol. 49, No. 5 (June 1993), pp. 14–23, especially p. 20. See also International Institute for Strategic Studies, *The Military Balance 1993–1994,* pp. 231–32.

12. IISS, *The Military Balance 1993–1994,* p. 231.

13. IISS, *The Military Balance 1993–1994,* p. 232.

14. "Science and the Citizen," *Scientific American,* Vol. 229, No. 4 (Oct. 1973), p. 47.

15. *World Armaments and Disarmament: SIPRI Yearbook 1981,* pp. 22–23.

16. Kosta Tsipis, "Cruise Missiles," *Scientific American,* Vol. 236, No. 2 (Feb. 1977), pp. 20–29.

17. For a detailed description of the technological aspects of a strategic defense system see James C. Fletcher, "Technologies for Strategic Defense," *Issues in Science and Technology,* Vol. 1, No. 1 (Fall 1984), pp. 15–29, or John A. Adam and Paul Wallich, "SDI: The Grand Experiment," *IEEE Spectrum,* Sept. 1985, pp. 36–64).

18. For an informed but critical examination of SDI see Robert Bowman's *Star Wars: Defense or Death Star* published in 1985 by the Institute of Space and Security Studies, 5115 Hwy A1A South, Melbourne Beach FL 32951.

19. Adam and Wallich, "SDI," *IEEE Spectrum,* Sept. 1985, p. 45.

20. For a detailed discussion of the agreement and how it has been maintained despite occasional violations, see James Eayrs, "Arms Control on the Great Lakes," *Disarmament and Arms Control,* Vol. 2, No. 4 (Autumn 1964), pp. 372–404.

21. Hans Wehberg, *The Limitation of Armaments,* trans. by Edwin Zeydel (Washington DC: Carnegie Endowment for International Peace, 1921), pp. 23–25.

22. Wehberg, *The Limitation of Armaments,* pp. 26–28.

23. *Encyclopaedia Britannica,* 15th ed. (1974), "Naval Ships and Craft," Vol. 12, p. 894.

24. Information about this treaty and the other treaties discussed in the text can be found in Sivard, *WMSE 1993*, pp. 34–36 and International Institute for Strategic Studies, *The Military Balance 1993–1994*, pp. 229–34. For the texts of these arms control agreements and the names of countries which have signed/ratified them see *1990 Edition, Arms Control and Disarmament Agreements: Texts and History of Negotiations*, U.S. Arms Control and Disarmament Agency (US ACDA, Washington DC 20451).

25. See US ACDA, *1990 Edition, Arms Control and Disarmament Agreements*, pp. 45–47.

26. For a record of the voting on this resolution see p. 19 of the booklet *The Test Ban Conference: Summary of the Proceedings and Analysis* written by Carolyn Cottom, Lisa Evanson, and Aaron Tovish and published by The U.S. Test Ban Coalition, 1000 16th St. NW, Suite 810, Washington DC 20036. For more information about this conference see the whole booklet mentioned in the previous sentence and also the March 1991 issue of *Global Action*, the newsletter of Parliamentarians for Global Action, 211 E 43rd St., Suite 1604, New York NY 10017.

27. International Institute for Strategic Studies, *The Military Balance 1993–1994*, pp. 233–34.

28. *Disarmament Newsletter* of the World Disarmament Campaign, Vol. 10, No. 3 (June 1992), p. 5. This newsletter was published by the UN Office of Disarmament Affairs, Room S-3150, United Nations NY 10017.

29. *Disarmament Newsletter* of the UN Centre for Disarmament Affairs, Vol. 11, No. 2 (Nov. 1993), p. 6. This newsletter was published by the Centre for Disarmament Affairs, Room S-3151, United Nations, New York NY 10017.

30. *Disarmament Newsletter* of the UN Centre for Disarmament Affairs, Vol. 11, No. 2 (Nov. 1993), p. 7.

31. Sivard, *WMSE 1993*, p. 35.

32. *Disarmament Newsletter* of the UN Centre for Disarmament Affairs, Vol. 11, No. 2 (Nov. 1993), pp. 2 and 13.

33. IISS, *The Military Balance 1993–1994*, pp. 250–51.

34. IISS, *The Military Balance 1993–1994*, p. 250.

35. IISS, *The Military Balance 1993–1994*, pp. 249–50 and *Keesing's Record of World Events 1993*, p. 39297.

36. Sivard, *WMSE 1993*, p. 35.

37. IISS, *The Military Balance 1993–1994*, p. 249 and Sivard, *WMSE 1993*, p. 35.

38. IISS, *The Military Balance 1993–1994*, pp. 246–47.

39. IISS, *The Military Balance 1993–1994*, pp. 247–49.

40. IISS, *The Military Balance 1993–1994*, p. 247 and Sivard, *WMSE 1993*, p. 35.

41. *The Interdependent*, Vol. 19, No. 3 (Fall 1993), p. 7. *The Interdependent* is a publication of UNA-USA, 485 Fifth Ave., New York NY 10017.

42. "The Grand Forks Pyramid," *Nation*, Vol. 221, No. 20 (Dec. 13, 1975), p. 613.

43. The text of the SALT II Treaty can be found in US ACDA, *1990 Edition, Arms Control and Disarmament Agreements*, pp. 267–300.

44. For a good summary account of these events leading up to the Intermediate Nuclear Forces (INF) Treaty, see *Keesing's Record of World Events, 1987*, pp. 35601–06. See also pp. 34971–74 in that same volume.

45. *Keesing's Record of World Events, 1987*, p. 35601 and *1988*, p. 35939.

46. *Keesing's Record of World Events, 1987*, p. 35602 and Sivard, *WMSE 1993*, p. 35.

47. *Keesing's Record of World Events, 1991*, p. 38320.
48. The provisions of START I are summarized in *Keesing's Record of World Events, 1991*, p. 38320.
49. *Keesing's Record of World Events, 1992*, p. 39169.
50. *Keesing's Record of World Events, 1992*, p. 39216.
51. *Keesing's Record of World Events, 1992*, p. 38890.
52. *Keesing's Record of World Events, 1992*, p. 38937 and International Institute for Strategic Studies, *The Military Balance 1993–1994*, pp. 229–30.
53. IISS, *The Military Balance 1993–1994*, p. 229.
54. IISS, *The Military Balance 1993–1994*, pp. 229–30.
55. *Keesing's Record of World Events, 1993*, p. 39393.
56. For details of this treaty see *Keesing's Record of World Events, 1993*, pp. 39296–97 and IISS, *The Military Balance 1993–1994*, pp. 230–31.
57. *Keesing's Record of World Events, 1990*, p. 37838.
58. *Keesing's Record of World Events, 1991*, p. 38027.
59. *Keesing's Record of World Events, 1991*, pp. 38313–14.
60. *Keesing's Record of World Events, 1991*, p. 38601.
61. *Keesing's Record of World Events, 1992*, p. 38922.
62. *Keesing's Record of World Events, 1992*, p. 38986.
63. *Keesing's Record of World Events, 1992*, p. 39301.
64. IISS, *The Military Balance 1993–1994*, pp. 245–46 and 252.
65. *Keesing's Record of World Events, 1992*, p. 38841.
66. IISS, *The Military Balance 1993–1994*, p. 247.
67. See Seymour J. Deitchman, *New Technology and Military Power: General Purpose Military Forces for the 1980s and Beyond* (Boulder CO: Westview, 1979).
68. Bernard Brodie, *War and Politics* (New York: Macmillan, 1973), p. 51.
69. See John Cox, *Overkill: Weapons of the Nuclear Age* (New York: Thomas Y. Crowell, 1977), pp. 62–66.
70. Barry E. Fridling, "Lasers Highlight Policy Blindspots," *The Bulletin of the Atomic Scientists*, Vol. 44, No. 6 (July/August 1988), pp. 36–39.
71. Philip Morrison and Paul F. Walker, "A New Strategy for Military Spending," *Scientific American*, Vol. 230, No. 4 (Oct. 1978), pp. 56–57.
72. Morrison and Walker, "A New Strategy for Military Spending," *Scientific American*, pp. 55–60. See also "Battlefield of the 1990s," *U.S. News and World Report*, Vol. 83, No. 1 (July 4, 1977), pp. 48–50 and "One Shot, One Kill: A New Era of 'Smart' Weapons," *U.S. News and World Report*, Vol. 102, No. 10 (March 16, 1987), pp. 28–35.
73. See John Bell's review of Manuel De Landa's *War in the Age of Intelligent Machines* (MIT Press, 1992) entitled "Smart Kills" in *The Bulletin of the Atomic Scientist*, Vol. 49, No. 5 (June 1993), p. 54.
74. See graphs in Deitchman, *New Technology and Military Power*, pp. 60, 81, 106, 131, 225, 244, and 252.
75. William Wilson, "Chemical and Biological Welfare," *In Depth: A Journal for Value and Public Policy*, Vol. 3, No. 2 (Spring 1993), pp. 112–13.

Chapter XII. Institutional Aspects of the Contemporary Situation

1. Schuman, *International Politics*, pp. 219–24.
2. Poland was unable to send a representative to the San Francisco conference but

was permitted to sign as the fifty-first charter member. The other charter members were Argentina, Australia, Belgium, Bolivia, Brazil, Byelorussian Soviet Socialist Republic, Canada, Chile, China, Colombia, Costa Rica, Cuba, Czechoslovakia, Denmark, Dominican Republic, Ecuador, Egypt, El Salvador, Ethiopia, France, Greece, Guatemala, Haiti, Honduras, India, Iran, Iraq, Lebanon, Liberia, Luxembourg, Mexico, Netherlands, New Zealand, Nicaragua, Norway, Panama, Paraguay, Peru, Philippines, Saudi Arabia, South Africa, Syria, Turkey, Ukrainian Soviet Socialist Republic, Union of Soviet Socialist Republics, United Kingdom, United States of America, Uruguay, Venezuela, and Yugoslavia. Byelorussian S.S.R. and Ukrainian S.S.R. were not really separate countries at that time but they were allowed separate votes as one of the compromises which made the U.N. possible.

3. For detailed information about the U.N. see Moshe Y. Sachs (ed.), *The United Nations: A Handbook on the United Nations: Its Structure, History, Purposes, Activities, and Agencies* (New York: Wiley, 1977) and *Everyone's United Nations: A Handbook on the Work of the United Nations,* 10th ed. (New York: U.N. Dept. of Public Information, 1986, distr. by Bernan-Unipub, 10033-F.M.L. King Hwy, Lanham, MD 20706).

4. *Keesing's Record of World Events, 1993,* p. R88. This article contains detailed information about the recent history and situation of Belau as of the middle of 1993.

5. For information about the difficult situation of indigenous peoples see Bernard Nietschmann, "Third World War: The Global Conflict over the Rights of Indigenous Nations" in *Cultural Survival Quarterly* (11 Divinity Ave., Cambridge MA 01238), reprinted in *Utne Reader,* Nov.-Dec. 1988, pp. 84–91 and then reprinted in Robert M. Jackson, ed., *Global Issues 92/93* (Guilford CT 06437, 1992), pp. 168–72. On the same issue see also Alan Thein Durning, "Supporting Indigenous Peoples" in Lester R. Brown and others, *State of the World 1993* (New York: W.W. Norton, 1993), pp. 80–100.

6. Even then problems may arise. For example, the U.S. has agreed to commit itself in advance to the jurisdiction of the Court, but the Connally Amendment to the Senate's acceptance of the Statutes of the International Court of Justice indicates that the U.S. will not accept this jurisdiction in cases which the U.S. (rather than the Court) decides fall within its domestic jurisdiction. Many other nations have also adopted "Connally-type" reservations to their acceptance of the Statutes.

7. For wording of Security Council Resolution 678 see *Keesing's Record of World Events 1990,* p. 37870.

8. For a detailed account of the Gulf War against Iraq see *Keesing's Record of World Events 1991,* pp. 37982–90.

9. For a review of U.N. peacekeeping operations up to 1985 see United Nations Department of Public Information, *The Blue Helmets: A Review of United Nations Peace-keeping* (New York: U.N., 1985). For a good historical behind-the-scenes account of the many conflicts where the U.N. has been involved see Max Harrelson, *Fires All Around the Horizon: The U.N.'s Uphill Battle to Preserve the Peace* (New York: Praeger, 1989). For a briefer review plus a critical discussion of issues related to U.N. peacekeeping efforts see Michael Renner, "Preparing for Peace" in Lester R. Brown and others, *State of the World 1993* (New York: W.W. Norton, 1993), pp. 139–57, especially pp. 150–56. For a brief but comprehensive overview of U.N. peacekeeping operations as of mid–1993 see International Institute for Strategic Studies, *The Military Balance 1993–1994,* pp. 253–60.

10. U.N. Dept. of Public Information, *The Blue Helmets.* See foreword by Javier Pérez de Cuéllar.

11. For a succinct but thorough history of developments in the Middle East since 1917 see *The Middle East,* 6th ed. (Congressional Quarterly, 1414 22nd St. NW, Washington, DC 20037, 1986), pp. 7–17.

12. Harrelson, *Fires All Around the Horizon*, p. 63.

13. U.N. Department of Public Information, *Everyone's United Nations*, 10th ed. (New York: U.N., 1986), pp. 124–26.

14. U.N., *Everyone's United Nations*, pp. 136–39; Harrelson, *Fires All Around the Horizon*, pp. 119–32; and U.N. Department of Public Information, *The Blue Helmets: A Review of United Nations Peace-keeping* (New York: U.N., 1985), pp. 213–57.

15. Harrelson, *Fires All Around the Horizon*, pp. 149–51 and U.N., *The Blue Helmets*, pp. 303–16.

16. U.N., *The Blue Helmets*, pp. 188–97.

17. U.N., *The Blue Helmets*, pp. 259–300.

18. U.N., *The Blue Helmets*, pp. 166–69.

19. Harrelson, *Fires All Around the Horizon*, pp. 181–84.

20. For a report on how this project got underway see Ethan Schwartz, "Namibia: Birth of a Nation," *The Interdependent*, Vol. 15, No. 1 (Winter 1989), pp. 1, 3.

21. *Keesing's Record of World Events 1990*, pp. 37296–97 and 37562–63.

22. See Robert Rotberg, "Namibia Eschews Intolerance," *The Christian Science Monitor*, Aug. 2, 1993, p. 18.

23. For a view of this project as it was beginning, see Ethan Schartz, "The U.N. Inching Toward Cambodia," *The Interdependent*, Vol. 16, No. 1 (Spring 1990), pp. 1–2, 6. For a view just before the elections, see Kathy Chenault, "Cambodian Campaign Closes Amid Concerns of Violence," *The Christian Science Monitor*, May 21, 1993, pp. 1, 4. For a view just after the elections, see Kathy Chenault, "Large Voter Turnout Bodes Well for Cambodians Tired of War," *The Christian Science Monitor*, June 1, 1993, p. 7.

24. Institute for Strategic Studies, *The Military Balance 1993–1994*, pp. 255–56.

25. See Kathy Chenault, "Cambodia Agreement Eases Pressure on UN," *The Christian Science Monitor*, June 17, 1993, p. 7.

26. See Kathy Chenault, "Cambodia: Victory at the Ballot Box, but Threat of War Lingers," *The Christian Science Monitor*, Oct. 6, 1993, p. 11 and "Cambodia Fights Back," *The Christian Science Monitor*, Dec. 23, 1993, p. 20.

27. For a table listing dates, budgets, and number of personnel in U.N. peace-keeping efforts as of the end of 1992, see Michael Renner, "Preparing for Peace" in Lester R. Brown and others, *State of the World, 1993*, p. 151. For a list of peacekeeping efforts being carried on in the middle of 1993, not only by the U.N. but also by other international organizations, see International Institute for Strategic Studies, *The Military Balance 1993–1994*, pp. 253–60. For a list of U.N. peacekeeping efforts in operation at the beginning of October 1993 see "The U.N.: Keeping the Peace the World Over," *The Christian Science Monitor*, Oct. 6, 1993, pp. 10–11.

28. *Keesing's Record of World Events, 1993*, pp. 39609, 39650–51, and R108–09 and *The Christian Science Monitor*, Oct. 6, 1993, pp. 10–11.

29. *Keesing's Record of World Events, 1993*, pp. 39582–83.

30. For a discussion of this point with Elliott Richardson, see "Our Man in Managua," *The Interdependent*, Vol. 16, No. 1 (Spring 1990), pp. 1, 6.

31. *Keesing's Record of World Events, 1989*, p. 37038 and *1990*, pp. 37236–37.

32. For details of the planning for this referendum see Marian Hout, "U.N. Prepares for Western Sahara Referendum," *The Interdependent*, Vol. 17, No. 3 (June–July 1991), pp. 1, 6. For information about obstacles the project ran into, see Leonard Doyle, "U.N. Stumbles in Western Sahara," *The Interdependent*, Vol. 18, No. 2 (Spring 1992), p. 3.

33. *Keesing's Record of World Events, 1992*, pp. 39128–29 and 39178.

34. International Institute for Strategic Studies, *The Military Balance 1993–1994*, pp. 257–58.

35. *Keesing's Record of World Events, 1992*, pp. 39225–26.

36. *Keesing's Record of World Events, 1993*, pp. 39356 and 39451.

37. See "Conflict in the Former Yugoslavia" in *Washington Newsletter*, Dec. 1992, pp. 1–6 (published by Friends Committee on National Legislation, 245 Second St. NE, Washington DC 20002-5795).

38. *Keesing's Record of World Events, 1991*, pp. 38373–76 and 38420–22.

39. FCNL *Washington Newsletter*, Dec. 1992, pp. 2–3.

40. *Keesing's Record of World Events, 1992*, pp. 38832–33 and International Institute of Strategic Studies, *The Military Balance 1993–1994*, p. 256.

41. *Keesing's Record of World Events, 1992*, pp. 38970–71.

42. *Keesing's Record of World Events, 1993*, pp. 39469–71.

43. See Trevor Rowe, "The Growth—and Limits—of U.N. Peacekeeping," *The Interdependent*, Vol. 18, No. 3 (Summer 1992), pp. 1, 6 and Edmund Piasecki, "South Africa: More Hard Lessons for U.N. Peacekeeping," *The Interdependent*, Vol. 19, No. 2 (Summer 1993), pp. 1, 6.

44. Based on summing up the costs of the various separate operations provided in "The U.N.: Keeping the Peace the World Over," *The Christian Science Monitor*, Oct. 6, 1993, pp. 10–11.

45. This idea is presented in Ronald J. Glossop's "Improving U.N. Peacekeeping," *Transnational Perspectives*, Vol. 15, No. 2 (1989), pp. 14–18, especially pp. 16–17.

46. See Institute for Strategic Studies, *The Military Balance 1993–1994*, pp. 258–60.

47. This 53-page booklet is available from the Department of Public Information, United Nations, New York NY 10017.

48. *Keesing's Record of World Events, 1992*, p. 39240.

49. See Jonathan Landay, "U.S. Troops Arrive in Macedonia to Keep Watch on Serbian Border," *The Christian Science Monitor*, July 7, 1993, pp. 1, 4.

50. Inis L. Claude, Jr., *Swords Into Plowshares: The Problems and Progress of International Organization*, 3rd ed. rev. (New York: Random House, 1964), p. 343.

51. Harrelson, *Fires All Around the Horizon*, pp. 215–16.

52. Sivard, *WMSE 1978–88*, p. 28.

53. Sivard, *WMSE 1991*, p. 20.

54. Russell M. Dallen, Jr., "Curtain Rises on 48th General Assembly," *The Interdependent*, Vol. 19, No. 3 (Fall 1993), p. 1.

55. Steven A. Dimoff, "Congress's Budget-cutting Fervor Threatens U.S. Standing at U.N," *The Interdependent*, Vol. 19, No. 3 (Fall 1993), p. 6.

56. "Cutting Unnecessary Military Spending: Going Further and Faster," *The Defense Monitor*, Vol. 21, No. 3 (1993), p. 1.

57. The texts of these documents plus a great deal of related information on human rights can be found in Robert Woito (ed.), *International Human Rights Kit* (World Without War Publications, 421 So. Wabash, Chicago IL 60605, 1977) and also in Burns Weston, Richard Falk, and Anthony D'Amato (ed.), *Basic Documents in International Law and World Order* (St. Paul MN: West, 1980).

58. Donald A. Henderson, "Smallpox—Epitaph for a Killer?", *National Geographic*, Vol. 154, No. 6 (Dec. 1978), pp. 796–805.

59. Article 71 of the U.N. Charter reads as follows: "The Economic and Social Council may make suitable arrangements for consultation with non-governmental organizations which are concerned with matters within its competence. Such arrangements may be made with international organizations and, where appropriate, with national organizations after consultation with the Member of the United Nations concerned." (*Everyone's United Nations*, p. 443.)

60. See *Everyone's United Nations*, p. 20.

61. St. Louis *Post-Dispatch*, July 14, 1986, pp. 1, 12.

62. *United Nations Monthly Chronicle,* Vol. 15, No. 6 (June 1978), p. 27, and Vol. 15, No. 7 (July 1978), p. 4.

63. *Washington Newsletter,* No. 397 (Nov. 1977) of the Friends Committee on National Legislation, 245 Second St. NE, Washington DC 20002, p. 6. Eisenhower made this comment in London on August 31, 1959.

64. *Esperanto,* No. 960 (Dec. 1985), pp. 201–04 and *Esperanto,* No. 1054 (Dec. 1993), pp. 201–03. *Esperanto* is published by the Universala Esperanto-Asocio, Nieuwe Binnenweg 176, 3015 BJ Rotterdam, Netherlands.

Chapter XIII. Legal Aspects of the Contemporary Situation

1. The discussion of international law in this chapter is confined to that part which deals with the relations between nations and which is called *public international law.* Not discussed here is that other part of international law, *private international law,* which deals with private persons and property in international situations where there are problems about which national government has jurisdiction and which national laws are applicable.

2. For a short discussion of the early development of international law, see Frederick L. Schuman, *International Politics,* 7th ed. (New York: McGraw-Hill, 1969), pp. 67–71. For a discussion of the principles of international law, see pp. 115–48 of the same work.

3. Article 10 of the League Covenant says: "The Members of the League undertake to respect and preserve as against external aggression the territorial integrity and existing political independence of all Members of the League. In case of any such aggression or in case of any threat or danger of such aggression, the Council shall advise upon the means by which this obligation shall be fulfilled." (From Schuman, *International Politics,* p. 711.)

4. The U.N. Charter reads as follows:

Article 41. The Security Council may decide what measures not involving the use of armed force are to be employed to give effect to its decisions, and it may call upon the Members of the United Nations to apply such measures. These may include complete or partial interruption of economic relations and of rail, sea, air, postal, telegraphic, radio, and other means of communication, and the severance of diplomatic relations.

Article 42. Should the Security Council consider that measures provided for in Article 41 would be inadequate or have proved to be inadequate, it may take such action by air, sea, or land forces as may be necessary to maintain or restore international peace and security. Such action may include demonstrations, blockade, and other operations by air, sea, or land forces of Members of the United Nations.

Article 43. 1. All Members of the United Nations, in order to contribute to the maintenance of international peace and security, undertake to make available to the Security Council, on its call and in accordance with a special agreement or agreements, armed forces, assistance and facilities, including rights of passage, necessary for the purpose of maintaining international peace and security. 2. Such agreement or agreements shall govern the numbers and types of forces, their degree of readiness and general location, and the nature of the facilities and assistance to be provided. 3. The agreement or agreements shall be negotiated as soon as possible on the initiative of the Security Council. They shall be concluded between the Security Council and Members or between the Security Council and groups of Members and shall be subject to ratification by the signatory states in accordance with their respective constitutional processes. (*Everyone's United Nations,* pp. 437–38.)

5. Woito, *International Human Rights Kit,* pp. 90–91, and Burns Weston,

Richard Falk, and Anthony D'Amato (eds.), *Basic Documents in International Law and World Order,* pp. 210–11 (for both, see note 16 for Chapter XII).

6. The U.N. General Assembly directed its Law Commission to "formulate the principles of international law recognized in the Charter of the Nürnberg Tribunal and in the judgment of the Tribunal." The seven principles formulated can be found in Woito, *International Human Rights Kit,* p. 76.

7. Schuman, *International Politics,* p. 147n.

8. *Keesing's Record of World Events, 1993,* p. 39490.

9. For a good introduction to the ideas and issues related to an international criminal court see Bryan F. MacPherson, *An International Criminal Court: Applying World Law to Individuals* (Monograph #10 published by Center for U.N. Reform Education, 418 Seventh St. SE, Washington DC 20003 in 1992). For more lengthy explorations of the issue see U.N. General Assembly—International Law Commission, *Historical Survey of the Question of International Criminal Jurisdiction* (Lake Success NY: U.N., 1949) and Julius Stone and Robert K. Woetzel (eds.), *Toward a Feasible International Criminal Court* (Geneva: World Peace through Law Center, 1970). For a very detailed inquiry into the issue see Benjamin B. Ferencz, *International Criminal Court: A Step Toward World Peace,* 2 vols. (Bobbs-Ferry NY: Oceana, 1980). For contemporary discussions of the pros and the cons of the issue and current developments see M.C. Bassiouni, "The Time Has Come for an International Criminal Court," *Indiana International and Comparative Law Review,* Vol. 1, Nos. 1–2 (1991), pp. 1–44 and Michael P. Scharf, "The Jury Is Still Out on the Need for an International Criminal Court," *Duke Journal of Comparative and International Law,* Vol. 1, No. 1 (1991), pp. 135–68.

10. For a more comprehensive overview of the evolution of international law see Benjamin B. Ferencz, *A Common Sense Guide to World Peace* (New York: Oceana, 1985), pp. 1–42.

11. For a book-length argument for this thesis see Francis Anthony Boyle, *World Politics and International Law* (Durham NC: Duke University Press, 1985).

12. Rules for warfare were first advanced by Hugo Grotius in his *On the Law of War and Peace* (1625). They have been developed by various conventions, the most important of which are the Geneva Conventions (developed at meetings in 1864, 1929, and 1949) and the two Hague Conventions (1899 and 1907). Other conventions such as the Convention on Genocide (1948) and the one protecting cultural property (1954) also apply to wartime situations. The laws of war also include rules about the treatment and obligations of neutrals. For a more detailed account, see "War, Laws of" in *Encylopaedia Britannica,* 15th ed. (1974), Vol. 19, pp. 538–42 and Schuman, *International Politics,* pp. 134–39.

13. See the Preamble and Article 2 of the U.N. Charter. *Everyone's United Nations,* pp. 429–31.

14. See *Everyone's United Nations,* p. 457.

15. Schuman, *International Politics,* pp. 220–21.

Chapter XIV. Reforming the Attitudes of Individuals

1. A moving plea for greater effort on the part of the U.S. in educating its people about other cultures and about world affairs can be found in Edwin O. Reischauer, *Toward the 21st Century: Education for a Changing World* (New York: Alfred A. Knopf, 1973).

2. For an eloquent and moving statement of this viewpoint, see Robert Muller, *The Birth of a Global Civilization* (published by World Happiness and Cooperation, P.O. Box 1153, Anacortes WA 98221, 1991).

3. A good brief introduction to the life and teachings of Gandhi is Louis Fischer's

Gandhi: His Life and Message for the World (New York: New American Library, 1954). For an overview of Gandhi's thought see Joan V. Bondurant, *Conquest of Violence: The Gandhian Philosophy of Conflict* (Princeton NJ: Princeton University, 1958) and the selections from Gandhi's writings in *All Men Are Brothers,* ed. by K. Kripalani (Weare NH: Greenleaf Books, 1982). For an introduction to the life and teachings of Martin Luther King, Jr., one might well begin with his own *Stride Toward Freedom: The Montgomery Story* (New York: Harper and Row, 1958). On pp. 102–07, King gives his own presentation of the basic principles of the philosophy of nonviolent resistance. For current information about teaching nonviolence contact the Martin Luther King, Jr. Center for Nonviolence, 1707 Rodney Drive, Los Angeles CA 90027.

4. For a philosophical discussion of this idea see Herbert Spiegelberg, "Ethics for Fellows in the Fate of Existence" in Peter Bertocci (ed.), *Mid-Twentieth Century Philosophy* (Atlantic City Highlands NJ: Humanities, 1974), pp. 193–210.

5. One such pledge, composed by Lillian Genser of Wayne State University in Detroit, goes as follows:

I pledge allegiance to the world, To cherish every living thing,
To care for earth and seas and air, With peace and justice everywhere.

6. For more information, contact Dorothy Schneider, P.O. Box 78189, St. Louis MO 63178-8189.

7. For more information about the UNICEF collection, contact U.S. Committee for UNICEF, 331 E. 38th Street, New York NY 10016.

8. The term "humatriotism" was formulated by Theodore Lentz of St. Louis. See Note 1 for Chapter IV.

9. *African Genesis* (New York: Dell, 1967), p. 256.

10. *Civilization and Its Discontents* (New York: Norton, 1930), p. 61.

11. *Multiple Loyalties: Theoretical Approach to a Problem in International Organization* (Princeton NJ: Princeton University's Center for Research on World Political Institutions, 1955), pp. 49–50.

12. An approach along these lines is suggested by William James in his essay "The Moral Equivalent of War" which is reprinted in Bramson and Goethals, *War: Studies from Psychology, Sociology, Anthropology,* pp. 21–31.

13. For more information about Esperanto, contact the Esperanto League for North America, Box 1129, El Cerrito CA 94530 or Universala Esperanto-Asocio, Nieuwe Binnenweg 176, 3015 BJ Rotterdam, Nederlando. It is worth mentioning that UNESCO has passed resolutions recognizing the value of Esperanto in 1954, 1985 and 1993. A recent informative article about Esperanto is Israel Shenker's "Doing Away with All Babble from the Tower of Babel" in *Smithsonian* Vol. 17, No. 10 (Jan. 1987), pp. 113–25.

14. See Mario Pei, *One Language for the World* (New York: Devin-Adair, 1958) for a book-length treatment of this issue.

15. For example, consider the contents of the book *Many Voices, One World* (London: Kogan Page; New York: Unipub; and Paris: UNESCO, 1980), which is a report of the International Commission for the Study of Communication Problems appointed in 1977 by Amadou-Mahtar M'Bow, Director-General of UNESCO, and headed by Sean McBride. This Commission analyzed language and communication problems only from the point of view of national governments and did not mention Esperanto or even the idea of a single international language for everyone. It is unbelievable that an international commission set up by a U.N. agency to study communication problems can manage not even to address itself to this crucial issue.

16. It is noteworthy that both the Boy Scouts and the Girl Scouts offer a merit badge for citizenship in the world to those scouts who fulfill the appropriate requirements as well as badges for citizenship in the community and citizenship in the nation.

Chapter XV. Reforming the Internal Operation of National Governments

1. Such views about the desirability of democracy as a way of reducing the likelihood of war go back at least to the eighteenth-century philosophers Rousseau, Montesquieu, and Kant. See Michael E. Howard, *War and the Liberal Conscience* (New Brunswick NJ: Rutgers University, 1978), pp. 23–28. For a recent statement of this view, see R.J. Rummel, "Political Systems, Violence, and War" in W. Scott Thompson and Kenneth M. Jensen (eds.), *Approaches to Peace: An Intellectual Map* (Washington: U.S. Institute of Peace, 1991), pp. 350–70.

2. Wright, *A Study of War*, Vol. 2, pp. 843–48.

3. For support of this statement on the basis of public reactions in the U.S. during the Vietnamese War, see Robert W. Tucker, *A New Isolationism: Threat or Promise* (New York: Universe Books, 1972), pp. 99–101.

4. Schuman, *International Politics*, pp. 220–21.

5. R.J. Rummel, "As Though a Nuclear War. The Death Toll of Absolutism," *International Journal on World Peace*, Vol. 5, No. 3 (July-Sept. 1988), pp. 27–43. The quotation is from p. 40.

6. Rummel, "As Though a Nuclear War," *Int'l Journal on World Peace*, p. 28.

7. Rummel, "As Though a Nuclear War," *Int'l Journal on World Peace*, p. 39.

8. Rummel, "As Though a Nuclear War," *Int'l Journal on World Peace*, p. 39.

9. Gene Sharp in *Exploring Nonviolent Alternatives* (Boston: Porter Sargent, 1970) lists 85 cases of nonviolent action (pp. 115–23) and indicates that slightly more than 60 percent occurred under dictatorships. With regard to success, Sharp says only that "in some of these cases the nonviolent actionists partly or fully succeeded in achieving the desired objectives" (p. 122).

10. For a collection of articles on nonviolent resistance, see Severyn T. Bruyn and Paula M. Rayman (eds.), *Nonviolent Action and Social Change* (New York: Irvington, 1979). A classic on all phases of nonviolent resistance is Gene Sharp, *The Politics of Nonviolent Action* (3 vols.) (Boston: Porter Sargent, 1973).

11. See Thomas Weber, "The Marchers Simply Walked Forward Until Struck Down," *Peace and Change*, Vol. 18, No. 3 (July 1988), pp. 267–89, especially pp. 276–79.

12. See Fred Halliday, "The Iranian Revolution: Uneven Development and Religious Populism," *Journal of International Affairs*, Vol. 36, No. 2 (Fall/Winter 1982/83), pp. 187–207, especially p. 190 and Ralph Summy, "The Efficacy of Nonviolence: Examining 'The Worst Case Scenario,'" *Peace Research*, Vol. 25, No. 2 (May 1993), pp. 1–19, especially pp. 8–9.

13 Richard Deats, "The Philippines: The Nonviolent Revolution That Surprised the World" in Robert L. Holmes (ed.), *Nonviolence in Theory and Practice* (Belmont CA: Wadsworth, 1990), pp. 203–06.

14. See Adam Roberts, *Civil Resistance in the East European and Soviet Revolutions* (Monograph #4 published by the Albert Einstein Institution, 1430 Massachusetts Ave., Cambridge MA 02138, 1992). See also Summy's comments in "The Efficacy of Nonviolence," *Peace Research*, Vol. 25, No. 2 (May 1993), pp. 9, 11, and 16.

Chapter XVI. Reforming the Policies of National Governments

1. For a carefully worked out and well-documented defense of this proposition see Bueno de Mesquita, *The War Trap* (New Haven CT: Yale Univ. Press, 1981).

2. For a discussion of this point see Walter S. Jones, *The Logic of International Relations,* 5th ed. (Boston: Little, Brown, 1985), pp. 282–86.

3. Since the term "transarmament" has been used to refer to both of these approaches, it will be less confusing if we do not use it for either. "Transarmament" is used to describe the shift from offensive to defensive weaponry by Dietrich Fischer, *Preventing War in the Nuclear Age* (Totowa NJ: Rowman and Allanheld, 1984), pp. 7–8, 26, 106, 108–11, 199, 221–22, while that term is also used for the shift from military to nonmilitary efforts by Gene Sharp, whose views are advanced by the Association for Transarmament Studies (see note 11 below).

4. Johan Galtung, *There Are Alternatives: Four Roads to Peace and Security* (Nottingham, England: Russell, 1984, distributed in the U.S. by Dufour Editions, Chester PA 19425), p. 173.

5. Galtung, *There Are Alternatives,* pp. 176–77.

6. Galtung, *There Are Alternatives,* pp. 177–78.

7. Fischer, *Preventing War in the Nuclear Age,* p. 67.

8. Galtung, *There Are Alternatives,* pp. 180–81.

9. Galtung notes that reliance on strictly defensive forces means that nations would not be able to do a great deal to help one another. See *There Are Alternatives,* pp. 180–81.

10. Galtung in fact proposes that civilian-based defense be used in conjunction with conventional military defense and paramilitary defense. See *There Are Alternatives,* pp. 177–80.

11. Gene Sharp, "Making the Abolition of War a Realistic Goal." This essay was originally published in the December 1980 newsletter of the World Without War Issues Center—Midwest. It was reprinted as a separate booklet by the Institute for World Order as a result of winning the Wallach Awards Competition for 1979–80 and is also reprinted in Carolyn M. Stephenson (ed.), *Alternative Methods for International Security* (Washington: University Press of America, 1982), pp. 127–40. See also Gene Sharp, "Civilian-Based Defense as a Peace Strategy," *Peace and Change,* Vol. 7, No. 4 (Fall 1981), pp. 53–58, and his "National Defense Without Armaments," *War/Peace Report,* Vol. 10, No. 4 (April 1970), pp. 3–10 (reprinted in Beitz and Herman, *Peace and War,* pp. 349–67). Gene Sharp's books explaining and defending the civilian defense idea include *Exploring Nonviolent Alternatives* (Boston: Porter Sargent, 1970); *The Politics of Nonviolent Action* (3 vols., Boston: Porter Sargent, 1973); *Social Power and Political Freedom* (Boston: Porter Sargent, 1980); *Making Europe Unconquerable* (London: Taylor and Francis, 1985); and *Civilian-Based Defense: A Post-Military Weapons System* (Princeton: Princeton Univ. Press, 1990). More succinct statements can be found in *National Security Through Civilian-Based Defense* published by the Association for Transarmament Studies, 3636 Lafayette Ave., Omaha NE 68131 and *Defense Without War? The Status of Civilian-Based Defense in the World Today* (Occasional Paper No. 6 published by Matsunaga Institute for Peace, University of Hawaii, 2424 Maile Way, Porteus 717, Honolulu HA 96822, 1993).

12. For a restrained but cogent response to Sharp's proposal, see Michael Walzer, *Just and Unjust War: A Moral Argument with Historical Illustrations,* pp. 329–35. See also Thomas C. Schelling, "Some Questions on Civilian Defense" originally printed in Adam Roberts (ed.), *Civilian Resistance as a National Defense* (Harrisburg: Stackpole, 1968), pp. 302–08 and reprinted in Beitz and Herman, *Peace and War,* pp. 368–74.

13. See Plinio Prioreschi, *Man and War* (New York: Philosophical Library, 1987). Relevant excerpts can be found in Melvin Small and J. David Singer (eds.), *International War: An Anthology*, 2nd ed. (Chicago: Dorsey Press, 1989), pp. 396–403.

14. Schuman, *International Politics*, p. 248.

15. Schuman, *International Politics*, p. 248.

16. *Everyone's United Nations*, p. 430.

17. US ACDA, *1982 Edition, Arms Control and Disarmament Agreements*, p. 159.

18. US ACDA, *1982 Edition, Arms Control and Disarmament Agreements*, p. 160.

19. *New York Times*, Sept. 21, 1961, p. 10. These same principles are incorporated in House Concurrent Resolution 392 introduced in the U.S. House of Representatives on August 5, 1982, by Congressman George Brown of California.

20. See his *An Alternative to War or Surrender* (Urbana IL: University of Illinois, 1962). A more recent statement by Osgood entitled "Disarmament Demands GRIT" is reprinted in Weston, *Toward Nuclear Disarmament*, pp. 337–44. It was originally published in *Planet Earth*, newspaper of Planetary Citizens, in Spring 1981.

21. The latter formulation is used by Osgood in his preface to the 1970 edition of *An Alternative to War or Surrender* and in "Disarmament Demands GRIT" (note 20).

22. Amatai Etzioni, "The Kennedy Experiment," *The Western Political Quarterly*, Vol. 20 (1967), pp. 361–80 (reprinted in Amatai Etzioni and Martin Wenglinsky (eds.), *War and Its Prevention* (New York: Harper and Row, 1970), pp. 215–42. Etzioni has also developed his own general presentation of the gradual-tension-reduction approach in his book *The Hard Way to Peace: A New Strategy* (New York: Collier Books, 1962).

23. Etzioni, "The Kennedy Experiment," *West. Pol. Quart.*, pp. 368–69.

24. Etzioni, "The Kennedy Experiment," *West. Pol. Quart.*, pp. 367–68.

25. For a succinct review of the issues and various views related to this question, see Stanley Hoffmann, *Duties Beyond Borders: On the Limits and Possibilities of Ethical International Politics* (Syracuse NY: Syracuse University, 1981), pp. 10–27. Hoffmann himself rejects the prevalent view. See pp. 190–91 of his book for a summary of his own position.

26. The work describing the classical experiments with boys on the value of cooperative projects in overcoming group antagonism is Muzafer Sherif's *In Common Predicament* (Boston: Houghton Mifflin, 1966).

27. See Robert Bowman, *Star Wars*, pp. 73–74, and Carol Rosin, "Cooperation in Space: An Alternative to Star Wars" in *Breakthrough*, Vol. 6, No. 2 (Winter 1985), pp. 1–4 (published by Global Education Associates, Suite 570, 475 Riverside Dr., New York NY 10115).

28. During the Cold War Detroit area teacher Henry Paley made the suggestion that a better way of securing mutual deterrence between the U.S. and the Soviet Union would be to have a million U.S. children in the Soviet Union and a million Soviet children in the U.S. as hostages who would be killed in case of a nuclear attack. To insure that the scheme would work, many of the children would have to be close relatives of decision-makers in both societies. Paley's idea was originally published in *The Metro Times* of Detroit in June 1984. The article is reprinted in Small and Singer, *International War: An Anthology*, 2nd ed., pp. 309–13.

29. See Joseph V. Montville, "Transnationalism and the Role of Track-Two Diplomacy" in Thompson and Jensen, *Approaches to Peace*, pp. 255–69, especially p. 262.

30. Montville, in Thompson and Jensen, *Approaches to Peace*, pp. 262–64.

31. Ziegler, *War, Peace, and International Politics*, pp. 297–98 and Schuman, *International Politics*, p. 141.

32. Schuman, *International Politics*, p. 156.

33. Schuman, *International Politics*, p. 154.

34. Robert L. Butterworth, *Managing Interstate Conflict, 1945–74: Data with Synopses* (Pittsburgh: University Center for International Studies, 1976), pp. 131–32.

35. Butterworth, *Managing Interstate Conflict,* pp. 94–96.

36. Butterworth, *Managing Interstate Conflict,* pp. 392–93.

37. Butterworth, *Managing Interstate Conflict,* pp. 235–37.

38. *New York Times,* Dec. 6, 1977, p. 8, and Jan. 26, 1978, p. 6.

39. *The Interdependent,* Vol. 10, No. 5 (Sept./Oct. 1984), p. 5.

40. Butterworth, *Managing Interstate Conflict,* pp. 341–44.

41. See *Time,* Vol. 114, No. 22 (Nov. 26, 1979), pp. 62–64.

42. For a succinct statement of the philosophy behind this conflict-management-using-international-organization approach to peace, see Robert L. Butterworth, *Moderation from Management: International Organization and Peace* (Pittsburgh: University Center for International Studies, 1978), pp. 1–14 and 120–26.

43. For a summary of the mostly unsuccessful efforts by regional organizations to manage international conflicts see Ziegler, *War, Peace, and International Politics,* pp. 202–07.

44. *Keesing's Record of World Events, 1991,* p. 37935.

45. *Keesing's Record of World Events, 1990,* p. 37871.

46. See Michael Renner, "Preparing for Peace" in Lester R. Brown and others, *State of the World 1993,* p. 156.

47. Butterworth, *Moderation from Management,* pp. 62–63. See pp. 33–71 for a detailed account of the record of the U.N. in managing various types of conflict situations.

48. Butterworth, *Moderation from Management,* p. 66.

49. Butterworth, *Moderation from Management,* p. 66.

50. Butterworth, *Moderation from Management,* p. 67.

51. This 53-page booklet is available from the Department of Public Information, United Nations, New York NY 10017.

52. See Michael Renner, "Preparing for Peace" in Brown and others, *State of the World 1993,* p. 154. For information on efforts to implement this proposal for a U.N. Surveillance System, contact War Control Planners, Inc., Box 19127, Washington DC 20036.

53. For further details of such a proposal see Grenville Clark and Louis Sohn, *World Peace Through World Law,* 3rd ed. enlarged (Cambridge MA: Harvard University, 1966), pp. xxv, 379–92, and 415–47.

54. For an editorial arguing that the U.S. should support this kind of individually recruited standing U.N. force see Michael Ignatieff, "The High Price of Gunboat Diplomacy," originally in the weekly "Observer" of London and reprinted in *World Press Review,* Vol. 40, No. 3 (March 1993), p. 13.

55. For a discussion of this idea see Ronald J. Glossop, "Improving U.N. Peacekeeping," *Transnational Perspectives,* Vol. 15, No. 2 (1989), pp. 14–18, especially p. 17.

56. United Nations Educational, Scientific, and Cultural Organization, *Peace Research: Trend Report and World Directory* (Paris: UNESCO, 1978–79), p. 26.

57. UNESCO, *Peace Research,* pp. 35–222.

58. UNESCO, *Peace Research,* pp. 21–24.

59. UNESCO, *Peace Research,* pp. 54–55, 79–80, 85–86, 87–93, 98–100, 126–27, 147–48, 166–67.

60. The address is U.S. Institute of Peace, 1550 M Street, N.W., Washington DC 20005.

61. Kenneth Boulding, *The Meaning of the Twentieth Century* (New York: Harper and Row, 1964), p. 103. Information about current efforts is available from the

International Peace Research Association, Paul Smaker, Antioch College, Yellow Springs OH 45387.

62. *War* (Homewood IL 60430: Dorsey Press, 1985), p. 159. This point is developed very well in the videotape "Good-Bye War," the final program of the series *War* written and narrated by Dyer for the Canadian Broadcasting Company in 1983.

Chapter XVII. Reforming the International System

1. See Silviu Brucan, "The Establishment of a World Authority: Working Hypotheses," *Alternatives: A Journal of World Policy,* Vol. 8, No. 2 (Fall 1982), reprinted in Weston, *Toward Nuclear Disarmament and Global Security: A Search for Alternatives* (Boulder CO: Westview, 1984) , pp. 615–28.

2. I am indebted to the Campaign for U.N. Reform, 418 7th St. SE, Washington DC 20003 for several of the ideas in this section. A good summary of proposals for reforming the U.N. is a report prepared by the Foreign Affairs and National Defense Division of the Congressional Research Service, Library of Congress, for the Committee on Foreign Relations of the U.S. Senate (96th Congress, 1st Session) entitled "Reform of the United Nations: An Analysis of the President's Proposals and Their Comparison with Proposals of Other Countries." This report was published in October 1979 by the U.S. Government Printing Office in Washington DC.

3. D. Evan T. Luard, *The Control of the Sea-Bed: A New International Issue* (London: Heineman, 1974), p. 35.

4. Luard, *The Control of the Sea-Bed,* pp. 30 and 114–46.

5. Luard, *The Control of the Sea-Bed,* pp. 139–42 and 146–49. The Conference, which met periodically from 1973 to 1982, was actually the third international conference on the law of the sea, the first having been held in 1958 and the second in 1960. The first conference, held in Geneva, generated four conventions covering matters such as definitions of terms, rights and responsibilities in the various "zones" of the ocean, conservation of the living resources of the high seas, and ownership of the continental shelf by the coastal state, but none of these conventions has been accepted by a majority of the nations of the world. For a history of the three law of the sea conferences, see Luard, *The Control of the Sea-Bed,* pp. 29–48, 83–96, and 127–68.

6. *The Interdependent,* Vol. 10, No. 5 (Sept./Oct. 1984), p. 5.

7. See Hilary French, "Strengthening Global Environmental Governance," in Lester R. Brown and others, *State of the World 1992,* p. 159 and "Milestone for Law of Sea Treaty," *The Interdependent,* Vol. 19, No. 4 (Winter 1993–94), p. 4. For up-to-date news related to the Law of the Sea Treaty and other aspects of ocean law see the monthly newsletter published by the Council on Ocean Law, 1709 New York Ave. SE, Washington DC 20007.

8. "The Struggle for Antarctica's Riches," *World Press Review,* Vol. 24, No. 12 (Dec. 1977), pp. 21–23.

9. In Dec. 1979 the U.N. General Assembly accepted the draft of an agreement covering the Activities of States on the Moon and Other Celestial Bodies and asked the Secretary-General to open the Agreement for signature and ratification. Article 11 of the Agreement declares that "the moon and its natural resources are the common heritage of mankind" and calls for the establishment of "an international regime . . . to govern the exploitation of the natural resources of the moon as such exploitation is about to become feasible." For more details see *Keesing's Contemporary Archives,* May 2, 1980, pp. 30226–28 and *The United Nations Treaties on Outer Space* (New York: United Nations Publications, 1984), pp 27–37.

10. Richard Hudson, "Time for Mutations in the United Nations," *Bulletin of the Atomic Scientists,* Vol. 32, No. 9 (Nov. 1976), p. 40.

11. Clark and Sohn, *World Peace Through World Law,* pp. 513–15 (see note 53 for Chapter XVI).

12. See Lionel Penrose, "The Elementary Statistics of Majority Voting," *Journal of the Royal Statistical Society,* Vol. 109 (1946), pp. 53–57.

13. Hudson, "Time for Mutations in the United Nations," *Bulletin of Atomic Scientists,* pp. 39–43. Hudson's later modification of his "Binding Triad" proposal can be found in *Global Report,* No. 18 (Nov./Dec. 1984) published by the Center for War-Peace Studies, 218 E. 18th St., New York NY 10003. It is reprinted in Small and Singer, *International War,* pp. 322–30. The latest version is given in *Global Report,* No. 36 (Fall 1992). There are other international organizations, such as the International Monetary Fund and the European Parliament, where voting is weighted rather than being one vote per nation, so establishing such a system in the General Assembly would not be without precedent.

14. There are a couple of exceptions to the principle that the U.N. and its various programs must be funded by contributions from national governments. For example, individual persons can contribute to UNICEF and to the U.N. Special Account, a fund used at the discretion of the Secretary-General, usually to help refugees.

15. For a detailed discussion of this idea, see Dieter Heinrich, *The Case for a United Nations Parliamentary Assembly,* published in 1992 by the World Federalist Movement (777 U.N. Plaza, New York NY 10017). For updated information contact Dieter Heinrich, 199 Pearson Avenue, Toronto, Ontario M6R 1G6 Canada or Jeffrey Segall, 308 Cricklewood Lane, London NW2 2PX, United Kingdom.

16. For details see Bryan F. MacPherson, *An International Criminal Court: Applying World Law to Individuals* (Monograph #10 published in 1992 by the Center for U.N. Reform Education, 418 Seventh St. SE, Washington DC 20003).

17. Norman Alcock et al., *1982* (Oakville, Ontario: Canadian Peace Research Institute Press, 1978), pp. 141, 146–60.

18. Alan Newcombe, "A World Peace-Makers Association of Nations," and Norman Alcock and Arnold Simoni, "Peacemakers Association of Nations." Copies of both these articles are available from Peace Research Institute–Dundas, 25 Dundana Ave., Dundas, Ontario L9H 4E5.

19. The information in this paragraph is from Beverly Woodward, "Nonviolent Struggle, Nonviolent Defense, and Nonviolent Peacemaking," *Peace and Change,* Vol. 7, No. 4 (Fall 1981), pp. 62–63, and Carolyn Stephenson, "Alternative Methods for International Security: A Review of the Literature" in the same volume. Johansen's proposal is described in Robert C. Johansen and Saul H. Mendlovitz, "The Role of Enforcement of Law in the Establishment of a New International Order: A Proposal for a Transnational Police Force," *Alternatives,* VI (1980), 307–37, especially 335–37. Those interested in learning more about present efforts to establish a nonviolent peacemaking force can contact Peace Brigades International, 333 Valencia St. Suite 330, San Francisco CA 94103 or METTA, P.O. Box 183, Tomales CA 94971, phone (707) 878-2369 or Peace Brigades International, Box 381233, Cambridge MA 02238, phone (617) 491-4226.

20. For a view of American history in the 1780s as a model for the formation of a federal world government, see Carl Van Doren, *The Great Rehearsal* (New York: Viking, 1948; republished by Viking-Penguin, 1986).

21. Clarence Streit, *Union Now* (printed privately in 1938; then published by Harper Brothers in New York in 1939 with an enlarged postwar edition by the same publisher in 1948). Streit's view is being promoted by the Association to Unite the Democracies, 1506 Pennsylvania Ave SE, Washington DC 20003. A study which is somewhat related to Streit's proposal is *Political Community and the North Atlantic Area* by Karl W. Deutsch and others (Princeton NJ: Princeton University, 1957; and New York: Greenwood, 1969).

22. Streit apparently had no qualms about the racial policies of the Union of South Africa since he includes that country in his list of places where federal democracy has been tried and worked (*Union Now,* p. 6) and includes it as one of the 15 founder democracies of the Union of the Free (p. 9).

23. It is worth noting that at present state governments in the United States likewise do not need to concern themselves with defense against possible attacks from other states and that after a world government had been established national governments would no longer need to maintain military forces for defense.

24. On the increasing size of political communities see Hornell Hart and Donald Taylor, "Was There a Prehistoric Trend from Smaller to Larger Political Units?" *The American Journal of Sociology,* Vol. 49, No. 4 (Jan. 1944), 289–301; Hornell Hart, *Can World Government Be Predicted by Mathematics? A Preliminary Report* (Ann Arbor MI: Edwards Brothers, Inc. lithoprinted in 1944, 16 pp.); and Hornell Hart, "The Logistic Growth of Political Areas," *Social Forces,* Vol. 26, No. 4 (May 1948), 396–408. If the "circumscription" theory of the origin of the state put forth by Robert Carneiro is correct, then the expanding of the world's population coupled with modern means of transportation and global limits on where people can successfully reside makes the creation of a single world state inevitable. See Robert L. Carneiro, "A Theory of the Origin of the State," *Science,* Vol. 169 (21 August 1970), pp. 733–38.

25. The idea of a world government brought about through the agreement of the leaders of all nations rather than by conquest seems to have been first advanced in 1623 by Parisian monk Eméric Crucé in a book entitled *The New Cineas* (trans. by C. Frederick Farrell, Jr., and Edith R. Farrell, New York and London: Garland, 1972). The idea of a world government brought about by consent has also been espoused by philosophers such as Rousseau, Kant, Bentham, and Russell and noted scientists such as Einstein. For a brief history of early advocates of world government, see Schuman, *International Politics,* pp. 203–06. For a more complete review which also covers more recent thinkers, see Finn Laursen, *Federalism and World Order: Compendium I* (Copenhagen: World Federalist Youth, 1970). Two of the more influential works about world federalism published during World War II were Mortimer J. Adler, *How to Think About War and Peace* (New York: Simon and Schuster, 1944) and Emery Reves, *The Anatomy of Peace* (New York and London: Harper and Brothers, 1945; republished by Peter Smith, Publisher, Gloucester MA, 1969). A significant proposal addressed to creating a minimal federal world government through modification or expansion of the U.N. is given in Clark and Sohn, *World Peace Through World Law* (see note 51 for Chapter XVI). For recent scholarly defenses of the world federalist position see John Kiang, *One World: The Approach to Permanent Peace on Earth and the General Happiness of Mankind* (One World Movement, P.O. Box 423, Notre Dame IN 46556, 1984), James P. Speer, *World Polity: Conflict and War: History, Causes, Consequences, Cures* (Q.E.D. Press, 155 Cypress St., Ft. Bragg CA 95437, 1985), Mortimer J. Adler, *Haves Without Have-Nots: Essays for the 21st Century on Democracy and Socialism* (New York: Macmillan, 1991) and Ronald J. Glossop, *World Federation? A Critical Analysis of Federal World Government* (Jefferson NC: McFarland, 1993). The world federalist view is promoted in the U.S. by the World Federalist Association, 418 7th St. SE, Washington DC 20003; the American Movement for World Government, 375 South End Ave., Plaza 400, #29P, New York NY 10004; the Campaign for World Government, P.O. Box 405, Winnetka IL 60093; and The Federalist Caucus, 1544 NW Dixon St., Corvallis OR 97330. Scholarly materials about world federalism are available from the Institute for Global Policy Studies, Leliegracht 21, 1016 Amsterdam, Netherlands. A recent book arguing for the world federalist position from a British point of view is *Prescription for Peace* by Henry Usborne (published by "Minifed" Promotion Group, Totterdown, Evesham, WR11 5JP, U.K., 1985).

26. Inis L. Claude, Jr., *Power and International Relations* (New York: Random House, 1962), pp. 214–15.

27. Lewis Richardson, in his historical study of wars from 1820 to 1945, concludes that once a single government is established over previously sovereign groups, the longer these groups are under a common government the less likely they are to go to war with each other. See *Statistics of Deadly Quarrels,* pp. xi, 189–90, 295–96, 311–13.

28. See Glossop, *World Federation?,* pp. 111–12, 161–63.

29. *Ibid.,* pp. 75–79, 120–21, 181–83.

30. For relevant details see Tad Daley, "Can the U.N. Stretch to Fit Its Future?", *The Bulletin of the Atomic Scientists,* Vol. 48, No. 3 (April 1992), 38–42 and Boutros Boutros-Ghali, *An Agenda for Peace* (New York: U.N. Dept. of Public Information, 1992).

31. Available from Prime Minister's Office, S-103; 33 Stockholm, Sweden, or from the World Federalist Association, UN Office, 777 U.N. Plaza, New York NY 10017.

32. See pages 1, 3, and 4 of *Global Report,* No. 36 (Fall 1992) published by the Center for War/Peace Studies, 218 E. 18th St., New York NY 10003.

33. See page 1 of *Global Report,* No. 36, for more information about this commission. A copy of the Final Report of the U.S. Commission on Improving the Effectiveness of the U.N. is available from one of the co-chairs of the Commission, Jim Leach, U.S. House of Representatives, Washington DC 20515.

34. See Harlan Cleveland, *The Third Try at World Order* (New York: Aspen Institute for Humanistic Studies, 1977) and Harlan Cleveland, *Birth of a New World* (San Francisco: Jossey-Bass, 1993). Cleveland's books provide recent statements of the functionalist approach. An earlier and very influential statement of the functionalist view is David Mitrany's *A Working Peace System* (London: Royal Institute of International Affairs, 1943). A later significant discussion of functionalism is Ernst B. Haas's *Beyond the Nation-State: Functionalism and International Organization* (Stanford CA: Stanford University, 1964).

35. See Speer, *World Polity* (note 25 above), pp. 170–76 for a detailed statement of the federalist view concerning the futility of the functionalist approach.

36. The creation of such an agency was proposed by Sri Lanka at the 1978 U.N. Special Session on Disarmament, and France proposed an international satellite agency to help monitor arms control agreements. See *Keesing's Contemporary Archives,* Oct. 20, 1978, p. 29263.

37. *New York Times,* Sept. 12, 1948, p. 30 and Sept. 13, 1948, p. 5.

38. Garry Davis now publishes a monthly magazine entitled *World Citizen News* available from NWO Publications, 113 Church Street, Burlington VT 05491. He has also organized a World Service Authority, 1012 14th Street NW, Suite 1106, Washington DC 20005, which issues WSA passports for use by stateless persons and refugees who often cannot get passports from any national government. Birth certificates, marriage licenses, and similar documents are also available.

39. The International Registry of World Citizens in Paris is at 66 Bd. Vincent Auriol, 75013 Paris, France, while the address in Palo Alto is 2671 Southcourt, Palo Alto CA 94303.

40. For information contact World Citizens Assembly, 2671 Southcourt, Palo Alto CA 94303.

41. Alan Newcombe and Hanna Newcombe, "Mundialization: World Community at the Doorstep" in Israel W. Charny (ed.), *Strategies Against Violence: Design for Nonviolent Change* (Boulder CO: Westview, 1978), pp. 314–30. For current information on mundialization contact Paul Dilse, 85 Bleecker St., Apt. 929, Toronto, Ontario M4X 1X1.

42. W. Warren Wagar, *Building the City of Man* (San Francisco: W.H. Freeman,

1972). For another expression of a somewhat similar approach, see Gerald Mische and Patricia Mische, *Toward a Human World Order* (New York: Paulist, 1977).

43. Joseph H.C. Creyghton, *Internationale Anarchie* (Amsterdam: De Brug-Djambatan, 1962). See also Johan M.L.F. Keijser (ed.), *Political World Union 1962–1981: A Documentary Appraisal* (The Hague: Working Group World Union, 1982) (available from Johan Keijser in care of Hesbjerg Peace Research Institute, Hesbjergvej 50, DK-5491 BLOMMENSLYST (Fyn, Denmark).

44. Jacques Maritain, *Man and the State* (Chicago: University of Chicago, 1951), pp. 212–16.

45. The Bertrand Russell Peace Foundation is located in Bertrand Russell House, Gamble St., Nottingham NG7 4ET, England.

46. Gerald H. Gottlieb, "The Court of Man," *Center Magazine,* Vol. 2, No. 1 (Jan. 1969) (Center for the Study of Democratic Institutions, 256 Eucalyptus Hill Dr., Santa Barbara CA 93103), pp. 20–31.

47. Gottlieb, "The Court of Man," *Center Magazine,* p. 25.

48. This endeavor is being coordinated by the World Constitution and Parliament Association, 1480 Hoyt St., Suite 31, Lakewood CO 80215. The newsletter is called *Across Frontiers.* A book promoting this effort and containing a copy of the proposed world constitution is Errol E. Harris, *One World or None: Prescription for Survival* (Atlantic Highlands NJ: Humanities Press, 1993).

49. For more information, contact One World Now, P.O. Box 1145, Houston TX 77251-1145, phone 1-800-5-EARTH-5.

50. The organization supporting the "Philadelphia II" project is One World, P.O. Box 2566, Monterey CA 93942, phone 1-800-646-3003.

51. See Hanna Newcombe, "Alternative Approaches to World Government — II" in *Peace Research Reviews,* Vol. 5, No. 2 (Feb. 1974). For a compilation of abstracts which deal with many books and articles addressed to the development of a just and peaceful world society, see Hanna Newcombe (comp.), *World Unification Plans and Analyses* (Peace Research Institute — Dundas, 25 Dundana Ave., Dundas, Ontario L9H 4E5, Canada, 1980). For Newcombe's own views see *Design for a Better World* (Lanham MD: University Press of America, 1983) and her four essays in *Hopes and Fears: The Human Future* (Toronto: Science for Peace/Samuel Stevens, 1992) which she edited.

52. The "world order" approach is promoted by the World Policy Institute (formerly the Institute for World Order), 777 U.N. Plaza, New York NY 10017. It publishes the quarterly *World Policy Journal.*

53. Part IV of this book is an attempt to give an overview of proposals for solving the war problem. For another overview see Carolyn M. Stephenson, "Alternative Methods for International Security: A Review of the Literature," *Peace and Change,* Vol. 7, No. 4 (Fall 1981), pp. 85–110. That article, along with other related articles, is also available in Stephenson (ed.), *Alternative Methods for International Security* (Washington: University Press of America, 1982).

Selected Bibliography

Adler, Mortimer J. *Haves Without Have-Nots: Essays for the 21st Century on Democracy and Socialism.* New York: Macmillan, 1991.

————. *How to Think About War and Peace.* New York: Simon & Schuster, 1944.

Barash, David P. *Introduction to Peace Studies.* Belmont CA: Wadsworth, 1991.

Baratta, Joseph P. *Strengthening the United Nations: A Bibliography on U.N. Reform and World Federalism.* New York: Greenwood, 1987.

Beitz, Charles R., and Theodore Herman (eds.). *Peace and War.* San Francisco: W.H. Freeman, 1973.

Boulding, Kenneth E. *Stable Peace.* Austin: University of Texas Press, 1978.

Bramson, Leon, and George W. Goethals (eds.). *War: Studies from Psychology, Sociology, Anthropology,* rev. ed. New York: Basic Books, 1968.

Brodie, Bernard. *War and Politics.* New York: Macmillan, 1973.

Bueno de Mesquita, Bruce. *The War Trap.* New Haven: Yale University Press, 1981.

Butterworth, Robert L. *Managing Interstate Conflict, 1945–74: Data with Synopses.* Pittsburgh: University Center for International Studies, 1976.

————. *Moderation from Management: International Organization and Peace.* Pittsburgh: University Center for International Studies, 1978.

Charny, Israel W. (ed.). *Strategies Against Violence: Design for Nonviolent Change.* Boulder CO: Westview, 1978.

Clark, Grenville, and Louis Sohn. *World Peace Through World Law,* 3rd ed. enlarged. Cambridge MA: Harvard University Press, 1966.

Claude, Inis. *Swords into Plowshares: The Problems and Progress of International Organization,* 4th ed. New York: Random House, 1971.

Cleveland, Harlan. *Birth of a New World: An Open Moment for International Leadership.* San Francisco: Jossey-Bass, 1993.

————. *The Third Try at World Order.* New York: Aspen Institute for Humanistic Studies, 1977.

Cooling, Benjamin F. (ed.). *War, Business, and American Society: Historical Perspectives on the Military-Industrial Complex.* Port Washington NY: Kennikat, 1977.

Dyer, Gwynne. *War.* Homewood IL: Dorsey, 1985.

Eckhardt, William. *Civilizations, Empires, and Wars.* Jefferson NC: McFarland, 1992.

Falk, Richard, and Samuel S. Kim (eds.). *The War System: An Interdisciplinary Approach.* Boulder CO: Westview, 1980.

————, ————, and Saul H. Mendlovitz (eds.). *Toward a Just World Order.* Boulder CO: Westview, 1982.

Ferencz, Benjamin. *A Common Sense Guide to World Peace.* New York: Oceana, 1985.

Fischer, Dietrich. *Preventing War in the Nuclear Age.* Totawa NJ: Rowman & Allanheld, 1984.

Fried, Morton, Marvin Harris, and Robert Murphy (eds.). *War: The Anthropology of Armed Conflict and Aggression.* Garden City NY: Natural History Press, 1967.

Ginsberg, Robert (ed.). *The Critique of War: Contemporary Philosophical Explorations.* Chicago: Henry Regnery, 1969.

Glossop, Ronald J. *World Federation? A Critical Analysis of Federal World Government.* Jefferson NC: McFarland, 1993.

Haas, Ernst B. *Beyond the Nation-State: Functionalism and International Organization.* Stanford CA: Stanford University Press, 1964.

Harris, Errol E. *One World or None: Prescription for Survival.* Atlantic Highlands NJ: Humanities Press, 1993.

Hoffmann, Stanley. *Studies Beyond Borders: On the Limits and Possibilities of Ethical International Politics.* Syracuse NY: Syracuse University Press, 1981.

Jervis, Robert. *Perception and Misperception in International Politics.* Princeton NJ: Princeton University Press, 1976.

Jones, Walter S. *The Logic of International Relations,* 5th ed. Boston: Little, Brown, 1985.

Keegan, John. *A History of Warfare.* New York: Alfred A. Knopf, 1993.

Lovell, John P. *The Search for Peace: An Appraisal of Alternative Approaches.* Pittsburgh: International Studies Association, Occasional Paper No. 4, 1974.

Mische, Gerald, and Patricia Mische. *Toward a Human World Order.* New York: Paulist, 1977.

Mitrany, David. *A Working Peace System.* London: Royal Institute of International Affairs, 1943.

Muller, Robert. *The Birth of a Global Civilization.* Anacortes WA: World Happiness and Cooperation, 1991.

Newcombe, Hanna. *Design for a Better World.* Lanham MD: University Press of America, 1983.

Osgood, Charles E. *An Alternative to War or Surrender.* Urbana: University of Illinois Press, 1962.

Rapoport, Anatol. *Fights, Games, and Debates.* Ann Arbor: University of Michigan Press, 1960.

Reves, Emery. *The Anatomy of Peace.* New York: Harper & Brothers, 1945.

Richardson, Lewis F. *Arms and Insecurity.* Pittsburgh: Boxwood, 1960.

―――――. *Statistics of Deadly Quarrels.* Pittsburgh: Boxwood, 1960.

Ringler, Dick (ed.). *Dilemmas of War and Peace: A Sourcebook.* Madison WI: Board of Regents of University of Wisconsin and the Corporation for Public Broadcasting, 1993.

Rummel, R.J. *Understanding Conflict and War,* 5 vols. Beverly Hills: Sage, 1975–1981.

Schuman, Frederick L. *International Politics,* 7th ed. New York: McGraw-Hill, 1969.

Sharp, Gene. *Civilian-Based Defense: A Post-Military Weapons System.* Princeton: Princeton University Press, 1990.

―――――. *Exploring Nonviolent Alternatives.* Boston: Porter Sargent, 1970.

Sivard, Ruth Leger. *World Military and Social Expenditures, 1993.* Washington: World Priorities, 1993.

Small, Melvin, and J. David Singer (eds.). *International War: An Anthology and Study Guide.* Homewood IL: Dorsey, 1985.

―――――. *Resort to Arms: International and Civil Wars, 1815–1980.* Beverly Hills: Sage, 1982.

Smoke, Richard, and Willis Harman. *Paths to Peace: Exploring the Feasibility of Sustainable Peace.* Boulder CO: Westview, 1987.

Stephenson, Carolyn M. (ed.). *Alternative Methods for International Security.* Washington: University Press of America, 1982.

Stoessinger, John. *Why Nations Go to War,* 5th ed. New York: St. Martin's, 1989.

Streit, Clarence. *Union Now,* enlarged ed. New York: Harper, 1949.

Thompson, W. Scott, and Kenneth M. Jensen (eds.). *Approaches to Peace: An Intellectual Map.* Washington DC: U.S. Institute of Peace, 1991.

Toffler, Alvin, and Heidi Toffler. *War and Anti-war: Survival at the Dawn of the 21st Century.* Boston: Little, Brown, 1993.

Waltz, Kenneth. *Man, the State, and War.* New York: Columbia University Press, 1959.

Walzer, Michael. *Just and Unjust Wars: A Moral Argument with Historical Illustrations.* New York: Basic Books, 1977.

Wright, Quincy. *A Study of War.* Chicago: University of Chicago Press, 1942; abridged ed. by Louise Wright, 1964.

Ziegler, David W. *War, Peace, and International Politics,* 3rd ed. Boston: Little, Brown, 1984.

Index

417

114, 116, 120–21, 128, 129, 267, 130, 131, 132, 136–37, 144, 147, 150, 152, 153, 161, 168, 190, 192, 194, 195, 209, 221, 233, 239, 240–42, 243, 252, 284–88, 289, 290–91, 307, 346, 347, 348, 352, 354, 362
democratic centralism 127, 150
Deng Xiaoping 167–68, 169
Denmark 29, 32, 155, 156, 185, 188, 251, 252, 285, 308, 331
depression, worldwide, of 1930s 32, 59
deterrence & deterrence theory 21, 195–98, 202–03, 305, 308, 335
"dictatorship," definition of 114, 116
dictatorship & killing of domestic population 287–88, 309, 351
diplomacy & diplomats 243, 258, 316–17, 323–25, 327
disarmament 253, 312–13, 334, 350, 356, 357
discrimination, principle of (combatants & noncombatants) 20, 40, 45–46
displaced aggression as a cause of war 59, 192
Djibouti 77
doctrinal nationalism *see* nationalism, doctrinal
Dollard, John 54
Dominican Republic 35, 76, 150, 231
double effect, principle of 20
Dumas, Lloyd 100–01
Dunant, Jean-Henri 247
Duvalier, Jean-Claude 294
Dyer, Gwynne 26, 333

E

"Earth Summit" *see* U.N. Conference on the Environment and Development
"East-West" conflict 170, 239, 240, 241
Ecazu, Costa Rica 331
Eckhardt, William 27, 42
economic assistance to LDCs 188, 244
Economic Community of West African States (ECOWAS) 236
economic competition between groups 62–65, 67–68, 90–91, 175–77, 181–87, 189–93
economic determinism *see* materialistic interpretation of history

economic development, approaches to 178–81
"economic ideology," definition of 113, 114
economic impact of military spending 99–101, 187–89
Ecuador 337
Egypt, Egyptians 28, 135, 171, 224, 226, 227, 229, 230, 315, 318, 323, 324
Einstein, Albert 98
Eisenhower, Dwight 86, 166, 216, 227, 253
El Salvador 35, 104, 143, 232, 299
Elizabeth II, Queen of Britain 324
"end of history" thesis 108, 131–32
Engels, Friedrich 88, 89, 121, 122, 123, 126, 127
England, English *see* Britain & British
English Channel 33
English language 254, 279
Environmental Modification Convention 208, 217
equality, principle of 16–17, 108–12, 114, 128–29, 166, 175, 184–87
equality of opportunity 17–18, 24, 138, 148–49, 184
Equatorial Guinea 288
Eritrea 7, 35, 77
Eskimos 56
Esperanto 159, 255, 278–79
Estonia 32, 157, 308
Ethiopia 32, 35, 77, 176, 187, 221, 224, 240, 267, 287
Europe, Europeans 28, 29, 30, 32, 33, 36, 37, 54, 64, 73, 74, 77, 78, 97, 99, 103, 108, 113, 127, 129, 132, 136, 137, 139, 140, 141, 142, 144, 146, 147, 149, 151, 152, 153–60, 161, 162, 164, 165, 169, 170, 175, 176, 177, 189, 194, 199, 210, 212–13, 217, 225, 230, 233, 236, 237, 238, 240, 250–51, 252, 259–60, 265, 278, 279, 288–89, 291, 294, 295, 301, 302, 303, 318, 320, 345, 346, 347, 350
European Atomic Energy Community (Euratom) 155
European Coal and Steel Community (ECSC) 155, 250
European Commission 156, 157, 159, 251
European Community (EC) 155–56,